Silver Girl

ELIN HILDERBRAND

Silver Girl

HODDER &
STOUGHTON

First published in Great Britain in 2011 by Hodder & Stoughton
An Hachette UK company

1

Copyright © Elin Hilderbrand 2011

The right of Elin Hilderbrand to be identified as the Author of the Work has been
asserted by her in accordance with the Copyright, Designs and Patents Act 1988.

A CIP catalogue record for this title is available from the British Library

Hardback ISBN 978 1 444 72388 5
Trade Paperback ISBN 978 1 444 72389 2
eBook ISBN 978 1 444 72391 5

Printed and bound by CPI Mackays, Chatham ME5 8TD

Hodder & Stoughton policy is to use papers that are natural, renewable and
recyclable products and made from wood grown in sustainable forests.
The logging and manufacturing processes are expected to conform to the
environmental regulations of the country of origin.

Hodder & Stoughton Ltd
338 Euston Road
London NW1 3BH

www.hodder.co.uk

For my daughter, Shelby Katharine Cunningham
I am at a loss for the words to describe you.
Graceful? Vivacious? Captivating?
All of these, yes, my love, and more.

PART ONE

MEREDITH MARTIN DELINN

They had agreed not to speak about anything meaningful until Meredith was safely inside the house on Nantucket. First, they had the highway to face. Meredith knew it too well, just like every other American with a home (or, in her case, three homes) between Maine and Florida. There were the ninety-three tedious exits of Connecticut before they crossed into Rhode Island and, a scant hour later, Massachusetts. As they drove over the Sagamore Bridge, the sun came up, giving the Cape Cod Canal a cheerful pink glaze that hurt Meredith's eyes. There was no traffic on the bridge even though it was the first of July; that was why Connie liked to do the drive overnight.

Finally, they arrived in Hyannis: a town Meredith had visited once with her parents in the early 1970s. She remembered her mother, Deidre Martin, insisting they drive by the Kennedy Compound. There had been guards; it was just a few years after Bobby's assassination. Meredith remembered her father, Chick Martin, encouraging her to eat a lobster roll. She had been only eight years old, but Chick Martin had confidence in Meredith's sophistication. *Brilliant and talented,* Chick used to brag shamelessly. *The girl can do no wrong.* Meredith had tasted the lobster salad and spit it out, then felt embarrassed. Her father had shrugged and finished the sandwich himself.

Even all these years later, the memory of Hyannis filled Meredith with a sense of shame, which lay on top of the disgrace Meredith had been feeling since her husband, Freddy Delinn, had been indicted. Hyannis was a place where Meredith had disappointed her father.

Thank God he couldn't see her now.

Although they had agreed not to talk about anything meaningful, Meredith turned to Connie, who had decided—against her better judgment—to shelter Meredith, at least for the time being, and said, "Thank God my father can't see me now."

Connie, who was pulling into the parking lot of the Steamship Authority, let out a sigh and said, "Oh, Meredith."

Meredith couldn't read Connie's tone. *Oh, Meredith, you're right; it's a blessing Chick has been dead for thirty years and didn't have to witness your meteoric rise and your even more spectacular fall.* Or: *Oh, Meredith, stop feeling sorry for yourself.* Or: *Oh, Meredith, I thought we agreed we wouldn't talk until we got to the house. We laid ground rules, and you're trampling them.*

Or: *Oh, Meredith, please shut up.*

Indeed, Connie's tone since she'd rescued Meredith at two in the morning was one of barely concealed...what? Anger? Fear? Consternation? And could Meredith blame her? She and Connie hadn't spoken in nearly three years, and in their last conversation, they had said despicable things to each other; they had taken a blowtorch to the ironclad chain of their friendship. Or: *Oh, Meredith, what have I done? Why are you here? I wanted a quiet summer. I wanted peace. And now I have you, a stinky international scandal, in my front seat.*

Meredith decided to give Connie the benefit of the doubt. "Oh, Meredith" was a quasi-sympathetic non-answer. Connie was pulling up to the gatehouse and showing the attendant her ferry ticket; she was distracted. Meredith wore her son Carver's baseball hat from Choate and her last remaining pair of prescription sunglasses, which fortunately were big, round, and very dark. Meredith turned her face away from the attendant. She couldn't let anyone recognize her.

Connie pulled up the ramp, into the ferry's hold. Cars were packed like Matchbox models in a snug little suitcase. It was the first of July; even at this early hour, the mood on the boat was festive. Jeeps were laden with beach towels and hibachi grills; the car parked in front of Connie's was a vintage Wagoneer with at least sixteen beach stickers, in every color of the rainbow, lining the bumper. Meredith's heart was bruised, battered, and broken. She told herself not to think about the boys, but all that led to was her thinking about the boys. She remembered how she used to load up the Range Rover with bags of their bathing suits and surf shirts and flip-flops, and their baseball gloves and cleats, the aluminum case that held the badminton set, fresh decks of cards, and packs of D batteries for the flashlights. Meredith would load the dog into his crate and strap Carver's surfboard to the top of the car, and off they'd go—bravely into the traffic jam that lasted from Freeport all the way to Southampton. Inevitably, they timed it badly and got stuck behind the jitney. But it had been fun. The boys took turns with the radio—Leo liked folk rock, the Counting Crows were his favorite, and Carver liked the headbanger stuff that would make the dog howl—and Meredith always felt that the hotter and slower the drive was, the happier they were to arrive in Southampton. Sun, sand, ocean. Take your shoes off, open the windows. Freddy did the drive on the weekends, and in later years, he arrived in a helicopter.

As Meredith looked on the summer revelers now, she thought, *Leo! Carver! Leo. Poor Leo.* For all of the years of their growing up, Leo had taken care of Carver. Protected him, schooled him, included him. And now, Carver was the one who would be supporting Leo, propping him up. Meredith prayed he was doing a good job.

A voice came over the loudspeaker, announcing the rules and

regulations of the boat. The foghorn sounded, and Meredith heard distant clapping. The good, fortunate souls headed to Nantucket Island on this fine morning were applauding the start of their summer. Meanwhile, Meredith felt like she was still three states away. At that very moment, federal marshals would be entering Meredith's penthouse apartment on Park Avenue and seizing her belongings. Meredith wondered with a curious detachment what this seizing would be like. To go with Connie, Meredith had packed one duffel bag of simple summer clothes, and one cardboard box of personal effects—photographs, her marriage license, the boys' birth certificates, a few of her favorite paperback novels, one particular spiral-bound notebook from her freshman year at Princeton, and one record album—the original 1970 release of Simon and Garfunkel's *Bridge Over Troubled Water,* which Meredith had no hope of ever listening to, but which she couldn't bring herself to leave behind.

She'd been permitted to take her eyeglasses, her prescription sunglasses, and her four-karat diamond engagement ring. The ring had been inherited from her grandmother, Annabeth Martin, and not bought with dirty money. There was a strand of pearls from Meredith's mother, a present on Meredith's graduation from Princeton, which fell into the same category, but Meredith had no use for pearls now. She couldn't wear pearls in jail. With a little forethought, she might have pawned them and added the money to the paltry sum she had left.

But what of her other possessions? Meredith imagined grim, strapping men in black uniforms with handguns concealed in their waistbands. One might lift the delicate Shalimar bottle off her dressing table and, unable to help himself, inhale the scent. One would strip her Aurora linens from Schweitzer off the bed. Those sheets were worth thousands of dollars, but what would the marshals do with them? Launder them, fold them, sell them off? They would take her Hostetler sculpture and the Andrew Wyeth sketches; they would clip the Calder mobile from the ceiling in the living room. They would go through Meredith's closet and box up the Louboutins and the Sergio Rossis; they would carry off her everyday dresses—Diane von Furstenberg, Phillip Lim—and her gowns—the Dior, the Chanel, the Caroline Herreras. The Feds had told Meredith that her belongings would be sold at auction and the proceeds funneled into a restitution fund for the fleeced investors. Meredith thought of her baby-blue Dior gown, which she had paid $19,000 for—a fact that, now, made her want to gag with disgust—and wondered who would own it next. Someone petite—Meredith was only five foot one and weighed a hundred pounds. That gown had been custom-tailored for her by John Galliano himself. Who would end up with Meredith's copper All-Clad sauté pans (never used, except occasionally by Leo's girlfriend, Anais, who thought it was a sin that Meredith didn't cook in her gleaming gourmet kitchen). Who would end up with the cut crystal whiskey decanter that Freddy had never poured a drink from, except in the final days before his exposure to the world. (It was the sight of Freddy throwing back three successive shots of a 1926 Macallan that put Meredith on high alert. A Pandora's box of accusations had cracked open in her mind: *No one knows how he does it. He says it's black magic, but it can't be legal. He's breaking the law. He's going to get caught.*)

Meredith knew the Feds would be most interested in what they found in Freddy's home office. Freddy had always kept the door to his office locked, a practice that began when the children were young and he wanted to keep them from interrupting him on the phone, though it continued into later years. The door had remained locked—both when he was in the office and when he wasn't—even against Meredith. If she wanted entry, she had to knock. She had testified to this in her deposition, but the authorities didn't believe her. Her fingerprints (literal) were on the doorknob. And her fingerprints (figurative) had been found on one illegal transaction. Three days before the collapse of Delinn Enterprises, Meredith had transferred $15 million from the company's "slush fund" into the personal brokerage account she and Freddy shared.

The federal marshals would also be interested in Freddy's den. Their decorator, Samantha Deuce, had masterminded the "gentleman's library" look with shelves of books on finance, antique piggy banks, and baseball memorabilia from Babe Ruth's stint with the Yankees. Freddy wasn't even a Yankees fan, but Samantha had likened him to Babe Ruth because, she said, they were both iconic men of their times. *Iconic men of their times.* Meredith had believed Samantha to be a maestro of overstatement.

Freddy had nearly always enjoyed his den alone; Meredith was hard-pressed to remember anyone else relaxing in the deep suede club chairs or watching the fifty-two-inch television. The boys didn't like hanging out in that room; even when the ball game was on, they preferred to watch in the kitchen with Meredith. There was a hidden dartboard in the back of the den that Meredith was sure had never been used; the darts were still in the bubble wrap.

The only person that Meredith could remember ever seeing in Freddy's den was Samantha. Meredith had come across Freddy and Samantha in that room a few years earlier. They had been standing side by side admiring a hunting print that Samantha had bought at Christie's. (The choice of this print was ironic, since Freddy didn't hunt and hated guns: his brother had been killed by an errant bullet in a training exercise in the army.) Freddy had been resting his hand on Samantha's lower back. When Meredith walked in, Freddy whipped his hand away so quickly that it called attention to the fact that he had been touching Samantha in the first place. Meredith thought of that moment often. Freddy's hand on Samantha's lower back: No big deal, right? Samantha had been their decorator for years. Freddy and Samantha were friends, chummy and affectionate. If Freddy had simply left his hand there, Meredith wouldn't have thought a thing about it. It was his startled reaction that made Meredith wonder. Freddy never got startled.

The ferry lurched forward. Connie had wedged her hunter-green Escalade between a Stop & Shop semi and a black Range Rover not so different from the one that Meredith used to drive to the Hamptons. Connie got out of the car, slamming her door.

Meredith panicked. "Where are you going?" she asked.

Connie didn't answer. She opened the back door of the Escalade and climbed in. She foraged in the way-back for a pillow, and lay across the backseat.

"I'm tired," she said.

"Of course," Meredith said. Connie had left her house at eight o'clock the night before, a scant four hours after receiving Meredith's phone call. She had driven six hours to Manhattan and had idled in the dark alley behind 824 Park Avenue, waiting for Meredith to emerge. There had been a reporter standing behind a Dumpster, but he had been smoking a cigarette and hadn't gotten his camera ready until Meredith was in the car and Connie was screeching out of the alley in reverse, like a bank robber in a heist movie. Meredith had ducked her head below the dashboard.

"Jesus, Meredith," Connie said. "And have you seen the *front* of the building?"

Meredith knew it was swarming with reporters, television lights, and satellite trucks. They had been there on the day Freddy was led out of the apartment in handcuffs, then again on the morning that Meredith had gone to visit Freddy in jail, and they had gathered a third time nearly two days earlier in anticipation of Meredith's removal from the building by federal marshals. What the public wanted to know was, where does the wife of the biggest financial criminal in history go when she is turned out of her Park Avenue penthouse?

Meredith had two attorneys. Her lead attorney's name was Burton Penn; he asked Meredith to call him Burt. He was new to her. Freddy had taken their longtime family lawyer, Richard Cassel. Goddamned Freddy, taking the best, leaving Meredith with prematurely balding thirty-six-year-old Burton Penn. Though he had, at least, gone to Yale Law School.

The other attorney was even younger, with dark shaggy hair

and pointy incisors, like one of those teen vampires. He wore glasses, and in passing, he'd told Meredith that he had an astigmatism. "Yes, so do I," Meredith said; she had worn horn-rimmed glasses since she was thirteen years old. Meredith had bonded more closely with this second attorney. His name was Devon Kasper. He asked her to call him Dev. Dev told Meredith the truth about things, but he sounded sorry about it. He had sounded sorry when he told Meredith that, because she had transferred the $15 million into her and Freddy's shared brokerage account, she was under investigation, and it was possible she would be charged with conspiracy and sent to prison. He had sounded sorry when he told Meredith that her son Leo was also under investigation, because he had worked with Freddy at Delinn Enterprises.

Leo was twenty-six years old. He worked for the legitimate trading division of Delinn Enterprises.

So why, then, were the Feds investigating Leo? Meredith didn't understand, and she was trying not to panic — panic wouldn't serve her — but this was her child. He was her responsible son, the one who got into Dartmouth and was captain of the lacrosse team and vice president of the Dartmouth chapter of Amnesty International; he was the one who had a steady girlfriend; he was the one who, to Meredith's knowledge, had never once broken the law — had never shoplifted a pack of gum, had never taken a drink underage, had never gotten a parking ticket.

"Why are they investigating Leo?" Meredith had asked, her bruised heart racing. Her child in danger, as surely as a three-year-old running out into traffic.

Well, Dev said, they were investigating Leo because another trader — a well-respected, ten-year veteran on the legitimate floor named Deacon Rapp — had told the SEC and the FBI that Leo was involved in his father's Ponzi scheme. Deacon testified that Leo was in "constant contact" with colleagues on the seventeenth floor, which was where the Ponzi scheme was headquartered. Freddy had a small office on the seventeenth floor, as well as a secretary. This came as a shock to Meredith. She had known nothing about the existence of the seventeenth floor, nor the secretary, a Mrs. Edith Misurelli. The Feds couldn't question Mrs. Misurelli because she had apparently been due months of vacation time and had left for Italy the day before the scandal broke. No one knew how to reach her.

Dev sounded especially sorry when he told Meredith that she absolutely could not be in contact with either of her sons until the investigation was cleared up. Any conversation between Leo and Meredith might be seen as evidence of their mutual conspiracy. And because Carver and Leo were living together in an old Victorian that Carver was renovating in Greenwich, Meredith couldn't call Carver, either. Burt and Dev had met with Leo's counsel, and both parties agreed there was too much chance for cross-contamination. Meredith should remain in one camp, the boys in another. For the time being.

"I'm sorry, Meredith."

Dev said this often.

Meredith peered at Connie, who had scrunched her long, lean form to fit across the backseat. Her head was sunk into the pillow, her strawberry-blond hair fell across her face, her eyes were closed. She looked older, and sadder, to Meredith—her husband, Wolf, had died two and a half years earlier of brain cancer—but she was still Connie, Constance Flute, née O'Brien, Meredith's oldest, and once her closest, friend. Her friend since the beginning of time.

Meredith had called Connie to ask if she could stay with her "for a while" in Bethesda. Connie had artfully dodged the request by saying that she was headed up to Nantucket for the summer. Of course, Nantucket. July was now upon them—a fact that had effectively escaped Meredith, trapped as she was in her apartment— and Meredith's hopes tanked.

"Can you call someone else?" Connie asked.

"There isn't anyone else," Meredith said. She said this not to invoke Connie's pity, but because it was true. It astounded her how alone she was, how forsaken by everyone who had been in her life. Connie was her one and only hope. Despite the fact that they hadn't spoken in three years, she was the closest thing to family that Meredith had.

"You could turn to the church," Connie said. "Join a convent."

A convent, yes. Meredith had considered this when casting about for options. There were convents, she was pretty sure, out on Long Island; she and the boys used to pass one on their way to the Hamptons, set back from the highway among rolling hills. She would start out as a novice scrubbing floors until her knees bled, but maybe someday she'd be able to teach.

"Meredith," Connie said. "I'm kidding."

"Oh," Meredith said. Of course, she was kidding. Meredith and Connie had attended Catholic schools together all through their childhood, but Connie had never been particularly devout.

"I guess I could pick you up on my way," Connie said.

"And do what?" Meredith said. "Take me to Nantucket?"

"You do owe me a visit," Connie said. "You've owed me a visit since nineteen eighty-two."

Meredith had laughed. It sounded strange to her own ears, the laugh. It had been so long.

Connie said, "You can stay a couple of weeks, maybe longer. We'll see how it goes. I can't make any promises."

"Thank you," Meredith had whispered, weak with gratitude.

"You realize you haven't called me in three years," Connie said.

Yes, Meredith realized that. What Connie really meant was: *You never called to apologize for what you said about Wolf, or to give me your condolences in person. But you call me now, when you're in heaps of trouble and have nowhere else to go.*

"I'm sorry," Meredith said. She didn't say: *You didn't call me, either. You never apologized for calling Freddy a crook.* Now, of course, there was no need to apologize. Connie had been proved right: Freddy was a crook. "Will you still come get me?"

"I'll come get you," Connie said.

Now, Meredith wanted to wake Connie up and ask her: Can you please forgive me for the things I said? Can we make things right between us?

Meredith wondered what the federal marshals would think about the mirror she'd smashed in the master bath. In a fit of rage, she'd thrown her mug of peppermint tea at it; she had savored the smack and shatter of the glass. Her reflection had splintered and fallen away, onto the granite countertop, into Freddy's sink. *Goddamn you, Freddy,* Meredith thought, for the zillionth time. The ferry rocked on the waves, and Meredith's eyes drifted closed. If there were beating hearts beneath the federal marshals' black uniforms, then she supposed they would understand.

CONSTANCE O'BRIEN FLUTE

They had agreed not to speak about anything meaningful until Meredith was safely inside the house on Nantucket. Connie needed time to digest what she'd done. *What had she done?* She had six hours in the car from Bethesda to Manhattan to repeatedly ask herself. The roads were clear of traffic; on the radio, Connie listened to Delilah. The heart-wrenching stories of the callers boosted Connie's spirits. She knew about loss. Wolf had been dead for two and a half years, and Connie was still waiting for the pain to subside. It had been nearly as long since Connie had spoken to their daughter, Ashlyn, though Connie called Ashlyn's cell phone every Sunday, hoping that one time she might answer.

Connie sent Ashlyn flowers on her birthday and a gift certificate to J. Crew at Christmas. Did Ashlyn tear up the gift certificate, throw the flowers in the trash? Connie had no way of knowing.

And now look what she'd done. She had agreed to go to Manhattan to pick up her ex–best friend, Meredith Delinn. Connie thought *ex-friend,* but inside Connie knew that she and Meredith would always be tethered together. They had grown up on the Main Line in Philadelphia. They attended Tarleton in the 1960s, then grammar school, then high school at Merion Mercy Academy. They had been as close as sisters. For two years in high school, Meredith had dated Connie's brother, Toby.

Connie fingered her cell phone, which rested in the console of her car. She considered calling Toby now and telling him what she was doing. He was the only person who had known Meredith as long as Connie had; he was the only one who might understand. But Toby and Meredith had a complicated history. Toby had broken Meredith's heart in high school, and over the years, Meredith had asked Connie about him, the way a woman asks about her first true love. Connie had been the one to tell Meredith about Toby's voyages around the world captaining megayachts, his hard-partying lifestyle that landed him in rehab twice, the women he met, married, and abandoned along the way, and his ten-year-old son who was destined to become as charming and dangerous as Toby himself. Meredith and Toby hadn't seen each other since the funeral of Connie and Toby's mother, Veronica, six years earlier. Something had happened between Meredith and Toby at the funeral that ended with Meredith climbing into her waiting car and driving away before the reception.

"I can't be around him," Meredith had said to Connie later. "It's too painful."

Connie hadn't been gutsy enough to ask Meredith exactly what had happened. But she decided it would be wisest not to call Toby, as tempting as it was.

Connie had seen Meredith on CNN back in April, on the day

that Meredith went to visit Freddy in jail. Meredith had looked gray haired and haggard, nothing like the blond, Dior-wearing socialite that Connie had most recently seen in the society pages of the *New York Times*. Meredith had been wearing jeans and a white button-down shirt and a trench coat; she had been ducking into a cab, but a reporter caught her before she closed the door and asked her, "Mrs. Delinn, do you ever cry about the way things have turned out?"

Meredith looked up, and Connie had felt a sharp rush of recognition. Meredith's expression was feisty. This was the Meredith Connie had known in high school—the competitive field-hockey player, the champion diver, the National Merit Scholarship finalist.

"No," Meredith said.

And Connie thought, *Oh, Meredith, wrong answer.*

She had meant to call Meredith in the days following. The press was brutal. (The headline of the *New York Post* read, *JESUS WEPT. BUT NOT MRS. DELINN.*) Connie had wanted to reach out and offer some kind of support, but she hadn't picked up the phone. She was still bitter that Meredith had allowed money to sink their friendship. And besides, Connie was too involved with her own melancholy to take on Meredith's problems.

Connie had seen a picture of Meredith, peering from one of her penthouse windows, published in *People*. The caption read, *At daybreak, Meredith Delinn gazes out at a world that will no longer have her.*

The paparazzi had caught her in her nightgown at the crack of dawn. *Poor Meredith!* Again, Connie considered calling, but she didn't.

Connie then saw the article on the front page of the *New York Times* Style section entitled "The Loneliest Woman in New York." It told the story of Meredith's ill-fated trip to the Pascal Blanc salon, where she'd been getting her hair colored for fifteen years. The newspaper reported that Meredith had been calling for an appointment at the salon for weeks, but she kept getting put off by the receptionist. Finally, the owner of the salon, Jean-Pierre, called Meredith back and explained that he couldn't risk offending his other patrons, many of whom were former Delinn investors, by having her in the salon. The article said that Meredith asked for an after-hours appointment, and he said no. Meredith asked if the woman who normally colored her hair could come to her apartment — Meredith would pay her in cash — and Jean-Pierre said no. The article also stated that Meredith was no longer welcome at Rinaldo's, the Italian restaurant where she and Freddy had dined at least twice a week for eight years. "They always sat at the same table," Dante Rinaldo was quoted as saying. "Mrs. Delinn always ordered a glass of the Ruffino Chianti, but Mr. Delinn drank nothing, ever. Now, I can't let Mrs. Delinn come to eat, or no one else will come to eat." The article had made one thing perfectly clear: everyone in New York City hated Meredith, and if she were to show her face in public, she would be shunned.

Awful, Connie thought. *Poor Meredith.* After she read the article, she picked up the phone, and, with numb fingers, dialed the number of Meredith's Park Avenue apartment. She was promptly informed by an operator that the number had been changed and that the new number was unlisted.

Of course.

Connie hung up, thinking, *Well, I tried.*

And then that very day, at one o'clock, Connie had been watching Fox News as she packed her suitcases for Nantucket. It was the day of Freddy's sentencing. The talking heads at Fox were predicting a sentence of twenty-five to thirty years, although Tucker Carlson mentioned how savvy and experienced Freddy's counsel was.

"His attorney, Richard Cassel," Carlson said, "is asking for seventeen years, which could become twelve years with good behavior."

And Connie thought, *Ha! Richard Cassel!* Connie had done beer bongs with Richard Cassel when she'd gone to visit Meredith at Princeton. Richard had tried to lure Connie back to his suite, but she had turned him down. He was such a casual aristocrat in his button-down shirt with the frayed collar, and his scuffed penny loafers. Hadn't Meredith told Connie that Richard once cheated on an exam? He was a fitting attorney for Freddy.

Connie's memories of Richard Cassel were interrupted by the announcement that Frederick Xavier Delinn had been sentenced to 150 years in federal prison.

Connie sat down for that. *A hundred and fifty years?* She thought, *The judge is making an example of him.* Well, Connie hated to say this, but Freddy deserved it. So many people had been left penniless; futures had been destroyed, kids were forced to drop out of college, family homes had been foreclosed on, eighty-year-old women had to get by living on Social Security, eating from cans. *A hundred and fifty years.* Connie thought, *Poor Meredith.*

Connie was angry with Meredith for her own personal reasons, but unlike everyone else, she didn't blame Meredith for Freddy's crimes. Meredith couldn't have known what Freddy was doing. (*Had* she? Okay, there was always room for doubt.) But when Connie closed her eyes and searched inside of herself for an answer, she thought, *There is no way Meredith knew.* There was *no way* Meredith would accept fraud in her life. She was a straight arrow. Connie should know: growing up, it had driven her crazy. And still, Connie wondered, just as the rest of the world wondered, how could she *not* have known? Meredith was a smart woman—she had been the class salutatorian at Merion Mercy, she had gone to Princeton. How could she be blind to the crimes going on under her own roof? So, she knew. But no, she couldn't have.

Connie had opened her eyes in time to see Freddy, looking gaunt and nauseous and wearing an ill-fitting suit, being led from the courthouse, back to his dungeon.

You bastard, she thought.

It was a few hours later that the phone had rung. The caller ID said, *NUMBER UNAVAILABLE,* which always stirred up hope in Connie, because any unidentified number might be Ashlyn calling.

Connie picked up. "Hello?"

"Connie? Con?" It was a woman's voice, so familiar, though Connie was slow to identify it. It wasn't her daughter, it wasn't Ashlyn, so there was an immediate stab of disappointment to experience before she realized...that the woman on the phone was Meredith.

"Meredith?" Connie said.

Meredith said, "Thank God you answered."

What had she done? Why had she said yes? The truth was, Meredith had been on Connie's mind for months. The truth was, Connie felt sorry for Meredith. The truth was, Connie had been closer to Meredith than to any other woman in her entire life—her own mother included, her own daughter included. The truth was, Connie was lonely. She yearned for another person in the room, someone who knew her, who understood her. The truth was, Connie didn't know why she had agreed, but she had agreed.

Connie had balked when she saw the throng of reporters outside Meredith's building. She had nearly cruised on past, but she knew Meredith would be waiting for her in the dark alley behind the building and that to abandon her there would be cruel.

When Connie pulled up, Meredith ran from the back door and leapt into the car. She was wearing the same white button-down blouse, jeans, and flats that Connie had seen her photographed in months earlier when she went to visit Freddy in jail. Connie barely waited for Meredith to shut the door before she hit the gas and reversed out. A photographer got a shot of the car departing; thankfully, Meredith's head had been down. Connie floored it up Park Avenue, although she didn't feel safe until they were off the FDR and on I-95. That was when Meredith had wanted to talk, but Connie had held up her palm and said, "Let's not discuss anything until we're safely in the house on Nantucket."

Though there was much, of course, that she wanted to know.

*   *   *

When the announcement came over the loudspeaker that the ferry was pulling into Nantucket harbor, Connie startled awake. Meredith was in the front seat, and there were two steaming cups of coffee—light, with sugar—snug in the console. Connie and Meredith drank their coffee the same way, a habit learned together at age six during tea parties with Meredith's grandmother, Anna-beth Martin, who unorthodoxly served the little girls real coffee from a silver pot.

Meredith was wearing a baseball hat and sunglasses. When she saw that Connie was awake, she said, "I got coffee. A guy in line stared me down, but he was a foreigner, I think. I heard him speaking Russian."

Connie said, "I don't want to burst your bubble..."

Meredith said, "Believe me, there is no bubble."

Connie said, "You're going to have to be incredibly careful. No one can know you're here with me. No one Russian, no one Swedish, I mean no one."

"Except for my attorneys." Meredith took a sip of her coffee. "They have to know where I am. Because I'm still under investigation. Me, and Leo, too."

"Oh, Meredith," Connie said. Connie found herself feeling both concerned and annoyed. Meredith should have told her this before she asked Connie to come get her, right? Would that have changed Connie's mind? And poor Leo, Connie's own godson, one of the greatest kids she had ever known. Still under investigation? But why? Connie refrained from asking the obvious: *Do they have anything to charge you with? Am I going to become some kind of accessory to conspiracy?* Instead, she said, "I almost called Toby last night, to tell him I was bringing you here."

"Toby?" Meredith said.

"Toby, yes."

"Do you mind if I ask where he is?"

Connie metered her breath. She said, "He's in Annapolis, running a wildly successful charter sail business. In the winter, he takes off and barefoots through the Caribbean."

"Meaning he sleeps with models half his age in Saint Barth's," Meredith said.

Connie couldn't tell if Meredith was being playful or bitter. She decided to go with playful. "I'm sure that's correct," Connie said. "He's never really grown up. But that's what we love about him, right?"

Meredith bleated. *Ha.* Connie felt the old ambivalence about Meredith and Toby's long-ago relationship return. There was jealousy—once Meredith had fallen in love with Toby, he had become far more important to Meredith than Connie was; there was guilt that Toby had so mercilessly trampled Meredith's feelings; there was disbelief that all these years later, Meredith still cared about him. Even after Meredith was married to Freddy and ludicrously wealthy with her twenty houses and her fleet of Rolls-Royces and a private jet for every day of the week, she always asked: How is Toby? Is he still married? Dating anyone? Does he ever ask about me?

"Listen," Connie said. It was weird having Meredith next to her like this. There was so much shared history—years and years and years, and many of those years they had been together every single day—and yet so much had changed. "I know you don't have anywhere else to go. But it's possible that this won't work. I'll be miserable, you'll be miserable, we won't be able to mend the friendship. You're under investigation, but *I* can't be under investigation. You understand that? If anything happens that I'm not comfortable with, you'll have to leave. You'll have to find your own way."

Meredith nodded solemnly, and Connie hated herself for sounding harsh.

"But I want to try it," Connie said. "I want to give you a place to rest your mind. I want to spend time with you. I'm not completely selfless, Meredith. I'm lonely, too. I've been lonely every hour of every day since Wolf died. Ashlyn has made herself a stranger to me. We don't speak. There was a misunderstanding at the funeral." Connie shook her head. She didn't want to think about that. "She has no idea how cruel she's being. She won't understand until she has children of her own."

"I'm sorry," Meredith said. "If it makes you feel any better, I'm not allowed to contact either of the boys because of the ongoing investigation. And although Freddy isn't dead, he might as well be."

There was symmetry in their situations, but Connie didn't want to contrast and compare to determine whose situation was worse. Thankfully, at that moment, the cars in front of hers started pulling off the ferry, and Connie edged the Escalade forward. As she did so, the panorama of Nantucket in the morning sun was revealed: blue sky, gray-shingled houses, the gold-domed clock tower of the Unitarian Church. Meredith had owned homes in glamorous places—before their falling out, Connie had been to visit her in Palm Beach and Cap d'Antibes—but for Connie, the vista of Nantucket Island was the most breathtaking in the world.

"Wow," Meredith whispered.

"Get down," Connie advised. "Just in case."

There were no cameras, no satellite trucks, no reporters—just the relaxed pace of a Friday morning in early July on Nantucket. There were tourists on Steamship Wharf and the usual crowd on "the strip"—people ordering sandwiches for the beach, renting bicycles, getting their surfboards waxed at Indian Summer. Connie drove past the Nantucket Whaling Museum. Wolf had loved the whaling museum; he had been a maritime buff, reading all of Nathaniel Philbrick's books and everything by Patrick O'Brian. Wolf's family had owned the land on Nantucket for generations, and when Connie and Wolf had the money, they tore down the simple cottage that sat on three acres of beachfront land and built a proper house.

The house was located in the hinterlands of Tom Nevers. When Wolf and Connie mentioned that they lived in Tom Nevers, people who knew the island said, "Really? All the way *out there?*"

It was true that Tom Nevers was "out there" by island standards. It was a six-mile journey down the Milestone Road, and it wasn't as chic as the village of Sconset, nor was it as prestigious as owning a home that fronted the harbor. Tom Nevers had no restaurants and no shopping; to get coffee and the paper, Connie had to drive to Sconset. Because Tom Nevers faced southeast, it was frequently blanketed in fog, even when the rest of the island was bright and sunny. But Connie loved the peace and quiet, the rugged, deserted beach, and the friendly seal that swam offshore. She loved the low horizon and the simplicity of the other houses. Tom Nevers wasn't glamorous, but it was home.

As soon as Connie turned into their long, dirt driveway (marked by a weathered wooden plank that said "Flute") she told Meredith it was okay to sit up.

"Wow," Meredith said again. The driveway was bordered on either side by eelgrass and wind-flattened Spanish olive trees. They drove on, and Connie wondered what Meredith was thinking. It had been a sensitive topic—long before the thing with Wolf and the money—that Meredith and Freddy had never deigned to visit Wolf and Connie here on Nantucket. Meredith had promised to visit the summer after she graduated from college; she had been on her way with her bus and boat tickets already booked, but she'd canceled at the last minute because of Freddy. And then once Meredith and Freddy were married, Meredith became wrapped up with her fabulous life in the Hamptons.

The house came into view, and the ocean beyond.

Meredith said, "My God, Connie, it's *huge*. It's *magnificent*."

Connie felt a bloom of pride, which she knew she should usher away. They had learned, hadn't they, that material things were evanescent. Meredith had once had everything in the world; now, she had nothing. And yet, Connie couldn't help feeling a certain satisfaction. It had forever been the case that Connie was considered the pretty one, Meredith the smart one. Connie had been given a life filled with love; Meredith had been given a life filled with fortune: money, places, things, and experiences beyond one's wildest dreams. Meredith's home in Palm Beach had once been owned by the Pulitzers. Meredith had hosted Donald and Ivanka for dinner; Jimmy Buffett had sung to her on her fortieth birthday. It was rumored that she even had a star in the heavens named for her.

In the face of this, wasn't it okay for Connie to feel pleasure that Meredith was impressed by the house? It *was* huge; it *was* magnificent.

It was, alas, empty.

That was the thought that met Connie when she opened the front door. Connie's footsteps echoed in the two-story foyer. The floors were made from white tumbled marble, and there was a curved staircase to the right that swept up the wall like the inside of a nautilus shell. The house had been Wolf's design.

Wolf was dead. He would never walk into this house again. This reality hit Connie anew in a way that felt unfair. It had been two and a half years; friends and acquaintances had told Connie that life would get incrementally easier, her sorrow would fade, but that day hadn't come.

Connie struggled for a breath. Beside her, Meredith looked very small and overwhelmed, and Connie thought, *We're a couple of basket cases. Me, once voted "Prettiest and Most Popular." Meredith, once voted "Most Likely to Succeed."*

Connie said, "Let me show you around."

She led Meredith through the foyer into the great room, which ran the whole length of the house, and flooded with rosy light at dawn. To the left was the kitchen: maple cabinets fronted with glass, countertops fashioned from blue granite. The kitchen had every bell and whistle because Connie was a gourmet cook. There was an eight-burner Garland stove, a porcelain farmer's sink, a wine refrigerator, double ovens, a custom-made extra-wide dishwasher, a backsplash of cobalt and white Italian tile that she and Wolf had found on their trek through Cinque Terre. The kitchen flowed into the dining room, which was furnished with a glossy cherrywood table and twelve chairs. Beyond a break for the double doors that led to the back deck was the living area, also decorated in white and blue. At the end of the room was a white brick fireplace with a massive mantel made of driftwood that Wolf's grandfather had found on their beach after Hurricane Donna in 1960.

"It's wonderful," Meredith said. "Who decorated?"

"I did," Connie said.

"I never decorated a thing in my life," Meredith said. "We always had Samantha." She wandered to the far end of the living room, where Wolf's barometer collection lined the shelves. "That always felt like a privilege, you know, to have Samantha pick things out for us, put things together, create a style for us. But it was phony, like everything else." She touched the spines of Wolf's books. "I like this so much better. This room is you and Wolf and Ashlyn."

"Yes," Connie said. "It is. It was. It's hard, you know." She smiled wistfully. She was happy not to be alone, but it was excruciating to hear Meredith repeating the things that Connie found it impossible to say. "Shall we go down to the water?"

It was particularly hard to be on the beach, because that was where she'd scattered Wolf's ashes two summers earlier in the presence of Wolf's brother, Jake, and his wife, Iris, and Toby, who had used the memorial on Nantucket as an opportunity for his last ridiculous bender. As Connie and Meredith left footprints in the wet sand— the tide was low—Connie wondered where the remains of Wolfgang Charles Flute were now. He had been a whole, warm, loving man with impressive height—Wolf was nearly six foot seven—and a baritone voice, a keen intellect, a crackerjack eye. He had been the owner of an architectural firm that built civic office buildings in Washington that were considered innovative, yet traditional enough to hold their own against the monuments. He had been a busy man, an important man, if not particularly powerful by Washington standards or wealthy by Wall Street standards. The best thing about Wolf had been the balanced attention he gave to every aspect of his life. He'd helped Ashlyn make the most dazzling school projects; he had mixed a shockingly cold and delicious martini; he had been a fanatic about the unicycle (which he learned to ride as an undergraduate at Brown) as well as paddleball, tennis, and sailing. He had collected antique sextants and barometers. He had studied astronomy and believed the placement of the stars in the sky could teach man about terrestrial design. Wolf had always been emotionally present in Connie's life, even when he was working on deadline. On days he had to work late—and there had been two or three a month—he sent flowers, or he invited Connie to come to his office for a candlelight dinner of Indian take-out. When Connie went out with her women friends, he always sent wine to the table and the other women cooed about how lucky Connie was.

But where was he now? He had died of brain cancer, and Connie had followed his wish to be cremated and have his ashes scattered off the beach in Tom Nevers. The ashes had broken down, disintegrated; they had become molecules suspended in seawater. The body that Wolf had inhabited, therefore, was gone; it had been absorbed back into the earth. But Connie thought of him as here somewhere, here in this water swirling around her ankles.

Meredith waded to midshin. The water was still too cold for Connie, but Meredith seemed to be enjoying it. The expression on her face fell somewhere between rapture and devastation. She spoke in a voice full of tears, though as the *New York Post* promised, her eyes remained dry.

"I never thought I'd put my feet in the ocean again."

Connie nodded once.

Meredith said, "How do I thank you for this? I have nothing."

Connie hugged Meredith. She was tiny, like a doll. Once, in high school, they had gotten drunk at a party at Villanova, and Connie had carried Meredith home on her back. "I want nothing," Connie said.

That was a lovely little *Beaches* moment down by the water, Connie thought, and it did feel good to have company and it did feel good to have Meredith indebted to her for life, but the magnitude of what Connie had done was now sinking in. Her best friend from childhood was married to the biggest crook the world had ever known. Meredith was *persona non grata* everywhere. She had millions of disapprovers and thousands of enemies. She was "still under investigation." The "still" made it seem like being under investigation was a temporary condition that would be cleared up, but what if it wasn't? What if Meredith was found guilty? What if Meredith *was* guilty?

What have I done? Connie thought. *What have I done?*

Meredith settled into her room—a simple guest room with white wainscoting and a small private bath. Both bedroom and bath were done in pinks, decorated by Connie herself with help from Wolf and the woman at Marine Home Center. The bedroom had French doors that opened onto a tight, Romeo-and-Juliet-type balcony. Meredith said she loved the room.

"My room is down the hall," Connie said. The "room" she was speaking of was the master suite, which comprised the western half of the second floor. There was the bedroom with its California king bed that faced the ocean; there was a bathroom with a deep Jacuzzi tub, glassed-in rainfall shower, dual sinks, water closet, heated tiles in the floor, a wall of mirrors, and a scale that generously dropped a pound or two. There were two enormous closets. (Last summer, Connie had finally taken Wolf's summer clothes to the hospital thrift shop.) And there was Wolf's study, complete with drafting table, framed oceanographic maps, and a telescope that had been positioned to view the most interesting summer constellations. Connie didn't have the emotional strength to show Meredith the master suite, and the fact of the matter was, she hadn't spent a single night in her own bed since Wolf died. Every night she had been on Nantucket, she had fallen asleep, with the aid of two or three chardonnays, on the sofa downstairs— or, when she had houseguests, on the bottom bunk of the third-floor bedroom, which she was pointlessly preserving for future grandchildren.

She didn't want to sleep in the bed without Wolf. The same held true at home. She couldn't explain it. She had read somewhere that the death of a spouse was number one on a list of things that caused stress—and what had she done that morning but invited more stress into her life?

"I have to go to the grocery store," Connie said.

Meredith said, "Would it be all right if I came along?"

Connie watched Meredith bouncing on her toes, as she used to on the end of a diving board.

"Okay," Connie said. "But you have to wear your hat and glasses." Connie was terrified of getting caught. What would happen if someone discovered that Meredith Delinn was *here,* living with *Connie?*

"Hat and glasses," Meredith said.

Connie drove the six miles to Stop & Shop while Meredith made a list on a pad of paper braced against her thigh. Connie's fear subsided and a sense of well-being sneaked up on her, which she normally only experienced after a very good massage and three glasses of chardonnay. She opened the sunroof, and fresh air rushed in as she turned up the radio—Queen, singing "We Are the Champions," the victory song of the Merion Mercy field-hockey team, which she and Meredith had both played on for four years. Connie grinned and Meredith turned her face toward the sun, and the car was a happy place for a moment.

In the store, Connie sent Meredith for whole-wheat tortillas and Greek yogurt while she waited at the deli counter. She sent Meredith for laundry detergent, rubber gloves, and sponges, but then Meredith was gone for so long that Connie panicked. She raced through the store with her cart, dodging the other shoppers and their small children, everyone moving at a snail's pace, drugged by the effects of the sea air and sun. Where was Meredith? Connie was hesitant to call out her name. It was unlikely that she'd left the store, so what was Connie afraid of? She was afraid that Meredith had been handcuffed by FBI agents. Meredith should rightly be in the aisle with the Windex and the paper towels, but she wasn't there, nor was she in the next aisle, nor the next. Connie had only had her old friend back for a matter of hours, and now she was missing. And Connie wasn't even sure that she wanted Meredith to stay—so why was she now panicking that Meredith was gone?

Connie found Meredith standing in the bread aisle, holding a bag of kaiser rolls.

Connie flooded with relief, then thought, *This is ridiculous. I have to get a grip.* "Oh, good," she said. "I thought I'd lost you."

Meredith said, "There was a *USA Today* photographer who staked out the Gristedes by my house, and there was a guy from the *National Enquirer* who frequented the D'Agostino down the street. I couldn't go shopping for eggs. Or toothpaste."

Connie took the rolls from Meredith's hands and dropped them in the cart. "Well, no one's following you here."

"Yet," Meredith said, adjusting her sunglasses.

"Right. Let's not press our luck." Connie headed for the checkout. She was grateful not to know anyone in the store. She and Wolf had made a conscious decision not to engage in Nantucket's social scene. They attended parties and benefits and dinners at home in Washington all year long, and Nantucket was a break from that, although Wolf still had a few friends on Nantucket from summers growing up. His parents and grandparents had belonged to the Nantucket Yacht Club, and once or twice a summer Wolf was called on to sail, or he and Connie were invited to a cocktail party or barbecue in the garden of a friend's ancestral summer cottage. But for the most part, Connie and Wolf kept to themselves. Although she had been coming to Nantucket for over twenty years, Connie often felt anonymous. She knew no one and no one knew her.

As they stood in line, Meredith handed Connie three twenty-dollar bills. "I'd like to chip in for expenses."

Connie considered waving the money away. The television

reporters had made it clear that—unless there was a cache of funds at some offshore bank—Meredith Delinn had been left penniless. "Do what you can," Connie said. "But there's no pressure."

"Okay," Meredith whispered.

On their way back to Tom Nevers, Connie noticed a commotion at the rotary. News vans were clustered in the parking lot of the *Inquirer and Mirror,* the island newspaper. Connie did a double take. *Were* those news vans?

"Get down," Connie said. "Those are reporters." She checked the rearview mirror. "CNN, ABC."

Meredith bent in half; she was as low as the seatbelt would allow. "You're kidding," she said.

"I kid you not."

"I can't believe this," Meredith said. "I can't believe they care where I am. Well, of course they care where I am. Of course the whole world needs to know that I am now summering on Nantucket. So they can make me look bad. So they can make it seem like I'm still living a life of luxury."

"Which you are," Connie said, trying to smile.

"Why couldn't you live someplace awful?" Meredith said. "Why couldn't you live in East Saint Louis? Why couldn't they be reporting that Mrs. Delinn was spending the summer in hot and dangerous East Saint Louis?"

"This isn't funny," Connie said. She checked her rearview mirror. The road behind them was clear. Connie checked again. "Well, guess what. They're not following us."

"They're not?"

Connie motored on. She felt the teensiest bit disappointed. "False alarm, I guess." She tried to think why there would have been TV vans at the rotary, and then she remembered a third- or fourth-tier news story, buried way beneath the sentencing of Freddy Delinn. "Oh, that's right!" she said. "The president is here this weekend!"

Meredith sat up. "You scared me." She was doing some audible

Lamaze breathing to calm herself down, and Connie remembered when Meredith was in the hospital after giving birth to Leo. Connie had taken two-year-old Ashlyn to the hospital to see Meredith and the baby. Freddy had been as proud as a goddamned rooster, handing out expensive (not to mention illegal) Cuban cigars; he'd pushed one on Connie, saying, "Go home and give it to Wolf. He's going to love it." Connie remembered feeling jealous that giving birth had come so easily for Meredith (Connie had slogged through twenty-three hours of labor with Ashlyn and she'd suffered a uterine rupture, which precluded her from having any more children). Meredith had said, "Thank God, Freddy got his boy and the hallowed Delinn name will live on." This had upset Connie; she had felt defensive that Ashlyn was a girl and that there would be no more children to carry on the hallowed Flute name. Feeling bad about this led to resentment that, while Connie had made the trip from Bethesda to New York to see Meredith in the hospital, Meredith hadn't made the reverse trip two years earlier when Ashlyn was born. It was amazing how memories intruded like that. It was amazing how Connie's mind held the good and the bad of every interaction, swirled together like children's paints. Meredith might only remember happiness that Connie had come, or recall the cute outfit that Connie had brought. When Meredith thought of Leo being born, she might only think, *Leo is under investigation.*

Connie turned into her driveway and parked in front of the house. Meredith scrambled to get the groceries out of the car.

"You go in and relax," Meredith said. "I'll get these."

Connie laughed. "You're not an indentured servant," she said. "But thank you for the help."

She flashed back to that day at the hospital. Meredith had allowed Ashlyn to hold her hours-old infant, even though the head nurse strongly advised against it. *It'll be fine!* Meredith had said. *Connie and I will be right here.* Meredith had snapped the pictures herself. She'd had one framed and sent it to Connie. And then, of course, she'd asked Connie to be Leo's godmother.

"It's nice to have someone else around," Connie said.

"Even me?" Meredith said.

"Even you," Connie said.

MEREDITH

At ten minutes to five, Meredith couldn't put it off any longer: she had to call her attorneys and give them her coordinates. She was still under investigation. She wasn't allowed to leave the country; the Feds had her passport. Burt and Dev needed to know where she was.

She sat on her bed and turned on her cell phone. This had become a suspenseful moment in Meredith's daily routine: Had anyone called her? Had anyone texted her? Would Carver and Leo break the rules and text her the *I love you* that she so desperately needed? Had any of Meredith's former friends found enough compassion in their hearts to reach out? Would she hear from Samantha? Had Burt or Dev called? Did they have good news or bad news? How bad was the bad news? Would this be the moment when Meredith received the worst news? Indeed, the reason Meredith kept her phone turned off was to limit the torture to this one moment, instead of living with it all day long.

There were no messages and no texts. This presented its own kind of misery.

She dialed the law firm and said a Hail Mary, which was what she always did when she dialed the law firm. She could hear the sounds of Connie making dinner downstairs.

Meredith had thought she might feel safer on Nantucket, but she was plagued by a low-grade terror. Nantucket was an *island,* thirty miles out to sea. What if she needed to escape? There would be no hopping in a cab uptown or downtown or across the bridge or through the tunnel into New Jersey. There would be no high-tailing it to Connecticut if Leo or Carver needed her. She felt both exiled and trapped.

Meredith had $46,000 of her own money. This was the savings that she'd tucked away in a CD earning 1.5 percent, from her teaching job in the 1980s. (Freddy had ridiculed her for this. *Let me invest it,* he'd said. *I'll double it in six months.*) But Meredith had kept rolling over the money in that CD for no reason other than personal pride—and how relieved she was now! She had something to live on, actual legitimate money that she'd earned and banked. Forty-six thousand dollars would seem a fortune to many people, she knew, but to her it felt like a pittance. She had run through that much in an afternoon of antiques shopping. *Disgusting!* she thought as the phone rang. *How had she become that person?*

The receptionist answered.

"May I speak with Burton Penn, please?" Meredith asked.

"May I ask who's calling?" the receptionist said.

Meredith cringed. She hated identifying herself. "Meredith Delinn."

The receptionist didn't respond. The receptionist never responded, though Meredith had called and spoken to this self-same receptionist dozens of times.

The phone rang. Although Meredith had asked for Burt, the person who answered the phone was Dev.

"Hi Dev," Meredith said. "It's Meredith."

"Thank God," Dev said. "I was just about to call your cell. Where are you?"

"I'm on Nantucket," Meredith said.

"Nantucket?" Dev said, "What are you doing on Nantucket?"

"I'm with a friend," Meredith said.

Dev made a noise of surprise. Clearly, he had been under the impression that Meredith didn't have any friends. And he was right. But Meredith had Connie. Was Connie her friend? Connie was something; Meredith wasn't sure what.

"What's the address there?" Dev asked.

"I have no idea."

"Phone number? Please, Meredith, give me *something.* The Feds want us to have contact information for you on the ground."

Meredith had written down the phone number at the house. She recited it to Dev.

He said, "First things first. I'm glad you're safe." Meredith smiled. Dev was one person, aside from her sons, who didn't want to see her jump off the George Washington Bridge. Her other attorney, Burt, would never have expressed this kind of sentiment. Burt didn't dislike Meredith, but he was detached. She was a case, a legal problem. She was work.

Dev said, "I heard from Warden Carmell at the MCC, and he said Mr. Delinn was shipped out on the bus at noon. Ten hours down to Butner. He's due to arrive tonight."

Meredith closed her eyes. When her attorneys had called her to tell her Freddy had been given the maximum sentence, Meredith hadn't been sure what they meant. She had turned on the TV and saw Freddy being led out of the courtroom in his light-gray suit, which no longer fit. The banner across the bottom of the screen read: *Delinn sentenced to 150 years.* Meredith had run for the kitchen sink, where she vomited up the half cup of tea she'd managed to ingest that morning. She heard a noise and she thought it was the TV, but it was the phone. She'd dropped the phone on the ground, and Burt was calling out, "Meredith, are you there? Hello? Hello?" Meredith hung up the phone and shut off the TV. She was done.

She had gone into her bedroom and fallen back onto her king-size bed. She had sixteen hours until federal marshals came to escort her from her home and she would have to give up the sheets, which were as crisp as paper, the luscious silk quilt, the sumptuous down-filled duvet.

One hundred and fifty years.

Meredith had understood then that Freddy had taken her hand

at the edge of a giant hole, and he had asked her to jump with him, and she had agreed. She'd jumped without knowing how deep the hole was or what would happen when they hit the bottom.

"Okay," Meredith said to Dev now, although obviously the fact that Freddy was going to prison for two or three lifetimes wasn't okay. She was so angry with Freddy that she wanted to rip her hair out, but the thought of him on that bus crushed her.

"The sticking point with your investigation..."

"I know the sticking point."

"They can't seem to get past it," Dev said. "Do you have anything to add?"

"Nothing to add," Meredith said.

"Anything to amend?"

"Nothing to amend."

"You know how bad it looks?" Dev said. "Fifteen million dollars is a lot of money, Meredith."

"I have nothing to add or amend," Meredith said. "I told it all in my deposition. Do they think I *lied* in my deposition?"

"They think you lied in your deposition," Dev said. "Lots of people do."

"Well, I didn't," Meredith said.

"Okay," Dev said, but he didn't sound convinced. "If you think of anything you want to add or amend, just call. Otherwise, we'll be in touch."

"What about Leo?" Meredith said. "Please tell me about Leo."

"I didn't hear from Julie today," Dev said. Julie Schwarz was Leo's attorney. It was her job, now, to help federal investigators find Mrs. Misurelli, and to prove that Deacon Rapp was lying. "And days that I don't hear from Julie are good days, much as I love her. It just means there's no news. And as they say, no news is..."

"Right," Meredith said. She wasn't going to utter the words "good news." Not until she and Leo and Carver were free and clear. And together.

Goddamn you, Freddy! she thought (zillionth and first).

A voice rang out from downstairs: it was Connie, calling her for dinner.

They sat at a round teak table on the deck and gazed out at the indifferent ocean. The ocean didn't care whether mankind lived or died or cheated or stole; it just kept rolling and tumbling over itself, encroaching, then receding.

Connie had poured herself a glass of wine. She said, "Meredith, do you want wine?"

"Do you have any red?"

"Of course I have red," Connie said, standing up.

"No, wait. I don't want it," Meredith said. The chicken was cooking on the grill, and it smelled far more delicious than anything Meredith had eaten in months. Meredith would have loved a glass of red to go with the chicken and the fresh, delicious salad that they were now eating—Connie had whipped up the vinaigrette while Meredith looked on, astonished—but drinking a glass of red wine would put Meredith right back at her usual table at Rinaldo's, next to Freddy.

"You're sure?"

"I'm sure." Meredith squinted out at the water. She saw a sleek, black head out about twenty yards. "Do you have seals?"

"That's Harold," Connie said. "Our seal. He's always here."

Meredith watched Harold swim through the breaking waves, then she noticed Connie's downcast eyes.

"Are you okay?" Meredith asked.

Connie took a sip of her wine and nodded, but her eyes were shining. *Our seal:* she was thinking about Wolf. Meredith wanted to take Connie's hand, but she wasn't sure how that kind of gesture would be received.

Connie sniffed. "Tell me something."

"What?" Meredith said.

"I don't know. Anything," Connie said. "We have to start somewhere."

Instinctively, Meredith checked her wrist. For her birthday in October, Freddy had given her a tiger-striped Cartier watch, but Meredith had been required to leave behind any personal effects purchased in the past twelve months worth more than three hundred dollars. She said, "Well, as we speak, Freddy is on the bus for Butner. He'll get there at ten o'clock tonight."

"Jesus," Connie said.

"What he did was awful," Meredith said. She swallowed, and wished for that wine, but she took a sip of ice water instead. Her glass of ice water had a paper-thin slice of lemon in it. Things at Connie's house were nice like that. What had Meredith done to deserve this? Freddy was, at that very moment, on some bus to North Carolina, his hands and feet shackled in heavy iron cuffs. The bus driver probably stopped for bathroom breaks every four hours or so. If Freddy couldn't hold it, he would wet himself, and the other prisoners would love that. Meredith tensed with worry, as she might have for one of her children. Freddy suffered from a weak bladder. Recently, Meredith wondered if this had been a side effect from carrying around so much stress, fear, and guilt. Maybe now that he'd confessed, his bladder was sturdier. "I went to see him in jail."

"I know," Connie said. "I saw it on TV. I mean, I saw you headed down there."

"It was a disaster," Meredith said. "In retrospect, I shouldn't have gone. But I wanted to see him."

After the police hauled Freddy away on the afternoon of December 8, Meredith had found herself thinking of him in the past tense, as though he were dead—but he was alive, only a few miles away at the Metropolitan Correctional Center, which was connected to the federal courthouse by an underground tunnel. Meredith could go visit him. But should she? As the weeks passed, she went back and forth on this question. Absolutely not. But yes, she had to; there were so many things to ask. She wasn't sure how it would look to the rest of the world. She couldn't decide. She asked her attorneys.

"Should I go see Freddy in jail?" she said. "Or should I follow my sons' example and cut him out of my life?"

They stumbled over each other trying to answer. Dev, she could tell, wanted her to forsake the old man. *What can he do for you now? He's ruined you along with everyone else.* Burt, on the other hand, was more orthodox.

"I'm not your publicist," Burt said. "I'm your attorney. So it's my job to tell you that you have a legal right to visit your husband." He handed her a sheet of paper. "Visiting hours are Mondays between nine and eleven. The visit can last up to an hour."

"Can I bring him anything? What does he need?"

Burt cleared his throat. "They're pretty strict about what will make it through security down there." The way he said this sounded vague. It sounded as if there were pages and pages of regulations, but Burt had yet to grow familiar with them. Had Burt ever *had* a client in jail before? Meredith wouldn't embarrass him by asking point-blank. "Quarters are good."

"Quarters?"

"Rolls of quarters," Burt said. "For the vending machines."

"For the vending machines," Meredith repeated. She thought about Freddy selecting a bag of Doritos or a package of Twinkies from a vending machine, and a part of her died. But what did she think he was eating in there? Salad caprese?

She decided not to go. The only way she could ever hope to save herself was to do what her children had done: denounce Freddy and the life they'd led together. When Leo and Carver found out about Freddy's crimes, they had roared in anger, and Freddy sat impassively, offering them nothing to combat the fact that they were the sons of a thief and a pathological liar. They had stormed out of the apartment, and Meredith understood now, though she hadn't at the time, that the boys had expected her to go with them. But she had stayed by Freddy's side, because that was where her rut had been dug for the past thirty years. She couldn't leave Freddy until this was figured out. Leo had said, *What precisely do you need to figure out, Mom? Dad is a thief. He's a criminal! He has committed financial genocide!* Carver said, *We're changing our name. You should, too.*

Meredith knew she should make a statement, do an interview with Barbara Walters, if Barbara would have her. Explain the truth as she understood it, even though nobody on God's green earth would believe her.

Weeks passed, then months. Meredith stuck to her resolve. Don't think about Freddy. Pretend Freddy is dead. But as the evidence materialized against her, and then against Leo, Meredith realized her best hope lay in going to see him. She needed answers. There was the matter of the money: The money the Feds knew about, and the money they didn't. He had to give it back—all of it. He understood this, right? How long had the Ponzi scheme been going on? Since the beginning? Had Delinn Enterprises *ever* been fully legitimate? Wasn't there some way to prove that Leo was innocent, that Deacon Rapp was lying about Leo? Couldn't Freddy give up the names of the people who had conspired with him in order to save his son? Meredith started scribbling out a list of questions. She had eighty-four. Eighty-four questions that required answers, including a question about why Freddy had been touching Samantha's back that day.

To the jail, Meredith had worn jeans and a white button-down shirt and suede flats and her trench coat, and she carried a clutch purse with two rolls of quarters inside. Her hair hadn't been colored in months, and there had been no trips to Palm Beach, so she was graying and her skin was the color of paste. She wore no makeup—she couldn't insult the American public by bothering with mascara—although she knew that by not prettying herself, she would invite the press to comment on how worn-out she looked. Well, she *was* worn-out. The mob of photographers and reporters was waiting for her, snapping pictures, sticking microphones in her face, but Burt and Dev were there to fend them off and hail her a cab.

Later, she would wish she'd stayed in the relative safety of her apartment.

There had been a terrific wait to get in to see Freddy, during which Meredith experienced thirty-one flavors of anxiety. Burt and Dev were with her—together, they were costing her nine hundred dollars an hour, though how she would ever pay them, she had no idea. Burt checked his BlackBerry with a compulsivity that unsettled Meredith. Dev paged restlessly through an outdated *National Geographic* from the sad, wobbly lounge table that was scarred with other people's initials. He then set the magazine down and studied the other denizens of the waiting room—the men and women who looked even more hopeless and lost than Meredith felt—as though he were going to put them in a novel. They didn't speak until Meredith was called to go through security, when both Burt and Dev wished her luck. They weren't going in with her. Security was another long and arduous process where Meredith and her clutch and trench coat were subjected to scrutiny. Meredith was patted down—roughly—by a female officer twice her size. The woman did everything but pick Meredith up, turn her upside down, and shake her. She didn't say so, but she must have recognized Meredith and felt the predictable contempt. At the end, she shoved Meredith, just for fun.

Meredith didn't protest. She was too nervous to protest because she was being escorted through locked doors and down long, stark hallways, to see Freddy. Meredith had promised herself she wouldn't break down. She would fight off sentimentality and longing. She would simply ask Freddy the questions she needed the answers to, maybe not all eighty-four—there wouldn't be time for that—but the top two or three: Where was the rest of the money? What could they do to clear Leo's name? How could she prove to the world she was innocent? At this point, Freddy was the only person who could help her.

When she finally did see Freddy, she lost her legs. The guard had her firmly by the arm and kept her upright.

Freddy! A voice inside her head was echoing down a long tunnel.

He was wearing an orange jumpsuit, just like the prisoners they'd seen on countless reruns of *Law & Order;* his hands were cuffed behind his back. His hair, which had been salt-and-pepper curls, was shaved down to the scalp, and nearly white. He was fifty-two; he looked seventy-five. But it was him just the same, the boy who had accosted her in the stacks of the Princeton book-store. They had been enrolled in the same anthropology course, and Meredith had picked up the last used textbook, thinking she would save her parents some money. Freddy had begged her for it. He'd said, *I can't afford a new textbook, so if you buy that one, I'll have to go without, and if I go without, I'll fail the course. You don't want me to fail the course, do you?* And she'd said, *Who are you?* And he'd said, *I'm Freddy Delinn. Who are you?*

She'd told him her name was Meredith Martin.

He said, *You're very pretty, Meredith Martin, but that's not why I'm asking you for the book. I'm asking you because I'm here on six different scholarships, my mother works at a bottling plant during the day and at Kmart as a cashier at night, and I need that used book.*

Meredith had nodded, taken aback by his candor. Growing up on the Main Line, she had never heard anyone admit to poverty before. She liked his black hair and blue eyes and his pale, smooth skin. She would have mistaken him for just another beautiful, ass-holish upperclassman had it not been for his humility, which pierced her. Meredith had found him instantly intriguing. And he had called her pretty! Toby had broken up with Meredith only a few months earlier, and he had so decimated her self-esteem that she'd been certain no one would ever call her "pretty" again.

She handed Freddy the used book and took a new book, at more than double the price, for herself.

This entire memory was encapsulated in a single moment as she looked at Freddy. Meredith thought, *I never should have given him that book. I should have said, "Tough luck," and walked away.*

The warden released Freddy's wrists from the cuffs so he could talk to Meredith on the phone.

Meredith found herself unable to speak. She didn't pick up the phone and neither did he. He had always believed that Meredith was smarter than he was—true—that she was classier, better bred, more refined. He had always treated her like a rare, one-of-a-kind treasure; he had lived in awe of her. Deep in her heart, she worried—God, how she worried—that he had started all of this as a way to impress her.

She picked up the phone. "Fred."

The guard standing behind Freddy helped him pick up the phone and put it to his ear.

"Fred, it's Meredith." Saying this made her feel idiotic, but she wasn't sure he recognized her. She had pictured him crying, apologizing; she had, at the very least, pictured him expressing his undying love.

He regarded her coolly. She tried to get the guard's attention to ask "Is he okay?" but the guard was staring off into middle space, perhaps willfully, and Meredith couldn't snag him.

"Fred," Meredith said. "I need you to listen to me. I'm in trouble and Leo's in trouble. They're trying to get me on a conspiracy charge." She swallowed. "They think I *knew* about it!" Freddy seemed to be listening, but he didn't respond. "And they think Leo was working with you on the seventeenth floor. Someone named Deacon Rapp told them this." Meredith watched Freddy's face for a flicker of recognition or interest. "Where is the rest of the money, Fred?" She had the list of eighty-four questions in her clutch purse—no one from security had even bothered to look at it—but if he could just tell her this one thing, then she could turn the information over to the Feds, and maybe that would get them off the hook. Even if there wasn't very much left—a few billion or hundreds of millions—to give the Feds this information would help her and Leo. There would be no helping Freddy at this point. "Please tell me where the rest of the money is. An offshore account? Switzerland? The Middle East? It does nobody any good hidden, Freddy."

Freddy removed the receiver from his ear and looked at it like it was something he might eat. Then he set the receiver down on the counter in front of him.

She said, "Freddy, wait! They're going to prosecute me. They're going to prosecute Leo. Our son." Maybe Freddy didn't care about Meredith; she had to acknowledge the possibility that, along with lying about everything else, he had been lying about his devotion to her. But he would never knowingly allow Leo to go to prison.

He stared at her. The Plexiglas between them reminded Meredith of being at the zoo. Freddy was watching her like she was some curious specimen of wildlife.

She tried another tack. "I brought you quarters," she said. "For the vending machines." She held up the quarters, the only thing she had to bargain with.

He tilted his head but said nothing.

"He had no intention of talking to me," Meredith said to Connie. "He wasn't going to explain himself, he wasn't going to give me any answers. He wasn't going to give me anything. He didn't care if I went to prison. He didn't care if Leo went to prison."

Connie said, "He's a bastard, Meredith."

Meredith nodded. She had heard people say this again and again. Her attorneys had said it. Even Freddy's attorney, Richard Cassel, had said it to Meredith, out in the hallway before Meredith's deposition: *You knew he was a bastard when you married him.* But it wasn't that easy. Freddy had been many things during the thirty years of their marriage and a bastard wasn't one of them. Freddy was smart and charming and driven to succeed like nobody Meredith had ever known. And he had made it clear that Meredith was part of his success. How many times had he said it? She was his winning lottery ticket. Without her, he was nothing. She, in turn, had done what any devoted wife would do: she had defended him.

He had returns of 29 percent in good years. Meredith reminded people that he had been the star of the economics department at Princeton. He delivered returns of 8 percent in down years, and people were even happier. Meredith said, "Freddy's got the magic. He understands the stock market like nobody else."

But those who weren't invited to invest with Delinn Enterprises had been jealous, then suspicious. He's lying. He's cheating. He's breaking the law. He's got to be; you just can't deliver returns like that in this economy. Although it was difficult, Meredith learned to snub these people. She took them off the lists of the benefits she was chairing; she had them blackballed from clubs. These actions, now, seemed abominable, but at the time, she had only been defending her husband.

Was Freddy a bastard? Yes—God, yes! Meredith knew it now but didn't understand it. She didn't understand how she had lived with the man for thirty years without knowing him. He had always been generous to a fault; he made good things happen for people. He called the dean of admissions at Princeton to get his secretary's son off the waiting list. He gave a pregnant woman his seat in first class, while he took her seat in coach—on a transatlantic flight! He sent Meredith's mother orchids every year on her birthday without a reminder from Meredith. Was he a bastard? Yes, but he had hidden it well. And that was part of the allure of Freddy Delinn—he came across as mysterious and unknowable. What was it Freddy was hiding in the deep recesses of his mind, behind his kind and generous facade?

Now, of course, Meredith knew. Everyone knew.

Things at the jail had ended badly. Freddy didn't say a single word. He stood up and offered his wrists to the guard like a well-trained monkey—and the guard, without so much as a glance at Meredith, shackled him back up.

"Wait!" Meredith said. She jumped up abruptly, knocking her chair over, and she slapped her palms against the Plexiglas.

"Freddy, wait! Don't leave. Don't you dare leave!" She felt a force on her arms, the guards grabbed her, and she struggled to break free. She shouted, "They're going to throw us in jail, Fred! Your family! You have to fix this! You have to tell them we're innocent!" The guard had her bent over in a half nelson. She screamed. "Freddy! Goddamn it, Fred, tell them!"

The guard led Freddy away. It was no use; there was no getting him back. He was going to let them drown. Meredith's body went limp in the guard's grip; she clapped her mouth shut. She had never, ever raised her voice in public. She thought, *He's drugged.* Or they'd given him a lobotomy or shock treatment. He'd been sitting right there, but he hadn't been himself. He would never willfully let his wife and son go to the gallows.

Would he?

As Meredith was led back down the depressing hallways from whence she'd come, she had to admit: she didn't know.

"So you still haven't spoken to him?" Connie said. "You haven't gotten any answers?"

"No answers," Meredith said. "My attorneys told me that Freddy has stopped speaking altogether. They're diagnosing it as a type of post-traumatic stress disorder."

"Give me a break," Connie said. "Freddy?"

It seemed unlikely. Freddy was tough. He had come from nothing. His father had left the family when Fred was in diapers, then Fred lost his only brother, but he had shored himself up. He didn't believe in things like PTSD. He was a pull-yourself-up-by-your-bootstraps kind of guy. He was a nothing's-gonna-happen-until-you-make-it-happen kind of guy. He had been so hard on the boys, Meredith remembered; they'd had to earn Fred's respect. There were no excuses for bad grades or bad behavior or a missed fly ball. There were no excuses if they forgot a "please" or a "thank you," or if they neglected to hold the door for their mother. *You kids have it so much easier than I had it. You don't even know. You don't know a thing.*

Burt and Dev had confirmed with prison officials that Freddy Delinn had completely shut down. He was spending time in psych, but they couldn't make him talk. He spoke to no one.

"Sometimes prisoners use this as a form of control over their captors," Burt said. "He's like that Indian in *One Flew Over the Cuckoo's Nest*."

So he was being willfully mute, Meredith thought. Which should not be confused with PTSD. He was pulling a Chief Bromden. Had Freddy even read *Cuckoo's Nest*?

"I don't know what to do," Meredith said to Connie. "Freddy is the only one who can save me, and he won't do it."

"Forget Freddy," Connie said. "You're going to have to save yourself."

That night, Meredith didn't sleep. *Goddamn you, Freddy,* she thought (zillionth and second). But she was sick with worry about him. By now, he would be getting adjusted to the horrors of his new, incredibly permanent home. What did it look like? What did it smell like? What did they feed him? Where did he go to the bathroom? Where did he shower?

And how were the boys? Meredith had seen some of the houses that Carver renovated—he favored glorious old Victorians in sad, sagging disrepair. He yanked out carpet and sanded down the long-hidden wood floors beneath. He drove around to architectural salvage places looking for glass doorknobs and stained glass windows. In Meredith's imagination, the boys were living in such a house; it smelled like polyurethane; every surface was coated with sawdust. Carver hung doors while Leo lay across a high-backed sofa, talking to Julie Schwarz on the phone. Meredith knew the Feds had seized his computer and were trying to back up Deacon Rapp's claims and link Leo to the bandits on the seventeenth floor. The Feds were still trying to track down Mrs. Misurelli in Italy so they could depose her. She, apparently, had been the gatekeeper upstairs. In this case, being "under investigation"

for Leo was a lot of sit around and wait. Maybe in his spare time—
and there would now be much of it—Leo helped Carver paint
bedrooms or shingle the roof or repoint the brickwork of the eight
fireplaces. Meredith was certain Anais was around; she had
remained steadfast. She would cook her famous veggie enchiladas
for Leo and Carver, and she would grow jealous about how much
time Leo was spending on the phone with Julie Schwarz.

Meredith was okay picturing the boys like this, although Leo was
a worrier and she knew he'd be having night sweats. For years when
he was a child, Leo had wandered into Meredith and Freddy's bedroom, afraid of the dark. He had a recurring dream about a scary
pelican. Now the scary pelican was real: It was Deacon Rapp, it was
the FBI, it was Freddy. Meredith couldn't stop the unbidden flashes
of Leo in prison, his head shaved, the other men coming after him
day and night with their sick desires. Leo was only twenty-six.

Fear gripped her like hands around the neck, the way it could
only happen in an unfamiliar room in the pitch black of night.
Take me if you must, Meredith thought. *But do not take my son.*

Connie had been right about one thing: Meredith was going to
have to save them herself.

But how? How?

In the morning, Connie said, "I'm going to the Sconset Market for
some muffins and the newspaper. And I'm going to the package
store for a case of wine."

Meredith nodded and tried not to seem like an eager, panting
dog. *Don't leave me here alone,* she thought. *Please.*

"I know you want to come with me," Connie said. "But Sconset
is a tiny village, and everyone who summers there has summered
there forever. Strangers are scrutinized. Someone will ask you
who you are, guaranteed. The Sconset Market is microscopic. So
you're going to have to stay here. We don't want anyone..."

"Right," Meredith whispered. "I know."

"I won't be gone long," Connie said.

*   *   *

Meredith took an old book-club selection of Connie's out onto the deck. She would read in the sun; this was what people did in the summertime. This was what Meredith had done for days on end all those years in Southampton. She had read by her pool, walked to the ocean, swam with the boys and watched them surf; she had pitched the Wiffle ball to them and chased after their grounders. She had thrown the Frisbee to the dog. She had cut flowers from the garden and had given instructions to their housekeeper, Louisa. She had invited people for dinner, and made reservations at Nick and Toni's, and dealt with the details of the various fundraisers she was chairing. Her life had been disgustingly easy; it had, in so many ways, been beneath her. *Brilliant and talented,* her father used to say. And yet, what had she done with it?

Goddamn you, Freddy, she thought (zillionth and third). She tried to concentrate on the words on the page of her book—it was about a woman in a small town who is murdered—but Meredith's mind was squawking. She lived with a bullhorn in her head, loudly announcing and reannouncing her fears; it was the internal soundtrack of extreme anxiety. There was medication for it, perhaps. Meredith wondered if Connie had anything. She didn't want to snoop, but a few minutes after Connie left the house, Meredith padded upstairs to the master suite. She just wanted to see it.

The door that led to the suite was closed tight, and Meredith wouldn't have been surprised or insulted if the door had been locked. After all, Connie was now rooming with the wife of the biggest crook in history. But the door was open, and Meredith tiptoed through the rooms. The bedroom had an arresting view of the ocean, and the bed was made up with Frette linens (Meredith checked, she couldn't help herself, though she knew she shouldn't care about things like thread count anymore). The closets were roomy. Wolf's closet was completely empty except for some padded hangers and a thick, nubby fisherman's sweater folded on the dresser. Meredith touched the sweater, then felt she had, somehow, crossed a line. She didn't look in Connie's closet, though she would have liked to—even as a schoolgirl, Connie had had a flair for fashion. However, Meredith couldn't help from peeking in the master bath—and that was when she saw the prescription bottles. There were four or five of them, and Meredith was sure that one of those prescriptions would help her. She eyed the brown bottles for a long, hot moment, then she made herself retrace her steps and leave the suite, shutting the door behind her.

She wondered if it was a bad thing that Connie had brought her to this beautiful house where she had nothing to do but think. If she had been scrounging half-eaten Big Macs out of a Dumpster, consumed with worry about her daily survival, she wouldn't have this much time to think.

And that might have been better.

Back on the deck, Meredith tried to read. The woman in her novel was worse off than she was; she had been murdered in the woods. The mother of that woman was worse off than she was. But then Meredith realized she *was* that woman. If Leo went to prison, he would be raped, beaten, and eventually killed. She was sure of it. But she had to stop thinking like this. The bullhorn blared in her head. Freddy was in Butner for all eternity. Meredith was here. How had she gotten here?

Before Meredith graduated from high school and attended Princeton and fatefully met Freddy Delinn in the stacks of the campus bookstore, there had been one presiding fact in Meredith's life, and that was that she loved her parents. She had loved her mother, Deidre, certainly, but she had been especially devoted to her father.

Meredith's father's name was Charles Robert Martin, but everybody called him Chick. Chick Martin was a respected lawyer in the downtown Philadelphia firm of Saul, Ewing, Remick, and Saul; he worked on the thirty-eighth floor of the high-rise known throughout the city as the "clothespin building," because of the Claes Oldenburg sculpture out front. Chick specialized in the laws of arbitrage, and although Meredith loved her father to distraction, she had never learned exactly what arbitrage was. (Fred had claimed to understand arbitrage inside out, but it was safe to say he had been bluffing about that.) The way her father explained it, he had very specialized knowledge about a certain portion of the tax code, and his law partners came to him with intricate and tricky questions that he would, after hours of research, produce the answers to.

Chick Martin made a handsome salary. The Martins had an impressive home in Villanova with white columns and black shutters and a wide green lawn in front and back. Inside the house, there were beautiful crown moldings, five working fireplaces, a butler's pantry, and a dumbwaiter that ran from the kitchen to the basement.

Chick Martin was a golfer—the family belonged to the Aronimink Country Club—and a rabid Philadelphia sports fan. He had season tickets to the Eagles, and he would very often be given box seats to see the Phillies at the Vet, or the Flyers or Sixers at the Spectrum. He once took Meredith to a car dealership to shake hands with Dr. J, and the two things that Meredith remembered about that event were that Dr. J's hand was so large it spread halfway up her forearm, and Chick Martin, whom Meredith had believed was the most important man in Philadelphia, had been rendered speechless by the presence of Julius Erving. Meredith had wanted to intervene on her father's behalf and tell Dr. J that her father was a tax attorney who specialized in the difficult, mysterious world of arbitrage, and that it should be Dr. J who was in awe of Chick Martin and not the other way around. Her father had brought a basketball for Dr. J to sign, which he had, in a sprawling script without even really paying attention, but Meredith's father was delighted. He mounted it on a pedestal in his office.

Chick Martin was a guy's guy. There were always other men

around the house at night and on the weekends—other attorneys and executives and business owners who played golf with Chick, or who accepted tickets to the Eagles, or who came over to the house on the last Thursday of every month for poker. Poker in the Martin household was a sacred affair that occurred in the game room and involved cigar smoking and subs delivered from Minella's Diner. On poker nights, Meredith's mother read in her bedroom with the door closed, and Meredith was supposed to do her homework upstairs and go straight to bed. Meredith always broke this rule. She wandered down to the game room, and her father would let her sit on his lap and munch on the dill pickle that accompanied his eggplant parm sub, while he played his hand. When she got older, he pulled up a chair for her and taught her how to read the cards.

The other men accepted Meredith's presence in the room, though she could tell they didn't love it, so she never stayed for more than three hands, and she never asked to play.

Once, when she was just out of the room, the door closing behind her, she heard Mr. Lewis, who was an estate attorney for Blank, Rome, say, "That's a good-looking daughter you got there, Chick."

And Meredith's father said, "Watch your mouth."

And George Wayne, who was a big shot at PSFS and a descendant of General Anthony Wayne, said, "Do you ever wish you'd had a boy, Chickie?"

And Meredith's father said, "Hell, no. I wouldn't trade Meredith in for a hundred boys. That girl is perfection. That girl owns my heart."

Hearing her father speak those words confirmed what Meredith already knew: she was safe. Her father's love was both a cocoon and a rabbit's foot. She would live a happy life.

And, indeed, she did. Her grades were excellent, and she was a natural athlete: she played field hockey and lacrosse, and she was a champion diver. As a diver, she made it to the finals in State College her junior and senior years; in her senior year, she placed third. She'd had interest from Big Ten schools, but she didn't want to carry the burden that a Division I athletic scholarship entailed. She wanted to be well rounded. She edited the yearbook and was a lector during morning chapel. She was *that girl* at Merion Mercy, the girl everyone admired and talked about with near-embarrassing praise.

Meredith was safe, too, because she'd had a best friend since the beginning of time, and that friend was Constance O'Brien. They met at preschool at Tarleton, although Meredith didn't actually remember *meeting* Connie. By the time their synapses connected time and circumstance in a meaningful way, they had already been friends for years, and so it seemed to both girls that they had always been together. They grew up a half mile from each other in the same kind of house, which is to say, Catholic, upper-middle class, civilized but not snobbish. The only difference between the two homes was that Connie's mother, Veronica, drank. And the way Meredith knew that Veronica O'Brien drank was because her own parents talked about it: Veronica went to the Mastersons' party, picked a fight with her husband, Bill, and battled it out with him on the front lawn. Veronica fell down and bruised her hip. She forgot to pay the neighborhood babysitter so many times that the babysitter refused to work there anymore. When Meredith was older, she heard about Veronica O'Brien's drinking from Connie. Her mother left a bottle of vodka in the second fridge in the garage and did three shots before Bill O'Brien came home from work. Veronica committed minor offenses like throwing away Connie's paper on Mark Twain, and major offenses like setting the kitchen drapes on fire. Connie and Toby had learned to keep their friends out of the house. But they took advantage of the money and the freedom their mother bestowed on them while drinking, and when they reached a certain age, they burgled their mother's wine and vodka and gin and drank it themselves.

Veronica O'Brien's drinking—though it did manifest itself in more insidious ways eventually—did little to hamper Meredith and Connie's childhood happiness together. They were twins, sisters, soul mates. As they got older, however, the peace was harder to keep. They were growing and changing; things grew nuanced. There was one twenty-four-hour period when Meredith and Connie didn't speak. This was right after Meredith told Connie that she, Meredith, had kissed Connie's brother, Toby, on the way home from Wendy Thurber's late-night pool party.

Meredith had dutifully reported every detail to Connie by 8 a.m., just as she would have if Toby had been any other boy—but this time, Connie was disgusted. Meredith and Toby? It was appalling.

Meredith had felt ashamed and confused. She had expected Connie to be happy. But Connie slammed the phone down on Meredith, and when Meredith called back, the phone rang and rang. Meredith kept calling until Veronica answered and pleasantly and soberly explained that Connie didn't want to talk right that second. Meredith should call back later, after Connie had had a chance to calm down.

Meredith was stunned. She hung up the phone and looked out her bedroom window down the street toward Connie's house. She would forfeit Toby, then. She would give him up. It wasn't worth ruining her friendship with Connie.

But here, Meredith faltered. She was a hostage to her feelings and, stronger still, her hormones. She had known Toby O'Brien just as long as she had known Connie, essentially her entire life. They had thrown water balloons at each other in the O'Briens' backyard on hot afternoons, and they had watched horror movies side by side in the O'Briens' shag-carpeted den, eating Jiffy Pop and Jax cheese doodles. Whenever they went somewhere in the O'Briens' Ford Country Squire—to Shakey's for pizza or to the King of Prussia Mall or downtown to Wanamaker's to see the light show at Christmas—Connie, Meredith, and Toby had sat three across in the backseat, and sometimes Meredith's and Toby's knees had knocked, but it had never meant a thing.

How to explain what happened? It was like a switch had flipped and in an instant the world had changed, there in the deep end of Wendy Thurber's pool. There had been a bunch of kids at the party—Wendy, Wendy's brother Hank, Matt Klein, whom Connie was dating (though secretly, because Matt was Jewish and Connie feared her parents would object), Connie, Toby, Meredith, a girl from the field-hockey team named Nadine Dexter, who was chunky and a little butch, and Wendy's runty next-door neighbor Caleb Burns. There was the usual splashing and roughhousing and dunking; all of the kids were in the pool except for Connie, who claimed the water was too cold. She lounged in a chaise wearing her petal-pink Lilly Pulitzer cover-up, and she braided and rebraided her strawberry-blond hair. Meredith impressed everyone with her dives. She had just perfected her front one and half somersault with one and half twists, which was a crowd pleaser.

As the party was starting to wind down, Meredith encountered Toby in the deep end. He had, as a joke, pulled at the string of her bikini top, the top had come loose, and her newly formed breasts— so new they were tender to the touch—were set free, bobbing for a second in the chlorinated water. Meredith yelped and struggled to retie her top while treading water. Toby laughed wickedly. He swam up behind her and grabbed her, and she could feel his erection against her backside, though it took a second to figure out what was happening. Her mind was racing, reconciling what she had learned in health class, what she had read in Judy Blume novels, and the fact that Toby was a seventeen-year-old boy who might just be turned on by her newly formed breasts. Immediately, there was a surge of arousal. In that instant, Meredith became a sexual being. She felt momentarily sorry for her father and her mother, because she was lost to them forever. There was, she understood, no going back.

Connie left the party with Matt Klein. They were off to make out and push at the boundaries of Connie's virginity, though Connie had said she was determined to stay chaste until her sixteenth birthday. Connie talked about her sex life all the time, and up to that point, Meredith had bobbed her head at what felt like the appropriate moments, not having a clue what Connie was talking about but not wanting to admit it. Now, suddenly, she *got* it. Desire.

She dried off and put her shorts and T-shirt back on, then a sweatshirt because it was nighttime and chilly. She took a chip off the snack table but refrained from the onion dip. Caleb Burns's mother called out from next door that it was time for him to go home. Wendy's brother Hank, who was friends with Toby, wanted Toby to stick around, hang out in his room, and listen to Led Zeppelin.

Toby was bare chested with a towel wrapped around his waist. Meredith was afraid to look at him too closely. She was dazzled by how he had suddenly become a different person.

Toby said, "Sorry, man. I have to head out." He and Hank did some kind of complicated handshake that they had either learned from watching *Good Times* on channel 17 or from hanging out on South Street on the weekends. Meredith knew that Toby would walk home—his house was nearby, hers a half a mile farther— not an impossible walk but not convenient either, in the dark. Meredith's parents had said, as always, *Just call if you need a ride home.* But if Meredith called for a ride, she would be missing a critical opportunity.

She said to Wendy and Nadine, who were both attacking the bowl of chips, "I'm going to go, too."

"Really?" Wendy said. She sounded disappointed, but Meredith had expected this. Wendy was a bit of a hanger-on; she was constantly peering over the proverbial fence at Meredith and Connie's friendship. "Where did Connie go?"

"Where do you *think?*" Nadine asked slyly. "She went to get it on with Matt."

Wendy's eyes widened and Meredith shrugged. Wendy had clearly not been introduced to her own sexuality yet, though Nadine had, in whatever form that had taken. (Another girl? Someone from the camp she went to in Michigan?)

Meredith kissed Wendy's cheek like an adult leaving a cocktail party and said, "Thanks for having me."

"You're walking?" Wendy said, sounding worried. "My dad can probably drive you."

"No, I'll walk," Meredith said.

"I can ask him."

"I'm fine," Meredith said. She hurried to the gate. Toby was strolling across the Thurbers' front lawn. He hadn't waited for her and she hadn't gotten out before him. She wondered if she had been imagining his erection, or if she had been flattering herself that the desire had been aimed at her. But if not her, then who? Not pathetic Wendy, and certainly not Nadine with her blocky shoulders and faint mustache. Meredith waved to the other girls and took off down Robinhood Road, trying to seem nonchalant. All this posturing! She wished Toby was behind her. Now it would look like she was chasing him.

When they were three houses away from the Thurbers' and four houses away from the O'Briens', Toby turned around and pretended to be surprised to find Meredith behind him.

"Hey," he called out in a kind of whisper.

She was at a loss for words. She waved. Her hair was damp and when she touched it, she could feel that it held comb marks. The streetlights were on, so there were pools of light followed by abysses of darkness. Across the street, a man walked a golden retriever. It was Frank diStefano, the roofer, a friend of Meredith's father. Oh, boy. But he didn't see her.

Toby stopped in one of the dark spots to wait for her. Her heart was tripping over itself like two left feet. She was excited, scared, nearly breathless. Something was going to *happen* between her and Toby O'Brien. But no, that wasn't possible. Toby was unfathomably cool, a good student and a great athlete, and he was as beautiful as Connie. He had dated the most alluring girl at Radnor—Divinity Michaels—and they had had an end-of-the-year breakup that was as spectacular as a Broadway show, where Divinity threatened to kill herself, and the school counselors and the state police were called in. (There had been simultaneous rumors circulating about Toby and the young French teacher, Mademoiselle Esme, which Connie called "completely idiotic, and yet not beyond Toby.") Earlier that summer, Toby had started "hanging out" with an Indian girl named Ravi, who was a junior at Bryn Mawr. Compared to those girls, what did Meredith have to offer? She was his kid sister's best friend, a completely known quantity, a giant yawn.

And yet...?

Meredith walked along the strip of lawn between the street and the sidewalk, and her feet were coated with grass clippings. She had her flip-flops in her hand and she stopped to put them on, partly as a stall tactic. She kept walking. Toby was leaning up against a tree that was in the front yard of a house where, clearly, no one was home.

"Hey," Toby said, as she approached. "Meredith, come here."

She went to him. He was the same person—sandy hair, green eyes, freckles—but he was new to her.

He seemed nervous, too, but with all of his experience with women, this was impossible.

He said, "Are you walking all the way home?"

She nodded.

He said, "Have you seen Connie?"

"No," Meredith said, gazing down the street. "She went somewhere with Matt."

"I don't know why she doesn't just tell my parents about him," Toby said.

"It's because he's..."

"Jewish," Toby said. "I know. But my parents won't care."

"I told her that," Meredith said. "She doesn't listen."

Toby put both his hands on Meredith's shoulders. "She doesn't listen to you? Her best friend?"

Meredith looked at Toby. This was, for sure, the first time she'd ever seen him. Everything had changed. She shook her head, pretending that she was caught up in the drama of Connie and Matt Klein, though she couldn't have cared less. Just as she was wondering if she should take a step closer to Toby, he pulled her in, as if for a friendly hug.

"Meredith," he said into her hair. Then he said, "Sorry about the pool. About pulling on your suit, I mean."

She could feel his erection again. Again, she thought about health class, Judy Blume, what she had heard other girls say. She was sick with desire. "Oh," she said. "That's okay."

He fumbled with her head, like it was a ball he was trying to get the correct grip on. Then he had one hand on her ear, and he was kissing her, deeply and desperately. And she thought, *Oh, my God, yes! Yes!*

They stood against the tree kissing for twenty minutes? Thirty minutes? They kissed until Toby's hands fell to her hips, he pulled her against him and groaned, and he played with the bottom edge of her sweatshirt as if considering whether or not to lift it, and although Meredith was thinking, *Yes, lift it, lift it,* she pulled away.

She said, "I really have to go. I have a long way to walk."

He said, "Will you go with me tomorrow night to see *Animal House*?"

"Yes," she said.

"Just you and me?" he said. "A date."

"Yes," she said.

He smiled at her and she saw his teeth, straight and white. She had known him through three years of braces and rubber bands. She had known him when his teeth fell out and he left them under his pillow for the tooth fairy. She waved and backed away and he said, "I'll pick you up at seven!"

"Okay!" she said. And she ran all the way home.

But then Connie was mad and wouldn't speak to Meredith on the phone. Meredith considered calling the O'Brien house again, asking to speak to Toby, and telling him the date was off. But Meredith couldn't make herself do that. She was in the grip of a romantic and sexual urge that wouldn't be denied. She liked Toby, and Connie would have to wrap her mind around that. Connie had Matt Klein; they had gone to third base, or nearly. Connie couldn't have Matt and expect Meredith to have nobody; that was unfair. Meredith was sorry it was Toby, but this was a matter of the heart, one beyond her control.

Meredith's eyes drifted closed. It was a welcome change to be thinking about something else, even if that something was Toby O'Brien. Sailing in Annapolis, seducing in Anguilla. At Connie's wedding, Meredith had been close. At Veronica's funeral, even closer. But Meredith hadn't allowed herself to get sucked back in. She had been lucky.

When Meredith woke up, Connie was lying in the chaise next to her, reading.

Meredith thought, *Oh, thank God. She came back.*

They went for a walk on the beach.

Meredith said, "I was thinking about Nadine Dexter and Wendy Thurber. Do you remember the night of Wendy's pool party?"

"Wendy *who?*" Connie said.

Meredith didn't say, *I was remembering the night I first kissed your brother.*

Meredith said, "I'm going in the water."

"Suit yourself," Connie said. "It's too cold for me."

Later, they took outdoor showers, and Meredith put on white shorts and a navy Trina Turk tunic, refugees from her Hamptons closet circa 2007. She went downstairs with her hair still damp. Connie was pouring herself a glass of wine. It was five o'clock. A day hadn't passed that quickly for Meredith since long before Freddy's arrest — but this mere thought triggered a heaviness. She pictured Leo and

Carver with plaster dust sugaring their hair and clothes, sitting on the wide front porch of the imaginary house, drinking a beer. They were okay, Meredith told herself. They were fine.

"Glass of wine?" Connie asked.

Meredith decided she would have a glass of wine; maybe it would help her sleep.

"White or red?" Connie said.

"White, please," Meredith said. She didn't want to think about the Ruffino Chianti, their usual table at Rinaldo's, Freddy saying, *Here comes your poison, Meredith*. Freddy didn't approve of Meredith drinking, and he rarely, if ever, drank himself. He didn't like losing control, he said. Of course, he hadn't always felt that way. He had been a social drinker in college and young adulthood, and then, as his business grew, he had transitioned into abstinence. Now, Meredith knew that you couldn't lie and cheat *and* drink, because what if you let something slip? What if you let the facade crumble? She thought of Freddy throwing back those three shots of Macallan and how shocked she had been. She had known something was wrong then, seventy-two hours before the rest of the world knew. Freddy had turned on her with wild eyes; she had seen the desperation. She thought, *We've lost all our money*. But so what? Easy come, easy go. Freddy had then pulled Meredith into the bedroom and had pushed her down and taken her roughly from behind, as though it were his final act. Meredith remembered feeling raw and panicky and electrified—this was not the perfunctory lovemaking she and Freddy had engaged in for the past decade or so (its lackluster nature owing to the fact, she had assumed, that he was preoccupied with work)—she remembered thinking, *WOW*. They were ruined perhaps, but they still had each other.

That was what she'd thought, then.

Connie handed Meredith a glass of chardonnay and said, "You can go out to the deck."

"Do you need help with dinner?" Meredith asked.

"Don't tell me you've started cooking?" Connie said.

"No," Meredith said. And they laughed. "I ate from cartons every night after Freddy left."

The words "after Freddy left" echoed in the kitchen. Connie poured a stream of olive oil into a stainless steel bowl and started clanging with her whisk.

Meredith said, "I'll go out."

She stepped onto the deck and took a seat at the round teak table. She hadn't heard from Burt and Dev; she never knew if that was good or bad. The sun spangled the water. Let's say good. She might be going to jail, but she wasn't going to jail today.

Out in the water, Meredith saw a sleek, black head, then its body and flippers undulating through the waves. Then she saw a second dark form, moving less gracefully. Meredith squinted; she was wearing her prescription sunglasses, which weren't as strong as her regular horn-rimmed glasses.

She called out to Connie. "Hey, there are two seals today."

"What?" Connie said.

Meredith stood up with her wineglass. She poked her head through the sliding door.

"There are two seals today."

"Really?" Connie said. "I've never seen two before. Only one. Only Harold."

"I saw two," Meredith said. "Harold found a friend."

She smiled at this.

CONNIE

When Connie checked her cell phone in the morning, she saw that she'd missed a phone call during the night. There was no message, just a clattering hang up. Connie checked her display, then gasped. The number itself was unfamiliar, but it was from the 850 area code:

Tallahassee. Which was where Ashlyn practiced medicine. So had Ashlyn called, finally, after twenty-nine months of silence? Connie's hopes were coy, afraid to show themselves. The call had come in at 2:11 a.m., but this told Connie nothing. Ashlyn was a doctor, and doctors kept absurd hours. Connie checked the number again. It was the 850 area code; that was certainly Tallahassee, and Tallahassee was where Ashlyn now lived. So, it was Ashlyn. Was it Ashlyn? Connie was tempted to call the number right back, but it was still early, not quite seven. Should she call at eight? Ten? Should she wait and call tonight? A call at two in the morning might mean Ashlyn was in trouble. Connie decided to call right back, but then she caught herself. This was an opportunity she couldn't afford to blow. She would wait. She would think about it.

Connie stepped out onto the front deck. There was low-lying fog, typical of early July: How many times had the town had to cancel the Fourth of July fireworks? *Ashlyn!* Connie thought. Was it possible? Connie was going out to get muffins and the newspaper from the Sconset Market, a pleasant errand, and now she would think about Ashlyn, a phone call out of the blue.

Connie didn't see the envelope until she had kicked it off the porch and down the stairs. What was it? She picked it up. Manila envelope, closed with a gold clasp, nothing written on it, thin and light, nothing particularly sinister, but Connie got an awful feeling. She thought, *Don't open it!* She thought, *Anthrax!* But that was ridiculous. This was Nantucket; it was a placid, foggy morning. She thought, *An envelope dropped on the porch?* She thought, *Something from the Tom Nevers Neighborhood Association.* They so often left her out because she was a summer resident, whereas most everyone else lived here year-round, but they'd remembered her this time. Potluck dinner or a community yard sale.

She opened the envelope and saw there was a photograph inside, a glossy color photo, five-by-seven, of Meredith, wearing her navy tunic and white shorts, standing on Connie's back porch, holding a glass of wine.

Connie shivered. She looked out at her front yard and thought, *What is this? Who put this here?*

She looked at the photo again. It had been taken the night before. Meredith was turned toward the sliding door and she was smiling.

All day they passed the photograph back and forth between themselves, and when one or the other of them wasn't looking at it, it sat on the dining table like a time bomb.

Meredith had blanched when Connie showed her the photograph. Someone had been out there taking her picture, but where? Meredith thought it was the same guy they'd seen by the Dumpster in the alley behind 824 Park Avenue—he must have followed them all the way from the city!—but Connie made her see this was unlikely, if not impossible. It was someone else.

"The only way they could have gotten that shot of you was from the beach," Connie said. "Did you see anyone walking on the beach?"

"No one," Meredith said.

"Or it could have been taken from the water," Connie said. "Did you see anyone in a boat? Or a kayak?"

"I saw the seals," Meredith said. "That was what I was smiling about, remember? Harold had a friend."

Connie said, "Harold's 'friend' was a photographer in a wet suit. Is that possible?"

"Oh, God," Meredith said. She approached the sliding glass doors, then backed away. "You know what scares me?"

Connie wasn't sure she wanted to know. What scared Connie was the whole thing. Someone taking the picture, someone leaving it for them on the front porch. A person trespassing on her property. Meredith couldn't stay here. She had to go. The whole thing was chilling. Someone was watching them.

"What scares you?" Connie asked.

"If it was just the paparazzi, they wouldn't have left the photograph for us. They would have published it, and we would have woken up this morning, and it would have been splashed across the front of the *Post*. HAPPY HOUR FOR MRS. DELINN."

"So if it wasn't the paparazzi, who was it?"

"Someone who wants me to know they know I'm here. One of Freddy's enemies. The Russian mob."

"The Russian mob isn't real," Connie said.

"There were Russian investors who lost billions," Meredith said. "There are a lot of people who want Freddy's head. And since they can't get to Freddy, they're coming after me." She looked at Connie. "I'm putting you in danger."

"No," Connie said. "You're not." But she was. She had to go. Connie racked her brain. Meredith had made it clear that she'd lost everybody else in her life. But Connie had friends. Maybe she could ship Meredith quietly off to Bethesda? She could live with Wolf's brother, Jake, and Jake's wife, Iris. Iris was a know-it-all busybody. She had a degree in psychology from the University of Delaware and she was constantly expressing concern over others' "general state of mind," and especially Connie's, since Connie had recently lost her husband and her daughter and, in Iris's estimation, wasn't doing terribly well. Connie would take great pleasure in inflicting Meredith on Iris, but she couldn't bring herself to inflict Iris on Meredith. There was Toby? God, no, that could backfire in any one of a hundred ways. Plus, if Meredith left, Connie would be alone, and the absolute best thing about the past two days was that, for the first time in years, Connie hadn't been alone.

Connie flung open the sliding door, and Meredith scurried to the other side of the room, as though she were a vampire, allergic to daylight. Connie went outside and stood on the deck. The jig was up. Meredith was here. Connie wanted to face the ocean and anyone hiding in it and shout, *She's here! Meredith Delinn is here!* The world could tell Connie she was unstable, insane, or just plain stupid, but at that moment, she made a decision: Meredith was staying.

*   *   *

Meredith was afraid to read on the deck. Meredith was afraid to walk on the beach. Connie sat on the deck herself. She peered at the water. Around noon, Harold appeared, alone. Connie watched him frolic in the waves, then felt lonely. She went inside and made turkey sandwiches.

"Meredith!" she called. "Lunch!"

Meredith didn't answer.

Connie went upstairs and tapped on Meredith's door.

Meredith said, "*Entrez.*"

Connie opened the door. Meredith was lying on her bed wearing her bathing suit and cover-up, reading.

"Come out on the deck and have lunch."

"No," Meredith said.

Connie wondered if Meredith was more frightened of the Russian mob or the FBI.

"No one is trying to hurt you. They're just trying to scare you."

"They succeeded."

"Well, they didn't succeed with me. I've been sitting on the deck all morning and nothing's happened."

Meredith said, "Someone knows I'm here."

Connie sighed. "What can I say? Someone knows you're here. You know, we might feel better if we called the police."

"We can't call the police," Meredith said. "Absolutely not."

"Why not?" Connie said. "You're scared, you feel threatened, you call the police; they write up a report, wave their guns, anyone watching us knows we've called the police, they get intimidated, they leave us alone."

"No one can know I'm here," Meredith said. "Not even the police. If this gets out, everyone's going to hate you."

"No one's going to hate me," Connie said, "and the police would keep it quiet." But she knew Meredith was right: the police talked to the fire department who talked to Santos Rubbish who talked to the guys at Sconset Gardener, and soon everybody on Nantucket knew that Meredith Delinn was hiding out at 1103 Tom Nevers Road. "Okay, we won't call the police. Just please come outside."

"No," Meredith said.

For dinner, Connie made cheeseburgers and salad. The cheeseburgers had to be cooked on the grill, which put Connie out on the deck with her back to the ocean. It was unnerving, she had to admit. She kept whipping around, but when she did, no one was there.

At Meredith's request, they ate inside. They needed a safe topic of conversation, which meant they had to venture pretty far back. Growing up, high school—but not Toby. Meredith again unearthed the names Wendy Thurber and Nadine Dexter, and once Connie had sifted through the archaeological ruins of her mind and figured out who these names belonged to, she hooted. Wendy and Nadine had been good, close friends. They had once been a part of Connie's everyday, though she hadn't seen them in over thirty years. What were Wendy and Nadine doing now? Meredith remembered Wendy as clingy and pathetic, and Nadine as a stout lesbian in the making.

"Yes, so do I," Connie said, although really it had been so long ago and Connie's memory was so poor that she was helpless to do anything but agree.

At nine thirty, Meredith said she was going upstairs. "It's my bedtime," she said, and Connie remembered that both Meredith and Freddy had always stuck to an early bedtime, as though they were children with school in the morning.

"Freddy's not here," Connie said, pouring herself a third glass of wine. "You can stay up with me."

Meredith said, "Are you afraid to stay up by yourself? Admit it, you are."

"I'm not *afraid* to stay up by myself, no. But I'd like company."

Meredith moved toward the stairs, meaning she didn't care that Connie wanted company (and yes, actually, Connie *was* a little afraid). She said, "I wonder what it's like for him."

"Who?"

"Freddy. In prison."

Connie was tempted to say something ungenerous. But instead she said, "I'm sure it's perfectly awful."

"I'm sure it is, too," Meredith said. "But what if 'perfectly awful' is something even worse than you and I can imagine?"

"Do you care?" Connie said.

Meredith didn't answer that.

"Do you still love him?" Connie asked.

"I'm going up," Meredith said, and Connie was glad. They had ventured way off their safe topics.

Connie's mind was on the phone call from Tallahassee. All Connie had to do was call the number back and *find out*—but she was afraid this new number would prove to be a dead end, and her hopes of reconnecting with her daughter would be crushed. The longer she held off calling, the longer the potential for reconciliation lived. And, too, Connie was afraid that she would call the number and Ashlyn would answer, and what would Connie say, after nearly two and a half years of silence? How would Connie keep from breaking down and crying, or breaking out and screaming—and in either case making things worse?

She finished her third glass of wine and then polished off Meredith's unfinished glass of wine as she did the dinner dishes. By that time, her fear had all but dissipated. She checked her cell phone again. The Tallahassee number was on her display. This was the moment.

She pushed the button that dialed the number. Then she steeled herself. One ring, two, three...seven, eight...voice mail. It was a computer-generated voice, one that gave no hint or clue who Connie had called. *Please leave a message.*

Connie took a breath. Leave a message? She left a message each and every Sunday on Ashlyn's cell phone and had never once gotten a response. Why expect that this would be any different?

And yet, she couldn't resist. She said, "Ashlyn, it's Mom. I see that you called. If you want to call me back, I'm here on Nantucket. As I'm sure you realize. If you call me back, I'll tell you something unbelievable." She paused. She couldn't stand using news of Meredith as a bribe, but she didn't have anything else to offer as enticement. "Call me back, please." She looked at the display of her phone, at the seconds ticking off, as if expecting her phone to answer. "Call me," she said again, and then she punched the phone off.

She shouldn't have left a message.

Had she sounded like she'd been drinking? She had slurred a little bit in there with the "As I'm sure you realize." Would Ashlyn notice?

Connie lay down on the sofa. She hated herself.

She didn't see the graffiti until she was in her car the next morning, on her way to the Sconset Market for the newspaper. It was the Fourth of July, and Connie was wondering if Meredith would want to go to see the fireworks that night. Probably not, definitely not, too many people. Then, Connie caught a glimpse of something unexpected, a color. A garish neon green. Huh? Connie looked in her rearview mirror and hit the brake as hard as she might have for an oncoming deer. She closed her eyes and tried to calm herself. She had a headache like a door repeatedly slamming. She opened her eyes. *Oh, my God.* She threw the car in reverse and backed all the way up to the house. She parked. She got out of the car. She studied the damage to her beautiful, beloved house.

Someone had spray painted, in letters that had to be six feet high, in a color that assaulted the eye, that noxious green, the word "*CROOK.*"

Connie couldn't believe it. She had to touch the paint on the gray shingles. The paint was still wet; some of it came off on Connie's fingertips. So, this had been done when? Late last night? Early this morning? Connie felt violated. She felt—if she could say this without sounding melodramatic—like she'd been raped.

Some depraved, hateful person had vandalized her home. He had trespassed onto her property—with extension ladders and what must have been ten cans of spray paint—and graffitied the front of her house.

CROOK. Meredith would be devastated. God, this was a hundred times worse than the photograph. Connie couldn't stand the thought of telling her.

She gave herself a minute to repeat the obvious things in her head: She should have known something like this would happen. The photograph had been a warning: *We know you're here. Now we're coming after you.* Freddy Delinn had enemies, dangerous people who had lost a lot of money. One of them, or a group of them, was behind this.

Connie touched the paint again. It would come off, right?

Inside, she found Meredith wearing a white nightgown, sitting in a chair at the head of the dining-room table as if waiting for a banquet to be served. A banquet of humiliation and sorrow, Connie thought. Meredith wasn't reading or drinking coffee. She was just sitting. Meditating, perhaps. When the screen door slapped shut behind Connie, Meredith startled. She looked up.

"Back already?" she said. "Did you forget something? Your wallet?"

Connie sat in the chair next to Meredith and took Meredith's hands in hers in her best imitation of a grief counselor. She had known this person since she was a child, since before rational thought or lasting memory. She had never imagined having to tell her something like this.

"I have to call the police," Connie said.

Meredith clenched her jaw. She nodded, though barely.

"Someone vandalized the house," Connie said. She tried to swallow, but her mouth was a sandbox. She was parched, hung over, heartsick. Her house! If Wolf had been alive to see this . . .

"What?" Meredith asked. Her hands were small and very cold.

"Green paint, big letters."

"What does it say?" Meredith asked.

"Crook."

Meredith hid her face in her hands. "Oh, God," she said.

Connie rubbed her back. She was tiny and frail. But no. She *wasn't* frail, and neither was Connie. "So I'm going to call the police."

"Okay," Meredith said.

Connie had thought they would send a lackey in a squad car, someone to witness the damage and write up a cursory report, especially since it was a holiday, but the chief of police came himself. He was a pleasant-looking middle-aged man with a short haircut, brown going gray around his ears. He was tall and impressive in his white uniform shirt, his crisp black pants, radio on his hip. When he climbed out of his car, he greeted Connie first, very kindly keeping his eyes off the vandalism.

"Mrs. Flute?" he said. "I'm Ed Kapenash, chief of police."

"Nice to meet you," she said.

Then he regarded the house. "Wow."

"I know," Connie said.

The chief, too, seemed most immediately interested in touching the paint. "The good news is that this appears to be water based, which is lucky for you. In the city, they have all kinds of nasty oil-based paints that never come out. You'd literally have to reshingle your house to have this gone. As it is, I can give you the name of a good power washer. I can pull some strings and see if I can have him out here today, assuming he hasn't gone fishing or to the beach with the rest of the world."

"Oh," Connie said. "Yes, absolutely. That would be wonderful."

"Okay," the chief said. "Your first priority will be getting the paint off your house, and our first priority will be finding out who did this."

"There's something I should explain," Connie said.

"And what's that?" he asked.

"Meredith Delinn is staying here."

"Meredith Delinn?"

"Yes. She's the wife of..."

"I know who she is," the chief said. "She's staying *here?*"

"She's a friend of mine from growing up," Connie said. "We've been friends forever."

The chief removed a pen from his back pocket and started taking notes. (What would he write? *BFF?*) He said, "Well, that explains things a little bit, doesn't it? Explains them but doesn't excuse them. We'll do what we can to find out who did this and to make sure it doesn't happen again. I'll start by putting a squad car on this road every hour throughout the night. Do you mind if I speak to Mrs. Delinn?"

"Um," Connie said. Meredith was still in her nightgown, and Connie was protective and suspicious. This guy *was* the chief of police, but what if he turned around and sold the story to the *National Enquirer*? "Just a minute. Let me ask her."

The chief nodded. "I'll call my power-washer connection from my car. I take it you'd like him here as soon as possible?"

"Yes," Connie said. "Thank you." She was trying not to look at the front of her house. That poisonous green, the absurd size of the letters, the ugly word. It was a scream, written on her house. *CROOK.* People had called Richard Nixon a crook. John Dillinger had been a crook. Bonnie and Clyde. But none of those people had been a crook like Freddy Delinn.

"Meredith?" Connie said. She saw that Meredith had gone upstairs and changed into what Connie thought of as her Doomsday outfit: her white button-down shirt, now a little wrinkled, jeans, suede flats. Already, it was too warm for the jeans. "The chief of police is here. He has questions for you. Is that okay?"

Meredith nodded.

"You don't have to talk to him," Connie said.

"I will."

Connie beckoned the chief inside, and the three of them sat at the dining-room table.

Connie said to the chief, "Can I get you some coffee?"

The chief held up a hand. "I've already had my three cups."

"Ice water then?"

"I'm all set, thanks," the chief said.

Connie brought a pitcher of ice water and three glasses to the table nonetheless. She poured herself a glass, returned to the counter where she sliced a lemon and put the slices in a shallow bowl. The three of them were sitting in a house that screamed CROOK, but there was no reason they couldn't be civilized.

"So," the chief said. "You're in luck. I've gotten hold of a man to do the power washing. He'll be here before noon today, he said."

"Excellent, thank you," Connie said.

The chief lowered his voice to speak to Meredith. He was responding to the situation, or to her pinched face, which was drained of all color. Or he was responding to her diminutive size — five foot one, a hundred pounds. Meredith had complained all her life that her petite stature caused people to treat her like a child.

"Do you have any idea who might have done this?" the chief asked her.

Connie couldn't help herself from interjecting. "Well, yesterday, something happened."

"What happened yesterday?" the chief said.

"Someone left an envelope on my front porch," Connie said. "And in the envelope was this photograph." She slid both the photograph and the envelope across the table.

The chief studied the photograph. "So you don't know who took this?"

Connie shook her head. "It was just left on our porch. Like someone was telling us they knew Meredith was here. It was creepy."

"Creepy," the chief agreed. "You should have called us then."

Connie felt a flash of triumph. Meredith cast her eyes down at the table.

"We figured out it was a photographer dressed as a seal,"

Connie said. "It was taken from the water, night before last, around six o'clock."

"And then it was left on your porch. You found it when?"

"Yesterday morning."

"Yesterday morning. And you didn't call the police. And now this morning you have this vandalism."

Meredith said, "I'm sorry. I should have let Connie call the police. She wanted to. But I didn't want anyone to know I was here."

The chief took a noticeable breath. "You'll forgive me for being indelicate and asking the obvious. Are any of your husband's former investors living on Nantucket that you know of?"

Meredith raised her face to the chief. Her expression was so blank, Connie was scared.

"Mary Rose Garth lost forty million. The Crenshaws lost twenty-six million; Jeremy and Amy Rivers lost nine point two million; the LaRussas lost six million and so did the Crosbys and so did Alan Futenberg. Christopher Darby-Lett lost four and a half million."

The chief scribbled. "These people live on Nantucket?"

"They're summer residents," Meredith said. "The Rosemans lost four point four, the Mancheskis lost three eight, Mrs. Phinney lost three five; the Kincaids, the Winslows, the Becketts, the Carlton Smiths, Linsley Richardson, the Halseys, the Minatows, and the Malcolm Browns all lost between two and three million. The Vaipauls, the McIntoshes, the Kennedys, the Brights, the Worthingtons..."

Connie sucked down a glass of cold water and tried not to let her surprise show. She had no idea so many of Freddy's investors were on this island. She and Meredith were sitting in the heart of enemy territory.

The chief left an hour later with a list of fifty-two names of Nantucket summer residents who had lost over a million dollars in

Freddy's scam. He couldn't question any of them without probable cause, but it was good to have the list to reference, he said. Of
course, he pointed out, it wasn't certain that the vandal was an
investor; there were all kinds of creeps in the world. The chief was
taking the photograph and the envelope with him. The main
thing, he said, was that Connie and Meredith should try to relax
while remaining vigilant. The house had an alarm system, though
Connie had never felt the need to set it. Nantucket—and Tom
Nevers in particular—was so safe! She would set it tonight; she
would set it from now on.

"And we'll send a squad car out like I promised," the chief said.
"Every hour on the hour throughout the night."

"Thank you," Connie said. She hated to see him go. He was the
first man to help her in this kind of practical way since Wolf had
died. And he was handsome. She checked for a wedding ring. He
wore a solid gold band—of course. Chiefs of police were always
happily married, with a couple of kids at home. That was as it
should be. Still, Connie was pleased with herself for noticing him.
It felt like some kind of progress.

Less than an hour later, there was a knock at the door, and both
Connie and Meredith froze. They were still at the dining-room
table, drinking coffee and letting their bowls of cereal grow soggy.
Meredith was talking in circles—mostly about the investors who
lived on Nantucket. She only knew a few of them personally. She,
of course, knew Mary Rose Garth (net loss $40 million); everyone
in New York society knew Mary Rose Garth, the anorexically
thin, sexually lascivious rubber heiress. She had served on the
board of the Frick Collection with Meredith.

And Jeremy and Amy Rivers (net loss $9.2 million) had been
friends of Meredith's from Palm Beach.

Meredith told Connie that she had met Amy Rivers during a
tennis clinic at the Everglades Club. Amy had a high-powered job
for a global consulting firm; she had gone to Princeton three years

behind Meredith, though Meredith didn't remember her. But they bonded over their equally pathetic backhands and their mutual admiration of the tennis pro's legs, and became casual friends. Amy traveled all the time for business—Hong Kong, Tokyo, Dubai—but when next she was in Palm Beach, she called Meredith to go to lunch. They sat out on the patio at Chuck and Harold's—very casual, very friendly—but at the end of the lunch, Amy bent her head toward Meredith as if to confide something. Meredith was wary. Palm Beach was a vicious gossip town. Meredith was okay with accepting confidences, but she never, ever told any of her women friends a single thing about her personal life.

Amy said, "I have money to invest. In the neighborhood of nine million. Do you think there's any way I could get into your husband's fund? I hear his returns are unbelievable."

"Oh," Meredith said. She felt a bit deflated. She had thought that Amy Rivers had chosen to befriend her because she recognized Meredith as being in a category above the run-of-the-mill Palm Beach matron. While it was true Meredith didn't teach anymore, she was extremely smart and capable. But now it seemed that what Amy had been after, really, was a way into Delinn Enterprises. The fact of the matter was, Meredith had no say in who was chosen to be an investor. People asked her all the time if she could "get them in" with Freddy; even the cashier at Publix, who had inherited money from her great-uncle, had asked. But when Meredith mentioned these people to Freddy, he always said no. He had some secret set of criteria for accepting investors that he wouldn't share with Meredith, and quite frankly, she didn't care. Still, for certain people, she agreed to ask. Although she felt a tiny bit stung by Amy Rivers, Meredith promised to lobby Freddy on her behalf. Amy clapped a hand over her mouth like she had just been named Miss America.

"Oh, thank you!" she said. "Thank you, thank you, thank you! Here's my card. You'll let me know what he says?"

When Meredith talked to Freddy about Amy Rivers, Freddy asked who she was.

Meredith said, "A woman I play tennis with at the Everglades. She's a consultant with Hackman Marr."

"Hackman Marr?" Freddy said, sounding interested.

"Yes," Meredith said. "And she went to Princeton, graduated in eighty-five. I had lunch with her today. I really like her."

"I'm sorry," Freddy said.

"Sorry about what? You mean you won't take her on?"

"No."

"Why not?"

"We don't take investors because we 'really like' them," Freddy said. "We take them on for other reasons."

"What other reasons?" Meredith asked. "She said she has nine million dollars." She handed Freddy Amy's business card. "Will you please think about it? For me, please?"

"For you, please? All right, yes," Freddy said. "I'll think about it."

And voilà! Freddy called Amy Rivers himself and invited her to invest, and Amy sent Meredith a huge bouquet of flowers. They became great friends, playing tennis and meeting for lunch, recommending books, talking about their kids. Amy never again mentioned Delinn Enterprises, Freddy, or her money. And then, of course, there was no money. Amy Rivers lost everything.

Meredith looked at Connie. "I could tell you dozens of stories like that."

Connie wasn't sure how to respond. She and Wolf, too, had been investors. She thought that all this talk about other investors might lead to an uncomfortable discussion of their own situation — but Connie was spared this by the knock at the door. It frightened her at first, and it certainly frightened Meredith, but then Connie realized it must be the power washer, and she hurried to greet him.

The man's name was Danforth Flynn; he told Connie to call him Dan. He was about fifty, with the lean body of a long-distance runner and a permanent sunburn. Again, Connie felt self-conscious.

This was the second time this morning that she had a handsome man show up to help her.

Dan Flynn regarded the front of the house and whistled.

"Did the chief explain?" she asked.

"He did."

"Can you get it off?"

He approached the front of the house and touched a shingle that had been painted. He rubbed his fingers together. "I can," he said. "What I want you to do is to go inside and close and lock all of the windows on this side of the house. This is going to take me a couple of hours, I'd guess. And it's going to be loud."

"No problem," Connie said.

"Okay," Dan Flynn said. "I'll get started. The tank of my truck holds four thousand gallons of water, but this job is so big I may need to hook up to your outdoor spigot to fill my reserve tank. Can you show me where that is?"

"I can," Connie said. "It's around here." She led him to the side of the house and showed him where her garden hose was coiled. He wasn't looking at the house, however—he was looking at the view of the ocean.

"You have quite a spot," he said. "In good old Tom Nevers. I forget how breathtaking it can be out here."

"Yes," she said. "The land had been in my husband's family since the nineteen twenties, but we only built the house fifteen years ago. And then my husband died in two thousand nine, so now it's just me."

"Funny," Dan said, still looking at the water. "My wife died in two thousand nine. Breast cancer."

"Brain cancer," Connie said.

They were quiet for a moment, and Connie couldn't help but think of her friend Lizbet who had, for two and a half years, been encouraging Connie to go to a support group so she could meet people who were going through the same thing she was.

Connie looked at Dan Flynn and smiled. "I'll go take care of those windows," she said.

"Great," he said.

Connie bounded into the house. She felt more energized than she had in months.

She closed the windows on the first floor and watched Dan move around his truck, turning knobs, pulling out a thick blue ridged hose. He was wearing jeans and a T-shirt and running shoes. He had a buzz cut, brown hair turning gray, and a day of growth on his face like that newly retired NFL quarterback, which she found sexy. Sexy? She couldn't believe she was thinking this way.

Connie caught sight of herself in the mirror. She had lost a lot of sparkle in the past two and a half years—but did she really look so bad for fifty? Her hair was still strawberry blond, more strawberry in the winter, more blond in the summer. She had her mother's good genes to thank for that because Veronica had gone to the grave at sixty-eight with a full head of natural red. Connie had green eyes, a light tan, some freckles, some sun spots. Her skin wasn't great; she had never been able to stay out of the sun. She was out of shape although she was very thin from skipping meals. Her nails were a mess, and her eyebrows. She needed to start taking care of herself again. She needed to exercise.

Ha! All this in response to the cute power-washing guy. Meredith was going to die laughing.

Connie went upstairs to close the second-floor windows. Dan had started working. The noise was incredible; it sounded like the house was being attacked by fighter jets. Connie hurried to shut all the windows. She could see Dan Flynn bracing the hose against his hip, shooting a stream of water at the house that was moving so fast, it looked solid. Dan's body was shaking like he was operating a jackhammer; all the muscles in his arms were popping. The whole thing was rather phallic.

"Meredith," Connie said. "Come here, you have to see this."

There was no response. Connie was pretty sure the paint was coming off. There were green puddles in the yard now, the color of radioactive waste.

"Meredith?" Connie called.

Connie finished with the windows facing the front of the house and, just to be safe, she shut the windows on either side of the house, even though those rooms would get murderously hot. The house had central air-conditioning—but, like the alarm system, Connie never turned it on.

She moved into the hallway. The door to Meredith's room was shut. Connie remembered the blank look on her face as she sat at the table, and the way she recited the names of the investors. (She had committed nearly three thousand of the names to memory, she said, as a kind of penance. It was how she'd filled her days in the New York apartment after Freddy had been taken away.)

Connie had a bad feeling. She knocked on the door.

"Meredith?" she said. No answer. She could have been sleeping. Connie really wanted to respect Meredith's privacy, just as she wanted her own privacy respected—it was the only way it was going to work with them living in the house together—but Connie was worried that Meredith would take pills or hang herself or slash her wrists with one of the disposable razors that Connie knew were under the sink in the bathroom.

"Meredith?" Connie said. No answer. Nothing. Just the percussive drone of the power washer.

She opened the door and gasped. Meredith was sitting on her bed, facing the door, wearing that same zombie-like expression. Her Louis Vuitton duffel bag was next to her on the bed.

"Jesus!" Connie said. "You scared me. What are you doing?"

She looked at Connie. "I have to leave."

"No!" Connie said.

"Yes," Meredith said. She stood up, grabbing her bag.

"You are *not* leaving," Connie said. She tried to wrest the leather handles from Meredith, but Meredith held fast. She was small, but she was tough; Connie remembered her on the hockey field, gripping her stick, biting down ferociously on her mouth guard.

"I'm leaving," Meredith said. "Your beautiful house was wrecked because of me!"

"It's not wrecked," Connie said. "Come see—this man named Dan Flynn is outside fixing it. The paint's coming off. We'll never even be able to tell it was there."

"But it *was* there," Meredith said. "*CROOK*. They think I'm him. They think I was in on it. They think I'm the one who stole their money. And I did in a way, didn't I? Because I had four houses, a yacht, a jet, seven cars, jewelry, clothes, antiques—and where did the money for all that come from? Well, technically, I stole it, didn't I?" She blinked, and Connie thought that this might be the thing that made Meredith cry, but behind her glasses, her eyes were dry. "But I had no idea. *No idea.* I thought Freddy was a genius. I thought he was beating the market, again and again and again. I was so..."

"Meredith—"

"Stupid! So blind! And no one believes me, and why should anyone believe me? I'm a smart woman with an Ivy League education. How could I not see something illegal was going on?" She glared at Connie. "Even you tried to tell me."

That was correct; Connie had tried to tell her. But Connie was in too generous a frame of mind to revisit that. "You were blinded," Connie said. "Blinded by love."

"Is that an excuse?" Meredith said. "Is that going to get me off the hook with the FBI, Connie? *Love?*"

Connie didn't know what to say.

"Do *you* believe I'm innocent?" Meredith said.

"Yes, Meredith. I believe you're innocent."

"And why is that? Why are you the *only person in the whole country* who believes I'm innocent?"

"Because I know you."

"I knew Freddy," Meredith said. "I thought I knew Freddy." She raised her head. "I should never have called you to come get me. I've put you in danger. Look what happened to your house. I'm drowning, Connie, but I'm drowning alone. I won't take you with me."

"Meredith!" Connie said. She had to shout to be heard above the din of the power washer. "YOU'RE STAYING. I WANT YOU TO STAY. I'M NOT WILLING TO LET YOU GO." She didn't say, *You have nowhere else to go,* because it wasn't about that. "I need you to stay for me, okay, not for you. I need a friend. I need companionship. And it has to be you. We're going to put what happened behind us; we're going to forget the things we said to each other. We need time for that. And we need to figure out how to prove you're innocent. We need the world to see you as I see you."

Meredith didn't move or speak for what seemed like a long time, but then, Connie watched her exhale. She relaxed her grip on the duffel bag and let Connie take it from her. Connie said, "I want you to come see what Dan the power-washer guy looks like." And she led Meredith to the window.

MEREDITH

Connie came home from the hospital thrift shop a few days later with a dark wig for Meredith, styled in two long pigtails. When Meredith tried it on, she looked like Mary Ann from *Gilligan's Island.*

"It's awful," Meredith said.

"Awful," Connie agreed. "But that's a good thing. We want mousy, and we want anonymous. And we need to do something about your glasses."

"I love my glasses," Meredith protested. "I've had my glasses since the eighth grade."

"I know," Connie said. "I remember the day you got them. But now, they have to go. We aren't going to stay inside all summer, and we aren't going to have you accosted by haters, and so you need to travel incognito. The glasses are a dead giveaway. When women dress up as Meredith Delinn for Halloween, they'll be wearing those glasses."

"Are women going to dress up as me for Halloween?" Meredith said.

Connie smiled sadly. "The glasses have to go."

Connie took Meredith's glasses to Nantucket Eye Center and had a new pair made. While Connie was gone with her glasses, Meredith was left helplessly blind. She desperately wanted to go outside and sit on the deck, but she was terrified to do so without Connie around. She lay upstairs on her bed, but she couldn't read without her glasses. She stared at the blurry surrounds of the pink guest room.

She was still back on the Main Line in the 1970s with her father and Toby.

Meredith's parents had been stunned when she told them about her date with Toby. For Chick Martin, the surprise had been mixed with something else. Jealousy? Possessiveness? Meredith feared her father would react the same way that Connie had. But he rose above whatever qualms he had about Meredith's burgeoning womanhood and acted the role of protective father. When Toby arrived on that first evening to pick Meredith up, Chick asked, "Do you have a clean driving record?"

"Yes, sir," Toby said.

"You will have Meredith home by eleven, please."

"Yes, sir, Mr. Martin," Toby said.

It took Chick a few months to adjust to Meredith's new persona. Meredith was the same on the outside — studious, obedient, loving toward both her parents, respectful of their rules, grateful for all they did for her — but something had changed. To her father, she supposed, it seemed like she was now focused on Toby. But really, she was focused on herself — her body, her emotions, her sexuality, her capacity to love someone other than her parents.

Whoa! Meredith couldn't remember ever feeling as alive as she had that summer she turned sixteen, when her romance with Toby raged in her like a fire. She was hot for him — that had been the popular turn of phrase at the time. Many times they skipped the movies and drove to Valley Forge Park and made out in the car. They touched each other through their clothes, and then the clothes started coming off in stages. And then arrived a night when Meredith was naked and Toby had his jeans at his knees and Meredith straddled him and...he stopped her. It was too soon, she was young, it wasn't time yet. Meredith had cried — partly out of sexual frustration, partly out of anger and jealousy. Toby had had sex with Divinity Michaels and Ravi from Bryn Mawr and probably also the French teacher, Mademoiselle Esme (though Meredith had never been brave enough to ask him) — so why not her?

"This is different," he said. "This is special. I want to take it slow. I want it to last."

"Plus," he said, "I'm afraid of your father."

"Afraid of my *father?*" Meredith wailed.

"He spoke to me," Toby said. "He asked me to respect you. He told me to be a gentleman."

"A gentleman?" Meredith said. She huddled, shivering, against the passenger-side door. The vinyl seats of the Nova were cold. She hunted for her underwear. She didn't want a gentleman. She wanted Toby.

Meredith went on a campaign to keep her father and Toby away from each other. But then Chick invited Toby over to help burn the piles of leaves in the yard, then go inside and watch Notre Dame trounce Boston College, and eat pigs in a blanket that Meredith's mother served along with a dish of spicy brown mustard. At the holidays, Toby was invited to the Martins' annual Christmas party, which was so crowded with reveling adults that Meredith was certain there would be an opportunity to sneak to her bedroom. But Toby would not be coerced upstairs.

Toby was also invited over on New Year's eve, a night that Meredith had traditionally spent alone with her parents. They always ate dinner at the General Wayne Inn and always saw a movie at the cinemas in Frazer, then they always returned home for a bottle of Tattinger champagne (Meredith had been given her first sip at age thirteen) and chocolate truffles while watching Dick Clark in Times Square on TV. Toby came along for all of it—the dinner, the movie, the champagne, the chocolates, and the ball dropping at midnight. At twelve fifteen, Chick shook Toby's hand and said, "I want you out of this house in one hour. Do you understand me?"

"Yes, sir."

"I'm not coming back down, so I'll need your word."

"You have my word, sir."

"Very good," Chick said. "Please tell your parents we say 'happy New Year.'" And he closed the door to the library with a click.

Meredith remembered sitting still as a statue on the library sofa, holding her breath, believing that it was some kind of trick. But then she heard her parents' footsteps on the stairs and their footsteps treading down the second floor hall above them. They were going to bed, leaving Toby and Meredith in the plush comfort of the library for a whole hour.

Toby approached the sofa cautiously. Meredith pulled him down on top of her.

Toby said, "Meredith, stop."

Meredith said, "He basically gave you his *permission*." She would not be deterred. It was a new year, and she was going to lose her virginity—not in the front seat of Toby's '69 Nova, and not in the grass of Valley Forge Park—but right here in her own house by the library fire.

Quietly.

*   *   *

In the spring, Toby graduated, but because he had underper-
formed on his SATs, he took a year off to boost his prospects
for college. During the summer, he and Meredith went to the
O'Briens' summer house in Cape May, where they sailed every
day and hung out on the boardwalk at night eating chili dogs and
kettle corn. They had their picture taken in a photo booth and
kept the strips in the back pockets of their jeans. They bought
matching white rope bracelets.

In the fall, Toby took two classes at Delaware County Community College and worked as a waiter at Minella's Diner. He was
around for everything Meredith's senior year, and although Meredith's parents grew concerned—was it a good idea for Meredith to
be so serious about someone in high school?—they had no grounds
for complaint. Meredith was at the top of her class at Merion Mercy,
and she was placing first and second in all her diving competitions.
She was a National Merit finalist, and everything else besides.

Because he worked at Minella's, Toby was sometimes the one
who delivered the subs to the Martin house for Chick's monthly
poker games, and one night, Chick invited Toby to come back
after his shift and join the game. This night fostered a new bond
between Chick and Toby; Meredith figured her father either liked
Toby, or he was embracing the if-you-can't-beat-'em-join-'em phi-
losophy. Chick invited Toby down to his law offices, and the two
of them went out for lunch at the City Tavern. He took Toby and
Meredith to Sixers games. He and Deidre and Toby and Meredith
went to see the lights at Longwood Gardens at Christmastime,
they went to hear the Philadelphia Orchestra at the Academy of
Music, they went out to dinner at Bookbinders and to brunch at
the Green Room in the Hotel du Pont.

"You do all this old-people stuff," Connie said. "How do you
stand it?"

"We like it," Meredith said. She refrained from telling Connie
that what she wanted most in the world was to marry Toby. She

pictured the two of them having kids and settling down on the Main Line, in a life not so different from that of her own parents.

To this day, Meredith couldn't explain how the whole thing fell apart, but fall apart it did.

Toby broke up with Meredith on the night of her high-school graduation. The O'Briens threw a huge party for Connie; the party was tented and catered and there was free-flowing alcohol for the adults, which inevitably trickled down to the teenagers. Toby was drinking Coke and Wild Turkey, but because Meredith's parents were in attendance, she was sipping lukewarm Tab. Connie was drinking gin and tonics like her mother. She had given up on her romance with Matt Klein and was now dating the star of the Radnor lacrosse team, Drew Van Dyke, who was headed to Johns Hopkins in the fall. Connie and Drew disappeared from the party at ten o'clock, and Toby wanted to ditch, too — he suggested skinny-dipping in the pool at Aronimink, then making love on the rolling hill behind the ninth tee. But this was too dangerous for Meredith; Chick was the president of the board at Aronimink, and if Meredith and Toby got caught, her father would be humiliated, which wasn't something Meredith was willing to risk. She told Toby she wanted to stay and dance to the band.

Toby said, "What are you, a hundred years old?"

It was true that the people remaining at the party were all older, friends of Bill and Veronica O'Brien.

"My parents are dancing," Meredith said. "Let's stay."

"I don't want to stay and dance with your parents," Toby said. "I'm getting kind of sick of your parents."

Meredith was aghast at this statement. She felt her cheeks grow hot.

"I'm nineteen," Toby said. "And you're eighteen. Let's go act our age."

Meredith glanced back at the dance floor. Her mother and father were jitterbugging.

"That looks like so much fun," Meredith said.

"It does not look like fun," Toby said.

Just then, a man approached Meredith. His name was Dustin Leavitt, and he worked with Bill O'Brien at Philco. Dustin Leavitt was a bachelor; he was tall and handsome and polished and charming—he was an *adult*—but he seemed to especially enjoy talking to Meredith. Over the winter, he'd seen her dive against Lower Merion—Dustin's niece swam the butterfly for Lower Merion—and that had been Meredith's best meet. She'd gotten 9's on her reverse one and a half pike and broken the pool record. *You're quite the shooting star,* Dustin Leavitt had said to her in the hallway of the school after the meet.

Since she'd arrived at the party, Meredith had felt Dustin Leavitt looking at her. Even Connie had noticed it. She'd said, "I think Dustin Leavitt has a thing for you."

And Meredith said, "Please shut up."

Connie said, "I'm serious. He's hot. And he's a *man.*"

Meredith knew he was fifteen years her senior. Thirty-three. It seemed impossibly old.

"Hey there, Toby," Dustin Leavitt said. "I'd love to take your girlfriend for a spin. Do you mind?"

Meredith was certain Toby would object, but he just shrugged. "Go for it."

"Meredith?" Dustin Leavitt held out his arms.

Meredith was uncertain. She was flattered by the gesture, certainly, but she didn't want to upset Toby. But she wanted to dance, and Toby was drinking and he was being mean. She let Dustin Leavitt lead her to the dance floor, and it was only when the song was over and Meredith and Dustin were flushed and perspiring, clapping for the band, that Meredith realized that Toby had left the party without her.

Meredith went home with her parents a while later, panicked and heartsick about Toby. She was afraid he'd left because he was mad or upset about her dancing with Dustin Leavitt. But when Meredith finally talked to him—she walked over to the O'Briens' house first thing the next morning, ostensibly to help clean up— he told her that he didn't care about her dancing with Dustin Leavitt. In fact, he said, it had come as kind of a relief.

"What does *that* mean?" Meredith asked. They were in the backyard under the tent. Toby was stacking the folding chairs, and Meredith was picking crumpled cocktail napkins out of the grass.

"I think we should break up," Toby said.

"Break up?" Meredith said. "You're breaking up with me?"

"I think I am," he said. He nodded once, definitively. "I am."

Meredith had sat down in the grass and cried. Toby stretched out beside her and leaned back on his hands. It was like he had changed overnight. He was distant and cool. He was leaving for Cape May in a few days, he said, to work as first mate on a sail-boat; he would be gone all summer, she knew that. Yes, she said, but she was supposed to visit him. Every weekend!

He said, "Right. But I think it would be better if I was free."

"Better for whom?"

"Better for me," he said. He went on to mention that, although he really liked Meredith's parents, he didn't want to *become* Meredith's parents. Not yet, anyway, and maybe not ever. "Besides," he said, "you're going to Princeton in the fall. You'll have so many amazing opportunities in front of you..."

"Jesus Christ!" Meredith screamed. She thought of the stories she had heard about Divinity Michaels locking herself in the janitor's closet and threatening to drink the ammonia. Now Meredith understood. "Don't patronize me!"

"Okay," Toby said. His expression was one of concern, but probably only because Meredith had taken the Lord's name in vain—which she never did—and he feared she was becoming a psycho like his other ex-girlfriends. "Geez, Meredith, I'm sorry. I can't change how I feel."

*   *   *

Meredith cried in her bedroom, she cried on the phone with Connie (who, if Meredith wasn't mistaken, sounded almost happy about the breakup), she skipped meals and her parents worried. Chick Martin took Meredith to the Villanova parking lot to practice for her driving test, but this turned into hour-long sessions of Meredith crying and Chick attempting to console her.

"I can't stand to see you hurt like this," Chick said. "Your mother and I feel so helpless. Do you want me to talk to Toby?"

"No," Meredith said. Her father could do many magical things, but he couldn't make Toby love her.

It took two days for Meredith's glasses to be ready, and when they were, the transformation was complete. She put on the dark wig with the pigtails and slipped on the new glasses, which had wireless rims. The lenses seemed to float before Meredith's eyes. They offered no definition the way her signature horn-rimmed glasses had.

"That's what you want," Connie said. "Trust me."

It was true that with the wig and the glasses, Meredith looked nothing like herself. From a distance, even Freddy wouldn't recognize her.

On Saturday morning, Connie suggested that they go shopping in town. Meredith declined. "Town" meant other people and she couldn't do other people.

"But you haven't even seen town," Connie said.

"I'll see it another time," Meredith said.

"Like when?" Connie said.

"When it's less populated," Meredith said. She was thinking of midnight in the middle of March. "When there's less chance of being recognized."

Connie argued that the more people were around, the less likely someone would notice Meredith. Plus, she and Wolf had always gone into town shopping on Saturday morning; it was what they did.

"Someone out there is watching me," Meredith said.

"The police checked the area. It's not like someone is watching you twenty-four, seven."

"It feels like it."

"It was a scare tactic, Meredith. That's how they want you to feel. But we're not going to let them win. We're going to live our lives. And if they're watching you today, then they're watching you shop in town."

Meredith had little room to argue, and she was desperate to get out of the house. Once they got to town, Meredith realized Connie was right: There was such a happy buzz on Main Street that no one had time to take notice of her. There were people everywhere—parents with children in strollers, couples holding hands, older men in pink polo shirts walking golden retrievers, women wearing Lilly Pulitzer skirts and carrying shopping bags from Gypsy and Eye of the Needle. Meredith used to be one of those women. Now, of course, she couldn't afford to buy a thing. But it was fun to be part of the crowd. She and Connie stopped at the Bartlett's Farm truck, and Meredith let her eyes feast on the fresh, organic produce nestled into sixteen square boxes on the tilted truck bed. It was a patchwork quilt of color—the purple cabbages, the green zucchini and cucumbers, the red hothouse tomatoes, the yellow summer squash. Connie bought some beautiful, tender lettuce and an armload of bright gladiolus that Meredith offered to carry. She felt lucky to be carrying flowers and shopping at farm trucks. She wondered what the boys were doing. She hoped Leo was with Anais, mountain biking or playing golf, momentarily free from anxiety. Poor Freddy had finished the first week of his one hundred and fifty year sentence. He was staring down an eternity of barbed wire and desolation. For all Meredith knew, this time next year, she would be in prison herself.

But she couldn't let herself think about that.

Connie led her around the corner and down the cobblestone streets to Nantucket Bookworks, where they browsed for a luxurious stretch of time. Meredith stayed away from the nonfiction shelves; already there were books about the evil empire of Delinn Enterprises. These books had been written quickly and must have contained hundreds of inaccuracies and suppositions. Meredith assumed at least one of the books contained background information about Freddy and possibly about her as well. But would they have gotten it right? Would they have written about Meredith's idyllic upbringing on the Main Line? Would they have written about how she adored her father? Would they have written about her good grades, her excellent test scores, her near-perfect reverse one and a half pike? Would they have wondered how a girl with so much on the ball had allowed herself to get mixed up with Freddy Delinn?

Meredith immersed herself in the novels. For some reason, fiction hit on the meaning of life so much more concisely than real life itself did. She browsed Atwood and Morrison, Kingsolver, Russo. She picked up a novel by Laura Kasischke that she'd seen written up in *Town & Country* months before. There was a shelf of classics, too: she could pick up the one Austen she hadn't read yet or *Pale Fire* by Nabokov. There were holes in her canon. One couldn't read everything, though Meredith could try. Now, she had the time. For one second on a sunny Saturday morning in a bookstore in Nantucket, her life seemed good, at least in that one aspect.

Then, she looked up. Connie had bought the new Barefoot Contessa cookbook and was waiting patiently, browsing at the travel section. Meredith had to make a decision. Would she buy anything? Yes, she would buy the Kasischke and *Persuasion.* She put the other books back where they belonged—Meredith wanted to follow the rules in even the smallest things now—and when she turned to the register, she saw Amy Rivers. Amy was holding a copy of Nathaniel Philbrick's *Mayflower,* asking the woman behind the counter if she could get it autographed by the author. Her voice was so familiar that Meredith panicked to the point of absolute stillness. Connie was waiting, they had other places to go, but Meredith couldn't move. Her disguise of wig and glasses wouldn't be enough. If Amy Rivers saw her, she would know her.

Amy Rivers sensed something, perhaps. She turned toward Meredith. Meredith bowed her head. Amy Rivers had left a message on the answering machine in the Delinns' Park Avenue apartment, a screaming, hysterical message in which she'd used the word "fuck" as every part of speech. She could not fucking believe it. Freddy was a lying, criminal bastard, an inexcusable fuck of a human fucking being. Then Amy lit into Meredith. Meredith had fucked her, fucking betrayed her. *And I thought we were fucking friends. What the fuck?* Meredith wanted to call Amy back, to remind Amy that it was *she* who had begged Meredith to get her in with Freddy. Meredith had given Freddy Amy's business card as a favor. Meredith had no idea Freddy was running a Ponzi scheme. She had no clue she was setting Amy up to lose all her money. Amy said herself that the returns were "unbelievable." Things that seemed unbelievable usually were. Amy was smart enough to know that. Where was Amy's due diligence? Why was this *Meredith's* fault?

Meredith felt Amy's eyes on her. She could see Amy's feet and legs. She was wearing her white Tretorns with the pink stripe, the same shoes she'd played tennis in at the Everglades Club. Meredith closed her eyes and counted to twenty. She felt a hand on her arm.

Connie said. "Hey, are you okay?"

Meredith looked up. Amy was gone.

"Yes," she said. And she went to the counter to buy her books.

That run-in was enough to send Meredith back to the refuge of Tom Nevers, but Connie was hot to keep going. They went into Stephanie's gift shop, and Connie read aloud all the funny sayings on the cocktail napkins, and Meredith faked a smile. She had let her guard down in the bookstore, and she'd nearly been assassinated. She had to remain aware at all times; she would never be safe.

They moved on: down the street, they gazed in the window of Patina at the tall, incredibly elegant Ted Muehling candlesticks.

"They're, like, eight hundred dollars apiece," Connie said.

Meredith didn't mention that in her life before, she would have waltzed right in and bought four or six of the candlesticks in different sizes. She would have filled them with the hand-milled beeswax candles that she bought at Printemps in Paris; she would have looked fondly on the candlesticks a dozen times over the next several days, feeling the buzz that buying fine, expensive things gave her. But by the end of the week, the buzz would be gone; the candlesticks would be just one more thing for Louisa to dust, and Meredith would have moved on to wanting something else—buying it, then forgetting it. It had been a shameful way to live, even when she'd believed the money she was spending was her own. She wondered if she would ever buy anything as frivolous as candlesticks again.

On to Vanessa Noel shoes. The shoes were glorious—suede and snakeskin, patent leather and sequined. There were sandals and slides and slingbacks and peep toes. Connie tried on a pair of pink slides decorated across the vamp with striped grosgrain ribbon. They fit perfectly; they made her legs look amazing. She was so tall, so slender. Meredith felt fifty stabs of jealousy, but she was used to feeling jealous about Connie's looks.

Meredith said, "They're fabulous. You should get them."

Connie said, "I think I will. But where will I ever wear them?"

Meredith said, "How about on a date with Dan Flynn?"

Connie looked at Meredith in shock, alarm, anger perhaps. Had Meredith overstepped her bounds? Connie was still singularly devoted to mourning Wolf. Meredith had noticed that Connie had been sleeping each night on the sofa under a blanket, and when Meredith asked her why, she said, "I can't sleep in the bed without him." Meredith found this a little strange. It had been two and a half years! But she'd said nothing. Now, she'd stuck her foot in her mouth.

But then Connie said slyly, "I *am* going to get them!"

While Connie was paying, Meredith picked up a pair of silver heels decorated with milky blue stones. Gorgeous, original—they would have matched a blue silk shutter-pleat dress that Meredith had left in her closet in Cap d'Antibes. These were shoes for a dress she no longer owned. They were on sale for $495.

No.

On the way back home, they stopped at Nantucket Looms where Connie bought a certain kind of wildflower soap that she liked, and then they passed Saint Mary's, the Catholic church. It was a gray-shingled building with white trim—just like every other building on Nantucket—and there was a simple white statue of the Virgin Mary out front. The Virgin held her hands out in a way that seemed to beckon Meredith in.

She said to Connie, "I'm going in to light a candle, okay?"

Connie nodded and took a seat on a bench. "I'll wait here."

Meredith entered the church and inhaled the vague scent of incense; a funeral Mass must have been celebrated that morning. She slipped three dollars into the slot, and even then, she felt a twinge—three precious dollars! She lit the first candle for Leo. It was a parent's job to keep his children safe, and Freddy had failed. He had so wanted the boys to join him in business, although it had been obvious from the beginning that he would only get Leo. Leo had worked preposterous hours, and he had made very little money compared to the people who worked on the abhorrent seventeenth floor. Surely the Feds realized this? If Leo was in on the Ponzi scheme, wouldn't he be rich, too, like the rest of them? Why would Freddy involve Leo in something illegal? How was it any different from giving Leo a handgun and forcing him to hold up a 7-Eleven?

Keep Leo safe, Meredith prayed.

She lit a candle for Carver. Carver was a free spirit; he'd had no interest in an office job, and Freddy, reluctantly, had let him go. Carver had asked Freddy for a loan in order to buy his first renovation project, and Freddy had said no. No handouts. So Carver had gone to the bank himself, and they gave him the loan because his last name was Delinn and nobody turned down a loan to a Delinn. And now, thank God, he wasn't involved; he was a carpenter, and he could keep a roof over his brother's head.

Keep Carver strong, Meredith prayed.

She struggled with the last candle, then decided she would light it for Freddy.

But she couldn't think of a word to say to God on his behalf.

She blessed herself and stepped back out into the sun. She was ready to go home. Her wig was starting to itch.

As they pulled into Connie's driveway, Meredith studied the front of the house. The paint had come off, but the power washing left the ghost of the word behind. If you looked closely, *CROOK* was still there — only instead of hideous green letters, it was marked by shingles that were paler than the others. Dan had come back that morning to do some touch-up work. They had missed him, but there were telltale puddles in the front yard. Dan had promised that, over time, the shingles he'd blasted would weather back to gray. In six months, he said, the damage would be completely gone.

Connie pulled her purchases from the backseat of the Escalade. "Dan was here," she said, eyeing the dripping eaves. "I can't believe we missed him."

Meredith was the first one to the front door. A business card was sticking out of the screen. She plucked it — it was Dan's card. On the back, he'd written, "Connie, call me!" Meredith felt a rush of adolescent excitement.

"Look!" she said. "He left this!"

Connie flipped the card over. Her expression was inscrutable. She said, "It's probably something about the house. Or about the bill."

Meredith felt a twinge of panic. The bill. She would pay it, but how much would it be? Four hundred? Six hundred?

"You're going to call him, though, right?" Meredith said.

"Not right now," Connie said.

Meredith didn't push it. Once inside, she extracted the bobby pins from her head and pulled off her wig. Ahhh. Her real hair, which could now only be described as blondish gray, was matted.

She tried to fix it in the mirror. Her glasses were truly awful. No man would ever leave a business card for her. But that was okay; that was absolutely for the best.

Meredith longed to go for a swim. There was the sunny deck, and there was the beach twenty stairs below. There was the golden sand and the cool, blue water. But unlike the center of town with all its busyness and crowds, being on Connie's property spooked her.

Connie said, "There's Harold."

"Where?" Meredith said.

Connie pointed offshore, and Meredith saw the sleek black head surface, then disappear. Yes, only one seal.

"How long has Harold been around?" Meredith asked.

"I was wondering that the other day," Connie said. "And I figured out this is the fifth summer."

"The fifth? Really?"

"Wolf saw him first when he was fooling around with his binoculars. The next summer, Wolf was sick, but we came here anyway, and Wolf spent a lot of time on the deck, wrapped in a blanket. He couldn't see very well by that point, but I would tell him every time I saw Harold. The following summer, Wolf had died, and we scattered his ashes here. Then last summer. And now this summer. So, five." Connie was quiet for a moment, then she said, "It's amazing how Wolf's death has put everything into two categories: before Wolf died and after Wolf died."

Meredith nodded. She certainly understood that: the before and the after.

"Let's have lunch," Connie said.

Connie wanted to eat on the deck, but Meredith refused.

"You're being ridiculous," Connie said.

"I can't help myself," Meredith said. "I feel exposed."

"You're safe," Connie said. "No one is going to hurt you."

"You don't know that," Meredith said.

Connie was holding two beautiful plates of food. "Okay, I'll eat inside one more time. But after this, I'm eating outside if I want to. I'm lying on the deck, just like I did the other day. I'm going for a swim."

"You won't swim until August," Meredith said. "Admit it, you think the water's too cold."

"The water is too cold," Connie said. "But I'll walk on the beach. And if they want to photograph me walking on the beach, so be it. I'll give them the finger. That's what you have to do, Meredith. Mentally give them the finger. Let them know they don't scare you."

"They do scare me," Meredith said.

Even inside, lunch was delicious: tuna sandwiches with hothouse tomato and the farm lettuce, great globs of mayonnaise, the subtle tang of mustard. They drank cold cans of sparkling Italian lemonade.

Connie had Dan Flynn's business card next to her plate. She said, "I'm sure he just wants to know where to send the bill."

Meredith said, "Call him and find out."

Connie made a face. Then she picked up the phone. Meredith stood to give her friend some privacy, and Connie snapped her fingers and pointed to Meredith's chair.

"Stay," she said. "I can't do this alone."

Meredith sat.

Connie said, in a bright voice, "Hi, Dan? It's Connie Flute calling. From Tom Nevers? Yes, it looks great. I'm so *relieved*. You're a lifesaver!" She paused and her green eyes widened. "Oh? Tonight you mean? Gosh, well...I have other plans tonight, I'm afraid. What about tomorrow night?" She bit her lower lip. "Okay, that sounds great. And would it be okay if Meredith joined us?"

Meredith waved her arms and shook her head so violently, she heard wind in her ears. *NO!*

"I can't leave her here alone," Connie said. "Especially not after what happened."

Meredith mouthed, "You go! I'll stay here!"

"Okay, that sounds perfect. Seven thirty, Company of the Cauldron. Wonderful. You'll come pick us up at six? So early, you're sure? You're sure it's not out of your way? Oh, don't lie—it's out of everyone's way! We could just meet you at the restaurant. Really? You're sure? Okay, okay, fine, drinks sound fun. So... we'll see you at six. Thanks, Dan! Bye-bye." She hung up.

Meredith said, "What the hell are you thinking?"

Connie collapsed in her chair. She fiddled with the bread crusts that were still on her plate. "He asked me out to dinner. To the Company of the Cauldron. Which is the most romantic restaurant on earth."

Meredith groaned. "I'm not going with you."

"You have to," Connie said.

"Oh, come on, Connie. Why?"

Connie massaged her forehead. "I'm not ready to date. Normally, I would have just told this guy I'm not ready—but if you come with us, then it won't be a real date and I'll be okay." Connie's cheeks were flushed and her green eyes were shining. She liked Dan. And why not—he was good-looking, he was the right age, he'd lost his wife. But Meredith knew that if she refused to go, Connie would call Dan back and cancel. How was this any different from Connie insisting that Meredith come with her to Radnor High School three afternoons a week to watch Matt Klein wrestle when they were in the eleventh grade? How was it different from driving with Connie past Drew Van Dyke's house in the middle of the night to make sure his car was in the driveway and not parked in front of Phoebe Duncan's house?

"This is high school all over again," Meredith said.

"That's what life is," Connie said. "It's high school, over and over and over again."

It would be nice if that were true, Meredith thought. In high school, no one died of prostate cancer. In high school, no one was operating a $50 billion Ponzi scheme. The fact that what was happening right now was like high school was something to rejoice about, she supposed.

"All right," Meredith said. "I'll go." She didn't *want* to be left in the house alone; it would absolutely petrify her. "Did he sound upset that you were dragging me along?"

"Not really," Connie said.

Right: men would do anything for Connie, including having dinner with the wife of the biggest robber baron in history.

"And what plans do we have tonight?" Meredith asked.

"Plans?"

"You told Dan you had plans tonight."

"Of course I did," Connie said. She stood to clear the table. "I couldn't let him believe we were *staying home*. Don't you know anything?"

Their "plans" for Saturday night included eating a goat cheese soufflé and Caesar salad for dinner—it was like something Meredith used to order at Pastis, and Connie had whipped it up herself. And after dinner, Connie invited Meredith upstairs to Wolf's study to look at the stars through Wolf's telescope.

"Wolf knew all of the constellations," Connie said. She pointed the telescope out the window. "I only know Orion, the Big Dipper, and Cassiopeia."

"I can find the Little Dipper," Meredith said. "And the Pleiades. And I know what the Southern Cross looks like." Meredith had seen the Southern Cross on a trip she and Freddy had taken to Australia. They had been staying in the northwestern seaside town of Broome, which was the remotest place Meredith had ever visited. Freddy had a friend from business school named Michael Arrow who owned a huge pearl farm in Broome. Michael had been an investor; he had lost the pearl farm, which had been in his family since 1870. Michael had been a good guy, open and likable; he had been a friend. Meredith wondered how Freddy felt about cheating Michael Arrow. *Goddamn you, Freddy!* she thought (zillionth and fourth).

What Meredith remembered about Broome was the open-air

movie theater Michael had taken them to. They had sat on swings and watched a movie under the stars. Meredith couldn't remember what movie they'd seen, but she remembered Michael saying, "And that beauty there? That's our Southern Cross."

Meredith wondered if she'd ever see the Southern Cross again. Freddy, most certainly, would not.

Through the telescope, the stars looked closer, though they were still just stars, just points of light that were millions of miles away.

Connie said, "Freddy bought you a star, didn't he?"

Meredith nodded but said nothing. Freddy had bought Meredith a star and named it Silver Girl, after the lyrics of a song that Meredith's father used to sing her. *Sail on Silvergirl, Sail on by, Your time has come to shine, All your dreams are on their way, See how they shine.* The song was "Bridge Over Troubled Water." Every time it came on the radio, Chick Martin would reach for Meredith's hand. *Oh, if you need a friend, I'm sailing right behind.* Chick Martin had bought the album for Meredith's birthday. He played the song before each of her swim meets. They had slow-danced to the song in the living room in the hour before Meredith's graduation. He had played the song on a cassette during every driving lesson after Toby broke up with her and left town for the summer. Meredith had played the song on her turntable again and again in the cold, lonely days after Chick Martin dropped dead of a brain aneurysm. She had the old album upstairs in her sole cardboard box; it was now, and always had been, her most precious possession. Even though technology had rendered the album all but useless, she couldn't bear to part with it.

Meredith had explained the meaning of the song to Freddy, and, years later, when NASA made it possible for private citizens to buy and name stars, Freddy had bought a star for Meredith and named it Silver Girl.

Whoa. That was hard to think about, for many reasons.

Meredith excused herself for bed.

*   *   *

Connie was so excited about the date with Dan Flynn that Meredith felt herself growing excited by osmosis. Connie spent all day on the deck in the sun, diligently applying SPF 15 to her face and keeping cucumber slices over her eyes like a movie star. Meredith watched Connie from the safety of the living-room sofa, where she lay reading a book. More than anything, she wanted to be outside, but she couldn't relax while worrying that someone might photograph her. The paparazzi in New York had been relentless, swarming the awning of Meredith's building for days. But this was more insidious—the hidden camera, the secret, gazing eye recording Meredith's every move. Whether or not there was anyone out there watching her didn't matter. Meredith felt self-conscious; she felt guilty. She didn't belong on a sunny deck on Nantucket.

She wanted to call Dev to see if he had any further news from Julie Schwarz about Leo's case. Had they discredited Deacon Rapp? Had they found Mrs. Misurelli? Meredith switched on her cell phone and held her breath as she waited for calls or texts to come in. Nothing. Then she realized it was Sunday and even Dev, as hard as he worked, wouldn't be in the office. He would be on a lake fishing somewhere, or strolling in Central Park. Hell, even the Feds—the nameless, faceless Feds—would be enjoying summertime today.

Meredith was borrowing a white linen dress from Connie; it was too long, it hit her midknee, but what could she do? She wished her skin had a little bit of color. She slipped on the dress first, then did her makeup, then put on her wig. It didn't matter what she looked like, she reminded herself. She was the sidekick here, the tagalong. She was Rhoda to Connie's Mary Tyler Moore. She was Mary Ann to Connie's Ginger.

Connie looked absolutely drop-dead gorgeous in a celadon-green silk sheath. She looked like a mermaid who lured sailors to their death. She had on sparkly silver Manolos (Meredith had once owned a nearly identical pair) and she wore Guerlain Champs-

Élysées and smelled like a garden in Provence. *Oh, perfume!* Meredith nearly asked Connie for a spritz, but she refrained. It didn't matter how she smelled.

There was a knock at the door, and Dan Flynn materialized in the foyer. He was a very handsome man to begin with, and he cleaned up incredibly well. He wore creased white pants with expensive-looking loafers and a blue-patterned Robert Graham shirt.

Connie floated down the hallway. From her perch on the stairs, Meredith could see Dan's eyes pop. It gave Meredith a vicarious thrill, watching Dan feast on the vision of her lovely friend. They embraced awkwardly, and Meredith suppressed a smile. Then Dan noticed Meredith and said, "And here comes my second date. Am I lucky or what?"

Connie and Meredith climbed into Dan Flynn's strawberry-red Jeep. The soft black top was accordioned down, and Dan said, "Here we go! Hold on to your hair!" This was a joke about Meredith's wig—and surprise!—Meredith laughed. She did, indeed, hold on to her hair. The wind and the sun in her face were intoxicating. Dan played some Robert Cray. Meredith felt relaxed for the first time in months. She had made a deal with herself in the upstairs bathroom that she wouldn't spend the evening musing about what the boys were doing, or about Freddy. Freddy, she had to assume, was fending for himself, and she, Meredith, was left to do the same. She was determined to be a sparkling dinner companion, witty and interesting—and not the complete downer that Dan Flynn, no doubt, expected.

"We're starting with drinks!" Dan said. "Champagne!" Yes, Meredith loved champagne, although it gave her a regrettable headache. They arrived at the Galley Restaurant, which looked out over Nantucket Sound; they took their champagne onto the sand, where they lounged across low-slung wicker furniture covered with creamy linen pillows. It was a scene straight from the south of France. Meredith listened to Connie and Dan talk about Nantucket—the way it was now, the way it used to be. Dan Flynn had been born and raised on the island, and his father before him and his father...back five generations. At one time, he said, his family had owned nearly a tenth of the land on the island, but they had sold some of it off and donated some to conservation. Dan was a fisherman and a clammer and the owner of twenty-five lobster traps. He owned the power-washing business, and he managed his family's fourteen properties, though his real job, he said, was to know everyone on the island and everything that was going on. In the off-season, he traveled. Just like the whalers of the 1800s, Dan Flynn had seen the world. He had ridden a motorcycle through China; he had backpacked through India, contracted malaria, and spent months convalescing, with the help of some psychedelic drugs, on the beach in Goa. He had hiked with his wife and three sons to see Machu Picchu.

Connie was beaming, and it looked like real Connie beaming and not fake, polite Connie beaming. Dan was a charmer and a gentleman. When Meredith tried to slip him a twenty-dollar bill for the drinks, he said, "Put that away. Everything tonight is my treat." Meredith felt a relief she would have found absurd only a year before: she didn't have to worry about money.

They left the Galley and stopped for another round of drinks at 21 Federal. Even Meredith, who knew next to nothing about Nantucket, had heard of 21 Federal—which meant she had to be on high alert. She would see someone she knew—but, she reassured herself, no one would recognize her. The wig, the glasses. Dan had been instructed to introduce her as Meredith Martin.

Dan knew everyone at the bar at 21 Federal, including both of the bartenders. He ordered more champagne. The bar was dark and sophisticated; the clientele was attractive and convivial. But it was in gracious, genteel places like this that the Delinn name got kicked around. These were the people who had lost money or who knew people who lost money. *We're changing our last name,* Carver had said. *You should, too.*

Meredith wondered if the boys had followed through with this.

Would Leo be able to change his name while under investigation? She worried that if they did change their name, they would slip away from her, and how would she ever find them?

She had to bring herself back. Stay present, no musing! The people next to her were talking about horses. Dan and Connie were talking about sailing.

Connie said, "My husband used to sail. And my brother, Toby, is a sailor."

Toby, Meredith thought. God, she remembered when Toby had seemed like the dangerous one.

Meredith excused herself for the ladies' room, even though this meant walking past people seated for dinner, people who might recognize her. She glanced surreptitiously at faces: she knew no one. She eyed the door to the ladies' room warily. Amy Rivers could be on the other side of that door.

She wondered if she would ever outlive this particular anxiety.

The ladies' room was empty. Meredith peed gratefully, washed her hands, adjusted her wig, and briefly studied herself in the full-length mirror. Somewhere in this disguise was a girl who had been able to execute a flawless reverse one and a half pike, a woman who had read all of Jane Austen's novels except for one, a daughter and a wife and a mother who had always acted out of love. She was a good person, though no one would ever see her that way again.

Goddamn you, Freddy Delinn, she thought (zillionth and fifth). Then she took it back, because that was how she was.

The Company of the Cauldron was, as Connie had promised, the most romantic restaurant on earth. The room was small, charming, cozy. It was lit only by candles and decorated with dried flowers, copper pots, antique farm implements, and kitchen utensils. There was a harp player, and the sound of the music made Meredith think that even if everything she'd been told about heaven turned out to be false, there had better still be a harp player. Dan knew the owners of the restaurant, and so they were given the table in the front window, where they could look across the cobblestone street. Connie and Meredith sat next to each other, and Dan sat across from them. There was a rustic loaf of bread on the table, and a dish of garlicky white-bean dip. Dan ordered a bottle of wine, and when the waiter left to fetch it, Dan reached for Connie's hand. Connie and Dan were holding hands, this was their date that Meredith was crashing, and yet Meredith didn't want to be anywhere else.

As their food arrived, the conversation grew more serious. Dan talked about his wife and her ten-year battle with breast cancer. Her name was Nicole, she found a lump when she was forty years old and her youngest child was four. She went through chemo, and then a double mastectomy, and then five years on tamoxifen. Nicole had taken every possible precaution, including putting herself on what Dan called "a nasty macrobiotic diet," and just when they thought she'd beat it—she was in great shape, doing long breast-cancer walks across the state—they found the cancer had metastasized to her liver. She was dead in two months.

"I'm so sorry," Connie said. Her eyes were shining with tears.

"The kids?" Meredith said.

"It was paralyzing for the boys," Dan said. "Especially my oldest. He ditched his plans for college, stole my old pickup truck, and lit out for California. I hardly ever hear from him."

That makes three of us who aren't in touch with our kids, Meredith thought.

Connie took a breath. "My husband died of prostate cancer that metastasized to the brain," she said. "But I can't talk about it. I'm just trying to survive each day."

Dan raised his wine glass. "To survival."

Amen, thought Meredith.

The three of them touched glasses.

The evening might have ended with the tiny, seductive chocolates that came with the bill, but Dan Flynn was one of those people who never stopped. (Freddy had always been in bed by ten o'clock, and preferably nine thirty. *The stress!* he used to say, when Meredith begged him to stay out later. *There's no way you'd understand!*) Dan pulled Connie and Meredith down the street to the Club Car. There was more champagne ordered for the ladies, while Dan drank a glass of port. Meredith was tentative at first — again, scanning the old Pullman car for people she knew. (On the way, Dan had told Meredith that this Pullman car had once been part of the train that ran from Nantucket town out to Sconset.) But Meredith was drawn to the back end of the car where a man played the piano and people gathered around him singing "Sweet Caroline" and "Ob-La-Di Ob-La-Da." At one point, Meredith caught sight of Dan nuzzling Connie's neck at the bar. This was the romantic end of their date; they would both want to be rid of Meredith soon. The piano player launched into "I Guess That's Why They Call It the Blues," and Meredith belted it out, thinking of Sister Delphine at Merion Mercy, who had trained Meredith's voice for four years in the madrigal choir. Now here she was, a rather drunk torch singer.

The piano player turned to Meredith. "You have a great voice," he said. "What's your name?"

She had to make up a name. She touched her wig. "Mary Ann," she said.

"Okay, Mary Ann, you pick the next song," he said.

She picked "I Will Survive" by Gloria Gaynor, since survival had become a sort of theme for the evening. A theme for the summer.

CONNIE

On Monday morning, Connie woke up and didn't know where she was.

Then she laughed, uneasily.

She was in her bed.

She was in her own bed, tucked between the crisp white sheets, her head sunk into a cloud of a pillow. Light spilled in through the windows. The ocean seemed so close it felt like the waves were lapping at the bottom of the bed.

Connie's head was heavy but not throbbing. She noticed water in the glass carafe on her night table, with a thin slice of lemon, just as she liked it. She had no recollection of fixing it herself. She looked circumspectly over her shoulder to make sure the other side of the bed was unoccupied.

Okay.

Her clock said 5:30. God love Nantucket, the Far East of the United States. Morning came early. Connie put a second pillow over her head, and closed her eyes.

When she reawoke at ten minutes to eight, she thought, *My God, I'm in my bedroom! I'm in my bed!*

She had done it. She had faced down some kind of demon and slept in her own bed. But this pride was quickly replaced by guilt. She had slept in her own bed when *not* sleeping in it had been a tribute, of sorts, to Wolf.

Connie pulled a feather pillow to her chest as memories of the previous night came back to her. She had held hands with Dan Flynn, and just that act—holding hands with a man—had felt sinfully good. All her life she had had boyfriends; in high school and college she left one for the next. She hadn't been alone for five minutes, she realized, until Wolf died. That she had survived for so long without male attention seemed amazing, like going without hot food or good books. At the Club Car, Dan had put his mouth on her neck, and something inside of her stirred, as if returning from the dead. She had to shake off the chill, but she was doing it; she was warming up! How long since she had given her physicality any thought? With Dan, all she wanted to be was a body.

Once they were home and Meredith had stumbled up to bed, Dan and Connie had gone into the kitchen—ostensibly for a nightcap—though what Dan had asked for was water. Connie didn't remember water, what she remembered was soft, deep kissing that sent her into the stratosphere.

And Dan, the gentleman, had kept it to just kissing. Connie had cried, she remembered that now, when she told Dan that she hadn't kissed a man since Wolf died. She had believed that her days of being kissed were over. Dan didn't offer a parallel sentiment. He didn't say that Connie had been the first woman he'd kissed since Nicole died, which probably meant he'd stanched the bleeding of his heart with the kindnesses proffered by other women. He'd had sex with a woman from Nicole's yoga class when she brought over a brown-rice casserole, or he'd allowed himself to be seduced by the children's twenty-one-year-old nanny. Men were different creatures. If Connie had been the one who had died, Wolf would never have spent two and a half years sleeping on the sofa. He would already be remarried to some younger, prettier, less seasoned version of Connie. Of that she was sure.

Connie drank down the water and slipped out of bed. She would leave it unmade; she liked the way it looked rumpled. Finally, the bedroom looked inhabited.

She brushed her teeth, washed her face, inspected her skin in the mirror. She was still pretty. Big whoop. She had always been pretty, but this morning she was grateful for her looks. Dan Flynn had kissed her. He had left it at kissing—maybe because he wanted to take it slow, or maybe because today was Monday and he was scheduled to work at a house on Pocomo Point at 8 a.m.

Yes, that was it. That was what he'd told her.

It was *Monday*.

Connie gasped. Oh, my God. Oh, my God. Oh, my God. She... she couldn't even say it. A realization came to her that was so slippery, it shot right out of her grip, ricocheted around, bounced, and oozed before landing with a big, ugly, stinky splat on the floor of her mind.

She hadn't called Ashlyn yesterday. It had been Sunday, and she hadn't called.

Connie looked at herself in the mirror with wide eyes. Her eyelashes stuck together with clumps of the previous night's mascara. She had gone on a date with another man, she had kissed that man, she had slept in her own bed for the first time in two and a half years. This was all noteworthy. Indeed, startling.

But overshadowing these developments: she had forgotten to call her daughter.

After the initial panic passed, Connie thought, *I wonder if Ashlyn noticed. And if she did notice, I wonder if she cared.*

Connie hadn't spoken to her daughter since ten days after Wolf's funeral, on the day that they settled Wolf's estate and took care of the accounting at their lawyer's office in Georgetown. Ashlyn had received a trust fund filled with stocks and government bonds — it was a portfolio that Wolf had been building for her for years — that was now worth between $600,000 and $700,000. And she had inherited Wolf's navy-blue Aston Martin convertible. Ashlyn had been able to contain her seething anger and bitterness until she had the money in hand and was seated behind the wheel of the car — and then she drove out of Connie's life.

Part of it was the curse of having a daughter who was a doctor. When Wolf was diagnosed with prostate cancer, Ashlyn had just graduated from Johns Hopkins University School of Medicine, and she was doing her residency in pediatric oncology at the Washington Cancer Institute at WHC. Wolf had been suffering from symptoms and ignoring them; he was too busy with work, and although beaming with pride about the accomplishments of his daughter, he himself didn't like to go to the doctor. He liked to allow his body to heal itself, no matter the suffering. This had been true through the decades that Connie had been married to him, with stomach bugs, ear infections, colds. The problem with Wolf's prostate had presented itself a little differently, interfering as it did with their sex life. Connie had been relieved when Wolf made an appointment with a urologist, and then when he got the news of irregularities with his prostate, she was alarmed. But the first oncologist they saw was a placid man who assured them that radiation would take care of the problem. Wolf would be tired; for a while, he would be incontinent and their sex life would be put on hold.

Ashlyn had been privy to what the doctors had told Wolf, and she had agreed with their treatment plan. She and Wolf had private phone conversations about his illness, and that was fine. Ashlyn had a shiny new medical degree and she wanted to show it off. She knew far more about cancerous cells than Connie did, even though cancer of the prostate wasn't something Ashlyn saw in ped onc. Connie and Ashlyn didn't discuss Wolf's illness except in the most general terms because it was *prostate* cancer, and despite the fact that Ashlyn was a doctor, Connie still believed Wolf's privacy should be respected.

As predicted, the cancer went away following radiation treatment. Wolf wore adult diapers for twelve weeks or so; when they went to the theater, Connie would carry a spare diaper in her purse and slip it to Wolf like a contraband package before he went to the men's room. It was a humbling time for Wolf, but a small price to pay for a clean bill of health.

And then life went back to normal. Wolf was given an Institute Honor Award from the AIA for a student union building he designed at Catholic University, and three enormous commissions followed, including a federal commission to design and build a new VA building in downtown D.C. Wolf had never been busier, but both he and Connie recognized the work and its compensation as a golden sunburst that would mark the pinnacle of his career. They had nearly $3 million in investments with Delinn Enterprises, and that money was growing exponentially—one month they had a return of 29 percent—and this, along with the award, the commissions, and Wolf's restored health, secured their sense of good fortune and well-being.

Wolf started experiencing splotchy vision at the same time that

Ashlyn brought a friend home for her parents to meet, a woman named Bridget.

Ashlyn and Bridget both lived in Adams Morgan, less than thirty minutes away from Wolf and Connie in Bethesda, but they decided to come and stay for the weekend. Connie, initially believing this to be a "country escape" for two overworked, stressed-out residents, took great pains to make the house welcoming. She made up the beds in both guest rooms and put dahlias in glass vases on the nightstands. She baked cranberry muffins and braised short ribs to serve with a mushroom stroganoff. She filled the Aston Martin with gas and mapped out the drive to the biggest pumpkin patch in the state of Maryland. She had bought two novels lauded in *Washington Post Book World* and had rented a handful of new releases from the video store.

What Connie *hadn't* done was to think about what this visit from Ashlyn and her closest friend might *mean*—until she saw them walking hand in hand, with their duffel bags, from the Metro station. Until she saw them stop in the middle of the brick path that led to Connie and Wolf's front door and face each other and share an intimate, whispered moment—Ashlyn was clearly reassuring Bridget that the weekend would be fine; her parents were open-minded, tolerant, liberal people, registered Democrats, pro-choice, anti-war—and then kiss.

Connie was watching them from the front window. She had been anticipating their arrival. And quite honestly, it was as if her heart were a teacup that fell to the floor and shattered.

Ashlyn and Bridget were lovers. The reason that Ashlyn had wanted to come spend the weekend wasn't to tell her parents this but, rather, to show them.

Connie straightened her spine. She tried a couple of smiles before she opened the front door. She needed to talk to Wolf, but he was on-site. The commissions had kept Wolf at work for ridiculously long hours, and although Connie hadn't complained, she now felt abandoned and resentful. She needed Wolf here. He should have been paying attention; he might have prepared Connie for this possibility. Was her daughter, her only child, a lesbian? Yes, it appeared so. Although girls, Connie thought, were more apt to experiment sexually, weren't they? Time to ruminate was running out; Connie could hear the girls' footsteps on the stairs leading to the front door. She could hear Ashlyn giggling. This didn't mean there would never be a wedding at the house on Nantucket as Connie had always dreamed. This didn't mean there would never be grandchildren. Connie *was* liberal; she *was* tolerant. She had taken women's studies classes at Villanova; she had read Audre Lorde and Angela Carter and Simone de Beauvoir. But was it still okay for Connie to say that this *wasn't* how she wanted things to turn out? This—Connie opened the door and saw Ashlyn and Bridget side by side, grinning nervously—wasn't what she wanted at all.

She got an A+ for trying in her own estimation. Connie smiled and hugged Bridget and fawned over her as though she were an adorable kitten Ashlyn had brought home. Bridget was Irish, from County Mayo, and she had an elfin quality about her—a pixie cut of black hair, freckles, and that accent, which stirred delight in Connie despite the circumstances. She was witty and, from what Ashlyn said, wickedly brilliant. She was exactly the kind of girl Connie would have wanted a son to bring home.

Connie plied the girls with oatmeal chocolate chip cookies—Ashlyn's childhood favorite—and a pot of tea—the lover was Irish—and she chattered like an idiot. An idiot mother who hadn't guessed her own child's sexual preference. (Had there been clues Connie had missed? In high school and college and even in medical school, Ashlyn had had *boyfriends*. Wolf had caught one young man climbing the rose trellis up to Ashlyn's bedroom in the middle of the night. And, as Wolf had shouted angrily at the time, that boy hadn't come to play tiddlywinks!) Connie knew she was transparent—at least to Ashlyn—and she was grateful when Ashlyn said that she and Bridget were going up to "their" room to unpack. This gave Connie a chance to escape to the sanctuary of her bedroom where she called Wolf to break the news.

He listened, but didn't comment. He said, "I know this is going to sound like a complete non sequitur, but I have a crushing headache. The pressure in my skull is so intense, it feels like I'm growing horns. Can this wait until I get home?"

That night, the four of them sat around the dining-room table eating the sumptuous meal that Connie had prepared, and Ashlyn and Bridget talked about the trip they were planning to London, Wales, Scotland, and finally to Ireland to visit Bridget's family.

So another mother can have her dreams trampled, Connie thought.

But what she said was, "That sounds terrific, girls!"

Ashlyn scowled, probably at the use of the term "girls." Why infantilize them? Why not refer to them as women or, better still, people? But Connie found it helpful to think of them as innocent girls: Ashlyn with her long, pale hair left loose except for a braid that framed her face and made her look like a Renaissance maiden, and Bridget with her shiny cap of black hair and her implike smile. They weren't so different from Connie and Meredith in high school—always together, palling around, being funny and affectionate with each other—were they?

Wolf didn't say much of anything during dinner. His head, he complained. And he'd already taken six hundred milligrams of ibuprofen. He excused himself before dessert. The girls settled on the couch to watch one of the DVDs Connie had rented and to eat apple brown betty and make some jokes about the whipped cream that Connie pretended not to hear as she cleaned up in the kitchen. She reminded herself that this was probably a phase. She prayed to God that she wouldn't be woken up by any female cries of ecstasy, and she cursed Wolf for being so self-absorbed. When she got upstairs, he was already in bed with the light off, a washcloth folded over his eyes.

Connie said, "I honestly can't believe it."

Wolf said, "I'm going blind, Con. I can't see a thing."

*   *   *

In the morning, Ashlyn took one look at her father and suggested he call his primary care physician. But it was Saturday, so that meant the emergency room. Wolf resisted. He would just take some more ibuprofen and lie down.

Ashlyn said, "Dad, your right pupil is dilated."

Wolf said, "I just need rest. I've been working like a demon."

And Ashlyn, caught up in the throes of romance, didn't push him the way she might have normally. She and Bridget were, at Connie's suggestion, off to the pumpkin patch in the Aston Martin. They were taking a picnic.

By two o'clock, Wolf was moaning. By three, he asked Connie to call an ambulance.

Connie changed into shorts and a T-shirt. She pulled her hair back into a ponytail. The house was still; Meredith was sleeping. Connie would go get the newspaper. She would drive around and clear her head. She would decide whether to call Ashlyn this morning or wait and see what happened. In her heart, however, Connie knew that nothing would happen. She could call or not call—it didn't matter.

Wolf had been diagnosed with prostate cancer that had metastasized to the brain. He had two tumors located in the frontal lobe and so, the oncologist said, Wolf's analogy about "growing horns" was apt. One of the tumors was operable; one was inoperable. The inoperable tumor was spread out, like a spilled drink on a table. They would give Wolf chemo and try to shrink the inoperable tumor. If they got it to a stage where it could be contained, they could go in and scoop out both tumors at once.

Wolf, over the course of the weekend, had seemed to accept his own mortality. "What if I decline chemo? What if I just let them be?"

The doctor said, "Severe headaches, which we can manage with medication. Blotchy vision, ditto. Depending on how aggressive the cancer is, you might have one year; you might have three."

Wolf squeezed Connie's hand. "Okay," he said.

"Chemo," Connie said.

"Let me think about it," he said.

Connie sat on the edge of the unmade bed. At dinner at the Company of the Cauldron the night before, Dan Flynn had told them about his wife's death. The basics of her illness were similar to Wolf's. The cancer disappeared then resurfaced—the same cancer—in a different place. Nicole had breast cancer travel to her liver. Wolf had prostate cancer travel to his brain. It seemed so unfair: the doctor declared you "clean," said you'd "beat it," and then one random, renegade cell traveled to a more hospitable location and decided to multiply.

Connie had never been able to share Wolf's story with anyone who hadn't lived through it with her. It was too Byzantine; it didn't make sense.

Wolf had refused chemo.

Part of this was because of the three commissions he was working on, including the new VA building. These buildings would, presumably, stand for decades and possibly centuries. It was architecture, he was the architect, and if he bailed out now because of debilitating treatment, he would lose control. The buildings would become something else—someone else's—even if they used his plans.

"It would be like Picasso handing his palette to his assistant, or to some other artist—Matisse, say—and asking that person to finish *Guernica*. You understand that, don't you, Connie?"

What Connie understood was that Wolf thought he was Picasso. So it was about ego.

"Not ego," Wolf said. "Legacy. I can finish these three buildings and complete my legacy, or I can go in for chemo and let my legacy slip down the drain. And there's no saying the chemo will save me. The chemo might shrink my tumor to an operable size, and then I'll die on the table."

"You have to have faith," Connie said.

"I have faith that I can finish the buildings," he said. "I can finish my life's work."

"And what about me?" Connie said.

"I love you," Wolf said.

He loved her but not enough to fight the disease. The work was what was important. His legacy. This was his argument, and Connie also knew that deep down, he was afraid. He didn't like doctors, he was distrustful of the health-care system, he feared chemo, and he feared having his head shaved, his skull cracked open, and his brain scooped out like orange sherbet or rocky road. Better to bury himself in the work and pretend like nothing was wrong. Numb his pain with Percocet and, later, morphine, and hope that his body healed itself. Connie had been married to Wolf for twenty-five years, but she, ultimately, had no say or sway in the matter. It was his body, his illness, his decision. She could either fight him or back him. She backed him.

Ashlyn was furious. She was, in turn, incredulous and disconsolate. She stormed Wolf's office, then his work sites, and lectured him. She set up an appointment for a second opinion that he agreed to go to and then skipped at the last minute because of a problem with his head mason. Ashlyn stormed the house and screamed at Connie.

"You're just going to stand by and let him die!"

Wolf died seventeen months later. He had gotten two of his commissions done and the third—the spectacular, complicated VA building—into its final phase.

Connie couldn't believe she had all but lost her only child over Wolf's death, but the fact was, Ashlyn had always been an intense, tricky kid. She was all or nothing. She loved you or hated you;

there was never any middle ground. Connie herself had grown up scattered, disorganized, fun loving, laid back. None of these words applied to Ashlyn. Ashlyn didn't accept compromise; she didn't take it easy on herself or others. Connie and Wolf had once met with a school psychologist who was concerned that Ashlyn was "preoccupied with perfection." She was eight years old, and when she held a crayon, a vein bulged in her forehead.

After Wolf died, Ashlyn's anger consumed her. Ashlyn *became* her anger. During the days when there was still dialogue, Connie had heard it all.

Ashlyn said, "You didn't encourage him to fight. If you're diagnosed with an illness like his — which was certainly treatable, if not curable — you battle it. You do whatever you can, you take the clinical trials, you go through seventeen rounds of chemo, you do what you have to do to stay alive."

"But you know your father didn't feel that way. His work..."

"His work!" Ashlyn screamed. Her eyes flashed in a way that frightened Connie, and Connie reminded herself that Ashlyn was hurting. All her life, Ashlyn had favored her father. She sought his attention and love as though they were the only attention and love that mattered. Connie had often been treated as the enemy, and if not an enemy then an obstacle that had been placed between Ashlyn and Wolf. Connie had remained steadfast, and sure enough, in college and medical school, Ashlyn had come back to her. There had been lunches and shopping trips and spa vacations (though no real heart-to-hearts, Connie saw now, there had been no chance for Ashlyn to reveal her emotional life). Ashlyn had remained closer with Wolf and that was fine. If anything, Connie had counted on Wolf agreeing to treatment for Ashlyn's sake. She had expected Ashlyn to save Wolf for both of them.

Connie said, "Your father was a thoughtful man. He made the choice that felt right to him. Surely, in your work you've seen other patients who refused treatment?"

"Those patients weren't my father."

Fair enough. Connie said, "I loved your father deeply. You know I did. I chose to respect his decision because I loved him, but don't you think it was hard for me, too? Don't you think it was damn near impossible for me to watch him slip away?"

"He chose his work," Ashlyn said. "Not you, not me."

"He was afraid of hospitals," Connie said. "He didn't even like putting on a Band-Aid. I couldn't imagine him hooked up to forty machines, lines sticking out of him, pumping him full of poison. I couldn't imagine him strapped to a table while they sawed open his skull."

"He would have done it if he loved us," Ashlyn said.

"That's not true," Connie said. "Because he did love us. He loved me, and he loved you."

"Yeah, but you know what it feels like?" Ashlyn said. She had been crying so hard that the half-moons under her eyes were pink, and her nostrils were raw and chafed. Such pale skin, pale hair, pale eyes. Ashlyn had fair and delicate looks, and people always assumed on meeting her that she would have a mild, milky way about her, but they were wrong. She was a force, driven, determined, and focused. Even in childbirth, she had wanted out. "It feels like he gave up on me because of how I am. Because of Bridget—"

"Honey!" Connie said. "No!"

"He gave up on me. Because there won't be a big wedding or an investment banker son-in-law. Because there won't be grandchildren. And you let him."

"Ashlyn, stop! That had *nothing* to do with it."

"For twenty-six years I strived to make you proud of me. High school, college, medical school—"

"We are proud of you—"

"But I can't help how I feel. I can't help *who I am*—"

Connie had tried to make Ashlyn see that Wolf's decision was just that—Wolf's decision. It had been supremely selfish, yes. But he had wanted to live and die on his own terms. It had nothing to do with Ashlyn or her relationship with Bridget. It might seem that way because of the timing, but no.

"But yes!" Ashlyn said. She wasn't going to back down. She was raging at Connie, and Connie felt a flash of anger at Wolf for leaving her behind to be raged at. After all, she had lost him, too. She was suffering, too. Connie should have backed off—she'd had twenty-six years of dealing with her daughter to know this was true—but instead Connie said, "You think Daddy didn't want to fight because he found out you were gay? You know what that sounds like to me, Ashlyn? That sounds like a heap of self-loathing."

Ashlyn reached out to smack Connie, but Connie caught her hand and held it tight. She was Veronica O'Brien's daughter, after all. She said, "Come to peace with yourself, Ashlyn, and then you'll be able to come to peace with your father's decision."

Connie didn't regret saying any of this, although she did regret what she said later, after the funeral. And she regretted not doing more when Ashlyn climbed into the Aston Martin. Connie should have laid her body down in front of the car. She should have chased after her.

Connie had found out—through Jake and Iris—that Ashlyn had taken a job with a hospital in Tallahassee. She had moved down there with Bridget. Jake and Iris claimed they only heard from Ashlyn sporadically, and they promised that when they had important news, they would let Connie know. (Most of the reason Connie didn't like Iris was because Iris knew more about her daughter than she did.) Connie continued to call Ashlyn's cell phone every week, and every week she was treated to voice mail.

The call that came to Connie's phone on the day the photograph of Meredith was left on the porch was the most promising lead Connie had had since Ashlyn drove away in the Aston Martin.

Connie descended the stairs to the front door. That she hadn't called Ashlyn yesterday now seemed like it might be a positive thing. *How can I miss you when you won't go away?* Ashlyn would, at the very least, be curious about her mother's lapsed communication. And maybe even worried.

Connie would wait a few days, then try again with the new phone number.

That decided, Connie felt better. She was moving on with her life, finally. She had experienced two Julys and two Augusts since Wolf died, but only now, today, did she feel like it was actually summertime. She would go to the Sconset Market and get the paper and some snickerdoodle coffee and freshly baked peach muffins. When Connie got back, Meredith would be awake, and they could deconstruct the night before minute by minute.

If nothing else, it was a wonderful distraction.

Connie stepped outside and knew immediately that something was wrong. Something with her car. It was parked in front of the house, the windows were intact, the body work was unscathed, at least on the side facing the house. But the car looked sick. It was sunken, listing.

Connie moved closer to inspect. "Oh," she whispered.

The tires had been slashed.

They had been sliced open in ragged gashes. And then Connie noticed a piece of paper tucked under the windshield wiper. She plucked it out, opened it up, read it.

In black marker it said, "Theif, go home."

Connie's first instinct was to crumple the note and throw it away, but they would need it as evidence for the police. The police again. Oh, her poor car. Connie spun around and surveyed her property. The day was bright and sunny, with enough breeze to make the eelgrass dance. This spot was idyllic. It had been safe, until she brought Meredith here. Now they were under attack.

Theif, go home.

Whoever wrote the note didn't know how to spell. So it was somebody young, or somebody stupid, or somebody foreign.

Or was it Connie who was being stupid? First her house, now her car. What would be next? Meredith and Connie had bull's-eyes painted on their backs. What if this escalated? What if they got hurt? Connie was placing her well-being on the line for Meredith's sake. But Meredith was her friend. They hadn't spoken for three years — those had been awful, lonely years — and now Connie had her back.

Theif, go home. Connie was assaulted by contradictory thoughts. Meredith had said horrible things to her; Meredith had put Freddy and his contemptible dealings before her lifelong friendship with Connie. Meredith was still under investigation — she knew more than she was telling, that was for damn sure. But Meredith had never stolen or cheated in her life. She was the only senior girl who never sneaked sips of the Communion wine; she was the only one who didn't cheat on her Good Friday fast — not a single Ritz cracker, not one chocolate chip from the bag her mother kept in the baking cabinet. Connie had watched Meredith march up the steps of Saint Mary's the other day, and she'd thought, *There is a woman who still believes in God. How does she do it?* Meredith's number one glaring fault was that she had always been so god-damned perfect, and nobody liked a perfect person. *Pull the stick out of your ass!* How many times had Connie wanted to shout *that* out over the years? Now that Meredith's perfection had come to a screeching halt, Connie loved her more. Just last night, Meredith had sung at the bar; she had been terrific fun, a good sport, and Connie had been shocked. She remembered Meredith's face as she belted out the song: shining with sweat, her glasses slipping to the end of her nose.

Theif, go home.

As far as Connie was concerned, Meredith *was* home.

Connie regarded her shredded tires. She understood how they had gotten to this point, but that didn't make it any easier.

She went back inside to wake up Meredith.

MEREDITH

Chief Kapenash inspected the four slashed tires, took the note as evidence, and gave Connie and Meredith his sincere apology. He'd had a squad car scheduled to cruise the road every hour, and last night it had made the run between midnight and 4 a.m. Before midnight, that particular officer had been called to break up a party of underage drinkers on the beach, and after four that officer had been called to a domestic dispute all the way out in Madaket. So the vandalism had taken place either while Connie and Meredith were out on the town or in the early-morning hours.

It didn't matter. Either way, Meredith was scared. Slashed tires: it seemed so violent. When she asked the chief what kind of tool could slash a tire, he'd said, "In this case, it looks like a hunting knife." And then there was the matter of the note. *Theif, go home.* It had been written in block letters, making it impossible to identify a male or female hand. (Meredith had secretly checked the handwriting against the handwriting on the back of Dan Flynn's business card. She liked Dan, and it seemed that Dan liked her, but in the world that Meredith now knew to be hiding all kinds of secrets, she wondered if Dan was asking Connie out so he could hurt Meredith. Thankfully, the handwriting didn't match up.) *Theif, go home.* The only clue they had to go on was the misspelling.

Dan showed up and changed all four tires. The labor for that was gratis, but Meredith offered to pay for the tires, which had cost six hundred dollars, and while she was at it, she threw in four hundred dollars for the power washing. She held out a thousand dollars in cash to Connie, her hand trembling.

Connie looked at the money and said, "Put it away."

"Please, Connie. You have to let me pay."

"We're in this together," Connie said. She then confided that, while changing the tires, Dan had invited her out on his boat on

Thursday. They were going to cruise around the harbor and check the lobster pots. "And you're coming with us."

"No," Meredith said flatly. "I'm not."

"You have to," Connie said.

"The man wants you to himself," Meredith said. "Last night was fine, but I'm not going to be a tagalong all summer."

"Well, I can't leave you here by yourself," Connie said. "Not after what happened this morning."

"I'm a big girl," Meredith said. "I'll be fine."

Connie grinned. It was amazing what a little romance did for a person. Her tires had been slashed with a hunting knife, and yet Connie was floating. Meredith thought she might insist one more time that Meredith come along, and if she had, Meredith would have agreed. She liked the sound of a boat ride—out on the open water, Meredith wouldn't be confronted with anyone she knew. And she was afraid to be left home by herself. She would spend the day behind locked doors, huddled on the floor of her closet.

But Connie didn't insist, and Meredith figured that Connie was ready to be alone with Dan. The phone in the house rang just then, and Meredith nearly jumped out of her skin. Connie hurried to get it—she may have thought it was Dan, or the police with a suspect. A few seconds later, she said, "Meredith? It's for you."

Leo! Meredith thought. *Carver!* But then Meredith chastised herself. She had to stop thinking like that. It was hope, ultimately, that would bring her down.

"Who is it?" Meredith asked.

"Some fifteen-year-old boy who says he's your attorney," Connie said.

Meredith took the phone. She felt a surge of jangly nerves. Good news? Bad news? Bad news, she decided. It was always bad news.

"Meredith?" the voice said. It was Dev. Meredith pictured his shaggy black hair, his vampire teeth, his rimless glasses. She hadn't made the connection before, but she realized she now wore the same kind of glasses as Dev. They looked far better on him.

"Dev?" she said.

"Hey," he said. His tone was soft, nearly tender. "How's it going?"

"Oh," she said. She thought for a moment that Dev had heard about the slashed tires and was calling to offer her some legal counsel—but that was impossible. "It goes."

"Listen," Dev said. "Burt and I had a meeting with the Feds. They're now convinced there is upwards of ten billion dollars stashed somewhere overseas. Freddy's still not talking. The Feds are willing to hold off pressing conspiracy charges on you, and possibly Leo also, if they get your cooperation."

Meredith sank into one of the dining-room chairs. From there, she could see the blue of the ocean. It was a dark, Yankee blue, different from the turquoise water in Palm Beach or the azure water of Cap d'Antibes. "What kind of cooperation?" Meredith said. She sighed. "I've already told you everything."

"I need ideas about where that money might be," Dev said.

"I thought I was clear," Meredith said. She took a metered breath. "I don't know."

"Meredith."

"I don't know!" Meredith said. She stood up and walked over to the window. "You were very kind to me back in New York. And I repaid you by being honest. I told the Feds the truth. Now they're trying to bribe me with my own freedom and, worse still, my son's freedom, which we deserve anyway, because I didn't know the first thing about what was going on. And you know and I know and Julie Schwarz knows that Leo didn't either. I wasn't privy to any of Freddy's business deals. They didn't interest me. I'm not a numbers person. I majored in American literature. I read Hemingway and Frost, okay? I did my thesis on Edith Wharton. I can give you a detailed explanation on the use of the outsider in *The Age of Innocence,* but I don't know what a derivative is. I don't properly know what a hedge fund is."

"Meredith."

"I don't know where Freddy put his money." Meredith was

screaming now, though in a low voice, so as not to alarm Connie. "There was an office in London. Have you checked there?"

"The Feds are investigating the people in London."

"I never once visited the London office. I didn't know *a single person* who worked there. And those were the bad guys, right?"

"Those were some of the bad guys," Dev said.

"I don't even know their names," Meredith said. "I was never introduced. I couldn't pick them out of a crowd of two. Freddy took me to London three times, and the first time we were college kids, backpacking. The other two times Freddy visited the office, and do you know where I went? I went to the Tate Gallery to see the Turners and the Constables. I went to Westminster blinking Abbey."

"What the Feds are looking for are buzzwords," Dev said. "Phrases. People's names. Things Freddy repeated that might not have made sense. One of the words that turned up in the files is 'dial.' Do you know the meaning of the word 'dial'?"

Meredith gave a short laugh. "That was the name of Fred's eating club at Princeton."

"Really?" Dev said. He sounded like he'd discovered a gold nugget in his sieve.

"Really," said Meredith. Freddy had been the king of the pool table at Dial. He had wooed Meredith with his dead eye, twelve ball in the right corner pocket. They used to get drunk on keg beer and raid the kitchen at Dial late at night, and Freddy would whip up his specialty—a fried chicken patty with a slice of tomato and Russian dressing. Nothing Meredith had eaten before or since had tasted better. Freddy had been able to let loose back then—drink too much, stay up late. He had those incredible looks—the black hair, the clear blue eyes. Meredith remembered asking him if he resembled his father or his mother. *I don't look like my mother,* he said. *And I never met my father, so I couldn't say.* What kind of name was Delinn, anyway? Meredith asked. Because it sounded French. *It's a French name,* Freddy said. *But my mother always said the old man was Irish. I didn't grow up the way you grew up, Meredith. I don't have a pedigree. Just pretend like I hatched from an egg.*

Devon said, "What about the word 'buttons'?"

"Our dog," Meredith said. Buttons had been a gift for the boys when they were ten and eight. Freddy had an investor who owned a kennel upstate, where the dogs consistently won awards. Freddy wanted a golden retriever. Meredith had lobbied to give the puppy a literary name—Kafka or Fitzgerald—but Freddy said it was only right to let the kids name the dog, and they named him Buttons. Meredith could still picture the boys and that tiny, impossibly cute butterscotch-colored puppy. Freddy had snapped pictures with this silly grin on his face. That night in bed, he'd said to her, *We'll give them cars on their sixteenth birthday and Rolexes when they turn twenty-one, but no present will ever beat the one we gave them today.*

And Meredith had to agree.

"Could it be a code word?" Dev asked.

"I suppose," Meredith said. "Freddy was very fond of the dog. He took him to work. They walked there, they walked home. Sometimes they detoured through the park. I used to take the dog to Southampton for the summer, and Freddy would get very depressed. Not without us, mind you, but without the dog."

"Really?" Dev said. Another gold nugget.

Meredith shook her head. This was a wild-goose chase. There was most certainly money hidden; Freddy was too cunning not to have buried millions, or even billions, but he would have hidden it where it would absolutely never be found.

"What about the word 'champ'?" Dev said. "That was a word that turned up frequently."

Oh, God. Meredith coughed, and fought off the urge to spit. *Champ?* Frequently? How frequently? "Champ" was Freddy's nickname for their decorator, Samantha, because her maiden name was Champion. (Meredith had always thought that the nickname was meant to be a jab at Samantha's husband, Trent Deuce, whom Freddy disliked and dismissed.)

"'Champ'?" Dev asked again. "Ring a bell?"

Meredith paused. "Where did this word 'champ' turn up? I'm curious. In his date book? His diary?"

"I really can't say," Dev said.

Right, Meredith thought. The information flowed only one way.

"Does the word mean anything to you?" Dev asked.

Meredith thought back to the day when she'd come across Freddy with his hand on Samantha's back. She remembered how he'd whipped his hand away when he saw Meredith. She could still see the expression on his face: What was it? Guilt? Fear? Despite this memory, which always made Meredith uneasy, she didn't want to turn Samantha over to the FBI. Samantha was Meredith's friend, or she had been. Plus, she was a decorator; she had nothing to do with Freddy's business or the Ponzi scheme.

Still, Dev was asking. She wasn't going to be the woman the media thought she was: a woman who lied to her lawyer. And there was Leo to think of. Leo!

"'Champ' was Freddy's nickname for our decorator. Samantha Champion Deuce."

"Oh, boy," Dev said quietly.

"She was a friend of Freddy's, but a better friend of mine," Meredith said. "She was our decorator for years."

"How many years?"

"Ten years? Twelve?"

"So there are lots of reasons why her name might turn up," Dev said. "Reasons that have nothing to do with the business."

"I guarantee you, Samantha didn't know a single thing about Freddy's business," Meredith said. "She used to call where he worked the 'money shop.' Like he was dealing in ice cream or bicycles."

"But now you understand what we're looking for?" Dev asked. "Words that have meaning. They might be a clue, a contact, a password. The money could be anywhere in the world. I spoke to Julie Schwarz..."

"You did?" Meredith said.

"Leo is making a list of words, and so is Carver. But they said we should ask you. They said Freddy talked only to you, confided only in you..."

"He was my husband," Meredith said. "But there are a lot of things I didn't know about him. He was a private person." For example, Freddy never told Meredith who he voted for in an election. She didn't know the name of the tailor in London who made his suits. She didn't know the password on his phone or his computer; she had only known that there was a password. Everything was locked up all the time, including the door to his home office.

"I understand," Dev said.

How could he understand? Meredith thought. Dev wasn't married. He hadn't slept beside someone for thirty years only to discover they were somebody else.

"This could help you, Meredith," Dev said. "This could save you. It could keep you out of prison. In a year or two, when all this is in the past, you could resume normal life."

Resume normal life? What did that even *mean?* Meredith was tempted to tell Dev about Connie's slashed tires, but she refrained. She was afraid it would sound like a cry for pity, and the image Meredith needed to convey now was one of strength. She would come up with the answer. She would save herself.

"I can't think of anything now," Meredith said. "You've caught me unprepared. But I'll try. I'll...make a list."

"Please," Dev said.

That night, Meredith was too afraid to sleep. She kept picturing a man with a hunting knife hiding in the eelgrass. Meredith rose from bed, crept into the hallway, and peered out one of the windows that faced the front yard and the road. The yard was empty, quiet. The eelgrass swayed. There was a waxing gibbous moon that disappeared behind puffy nighttime clouds, then reemerged. At three fifteen, a pair of headlights appeared on the road. Meredith tensed. The headlights slowed down at the start of Connie's driveway, paused, then rolled on. It was the police. The squad car parked in the public lot for a few minutes, then backed up and drove away.

She would make a list of words, the way Dev had asked. *Resume normal life* meant life with Leo and Carver. Leo would be safe and free, and the three of them—including Anais, and whatever young woman Carver fancied at the moment—would have dinner together at the sturdy oak table in Carver's imaginary house.

Meredith would come up with the answer.

Atkinson: the name of the professor who taught the anthropology class that brought her and Freddy together.

Meredith had given Freddy the used textbook. With that bond between them, they gravitated toward each other on the first day of class. Meredith and her roommate, a girl from backwater Alabama named Gwen Marbury, sat with Freddy and his roommate, a boy from Shaker Heights, Ohio, named Richard Cassel. The four of them became something of a merry band, though they hung out together only in that one class. When Meredith saw Freddy elsewhere on campus, he was usually in the presence of a stunning, dark-haired girl. His girlfriend, Meredith assumed, another upperclassman. It figured. Freddy was too funny and smart, and too beautiful himself, to be available. Through Gwen Marbury, who was far more interested in the social politics of Princeton than in her studies, Meredith learned that the girl's name was Trina Didem, and that she was from Istanbul, Turkey. Trina was a dual major in economics and political science. Again, it figured: ravishing, exotic, and brilliant, someone destined to be a far-flung correspondent on CNN or the head of the Brookings Institution or secretary of state. Meredith's crush on Freddy intensified the more she learned about Trina, although Meredith realized that what she was experiencing was nothing more than a freshman crush on a particularly cool upperclassman. It was also a way to stop thinking about Toby at the College of Charleston drinking yards of beer with all the sweet, blond southern girls. But Meredith cherished her time in class with Freddy and Richard and Gwen—the three of them cracked jokes about the clicking language of the Khoisan tribe, and they speculated on the advantages of a matriarchal society—and when class was over, Meredith continued her anthropological study of Trina Didem. Trina waited for Freddy outside on the stone steps of the building so she could smoke her clove cigarettes. She, Trina, wore a black suede choker at all times, as well as dangly earrings made from multicolored stones. She wore tight, faded jeans, and she carried a buttery soft Italian leather bag. Really, Meredith thought, she probably had a crush on Trina as well as Freddy. Trina was a woman, whereas Meredith was a girl trying to become a woman.

At the beginning of December, a knock came on the door of the anthropology classroom. Professor Atkinson stopped lecturing and swooped over to answer the door with a perplexed look on her face, as though this were her home and these were unexpected guests. Standing at the door was Trina Didem. Professor Atkinson looked first to Freddy, perhaps thinking there was going to be some kind of lovers' spat right in the middle of their discussion of Dunbar's number. But Trina, it seemed, was there on official business. She read off a slip of paper, in her lilting English. She was looking for Meredith Martin.

Meredith stood up, confused. She thought perhaps Trina had learned of her crush on Freddy and had come to call her out. But a second later, Trina explained that Meredith was needed in the Student Life Office. Meredith collected her books. Freddy reached for her hand as she left. It was the first time he'd ever touched her.

Meredith followed Trina out of the building. She was so starstruck in Trina's presence that she was unable to ask the obvious questions: *Why did you pull me out of class? Where are we going?* It looked, from the path they were taking, like they were headed for the office of the dean of students, which differed slightly from the Student Life Office that she'd been promised. Or maybe they were one and the same—Meredith was still too new to campus to know. Trina took the occasion of being outside in the cold, crystalline air to light a clove cigarette. Because she was a step or two ahead of Meredith, the smoke blew in Meredith's face. Somehow, this snapped Meredith back to her senses. She said, "You're Freddy's girlfriend, right?"

Trina barked once, then blew out her smoke. "Not girlfriend. Freddy is my English tutor." She blew out more smoke. "And my economics tutor. I pay him."

Meredith felt her own lungs fill up with the cloying, noxious smoke—it tasted to Meredith like burning molasses, and her grandmother's gingerbread cookies, which she detested—but she didn't care because she was so excited. Freddy was Trina's *tutor!* She *paid* him! Meredith couldn't wait to tell Gwen.

Meredith's elation was short-lived. Once they were in the plush office belonging to the dean of students, which was empty but for the two of them, Trina closed the door. Meredith remembered an Oriental rug under her feet; she remembered the brassy song of a grandfather clock. She noted that Trina had extinguished her cigarette, but an aura of smoke still clung to her. Up close, she could see that Trina had speckles of mascara on her upper eyelids.

What's going on? Meredith wondered. But she wasn't brave enough to ask. It was definitely something bad. She fleetingly thought of how ironic it would be if she got kicked out of school right at the moment that she had learned Freddy was unattached.

Trina said, "The dean is in a meeting across campus. I'm an intern here, so they sent me to tell you."

Tell me what? Meredith thought. But her voice didn't work.

"Your mother called," Trina said. "Your father had a brain aneurysm. He died."

Meredith screamed. Trina moved to touch her, but Meredith swatted her away. She could remember being embarrassed about her screaming. She was screaming in front of Trina, whom she had considered a paragon of Ivy League womanhood. And what news had Trina, of all people, just delivered her? Her father was dead. Chick Martin, of the eggplant parm subs and the monthly poker games; Chick Martin, the partner at Saul, Ewing who specialized in the laws of arbitrage; Chick Martin, who had believed his daughter to be brilliant and talented. He had suffered a brain aneurysm at work. So arbitrage had killed him. Arbitrage was tricky; it had a million rules and loopholes, and while trying to decipher the code that would bring him to his answer, Chick Martin's brain had short-circuited. He was dead.

But no, that wasn't possible. Meredith had just been home for Thanksgiving break. Her father had been waiting for her at the Villanova train station. He had wanted to come get her at the university, but Meredith had insisted on taking the train—New Jersey Transit to 30th Street Station, SEPTA to Villanova. *That's what college kids do, Daddy!* Meredith had said. *They take the train!*

Both of her parents had coddled her over break. Her mother brought her poached eggs in bed; her father gave her forty dollars for the informal class reunion that was taking place on Wednesday night at the Barleycorn Inn. Her parents brought her along to the annual cocktail party at the Donovers' house on Friday night, and as a concession to her new adult status, her father handed her a glass of Chablis. He introduced her to couples she had known her whole life as though she were a brand-new person: *My daughter, Meredith, a freshman at Princeton!*

Chick Martin, Meredith's first and best champion, the only champion she'd ever needed, was gone.

Meredith stopped screaming long enough to look at Trina, thinking how she *hated* her, *hated* the smell of clove cigarettes, *hated* the city of Istanbul, *hated* the beauty and sophistication that was masking the sadism required to deliver this kind of news. Meredith said, "No, you're wrong."

Trina said, "I'll walk you back to your suite so you can pack your things. We've called for a car to take you home."

The world had stopped being safe on that day. As happy as Meredith had ever been in her life, she had never been *truly* happy again.

Her father was gone; her father's love for her was gone. She thought back to the driving lessons in the university parking lot, her father saying, *I can't stand to see you hurt like this.* The pain Toby had caused Meredith was one thing. This pain, now, was quite another.

Seven hundred and fifty people attended Chick Martin's funeral — his law partners, his poker buddies, friends, neighbors, Meredith's teachers, everyone she had ever known, it seemed. Connie was there and Connie's parents, but not Toby — he was entering finals at the College of Charleston and said he couldn't get away.

Dustin Leavitt came to the funeral.

Dustin Leavitt? Meredith saw him approaching the church as she waited for the hearse out front with her mother and grandmother. There were so many people from so many parts of Meredith's past in attendance that she had a problem pinning names to faces. When she saw Dustin Leavitt, she registered his good looks and she thought he was someone she knew from Princeton — a professor? a graduate student? then it came to her — Dustin Leavitt, thirty-three-year-old coworker of Mr. O'Brien's at Philco, whom she had danced with at Connie's graduation party. She had forgotten all about him.

He took her hands. Despite the fact that so many people had held, pressed, or squeezed Meredith's hands, they were ice cold. Meredith hadn't given a thought to her appearance in days, and now she worried that she looked like a red-nosed, wild-haired troll. She didn't own a black dress, so she was wearing a black cashmere turtleneck and a gray pinstriped skirt. Black tights, awful black flats. She had stupidly put on mascara, which now trailed in sooty streaks down her face.

"Hi!" Meredith said, trying to sound normal, as though she had come across Dustin Leavitt sitting at a booth in Minella's Diner and not on the steps of Saint Thomas of Villanova on the occasion of her father's funeral. She felt embarrassed by her situation, and then ashamed about her embarrassment.

Dustin Leavitt said, "I'm sorry for your loss, Meredith. Everyone knows how much your father loved you."

"Oh," Meredith said. She welled with fresh, hot tears. Dustin Leavitt hesitated. Meredith knew she was making him uncomfortable, so she tried to smile and wave him on. He squeezed her bicep—it seemed to her he had also done this after the Lower Merion swim meet—and then he disappeared into the dark mouth of the church.

Meredith saw him later at the reception at Aronimink, and still later, at the after-reception, which was an impromptu event held at the O'Briens' house. Meredith's mother and grandmother had gone home, but Meredith had stuck with Connie, and Veronica and Bill O'Brien, and the other mourners who were for the most part all drunk, but because of the early hour—six o'clock—and because of the meager, WASPy offerings of the luncheon at Aronimink, thought that more drinks and pizza and cheese steaks at the O'Briens' sounded better than going home. Meredith had little recollection of anything that had transpired that day—she had taken a pill at 9 a.m. to settle her nerves—and by the time she reached the O'Briens', she was drunker than either Connie or Veronica, which was saying something. She believed she finally understood alcohol's true purpose—to eradicate conscious and deliberate thought when such thought was too agonizing. Dustin Leavitt did his part in providing comfort by bringing Meredith a tall flute of very cold champagne.

"People think champagne is best for celebrating," he said. "But I like it for misery, myself."

Meredith knew she had a witty response to that somewhere inside her, but it was buried beneath a pile of her broken childhood memories, and she couldn't snatch it out. She raised her glass to Dustin Leavitt's handsome but increasingly blurry face and said, "To misery."

They touched glasses. They drank. In the dining room, where the table was laden with pizza boxes and foil-wrapped subs and cardboard boats of curly fries, Connie was huddled in the arms of Drew Van Dyke, who had come home from Johns Hopkins in order to be with Connie during her time of need. After all, her best friend's father had died. Meredith felt a surge of confusion. Certainly Connie had loved Chick Martin; because Meredith and Connie were so close, Connie had been like an adopted daughter to Chick. But Meredith suspected that for Connie and Drew, this funeral was just a bonus opportunity to travel the two hours to see each other and have sex. And why did Connie have someone here to comfort her, but not Meredith?

Toby should be here, Meredith thought. He should be here for her father. He should be here for her.

Meredith looked at Dustin Leavitt. "Get me out of here," she said.

"Gladly," he said.

They walked out the front door together without explanation or excuse, and no one fussed. Meredith had the leeway granted to the newly bereaved, maybe — or maybe nobody noticed.

She followed Dustin Leavitt out to his car, a Peugeot sedan. He opened the door for her. She got in, humbled once again by her hideous outfit, and to make matters worse, over the course of the day she'd worked a hole into the foot of her tights so that her big toe stuck through the material. This bothered her the way a ragged fingernail or loose tooth might.

Dustin said, "Any place special you want to go?"

Meredith shrugged.

He said, "My place okay?"

"Sure," she said.

She watched out the window as they drove. The town of Villanova looked the same as it had her whole life, but it was different now because her father was gone. They passed the train station where, until the day before, Chick Martin's car had remained in the parking lot, as if waiting for him to come home. How many times had Meredith ridden the bus home from school and seen her father's bronze Mercedes in that parking lot?

Dustin Leavitt took roads that led them to the expressway, and Meredith felt the first stirrings of panic. "Where do you live?" she asked.

"In King of Prussia," he said. "Over by the mall."

The mall, okay, yes the mall was familiar, but in her childhood naïveté, Meredith had thought that King of Prussia *was* the mall. She hadn't realized it was also a place people might live.

She had no energy or desire for conversation; she didn't want to ask Dustin Leavitt about his family or his job or his hobbies, and she certainly didn't want to talk about herself.

He pulled into an apartment complex. Three tall buildings, twenty or thirty stories, formed a semi-circle. They walked into the center building. On the ground floor was a Chinese restaurant. Through the window, Meredith saw people whose fathers had *not* died that week drinking electric-blue cocktails out of fishbowls.

Dustin Leavitt pulled out his keys, opened his mailbox, removed a sheaf of letters, and flipped through them. This simple, everyday act jolted Meredith like ice cubes down her back. What was she doing here? Who was this man? What would happen next?

Next, they would get into the elevator. Dustin Leavitt would push the button for the eighteenth floor. Dustin would step off. What choice did Meredith have now but to follow? The hallway was carpeted in maroon wall-to-wall that held the paths of the vacuum cleaner. It smelled like cigarettes and litter boxes and soy sauce. Meredith was disgusted. Her drunkenness started to assert itself. She feared she was going to vomit. Dustin Leavitt unlocked the door to apartment 1804. The apartment was dark.

Dustin said, "Good, my roommate isn't home."

Roommate? thought Meredith. She was the one with a roommate. Gwen Marbury. Meredith hadn't known what to expect from Dustin Leavitt; she supposed she'd expected that he would own a house, like Mr. O'Brien, minus the wife and children. Dustin was thirty-three years old. She certainly hadn't expected a crummy apartment and a roommate.

He opened his refrigerator, and it illuminated the kitchen. He said, "Would you like a beer?"

"Sure," Meredith said.

He handed her a bottle of St. Pauli Girl. She took the tiniest sip, mainly to block the ambient smells of the apartment. Dustin opened a beer for himself, loosened his tie, and walked down the dark hall. Meredith faltered. Now, it seemed, would be the time to excuse herself. But she had *asked* him to take her away from the O'Briens' house, and when he said, "My place okay?" she had said yes. She was far from home with no way back. She followed.

The next thing she knew, they were kissing on the bed. Dustin Leavitt was on top of her. His hands were fighting to get her tights down. Her shoes had fallen off, her big toe was protruding from the foot of her tights. Meredith couldn't decide whether to help Dustin or resist him. Meredith wished she were anywhere else. How could she stop him? She had asked for this.

He yanked off her tights. He put his finger in her. It hurt. She hadn't been with anyone since Toby, way back in June.

"Tight," he said.

Meredith was afraid she was going to vomit. Dustin Leavitt put on a condom; Meredith breathed in and out through her mouth, willing herself not to get sick. She would not think about the cheese steaks with cold, congealed onions on the O'Briens' dining-room table. She would not think about cat turds lying in kitty litter. She would not think about her father, collapsed on his desk, bleeding from one eye.

Dustin Leavitt entered her.

This, Meredith thought, *is what happens when a girl loses her father. She gets date raped.*

And then blames herself.

*   *   *

Meredith stayed home through Christmas, playing and replaying "Bridge Over Troubled Water" on her turntable. *If you need a friend, I'm sailing right behind.* Relatives and neighbors came to put up the Christmas tree and fix lovely meals that Meredith and her mother didn't eat. The holiday was a brightly wrapped box with nothing inside. Toby called, but Meredith refused to talk to him. She asked her mother to take a message.

"He sends his condolences," her mother said. "He said he loved Chick and will remember him fondly."

Condolences? Fondly? What kind of lexicon was this? Toby loved Chick, but he no longer loved Meredith. Meredith was furious. She thought about calling Toby back and telling him she'd slept with Dustin Leavitt. Would he care?

Meredith asked Connie about this when they met for beers at Bennigan's. Connie was noncommittal and dismissive about Toby.

"Try to forget about him," Connie said. "He's a lost cause."

Meredith would try to forget about him. To distract herself, she studied. In a rare form of torture, Princeton held finals after Christmas. Meredith went back to campus and, despite the fact that she was a shadow of her former self, she slayed her exams: A's across the board.

Freddy approached her in the first week of the new semester.

"I heard about your father," he said. "I'm sorry."

This was said with more gravitas than Meredith was used to encountering in her peers. Connie had hugged her and listened to her at home, and her roommate, Gwen, had hugged her and listened to her here, but Meredith could tell they didn't get it. She felt their pity, but not their empathy. They treated her like she had an illness. And Gwen, who hated her own father, even sounded a little envious.

But when Freddy spoke, Meredith sensed a deeper well.

"Thank you," she said. "Trina told you?"

"Gwen, actually," he said. "But when Trina showed up at class,

I knew it wasn't good news. She's pretty much known as the Grim Reaper around here."

"Yeah," Meredith said. She would be only too glad if she never saw Trina again. She remembered back a few weeks when Trina's clothes and accessories and mannerisms had been of the utmost interest to her—it was amazing how that had changed. Even Meredith's attraction to Freddy had paled when compared to the real love of Meredith's life. The steady, unconditional, fortifying love of Meredith's father was gone forever. It wasn't fucking fair, it was *not* fucking fair! Meredith, that week, had been alternating between devastated melancholy and door-kicking, hair-pulling anger.

Meredith and Freddy walked together for a while in silence. Meredith didn't know where Freddy was going, but she was headed to the east side of campus to the Mental Health Services building where students could receive free counseling. Meredith saw a woman named Elise, and did little more than sob through her fifty-minute sessions.

Freddy said, "My brother, David, died last year. He was in the army, and he was shot during training. A total, pointless mistake. Some complete asshole discharged his weapon when he wasn't supposed to, and my brother is dead."

"Oh, God," Meredith said. She had heard dozens of stories of untimely deaths in the weeks since her father died, and she had yet to figure out how to respond. She knew people were trying to create some kind of interpersonal connection by sharing their own losses, but Meredith took self-indulgent pleasure in believing that her loss was unique—and far worse—than anyone else's. But Freddy's story did indeed sound both sad and bad. A brother shot accidentally while training to defend our country? Shot by one of his own? Meredith wanted to say the right thing, but she didn't know what that was. She decided to give him a question he could answer. "How old was he?"

"Twenty-three."

"That's really young. Were you close?"

Freddy shrugged. "Not really. But he was, you know, my *brother.*"

"That must have been hard," Meredith said, then hated herself. She sounded just like Connie, or Gwen Marbury!

Freddy didn't respond and Meredith didn't blame him, but he did walk Meredith all the way to the Mental Health Services building. She thought of detouring so he wouldn't guess where she was headed, but then she decided it didn't matter if he knew. As soon as her destination became clear, he said, "I came here a lot last year. It helped. Is it helping you?"

"No," Meredith said.

"It takes a while," Freddy said. He locked eyes with her, and only then did Meredith remember that he had reached for her hand as she was called from the classroom. And in that moment, she recognized Freddy, much the way she thought the Virgin Mary must have recognized the angel Gabriel; it felt no less mystical. Freddy was a different person from the cool upperclassman she'd had a crush on. He was the person who had been sent to collect her. As Freddy held her gaze outside the dour and depressing Mental Health Services building, Meredith thought, *I'm yours. Take me.*

"I'll come back and pick you up in an hour?" Freddy asked.

"Yes," she said.

They had been inseparable from that point forward.

For many years, Meredith had believed that Freddy had been sent to her by her father. She had believed this right up until December of last year, when she, with the rest of the world, learned of Freddy's crimes. Even now, when she thought about Freddy's betrayal, it took her breath away. Other people had lost money. Meredith had lost faith in the one person she believed had been sent to save her. He, Freddy Delinn, was Dustin Leavitt, a man who would rape a drunk eighteen-year-old girl who had just lost her father. He was the man with the hunting knife. He was not an emissary from her guardian angel–father, but rather an emissary of the devil, come to ruin her life.

Meredith heard a door open down the hall.
Connie said, "Meredith, is that you?"
"Yes."
"Are you all right?"
All right? She would be all right if she didn't think, if she didn't remember. She felt a hand on her shoulder. Connie was there, her long hair tangled and even more beautiful in sleep.
"Meredith?"
"Yes," Meredith said. And she let Connie lead her back to bed.

CONNIE

Connie spent all morning trying to convince Meredith to come along. It was a brilliant day—sun, blue sky, a touch of a breeze. Days didn't get any better than this.

"Nothing you can say will change my mind," Meredith said. "I'm not going."

"I don't want to go alone," Connie said. She gazed at the ocean. "I'm scared."

"There, you admitted it," Meredith said. "Do you feel better?"

"No," Connie said. "I want you to come. If you come, I'll feel better."

"How are you going to know how you feel about this guy if you never spend time alone with him?"

"I'm not ready for time alone with him," Connie said. She thought about the kissing. It had been wonderful, but that, somehow, only added to her fear. "I'm going to cancel."

"No, you're not," Meredith said.

"I'll tell him we can picnic here, on the deck," Connie said. "I'll tell him we can swim here, on this beach, with Harold."

"No," Meredith said.

"That way we can all be together."

"No!" Meredith said.

"Meredith," Connie said. "I haven't asked you for anything since we've been here."

"Okay, wait," Meredith said. "Are you really going to play that card?"

Connie could barely believe it herself. "Yes," she said.

"Well, then, I can't say no, can I?" Meredith said. "You saved my life. You brought me here. You're sheltering me despite physical damage to your house and your car. I'm indebted to you. And so I *have* to go with you on your date." She put her hands on her hips. She was tiny in stature but imperious. Connie could tell she was trying not to smile.

"Yes," Connie said. "Thank you."

Meredith said, "I'll go put on my wig."

While Meredith was upstairs, there was a knock at the door. Connie practically ran to open it. She was *so* much more relaxed now that Meredith had agreed to come along, emotional arm twisting notwithstanding. Connie's fear and anxiety floated away. They were going on Dan's boat. They were going to have fun!

Connie flung open the door. Dan was holding a bunch of wildflowers that Connie recognized as coming off one of the farm trucks that parked on Main Street.

"For you," he said, handing her the flowers.

"Thank you!" she said. "That's sweet."

He smiled. He was so handsome with his sunglasses perched in his short, ruffled hair. Connie leaned in to kiss him. She meant it to be a quick, thank-you-for-the-flowers kiss, but he closed his eyes and made it a longer kiss. And even as Connie was liking it, loving it, she thought, *No, I can't do this. I'm not ready for this.*

She pulled away. She said, "Meredith has decided to come with us today."

"Oh," Dan said. "Terrific."

"It's not terrific," Meredith said, coming down the stairs. She was securing her wig with bobby pins. Connie threw her a warning look. Meredith was coming with them because Connie needed her, but she couldn't let Dan know she was coming because Connie needed her. This was the logic of high school, Connie knew, but just because they were older didn't mean they had outgrown the rules.

Meredith said, "I'm an egregious interloper. A third wheel. But the fact is, I don't feel safe alone in the house all day." She smiled sheepishly at Dan. "I'm sorry."

"Don't be sorry," Dan said. "It's fine."

"Just fine," Connie said.

It was one of those days that made you feel lucky to be alive—no matter if you'd lost a spouse to cancer, no matter if your only child no longer acknowledged your existence, no matter if your husband had lost $50 billion in a Ponzi scheme and you were hated by everyone in America. The back of Dan's red Jeep was loaded with life jackets and fishing poles, and Connie wedged in her cooler, which contained a couple bottles of wine and enough picnic lunch for ten people. Connie sat up front next to Dan, and Meredith stretched out in the backseat and closed her eyes in the sun. Dan played Marshall Tucker's "Heard It in a Love Song," and they all belted out the words at the tops of their lungs.

Dan pulled into the parking lot at Children's Beach. Children's Beach was a green park with a band shell, a playground, and an ice-cream shack fronted by a small beach right on the harbor. Connie tried to keep her emotions in check. She hadn't been to Children's Beach since Ashlyn was a little girl. There had been a few summers when Connie had brought Ashlyn here every day— Ashlyn had gone down the slides, complaining if the metal was too hot on her legs, and Connie had pushed Ashlyn on the swings, back and forth a thousand times. In those days, the ice-cream shack had been a breakfast joint with the best doughnuts on the island. God, it hurt to think about it. Connie had brought Ashlyn here on days that Wolf had been asked to sail, and then they'd walked to the Yacht Club to meet him for lunch, and Connie's only worry had been that Ashlyn might misbehave.

Dan sprang into action, and Connie and Meredith followed suit. He took the fishing poles, the beach towels, a gas can. Connie took one end of the cooler and Meredith took the other. Meredith, too, had an eye on the action at Children's Beach—the mothers trying to get their toddlers to eat one more bite of peanut butter and jelly, the kids building sandcastles, the orthopedist's dream that was a twenty-foot-high cone-shaped climbing structure on the beach—but she snapped out of her reverie. Was she thinking about Leo? Meredith took three life jackets in her free hand. Connie grabbed her beach bag.

Dan's boat was moored along the dock. They walked down to the boardwalk in front of the White Elephant Hotel and climbed aboard.

It was a beautiful boat, a Boston Whaler Outrage with dual engines off the back. Connie fell in love with it immediately. It had a horseshoe of cushioned seating in the back and up front, and room for two behind the controls under a bimini. Toby was a sailor—a skill learned in summer camp in Cape May and then honed at the College of Charleston—and Wolf had been a sailor as well, but Connie had never warmed to the sport. Sailing was so much work, a combination of physical work and intellectual work, and it required luck. Connie loved being out on the water, but it was much easier to do it Dan's way—turn a key and inhale those exhaust fumes.

Connie helped Dan gather the rope that tethered them to the slip. He guided the boat out into the harbor. Meredith was sitting up front, waving to the people on other boats. Connie joined her.

Meredith was beaming. Beaming! She felt comfortable enough to wave to people.

Connie said, "You're glad you came, aren't you?"

"Shut up," Meredith said. She raised her face to the sun and grinned.

"Where do you want to go?" Dan asked. Connie was sitting next to him behind the controls.

"Anywhere," Connie said. "Everywhere." She was happy-giddy, if a teensy bit uncomfortable to be sitting next to him in the girl-friend seat. But it was nice, too, to be able to just go where they wanted as fast as they wanted without worrying about the main-sail or the jib. She had never sat next to Wolf on a boat. When they sailed, he was always moving, always monitoring.

They cruised up harbor, past the huge homes of Monomoy and the huger homes on Shawkemo Point. Dan singled out certain houses and told Connie who owned them — this famous author, that captain of industry. The island looked especially verdant and inviting today. The houses seemed to be stage sets for summer: flags were snapping, beach towels hung from railings. Meredith scanned the land, one hand shielding her eyes, and then lay back in the sun with her glasses off and her eyes closed.

They tooled up to Pocomo Point, where they came across a fleet of Sunfish with white sails — kids learning the basics.

Dan said, "As soon as we're out of their way, we'll anchor and go for a swim."

He stopped the boat in a beautiful, wide-open spot. Great Point Lighthouse was visible to the northwest and the handsome Wau-winet hotel was due north. Without the noise of the engine, the only sound was that of the waves slapping the side of the boat, and Connie suddenly felt anxious.

"Let me pull out the wine," she said.

"It's dazzling here," Meredith said.

"We'll swim," Dan said. "And then we can have lunch." He looked at Meredith. "Do you swim?"

"Yes," she said. "I do."

Connie pulled the cork from a cold bottle of chardonnay. She felt her blood quicken. She couldn't pour fast enough. She wasn't sure what was wrong with her. "Meredith was a champion diver in high school. She came in third at the state finals our senior year."

"Really?" Dan said. "Well, then, I have a surprise for you."

Connie filled a red Solo cup with chardonnay and guzzled the top third of it down. A cool burn slid down her throat, and she felt her muscles go slack.

"Wine?" she asked Dan.

He was moving the cooler and rearranging some other things at the stern and he said, "I'll get a beer, in a minute."

Typical man with his beer, Connie thought. Wolf had been a wine drinker. It had been one of the many elegant things about him. Connie took another sip. How often did men like Wolf come along?

"Meredith, wine?" Connie asked.

"No, thank you," Meredith said.

Dan pulled something out of the back of the boat—a long white springboard. A diving board.

"There we go," he said proudly.

"Oh, my God!" Connie said. "Meredith, a diving board!"

Meredith made her way to the back of the boat. She saw the springboard and put her hand to her mouth.

Dan said, "I got it for my kids. They love it." He climbed up onto it, stripped off his T-shirt, which he threw into the well, and took a couple of test bounces. Then he approached the end of the board and did a soaring swan dive. He surfaced and rubbed at his eyes. "Your turn!" he called to Meredith.

Meredith looked at Connie. "I haven't dived in years."

"You were the best at Merion Mercy," Connie said. "You held all those records."

Meredith was pulling the bobby pins out of her head—off came the wig. Meredith's real hair was matted underneath, and she shook it out.

"I can't believe I'm going to dive," she said. "Will I remember how?"

"Isn't it like riding a bike?" Connie asked. She drank some more, and a feeling of well-being settled over her. Her arms tingled; there was a golden glow in her chest.

"I guess we'll see," Meredith said. She shed her cover-up and climbed onto the board. She walked to the end, then walked back. She gave it a few test bounces. Then, she composed herself at the back of the board, and, like a gymnast, she took one, two, three choreographed steps, bounced impossibly high, and folded her body into a perfectly straight up-and-down front dive. It was a thing of beauty. Connie blinked. She had gone to all of Meredith's home meets in high school, and what struck her watching Meredith dive now was the time warp.

Dan whistled and clapped and shouted. Meredith surfaced, her hair wet and slick, and swam easily over to the ladder on the side of the boat.

Meredith said, "Just like riding a bike."

Connie said, "Do another one. Do something fancy. Really show him." She remembered Meredith once telling a reporter from the *Main Line Times* that a simple front dive or a reverse dive was the hardest to execute because her body wanted to flip and twist. Her body, she said, craved degree of difficulty.

Meredith climbed back up onto the board. She did a front one and a half pike. Her pike wasn't as tight as it had been in high school, but that was to be expected.

Dan grabbed a towel and sat next to Connie. "Man," he said. "Did you see that?"

"I told you," Connie said. She drank her wine. She had two inches or so left in her cup. Another glass like that and she'd be ready for some food.

Meredith climbed back up onto the board. She walked out to the end with regal bearing and turned around.

Back dive. Her entry was perfect, her toes pointed, though she didn't get the height she'd gotten in high school. God, Connie could remember the way Meredith had seemed to float in the air, the way she had seemed to fly.

"Do another one!" Connie said.

"I don't know," Meredith said. She mounted the board and did a backflip with a half twist.

Dan put his fingers in his mouth and whistled.

Connie said, "That was too easy!" Connie remembered Meredith stretching on the blue mats that the coaches laid out alongside the diving well. Meredith could put her face flush to her knees, her arms wrapped around her thighs. It hurt now just thinking about it.

Meredith did a simple inward dive. Then a reverse dive. Then, without any warning, she approached the end of the board and whipped into a front two and a half somersault, tuck. Dan hooted, and Connie wondered if she should feel jealous. She had been an aggressive field-hockey player in high school, but that didn't inspire this kind of admiration. Connie touched Dan's shoulder, to remind him that she was still there. "Are you ready for that beer?"

He said, "Aren't you going to try?"

She filled her cup with wine—glug, glug, glug—and didn't quite catch his meaning. Meredith executed something else; Connie only looked up in time to see Meredith's legs enter the water. The key to a good entry was as little splash as possible.

Connie said, "Excuse me?" She corked the wine and stuck it back in the cooler.

"Aren't you going to take a turn on the board?" Dan asked.

"Oh," Connie said. "I don't dive like that."

"Come on," Meredith said. "The water's nice."

"Come on," Dan said, standing up. He climbed onto the board. "You must be hot."

She was kind of hot, yes, but she didn't like being pressured into things. And she still found the water too cold for swimming. But now if she said no, she would seem prissy and high maintenance or, worse, she would seem old. She would jump off the board once, she decided, and then she would drink that wine.

Dan did another swan dive and waited, treading water, for Connie to have a turn. Connie bounced on the board, testing it, as she'd seen Dan and Meredith do, but the board had more spring than she anticipated—either that or her legs weren't as steady as theirs—and she lost her balance and had to windmill her arms like some vaudeville act just to keep from falling.

"Whoa!" she said. "Okay." She steadied herself and proceeded to the end of the board. In the distance, she saw Great Point Light. Seagulls flew overhead, a few wispy clouds scudded by. She didn't want to jump. She liked it here, perched over the water, surveying.

She bounced, placed her arms over her head, and dove, hitting the water much sooner than she expected, and harder. Her chest, where she'd been holding that golden chardonnay glow, stung. And she had water up her nose. Her nasal passages buzzed and burned, and the burn trickled down her throat. Connie wiped her eyes, adjusted her bathing-suit top, pawed at her hair.

"There you go!" Dan said. "Great job!" But Connie felt he was being patronizing.

"The water's freezing," Connie said, though it wasn't, really. She wanted to get back on the boat. But here came Meredith again.

She said, "Okay, last one."

"What's it going to be?" Dan asked.

Meredith ran for the end of the board, bounced, and launched herself into another front one and a half pike, though her pike was loose, and she entered early, making a big splash. Despite this, Connie gave Meredith two hands up: a ten. Meredith jerked her head toward her shoulder. "Water in my ear," she said.

It was only swimming back to the ladder that Connie noticed the name of the boat written in gold script. *Nicky.*

Nicky? Connie thought. And then she realized: Nicole, the wife. Nicky.

She felt ten kinds of sad as she pulled herself aboard.

It was nothing a second and then a third glass of wine couldn't cure. Dan cracked a beer, and Meredith drank a diet Nantucket Nectars iced tea. Connie didn't love the fact that she had been bullied into the water, but she did love drying in the sun and feeling the saltwater evaporate off her skin.

Meredith's wig lay on the seat next to Connie like some kind of poor, abandoned animal. Connie held it up with two fingers.

"I wish you didn't have to wear this," Connie said.

"Here, give it to me," Meredith said.

"I wish people would just leave you alone," Connie said. She could feel the wine circulating around her brain, embalming it. "Leave *us* alone."

There was an awkward silence. Meredith jerked her head again, still trying to drain her ear. Connie hoped she hadn't heard; the words had come out wrong.

Dan said, "I don't know about you, but I'm ready for lunch."

Lunch, yes! Connie enthusiastically pulled lunch from the cooler. There were two kinds of sandwiches: chicken salad on wheat, or roast beef and Swiss with horseradish mayo on rye. There was potato salad that Connie had made from scratch, as well as a chilled cucumber soup with dill. There was a fruit salad of watermelon, strawberries, and blueberries. There were chocolate cupcakes with peanut-butter icing.

"Amazing," Dan said. He had one of each kind of sandwich, a whopping portion of potato salad, a cup of soup. "You made all this yourself?"

"Meredith dives," Connie said, "and I cook." She felt like perhaps this evened things out. She took a bite of her chicken-salad sandwich. "Did your wife like this boat?"

Dan nodded. "Loved it."

"You named it for her?" Connie asked. Her voice sounded confrontational to her own ears, though she wasn't sure why. Clearly the boat was named for his wife, and why should that matter? It was his boat, he'd had it a long time, longer than the past ten days, which was how long he'd known Connie. And there was nothing between him and Connie anyway except for a handful of great kisses. But still, wasn't it a little weird to take a woman that you'd kissed a few times out on a boat named for your dead wife?

"We used to have a boat," Meredith said wistfully. She said this without irony, as if everyone in America hadn't heard about Freddy's megayacht, *Bebe,* which had cost him $7 million of his clients' money. She smiled at Dan. "But it didn't have a diving board!"

In the afternoon, they motored to the end of the jetty. There were seals lounging on the black rocks, and Connie thought of Harold.

Dan said, "We're going out to check the lobster pots."

"Oh, yes," Connie said. She had finished one bottle of wine by herself and had eaten only part of half a sandwich, so she was pleasantly buzzed. She had achieved a perfect state of equilibrium. She was happy and lighthearted, without a care in the world. She debated opening a second bottle of wine but decided against it — she was, after all, the only one drinking. Dan had drunk one beer and Meredith had stuck to diet iced tea. But when Dan pulled back on the throttle and the horsepower kicked in, Connie wished she had a drink. If she stopped drinking now, in this sun, she might fall asleep, and if she fell asleep, she'd wake up with a headache. The boat was ripping along, skimming the water, and when they encountered wake from the high-speed ferry, which passed them on their starboard side, the front of the boat slammed against the chop, and a fine mist splashed over the side. Meredith was facing front, as still and alert as the maidenhead on a whaling ship; she hadn't replaced her wig, and her glasses were off. She didn't seem to mind getting wet.

Connie had been sitting next to Dan behind the controls, but she made a move to the stern to see if reaching into the cooler was feasible. But as soon as she stood up, the boat hit a wave and Connie fell against the gritty floor of the deck and scraped her knee. There was blood. She crawled to the safety of the cushioned seats and held on to the back rail for dear life. Dan hadn't noticed her fall, which was a good thing, though he would notice the blood on his deck. She inspected her knee. It stung. They crossed the wake of another, bigger power yacht, and the front of the boat slammed again; there was more spray up front. Connie couldn't reach the cooler; it was wedged under the seat, and even if she could get to it, the motor skills required to open the wine were beyond her under the circumstances. She would have to wait until they stopped or slowed down.

Their speed was breathtaking. Connie squinted at the boat's speedometer: one hundred knots, or nearly. Was that equivalent to a hundred miles an hour? She couldn't remember. Dan was a cowboy behind the wheel of a boat, whereas Wolf, while sailing, had been an orchestra conductor. But, Connie reminded herself, she wasn't looking to replace Wolf. She wasn't looking for anything except a respite from her misery. She liked motor boats, she reminded herself. Up front, Meredith seemed completely unfazed by the speed. Connie needed to loosen up.

And then, suddenly, Dan downshifted, and the boat slowed. Sticking out of the sparkling water, Connie saw tall buoys on stakes. Dan maneuvered the boat toward the buoys and cut the engine.

"Okay!" he shouted. He scrambled for the ropes and, like an experienced rodeo hand, lassoed a buoy with a green stripe. He seemed busy, so Connie made a move for the cooler, feeling like a pirate trying to pilfer from the treasure chest. She unwedged the cooler and had just gotten the second bottle of chardonnay in her hands when Dan said, "Quick! I need help here!" He was barking orders, just as Wolf tended to when he sailed. *Men,* Connie thought. She had her eyes on Dan — did he really expect *her* to help him with the lobster traps? — but her hands were rummaging for the corkscrew.

"Help!" Dan called again.

Meredith appeared beside him to help him pull up the ropes. Connie could see she was needed as well, so she abandoned the wine in the cooler and hurried over. Heave, ho—they yanked and rested and yanked and rested. Dan's forearms were straining with the effort, and Connie got the feeling that she and Meredith weren't contributing much in the way of strength. Finally, the heavy wooden trap broke the surface of the green water and Dan said, "Back up!" He hauled the trap up over the side of the boat and Connie and Meredith helped him maneuver it onto the deck.

Dan exhaled and wiped at his forehead. He looked at Connie and thought to smile. He was handsome, he had kissed her, but he was a complete stranger to her. She was glad Meredith was here.

"Wow," Meredith said. She crouched down to inspect the contents of the trap, but Connie didn't want to get too close. She could see thirty or forty blackish-green lobsters crawling all over in a panicked frenzy, like kids at a rock concert. The shells clicked against one another and some of the antennae stuck out of the slats. Lobsters were a lot like cockroaches, Connie decided, with their armored carapaces and their prehistoric ugliness. Still, she thought, delicious. She loved lobster salad, steamed and cracked lobsters with drawn butter, lobster bisque...

"So many!" Connie said admiringly. "What will you do with them?"

"Well, three lucky ones will be our dinner tonight," Dan said. "And the rest I'll sell to Bill at East Coast Seafood."

Meredith said, "I feel sorry for them."

Dan nodded. "Typical female answer. My wife felt sorry for them, too. She used to beg me to let them go."

Connie felt like she should chime in with her own expression of sympathy on the crustaceans' behalf, but she didn't care. She said, "Do you need our help?"

"No," Dan said. "But I have to band these guys and put them in coolers. And then I'm going to fish for a few minutes. Are you ladies okay to kick back here for a little while?"

"God, yes," Connie said. Now that he had basically given her permission, she opened the wine and poured herself a hefty cup. She said, "Meredith, do you want wine?"

"No, thanks," Meredith said. She was standing by the trap, watching Dan as he put on heavy work gloves and pulled the lobsters out one by one, securing thick blue rubber bands on each claw. He then set the disenfranchised lobsters in an industrial-size white cooler that he had pulled out from the hold. Meredith seemed mesmerized by this work. Well, it wasn't anything she would have seen on the French Riviera.

Connie took her wine up to the bow, and lay back in the sun.

Despite her best intentions, she must have fallen asleep because when she next looked up, the lobster trap was gone and the cooler with the lobsters had been tucked under the seats at the stern. Dan had his fishing pole out, and Connie saw that Meredith held the other fishing pole; she was standing next to Dan, reeling in her line.

Connie sat up. She had to pee.

She heard Meredith say, "So there was one time at the pool at Princeton where I dove like that for Freddy, only I was better then because I was younger and I had just been in training. And I was thinking that Freddy would be impressed, that he would think I was so talented, so athletic, so limber—I mean, even from a *sexual* standpoint it should have turned him on, right? But instead of being impressed, he...well, I didn't really understand his reaction. He was nonplussed. He didn't like watching me dive for some reason. And so I stopped doing it. There were times in subsequent years when we were at someone's pool and there was a diving board and I would whip out a front two and a half like I did today—it's a deceptively easy dive—and Freddy would seethe.

He accused me of showing off. He was threatened by my diving. I should have seen that as a sign." Meredith cast her line back out; her reel whizzed. "Why didn't I see that as a sign?"

Dan laughed. "Hindsight," he said.

"Hindsight in my case was worth about fifty billion dollars," Meredith said.

Connie reached for her wine. It was warm. She ditched it over the side and stumbled to the back of the boat for more.

Dan and Meredith were so deep in conversation that they didn't even notice she was awake. She poured another cup of wine and wondered if Dan *liked* Meredith, then decided not. All their lives, boys had enjoyed talking to Meredith—she was smart, quick, funny—but Connie was beautiful and that had always trumped smart.

Even Freddy Delinn had once—yes, he had once made a pass at her. Connie had banished that memory—she thought, permanently—from her mind.

She secured her wine in one of the round cup holders situated conveniently around the boat, then she climbed up onto the side and dove in. Smack! Again, the water came too fast. Her chest burned and her scraped knee stung. She let herself drift down into the cool depths and she peed, sweet release. She knew there was sea life below her—all of those lobsters for starters and probably a lot of other sinister creatures. That far out, maybe even sharks. But the wine and the nap gave Connie a lethargy that made her want to float beneath the surface for a minute.

Seven or eight years earlier, Freddy had brought Connie a cocktail on the deck of the house in Cap d'Antibes. Wolf had been out jogging, and Meredith had run into town to an antiques store to take a second look at something she'd wanted to buy. That part of the story made sense in Connie's memory, but Freddy bringing her a cocktail—a very cold, very crisp gin and tonic with lots of lime—had been a surprise, because Freddy didn't drink. So the drink was a flirtation; Connie had sensed that right away. And there was something about the look on Freddy's face when he brought it to her. Connie had always felt insecure when visiting the Delinns—in Manhattan, in Palm Beach, in France—because of money, she supposed. It was impossible, in the face of all that money, to feel that one measured up. And so, to compensate, Connie flaunted her beauty. On the evening that Freddy brought her the drink, she was already dressed for dinner. She was wearing a long patio dress in an orange and pink paisley; the dress had a plunging neckline, putting her breasts on display. At home in America, Connie would only have worn that dress privately, for Wolf. But this was the south of France, where everyone seemed determined to show off what they had.

Freddy was still in his robe. He had looked appreciatively at Connie's breasts, and he let Connie catch him looking, which seemed a brazen thing to do. He gave her the drink, she sipped it, they leaned together on the railing that looked down the cliff over the Mediterranean.

Then he turned toward her and she meant, as a grasp at light conversation, to ask him what his ethnic background was. The name "Delinn" was French, right? But just then, Freddy said, "You're an incredibly beautiful woman, Constance."

Connie was rendered speechless. She nodded, though barely. She wasn't struck by Freddy's actual words—people had been telling her she was beautiful her whole life—but by how he said it. He had said it with *intent,* as though he meant to carry her up to his bedroom and make love to her right that second. He had used her full name, Constance, which made her feel sophisticated. And then he leaned in and kissed her, and with one deft hand, he cupped her breast, which was thinly sheathed behind the silk of her dress. She felt a stab of arousal and she made a gasping noise. She and Freddy separated and stared at each other for a fierce, hot second, then Connie left the deck. She took her drink up to the guest room, where she sat on the bed, waiting for Wolf to return.

Even now, what struck Connie about that encounter was Freddy's confidence, his authority, his sense of entitlement as he reached out to kiss her and touch her body. He had no qualms about putting his hands on something that did not belong to him.

Connie felt arms close in around her, and she squirmed, confused and afraid. She was being pulled to the surface.

"What?" she choked.

Dan was in the water next to her, holding her roughly under one arm. "Thank God," he said. "I thought you were drowning."

"Drowning?" she said.

"You fell in dangerously close to our lines," he said.

From the side of the boat, Meredith waved. "Are you okay?"

"I didn't fall," Connie said. "I dove in."

"All I saw was the splash," Dan admitted. "But you've had so much wine, I was worried."

So much wine? Connie thought.

"I'm fine," Connie assured him. She swam away from him, toward the ladder on the back of the boat. There was the name again. *Nicky.* What a weird afternoon.

They stayed on the water until well after five o'clock. The sun mellowed in its slant, and Connie, despite the fact that she was being watched like a teenager, finished off the second bottle of chardonnay, though not by herself. As they motored back into the harbor, Meredith agreed to a glass. Connie and Meredith sat in the bow of the boat together, and Dan turned on some Jimmy Buffett, and the gold dome of the Unitarian Church glinted in the sun, and Connie decided that it had been a good day.

Meredith turned to Connie as Dan was tying the boat up in the slip and said, "You were right. I'm glad I came."

Once on land, they made a plan. Dan would drop them at home and return at seven o'clock for a lobster dinner.

Connie liked this idea. What she liked, she realized, was being back on her home turf. She started by making herself a very tall, very cold, very citrusy gin and tonic—reminiscent of the one prepared for her by Freddy Delinn—and carried it with her into the outdoor shower. When designing the shower, Wolf had built a special shelf for Connie's dressing drink, a feature that was, in her mind, the utmost in civility. She took a long shower, then wrapped herself in a towel, freshened her drink in the kitchen, and headed upstairs to dress.

Meredith popped out of her room and said, "I checked around the house and the car. Nothing happened while we were gone."

Connie waved a dismissive hand. "Of course not."

She put on a white cotton sundress and let her hair dry naturally. She moisturized her face—she had gotten a lot of sun—and applied mascara. Her hand wobbled with the wand, and the makeup smudged, and Connie cursed and got a cotton ball to wipe the mess away and start over.

Downstairs, in the kitchen, she put out crackers and Brie and a hunk of good cheddar and a jar of truffled honey. She poked a fork into three baking potatoes and accidentally stabbed her palm. She turned on the oven, though she hated to do it on such a warm evening. She refreshed her drink, and Meredith appeared and Connie said brightly, "Tanqueray and tonic?"

Meredith said, "I'll stick to wine."

Connie realized there was still a bottle in the cooler. She hadn't emptied the cooler; the picnic things were still in there, now sitting in two inches of water. She pulled out the container of potato salad and the thermos of soup. Were the sandwiches okay? Veronica, Connie's mother, would have tossed them. She couldn't abide leftovers, especially not in the form of sandwiches that, however well wrapped, would be a touch soggy. But Wolf had been raised in a more abstemious household with parents from the Depression era, and he never threw food away. So, in Wolf's honor, Connie put the sandwiches in the fridge.

She said to Meredith, "I wish we had blueberry pie. One should always have blueberry pie with a lobster dinner, but I don't have time to run out and get a pie now. So we'll have to eat these cupcakes for dessert." Connie pulled the plastic wrap off the top of the cupcakes, and the icing smeared. She wondered briefly what her mascara looked like. *You're an incredibly beautiful woman, Constance;* that was what Freddy had said so many years earlier, but no woman was beautiful with smudged makeup. Freddy's voice had been serious and stagy, as though he were a movie star born and bred, instead of some poor kid from upstate New York. The icing on the cupcakes—peanut-butter icing—was an unfortunate shade of brown, Connie realized now. It looked like…

She still had to shuck the corn, put on water for both the corn and the lobsters, tear greens for a salad, whip up a dressing, and clarify three sticks of butter. She gulped the rest of her drink and poured another and squeezed what was left of the lime into it. She heard someone say, *Really, Connie, another drink?* And she looked up, thinking it was Meredith, but Meredith was at the back door watching Harold frolic in the waves. Meredith had washed her hair and put on her white shorts and navy tunic. She hadn't worn that outfit since the evening she'd been photographed in it, so Connie was happy that she felt okay putting it on, and besides, she looked good. The sun lit her up like a statue. This had been Wolf's favorite time of day. The room was starting to spin, but no, Connie didn't have time. Water for lobsters and corn, salad dressing, set the table. Find the lobster crackers and picks. She wished they had blueberry pie.

At the stroke of seven, there was a knock at the door. Dan was one of those prompt people. Wolf, too, had strived for promptness, but Connie consistently made him late. She came by it honestly; her parents had been late to absolutely everything. *Late to my own funeral,* Veronica used to say. Wolf would get so mad, and as much as Connie didn't like to think about it, she and Wolf had fought.

Connie took a fortifying gulp of her drink despite the fact that her vision was blurring and her heels kept slipping off the backs of her espadrilles. The water for both the corn and the lobsters was boiling—too early, if they were to enjoy a proper cocktail hour—but the salad looked crisp and fresh, and the salad dressing was complete, though Connie's fingertips now smelled like garlic. Meredith had set the table for three.

Dan knocked again. Connie hurried to the front door and nearly turned her ankle. Stupid shoes.

She opened the door and there was Dan, showered and handsome in a white shirt and jeans, which was Connie's favorite outfit on any man. He was holding a bakery box in one hand and a large paper bag that contained the lobsters in the other hand. He held out the bakery box.

"For dessert," he said.

Connie took the box. It was a blueberry pie.

"Oh!" she said. She looked at Dan, thinking, *This is incredible, the man read my mind.* It was more than a lucky guess; it had to be fate. They were simpatico. Dan knew that a lobster dinner needed blueberry pie. "Thank you!"

She took a stutter step backward and nearly lost her balance, but Dan grabbed her arm. She said, "Whoa, geez, these shoes. I'd better take them off before I break my neck. Come in, hello." She moved in to kiss him, hoping for a kiss like the one he'd given her that morning, but this kiss was perfunctory and dry. He seemed somewhat less enchanted by her than when he'd arrived to pick them up for the boat trip. Quite possibly, Connie thought, he didn't even want to be here. Quite possibly, he'd only come out of a sense of obligation, because he had the lobsters.

As Connie headed back into the kitchen, she tried to figure out what she'd done that day to put him off. Maybe he'd decided he just didn't like her. She liked *him;* she liked that he was prompt. She liked that he had brought blueberry pie.

She said, "Can I get you a drink?"

He said, "Sure. Do you have any beer?"

Beer again. Connie hadn't thought about beer. She checked the fridge and found two green bottles of Heineken in the back, thank God, bought by one of her houseguests, probably Toby, before he quit for good. Toby used to drink beer even after his first try at rehab, because he claimed beer wasn't alcohol. Drinking beer was like drinking juice, Toby said. It was like drinking milk. Toby was an alcoholic, as purely and classically as their mother, Veronica, had been, but he'd beaten it now. He was sober. Connie pulled a beer out, opened it, poured it into a glass and watched it foam all over her counter.

Dan was out on the deck with Meredith, admiring the water. Meredith pointed out Harold's dark head. She said something and Dan laughed. Connie wondered again if Dan liked Meredith. Maybe they would be a better couple. But that was silly. Connie was glad to see Meredith outside on the deck. She hadn't ventured out to the deck since the photograph. Connie supposed she felt safer with Dan around. A man.

Connie joined them outside. She handed Dan his beer, and the three of them did a cheers.

"Thank you for a perfect day," Meredith said.

Connie took a breath to chime in but she couldn't think of what to add, so she just smiled. At Merion Mercy Academy, it had been popular to practice walking with a textbook balanced on one's head to promote good posture. Connie felt like she had a book balanced on her head now, one that was in danger of sliding off and hitting the ground. Or maybe it was her head that was threatening to fall off.

Dan said, "Well, thank you for joining me. It wouldn't have been much fun alone."

Connie nodded. Yep. She realized she was still holding her gin and tonic. She thought she had switched to wine. Meredith's wine glass was empty; she needed a refill. Connie would fetch the bottle.

Dan said, "I think the highlight was watching you dive!"

Connie nodded. Yep. Great watching Meredith dive. Meredith was a fantastic diver — champion, had been.

Meredith said, "That *was* fun! Of course, I used to be much better."

"When you were younger," Connie said. Her voice sounded funny to her own ears. Had those words made sense? Meredith and Dan were both looking at her now. "I used to go to all of Meredith's meets. Every one, every meet, every single meet."

They were still looking at her. Okay, what? She didn't want to know. She wanted to go get the bottle of wine. She would pour her gin and tonic down the sink. She picked up a cracker and cut a messy piece of Brie. Food! Connie devoured it. She'd had nothing to eat since the half of the half sandwich on the boat.

Dan said, "Do you need help with the lobsters?"

"No, no," Connie said, her mouth still full. She made some hand motions indicating *I've got it, I'll go in now and take care of things, you two stay here.*

The two pots on the stove were at such a rolling boil that their lids chattered. The bag with the lobsters was on the counter. Connie didn't want to do the lobsters, she realized. Wolf had always done the lobsters, and last summer, Toby had done them. Wolf, Toby, Freddy Delinn. How long would the lobsters take? Should she get Dan or just drop them in herself? She needed to clarify the butter. Meredith and Dan looked happy out on the deck; they were talking. They were enjoying their cocktail hour. So what if Connie was slaving in the hot kitchen? So what if Meredith was a great diver? Graceful and all that? Sexually limber. Who had said that? Connie took off her shoes. Ahhh, now that was a good idea. Wine. Connie poured herself a glass of wine and she should refill Meredith's glass also. She would, as soon as she was done with the butter. She went to pour her gin and tonic down the drain, but there was only a scant inch left, so she drank it.

She put the butter in the pan and turned on the burner.

Late for my own funeral, Veronica used to say. Veronica had died of cirrhosis of the liver. This had surprised no one. And then, at her funeral, something had happened between Meredith and Toby; Connie was sure of it.

Toby, Wolf, Freddy Delinn, Dan. Danforth Flynn, that was a nice name.

The butter was melting and Connie decided she would just do it: She dumped the lobsters into the boiling water. One, two, three. She secured the lid. There was a barely discernible high-pitched noise: the lobsters screaming. But no, that was a myth. It was the sound of air escaping the shells, or something.

Wine for Meredith. The butter was melting. What about the corn? The corn would only take five minutes.

And then Connie remembered her cell phone. She hadn't checked her cell phone since early that morning, before Dan arrived. What if Ashlyn had called?

Connie hurried up to her bedroom to grab her phone. Danforth Flynn, Freddy Delinn, Wolf, Toby. Her phone showed no missed calls. No missed call from Ashlyn. Never a call from her headstrong daughter, but why not?

Connie checked her texts: there was one unread text, which probably meant her cell-phone carrier had sent her a reminder that her bill was overdue. Connie held her arm straight out so she could read the display. The text was from Toby. It said: *Sold the boat to the man from Nantucket. Will be on island in 3 weeks, OK?*

Toby would be on island in three weeks? The man from Nantucket? Who was that? It was a joke, but Connie had forgotten the punch line. Toby was coming in three weeks! Her handsome, funny-fun-fun brother! Sold the boat? That just wasn't possible, unless he was buying a bigger boat or a faster boat.

Connie pushed the buttons that would reply to Toby. She had never really gotten the hang of texting, but maybe she should, maybe if she texted Ashlyn, Ashlyn would respond.

OK? he asked. Connie punched in: *OK!* Then she remembered about Meredith. She couldn't let him walk into that surprise party unwarned. What she wanted to say was *You won't believe this but Meredith Delinn called me up and asked me to throw her a lifeline, and I did, and guess what? It's been great. Except for the paint on the house. And the slashed tires.* But that was far too long for a text, especially when Connie couldn't see the buttons clearly. While she was getting Meredith's glasses replaced, she should have picked up a pair for herself. Connie left the text at *OK!* But then she thought to add *LOL!* which her friend Lizbet had told her meant "laugh out loud."

Connie sent the text. Then she hurried downstairs. She had a lot of pots on the stove.

The kitchen was hot. Connie rescued the butter from the stove. She dropped the corn into the second steaming pot and turned off the heat under the lobsters. She drizzled the dressing over the greens and tossed them. She poured the butter into a small ceramic pitcher. Her bare feet felt good against the cool floor. She had to pour Meredith more wine.

She hadn't lost anything, she reminded herself. There was no Ashlyn now, but there had been no Ashlyn before. She would try texting.

"Okay, we're ready!" Connie said.

Why was the kitchen so hot? The oven was on, that was why. But Connie had forgotten to put in the potatoes. Goddamn it— there they sat on the counter, in plain sight. She'd just overlooked them. *Laugh out loud,* she thought. But tears sprung to her eyes.

Meredith came in from the deck and said, "What can we do to help?"

Connie dissolved in sobs.

Meredith said, "Connie, what's wrong?" She sounded genuinely alarmed. But she wouldn't understand. Meredith, quite famously, had made it through a national crisis without shedding a single tear.

"I forgot to put in the potatoes," Connie said.

*   *   *

Connie recalled only snippets of dinner. She allowed Dan to lead her to her chair, and he cracked open her lobster and pulled the meat from it, as though she were a child. Her corn lay on her plate untouched. Her shoulders caved in, like her bones were melting, and Meredith rose and brought her a sweater. There was bright banter between Dan and Meredith, on what topic, Connie couldn't tell. The salad was weepy with dressing. Connie could only manage one bite.

"Eat!" Meredith implored her.

In the place where Connie expected to find her wine was a glass of ice water with a slice of lemon. She drank it gratefully, remembering how they used to pull this very same trick with her own mother and how Veronica usually fell for it, but one time spit the water all over the table and demanded her gin. Connie's eyes were closing, her head bobbed forward like it used to sometimes in the movie theater, when Wolf took her to the long, harrowing arthouse films he liked. She was hoping that either Meredith or Dan would have the foresight to put the blueberry pie in the oven to warm it up, though she was doubtful about this. She was the only one who thought of such things. But she was far too tired to stand up and tend to it herself.

Ashlyn didn't realize how cruel she was being. She wouldn't understand until she had children of her own. She may not have any children of her own, ever. And whereas this would be a shame, it would also be a blessing. Wolf, Toby, Freddy Delinn, Danforth Flynn. Connie's head fell forward to her plate, but she snapped it up again, alert and conscious. She stared at Meredith. Did Meredith know what Freddy had said and done to Connie in Cap d'Antibes? Certainly not. That man told her nothing.

Connie felt a pressure in her armpits. She felt herself being lifted. She was in Dan's arms. She could smell him; she could feel the weave of his white shirt. Linen. Who ironed for him, she wondered, now that his wife was dead? She was floating, much the way she'd been floating in the water today.

She heard the words "a lot to drink."

Meredith said, "And she barely ate anything."

She landed in softness, too novel yet to be familiar. Her bed, as lovely and luxurious as a bed in a five-star hotel. She felt a kiss on her cheek, but the kiss was feminine. It was Meredith.

Connie's eyes fluttered open. It was still light outside. There was something Connie wanted to tell Meredith, but Connie couldn't stay awake another second.

She said, "Wolf's dead." The words sounded funny, garbled. Had they made sense?

Meredith said, "I know, honey. I'm sorry."

MEREDITH

When Meredith awoke the morning after the boat ride, her body ached. Specifically, her torso: the spaces between her ribs were stretched and sore.

The diving.

Meredith felt guilty even thinking it, but yesterday had been a good day. Was this possible, really, considering her current circumstances? Certainly not. But yes. Yes. It had been a day when Meredith had been present in every moment. She had thoughts about Freddy but those thoughts had been intentional; they hadn't sneaked up on her. She had thought about the boys, too, but the day had been so brilliant in its every aspect that Meredith's thoughts about Leo were more optimistic than usual. She wondered what Leo and Carver were doing and decided that they were most likely enjoying the weather and not wasting their precious hours thinking about Deacon Rapp.

The good times had started with the diving board. Meredith had felt herself transform as she pulled off her wig and climbed onto that board. She hadn't taken a dive in years—decades—and while she expressed doubts to Connie about her ability to flip and twist and enter the water headfirst, inside she knew she could do it. There were dives still trapped inside of her, dives that had been waiting for thirty years to get out.

Meredith had been meant to dive at Princeton; it was one of the things that led to her admission. Coach Dempsey had one other diver—a junior named Caroline Free who came from California and who was breaking all kinds of Ivy League records. But Caroline Free would graduate, and Coach Dempsey wanted to bring Meredith up in her wake. But when Meredith's father died, Meredith lost all interest in diving. It was amazing how one of the most important things in her life suddenly seemed so pointless. Coach Dempsey understood, but he came right back to her sophomore year. By sophomore year, Meredith was ready. She had gained ten pounds her freshman year from the beer and the starchy food in the dining hall and the late-night fried chicken sandwiches with Russian dressing that Freddy made for her in the Dial kitchen. Back home in Villanova for the summer, she had returned to the Aronimink pool and swum laps alongside her mother, wearing one of her mother's hideous bathing caps festooned with lavender rubber flowers over the right ear. The laps had worked; Meredith was back to her slender, petite self, and she meant to stay that way. Plus, she wanted to dive. She missed it; it was part of who she was.

When she told Freddy, he went straight to work talking her out of it. If she dove for the Princeton team, he said, it would be all-consuming. There would be early-morning conditioning practices and regular afternoon practices. There would be home meets and, more sinisterly, *away* meets—whole weekends at Penn and Columbia and Yale with the squeaky-skinned, green-haired members of the swim team. He predicted that Meredith would miss the Dial holiday formal—a look at the team's schedule confirmed this—and with Meredith gone, Freddy would have to find another date.

Meredith took the opportunity to ask him who he'd taken to the formal the year before.

He said, "Oh, Trina."

"Trina?" Meredith said.

Freddy studied her to see if there were going to be any mildly annoying follow-up questions. They had, of course, talked about Trina early on in their relationship, and Freddy had corroborated Trina's story—though it had felt to Meredith like the *corroboration of a story*—that Trina was his tutoring student and not much else. Those had been Fred's exact words, "not much else." Now, Meredith found he had taken her to last year's formal! She didn't think she even needed to ask the annoying follow-up questions.

He said, "I didn't have anyone else to ask, and she was good for things like that. She presents well."

Meredith knew she shouldn't care about something as frivolous as the Dial holiday formal, but she did. Holiday formals at the eating clubs were glamorous events with twinkling lights and French champagne and sixteen-piece orchestras playing Frank Sinatra. The prospect of missing the formal and of Freddy going, instead, with Trina was enough to seal the deal: Meredith met with Coach Dempsey and gave him her regrets. He begged her to reconsider. Princeton *needed* her, he said. Meredith nearly buckled. She loved the university with near-militant ferocity; if Princeton needed her, she would serve. But Freddy laughed and said that Dempsey was being manipulative. Freddy was the one who needed her. This was his senior year. He wanted to spend every second of it with Meredith.

Meredith gave up the diving. Her mother, as it turned out, was happy. She had feared that diving would distract Meredith from her studies.

Meredith hadn't dived in any structured or serious way again. Freddy didn't like her to. He was jealous that she excelled at something that had nothing to do with him. He wanted Meredith to focus on sports they could do together—swimming, running, tennis.

And so, that was where Meredith put her energies. She and Freddy swam together in the Hamptons, in Palm Beach, in the south of France—which really meant that Meredith swam in the ocean or did laps in their sapphire-blue, infinity-edge pools while Freddy talked to London on his cell phone. They had played tennis regularly for a while, but ten years into the marriage, Freddy was far too busy to ever make a court time, and Meredith had been left to play tennis with women like Amy Rivers.

Diving from Dan's boat the day before had been a pleasure long overdue. How many other forty-nine-year-old women could pull off a front two and a half somersault? Meredith could have gone even further; she had been tempted to do her front one and a half with one and a half twists, but she didn't want to seem like a show-off, and she didn't want to injure herself. Dan Flynn had been impressed by her diving, which was gratifying, and Connie, reverting to high-school type, had been proud and proprietary. *I used to go to all of Meredith's meets.* It was fun to remember those meets, especially home meets where Connie always occupied the same seat in the pool balcony and used hand signals to assess Meredith's entry into the water. *A little over. A little short.* Two palms showing meant *Perfect 10!* There had been one meet when they had been down a judge, and after much conferring, Meredith convinced both team coaches to allow Connie to fill in. Connie knew the dives inside and out, and Meredith knew Connie would be fair. Connie had ended up being harder on Meredith than the other two judges, but Meredith won anyway.

To dive again had been to return to her real, deep-down, pre-Freddy self. But there had been other great things about yesterday— the sun, the water, the boat, the lunch. Meredith had loved being on the boat, feeling its speed and power, enjoying the salty mist on her face. She was, for the first time since everything happened, buffered from the outside world. She had enjoyed talking with Dan about lobstering, and he had asked her if she wanted to fish with him. Yes, certainly—she wasn't going to let a single opportunity get past her. At the end of the afternoon when the sun was mellow and golden and the water sparkled and Meredith was enjoying a cold glass of wine with Connie and there was the promise of a real, true lobster dinner ahead, Meredith had realized that she could experience happiness. Fleeting, perhaps, but real.

Even dinner was lovely—to a point. Dan appeared with the lobsters and a blueberry pie—he'd granted Connie's one wish without realizing it—and when they were out on the deck, Meredith couldn't thank him enough.

While Connie was in the kitchen pulling dinner together, Dan said, "I hope you won't think I'm too forward in saying this, but you're nothing like I thought you'd be."

This might have suggested a thorny conversation ahead, but Meredith had spent enough time with Dan to know that he wouldn't try to stick it to her. The bizarre thing was being faced with her own notoriety. Freddy had turned her into a public persona. People like Dan Flynn, a power washer on Nantucket Island, had formed an impression of "Meredith Delinn" without knowing her. Everyone in America had.

She cocked her head and said, "Oh, really? And how did you think I'd be? Tell me the truth."

Dan said, "I thought you'd be a society bitch. A fallen society bitch. I thought you'd be materialistic, demanding, entitled. I thought, at the very least, that you'd be bitter. Self-absorbed. A fun-sucker."

"A fun-sucker?" Meredith said. "Me?"

"Now, I'm not going to pretend I *know you* know you. I mean, we've only been on two dates, right? Sunday night and today."

Meredith glanced back at Connie in the kitchen. "Those weren't properly *our* dates..."

"Point taken," he said. "But I got to know you a little bit, right? And I think you're a wonderful woman, Meredith. You're smart, you're interesting, and you're a hell of a good sport."

"Well, thank you," Meredith said.

"You're an accomplished diver, you can cast a fishing line... does the world know this about you? No, the world sees you as... what? The wife of Freddy Delinn. A possible conspirator in his crimes..."

"I wasn't a conspirator," Meredith said. She hated herself for even having to say this. "I knew nothing about his crimes, and neither did my sons. But there are still people I have to convince of that."

"I believe you," Dan said. "I more than believe you. I know you're innocent in this. I can tell... because of how you are."

"Well, thank you," Meredith said. She said this to end the conversation while things were still relatively light. But she was tempted to remind him that he *didn't* know her and that he couldn't accurately tell anything about her. She was tempted to say that none of us knows anyone else—not really. If there was one person Meredith had thought she had known in this world, it was Freddy Delinn, and she had been wrong.

As soon as they settled at the table, it became clear that Connie was drunk. Dan glanced at Meredith, and Meredith made a helpless face. She felt responsible and embarrassed. She had noticed Connie drinking wine on the boat, a lot of wine, two bottles minus the one glass that Meredith had had, but she'd said nothing. What would she have said? Connie was a grown woman and she liked her wine. Some women were like that; they drank chardonnay like water, and it had no obvious effect. Meredith was comforted by the fact that Connie drank wine. Connie's mother, Veronica, had been an abuser of gin and could be found at any time of day with a Tervis tumbler at her elbow. There were always half-filled bottles of tonic around the kitchen and lime wedges in various stages of desiccation on the cutting board and in the sink drain.

Of course, Connie liked her gin, too. (Meredith decided there must be an inherited predilection for the juniper berry, because no one would have grown up watching Veronica destroy herself like she did and then voluntarily *choose* to drink gin.) Meredith had watched Connie pour herself a gin and tonic at the kitchen counter, but she didn't comment. It was, after all, cocktail hour. Furthermore, Meredith was in no position to judge or scold. Connie had saved Meredith's life; she had brought Meredith to this place and had put her in a position to have a wonderful time today. If Connie wanted to drink, Meredith wasn't going to pester her.

Now, though, Meredith felt negligent. Dan helped Connie into her chair, and she slumped. He pulled the meat from her lobster. Meredith pulled the meat from her own lobster thinking that the best idea was to act normal and see if they could make it through the meal. Meredith fetched Connie a glass of ice water with a paper-thin slice of lemon, the way she liked it. Then she helped herself to an ear of corn and some salad. She was impressed that Connie had been able to pull dinner together in her condition. Meredith could take a few pointers from Connie in the kitchen. There would come a day in the not-too-distant future when she would have to prepare her own meals, and she had never learned to cook. She was ashamed of this. Her mother had been a classic housewife of her era—veal saltimbocca, chicken and dumplings on Sundays, the best tuna salad Meredith had ever eaten. Meredith could microwave hot dogs, and she could fry or scramble an egg; that was how she'd managed when Leo and Carver were small. And then, magically, overnight it seemed, there was money to go to restaurants every night and hire a cook for breakfast, lunch, snacks, and any dinner party that Meredith wanted to throw.

But Meredith couldn't let her mind veer off this way. The meal before her was enticing, yet simple. Surely with a little instruction, Meredith could one day manage this?

"Cheers!" Meredith said.

Dan met her glass with a clink, and Connie, too, reached for her glass, but hesitated, realizing it was ice water. She succumbed, picking up the water and touching glasses with both Dan and Meredith.

"This looks delicious!" Dan said. He was using the too-loud, overly cheerful voice that one used with the infirm.

Connie made a move on her salad. Meredith said, "Eat!"

Meredith dug into her lobster. Her face was pleasantly warm and tight from the sun. There was no conversation, but that seemed okay. They were all busy eating.

Meredith said, "Boy, being out on the water really gave me an appetite!" She eyed Connie. Connie cut a piece of lobster, dragged it long and lavishly through the clarified butter, then left it impaled on the end of her fork, dripping onto the tablecloth.

"Eat up, Connie!" Meredith said. She felt like she was talking to a five-year-old.

Dan was eating ravenously, probably trying to get as much food in him as he could before this dinner came to its untimely end. Meredith wanted to say something that would ensure Dan would come back.

She said, "So what else should I do while I'm here on Nantucket?"

"Well, you have to go to Great Point," Dan said.

"How do I do that?"

"You need a four-wheel drive—the Escalade would work—and a beach sticker."

"Do you go to Great Point?" Meredith asked.

"Every chance I get," Dan said. "The fishing is great. And the clamming on Coatue."

"I'd love to go clamming," Meredith said.

"I'll take you sometime," Dan said.

"That'll be fun," Meredith said. "Won't it, Con? Clamming with Dan?"

Connie's head fell forward, and at first Meredith thought Connie was agreeing with her, but Connie's head dropped dangerously close to her plate before she caught herself and snapped her neck back. She came to for a second, though her eyes were glazed over and, Meredith noticed, she had salad dressing in her hair. Okay, Meredith hated to be a fun-sucker, but she was going to call the game.

She gave Dan a look, and Dan nodded. He picked Connie up, and together they delivered Connie to her bedroom. She sighed as she hit the mattress. Dan retreated, but Meredith stayed to tuck Connie in.

By the time Meredith got downstairs, Dan was standing by the front door, ready to leave.

"Don't you want to stay and finish your dinner?" Meredith said.

"I'd better go," he said. "It's been a long day."

She couldn't argue with him about that. "Do you want to take the pie, or ... ?"

"No, no, no," he said. "You ladies enjoy it."

Something about the way he said this made Meredith worry they would never see him again. She panicked. She said, "I know Connie really likes you. She's just ... going through some stuff. Her grief, you know ... and then, as if that's not enough, *I* show up. And all of the things that have happened since we've been here. She's under a lot of pressure."

He held up his palms. "I get it," he said. "I've been there."

Oh, no, Meredith thought. He was slipping away. This was upsetting. Meredith wanted him to stay—and if he had to leave, then she wanted to make sure he'd come back. For Connie's sake, certainly, but also for her own. He'd become sort of like a friend.

Meredith opened the door for him. She said, "Well, thank you again. For everything. It was ... the best day I've had in a long, *long* time."

These words weren't lost on him. He smiled. "You're welcome, Meredith. You're very welcome." He moved in to hug her, and as he pulled away, he said, "Keep your chin up."

Oh, no! That sounded like a permanent good-bye. Dan stepped outside. Meredith didn't know what to say, so she said, "Okay, I will." Once he was in his Jeep, she closed the door.

Now, Meredith touched the sore muscles between her ribs and decided she needed some Advil. But Connie would be feeling way worse this morning than Meredith did. Meredith eased herself out of bed and headed downstairs to see about her friend.

* * *

Dan didn't call for three days, and then four. Connie was pretending not to notice, but Meredith was certain she did. She asked Meredith how humiliating her behavior had been at dinner. The last thing she remembered, she said, was taking a bite of salad. "And it was overdressed!"

As if soggy salad was the problem.

Meredith tempered her response, though she felt flashes of fury: Dan Flynn was a quality person who could probably do them both a lot of good, and Connie had frightened him away.

She said, "Not humiliating at all. You were tired."

"I was drunk."

"You have a lot on your plate," Meredith said. "Emotionally speaking."

"True," Connie said. "Do you think Dan realizes that? Do you think he'll give me a free pass for one shabby drunken night?"

"Of course I do," Meredith said.

But the phone didn't ring. Meredith and Connie went about their days quietly. Meredith got a little braver. She ventured out onto the deck for half-hour stretches, she went for short walks on the beach with Connie. She took her first incredibly delightful outdoor shower and stayed in until the hot water ran out. On Saturday morning, Meredith and Connie went into town, and Meredith could tell Connie was hoping they'd run into Dan. Meredith found she wanted to run into Dan herself. Imagine that! Instead of fearing a chance encounter, she was seeking one out. She and Connie walked along with their eyes peeled. When they passed 21 Federal, they fell into a glum, respectful silence, as if for the newly deceased.

Then Connie said, "You know, I think Dan liked *you*."

"What?" Meredith said.

"I think he liked you."

"Connie," Meredith said. "I am the least desirable woman in all the world." She lowered her voice to a whisper. "First of all, I am married to Freddy Delinn. Second of all, look at me." She was glad her point would be underscored by the fact that she was wearing her thrift-shop wig, which was growing ratty. "No one *likes* me. No one will ever *like* me again."

"I think Dan liked you," Connie said. "As a person. I think he liked the way you were."

"I think he liked the way *you* were," Meredith said.

"Then why isn't he calling?" Connie asked.

Connie came up with an answer. Dan wasn't calling because she, Connie, was a hag. Since Wolf died, she had let herself go. She needed her nails done, she needed her eyebrows and bikini line waxed.

"We're going to the salon," she said.

"I can't," Meredith said.

"Of course you can," Connie said. "Wear your wig."

"It's not that easy," Meredith said.

"Of course it's that easy. We've been out to places a lot more public than the salon, and you've been fine."

"I know," Meredith said. "But I can't go to the salon." The salon was the equivalent of swimming in shark-infested waters. It was like negotiating a minefield on a pogo stick on Friday the thirteenth. The Pascal Blanc salon had been the first place to publicly denounce Meredith—and it didn't get much more public than the front page of the *New York Times* Style section. Surely Connie had seen the article?

"In case you haven't gotten it by now," Connie said, "I don't like going places without you."

"I'm going to have to beg your indulgence here," Meredith said. "I can't do the salon."

"You have to get back up on the horse," Connie said.

"So you saw the article?"

"I saw the article," Connie said. "And do you know what I thought when I read it? I thought, 'Meredith Martin is the best woman your salon has ever seen. It's your loss, Pascal Blanc.'"

"Really, it was my loss," Meredith said. "I'm as gray as Whistler's mother, and the salon got to broadcast how morally superior they were by keeping me out in the name of protecting their other clients, who might be upset by the sight of me."

"Don't you want to get your hair done?" Connie asked.

God, the answer to that question was yes. Since she'd started to go gray at forty, every six weeks she'd had her hair restored to the natural color of her youth — soft baby blond. This was, she knew, unspeakably vain of her — though it had more to do with how she felt inside, and especially now. The real Meredith Martin was blond. She was a brilliant and talented eighteen-year-old girl with an impossibly bright future.

"I can't get my hair done," Meredith said. "If I go to the salon, I'll have to wear my wig."

"So you'll go with me, then," Connie said. "And wear your wig. You can get a manicure and a pedicure. My treat."

"It's not about the money, Con." Though it was about the money, in addition to everything else. In Palm Beach, Meredith used to get a manicure and pedicure every week to the tune of $125. And she always left a $50 tip. So, $175 on her nails, $100 on a weekly massage, and $250 every six weeks for hair. All that money, and she hadn't blinked an eye. She was shamed by it now.

"It's not about the money," Connie said, "because it's *my treat.* Manicure and pedicure. Please? It's no fun going to the salon alone."

"I can't," Meredith said. "Women who are under investigation don't go to the salon. Women whose children are under investigation don't go to the salon. Women whose husbands are serving one hundred and fifty years in federal prison do not go to the salon."

"I understand you feel that way," Connie said. "But it's not that big a deal. It's a manicure and a pedicure. Something to make you feel pretty. Something to take your mind off things. I can go alone, but I really want you with me. And no one's going to hurt you, I promise."

*   *   *

Connie secured appointments for Friday afternoon. In the car, Meredith thought she might hyperventilate. She used her Lamaze breathing; it had been much more helpful for her Freddy-induced anxiety than it ever had for the births of her two children. Connie eyeballed her.

"Do you just want to bag and go home?" Connie said.

"No," Meredith said. "We're going." It had become some kind of stupid hurdle she now felt she had to jump. It was a test. And, Meredith reminded herself, she had never failed a test in her life.

The RJ Miller salon was inviting and unpretentious. There was jazz music playing, and the place smelled deliciously of hair product, acetone, cappuccino. It was a hive of activity, and Meredith quickly ascertained that this might work in her favor. The women who were lined up in the chairs were all glamorous—as glamorous as the women in Palm Beach or Southampton. They were suntanned and Botoxed; they wore Lilly Pulitzer skirts and Jack Rogers sandals. The type was familiar—it was Meredith's type, her exact genus and species—but she didn't recognize a soul. And no one turned to look at Meredith in her ugly wig and boring glasses. She was as exciting as a reference-room librarian. More than a few women turned to gaze at Connie; she was bewitching that way.

Connie checked them in with the receptionist, who had a cascade of sumptuous golden ringlets. She introduced Meredith as "Mary Ann Martin." The receptionist barely took notice of her, except perhaps to secretly wonder why Meredith wasn't there to have something done about her atrocious hair. It was a relief to be overlooked, but Meredith couldn't help reflecting on the Pascal Blanc salon in the days when Freddy's fund was returning at nearly 30 percent. When Meredith walked in, the room all but burst into applause. Meredith had been grounded enough to know that the ass-kissing had nothing to do with her and everything to do with money, but even so, she'd believed that the staff of the salon had liked her. She was a real person, despite her many millions. And yet, not a single one of the salon staff or the women she befriended at the salon had stood up for her. She had to admit, it had surprised her that, apparently, in the thirty years that she'd been with Freddy, she hadn't made one true friend; she hadn't forged one single human connection that could withstand the seismic aftershocks of Freddy's collapse. Absolutely everyone had forsaken her—except Connie.

"This way," the receptionist said. She led them into the spa room and showed them each to a pedicure tub. Meredith started to climb up on a perch, then realized she had forgotten to pick a color. She chose a dark purple. *Paris at Midnight.*

Meredith had experienced Paris at midnight more than once— any time they flew to Cap d'Antibes, they flew to Paris and then drove down to the coast in a Triumph Spitfire that Freddy kept in the hangar at Orly. Often, Meredith had shopping to do in Paris— she liked to stop at Printemps for candles and table linens, and at Pierre Hermé for boxes of colorful macarons.

Her life had been one of disgusting consumption. How had she not seen that?

The nail technician appeared. She introduced herself as Gabriella. She asked Meredith—whom she called "Marion"—if she would like a cappuccino. Meredith, feeling courageous, said yes.

Gabriella had some kind of accent, Eastern European or Russian. Meredith had known the names and life stories of all of the girls who had worked at Pascal Blanc. Her regular manicurist, Maria José, had a son named Victor who went to public school in Brooklyn. Meredith had once gone to see Victor in his high-school musical; he played Mr. Applegate in *Damn Yankees.* Meredith went because she loved Maria José and she wanted to be supportive, but Maria José was so ecstatic that *Meredith Delinn* would travel all the way to Red Hook to see Victor that Meredith's presence overshadowed Victor's performance, and Meredith ended up feeling guilty. When Meredith had explained this to Freddy, he'd kissed her cheek and said, *Ah, yes, I know. It's hard being Meredith Delinn.*

Here, at RJ Miller, Meredith didn't talk to Gabriella. She hid behind a copy of *Vogue*—which was filled with the cool and lovely things she could no longer afford—and tried to enjoy the pampering. She monitored the comings and goings of the salon over the top of the magazine. Every time a woman entered the salon, a chime sounded, and Meredith seized up in fear. Once, she jerked her foot, and Gabriella said, "Oh, no! I hurt you?"

"No, no," Meredith said. She closed her eyes and leaned back, listening to the sticky, slapping sound of Gabriella rubbing lotion into her feet and calves.

Next to her, Connie was blissed out. She said, "This is sublime, is it not?"

"Mmm," Meredith said. It was sublime in theory, though Meredith couldn't relax. She wanted to get it over with and get the hell out of there. She bent forward in anticipation, watching the final steps of her pedicure like she was watching a horse race. Gabriella slid Meredith's feet into the ridiculously thin foam-rubber flip-flops and gently inserted the stiff cardboard toe separators. She painted Meredith's nails with two coats of Paris at Midnight and a shiny top coat. Finished!

Meredith practically jumped off her perch. Gabriella said, "You in hurry?"

Meredith gazed at Connie, whose eyes were at half mast, like some college kid who had smoked too much dope.

"No," Meredith said guiltily.

Gabriella invited Meredith—again calling her "Marion"; Meredith almost didn't respond—over to the manicure table. The manicure table was trickier. There were no magazines to hide behind; it was face-to-face business. Gabriella started working on Meredith's hands and tried to make small talk.

"I like your ring," Gabriella said, fingering Meredith's diamond. Freddy had been dirt poor when they got married, too poor to buy a ring, so he'd been happy about Annabeth Martin's enormous diamond. There had been times, in those early years, when Meredith had overheard Freddy telling people that he'd bought it for her, or letting them assume so.

"Thank you," Meredith said. "It was my grandmother's."

"Are you married?" Gabriella asked.

"Yes," Meredith said. "No. Well, yes, but I'm separated."

Gabriella took this news in stride. She didn't even look up. Maybe she didn't understand "separated." She certainly didn't understand the kind of separated Meredith was talking about.

"So you live on the island, or you just visiting?"

"Just visiting," Meredith said.

"From where? Where you live?"

Meredith didn't know what to say. She defaulted. "New York."

Gabriella brightened. "Yes? New York City? We have many clients from New York City."

"Not New York City," Meredith said quickly. "I live upstate."

Gabriella nodded. She pushed at Meredith's cuticles. Since everything that had happened with Freddy, Meredith had reverted to her childhood habit of biting her nails. She remembered her grandmother dipping her fingertips in cayenne pepper to get her to stop. This would certainly be considered child abuse now.

Gabriella said, "Upstate? Where upstate?"

Meredith didn't want to answer. Gabriella couldn't have cared. Upstate had none of the sex appeal that the city had; they were like two different nations. But the question had been asked in earnest, and it required some kind of answer.

Meredith defaulted again. "Utica," she said. This had been the town where Freddy grew up, though he hadn't been well off enough to live in Utica proper. He had been raised—if you could call it that—in the sticks outside of Utica.

"Really?" Gabriella said. This came out as "Rilly!" Gabriella's voice was loud enough that conversation in that part of the salon came to a momentary halt. "My boyfriend, *he* come from Utica.

Perhaps you know him? His name is Ethan Proctor." She said his name carefully as though she had practiced long hours to pronounce it correctly.

"No, I'm sorry," Meredith said. "I don't know Ethan Proctor."

"But same, from Utica, yes?" Gabriella asked.

"Yes," Meredith said. Gabriella was transforming Meredith's nails from ragged, splintery edges to smooth half-moons. Her hands needed this, but Meredith had to turn the conversation around so that Gabriella was the one talking about herself, otherwise Meredith was going to find herself in trouble.

Gabriella leaned forward and lowered her voice, in the perfect stereotype of gossiping manicurist. "Of course you know who used to live in Utica long time ago?"

No, thought Meredith. *No!*

"Who?" she whispered.

"Freddy Delinn."

Meredith felt her nose twitch, and she thought she might sneeze. This was her goddamned stupid idiotic fault for saying Utica instead of making up the name of a town. Pluto, New York. Why hadn't she said Pluto?

"You know who I mean, Freddy Delinn?" Gabriella asked. "Monster psychopath, steal everybody's money?"

Meredith nodded. Monster psychopath, curled up next to Meredith in bed by nine thirty every night, buying the children a golden retriever puppy, resting his hand on Samantha's back, then snatching it away as though it had never been where it was not supposed to be. This was the boy who had walked her to Mental Health Services and had offered to come back and pick her up. He had talked her out of diving for the Princeton swim team so she could be his date at the holiday formal. He had been master of the fried chicken sandwich, king of the pool table. When, exactly, had he become a monster psychopath? The Feds thought 1991 or 1992, so when the kids were eight and six, right around the time Meredith was set free from the kitchen. No more making mac and cheese from a box.

They could go out for dinner—to Rinaldo's or Mezzaluna or Rosa Mexicano—every single night! Monster psychopath stealing everyone's money. Meredith thought it might be hard to hear Freddy called a monster psychopath by Gabriella the Bulgarian or Croatian manicurist, but all Meredith could think was that it was true.

"Where are *you* from, Gabriella?" Meredith asked.

Gabriella didn't answer. Gabriella hadn't heard her because Meredith's voice was nothing more than a strangled whisper. She may not have spoken at all, in fact; she may have only been thinking those words, desperate to change the subject, but had not actually managed to utter them.

Gabriella said, "There is girl? Here on Nantucket? Like me, also from Minsk?"

Minsk, Meredith thought. *Belarus.*

"She clean houses. She ask her boss, man who own house where she is cleaning, if he can invest her money with Freddy Delinn because man has account with Freddy Delinn, and man says, 'Okay, sure,' he will ask if she can also invest. And Mr. Delinn say, 'Yeah, sure.' So my friend invest her *life savings*—one hundred thirty-seven thousand dollar—with Freddy Delinn and now, all of it gone."

Meredith nodded, then shook her head. The nod was meant to acknowledge the story; the shake was meant to say: *That is a hideous, awful, sickening tragedy, caused by my husband. That money, your friend's life savings, that hundred and thirty-seven thousand dollars, could have been the same money I spent at Printemps on hand-milled candles. It could have been used to put gas in the Spitfire on the way to Cap d'Antibes. But what you have to understand, Gabriella, is that although I am guilty of spending the money in lavish and inexcusable ways, I didn't know where it came from.*

I thought Freddy had earned it.

Gabriella, perhaps picking up on something in Meredith's body language, or in the pheromones she was giving off, which were broadcasting FEAR, said, "Did you know Freddy Delinn?"

"No," Meredith said. The denial came easily and automatically, the same way it must have come to the disciple Peter. Meredith tried to convince herself that she wasn't lying. She didn't know Freddy; she had never known Freddy.

She met up with Connie again as they sat side by side at the nail dryers. Connie still seemed a little dazed, and Meredith wondered briefly if she was drunk. Had she been drinking at home before they left? Meredith didn't think so, but then again, Meredith was oblivious. She should have made a vow to *pay attention* to the next person she became close to, but she hadn't dreamed there would ever be such a person. She would pay closer attention to Connie, starting right now.

"Isn't this *heavenly?*" Connie said. She wasn't drunk, Meredith decided. She just had the nature of an addict, and the whole calming, peaceful, restorative atmosphere of the salon had permeated her skin and made her high.

"My nails look better," Meredith said matter-of-factly. She wouldn't tell Connie about her conversation with Gabriella, she decided. It was Meredith's own fault for mentioning Utica. Freddy was so infamous now that the details of his life were known to everyone. The story about the housekeeper losing her life savings had gutted Meredith—that was how she felt every time, like she was being sliced open—although Meredith wondered about the mysterious relationship between housekeeper and man of the house. What kind of person would go to Delinn Enterprises on behalf of his housekeeper? Was it the same as Meredith going to see the school play of her manicurist's son, a show of interest, a way of proving to himself that there was no class difference between him and his housekeeper—they could both invest with Freddy Delinn?

"I still have to get waxed," Connie said.

"Oh," Meredith said. She desperately wanted to leave.

"It should be quick," Connie said.

*   *   *

Meredith decided the safest thing would be to wait for Connie in the car. She told Connie this, and Connie said, "What are you, a dog? Wait right here and read *Cosmo.* I'll be out in a minute."

"I'd feel safer in the car," Meredith said.

"Okay, fine," Connie said. "Do you want to make an appointment for hair?"

Yes, Meredith thought. *But no.* This visit had gone fine—sort of—though her manicurist had called Freddy a monster psychopath to her face and Meredith had had to deny knowing him and she'd been force-fed that unsettling story about the housekeeper.

Could she do hair?

Vanity won out over fear: she made a hair appointment. The receptionist with the ringlet curls said, "You want cut and color?"

"I do," Meredith said. She touched her wig. The receptionist watched her. The receptionist certainly realized Meredith was wearing a wig, but she punched Meredith's information into the computer anyway and handed her a little card. Tuesday at four o'clock.

Connie disappeared into the waxing room. Meredith gave Gabriella a tiny manila envelope that held twenty dollars. This, she reassured herself, was her own money earned years before, *not* the money Freddy had pilfered from the housekeeper.

Meredith headed out of the salon. She was moving down the steps, watching her feet as she went. Paris at Midnight was a dynamite color. Her feet hadn't looked this good in months.

She raised her head, searching for Connie's car in the parking lot. She often caught herself looking for one of her own cars—the black Range Rover they drove to Southampton, or the Jaguar convertible that they drove in Palm Beach, a car that most closely resembled a woman's shoe. She didn't miss the cars at all; she wondered if Freddy did. She decided not. Freddy, ironically, hadn't cared much for material things, only the money and the power it brought. He liked being able to buy a $70,000 Range Rover, but he didn't love the Range Rover itself.

Meredith was so caught up in this thought—if she explained it to Connie or Dan, would they understand?—that she had to stop in the middle of the parking lot and remind herself: green Escalade. She spotted the car, but she was distracted by the sight of a woman chaining up a classic turquoise and white Schwinn at the bike rack while smoking a cigarette. Something familiar about the woman.

The woman turned, plucked the cigarette from her mouth, and blew smoke in Meredith's direction.

Amy Rivers.

Meredith started to shake. She backed up a few steps, thinking it was possible that Amy hadn't seen her, although there had been one split second of what Meredith feared was mutual recognition. Meredith spun back toward the salon and hurried up the stairs. In her haste, one of her flimsy flip-flops ripped off her foot. She had one bare foot, but she didn't care. She went back into the sweet-smelling, air-conditioned cool of the salon and thought, *Get Connie.* Was there another way out of this place? There was a front door. Meredith could walk out the front door, and Connie could drive around and pick her up.

The receptionist noticed Meredith and said, "Oh, did you forget your shoes?"

Yes, all of a sudden, Meredith realized she *had* forgotten her shoes, a fact that was only going to slow her down. Gabriella walked out of the spa room holding Meredith's suede flats, the same shoes she had gone to visit Freddy in—they were now, officially, bad-luck shoes—and at the same time, Meredith heard the chiming noise that meant someone was entering the salon. She was so nervous she feared she would pee all over the salon floor.

A voice said, "Meredith?"

And Meredith thought, *DO NOT TURN AROUND.*

But forty-nine years of Pavlov-like conditioning prevailed, and Meredith responded automatically and found herself face to face with Amy Rivers.

Amy was wearing a light-blue polo shirt and white shorts and her Tretorns. Her hair was in a ponytail; she was tan. The strange thing was how *familiar* she was to Meredith. It didn't seem right that someone so familiar—Meredith had eaten lunch with this woman countless times; she had hit thousands of tennis balls beside her—should be so threatening. She had been Meredith's *friend*. But that was how the world worked. It wasn't the bogey-man in the closet you had to fear; the people you liked and cared about could hurt you much worse.

"Nice wig," Amy said. She reached out to touch it—possibly, to tear it off—but Meredith backed away.

Meredith said nothing. Gabriella was still holding Meredith's shoes. Very slowly, like she had a gun trained on her, Meredith reached out for her shoes. Amy's eyes flickered to Meredith's feet, then over to Gabriella.

"You gave this woman a pedicure?"

"Yes," Gabriella said, a touch of Russian moxie in her voice.

"Do you know who she is?"

Gabriella shrugged, now seeming less certain. "Marion?" she said.

"Ha!" Amy said, announcing Gabriella's gullibility. Turning back to Meredith, she said, "Did you get the message I left you?"

Meredith nodded.

"Your husband stole all my money," Amy said. "Over *nine million* dollars. And I'm one of the lucky ones because I still have a job and Jeremy has a job, but we had to sell the house in Palm Beach, and we had to pull Madison out of Hotchkiss."

"I'm sorry," Meredith whispered.

"But like I said, I'm one of the lucky ones. I honestly don't know how you can move about like a regular human being—summer-ing on *Nantucket,* getting *pedicures*—when you have ruined so many lives. People are *broke* because of you, Meredith, and not only broke but *broken*. Our neighbor in Palm Beach, Kirby Delar-est, blew his brains out. He had three little girls."

Meredith closed her eyes. She knew Kirby Delarest. He was an investor with Freddy; he and Freddy had been friendly acquaintances, if not actually friends, because Freddy didn't have any friends. But Kirby Delarest had swung by the house on occasion. Meredith had once happened on Freddy and Kirby barbecuing steaks by the pool midday, drinking a rare and expensive bottle of wine that Kirby had bought at auction, and smoking Cohibas. Meredith had found this odd because Freddy never drank and certainly not midday during the week, but Freddy had been effusive on that day, saying that he and Kirby were celebrating. *Celebrating what?* Meredith had asked. Because of the cigars, she thought maybe Kirby's wife, Janine, was expecting another baby. Meredith had said, *Is there something I should know?* Freddy had taken Meredith in his arms and waltzed her around the flagstone patio, and he said, *Just dance with me, woman. Love me. You are my winning lottery ticket. You are my lucky charm.* Meredith had been curious, bordering on suspicious, but she decided to just enjoy it. She didn't ask anything else. She supposed Freddy and Kirby were toasting the occasion of yet more money, a good deal, a correct gamble, some more unbelievable returns. Kirby had been a tall, lean man with white-blond hair, and he had an accent she couldn't place. It sounded European — Dutch, maybe — but when she asked him, he claimed he hailed from Menasha, Wisconsin, which did explain his amiable nature and his Scandinavian good looks, as well as Freddy's affinity for him. Fred loved midwesterners. He said he found them to be the most honest people on earth.

Meredith hadn't heard the news that Kirby Delarest shot himself, because there was no one to tell her. Samantha had decorated for Kirby and Janine Delarest; Freddy and Meredith had made the introduction. Meredith wondered if Samantha knew.

Gabriella and the receptionist stood watching. Meredith then realized the salon was silent, except for Billie Holiday crooning.

"I'm sorry," Meredith said. "I had no idea."

"No *idea?*" Amy said. She took a step toward Meredith, and Meredith could smell the cigarette smoke on her. Meredith hadn't known Amy was a smoker; possibly it was a stress-induced habit, caused by Freddy.

"No," Meredith said. "No idea. About any of it."

"You expect me to believe that?" Amy said. "Everyone knows you and Freddy were connected at the hip. Everyone knows you two were living out some kind of sick love story."

Sick love story? Meredith had no response for that.

"And your son?" Amy said.

Meredith snapped her head up. "Don't," she said. What she wanted to say was, *Don't you dare say one word about Leo.*

"They have hundreds of pieces of evidence against him," Amy said. "Someone in my company knows that cute little lawyer of his, and supposedly even she says it's a lost cause. Your son is going to spend the rest of his life in prison."

"No," Meredith said. She closed her eyes and shook her head. No, there weren't hundreds of pieces of evidence against Leo. Julie Schwarz was a superstar; she would never have spoken out against her case, her client. *Leo!* If there were hundreds of pieces of evidence against Leo, Dev would have told Meredith.

"Yes," Amy said. "Yes, absolutely. My sources are reliable. Your family is going to be flushed away, Meredith. Like turds."

Meredith opened her mouth to speak—and say what? *You're wrong. Leave me alone.* Or again, *I'm sorry*—but the receptionist took the occasion of Meredith's loss for words to step in. "Are you ready to be shampooed, Mrs. Rivers? We have to keep things moving or we'll get backed up."

Amy laughed. "Do you know who this woman is?"

The receptionist seemed baffled. Gabriella said in a weaker voice, "Marion?"

"It's Meredith Delinn," Amy said.

That night, Meredith went up to her room without any dinner. Connie protested. She had salmon steaks marinating and ready to grill, and corn on the cob from Bartlett's Farm. "You have to eat something. I'm going to make you a winner dinner."

The winner dinner was the problem. The dazzling house over-looking the ocean was the problem. The beautiful life Connie had allowed Meredith to share was the problem. Amy Rivers was cor-rect: How could she continue to live a life of privilege when so many people had lost everything? Kirby Delarest—the kind-hearted midwesterner whose three little blond girls always wore matching Bonpoint outfits to dinner at the Everglades Club—had shot himself. Meredith occasionally took solace in the fact that Freddy hadn't murdered or raped anyone. But now Kirby Delarest's blood was on his hands. Seen through Amy's eyes, Fred's crimes seemed more reprehensible—as though Meredith had opened a basement door and found thirteen thousand dead bodies stacked one on top of the other.

She couldn't eat a winner dinner.

"I can't eat," she said.

Connie said, "Come on, you've just had a bad day."

A bad day. A bad day was when Meredith got an A- on her French quiz and her mother made chicken à la king with tinned mushrooms for dinner. A bad day was when it was raining and Meredith had both boys in the apartment pulling each other's hair and ripping pages out of their picture books and refusing to go down for a nap. What had happened with Amy Rivers in the salon hadn't been a *bad day.* It had been a moment Meredith would never forget. Amy had forced Meredith's face to the mirror and shown her the truth: She was ugly. She could try to hide, but once people discovered who she really was, they would all agree. Mere-dith was a despicable human being, responsible for the downfall of thousands. Responsible for the trajectory of the nation's econ-omy into the Dumpster. Gabriella, on hearing the name *Meredith Delinn,* had blanched and said, "But you told me you not *know* Freddy Delinn! Now you say he your husband?"

"She lies," Amy said. "Lies, lies, lies."

The receptionist had backed away from Meredith slowly, as though there were a tarantula sitting on her shoulder.

Meredith whispered, "Cancel my hair appointment, please."

The receptionist nodded; her face showed obvious relief. She banged on the computer keyboard with hard, eager strokes, deleting Mary Ann Martin.

As Meredith moved to the door, Amy said, "You can enjoy your Nantucket summer vacation, Meredith, but you'll pay. The other investors are clamoring for your head. You and your son are going to end up just like Freddy, moldering in jail where you belong."

Meredith had sat in the scorching hot interior of Connie's car like a dog—a dog that would have expired if he'd been left in the car for the length of this appointment—but Meredith had made no move to put down the window or turn on the AC. She didn't care if her brain boiled. She didn't care if she died.

Moldering in jail where you belong. You and your son.

Amy was right: On some level, it *was* Meredith's fault. She was, at the very least, responsible for Amy's loss. She had begged Freddy to take Amy on as a client. *For me, please?* And Freddy had said, *For you, please? All right, yes.* But Meredith hadn't known. They could surgically remove her brain and scour its nooks and crannies, and only then would they realize she hadn't known a thing. Back at the very beginning, Meredith had offered to take a polygraph test, but Burt had told her that with certain kinds of people, polygraph tests didn't work. Meredith didn't understand.

"With pathological liars, for example," Burt had said. "They are so convinced their lies are the truth that nine out of ten times they beat the machine."

Was he calling Meredith a pathological liar? No, no, he insisted. But there had been no polygraph test to announce her innocence.

And there *were* certain things Meredith was guilty of: She was a coward; she had lived a life of submission. She had never asked

Freddy where the money was coming from. Or rather, at a certain stage, she had asked him, and he hadn't given her a straight answer or any answer at all, and she hadn't demanded one. She hadn't picked the lock to his home office under the cover of darkness and gone through his books with a fine-tooth comb the way she should have.

Eleanor Charnes, the mother of Alexander, Leo's friend from Saint Bernard's, had put a rumor out through the school that Freddy's business was crooked, and Meredith had subtly seen to it that Eleanor wasn't invited to the Frick benefit or to the Costume Institute Gala at the Met.

Phyllis Rossi had insisted her husband pull $25 million out of Delinn Enterprises because she'd chatted with Freddy at the Flagler Museum in Palm Beach, and she said she found his answers about his business "evasive." Meredith had blackballed Phyllis for membership to the Everglades Club.

And then, of course, there was what she'd done to Connie.

Meredith was guilty of those things. But Leo—Leo wasn't guilty. (Was he? Oh, God. Oh, God. *Hundreds of pieces of evidence.* From which "reliable sources" had Amy heard this? What did this mean?) When Amy had said Leo's name, Meredith wanted to bare her teeth and snarl. *Don't you tell lies about my son.* Amy Rivers was another scary pelican from the nightmares of Leo's childhood.

Meredith's vision started to splotch. She was going to pass out, but she didn't care.

Connie came rushing out of the salon. When she opened the door, clean, fresh air blew into the car.

"Jesus!" Connie said. "What *happened?*"

Meredith told her, sparing no detail.

Connie said, "This is the woman you told me about? The one from Palm Beach?"

"Yes. I knew she was on the island. I saw her at the bookstore, but I didn't think she recognized me."

"Those things she said about Leo?" Connie asked. "They're not true, are they?"

"They're not true," Meredith whispered. They couldn't be true. They couldn't be.

"I'd like to go back in there and rip her face off," Connie said.

Meredith stared out the window. They were on Milestone Road, on their way home to Tom Nevers. There were trees and more trees. People riding bicycles. Normal people.

"The wig didn't work," Meredith said. "She knew me instantly."

"Because you used to be friends," Connie said. "Let me ask you this: Do you think she's the one who took your picture? Vandalized the house? Slashed my tires?"

The thought had crossed Meredith's mind. Amy was certainly angry enough to do those things, but the spray painting especially seemed juvenile and beneath her. The first word that Meredith would use to describe Amy Rivers was: "busy." She was always rushing from one commitment to another. Her day was overscheduled. When she had lunch with Meredith, she always left ten minutes early and was already five minutes late for the next thing. Seeing Amy on a bicycle had thrown Meredith. In Palm Beach, she whipped her black Audi into the parking lot of the Everglades Club and screeched out. In Meredith's mind, Amy Rivers was too busy to plan and execute that kind of vandalism. Surely she had bigger things to worry about?

But maybe not.

She would never have misspelled the word "thief." Unless she was trying to throw the police off her trail.

Possible?

"I don't know," Meredith said.

Once Meredith retreated to her room, she dialed Dev at the law firm, while praying a Hail Mary. It was six o'clock on a Friday evening. What were the chances Dev would be at his desk? Meredith got the firm's recording, which meant the miserable receptionist had left for the weekend. She was probably already in her seat aboard the Hampton Jitney. Meredith entered Dev's extension. He answered.

"It's Meredith."

"Hey, Meredith—"

Meredith launched into what Amy Rivers had said. It wasn't true, was it? There weren't hundreds of pieces of evidence against Leo?

Dev was quiet. Meredith felt like she was free-falling.

"I'm not Leo's attorney," Dev said. "Honestly, I'm not sure what kind of evidence is amassed against him. There's something, Meredith. I mean, we knew that, right? Otherwise he wouldn't be under investigation. But right now, from the sounds of it, nothing they have is strong enough to stand up in court—otherwise, they would have charged him. And he hasn't been charged. Julie is hunting down this Misurelli woman, the secretary. She said she'd fly to Padua herself if she had to. Julie has a phenomenal legal mind. And she has the eye of the tiger. Leo is in good hands, Meredith. There's nothing you can do except tell yourself that Leo hasn't been charged and he's in good hands." Meredith heard Dev swallow. "Okay?"

"Okay," Meredith said. Dev promised he would talk to her after the weekend, but if she needed him in the meantime, she had his cell number.

Meredith said good-bye and hung up, then turned off her phone. Deep breath: Not charged with anything. In good hands. Phenomenal legal mind. Amy Rivers was lying. *Your family is going to be flushed away. Like turds.*

My God, Meredith thought.

Later, Connie grilled the salmon, and the smoke floated in the open balcony doors and made Meredith's stomach rumble. She should just go down; she was being childish. Without Meredith downstairs, Connie might drink too much. She might obsess about the reason Dan hadn't called, or she might fall deeper into self-pity about Wolf and Ashlyn.

Meredith should go down. But she couldn't.

A little while later, Meredith heard a rustling outside her room. A piece of paper shot under the door.

It said, "Your dinner, Madame."

Meredith opened the door and despite her prevailing sentiment that all she should be eating was stale bread smeared with rat guts, she took the beautiful plate—rosy salmon glazed with some kind of mustard dill sauce, grilled asparagus, and a pearly ear of Bartlett's Farm corn already buttered and salted—and sat on her bed and devoured everything.

Meredith flipped the note over and wrote, "It was delicious. Thank you." She wanted to add, *I love you,* but she and Connie hadn't completely cleared the air between them yet. Soon, maybe. Meredith left the note out in the hallway, then shut her door and lay on her bed. It was still light outside, and her book was right there, but she couldn't read. She hadn't shut herself away to block out Connie. She had shut herself away because she needed to think.

Hundreds of pieces of evidence. Eye of the tiger. In good hands. Hasn't been charged. Fly to Padua. Spend the rest of his life in prison.

Sick love story. That was another phrase that bothered Meredith.

If Meredith were very honest with herself, she would admit that, in some way, the beginning of her love affair with Freddy had been entangled with the end of her love affair with Toby. Meredith had spent her first semester at Princeton seeking out the "amazing opportunities" Toby had promised she would have when he broke up with her. She had wanted Toby to be right. She had wanted Princeton to be so scintillating that she forgot she ever knew a boy named Toby O'Brien. And the person she fixed her attentions on was Freddy. Then her father died, and Toby missed the funeral, and Meredith had allowed herself to be used by Dustin Leavitt. And when Meredith returned to school feeling as lonely as she ever had in her life, there was Freddy. Her answer. He was a pool, and she dove in.

Freddy became the president of Dial his senior year while Meredith moved into a suite with Gwen Marbury and born-again-Christian twins Hope and Faith Gleeburgen, who had been matched with Meredith and Gwen because there had been no other choices for either pair. The Gleeburgens seemed perfectly nice. Although what did Meredith know; she was never in the suite. She spent every night with Freddy.

Meredith didn't have friends other than Gwen Marbury, though Gwen, too, fell away. Gwen had dated Richard Cassel for a while in an attempt to remain close with Meredith and Freddy; she had entertained notions, perhaps, of *becoming* Meredith and Freddy, but Gwen and Richard weren't a good match and they broke up. Richard later told Freddy, "You can take the girl out of the trailer park, but you can't take the trailer park out of the girl," which was a hideous thing to say—but that was Richard Cassel for you: an unapologetic snob.

After Freddy graduated, he received a job offer from Prudential Securities in Manhattan. Meredith couldn't stand the thought of being without Freddy; she couldn't stand the thought of Freddy in Manhattan with all the professional women in their snug power suits, meeting for drinks at the South Street Seaport after work. He would turn his blue gaze on someone else; this new girl would light up, fall at his feet, do his bidding. It made Meredith physically ill to think about. She started vomiting after nearly every meal in the spring of her sophomore year. Freddy thought she was bulimic—but no, she insisted, she was just sick with worry about losing him. They went to Mental Health Services together and saw a counselor, like a married couple. The counselor thought some separation would be good for both of them, but for Meredith in particular.

"It seems like you're in danger of losing yourself," the counselor said. "Freddy has basically subsumed you."

"That's bullshit," Freddy said. "We don't need separation." If he had been thinking the same thing when he walked in there, hearing the words come out of the therapist's mouth propelled him in the opposite direction.

"Then why are you leaving?" Meredith asked.

Well, Freddy pointed out, he had loans to pay back, lots of loans, which was something that Meredith, coming from her privileged background, would know nothing about. The Prudential job paid good money; he couldn't just walk away from it.

"Fine," Meredith said. "Then I'll drop out of school and come to Manhattan with you."

"Now, do you see how self-destructive that is?" the therapist asked.

The solution arrived in the form of a well-paying internship, offered to Freddy by the head of the economics department, who was writing a new textbook and needed a research assistant. Freddy, in his years at Princeton, had been known as an econ whiz. He understood the way money worked, what drove the markets, what slowed them down. He had been watching the stock market, he said, since he was twelve years old. At Dial, he was voted "Most Likely to Become a Wall Street Legend."

Now, Meredith blinked. She was sitting on the edge of her bed, watching the sun sink into the ocean. *Most Likely to Become a Wall Street Legend.* Well, that prediction had come true, hadn't it?

The summer between Meredith's sophomore and junior year, Meredith convinced Freddy to go backpacking through Europe. They rode the Eurail; they slept in cheap hotels and pensiones. Meredith had planned their itinerary of cities—Madrid, Barcelona, Paris, Venice, Florence, Vienna, Salzburg, Munich, Amsterdam, London—as well as the itinerary within each city. She wanted to see the churches and the art museums and every place that had literary significance—Anne Frank's house in Amsterdam, Shakespeare and Company in Paris. Meredith explained to Freddy the importance of Giotto's frescoes and the difference between the Gothic and the Romanesque. Freddy took notes in a tiny reporter's pad. At first, Meredith thought he was making fun of her, but as they squeezed into a twin bed at night, he insisted his interest was sincere. She was the one who had read the Yeats and taken the art-history courses; she was the one who could speak French. He was just an uncultured kid from a house with pasteboard walls in upstate New York, trying to keep up with her.

Before they left, Freddy had told Meredith that he had no money for such a trip. He had put all of his graduation money—which consisted of a check for a hundred dollars from his mother, a thousand-dollar cash award from the economics department, and a thousand-dollar leadership award from the alumni of Dial— toward his student loans. Meredith had assured him that she had enough money for both of them. And, true to his word, Freddy ran out of money right away. He spent the bulk of what he'd brought at a nightclub in Barcelona. Neither Freddy nor Meredith had wanted to go to a nightclub, but they'd met some chic Catalan university students on the Rambles who had talked them into it. Once they were in the club and were charged an exorbitant sixteen dollars for two beers, Meredith suggested they leave, but Freddy decided he wanted to stay. The university students secured a table near the dance floor and ordered several bottles of Cava. Meredith and Freddy danced awkwardly to the house music, and then sat back down at the table, talking to the university students in English. Freddy reverted to his tutoring days, correcting everyone's tenses. Meredith grew drunk and combative—she wanted to leave—but Freddy kept putting her off. One of the students was a dark-haired girl who looked like Trina. This girl asked Freddy to dance. Freddy glanced at Meredith and quickly said no, but Meredith felt com- pelled to say, "Don't be stupid, Fred. Go dance with her." So Freddy and the girl danced, and Meredith excused herself for the ladies' room—where everyone was snorting cocaine or shooting it into their ankles—and threw up. She rested her face against the grimy tiles of the floor by the evil-smelling toilet and decided that this was the lowest point of her life, short of her hour in Dustin Leavitt's apartment. She hadn't thought such a base feeling was possible when she was with Freddy, but there it was, and furthermore, she was pretty sure she was going to lose Freddy to the Spanish girl. He would marry her and enjoy a life in the Catalan countryside helping the girl's father with his olive farm. Meredith was only roused from the floor by someone aggressively kicking the door to her stall and bellowing something in German. When Meredith got back to the table, Freddy was standing. They were leaving, he said. Meredith had never been so relieved.

When they got outside, however, Freddy told Meredith that he'd paid the bill and that the bill had been three hundred dollars, and that he was, at that point, effectively broke.

Meredith wasn't used to being angry with Freddy. Upset, frustrated, jealous, yes, but not angry. She didn't know how to express what she was feeling.

She said, "Why did you pay the bill? Did they *ask* you to?"

He shrugged. "No. I wanted to."

"But now you have no money."

He gave her a hangdog expression. "I know."

And she thought, *I can't believe you, Freddy. How irresponsible!*

And she thought, *He did it to impress the girl who looked like Trina.*

Then she thought, softening, because there was something about Freddy that always made her excuse him, *He did it because he's naturally generous and he wanted to make those strangers happy.*

She did not think at the time (though she certainly thought it now), *He wanted their admiration, he wanted control. He wanted to walk out of there a big man.*

When Meredith became a senior in college, Freddy left Princeton. He had taken one year off to stay with Meredith, but he couldn't take two. Prudential had come back to him with another job offer at a bigger salary. It seemed that saying no to them and working with a famous economist had boosted his value, and Freddy couldn't turn them down again. His loans beckoned.

Meredith wasn't happy, but she agreed that he should go. It was only one year. She could make it.

She scheduled all of her classes on Monday, Tuesday, and Wednesday, so that by Wednesday night, she could be on a train headed for the city. Freddy, as a perk in the package Prudential had offered him, was living in a condo on East 71st Street. The condo was well beyond his means; it was, essentially, a free sublet from another Prudential trader who was spending a year with a Swiss bank in Zurich.

Meredith gasped. That trader had *remained* in Zurich; he had become a higher-up with a Swiss bank. A Swiss bank, where, possibly, Freddy had hidden money. Which bank was it? She'd asked, but had Freddy ever told her? She needed to remember so she could tell Dev. And what had that trader's name been? *Thorlo* was the name that popped into Meredith's mind, but that wasn't quite right. *Ortho?* No. Meredith had spent a large chunk of her senior year living among this man's possessions. She remembered that he had a Danish mother who had filled his apartment with sleek, modern furniture. She remembered a tall Norfolk pine that it had become her responsibility to keep watered; she remembered a rocking chair made from smooth, blond wood. She remembered a folk statue of a little man with a funny Alpine hat, his hair fashioned from gray cotton. The statue's name had been Otto—was that the name Meredith was remembering? But what, then, had the trader's name been? She racked her brain. This might be the name that could save her. *Thorlo, Ortho.* She had *lived* in this man's apartment. She had chopped celery with his special, sharp knives and had stuck the celery in the Bloody Marys she made for herself and Freddy every Sunday morning. Back in those days, she and Freddy had gone out on the weekends. They went to bars, they danced. Freddy had once gotten so drunk that he climbed up on the bar, gyrating his hips to "I Love the Nightlife." That had been a fun year, Meredith's senior year of college, though college had nothing to do with it; it was her life in the city with Freddy that mattered. Half the time, they enjoyed doing adult things: every Sunday, Meredith would make Bloody Marys and they would get bagels and lox from H&H and they would read the *Times*. And the other half of the time, they were drunk at the Mill on 85th Street. Meredith threw "cocktail parties" for the guys from Dial who had graduated with Freddy and were now living in the city with their various girlfriends. Meredith served shrimp cocktail and Armenian string cheese and pigs in a blanket with spicy brown mustard, just like her own mother had.

She remembered entertaining Richard Cassel and his new girl-friend Astrid, who worked as an editorial assistant at *Harper's Bazaar.* Astrid had shown up wearing a Diane von Furstenberg wrap dress, one of the originals, and a pair of Oleg Cassini heels. A familiar insecurity returned to haunt Meredith, who was wear-ing a khaki skirt and a cable-knit cardigan sweater. Astrid, like Trina, was sophisticated in a way that Meredith feared she would never be. And to boot, the night Richard and Astrid came to the apartment was the night that Richard planned to propose. He had a ring from Tiffany's in his jacket pocket; he was going to present it to Astrid after their dinner at Lutèce. It was all so exactly what Meredith wanted for herself that she had been overcome by nau-seating jealousy. (The coda to that story was that Richard and Astrid did get married, did have five children, the second of whom was born with cerebral palsy, and Richard did step out of the mar-riage, having a long affair with an unhappy married socialite, whom he then married and divorced in short order.)

There was something incomparably romantic about an engage-ment, Meredith thought, which didn't translate to marriage.

She and Freddy had had a lot of crazy sex that year on the impeccable white sheets of the Danish bed. Meredith had slept on this trader's sheets, and still she couldn't remember his name.

Thorlo. No, that was the brand of thick socks that she and Freddy had worn while hiking in the Alps. She was getting confused.

*   *   *

The night purpled. Meredith heard water gurgling through the pipes; Connie was running the dishwasher. Meredith's dirty dishes sat on her dresser. She would take them down in the morning and wash them herself. She brushed her teeth and changed into her nightgown. She listened to the waves. She had done so much thinking that Amy Rivers now seemed very far away. Amy Rivers was decades in Meredith's future.

Meredith graduated from Princeton with honors, but not Phi Beta Kappa as she had hoped. She had studied on the train between Princeton and New York, and all day Thursday and Friday while Freddy was at work—but she was away from the precious resource of the Firestone Library, and there had been times when she had been quick or lazy with a paper because she wanted to be with Freddy, or she was hung over from too much fun in the city. Still, her mother beamed with pride, and she had the news of Meredith's graduation from Princeton published in the *Main Line Times* and the Aronimink newsletter. She took Meredith to dinner at the Nassau Inn and gave her a string of pearls and a check for $5,000. A week after graduation, Meredith found that she had been chosen for a teaching program which placed top university graduates into failing school systems and that there were openings in Appalachia, Brownsville, Texas, and New York City. Meredith would go to New York, no question. If there hadn't been a position in New York, she would have abandoned the idea of the teaching program altogether, even though teaching English was all she'd ever wanted to do.

But, thankfully, she didn't have to worry. She had her degree and a job in New York City. She would be with Freddy!

There was more rustling outside the door. Meredith heard Connie sigh at her note. Another note floated under the door. Again, Meredith waited until she heard Connie retreat. The note said, "Your dessert, madame. Sweet dreams!"

Meredith opened the door. A square of something creamy on a graham cracker crust. Cheesecake? She brought the dessert to bed with her, tucked herself under the summer blanket, and tasted a forkful. It was tart: key lime. Key lime put Meredith back in Palm Beach with Amy Rivers, but no, she wouldn't let herself travel that mental highway. Stay present, find the answer. What was the name of that trader?

Meredith wanted Freddy to propose. It was all she thought about. Why? She wondered now. Why, why, why? What about him had been so irresistible? So impossible to let go? His blue eyes? His cutting wit? His natural, easy confidence despite the fact that he came from absolutely nothing? His brilliance in economics? His early success in the financial world? His innate generosity? His burning desire to be the man who took care of things, who solved problems, who made people happy? Was it the way he held Meredith, touched her, talked to her? Yes, now she was getting closer. It was the way he believed her to be a delicate treasure, no less precious than the crown jewels that they had seen together at the Tower of London. Freddy was devoted to her. He wasn't going to leave her the way Toby had. He wasn't going to sail off into the sunset in search of his freedom. He didn't see the allure of a different woman every night. He was singular in his desire. He wanted Meredith. It was intoxicating.

And then, just as soon as Meredith became cozy and secure in Freddy's constancy, Prudential sent Freddy on a two-week trip to Hong Kong. He let it slip that there was talk of moving him permanently to Hong Kong. This gave Meredith emotional seizures. She had just moved into Freddy's sublet, very much against her mother's wishes. (Her mother didn't like how it "looked," the two of them living together.) Meredith would begin her teaching job in September. What would she do if Freddy moved to Hong Kong?

She would move to Hong Kong as well.

She had wanted to go with him on the trip — she could use her graduation money—but Freddy said no, this was work. This was something he had to do himself. Girlfriends weren't welcome.

"How do you know?" Meredith said. "Did you ask?"

"I just know."

Meredith spent two weeks in the hot, dirty, miserable city while Freddy was in Hong Kong. Connie called and invited Meredith to Nantucket. Connie had just begun dating a man named Wolf Flute, whose family had a cottage on the beach. The place was simple but it had four bedrooms. Meredith could stay for a week, or longer.

Meredith had said no.

She stayed in the apartment, she ordered in Chinese food, she read books in the blond wood rocking chair (*Sophie's Choice; Goodbye, Columbus*); she pined for Freddy. Freddy called three times, but the connection was bad. Meredith heard the words "Victoria Peak," "Hollywood Road," "the Peninsula Hotel." She heard the excitement in his voice. One of the partners had taken Freddy on a junk to another island where they had gone to a seafood restaurant. They picked a fish out of the tank, and twenty minutes later it was sautéed, sauced, and garnished in front of them. Freddy had never been anywhere like Hong Kong. Before meeting Meredith, he had never been anywhere at all.

Meredith hated Freddy, she decided. He was going to leave her behind just the way Toby had, but she wasn't going to let that happen. She was going to preempt him. The next time the phone rang and Meredith suspected it was him, she didn't answer. The phone stopped ringing, then started up again. Meredith smiled vengefully but didn't pick up. She left the apartment for the first time in days. She would go for a walk in the park, then take herself to the Belgian place for *moules et frites*. When she walked out of the apartment, the phone was still ringing.

She calmed down, then revved up again. She screamed at the folk statue named Otto. She lunged at Otto with one of the sharp Danish knives. She wrote "Fuck you" in soap on the bathroom mirror; Freddy would find it when he returned, but Meredith wouldn't be around to witness his reaction. She was going to Nantucket to visit Connie after all. Connie had told her about a party called the Madequecham Jam—hundreds of people partying on the beach! All Meredith needed to bring was a bikini.

Meredith packed a bag. She was taking the Chinatown bus to Boston, and a second bus from Boston to Hyannis, and a two-hour ferry from Hyannis to Nantucket. It was a longer journey than Meredith had anticipated; the mere thought of it exhausted her, but at least she wouldn't be sitting around the apartment, *waiting,* when Freddy got home.

She had been at the door, she remembered, ready to leave for the bus station, when there was a knock. She peered through the peephole. It was Western Union, with a telegram.

"Meredith Martin?" the man said.

She accepted the telegram, her hands shaking. She had never received a telegram before. The only people she had known to receive telegrams were mothers whose sons had died in Vietnam. So this said what? That Freddy had died? He'd been hit by a bus while crossing the street in opposite-side traffic? Or maybe it was a telegram *from* Freddy, saying he wasn't coming back. They were placing him permanently in Hong Kong, and he wanted Meredith to send his things. Maybe he'd meant to tell her this over the phone, but she hadn't answered.

Whatever the telegram said, it wasn't good.

She thought about leaving the telegram behind in the apartment. But what kind of person had the willpower to leave an envelope like this—a telegram just screamed urgency—unopened?

She opened it by the front door. It said:

MEREDITH STOP I CAN'T LIVE WITHOUT YOU STOP
WILL YOU MARRY ME? STOP
FREDDY

She read it again, then a third time, her heart lifting like a balloon. She jumped up and down and whooped. She was laughing
and crying and thinking, *Goddamn it, someone should be here,* but
no, this was better somehow. He'd surprised her, really shocked
her, snatched her from despair, saved her from going to Nantucket, and, most likely, doing something regrettable.

This was the right thing. This was absolutely the only thing.
There was no decision. The answer was yes.

There had only been one bump in the road before Meredith and
Freddy got married, and that arrived in the form of Connie's own
shotgun wedding, which was thrown together in December once
Connie learned she was pregnant.

Meredith had been the maid of honor. She wore a red velvet
cocktail dress, red stiletto heels, and Annabeth Martin's diamond
engagement ring. She and Freddy were living together in the sublet apartment; Meredith was in the throes of her first year of teaching at Gompers. Meredith knew she would see Toby at the
wedding, but she was ready for him.

But then Freddy couldn't go. Work needed him. He was low
man on the totem pole at Prudential; he had no choice.

And so, Meredith faced Toby alone. Toby was tan from having
sailed somewhere impossibly glamorous—Ibiza or Monaco—
and he'd brought, as a date, a girl from his crew. The girl's name
was Pamela; she was taller than Meredith, and beefier, and she
had red, calloused hands. Meredith found her pushy; she offered
to help Connie with her train and her bouquet when they had just
met the day before.

Connie had said, *Oh, don't you worry about it. I have Meredith
here to help me.*

Meredith had thought, All right, Pamela was cute enough,
friendly enough, but not the person she'd expected Toby to
choose. Toby was effusive with his attention toward his sister and

his mother and Pamela; for the ceremony and the first part of the reception, he ignored Meredith completely. She, meanwhile, couldn't keep her eyes off him. He exuded his usual healthy, outdoorsy energy; the tuxedo seemed to be reining him in. The green satin bow tie he'd chosen made his eyes seem greener. Inwardly, Meredith cursed him. Goddamn him for being so luminous all the time. He spun Pamela around the dance floor. He gave a very sweet and funny toast to Wolf and Connie, and Meredith had to admit that freedom did suit him.

The band played "The Best of Times" by Styx, which was Meredith and Toby's number one song as a couple, and Meredith realized she had a choice: she could go to the bar for another fuzzy navel, or she could hide in the ladies' room and cry.

Toby intercepted her on the way to the ladies' room.

"Dance with me," he said.

"You haven't talked to me once all night," Meredith said.

"I know," he said. "I'm sorry. Dance with me."

Meredith thought back to the night of their breakup. She nearly said, *I thought you didn't like to dance.* But instead she let Toby lead her to the dance floor. She fit right into his arms in a way that felt unholy. *Freddy,* she thought. *I am engaged to Freddy.*

Toby hummed in her ear. They used to listen to this song in Toby's Nova when they made love. A long time ago. But not so long: five years. Meredith said, "It's weird that they're playing this song."

Toby said, "I made a request."

Meredith pulled away. Toby had requested their song to the band?

"What about Pamela?" she said.

"She's just a friend. And she doesn't seem to mind."

Meredith craned her neck. Pamela was at the bar, draped all over Wolf's brother.

"I don't get it," Meredith said. "You know I'm engaged? You know I'm getting married in June?"

"I know. I heard," Toby said. "But I just thought..."

"Thought what?" Meredith said.

"I needed a way to break the ice," he said.

"Break the *ice?*" Meredith said. "When I hear this song, Toby, I *hurt.*"

"I know," Toby said. "I hurt, too."

"Why would *you* hurt?" she asked. "*You* broke up with *me.*"

"Meet me later," Toby said. "Please, Meredith? Meet me at the Wayne Hotel."

She glared at him. "You have *got* to be kidding me."

"At the bar," he said. "So we can talk?"

"About what?" she said. But he didn't respond. He tightened his grip on her. He was humming again. *The best of times are when I'm alone with you.*

Meredith had half a mind to storm off the dance floor, but she couldn't make a scene at Connie's wedding; Connie's wedding was shrouded in enough scandal as it was. So she finished out the dance with Toby. The horrible truth was, she still had feelings for him; the horrible truth was, he did have the first and best piece of her heart; the horrible truth was, it felt electrifying to be in his arms. But would Meredith meet him at the Wayne Hotel? She hesitated. One second, two seconds, ten seconds. Then she thought, *No way. I won't do it.* The next song, she returned to her seat, and Wolf's brother, Jake, asked her to dance. Meredith watched Toby and Pamela throw back shots of tequila at the bar.

Meredith thought, *I have to get back to New York. I have to get back to Freddy.*

Freddy and Meredith got married the following June at Saint Thomas of Villanova, the same church where Chick Martin's funeral Mass had been held. There were a hundred and fifty people in attendance, and if Meredith had one complaint, it was that the church looked empty compared to the crowd that had packed in to pay their respects to her father.

Connie served as Meredith's matron of honor, even though

Ashlyn had been born in April and Connie was still nursing her. Richard Cassel had served as Freddy's best man. Bill and Veronica O'Brien were there, though Toby had declined. It had taken courage for Meredith to invite him, but after what had happened at Connie's wedding, she decided it would be a good idea for Toby to watch her getting married to somebody else. Surely, she wasn't the only bride to feel this way? Toby sent a note that said, "Sailing in the Lesser Antilles! Wishing you the very best!" Meredith was disappointed, but she realized he probably wouldn't have come if he'd been down the street.

Annabeth Martin came in a wheelchair and was tended to most of the night by Meredith's mother, both of them glowing with happiness. This was as it should be; Meredith married right out of college—just as they both had—to a man who was going places.

Freddy's mother came to the ceremony but didn't stay for the reception. She claimed she had to get back to Utica that night so she could get to work in the morning.

"Work?" Meredith said. "On Sunday?"

"At the store," Freddy said. He meant Kmart.

Meredith had only met Mrs. Delinn for the first time earlier that day. She was soft bodied, and her skin was the blue-white of an undercooked egg. Her hair was thinning and had been badly dyed the color of Bing cherries. She had watery blue eyes—lacking the intense cobalt pigment of Freddy's eyes. Generally Meredith thought Mrs. Delinn seemed worn out and run down, as though the effort of making it to this moment in her life had nearly killed her. She was oddly deferential to Meredith and kept saying how much she appreciated being invited.

"Of course," Meredith said. "You're Freddy's mother."

"You'll take care of him," Mrs. Delinn said. It was a statement, not a question. "You'll love him. He'll pretend like he can get along without it, but he can't. Freddy needs his love."

Meredith walked down the aisle by herself. She felt the absence of her father; her whole left side was numb. Everyone in the church was beaming at her. She was glad they were there, but the only person who mattered was the man at the altar, his eyes flashing, his face radiating promise. When she was ten steps or so from the altar, he came for her; he took her by the arm and walked her the rest of the way. The crowd in the church gasped at first, and then ahhhed.

Freddy leaned in and whispered, "You looked lonely."

She said, "Yes, but not anymore."

He said, "Never again."

Meredith set down her dessert plate. The ache in her heart could not be described.

She was tired, and in many ways, she was defeated, but she was still herself, Meredith Martin, so she slid out of bed and went into the bathroom to brush her teeth a second time.

She fell asleep remembering the dancing at her wedding. She and Freddy had taken lessons in the city, and they had been synchronized in the way they moved together. It had been a great party—at one point, every single guest had been out on the dance floor. Even Annabeth Martin in her wheelchair; even Wolf holding tiny baby Ashlyn. At one point, Meredith had been in a circle of Freddy's friends—the old guys from Dial, the new guys from Prudential—and now, as Meredith pictured it in her mind, there was someone she didn't recognize in the circle, a tall, lean man with the white-blond hair of a Scandinavian. Meredith turned to Gwen Marbury, while at the same time thinking, *Gwen Marbury wasn't at my wedding,* and asked, "Who is that guy?"

"That guy?" Gwen said. "That's Thad Orlo."

Meredith startled awake. Her eyes snapped open. *Thad Orlo!*

Meredith woke up at daybreak and wondered what time she could reasonably expect Dev to answer his cell phone. Eight o'clock? Seven o'clock? She didn't want to be the lunatic client who called him at dawn. But she wanted to tell him about Thad Orlo. It was something real; it was the name of a Swiss banker. She took a measured breath. She couldn't tell if she was anxious because she was sure this information would help, or if she was worried it wouldn't help. She had to find the answer. *The other investors are clamoring for your head. Your family is going to be flushed away.* She needed to find the key that would set her and Leo free.

She turned on her cell phone and waited with the predictable anxiety to see if anyone had called overnight. Amy Rivers had her number. It was conceivable that she had left an abusive voice mail, elaborating on the hateful things she'd said the day before. But the phone booted up silently, giving Meredith nothing but the time. It was 6:09. Unable to wait another minute, she dialed Dev, and he picked up on the first ring.

"Allo?" he said. He sounded funny, but of course he sounded funny, it was still basically the middle of the night.

"Dev, it's Meredith."

"Hello, Meredith." He sounded out of breath.

"Did I wake you?" Meredith asked.

"No," he said. "I'm running. Riverside Park."

Riverside Park was in the same city where Meredith had spent most of her adult life, but she hadn't been there in twenty years or more, since one of the boys had a little friend from school who lived on the Upper West Side, and the other mother (whose name was lost to Meredith) and Meredith would take the boys to the playground there. Meredith liked thinking of Dev running on those paths by the Hudson. She liked thinking of him unchained from his desk.

"I'm sorry to bug you," Meredith said.

"Is everything okay?" Dev asked.

"I'm calling because I thought of something that might help," Meredith said.

"Oh, yeah?" Dev said.

"A million years ago," she said, "and I'm talking nineteen eighty-two, nineteen eighty-three..."

Dev laughed. Meredith counted back to make sure that Dev would have been *alive* in those years.

"It was my senior year at Princeton, and Freddy was living in New York City working for Prudential Securities."

"Which division?" Dev asked.

"Oh, God, I have no idea," Meredith said. Even as much as she had loved Freddy back then, she hadn't bothered to find out exactly what he did for work. She didn't care; she had never cared, just as Freddy had never cared about the distaff family lines in Faulkner. "Trading? Derivatives? Don't you guys have that kind of information at your fingertips?"

"I don't," Dev said. "The SEC might, though."

"We lived in a sublet of a man named Thad Orlo." She paused. She could hear the thwack of Dev's sneakers on the pavement, a siren, taxi horns, a barking dog. "Has that name come up in the investigation?"

"I'm not supposed to say," Dev said. "But no, I don't think so."

"Thad Orlo was working for Prudential, but he was spending a year in Switzerland, at some Swiss bank, perhaps a bank affiliated with Prudential? Anyway, I never actually *met* him because while we were in New York, he was in Switzerland—that was the whole idea—but I asked Freddy about him from time to time in subsequent years. Freddy told me that Thad Orlo had stayed on with the bank in Switzerland, but when I asked which bank it was, Freddy said he couldn't remember. Now, what this really meant was that he didn't *want* to tell me because if there was one thing about Freddy, he remembered *everything*. And then there was another time—" this, Meredith remembered just as she was saying the words—"when I asked Freddy what had ever happened to Thad Orlo. I was asking because we had, you know, *lived* in his apartment with all of his furniture and all of his stuff—every

time I saw a certain kind of Danish design, I thought of him—
and at first Freddy pretended not to know who he was at all, which
was absurd, and then once he copped to the fact that he did
remember him, he started asking *me* in this paranoid way about
why I wanted to know about Thad Orlo. And I can remember saying, 'Freddy, I'm sorry. I was just wondering!' "

Dev was breathing hard. Maybe he was crushed at how underwhelming this tip was. Maybe he was wondering why she hadn't
just waited until he was in the office. But the more Meredith
thought about it, the more convinced she became.

"Yes," she said. "He was defensive and angry when I asked him
about Thad Orlo. You should check it out. You should find Thad
Orlo."

"But you don't know which bank?"

"I don't. Freddy most certainly does, even though he lied and
told me he didn't."

"But Freddy's not speaking. At all."

"Still?" Meredith said. She didn't want any news about Freddy.
But she did.

"Still."

"Well, can't you find him anyway?" Meredith said. She had figured the SEC had huge databases crammed with names, and connections between those names. It was impossible, in this day and
age, to stay anonymous, right? "Can't you google him?"

"I'll do that first thing on Monday," Dev said. "Do you know
anything else about this guy?"

"His mother was Danish," Meredith said, but then she wondered if she knew this for sure, or if she had just assumed it,
because of the furniture. "I think."

"Where was the apartment?" Dev asked.

"Seventy-first Street," Meredith said. But she couldn't remember if the building had been between Lexington and Third, or
Third and Second, and she certainly didn't remember the number
of the building. She had lived there for nearly two years, but the

address eluded her. She was old enough now that this sometimes happened. The salient details of her past evaporated.

"Okay," Dev said. "I'll check out everything you just told me."

"And you'll tell the Feds?"

"I'll tell the Feds."

"You'll tell them I'm helping? You'll tell Julie Schwarz and Leo I'm helping?"

"Yes, Meredith," Dev said. She couldn't discern if his breathlessness was due to his fast pace or the beauty of the Hudson in the morning light or exasperation. "I'll tell everyone you're helping."

CONNIE

Connie had been certain Dan would call. She knew she had *not* put on a good show that night at dinner; she had been drunk, and Connie had had enough experience with her own mother to know what that looked like. But she hadn't heard from Dan in nearly three weeks. Their relationship had been progressing, and then, boom, it just ended. Connie wasn't good at handling rejection. It was, as her sister-in-law Iris would say, messing with Connie's general state of mind.

She hadn't heard from Ashlyn, either, even though Connie had tried texting. *Please call. It's Mom.*

She had also resumed her habit of leaving messages on Sundays. It was pointless, Connie knew, as pointless as prayer: she was talking to someone who may or may not be listening.

The only person Connie heard from was Toby. He sent a text that said: *I'll be there the 5th or 6th, OK?*

Connie hadn't been quite sure what that text was referring to, until she scrolled back and saw the text saying that Toby had sold the boat to the man from Nantucket, and he would be on island in three weeks, OK? And she had responded, *OK! LOL.*

Connie groaned. Nothing about this was laugh out loud. She had to tell Toby that Meredith was here. She had to tell Meredith that Toby was coming. Which one of them would be more upset? Connie decided to keep quiet about it for now. She was afraid if she told Toby that Meredith was here, he wouldn't show up. And Connie desperately wanted to see him. She was afraid that if she told Meredith that Toby was coming, Meredith would pack her things and leave. Or perhaps worse, she would get her hopes up, and then at the last minute, Toby would call to say that he wasn't selling the boat after all but was, instead, sailing down to Venezuela to meet some girl named Evelina for a cup of coffee.

Connie looked at the text again. The fifth or sixth? Well, they had nothing going on. They never had anything going on. She responded, *OK.* But left off the *LOL.*

Connie decided to ambush Dan at Stop & Shop. He had told her in passing that when the island got crazy-busy in August, he went to the grocery store midweek at six o'clock in the morning.

Connie hadn't expected to bump into him on her first attempt. "Midweek" could mean Tuesday or Wednesday or Thursday. And "six o'clock" could mean six thirty or seven. But when Connie pulled into the parking lot at ten minutes past six on Wednesday morning, the strawberry Jeep was there. Connie felt a jolt of nervous excitement and an irrational sense of collusion: the mere fact that Dan was here when he said he would be seemed like a good sign. Connie began muttering to herself. *Calm down. Hurry up! You have to catch him before he leaves. This is so obvious, but only to you. He'll think it's a random coincidence; everyone has to go to the store. He gave you the tip for the best time to go, why wouldn't you take him up on it?* She grabbed a cart, she had a list; this was a legitimate trip to the store. Connie had invited Meredith along the night before saying, *Hey, I'm going to the store bright and early if you want to come.* But Meredith had said no; she had said no to every outing since that woman had accosted her at RJ Miller. Connie said, *Meredith you just can't spend the rest of the summer in the house. It's August now, the best month.* And Meredith said, *No, it's not safe.* Connie said, *But it is safe. The vandalism has stopped. You let that woman have her say; that was all she wanted was to have her say. She's not going to do anything else to you. She's not going to stone you.*

But Meredith wouldn't be moved. She was stubborn like that. Connie had not forgotten.

The store was chilly, the produce section like an icebox. Connie was on a mission here. She had to find Dan first, then worry about her groceries. But if she bumped into him in the middle of the store with an empty cart, it would announce the obvious.

Connie tossed a netted bag of limes into her cart.

Connie zipped through the store, checking down each aisle. There was a blond woman with two little boys in their pajamas, a man in a suit and tie—a Jehovah's Witness, perhaps? someone headed to a funeral?—and then she found Dan, looking positively edible in khaki shorts and a T-shirt and flip-flops, standing in front of the healthy cereal. He didn't see her. Connie could back up, retreat to produce, chicken out. But this was her chance. She had gotten up at daybreak to shower and do her hair. She was bright-eyed, she smelled good, she was wearing a pretty pink cotton halter dress.

She pushed her cart forward. "Dan?" she said.

He turned. The expression on his face was...complicated. It was many expressions at once. He looked surprised, happy, wary, perplexed, caught.

He said, "Connie, hey!"

"Hey," she said, trying to sound upbeat, despite his obvious lack of enthusiasm. "Well, I took you up on your tip about the grocery store at this hour, and you were right! The store is empty. It's clean, and everything has been restocked."

"See?" he said. "I told you." He plucked a box of Kashi off the shelf and put it in his cart. Connie looked at his other groceries — taco kit, ground beef, tomatoes, Triscuits, Starbucks coffee, avocados, six boxes of pasta, celery, plums, two large bottles of V8 Splash. She wondered if she had caught him stocking up for a party to which she hadn't been invited, until she remembered that he had teenagers at home.

"So," she said, "what have you been up to?"

Now it was his turn to cast his eyes into her cart, where he saw the lone bag of limes.

Connie wished she had picked something else as her token item.

And sure enough, when he looked at her again, his face said it all — limes for gin. She had been so drunk; she had started drinking on the boat in a way that had quickly become antisocial, and she had continued to drink until she fell face-first into her dinner. And what did she put in her cart to underscore the fact that she was a drunk? A bag of limes. Connie thought she would die of mortification right then and there.

"Oh, you know," he said. "The usual."

The usual: It was such a nonanswer. It was a blow-off. Connie should retreat. She had to accept that this relationship, friendship, whatever it was, was dead in the water. But she didn't want to.

"Have you been out on your boat?" she asked.

"Every Thursday and Sunday," he said. "Have to keep after the lobster traps."

The lobster traps, containing the lobster Connie hadn't eaten, hadn't even tasted.

"Mmm," she said. "What about the Galley? Have you been back to the Galley?"

He didn't answer that question, which meant what? He hadn't been to the Galley, or he'd been to the Galley with another woman?

He said, "How are you doing? How's Meredith?"

Connie wasn't surprised to hear him ask about Meredith. He

loved Meredith. She knew it! But that was her fault. She had dragged Meredith along on both of their dates, and on the second date, Meredith and Dan had bonded over what to do about drunk Connie.

"We're fine," Connie said. "Meredith is good." Lies, all of it lies. They were drowning. They needed someone to save them. "We were wondering why you haven't called." That was good, Connie thought, using the pronoun "we," implicating Meredith as well. Poor Meredith, who refused to leave the house. Connie had even suggested going to Mass so she could light a candle for Leo, but Meredith said no.

Dan smiled. "Why haven't I called?" he said. "Well, you ladies seem to have your hands full."

"We do have our hands full," Connie said. "They're full of despair and grief and loneliness. That's why we miss you. You were fun. I haven't seen Meredith smile like that since…"

"Well, good," he said.

"And I like you, too," Connie said. It felt like a bold admission, but this was a positive—the barrier of small talk had been knocked down. She was going to say what was on her mind. "I thought you'd call; I thought we'd go out again."

"Is that what you want?" Dan said.

"Yes," Connie said.

Dan nodded thoughtfully. "I think you're a beautiful woman, Connie. And I know you've just lost your husband, and I understand the kind of grief you're experiencing…"

"It's my daughter, too," Connie said. "My daughter doesn't speak to me. We had a falling out after Wolf died." Connie couldn't believe she was blurting out True Confessions here in aisle ten of the supermarket. "I think if my daughter hadn't abandoned me, I'd be doing a lot better…"

"I understand that, too," Dan said.

"Do you?"

"My son Joe took off cross-country a few weeks after Nicole

died—he stole my truck—and I've only heard from him once, by e-mail, and he was asking for money. And I sent it to him, despite how infuriated the request and his exodus in general made me. Because he's my son."

Connie nodded.

Dan said, "I told you about Joe at dinner at the Cauldron."

You did? Connie thought.

Dan said, "You don't remember, do you? Because you were drinking, maybe. Well, we were all drinking that night. But your drinking, if I may be so bold, seems to be in defense of something. You're afraid of me, or of intimacy, or the idea of intimacy. You're afraid to start dating someone, you're afraid of talking to someone, and that's why you brought Meredith along both times I asked you out. I get it, Connie: you're not ready. But I'm not ready for someone who's not ready. Does that make sense?"

The store Muzak was playing "Beautiful Day." Before she could talk herself out of it, she said, "Do you want to go somewhere? For coffee, maybe, or a walk on the beach?"

Dan pulled his cell phone out of his back pocket and checked the time. He said, "I have to be in town at eight."

Connie waited.

He said, "Okay, let me finish my shopping. I have time for a walk on the beach. A short walk."

They went to Monomoy, where the sand was thick and marshy and the air smelled of fish and seaweed and things decomposing, though with the sun coming up and the vista before them of the harbor filled with boats, Connie couldn't imagine anyplace more alluring. So she had the setting, and she had the man, temporarily, but she wasn't sure what to do. She was appalled at herself for suggesting this outing. (She wouldn't candy coat it: she had forced him.) Her whole life she had been pursued by boys, then guys, then men. She had been the adored wife of Wolf Flute for more than half her lifetime, but now Wolf was gone, so who was she? It was as though he had taken Connie with him. She was nobody's wife.

She was dangerously close to being nobody's mother.

Connie's feet made a sucking sound as she walked in the wet, dense sand at the shore line. The way Dan had said "a short walk" made her self-conscious. Already Connie thought about turning around so as not to hold this man up any longer. But she was intrigued by what he'd said about his son Joe stealing his truck, taking off for California, e-mailing to ask for money.

"Tell me about Joe," she said. She felt embarrassed that Dan had, apparently, already *told* her about Joe and she had no recollection.

"Oh, man," he said. "We're getting heavy, deep, and real right away?"

"I'm sorry," Connie said. "But I hear the clock ticking. And I really want to know."

"Joe," Dan said. "Joe, Joe, Joe." He was staring out at the water, and this gave Connie a chance to study him. He was so handsome that it made her a little queasy. She liked his short, clipped hair, the brown and the gray; she liked his blue-hazel eyes, the scruff on his face, his Adam's apple, the supple, tense form of his runner's body. Dan took care of his body, Connie could tell. He was going to make it last, and at their age, there was something very appealing about that.

"Just saying the kid's name makes me anxious," Dan admitted.

Connie knew this feeling. God, did she! Every time Connie thought or said the name "Ashlyn," her blood pressure rose. Every time someone else said the name "Ashlyn" — especially someone like Iris — Connie felt like she had a gun trained on her. She was excited to have this phenomenon described by someone else.

"Joe was named for Nicole's dad," Dan said. "So, from the beginning, it was like he belonged to her. Only her." Dan stopped, picked up a round, flat rock, and skipped it a dozen times across the shallows. He grinned at Connie. "I am an excellent skipper of stones."

"Indeed, you are," Connie said. It seemed like he was trying to impress her, which was a good sign.

"If you believe in things like that," Dan said. "That a child can be more aligned with one parent than the other just because of how they're named. I'm not sure I believe it, but I don't know; all three boys were inordinately fond of their mother. On some level, I understood it. She was their *mother,* and she was very nurturing. She was a nutritionist by trade. She worked with the common-wealth on state-mandated school lunches, and locally she worked with the private schools and the Boys & Girls Club and the Boost-ers. She made sure there was fresh fruit for sale at high-school football games. It sounded ridiculous, but somehow she made it work. It would be a clear autumn afternoon, and next to the snack bar that, by tradition, sold hot dogs and Doritos, there would be a wooden basket of red, crisp apples. Somehow she got the funding for a juice press, and one of the old-timers from the retirement community would be there turning the apples into juice." Dan shook his head. "The kids loved it; the parents loved it. Nicole was written up in the paper. A local hero."

Connie smiled. "So your kids loved her even though she made them eat spinach?"

"They ate spinach for her, they ate kale, they ate *okra,* for God's sake. I used to try to sneak them licorice and Milky Ways, but they would never eat candy. 'Mom would freak out,' they said. I offered them Fritos and Happy Meals. My middle son, Donovan, said to me once, 'Filled with trans fats!' Nicole had them brainwashed; they were her . . . disciples, and not just about food. About everything. No matter what I did, I couldn't compare. I had a flexible work sched-ule so I made it to every single one of their ball games, but the only question they asked when they scored the game-winning basket was, 'Did Mom see it?' It used to drive me bonkers, and when I complained to Nicole about it, she accused me of turning our par-enting into a competition, which wasn't healthy for anyone."

"So then she got sick . . ." Connie said.

"Then she got sick," Dan said. "And it was a complete crisis. We didn't tell the kids any more than they needed to know, but they clung to Nicole even tighter. And during the first battle when it looked like we might lose her"—here, Dan stopped talking and drew a few breaths—"I thought that maybe the boys had intuited that illness would claim Nicole, and they were jamming all their love in while they still had a mother to love."

Oh, God. Sad. Tears stung Connie's eyes.

"I mean, Charlie was only four when Nicole got diagnosed, so basically from his earliest memory, he'd been in danger of losing her."

"Right," Connie said.

"This is a long way of saying that all three boys were closely aligned with Nicole—but especially Joe. All three kids had the predictable struggles with Nicole's illness. But the problem with Joe happened when Nicole got diagnosed the second time, with cancer of the liver. The prognosis was bleak. It was, well, it was fucking terminal was what it was, and Nicole knew that, and Joe and Donovan and probably even Charlie knew that. Nicole had always been into holistic medicine and alternative treatments. But the pain with liver cancer took her by surprise. She got a doctor's prescription for..."

"Marijuana," Connie said.

"Marijuana," Dan echoed. "And I'm not going to lie to you. I was surprised Nicole would even consider it. She was such a health nut. She did yoga. Even after the liver diagnosis, I'd find her in downward dog, and she drank these revolting shakes with wheatgrass and God knows what else. But for the pain, she smoked weed. Pure, medical-grade ganja. So her last months with us, she was always high." He cleared his throat. "That might have bothered me in and of itself. But what really got me was that Joe started smoking it with her."

"He did?" Connie said.

"She allowed it," Dan said. "She encouraged it."

"Encouraged it?"

"She was lonely. She wanted to be less lonely, and having Joe with her in her sick room smoking with her made her feel less lonely. Never mind that the kid was only seventeen, a senior in high school. Never mind that smoking dope for him was illegal. They were communing on a 'higher' level—that was her joke. She made it sound okay, she made it sound beautiful. But for me it was *not* okay, and it was certainly *not* beautiful."

"No," Connie said. "I imagine not."

"It led to some pretty destructive conversations at the end of Nicole's life. She was so worried about the boys. They were her sole focus. What about me, I asked her, your husband of twenty years? She said, 'You'll remarry. You'll find another wife. But the boys will never have another mother.'" Dan looked at Connie. "I can't tell you how that hurt me. I was being dismissed. The boys were her flesh and blood; I wasn't. I was cast as some kind of outsider, and then it occurred to me that I'd always been an outsider." Dan picked up another stone and sent it skipping; it hopped like a bean in a hot pan. "The dying can be so fucking righteous. At some point, Nicole passed into this place where she felt she could say whatever she wanted, no matter who got hurt, because she was going to..."

"Die," Connie said.

"Die," Dan said.

Nicole died, Dan said. (Connie was interested by his tone of voice. He said it like he still couldn't believe it, which was how Connie felt about Wolf.) Donovan and Charlie handled it okay. Joe did not handle it okay. He continued to smoke dope in the house, in front of his brothers, and Charlie was only twelve. Joe had "inherited" a huge stash from Nicole, Dan said. Dan hunted all over the house for it but couldn't turn it up. There were fights. Dan was angry about the marijuana; Joe was angry at Dan for picking fights with Nicole about the marijuana.

"She was dying and you were yelling at her," Joe said.

"What she did was irresponsible," Dan said. "Letting you smoke."

"The marijuana was for the pain," Joe said.

"Her pain," Dan said. "Not your pain."

Joe continued to smoke—though, in a small concession, not in front of his brothers. He had been accepted to Boston College, but after Nicole died, he decided to defer a year. He talked about going to California and working on a campaign to legalize marijuana. Dan told him that no way in hell was Flynn family money going to be spent subsidizing a drug odyssey in California. If Joe wanted to go, that was his choice, but he had to pay his own way.

Joe's answer to this was to steal Dan's pickup truck while Dan was out on his boat. He put it on the ferry and was halfway across the state of New York before Dan figured out what had happened. He could have had Joe tracked down and arrested, but Dan knew Joe was in possession of marijuana, and despite his anger and his hurt, he didn't want to see his kid go to jail.

"And so that was it," Dan said. "He's gone, he's in California, he contacted me the one time for money. He sent a goddamned e-mail. I said to myself, If he has the stones to call and ask me for money, that's one thing, but I will not answer a goddamned e-mail. But then, of course, I did."

"Does he talk to his brothers?" Connie asked.

"He might, but they don't tell me. In our house, his is the name that shall not be spoken."

"But you'd welcome him back?" Connie asked.

"In a heartbeat," Dan said.

They had turned around at the part about Nicole being prescribed marijuana, and now they were headed back. Connie was afraid to ask what time it was. She didn't want this walk to end.

"Do you feel better, telling me?" Connie asked.

"You know?" he said. "I do. You may be the only person I've told the story to that way—start to finish like that. That's the problem with growing up in a place like Nantucket and still living here. Everyone feels like they already know what happened because they were right there watching it. Most people think Joe is a pot-head who stole my truck and lit out to California to live a life even more liberally oriented than his mother's had been. But those people bother me because it wasn't *entirely* Joe's fault. I'm to blame as well, and Nicole is to blame, although *no one* wants to blame Nicole because she's dead. I haven't had a chance to step far enough away from what happened to see it clearly." He laughed sadly. "That's the problem with an island."

"I guess," Connie said.

"So tell me about your daughter," Dan said.

"Isn't one tale of woe enough for one day?" Connie said. "No, I would tell you but I don't want you to be late for work."

"Work can wait," Dan said. He sounded like he meant it, and Connie felt something unfamiliar bloom inside her. Wolf had been the most wonderful man she'd ever known, but those words—*Work can wait*—had never once crossed his lips. Now, if Wolf were here to defend himself, he would point out that power washing and caretaking and lobstering were not the same as being a nationally renowned architect.

Connie ceded this point to him silently while still feeling plea-sure about being put first. "I'll tell you another time," she said.

"No, tell me now. Please," Dan said. "Otherwise I'm going to feel like I failed. Like I didn't allow you to climax."

Connie froze, shocked. Had he really just said that? The idea of her and sexual climax in the same sentence was much more for-eign than it ought to have been. But not wanting to call attention to that fact, Connie laughed.

Dan said, "I'm sorry. That was *very* inappropriate."

She said, "You caught me off guard. But I like that."

"I like that you like that," Dan said, and he took her hand.

They had about a hundred yards of beach left before they reached their shoes, and they were holding hands. Just a little over an hour before, Connie had been sure she was being given the brush off in aisle ten, and now they were holding hands. And Dan had made a joke about bringing Connie to climax. She wasn't sure she had the concentration to proceed.

"Okay, remember what you said about naming Joe after Nicole's father and then feeling like he belonged to her? Well, in my case..." Here, she drifted. She was about to revisit emotional territory she had decided to abandon decades ago. Why go back? Well, on the one hand, Dan had been achingly honest with her, and she wanted to reciprocate. But, on the other hand, she didn't know if she could *be* achingly honest. "I got pregnant with Ashlyn by accident. Wolf and I had been dating for less than six months, and he invited me here to Nantucket for a week, which turned into two weeks. And I'm pretty sure that Ashlyn was conceived in the back of a pickup truck at the Madequecham Jam."

"No way!" Dan said. "You were at the Madequecham Jam? What year are we talking about?"

"Eighty-two," Connie said.

"I was there," Dan said. "I was definitely there. How's that for weird?"

Weird, yes. Though, now that Connie thought about it, it wasn't terribly surprising. Everyone in the universe, it seemed, had been at that beach party. There were hundreds of girls in bikinis and Ray-Ban Wayfarers and guys bare chested wearing board shorts. The soundtrack was Journey and Springsteen and Asia. There were volleyball nets and horseshoes and kegs sitting in tubs of ice, and hibachis with burgers and dogs, and actual dogs catching Frisbees and chasing after tennis balls. There were chicken fights in the water—Connie and Wolf had participated and won handily, Wolf being so tall and Connie so ruthless. The jam had started in the morning and continued on late into the night—there were bonfires and guys strumming guitars and people singing and more beer, all taking place in a miasma of marijuana smoke. Couples drifted off to have sex in the dunes. Wolf and Connie had tried to have sex in the dunes but found them occupied, so they had nestled down in the back of a pickup truck owned by one of Wolf's buddies. Connie didn't remember the sex, though there were things about that night that remained with her—the stars in particular, the obscure constellations that Wolf pointed out: Cygnus, Lyra, Draco. Connie had felt pinned to the earth, one small person, negligible compared to the ocean and the sky, yet she was in love with Wolf Flute, and this made her feel significant in the turning world. Love made her matter. These were deep drunken thoughts. Connie had no idea she was conceiving a child. But yes, looking back, that had been the night. Connie had been nominally "on the pill," though she was lazy about taking it, and she had, in fact, forgotten her pill pack back at her parents' house in Villanova.

The gravity of what had happened that night didn't present itself to Connie until over a month later—Labor Day weekend. She was back on Nantucket with Wolf, only this time his entire family was vacationing at the cottage, as was their tradition. The Flute family believed that the final weekend of summer was superior to all other weekends, and that the last family to leave Nantucket for the season won some kind of intangible prize. (The Flutes regularly stayed until the Tuesday or Wednesday after Labor Day. As a child, Wolf had consistently missed the first day of school, and he'd been two weeks late matriculating at Brown.) In the house that weekend was Wolf's brother, Jake, Wolf's parents, and Wolf's grandparents. It was a weekend that included sailing and badminton, a lobster bake on Saturday, and lobster bisque made from the shells on Sunday. (It was a Yankee household; nothing went to waste.) The Flutes were athletic, hearty, seafaring people, but they weren't drinkers. The only person to have a drink at dinner was Wolf's grandmother, and that drink was a tiny glass of cream sherry. The rest of the family drank ice water or unsweetened iced tea, and Wolf and Connie complied. This being the case, Connie couldn't fathom the reason for her queasy stomach or leaden exhaustion. And yet, as she faced the first incarnation of the lobster and then the second, she had raced to the cottage's lone bathroom—which was no bigger than the bathroom on a ship and had to be shared among the seven of them—and vomited. The times when she wasn't expected at the family table or on a boat or on the beach for some camp game, Connie flopped across her spinsterish single bed in the third-floor guest room originally designed for the governess or nanny, and slept the heavy, sweaty sleep of the dead.

Near the end of the weekend, she awoke to Wolf rubbing her back. "You're sick," Wolf said. "My mother heard you retching in the bathroom. Why didn't you tell me?"

Connie buried her head under the feather pillow. She hadn't said so because she didn't want to ruin Wolf's family vacation or bring light to her infirmities (the fact that Mrs. Flute had heard her "retching" mortified her). She hadn't said so because, part of the time, she felt just fine. She hadn't said so because somewhere inside her, the knowledge lurked: she wasn't sick.

"I'm not sick," she told Wolf.

"You're not?" he said.

"I'm pregnant."

Wolf didn't react one way or another to this news, and Connie was glad. She couldn't handle anger or despair, and she couldn't handle joy. She thought nothing about the situation other than she had finally gotten what she deserved. She had been sleeping with boys since Matt Klein in eleventh grade, and she had never been assiduous about birth control. She had expected the boy-guy-man to be assiduous, and when she discovered they often weren't, it was always during the height of passion and she sometimes—too many times—took her chances. It was amazing she hadn't gotten pregnant before this.

When Wolf finally did speak—it took him so long that Connie had drifted off back to sleep—what he said was, "Wow. Okay. Wow."

The word "wow" bothered her. Connie had no intention of keeping this baby. She was only twenty-two years old, Wolf five years older. Wolf had a job as an architect with a firm in D.C., and he had a small apartment in Dupont Circle, but Connie still lived at home with her parents. She had been renting an apartment in Villanova, but one of her roommate's drunk boyfriends had punched a hole in the plaster and they lost the security deposit and Connie's parents had insisted that she live at home and save money until she proved she was responsible enough to live on her own. She had been working as a waitress at Aronimink and had, in fact, waited on her own drunk parents and her own drunk parents' drunk friends, a situation that Connie found humbling enough to bring her to tears. She couldn't handle caring for her own apartment, and she could barely handle her menial job, so how was she supposed to handle having a baby?

"I didn't want to have a baby," Connie said to Dan now. "I was just a kid; I still had living to do, a lot of living. I wanted to travel to Europe the way Meredith had done; I wanted to be the maid of honor in Meredith's wedding and look hot in my dress. I wanted to discover myself, live up to my potential. I had a degree from Villanova in sociology, and I wanted to prove the people wrong who said such a degree couldn't be put to use. Whatever, I didn't want a baby."

"And your husband?"

"My boyfriend?" Connie said. "Yes, he decided he wanted a baby."

Wolf had been as adamant about having the baby as Connie was adamant about not having the baby. He had been raised Protestant, but the first thing he did was to appeal to Connie's Catholic faith. Hadn't she been taught to believe in the sanctity of life? Yes, of course. But everyone made mistakes, and Connie had reconciled herself to the fact that this abortion was going to be her one grave mistake. She had her own accounting system as far as God was concerned, a system of checks and balances. She had lived cleanly up until that point—premarital sex aside—and she figured that even if she did commit this one mortal sin, she could dedicate the rest of her life to good works and still come out okay.

She would get her MSW and become a social worker on the terrifying streets of North Philadelphia. She could fight homelessness and teen pregnancy.

Wolf said, "I'm not okay with you killing a living thing that God created."

Connie couldn't believe he was taking this kind of hard-line moral position.

"It's an embryo," she said.

"It will turn into a person," Wolf said. "A boy or a girl. A man or a woman. Our child. Our first child, the next generation of my family... The future of the Flutes is *right here.*" He rested his hands on her abdomen.

She got it then. Wolf was under the intoxicating influence of the family weekend. He felt the pressure of his parents and his grandparents; he wanted to do his part in sustaining the dynasty, continuing the family line. Connie shook her head, looked away.

They didn't do anything for a week, then another week. Connie returned to Villanova, to her job waiting tables at Aronimink, a job made harder by her condition. The smell of eggs—unavoidable at brunch—made her hurl, and she could no longer join the rest of the staff for late-night benders at the bar. Well, she *could,* she reasoned, since she wasn't keeping the baby. But she didn't.

She and Wolf talked every night on the phone. He said he loved her. He said he wanted to marry her.

"I knew if I had an abortion, I would lose Wolf," Connie said. "And I didn't want to lose Wolf. I was madly in love with him. I wanted to marry him. But I wanted to marry him properly, in good time, and I wanted to be married to him for a while before we had children. I made this argument, but the man would not be moved. He wanted the baby. He was so sure about it that I finally felt secure enough to agree. He promised me everything would be okay. He promised me everything would be better than okay."

Connie and Wolf got married at Christmas in a small ceremony in Villanova. Meredith wore a red velvet cocktail dress and served as maid of honor. Freddy couldn't attend because of a work thing. Toby showed up with a nineteen-year-old girl who had crewed on one of his boats, but there had been one song when Toby had danced with Meredith, and the girl—Connie had forgotten her name—had thrown herself at Wolf's brother, Jake. Overall, however, the wedding was lovely. Connie wore a demure shade of ivory—according to Veronica, anything lighter would have been in poor taste—but what Connie remembered was looking longingly at the flutes of champagne, and longingly at Meredith's twenty-four-inch waist, and wishing that she wasn't pregnant.

Connie and Dan were sitting on the bottom step of the stairs of the public landing. They were still holding hands, and although Connie knew that it must be long past eight, Dan seemed in no hurry to get anywhere. This seemed like true luxury: being with someone who was content to listen. Connie suddenly believed that rehashing the past like this was going to lead her somewhere. But even if it didn't lead her anywhere, it felt good.

"When the baby came, there were complications," Connie said. "Ashlyn rotated during labor, her leg got stuck, I was howling in pain—though just like they all promise, I can only remember the howling, not the pain. At some point during this, my uterus ruptured, and I was rushed into surgery. When this kind of thing happened in the Middle Ages, the baby died and the mother died. But I was at Washington Hospital Center. They were good; they did a Cesarean, pulled Ashlyn out and stopped me from bleeding internally."

"Jesus, Connie," Dan said. He squeezed her hand, and Connie felt a rush of pure ecstasy, then chastised herself for using her most grisly story to get sympathetic attention. But it was true. It had happened; she had survived.

"I was convinced that the complication with the pregnancy was my punishment."

"Punishment for what?" Dan said. "You didn't terminate the pregnancy."

"Punishment, I don't know...for being me, maybe, for all of my transgressions. For *wanting* to terminate the pregnancy."

"Oh, come on, you don't believe that," Dan said.

"I believed it at the time. Ashlyn and I have had a difficult relationship from the get-go. Since her birth. Since conception."

Dan laughed. "You're as insane as I am."

"I know," Connie said. But even when Connie and Ashlyn were getting along, Connie was always holding her breath, waiting for the other shoe to drop. And it always did: Ashlyn said something cutting, cruel, dismissive. If Ashlyn was unhappy, Connie was blamed, and Connie accepted the blame. She would always feel guilty about not wanting to have Ashlyn in the first place.

"Wolf adored Ashlyn," Connie said. "She was his pride and joy. And, in her eyes, he could do no wrong."

Dan said, "Sounds familiar, in a way. Our kids bonded more closely with our spouses than they did with us. But that doesn't mean we failed, Connie."

But Connie *had* failed. She had always given a hundred percent, but there were times when she had resented it. Ashlyn was an amazing, brilliant child, but emotionally, she was made of granite. She was still, today.

Connie decided she would stop there; she didn't want to say anything more. But Dan was curious. "So why the rift?" he said. "What happened?"

"Mmm," Connie said.

She didn't want to tell him what happened.

But this was her chance to speak. Connie started by telling Dan the easy things: high school, college, medical school. Ashlyn excelled on all fronts. They were a happy family. Even when Wolf was diagnosed with prostate cancer, they were united. But then came Ashlyn's trip home with Bridget. The discovery of Ashlyn's sexual orientation converged with the discovery of Wolf's brain tumors. Wolf refused treatment because of his commissions; Ashlyn thought it was a rejection of her. She should have been angry at

Wolf, but she'd directed her fury at Connie, of course, because Connie was the one who remained.

"And then at the funeral…" Connie said. She closed her eyes. Was she going to tell Dan what happened at the funeral? She took a breath of soupy, marshy air. "I was as supportive as I could be about Ashlyn's relationship with Bridget. I mean, I wasn't exactly *happy* about it, but I was happy that Ashlyn was happy. I was happy that Ashlyn had someone, that she wasn't alone."

Still, Connie thought, she should have done a better job acting happy about it. Ashlyn and Bridget had sat together in the front pew of Saint Barnabas Episcopal Church, holding hands. And this had *bothered* Connie. Wolf was dead, Connie was in the worst emotional shape of her life, she had a church filled with everyone she had ever known, as well as many, many people she didn't know, and her daughter was holding hands with another woman in the front pew. Connie had glowered at Ashlyn the same way that her own father had glowered at her when she walked through the King of Prussia Mall with her hand in the back pocket of Drew Van Dyke's Levis. Connie had wanted to lean over and whisper: *Cool it with the PDA. Reverend Joel is watching. Your great-aunt Bette is watching.* But unlike her own father, who might have made a scene, Connie held her tongue. She was, at that point, proud of herself.

During the reception at Jake and Iris's house in Silver Spring, Ashlyn and Bridget slipped away. Connie noticed them leave the room, still ostentatiously holding hands, but Connie was tied up with a bridge partner of Iris's who had just lost *her* husband to emphysema. Connie discovered Ashlyn and Bridget later, on her way to the bathroom. Connie had headed upstairs in an attempt to escape awkward conversation with the mourners who were standing in line for the first-floor powder room. She found Ashlyn and Bridget standing in the doorway of one of the guest rooms. Bridget had her hands on either side of Ashlyn's face, and they were kissing.

Connie had relived this moment many times in her imagination, wanting the outcome to be different from what it had been. She had seen Ashlyn and Bridget kissing—lips, tongues, hands, shifting bodies—and she had cried out, "Jesus Christ, Ashlyn! Stop it! Stop it right now!"

Ashlyn had turned to her mother, her expression one of humiliation and anger and defiance, and she had raced down the stairs and out of the house. And Bridget had followed her.

Later, Connie tried to apologize. She had called Ashlyn's apartment but got voice mail. She considered contacting Ashlyn at the hospital, but it took her several days to build up the courage to do this. She told herself that the more time she put between her outburst and her inevitable conversation with Ashlyn about it, the better. However, when Connie finally made it to the hospital, she was informed that Dr. Flute had tendered her resignation.

It was only at the lawyer's office when they settled the particulars of Wolf's will that Connie learned that Bridget had been offered a prestigious fellowship at a large university hospital, and that Ashlyn was going with her. Ashlyn refused to say where the hospital was. Ashlyn didn't speak directly to Connie at all, except to laugh spitefully when Connie offered her apology.

"I didn't mean anything by it," Connie said. She had convinced herself that her reaction was no more or less severe than Bill O'Brien's would have been had he found Connie and a boyfriend kissing at the top of the stairs during a funeral reception. (What would he have said? She tried to channel him, channel any parent. *What are you doing up here? This is neither the time nor the place!*) But the slippery, stinky truth of the matter was that the time and the place had little to do with what made Connie react as she did. It had discomfited her to witness her daughter kissing another woman. It had made her... squeamish. Did that make Connie a bad person? Wasn't it, on some level, understandable?

"You two took me by surprise," Connie said. "I didn't expect to find you there. And I was very emotional that day. Ashlyn, I'm sorry."

Ashlyn had treated Connie to derisive laughter, and then once in the Aston Martin, a car Wolf had adored, Ashlyn drove away.

"And that's the last I heard from her," Connie told Dan. "I found out that she's practicing medicine in Tallahassee. She's working at some community health clinic, I guess. Her career is secondary to Bridget's. So maybe that's why she won't talk to me, maybe she's ashamed of what she's settled for. Of course, she was angry before the funeral. She holds me responsible for Wolf's death."

Dan put his arm around Connie and squeezed her, but the predictable tears didn't come. It was just like Dan had said: In talking about it, finally, with someone who was essentially a complete stranger to the situation, she was able to gain some distance. She was able to look at herself as someone who had lived through that story. Had it sounded awful to Dan? *Jesus Christ, Ashlyn!* It was nothing Connie hadn't said to her daughter a dozen times over the years in extreme anger or frustration—in response to nail polish spilled on the Persian rug, or a badly broken curfew, or the atrocious state of her bedroom. Had it sounded like the rejection of Ashlyn's sexuality? Had it sounded like a shout-out against tolerance? Did Dan think she was a bigot? Connie had never quite known how to grapple with her outburst—because there had been something in her tone of voice, some emotion that she couldn't name. Anger? Embarrassment? Disgust? Certainly not. But maybe, yes, just a little bit. And now Connie was being punished. She was being punished for not celebrating the fact that her daughter was in love with another woman.

She had learned her lesson. Connie would give anything—her house, her money, her right arm—*just to hear Ashlyn's voice.*

Dan cleared his throat. "That's difficult stuff," he said.

"It's the most difficult stuff I've got," Connie said. She laughed a little. "Remember, you asked for it."

"I'm not sure I know what to say, except I know how you feel. Sort of. I have an inkling."

They sat in silence a few seconds. Connie's mind was racing, she could feel this time coming to an end. She wasn't sure she could just get in her car and drive away after having given this man her most intimate confidence. The sun was high, it was hot, Connie needed water, shade, a swim. But she would sit here and freckle and burn as long as she could be beside Dan.

"You're missing work," she said.

"That I am," Dan said happily. He pulled her up by the hand. "Come on, I'm taking you to lunch."

It was only nine thirty, a little early for lunch they both agreed, though Connie had been up since five, so to her it felt like midday. She left her car in the parking lot there in Monomoy and climbed into Dan's Jeep. She was trembling, either from heat stroke or relief. She had told him the worst of it, and he still wanted to be with her.

"I'd better get these groceries home," he said. "We'll swing by my house, if that's okay with you?"

"Okay with me," Connie said.

They drove back to Milestone Road and Dan turned on to Sheep Commons Lane. He pulled into a circular driveway. The house had gray shingles and white trim, just like Connie's house, and a crisp brick chimney and a front porch with a nice-looking swing, and a ten-speed bike leaning against the railing. Connie gazed into a lush, landscaped side yard with a stone bench among the hostas.

"I'm just going to run in," Dan said, hoisting groceries out of the back.

"Yes," Connie said. In her head, she was singing, *He wants to be with me!* If only she'd known earlier this morning how her trip to the store would pan out, she wouldn't have panicked. If only she'd known the past weeks, when she was moping around the house. Connie couldn't wait to tell Meredith! Then she realized that Meredith had been in the house alone for hours, and that she had no idea where Connie was. Should Connie call? She rummaged through her bag. She didn't have her cell phone; it was in the kitchen, charging.

Meredith would be fine, Connie decided. Meredith wasn't a child.

Dan reappeared. He said, "Good thing you didn't come in. My son Donovan was sitting on the sofa in his underwear eating cereal and watching *Pimp My Ride.* It wasn't something I would have wanted you to see."

Dan drove out the Polpis Road to Sconset, taking meandering detours to travel across the acres of land that belonged to his family. They owned large plots in Squam and Quidnet; there were fourteen homes in the family trust, and Dan was in charge of the rentals and the upkeep. Dan told Connie about the Wampanoag Indian tribes who had populated Nantucket long before the Coffins and Starbucks came aground in the seventeenth century.

"And the Flynns," Connie said.

"In eighteen oh five," Dan said. "We were latecomers."

They ended up at the Summer House for lunch a little before noon. Dan had carte blanche at the restaurant by the pool because he did their power washing every spring. He and Connie sat in chaises in the sun and a waiter came to take their drink order. Dan ordered a beer, leaving Connie open to order wine, which she most definitely wanted, but no, she thought, she wouldn't. She didn't have to. She ordered an iced tea.

Dan delivered Connie back to her house at two thirty. He had blown off his morning appointments, but at three o'clock he had duties that couldn't be ignored. Connie was dizzy with happiness. They had laughed by the pool at the Summer House; they had talked until they both felt drowsy and napped. Dan had, unceremoniously, thrown Connie into the pool—cotton sundress and all—and Connie had found this funny and charming, which meant she must really be crazy about the man, because what fifty-year-old woman enjoyed being thrown into a pool with her clothes on? (And the careful job she did with her hair was ruined.) As they dried off, they ordered soft-shell crab sandwiches and a side of French fries, and they split a crème brûlée for dessert, and Connie thought about how nice it was to be out in the world, among other people. And then she thought about Meredith and felt guilty, and so when Dan said he had to take her home, she was eager.

"But if you're free, I'd like to take you to dinner tonight," he said. "And afterward, I'd like you to spend the night."

Connie nodded. "Yes," she whispered. It was an indication of how mature they were—or did she mean old?—that Dan had made his intentions clear. It eliminated posturing and guesswork. They had both been married before; Connie was going to assume that Dan had had lovers since Nicole's death. He knew what to do and she was grateful.

He dropped her at the front door and she stood on the porch waving until he drove away.

She hadn't had a single drink, but she felt drunk.

She found Meredith lying on the sofa, reading Jane Austen. She was wearing her bathing suit and her cover-up. Her sunglasses were perched on top of her head while she wore her regular glasses, but Connie knew that Meredith hadn't spent one second outside. She was braver now than she'd been that first week, but she wouldn't have ventured outside when she was alone at the house.

"Hey!" Connie said.

Meredith didn't look up. Connie got a sour feeling in her stomach.

"Meredith?"

She didn't move. She didn't tilt her head or twitch her leg. Connie waited. Meredith turned the page. She was near the end of her book. Maybe she was engrossed. Meredith could be such a nerd when it came to books. Then Connie remembered that Meredith had left thirty dollars and the titles of two novels written on a piece of paper on the kitchen counter, and Connie had promised that she would run to Bookworks today to pick them up. Meredith was too afraid to go along, but she really wanted the books; they were important to her. So was that why Meredith was mad, because Connie had forgotten to get the books? Okay, fine, Connie would go right now. She stepped into the kitchen — the money and the list were still there and Connie snapped them up — then she realized that she'd left her car in Monomoy. Shit. Well, she and Dan could remedy that tonight. She could pick up her car after dinner and drive it to Dan's house. Perfect.

Connie said, "Meredith, is everything okay?"

Meredith's head popped up. "You left here at six o'clock this morning saying you were going to the grocery store."

"I know," Connie said. "I'm sorry."

"I was worried, then panicked, then pissed off, because I realized around lunchtime that you must have had other plans and lied to me about them. Am I right?"

"I didn't have other plans," Connie said. "I went to the grocery store." She was speaking very slowly, scrambling in her mind for the right words. She had known Meredith wouldn't take this news well; she had been left in the house alone for almost nine hours. "I bumped into Dan. At the store."

Meredith turned her face toward Connie at the mention of Dan's name, although it was impossible to tell what she was thinking. At this moment, Connie remembered why they hadn't spoken for three years. Meredith was formidable when she was at odds with you. Connie thought back on their fight over the phone. Oh, boy — had they been at odds.

"It was a fluke," Connie said. She sounded like she was insisting. "We talked for a while, and then we went for a walk on the beach, and then we went to lunch at the Summer House, and then he brought me home."

Meredith sniffed, but she wasn't crying. Meredith didn't cry.

"Meredith? Say something."

"It sounds like you had a lovely day."

Connie sat down on the coffee table. She decided she wasn't going to lie to the woman to make her feel better. "It *was* a lovely day. We talked about Ashlyn, and about Dan's son Joe. We went for a drive around the island and ended up at the Summer House. You can have lunch by the pool there and the *Rosa rugosa* are in bloom and you can see the ocean. We had soft-shell crab sandwiches and these French fries that were to die for. Dan threw me in the pool."

"How much wine did you have?" Meredith asked.

Connie paused. It was an unkind question. But Connie wouldn't take the bait. She had learned a thing or two from her other fight with Meredith. Meredith was feeling bad, and she wanted Connie to feel bad, too.

"Are you mad at me?" Connie asked. "Are you mad that I went out with Dan?"

Meredith didn't answer.

"Do you have feelings for Dan, Meredith?" Connie asked. This hadn't crossed Connie's mind before; she had only been worried that Dan had feelings for Meredith.

"No," Meredith said. "I do not have feelings for Dan. Other than thinking he is a very nice guy. And much to my surprise, I've had fun when the three of us were together. The fact that the two of you went out and had fun together without me stings a little, yes. Especially since I didn't know where you were. Now, I get it. You're an adult; this is your house. I'm living here only because you have an open mind and a kind, merciful heart. You can come and go as you please and see who you want, obviously. And I can sit here alone and feel scared shitless and sorry for myself."

"Oh, Meredith," Connie said. Life was, as she continued to believe, high school over and over again. Connie could have gotten snippy and defensive—this *was* Connie's house, she did have every right to act spontaneously without calling home to check in with Meredith; Meredith was living there in the first place because of Connie's good graces—but looking at Meredith now, she got it. "I hate to tell you this, but I'm going out with Dan tonight. For dinner."

"By yourself?" Meredith asked.

Connie nodded.

"Where?"

"The Ships Inn," Connie said. "And Meredith?"

"What?"

"I'm spending the night at Dan's house. He asked me, and I said yes."

Meredith turned back to her book. That was preferable, Connie understood, to Meredith acting shocked and calling her a slut. Connie stood up. She thought, *I'll bike out to Monomoy, get my car, drive to Bookworks and get Meredith those books. She'll have them for tonight.* She thought, *And I'll get the groceries! I'll make something delicious for Meredith's dinner.*

She looked at Meredith, who now had the book tented over her face—though she wasn't crying, never crying—and thought, *How do I fix this?*

MEREDITH

It wasn't until nine o'clock or so that Meredith realized that Connie hadn't gone to the grocery store, or had gone not only to the grocery store. At first, Meredith assumed Connie had tacked on other errands: She went into town to shop at the farm stand or she went to the liquor store. Or she had revisited Vanessa Noel for shoes, or Erica Wilson or David Chase for a new dress or new white jeans or a new pretty top. It made sense that Connie would prefer to go shopping without Meredith. Meredith couldn't afford anything—and she wouldn't leave the house, anyway.

When, at noon, Connie still hadn't returned, Meredith thought, Okay, maybe she went out and did all those other things and then went to Mass (unlikely) or to the Whaling Museum (on such a fine day?). Meredith called Connie's cell phone from the house and another phone rang simultaneously, and Meredith was confused until she realized that Connie's cell phone was right there in the kitchen. Which explained why Connie hadn't called, but this didn't make Meredith feel any better.

At one thirty, Meredith gave in to suspicion first, then fear. Her suspicion was that Connie had another friend or group of friends that she was secretly meeting. The mere idea of this hurt Meredith, but after a few minutes, Meredith rejected this theory. Connie had never mentioned other friends on Nantucket, and if she had had other friends, she would have called on them before now. This left Meredith with only fear, and her fear was that Connie's long absence meant she had met with foul play which had been intended for Meredith. Amy Rivers had run her car off the road, or someone had accosted her in the parking lot of Stop & Shop and hurt her somehow. She was in the hospital, or someone had kidnapped her and she was, at this very second, sitting in someone's kitchen bound by ropes to a Stephen Swift stool.

As soon as the Stephen Swift stool appeared in her field of vision, Meredith knew she was being ridiculous. Connie hadn't met with foul play. So where was she?

When Connie did eventually arrive home at two thirty and told Meredith that she had bumped into Dan at the grocery store and they had spent the day together, Meredith was furious. Here, Meredith had spent eight hours worrying while Connie was getting her heart's desire. Connie had been the one to drag Meredith along on both of her dates with Dan—one of them quite long— and not only had Meredith enjoyed herself but she had gotten used to the idea of the three of them being together. So to have them suddenly assert their couplehood was a shock.

Now, Connie had left for her date, dressed in a stunning pink and orange Herve Leger bandage dress that very few women even twenty years younger could pull off, and her new Vanessa Noel heels. She gave Meredith the novels that Meredith had requested from Bookworks—Connie had ridden her bike to Monomoy to get her car to go to the bookstore. She had made this effort because she felt guilty. Connie had also made Meredith supper: a chopped salad with hard-boiled eggs, bacon, blue cheese, avocado, and grilled shrimp. Before she left, Connie locked all the doors and set the alarm. Then she hugged and kissed Meredith good-bye, and when Dan's Jeep pulled up, she disappeared out the front door.

Meredith felt resentful, mostly because Connie had left her nothing to complain about.

Alone, Meredith thought. *Alone, alone.*

The phone in the house rang, and Meredith gasped. She and Connie had watched too many scary movies as teenagers; all she could think was that someone out there knew she was alone. She forced herself to check the caller ID—because what if it was Connie or one of the boys?—and Meredith saw that it was the law firm.

She picked up the phone.

"Meredith, thank God."

"Hi, Dev," she said.

"I just called your cell phone three times, and I sent you a text. Did you get it?"

"No," Meredith said. "I—"

"You need to keep your phone *on,* Meredith," Dev said. "What's the point in having it otherwise?"

Should she try to explain to him that by turning it off, she saved herself twenty-three and a half hours of worry about who was or was not calling her?

"Thank God you gave me the landline," Dev said. "Because things are starting to happen."

"Like what?" Meredith said. She sat on the very edge of the sofa. She couldn't let herself get too comfortable.

"Well, I have good news and I have bad news."

Meredith clenched her fists. "What?"

"The good news is from Julie Schwarz. The Feds have determined that this guy Deacon Rapp, the so-called legitimate trader who was fingering Leo, was, in fact, in on the Ponzi scheme himself."

"You're kidding!" Meredith said.

"He was trying to feed Leo up to the Feds in his place, which was a logical move since Leo is Freddy's flesh and blood. But after examining the so-called hundred pieces of evidence, the Feds caught on to this guy. They have a paper trail on him now that's miles long, and without his deposition, there's nothing implicating Leo. Leo's computer was clean, and they found no communication between Leo's office and the fiends on the seventeenth floor."

"Thank God," Meredith said.

"Even better, they found this woman, Freddy's supposed secretary on the seventeenth, Mrs. Edith Misurelli. They got her arriving at JFK from Rome and took her in directly for questioning. She said straight out that Leo Delinn had been denied access to the seventeenth floor, by . . . guess who?"

Meredith was shaking. "Who?"

"Your husband. Freddy forbade Leo from ever entering the offices where the dirty deeds were done. According to Mrs. Misurelli, Leo never once set foot on that floor."

"Oh, my God," Meredith said. She felt a wash of relief, like cool water over her burning concern. "So Leo is off the hook?"

"Unless something unforeseen comes out, yes. The Feds are finished looking at Leo. They're looking at this Deacon Rapp kid who had *thirty-one million bucks* squirreled away. He was in cahoots with his uncle, who deposited the money in four banks in Queens."

"So I can talk to Leo?" Meredith said. "I can call him?"

"Now for the bad news," Dev said. "Leo has been cleared. And this pisses off the investors and their lawyers, why? Because they want to hold another Delinn accountable. So who are they going to focus on now?"

"Me," Meredith said.

"You."

She stood up. *The other investors are clamoring for your head.* She walked over to the bookshelves and stared at Wolf Flute's collection of barometers. Oh, the hours Meredith had spent acquiring and collecting things, instead of worrying about her own freedom.

But Leo is free, she thought. *Leo is free!* She allowed the massive weight of those worries to slide off her shoulders, which felt amazing, but nothing felt as good as dropping the insidious nugget of doubt that Meredith herself had felt about Leo. She had never believed that he'd been involved in the Ponzi scheme, but she'd feared, deep down, that he might have known about it and been too loyal to his father to turn him in.

This mysterious woman, a secretary of Freddy's that Meredith hadn't even known existed, had provided the only palatable answer: Freddy had forbidden Leo from visiting the seventeenth floor.

In light of this new information, did Meredith care about her own fate? Hadn't she said she would sacrifice herself if Leo was set free?

"That brings us to the sticking point," Dev said.

"The fifteen million," Meredith said. Her voice sagged. Hadn't they gone over this? "Are you going to ask me about the fifteen million?"

"Do you have anything else to say about it?" Dev asked. "Anything?"

"No," Meredith said.

"Are you sure?"

"I told them already," Meredith said.

"Okay," Dev said. "Then all you can do is to keep thinking of places where that money might be, where the Feds might look. But you shouldn't contact Leo or Carver until you're cleared. It's more imperative now than ever, okay?" He paused. "Hey, but the good news is that Leo is free."

Meredith closed her eyes. She had refused to say the words before, but she would say them now. "Yes," she said. "That is good news."

Meredith set down the phone. Leo was free. There would be a quiet celebration at Carver's house tonight, possibly just Carver and Leo and Anais sharing a meal, listening to music, and laughing for the first time in months.

Meredith poured herself a glass of wine. She yearned to step out onto the deck, but she couldn't risk the exposure. Leo was free, but she was still in peril, possibly more so than before. Meredith wished Connie were here. Meredith looked obliquely out the glass doors. She saw Harold's dark head emerge in the smooth green glass of a cresting wave, then disappear. Only one seal.

Meredith's new novels were lying on the table. She could allow herself the pleasure of cracking one open, but the experience would be wasted on her. There was too much to think about.

The Feds thought they knew her, the investors thought they knew her, the American media thought they knew her: Meredith Delinn, wife of financial giant Frederick Xavier Delinn, mother of two privileged sons, socialite. They thought she sat on boards, they thought she organized charity galas, they thought she shopped. And whereas she had indeed done those things, there had been other things as well. Worthy things.

Meredith had taught English at Samuel Gompers High School in the Bronx for five years. It had been hard work, frightening work, frustrating work — Meredith challenged any federal agent or any soft-handed cubicle-sitter at the SEC to give it a try. She had forced tenth graders to read; some of them she had *taught* to read. She had thrown Carson McCullers's novel *The Member of the Wedding* at them. For some kids, the book was like a blanket over their heads — they couldn't see a thing. But for some kids, that book was a bright portal that led them to other books. Meredith read a poem to her classes every day, and some days no one was listening—they were too busy talking about the Knicks or Hector Alvarez's new Corvette or doing smack. And some days they said, *We don't give a shit about no red wheelbarrow or no white fucking chickens.* But some days, Meredith read Gwendolyn Brooks or Nikki Giovanni, and more than half the class looked mildly engaged. "A Boy Died in My Alley" got a response of *Hey, man, that's like Lippy Magee getting knifed behind the free clinic.* And Meredith said, "Okay, everybody take out a pencil."

She made a pittance, she took the subway, she was exhausted when she got home to the apartment—and sometimes Freddy was still at work. When Meredith got pregnant, she worried as she rode the 6 train uptown, and she was more exhausted when she climbed the four flights of stairs with bags from D'Agostino's. She thought about quitting, but then Freddy announced that he was leaving Prudential and starting his own hedge fund. Why should he be working so hard to make money for a huge corporation when he could be making money for himself?

Meredith stayed at Gompers another year, then another year after that. They needed the health insurance. Freddy was having a hard time making the new business fly. Meredith got pregnant again. They didn't have space for another child, and they couldn't afford to move.

One night, with her belly hugely swollen, and Leo, at eighteen months, wailing in his crib, and Freddy out with some potential investors, who in the end never seemed to want to invest, Meredith lay in the bathtub and cried. She thought of her father saying, *Brilliant and talented, that girl can do no wrong.* Had he been lying? And if he was telling the truth, then what on earth was she doing here?

Meredith drained her glass of wine and stared at her beautiful salad. Could she bring herself to eat anything?

It was getting dark, and Meredith knew she should turn on some lights, but she had the dreadful feeling that if she turned on the lights, the person who was watching her would see her in the illuminated room eating alone. She picked at the salad in the gathering dark—not because she was hungry, but because Connie had made it for her. Connie was such a good cook, a good friend, a good person. Meredith had said all those beastly things to her years ago, but Connie hadn't mentioned it once. Meredith hoped Connie was having fun tonight; she and Dan would still be at dinner. If Meredith had a legitimate scare, she could still call Connie's cell phone. She could call now, but not later.

In those years, Leo and Carver went to day care, which bothered Freddy, but there was no money for a nanny. They moved to a two-bedroom apartment on East 82nd Street, but it was still a walk-up. Freddy used to leave the apartment before the boys were awake and get home after they were asleep. He lost weight. Meredith begged him to have a milkshake with his lunch, she begged him to see a doctor, but for Freddy there was only work and more work. Getting the company up and running. Attracting clients. How would he attract clients? He worked on the weekends. Meredith was left to handle everything at home. She couldn't do it. She couldn't have two little kids and run a household and grade thirty essays and do lesson plans. Carver was already showing signs of anxiety disorder; he screamed and cried when Meredith dropped him off at day care, and he screamed and cried when she picked him up.

And then Meredith got pregnant again.

She was waiting for Freddy in the apartment when he got home from work, waving the pregnancy test in her hand like a wand: a wand that was going to reveal everything that was wrong with their life. She wanted things to be easier; she wanted things to be different. Her job was hard. That very day Meredith had come across two girls fighting in the bathroom, and one of the girls had a razor blade concealed inside her lower lip. The most disturbing thing was that Meredith had known how to restrain the girl and where to look for the blade. Why should she know such things?

She wanted to leave Gompers at the end of the year. She hated the commute on the subway. She hated dropping the boys off at the dreaded day care. Carver clung to the front of Meredith's shirt; he clawed for her glasses. The workers had to peel him off her. And now she was having a baby.

She stared Freddy down. She loved him, but this was not the life she'd expected.

"I'm taking the children," she said. "And I'm going to my mother's." She was disappointed at how cliché this sounded, but what was *not* cliché was the thought of sleeping in her childhood home, the big white Colonial in Villanova with the expansive back yard where the boys could run through the sprinkler and play on the swings. Meredith would have an extra set of hands. She would enroll the boys at Tarleton.

Freddy, Meredith remembered, had seemed to shrink. Then, he smiled. "Another baby?" he said.

"Another baby," Meredith said, and she smiled, too, in spite of herself. But then she hardened. "I mean it, Fred. I'm leaving. Until things change, I'm going home."

"You're not going anywhere," Fred said. "You're going to stay right here, and I'll make things better. I will take care of everything."

The SEC and the Feds postulated that Freddy had been operating his Ponzi scheme for at least a decade, but when Meredith looked back, she knew with gut-rotting certainty that it had started the year after Meredith threatened to leave. Because Freddy was good to his word: everything got better. Instead of schlepping all the way to the Bronx every morning, Meredith stayed home with the boys. She delivered Leo to a summer preschool program at the Catholic church, she took Carver for a chocolate milk at E.A.T. Café, then home to play blocks, watch *Sesame Street*, take a nap. One sweltering day in the middle of the summer, Meredith was headed down the building's stairs in her flip-flops, and she missed a step. She fell all the way to the landing. She was hurt, but not *hurt* hurt; however, she decided to call off their outing to the deliciously cool, air-conditioned halls of the Museum of Natural History. By the time she got upstairs to the apartment, she was bleeding.

She was only twelve weeks along, and she'd barely told anyone about the pregnancy (her mother, Connie, the principal at Gompers, who asked why she wasn't coming back), but still, the miscarriage struck Meredith as a tremendous loss. She was positive the baby would have been a girl, whom she would have named Annabeth Carson after her grandmother and Ms. McCullers.

Freddy had taken the miscarriage in stride, and when Meredith accused him of being unfeeling, he said, "We can't both be basket cases. We have the boys to think about. And we'll get pregnant again, sweetheart. Don't worry. We'll have our little girl." He held Meredith, and he said these encouraging things, but when his cell phone rang, he switched right into work mode.

It was that autumn, Meredith remembered, that the money started rolling in. They got full coverage with Blue Cross and Blue Shield. They pulled Leo out of the Catholic preschool and sent him to Saint Bernard's. Freddy wasn't home any more often, but when he was home, he was happier. He had solved the problem of attracting clients. It seemed the way to attract clients was to tell them they *couldn't* invest in Delinn Enterprises. Delinn Enterprises was only looking for certain kinds of investors; many people got turned away. Freddy had investors banging down the door. He put back on the weight he'd lost, and twenty pounds besides. He ordered lunch in every day: reuben sandwiches, lobster bisque, omelets with goat cheese and smoked salmon. He had business dinners at Gallagher's and Smith & Wollensky. He had no time for exercise. He got his first gray hair at age twenty-nine. Meredith had wanted to pluck it, but he wouldn't let her. He wanted to look older, he said. He needed gravitas, he said.

After the New Year, they moved to a three-bedroom apartment

with an eat-in kitchen in the East Sixties. It was a doorman build-ing. They bought a car and kept it in the garage. They began rent-ing a house in Southampton for two weeks a summer.

In September, Carver joined Leo at Saint Bernard's. Meredith tried to get pregnant again but didn't have any luck. She suspected that Freddy's sperm were too stressed to swim. Freddy gave Mer-edith carte blanche to hire a nanny and a cook, even though they ate out almost every night. With both kids in school and a Filipino nanny, Meredith was free to go back to work. Gompers, or any other public school suddenly seemed out of the question, and before she knew it, working at all seemed out of the question. Freddy declared that business was gangbusters, and he whisked Meredith down to Palm Beach for the weekend, leaving the kids with Cecelia, and they loved Palm Beach so much that Freddy wanted to look at property. *To buy.*

Meredith's life became consumed with managing all that she suddenly had: The boys, their needs, their sports, their school func-tions. There was yet another new apartment—the penthouse at 824 Park Avenue—that they had bought, as well as a house in Palm Beach, the Pulitzers' former house. Freddy had snapped this up at auction "for a steal," he said. (As a testament to her remove from Freddy's financial dealings, Meredith never learned how much the Pulitzer house had cost them.) The Frick Collection asked Meredith to serve on its board of directors, and she was on the Parent Action Committee at the boys' school, which allowed Meredith to meet other busy, important people who each seemed to want to get her involved in something else. She and Freddy had *things* to attend—events, benefits, dinner parties, nights at the symphony and the Metropolitan Opera. There wasn't time for Meredith to work. She was too busy being Mrs. Freddy Delinn.

Meredith washed her dinner dishes. The house was dark now; she had to use the light over the sink or risk breaking a glass.

She saw that there was a single cupcake under plastic wrap resting on a saucer. It looked suspiciously like a vanilla-bean cupcake with strawberry icing from the bakery at the Sconset Market. *Connie is an angel,* Meredith thought. Or Connie felt worse about leaving Meredith alone than Meredith realized.

Meredith ate the cupcake standing up at the counter, wondering about the moment when she'd realized they were really... rich. It was probably a quiet moment—a nondescript afternoon walking home from lunch at Le Cirque with the likes of Astrid Cassel or Mary Rose Garth, when Meredith stopped in to Bergdorf's and bought—who knows?—a $2,000 powder-pink Chanel cardigan and didn't keep the receipt. Or it was something more momentous, such as her first trip to Paris with Freddy since their backpacking adventure. He had booked a suite at the Hôtel de Crillon. They had eaten at Taillevent, and in the Jules Verne restaurant at the top of the Eiffel Tower (Meredith could have skipped the Eiffel Tower, but not Freddy). The highlight of that trip wasn't the hotel (though they laughed, remembering the hostel they had stayed at in the sleazy eighteenth *arrondissement* their first time through) or the dining (they remembered how they ate a baguette and Camembert while sitting on the floor of their room in said hostel), but a private tour that Freddy had arranged at the Musée d'Orsay. When he told Meredith they were going on a private tour, she thought that meant they would have their very own English-speaking guide. But what it meant was that at six thirty, half an hour after the museum closed, they stepped through a discreet door and were met by the museum's curator, who was trailed by a waiter with a bottle of vintage Krug. The curator proceeded to give Meredith and Freddy a *private tour* of the museum, with special emphasis on Pissarro, who had been Meredith's favorite painter ever since she attended a Pissarro exhibit with her father at the Philadelphia Museum of Art when she was fifteen years old.

Champagne, the whole museum hushed and waiting for them, the erudite curator with his elegantly accented English. Yes, on that day, Meredith understood that they had become rich.

*   *   *

Meredith checked the back door: locked. She checked the front door: locked. She checked the alarm: activated. The windows were shut and locked; the air-conditioning was on. Meredith toyed with the idea of turning on the TV. Other voices in the room might ease her anxiety. But Connie never turned on the TV and Meredith wouldn't, either. She might inadvertently come across something in the news she didn't want to see, or "Frederick Xavier Delinn: The Real Story" on E!

She went upstairs.

She couldn't help feeling like a woman in a horror film, one who met her unsuspecting end in the doorway of a dark room. She wasn't sure how to shed this feeling and relax. She was safe. Nothing had happened to the house or the car in weeks. It was now August; for all Meredith knew, Amy Rivers was gone. She, Meredith, was safe. The doors were locked, the alarm set.

She needed to sleep. And what that really meant was that she needed a sleeping pill. She knew Connie had something. Meredith had seen the prescription bottles.

She felt her way into Connie's bathroom. She needed to turn on the light. But this was okay, this was Connie's light. Whoever was watching from outside would see Connie's light go on and believe that Connie was home. Meredith switched on the light. The prescription bottles were right there where Meredith remembered seeing them. She checked the labels: Ambien, Lunesta, Ativan, Prozac, Seraquil, Zoloft. Connie had cornered the sleep-aid/anti-anxiety market. Meredith shook each bottle; they were all full.

Meredith debated between the Ambien and the Lunesta. She chose Ambien; she took two pills. She took two Ativan as well, for a later time when she might really need them. She took the Ambien immediately, with tap water.

This was stealing. God, how she *hated* that word. She would make this right; she would tell Connie she'd taken two Ambien and then it would be borrowing. She told herself that she would also confess to Connie about the Ativan, although she knew she wouldn't. Unless Connie counted her pills, she would never know, and plus it was only two Ativan, completely harmless.

So that was how stealing worked, right, Freddy? You "borrowed" a little something, no one would ever know; you were dealing out returns of 22, 23, 25 percent, everyone was happy. You could roll on like this indefinitely. You would be dead before anyone caught you.

Meredith acted like a thief, putting the bottles back exactly as she had found them, lifting them again to see if there was a noticeable difference in their weight.

As she tiptoed back down the hallway, she heard a *thump, thump, thump* and a squeak. She stopped in her tracks. Squeak. A prolonged squeak. A squeaky wheel.

Blood hammered in Meredith's ears. She was hot with panic and afraid she would vomit up her dinner—as well as the pills she'd just taken. She sucked in a breath. She was either imagining things, or Connie was home, or the police were wandering around, doing a check. (Had the police continued to do their surveillance? Meredith should have asked Connie to call them.)

She heard another thump, a definite thump this time, and Meredith thought, *Okay, now what do I do?* Her instinct, as when she saw Amy Rivers at the bookstore, was to freeze. She closed her eyes and remained as silent and still as an animal in the woods and hoped that the predator moved on.

Another thump, more squeaking. The noise was coming from outside. There were people outside, people at this house, way out in deserted Tom Nevers. Part of Meredith wanted to look out the window and find out what was going on. It might be the police, and if it wasn't the police, it would be something she would have to describe to the police. But Meredith was afraid of being seen.

The hallway, she decided, was safe. It had no windows, and the rug was velvety soft. Meredith laid her head down. She wanted a pillow, but she was too afraid to venture into her room or back into Connie's room to fetch one. They were coming to get her. And didn't she deserve it? Three days before Delinn Enterprises was exposed as a Ponzi scheme, Meredith had transferred $15 million from the company slush fund to her and Freddy's personal brokerage account. Meredith had made it clear in her deposition: Freddy had asked her to transfer the money, and she had transferred it. She had thought nothing of it—until that afternoon, freshly home from the bank, when she saw Freddy throwing back the 1926 Macallan. At that moment she realized the $15 million wasn't meant for a house in Aspen (Carver had been pressuring Freddy because he loved to snowboard) or for a Roy Lichtenstein (Samantha had a line on one for sale), as Meredith had believed it might be. The $15 million was a levee against the flood. But by the time Meredith realized this, the money had been moved. Meredith had done it at Freddy's behest; he had made her an unwitting conspirator. And now, investors were clamoring for her head. And now, quite possibly, she was going to prison.

But Meredith's first crime was that she had threatened to leave Freddy; she had threatened to take his children away. She had attacked his manhood; she had made it clear the life he was providing wasn't good enough. She didn't want to work; she wanted to stay home. She didn't want to drop her kids at day care; she wanted a nanny. She didn't want to ride the subway; she wanted cabs. That wasn't what she'd been saying, but that was what Freddy heard— and he set out to find a way to give those things to her.

There was another noise, louder than the others, that came from out front. A *BAM,* that was how Meredith would describe it; it sounded as though someone had dropped a large package on the front porch. But maybe that was Connie? Meredith waited. It was quiet for one minute, then two.

Meredith felt the sleeping pills sprinkle their fairy dust over her graying head. Her eyes drifted closed. The rug was velvety soft.

*   *   *

Meredith awoke to the first pink light of day. Her body ached from sleeping in a pile on the floor, but she noted the daylight with relief. She had made it to the morning.

She felt okay to move around the house. The terror of the night before had faded, although there was still some residual fear, worry, concern, anxiety, something picking at Meredith's corners. She had survived, but she wasn't safe. Something had happened in the night, she was sure of it, though it might have been her imagination. It had *not* been her imagination. But it if *were* her imagination, how grateful she would be!

She descended the stairs. At least she hadn't interrupted Connie and Dan's romantic evening.

The downstairs was clean and unchanged, the great room suffused with light. With trepidation, Meredith peered out at the back deck. It looked okay, right? But there was a trail of something dark, something Meredith didn't like the looks of. Meredith felt groggy and cottonmouthed. She needed water first, then coffee. Connie always made the coffee and, sure enough, when Meredith checked, the coffee machine was all set up and ready to go.

There was a trail of something dark on the deck. Oil, she thought. Though she knew better.

She didn't like the way she was feeling. She should call the police. And say what? That she'd heard noises? That there was a suspicious trail on the deck?

Have you looked around? the police would ask.

And Meredith would say, *No, I'm too afraid.*

She picked up her cell phone and turned it on. It chimed three times with messages. But when Meredith checked, she saw these were the messages left by Dev the previous evening. So there was nothing new. She got a glass of ice water, which she drank to the bottom. The coffee was brewing; the sunlight was filling up this room exactly the way Wolf Flute had intended.

Meredith moved toward the front door. But no, the front door

256   Elin Hilderbrand

was too scary. Meredith was thinking of the worst, and the worst she was thinking about was a bomb. Something had been dumped or thrown on the front porch, of that she was fairly sure. Special delivery for Meredith Delinn.

Call the police! Nantucket had little or no crime (or at least this had been the case before she arrived); the police would welcome something to do on this Thursday morning.

Have you looked around?

The front door was too scary. If she opened the front door, the bomb would detonate. There would be a fiery explosion or a lethal spray of nails or a leak of radioactive waste.

Meredith peered out the window of the sitting room, from which she could see part of the front porch obliquely. And yes, Meredith saw a spill of something dark. *Oh, God!* She was really shaking now, she was moving to the front door, she would open it just a crack, she would peek through her fingers, not enough to see, just enough to confirm her awful suspicions.

The door was triple locked, and she had to disengage the alarm before she could open it. That required the code, which was Ashlyn's birthday: 040283, a date Meredith had known for, well, nearly thirty years, but had trouble remembering in her present state. She turned the alarm off; the house was unsealed. She stood behind the door and pulled it open with a sucking sound, and she peeked—her eyes were mostly closed—but she saw what she needed to see. Flippers, whiskers, a ghastly, gaping red smile.

Harold lay on the front porch with his throat cut.

Meredith slammed the door shut and locked it. She was hyperventilating. Not a bomb, but in many ways worse. From her cell phone, she called the police and gave the address, then she said, "I have found a dead sea mammal on my front porch."

"On your front porch?" The dispatcher said.

"A seal," Meredith said.

"A dead seal?" The dispatcher said. "Really? On your porch?"

"Can you send someone, please?" Meredith said. And then she

said, "This is Meredith Delinn." She wasn't sure if the dispatcher would know her name, but of course she did, everyone in American knew her name.

The dispatcher said, "Yes, Mrs. Delinn. We'll send a car out now."

Meredith slid to the floor and understood that her mistake wasn't in threatening to leave Freddy. Her mistake was in not leaving.

PART TWO

CONNIE

Connie drove to the town pier alone, thinking that she had another fifteen minutes of peace before her summer detonated. When she'd told Dan what she'd done—or, more accurately, *not done*—he'd said, *Don't worry about it. With what we've been through, it can't be a big deal, can it?* But he might only have been saying that to make Connie feel better.

Town pier, eleven o'clock in the morning on a stunning summer day. The pier was crawling with families carrying coolers and fishing poles and clam rakes, clambering aboard motor boats to putter out to Coatue and Great Point. Connie was astonished how relaxed and happy these people seemed. Connie was sick with anxiety. Sick! She had followed her gut, and now she had to hope for the best.

Eleven o'clock, he'd said. But she didn't see him anywhere. Typical. It was Veronica's gene passed down: *Late for my own funeral.*

Connie walked the dock, checking out this boat and that boat, looking but not seeing, her heart thundering, her stomach sour like she'd eaten a dozen lemons for breakfast. Then she saw him, the square shoulders, the bowlegged lope. Unmistakable. The sun was a bright halo around his head.

Toby!

He was wearing a green polo shirt, a pair of khaki shorts, deck shoes without socks (did Toby even *own* socks?), aviator sunglasses. He was tan. (Toby and Connie were alike in many ways, but Connie freckled while Toby was now, and always had been, a bronze god.) He still had a full head of sandy hair, and his weight seemed stable. In the past, Connie had seen him both gaunt and underfed, and bloated and heavy. He whooped and gave her a big hug, lifting her right off the dock, and Connie was reminded that, when sober, he was just like a Saint Bernard puppy, all boundless love and enthusiasm. He had been sober now for nearly two years—or so he claimed.

"I called your bluff!" he said. "I'm here!"

"Hey, brother," Connie said. He set her down and they kissed. He tasted clean, he smelled clean—not too minty the way he used to when he was drinking.

"This weather is amazing!" he said. He hoisted the canvas duffel bag he had owned literally his entire adult life over his shoulder. It was sky-blue with his monogram; it had traveled with Toby all over the world. "Maryland is brutally hot. We haven't had a lick of wind all summer. So I took that as a sign. This guy Roy Weedon has been asking me about my boat for years, and when the offer came from the Naval Academy, I thought, Now's the time to sell her."

"I can't believe she's gone," Connie said. Toby had saved for *Bird's Nest* for nearly ten years, and she was the most exquisite sailboat Connie had ever seen. A classic. The Jackie O of sailboats, the Audrey Hepburn of sailboats. Toby had run the number one sailing charter in the state of Maryland, which gave him the freedom and the cash to island-hop in the Caribbean all winter long. "I can't believe you sold her. You know you'll never be able to get her back, right? You know you'll never find another boat like her?"

"I do know that," Toby said. "But I can't be at the mercy of the wind or the economy, anymore, Con. And the gig at the Naval Academy was too choice to turn down. The premier collegiate sailors in the country will soon be under my tutelage."

Right. When they'd talked on the phone the day before, Toby

had confessed that the charter business had suited him because it left him free to do other things—primarily drink and chase after other men's wives. He needed something more stable, more serious. He had to think of his son, Michael. He needed health insurance, retirement benefits. He needed to grow up, finally.

"Want to take one last look at her?" Toby asked.

"Won't that be sad for you?" Connie asked.

"I've made my peace with it," Toby said. "Come on, she's down here."

Connie was grateful for anything that delayed their arrival back at home. She followed Toby down the dock. And there she was—*Bird's Nest*—thirty-three feet of polished wood, rope, canvas, and nickel. There was a guy on her, tying up the sails. He looked too young to be the new owner.

"Is that the man from Nantucket?" Connie asked.

Toby laughed. "You're funny, Con."

They ambled back to the car. He was going to think she was funny for another second or two. "So how are you doing?" Connie asked. The ride to Tom Nevers would only take twelve or thirteen minutes, so she had to work fast. "Are you sober?"

"Sure," Toby said.

"Sure?" Connie said. "What kind of answer is that?"

"Geez, Con," Toby said. "Are you riding me already? Can't we just ease into it?"

"No," Connie said. "We can't just ease into it." She wouldn't be lulled by his boyish, gee-whiz charm, though this seemed to work on everyone else. Wolf, despite the fact that he had seen Toby at his very drunkest and most pathetic, had absolutely adored his brother-in-law. The two of them could tell sailing stories for hours, and when Toby visited Nantucket, they used to race each other in Indians. It was the highlight of Wolf's summer—chasing Toby up the harbor and back again—and then settling with a cold beer at the Rope Walk so they could talk about the sail, tack by tack, afterward.

"Okay," Toby said. "I've been sober for twenty-two months. But

I don't take it for granted. I fell off the wagon once, early on." He squinted out the side window. "The evil combination of Marlowe Jones and the Treaty of Paris."

"Ah," Connie said. The Treaty of Paris was Toby's former watering hole. Marlowe Jones was the lonely wife of the Annapolis district attorney. Evil combination indeed.

"But like I said, that was nearly two years ago. I've come to terms with my relationship with alcohol. I inherited the disease. You're lucky you didn't."

Connie felt a complicated mix of emotions. She was ashamed, thinking of how drunk she'd gotten the day of the boat ride with Dan. But what that had taught her was that she *wasn't* immune; she had to watch herself. A part of Connie stupidly mourned the old Toby, the Toby who had been Connie's boozy, fun-loving comrade. Two years earlier, when Toby had come for Wolf's memorial service, he'd hit every bar downtown and had been dropped off at Connie's house in a cab, a sloppy-if-happy drunken mess. Then he and Connie had stayed up drinking wine on the deck until sunrise. Jake and Iris had found them passed out on the outdoor furniture in a dead-on reprise of their own parents.

Toby's not good for you, Iris, with her degree in psychology, had said. *You're not good for each other.*

"Are you dating anyone?" Connie asked him. "Other than Marlowe Jones?"

"I'm not dating Marlowe," he said.

"She's still married to Bart?"

"Still married to Bart. It's one of the worst marriages I've ever seen, but it just won't die."

"Like mom and dad," Connie murmured.

"Exactly," Toby said.

"And there's no one else?" Connie asked.

"No," he said. "Nobody special."

It might have been better if he'd been dating someone, Connie thought. But Toby's romantic life was impossible to keep track of.

There were always women, but rarely anyone who lasted more than a few weeks. Toby had been married twice. He'd met his first wife, Shelden, crewing on the boat *Cascade,* which was the boat he captained before *Excelsior.* Shelden had family money, much of which she spent financing Toby's lifestyle—the drinking and carousing in places like Portofino and Ios and Monaco. It wasn't hard to see why Shelden left—at that time, Toby was at his most uncontrollable and irresponsible, and Shelden was bankrolling all of his bad behavior. He would go to the most popular waterfront bar, buy a round for everyone in the place, and then arrive back at *Excelsior* with fifteen people ready to party until three in the morning.

Several years later while working in Norfolk, Virginia, Toby met Rosalie, who was a shore-bound single mother of two small children. Toby was like some kind of romantic hero who sailed in to save her—though "saving" her turned into getting her pregnant, marrying her, then making her so miserable and doing such a piss-poor job as a father and stepfather that Rosalie fled back to her family in New Orleans. Toby's son, Michael, was now ten. Rosalie had remarried a coach with the New Orleans Saints, a guy who Toby liked and admired. "The guy is so responsible," Toby said, "I want him to be *my* dad." There had been trips to New Orleans where the whole blended family—Rosalie and the coach had children of their own now—went to JazzFest and took river cruises.

"How's Michael?" Connie asked.

"He's great," Toby said. He flipped open his phone to show Connie a picture. She glanced at it quickly: Michael in a baseball hat. "He's a U-eleven all-star in Little League, and he's doing Pop Warner again in the fall. Starting QB. Kid's a natural athlete. Quick hands."

"Takes after his aunt," Connie said. She saw Toby staring at the picture. "Do you wish you saw more of him?"

"Huh?" Toby said. He flipped the phone closed. "Yeah, of course. I lobbied for him to come to Annapolis for two weeks, but he had camp."

"He still could have come for a little while," Connie said. "Did you ask Rosalie?"

"Of course I asked Rosalie," Toby said. "She said he had camp."

Connie shook her head, thinking, *Did you not fight to see your son?*

Toby said, "Michael's fine; he's happy, I'm happy he's happy. We Skype each other."

"Skype?" Connie said.

"Connie, it's fine," Toby said. And he did, indeed, sound fine.

Growing up, Toby had always been the better kid, at least in Connie's mind; possibly, this was a notion she'd gotten from her parents. Toby was the golden-haired son, the gifted athlete. He'd shown promise as a sailor during their summers at Cape May, but there was also football, basketball, and lacrosse. At Radnor, he'd been captain of all three varsity teams. He had always been kind and generous to Connie, perhaps because he understood that Connie wasn't as lucky as he was. She was smart, but he was smarter and better liked by his teachers. Connie was beautiful, but because she was a girl, this beauty was seen as a problem and not as a positive as it was for Toby. Connie's beauty required that she go to Merion Mercy, an all-girls Catholic school, instead of the super fun, incredibly social, less stringent public school that Toby attended. Connie's beauty led to boys sniffing around the house, none of whom her parents approved of.

When, in high school, Toby started drinking—going to keg parties out in the fields or stealing fifths of gin from their parents' liquor cabinet and drinking in the car on the way to South Street— it was treated as a rite of passage. When Connie started drinking, she was grounded for weeks, and she heard incessantly about the damage to her "reputation" from, of all people, her mother.

In general, growing up, Connie had resented Toby and worshipped him, hated him and wanted, more than anything, to *be* him.

Connie thought, *I have to tell him. Now.* But then Toby said, "How are you, Con? Are things any better?"

Are things any better? Connie didn't love the phrasing of this question, acknowledging as it did that things for Connie had been pretty bad. Well, they *had* been bad. Connie had been depressed about Wolf and about Ashlyn. But she resented the accusation that her life needed improvement—because, as an adult, Connie had been happy. She had the glowing marriage, the gracious home, the prestigious husband, the brilliant child.

"They're better," Connie said. The good news was, she could say this honestly.

"Are you seeing anyone?" Toby asked.

"Sort of," Connie said. She felt that as soon as she came right out and said, yes, she was seeing someone, the bubble would burst and Dan Flynn would vanish into thin air.

Because of the incident with Harold, her date with Dan had been overshadowed. But now she grew warm just thinking about it—Dan at dinner, holding her hand; Dan in bed, bringing her back to life. She felt Toby eyeing her.

" 'Sort of?' " he said. "What does that mean?"

They climbed into Connie's car, and Toby threw his duffel bag in the backseat. "It means yes, there's someone, but I don't know what's what yet, okay?"

Toby said, "Okay, sorry. Don't get all touchy on me."

"Oh, God," Connie said. She managed to fit the key in the ignition, but she didn't turn it. "There's something I have to tell you."

Toby raised his eyebrows at her. There was the look, so familiar, so condescending, as though he were sure she was about to make something out of nothing, typical female member of the family, drama queen like their mother. *Well, let's see then,* Connie thought. *Let's see how he likes it.*

"Meredith's at the house."

Yep, she got him. His eyes widened. The whole arrangement of his face changed. But she could tell he didn't quite believe her.

"You're fucking kidding me."

"Not kidding."

"Meredith Martin?"

"Meredith Delinn, yes."

Toby jerked his head, like he was trying to get water out of his ears. "She's..." He looked out the passenger-side window at the hot, shimmering grid of the town parking lot. "Wow."

"Yeah, I'm sorry," Connie said. "I was afraid if I told you, you wouldn't come."

"How long has she been staying with you?"

"All summer."

"You're fucking kidding me."

"Not kidding."

"So...I mean, the husband's in jail. So what is Meredith doing?"

"She's trying to figure out what to do. She's under investigation, I guess; she talks to her lawyer all the time. But the thing is... she's still *Meredith*."

"So you're telling me she didn't know what the husband was up to?"

"I'm telling you that, yes."

"I never met the guy."

"I think that was probably by design."

"But I could tell he was a class-A jerk. Typical Wall Street greedy banker hotshot."

"He was anything but typical," Connie said. And then, because it sounded like she was defending Freddy Delinn, she redirected the conversation. "So, are you okay with seeing Meredith?"

"Am I okay with seeing Meredith? Sure, of course." Toby's face was coloring. He was flustered.

"The last time you saw her was...?"

"Mom's funeral," Toby said. "And that ended badly. Are you sure Meredith is okay with seeing me?"

Connie rested her forehead against the top of the steering wheel. She turned on the car; she needed the air-conditioning. "She doesn't know you're coming."

Toby stared at her. "You're fucking kidding me."

"Not kidding." Connie backed out of her parking spot, thinking, *This whole situation is a tightrope walk.*

"Her head is going to spin," Toby said. "I hope you're ready."

"Don't flatter yourself," Connie said.

"I'm serious."

"After what we've been through this summer, seeing you will come as a very minor shock," Connie said. God, how she prayed this was true. She pulled out onto the road. "I'm sorry if that's a blow to your ego."

Connie spent her minutes on Milestone Road telling Toby about the highlights of the summer. Spray paint, slashed tires, Harold, their beloved seal, dead.

"You should have called me, Con," Toby said. "I would have come up sooner."

"We've been managing," Connie said.

"That sounds like a lie," Toby said.

"Only a partial lie," Connie said. She pulled into the driveway. "Here we are." Toby was looking at the front of the house. There was still a faint outline of the word *CROOK* on the shingles, but a few weeks of sun and sand had done its work. And Dan had used his power washer on the front porch to blast away all vestiges of Harold's blood and bodily fluids. All outward signs of terror had been wiped clean.

Toby adjusted his sunglasses and touched his hair, and with what sounded like a deep breath, he grabbed his old blue duffel bag out of the backseat. How did he feel? Did he have butterflies? Connie thought Toby might mask his nerves with small talk — *the house looks great* — but he was as silent as a monk.

When they walked in, Meredith was sitting at the head of the table. She saw them and stood up. She was wearing white shorts and a black tank top and she was in bare feet. Her hair was in a ponytail. She wasn't wearing any makeup, but her face was tan. She looked, graying hair aside, like she was sixteen years old— tiny and compact, a blue-eyed elf.

When she saw Toby, her eyes narrowed. She poked at her glasses, and Connie wanted to say, *Sorry, he's real.* Meredith looked at Connie, and then back at Toby. Connie had known Meredith since the age of four, but she had no idea how the woman was feeling right now.

Connie said, "Look who I found at the town pier."

Toby dropped his duffel and took a few strides toward her.

Meredith glared at Connie. "Do I seem like a woman who needs more surprise news?"

Toby stopped in his tracks.

Connie opened her mouth.

Meredith raised her face to the ceiling and let out a squawk. "Waaahhhhhh!!" Then she faced Toby. "Hello," she said.

He smiled nervously. "Hello, Meredith."

She took a baby step forward, and he opened his arms and they hugged. The hug was brief, but Connie thought it was real. Knowing each other for nearly fifty years counted for something. Connie wanted them both here, and somehow, by virtue of her own scatter-brained negligence, she had managed to get them in the same room.

She was proud of herself for that.

MEREDITH

Meredith felt the same way now that she'd felt at Connie's wedding. And Veronica's funeral. She couldn't bear to be near him; she only wanted to be near him. She was at a standoff with herself.

"How long are you staying?" she asked him.

"I don't know," he said. "How long are you staying?"

"I don't know," she said. She was angry enough at Connie to threaten to leave right that second—but where on earth would she go?

"Does anyone want lunch?" Connie asked brightly.

He looked good, but this only vexed Meredith further. She couldn't find her balance. There was so much she was dealing with already, and now Toby. Here, in person. He was wearing a green shirt and khaki shorts. His hair was the same, his face was the same but older, with lines and sun spots, but he was still a gorgeous golden lion of a man. Were they actually the same people who had kissed against the tree on Robinhood Road? Were they the same people who had made love in the Martin family library? There were two answers to that as well: They were. And they weren't.

"I'd love some lunch," Toby said.

"Meredith?" Connie asked.

"No, thanks," Meredith said. She could barely breathe, much less eat. "I might go up and lie down."

"Don't let me chase you away," Toby said.

"You're not..." Meredith wasn't quite sure what to say. *You're not chasing me away. You don't have the power to chase me away. You don't have power over me at all.* She was light-headed now. She said, "We've had a rough couple of days, as I'm sure Connie's told you. I'm exhausted."

"Stay down here with us," Connie said. She was already in the kitchen, toasting bread for sandwiches, slicing a lemon for the iced tea. "Even if you're not going to eat, come sit outside."

"You guys enjoy your lunch," Meredith said. "Catch up with each other. Do the brother-sister thing."

"Meredith," Connie said. "Stop it."

Toby put his hands on both her shoulders. Meredith closed her eyes and tried not to think. "Come out with us," he said. "Please."

The three of them sat at the outside table. Connie and Toby were eating sandwiches worthy of the front cover of *Bon Appétit.*

Meredith's stomach complained, but she would sustain her hunger strike. She sipped at her iced tea. Her back was to the ocean. She couldn't stand to look at the water. Thoughts of Harold with his throat slit, blood everywhere, as thick and viscous as an oil spill, pervaded.

"So...I'm here because I sold my boat," Toby said.

Meredith nodded.

"I've had her almost twenty years, so it was hard," he said. "But I tell myself that, ultimately, she was just a thing."

Just a thing. Well, Meredith could identify there. She had lost so many things: the Range Rover, the Calder mobile, the Dior gown. Did she miss any of them? Not one bit.

"It's hard imagining you without a boat," Connie said.

Meredith nodded again. Whenever she'd thought of Toby over the years, she'd thought of him in the cockpit of a sailboat, ropes in hand, the sun on his face. She'd thought of him toting all of his worldly possessions in the very same blue duffel bag he'd walked into the house with today. His parents had given him that duffel bag when he graduated from high school; Meredith had been sitting right beside him when he opened it. Little did she know then, it would become a symbol for Toby's life: He wanted to be able to carry everything he owned with him in that bag, so that he was free to get up and leave, move on to a new place, new people. No commitments.

But yes, one commitment, right?

"Tell me about your son," Meredith said.

"Michael is ten now," Toby said. "He lives in New Orleans with his mother and her new husband."

"Ten is the best age," Meredith said. All of her ached: her past, her present, her future. Because, suddenly, there were her memories of Leo and Carver at ten. Leo had asked Meredith and Freddy for a pair of Ray-Ban sunglasses, and Freddy had made him earn the hundred and thirty-nine dollars by doing jobs for Father Morrissey at the church. Meredith had gone to check on him and found him on his hands and knees, scraping candle wax off the wooden floors. Meredith had instinctively gotten down on her hands and knees to help, and Leo had said, *Don't, Mom. This is my job.* And reluctantly, Meredith had stood up and left him to it.

Carver had started surfing at age ten. He wore a leather choker with a white shell woven into it, and green and black board shorts that reached past his knees. Meredith could picture him so clearly—his young, tanned back, the emerging muscles under the smooth, clear skin of a boy, a boy whose voice had yet to change, a boy who still called her Mommy.

Mommy! Watch me!

"How old are your sons now?" Toby asked.

"Leo is twenty-six and Carver is twenty-four. They're in Connecticut. Leo has a girlfriend named Anais."

Toby nodded. The shirt made his eyes look very green.

Mommy! Watch me!

"Leo was working for Freddy, and he was under investigation for months. But my lawyer called a couple of days ago to say he's been cleared."

"That's good news," Toby said.

"The best news," Connie said. She swatted Toby. "Leo's my godson, remember."

"I'm sure you did a great job with the spiritual guidance through this crisis, Aunt Connie," Toby said.

"I was a basket case about it," Meredith said. "Your kids come first, you know."

"I know," Toby said.

"I'm still under investigation, however," Meredith said. She smiled weakly. "So enjoy me now, because I might be whisked off to jail at any moment."

"Meredith," Connie said.

"I don't mean to be maudlin. We've been having a pretty good summer, considering."

"Except for the dead seal," Toby said.

"Harold," Meredith said. "He was like our pet and they murdered him."

"And don't forget the slashed tires and the spray paint," Connie said. "Meredith spent the first part of the summer hiding inside."

"Wow!" Toby said. "There's a lot to talk about, but it's all really painful!"

Meredith stood up. Every time he opened his mouth, she thought about what had happened at Veronica's funeral. It made her dizzy. "I'm going upstairs to nap," she said.

"Please stay," Connie said.

"I can't," Meredith said. She realized this sounded harsh, so she said, "I can hardly keep my eyes open."

"Okay," Connie said. "If you're sure." She reached for Meredith's hand. Connie was being very sweet. Certainly she was worried that Meredith would be mad. Was Meredith mad? She was something. She needed time to process this.

She went upstairs to her bedroom, and cracked open the doors of her Romeo and Juliet balcony. She could hear the murmur of Toby's and Connie's voices. What were they saying? Meredith wanted to know. She stood in the stripe of sunlight between the doors and listened. Connie said, "Well, you didn't show up at Chick's funeral..."

"...always felt bad about that. But I was a kid..."

Meredith flopped on the bed. Her memories of Toby and her father were all jumbled up. One moment, she'd had them both. She lost one first, then the other, and like that, her childhood ended. She thought about her father and Toby in the front yard raking leaves, or in the den watching football. She thought about her father taking Toby aside for "the talk." *Respect my daughter. Be a gentleman.* She thought about Chick inviting Toby to sit in on the poker game and how thrilled Toby was to be included. It had been his passage into manhood. She thought about Chick and Toby heading off to the roast-beef station during brunch at the Hotel du Pont. She thought about her graduation from Merion Mercy. She had stood at the podium to deliver her salutatorian's speech, and when she gazed out at the audience, she found Veronica and Bill O'Brien, Toby, and her father and mother, all in a row. She'd day-dreamed about her wedding day at that moment. Her inevitable marriage to Toby. But less than twenty-four hours later, Toby had packed up his proverbial bag and announced that he was moving on, leaving Meredith behind. Meredith remembered the driving lessons with her father in the gathering dusk of the Villanova park-ing lot. The smell of hot asphalt and cut grass, the shouts of the few university students who remained for the summer, the unbearable knowledge that Toby was at the beach, and that the mainsail and the jib and his freedom were more important to him than she was. Chick Martin had said, "I can't stand to see you hurt like this," and at a loss for further words, he'd played the Simon and Garfunkel song over and over again. *Sail on Silvergirl, Sail on by.*

Meredith sat up. She couldn't sleep. She yanked her lone card-board box from the closet and unfolded the flaps. On top were the photographs. Meredith pulled out the one of her and Freddy at the Dial holiday formal. They looked like kids. Freddy had weighed 165 pounds, and his black curly hair went past his shirt collar. There was a picture from their wedding day. Freddy's hair was cut short then, in the manner of all stockbrokers. Those were the days of his first suit from Brooks Brothers, a huge extravagance. For their wedding, he'd rented a tux. When federal marshals stormed their penthouse on the first of July, they would have found six tuxedos and fourteen dinner jackets in Freddy's closet.

Meredith could have spent all day on the photos, but she was looking for something else. She dug down to the paperback novels that were on top of the boys' yearbooks that were on top of the copy of her Simon and Garfunkel album. Meredith pulled out the record sleeve and there, in her father's handwriting, it said: *For my daughter, Meredith, on her sixteenth birthday. You always have been and always will be my Silver Girl. Love, Dad, October 24, 1977.*

She'd had her wedding to Toby all planned. Her first dance with Toby was going to be to "The Best of Times," and her dance with her father was going to be to "Bridge Over Troubled Water."

Meredith stared into the dim, nearly empty closet. She couldn't remember what song she and Freddy had danced to at their wedding. Freddy didn't care much about music. Freddy only cared about money.

And yet, years and years later, he'd bought her a star and he'd named it Silver Girl, after the song. It had always bothered Meredith that he named the star Silver Girl—because he never knew her father, and he'd never heard her father play that song for her. The name and the song and the story were Meredith's, Freddy was only a guest to it, and yet in buying that star, he co-opted the song and made it his own. He stole the name from Meredith in order to give it back to her as something else.

Meredith rummaged through the cardboard box to the bottom, where she found a manila envelope that held her important documents. She had taken only the lasting things: the children's birth certificates, her marriage license, her Princeton diploma—and, for some reason, the certificate for her star. She pulled it out. It was on official-looking cream-colored paper and it said "NASA" across the top.

She had received the star for her forty-fifth birthday. Freddy had booked a private room at Daniel. He had invited thirty people—New York friends only—Samantha and Trent Deuce, Richard Cassel and his new girlfriend (young), Mary Rose Garth and her new boyfriend (younger), their favorite neighbors from the building, and some people that Meredith and Freddy didn't know all that well but whom Fred had probably invited in order to fill the room. The dinner had been elegant, everyone else got bombed on the extraordinary wines, but Meredith stuck to her glass and a half of red, and Freddy stuck to mineral water. And yet, he had been more effusive than usual, a manic, overeager master of ceremonies. Something was happening after the meal, Meredith picked up on that, and it had to do with her birthday present. Meredith experienced a flutter of curiosity; for her fortieth birthday, Freddy had arranged for Jimmy Buffett to sing to her on the beach in Saint Barth's. She thought this year would be something like that—Elton John, Tony Bennett. They had all the tea in China and so purchasing gifts for each other was a challenge. What could Freddy give her that would be creative and meaningful and unique, that she wouldn't just go out and buy for herself?

Right after Meredith blew out her candles, Freddy chimed his spoon against his water glass.

"Attention, attention!" Everyone quieted down to listen.

"It's Meredith's birthday," Freddy said. He mugged, the room chuckled. Meredith thought about the things she really wanted. She wanted her children to be happy and successful. She wanted more time with Freddy. She remembered looking up at his salt and pepper curls, his piercing blue eyes, his fine-cut suit, and thinking, *I never see this man. I never spend time alone with him.* She remembered hoping that her present was everyone else in the room going home.

But no. There was some elaborate presentation of an envelope on a silver tray by one of the waiters, which Freddy opened with the nervous suspense of an Oscar presenter, and he announced that he had bought his wife, Meredith Martin Delinn, a star in Bode's Galaxy. He had named the star "Silver Girl," after a song Meredith's father had sung to her as a child.

Teenager, Meredith thought.

A star? she thought.

Where is Bode's Galaxy? she wondered.

"So when you look up in the sky," Freddy said, "you'll know that one of those stars out there belongs to Meredith."

He kissed Meredith and presented her with a certificate from NASA, and everyone in the room applauded, and the waiters moved around the room with star-shaped chocolate truffles and bottles of port from the year of Meredith's birth.

Meredith kissed Freddy and thanked him.

He said, "What do you think? I promise you are the only woman on the Upper East Side with her own star."

Meredith had kept the NASA certificate, although in truth, she had barely glanced at it. She was ambivalent about the name of the star, and she felt abashed at the grandiosity of the gesture, and in front of all those people, some of them perfect strangers. How much money had Freddy spent on this star? She wondered. A hundred thousand dollars? More? Wasn't it the equivalent of throwing money away, since the star wasn't something Meredith would ever see in this lifetime? Wasn't Freddy basically announcing that since they could afford anything on God's green earth, he had to move into the heavens to find a surprise for Meredith?

These things had all bothered Meredith, but what had bothered her the most was the way he'd acted. His posturing, his showmanship. There were times—and this was one of them—when Freddy came across as a charlatan, rolling into town with his cart of magic potions meant to cure this or that, tricking the innocent townspeople, disappearing with their money, leaving them with a handful of placebos and a vial of sugar water.

Meredith studied the certificate. There was no seal on it, nothing engraved or embossed. Meredith hadn't wondered about this at the time Freddy gave it to her, although now it seemed clear that this *wasn't* a NASA document at all—but, rather, something that Freddy had printed up himself on his computer. She shook the paper in fury. How had she not *seen* this? She hadn't studied the document closely at all. As with everything else Freddy told her, she'd accepted it on blind faith.

And now it was painfully clear that it was a fake. If she had only *looked at it,* if she had only *opened her eyes,* she would have seen that. This was something Freddy did himself on the computer. She wanted to rip up the certificate—*Goddamn you, Freddy!* She thought (zillionth and sixth). But it might be evidence. Meredith pulled out her cell phone and called Dev.

"I think I have it this time," she said. "Check for the name 'Silver Girl.'" Then she caught herself. "Or, that may be the name of a star registered with NASA."

"Huh?" Dev said.

"Freddy said he bought me a star," Meredith said. "But now I think he was lying about it." Of course, he was lying about it: the certificate had been printed on ivory cotton bond paper, the same paper Freddy kept in his office.

"When was this?" Dev asked.

"Two thousand and six," she said. "Did you find Thad Orlo?"

"I'm not allowed to say," Dev said.

"Not allowed to say? I gave you the information."

"We're getting closer, we think," Dev said.

Meredith noted how he now included himself as a "we" with the Feds. "Well, use the name 'Silver Girl,' and cross-reference it with what you've already got. Or what the Feds have got."

"Does the certificate say anything else?" Dev said. "Does it have a number on it? The Feds are looking for account numbers. Preferably nine digits."

"Yes, it has a number," Meredith said. In the upper-right corner, in Freddy's own handwriting, was a number—ten figures, not nine, and three of the figures were letters. In Freddy's own handwriting, in Flair pen. This was it, this was a real clue, this stupid star, her supposed *birthday present!* Freddy had hidden information here. He had given the information to her, but had he ever expected her to figure it out? God, Meredith was a dismal failure at seeing what was right there in front of her face. Meredith read the number off to Dev. "Zero, zero, zero, four, H,N, P, six, nine, nine."

He said, "Do those numbers mean anything to you?"

"Nope," Meredith said.

"It's probably just an account number from the bank. Maybe one of the zeros is extraneous; maybe one of the numbers is a dummy number. Thank you for this, Meredith. This is good stuff."

"But you don't know for sure if it's good stuff," Meredith said. "The Feds have to check it out, right? But can you please tell them I'm trying?"

"Oh, Meredith," he said. "We all know you're trying."

CONNIE

Meredith and Toby had been under Connie's roof for nearly twenty-four hours—and was it awkward?

Yes.

There had been a strained exchange at lunch. Meredith had lasted ten or twelve minutes before she went to hide out upstairs.

Toby had said, "Should I just leave? I have an open-ended ticket back to BWI. I can go anytime."

Connie said, "You just got here. I haven't seen you in aeons. I want you to stay."

"Okay," Toby said uncertainly.

"She'll get over it," Connie said.

"You think?" Toby said.

When Meredith descended at five o'clock, she looked even more unglued than she had at noon.

Connie said, "Everything okay?"

Meredith turned on her. "Okay?" she said.

"I'm sorry," Connie said. "I didn't mean to spring it on you. I honestly didn't think he'd show. You know how unreliable he is."

"That I do."

At that moment, Toby materialized out of nowhere. "Who's unreliable?" he said.

They had to do something about dinner. Connie didn't feel like cooking, Meredith didn't want to go out, Dan called to say he was spending the night at home with his boys but that he'd come by in the morning to take the three of them to Great Point. Connie told Meredith this. Meredith had been talking about going to Great Point for weeks, but Meredith just frowned and said, "Fine."

They decided to order pizza with sausage and onion, which was the kind of pizza they'd eaten all through high school. If Connie closed her eyes, she could see their booth at Padrino's, herself and Matt Klein on one side, Meredith and Toby on the other, the pitcher of birch beer and four brown pebbled plastic glasses between them, Orleans on the jukebox singing "You're Still the One."

Connie whipped up a salad, and when the pizza came, they sat down to eat. But the conversation was stilted; Meredith was off in her own thoughts someplace. It was as different from Connie's memories of Padrino's as a dinner could be.

Not to be defeated, Connie suggested that they go into the sitting room to watch a movie. Was this too obvious? How many hundreds of movies had the three of them watched together in the O'Brien basement? Toby was game, and Meredith agreed reluctantly. Connie took the easy chair and Toby sat on the sofa, and Meredith glanced at the spot on the sofa next to Toby. Toby patted the cushion. "Come sit here."

But Meredith said, "I'll be fine on the floor." She sat cross-legged on the Claire Murray rug, her back straight, her chin high. Annabeth Martin's influence, or all that diving.

Connie said, "Meredith, you *can't* be comfortable."

Meredith said, "I'm fine."

They deliberated over which film to watch, which was to say that Connie and Toby deliberated with the understanding that whatever they picked, Meredith would deem it "fine." They had agreed on *The Shawshank Redemption,* but then at the last minute, Toby cried out, "Oh, no, let's watch *Animal House.*"

Very slowly, Meredith turned to him. "You're kidding, right?"

"Come on," he said. "Don't you remember?"

"Yes," Meredith said. "I do remember." And then, slowly as smoke, she rose and drifted out of the room. "Good night," she said, once she was on the stairs. "I'm going to bed."

Connie waited until she heard the door of Meredith's bedroom click. "Do I even ask?"

"First date," he said.

"Why are you torturing her?" Connie said.

"I'm not torturing her," he said. "I thought she'd find it funny."

"Yeah, she was just cracking up."

Toby said, "So what happened between the two of you?"

"What happened between the two of *you?*" Connie said.

"Work in progress," Toby said.

Connie shook her head.

Toby said, "I know the two of you had a big fight. I noticed she didn't show up at Wolf's funeral, but you never told me what happened. And I was too much of a drunk to ask."

"It's water under the bridge," Connie said.

"Tell me," Toby said.

"Oh..." Connie said. She hadn't talked to anyone about her fight with Meredith except for Wolf. Ashlyn and Iris and her friend Lizbet knew there had been a rift, but Connie hadn't wanted to share the details. It was nobody's business, and the break from Meredith had been exquisitely painful. But Connie was sick to death of taboo subjects. If she had told Dan what happened with Ashlyn at the funeral, then she could tell Toby about her phone call with Meredith.

"A few months before Wolf died," Connie said—Wolf had still been working, but the doctors weren't pulling any punches; this was it, Wolf wouldn't be getting any better—"he scrutinized all of our financial paperwork." Wolf had pored over the statements and stock reports for most of a Sunday afternoon, and Connie remembered feeling annoyed and churlish. It had been a glorious September day, and she had wanted to go for a walk with Wolf while he was still able, but he was tied to the paperwork spread out all over the dining-room table. They should go out and embrace the day; they had Gene, their accountant, to worry about the finances, didn't they? Wolf had long since given up reading—the effort made his eyes ache—and even at job sites, he had an assistant read him the measurements off the plans. So how much of those columns of figures did Wolf understand? But he was determined. Connie went for the walk by herself and came home watery eyed and sneezing from hay fever.

"Wolf asked me to sit down. He presented me with a pile of statements from Delinn Enterprises, which had been printed on a dot-matrix printer. I had never laid eyes on the actual statements before. I said to Wolf, 'Jesus, we should donate these to the Smithsonian.'"

We're going to pull this money out tomorrow, Wolf said.

What?

Get out of Freddy's thing. Gene loves it, but he can't explain to me how it's done, and in all the years I've known Freddy, he's never been able to explain it to me in any way that makes sense.

It's black magic, Connie had said lightly. This was Freddy's answer whenever someone asked him about the formula for such fantastic returns, even in years when there was a down market.

It's black all right, Wolf said. *I'm sure he's breaking the law.*

Freddy?

Yes, Freddy. I like the guy; I've always liked him. God knows, he's generous to a fault. And I love Meredith and the boys, but something isn't right with that business. Whatever he's doing, the SEC is going to catch him, but we're not waiting around for that to happen. We're getting out of this tomorrow.

Tomorrow? Really? Don't you want to talk to Gene about it before . . .

Connie. Wolf had put his hand over her hand and tried to look at her, but his gaze had been off, as it occasionally was then. He couldn't always focus. Connie's eyes had filled with hot tears that had nothing to do with ragweed. She was losing him. The liquidation of the Delinn Enterprises account was one step taken in preparation for Wolf's death. *We're getting out of that fund tomorrow.*

Okay, Connie said, though she was skeptical. The returns were so good and they had been so lucky to be allowed to invest when so many others had been turned away. But she had backed Wolf on more radical decisions that this; she would back him now. *Do you think Freddy will be mad?*

Mad? Wolf said. He had seemed amused by this idea. *We only have three million in our account. That's a drop of water in the ocean of Delinn Enterprises. Freddy won't even notice.*

"But as it turned out," Connie said to Toby, "Freddy *did* notice. He left messages at Wolf's office—and then once he found out that Wolf was on-site all the time, he ambushed Wolf's cell phone." But Connie had only discovered this days later when, reaching a point of extreme frustration, Freddy called the house.

Pulling out your money? Freddy ranted. *What the hell?*

Freddy had sounded livid, which perplexed Connie. It was only $3 million. Why did he care? She said, *We have so little money with you. Compared to other clients of yours, I mean. You won't miss us.*

Won't miss you? Freddy said. *Do you know how proud I am to be able to tell people that Washington architect Wolf Flute is a client of mine? I have hundreds of clients in Hollywood—I have Clooney's money and Belushi family money—but I get more pleasure out of mentioning Wolf Flute's name than anybody else's.*

Really? Connie said. She hadn't known how to react to this. Freddy wanted Wolf to stay invested so Freddy could drop his name and lure other architects, or other prominent Washingtonians, to invest? Could this possibly be true? And if it were true, would Wolf be flattered or annoyed?

"So I hung up with Freddy, promising that Wolf would call to explain. Wolf then told me that he didn't want to explain. It was a free country, he said, and he was pulling our money out of Delinn Enterprises. I had no choice but to throw the Meredith friendship card. And Wolf told me that if I was worried about what Meredith thought, I would have to call her myself."

"So what did you do?" Toby asked.

"I called her," Connie said.

Meredith had answered on the first ring, as though she had been standing around her apartment waiting for the call.

Meredith?

Constance.

You heard?

I heard something, Meredith said. *But I didn't believe it.*

Connie had sighed. She had hoped that Meredith would make this easier. She had hoped that Meredith would take the news in stride and do her part to smooth things over with Freddy. *Wolf really felt we had to pull our money.*

That's what Freddy told me. But why?

Well, Connie said. Did she tell Meredith the truth here? Certainly not. *I don't know why, exactly.*

You're lying to me, Constance, Meredith said.

I'm not lying, Connie said. *Wolf has his reasons, but I'm not sure what they are.*

Wolf is sick, Meredith said.

Connie raised her hackles. *Yes,* she said. *I know.*

He has brain cancer, Meredith said.

Well, that doesn't mean he's stupid, Connie said.

He's making a stupid mistake, Freddy says.

Of course, Freddy would say that, Connie said. *It's Freddy's fund. Freddy wants us to stay in. He made that perfectly clear.*

So then, what's the problem? Are the returns not good enough?

They're good enough, Connie said. *Wolf feels like they're too good.*

What does that mean? Meredith asked.

Our accountant can't explain how Freddy's doing it, Connie said. *Nobody can.*

Well, of course not, Meredith said. *Otherwise, they'd be doing it themselves. Freddy is a genius, Connie.* Here, Connie could mouth along to Meredith's words, they were so predictable. *He was an econ whiz at Princeton. He understands the market like nobody else. Do you know how many people who ask to invest with Freddy he turns down?*

Wolf thinks it smells funny, Connie admitted.

Smells funny? Meredith said. *Are you accusing my husband of something?*

I don't know, Connie said. She had used an apologetic voice when she said this. She used a please-don't-let-our-husbands'-business-tear-us-apart voice. *Wolf's just concerned.*

Because he thinks Freddy is breaking the law, Meredith said.

I said, I don't know.

You do know that Freddy works in a highly regulated industry?

Connie opened her mouth to speak, but Meredith said, *God, I HATE it when people call Freddy a crook. He's excellent at what he does, he's better at it than anyone else, and that makes him a crook?*

All I'm saying is that Wolf wants our money out. Connie's voice was tougher with that statement. She had never put herself up against Freddy in Meredith's eyes, and now, she could see, she was going to lose. If Meredith was going to champion Freddy, then fine—Connie would defend Wolf. She thought of sitting on Wolf's shoulders during the chicken fights at the Madequecham Jam. Hadn't she been ruthless? Hadn't they won every single time? *We want our money out. We want a check in the morning!*

A check in the morning? Meredith said. *So that's your decision? You're done with Freddy?*

Done with Delinn Enterprises, yes, Connie said. She said this to make a distinction between the business and the friendship. The awkward fact was that Connie and Wolf had a vacation planned to Cap d'Antibes with Meredith and Freddy two weeks hence. What would they do about that?

Meredith was the one to ask. *What about France?*

The trip to France would most likely be Wolf and Connie's last trip together, and Connie had been desperately looking forward to it. But how could they go to France now?

We're not coming to France, Connie said.

Here, Meredith paused. *You're not coming to France?*

I don't see how we can…now, Connie said. What she meant was: *How can we all sit around and eat pâté and drink wine when you've both made such a brouhaha about us pulling out our money? How can we accept hospitality from a man whom we've essentially labeled a crook?*

Meredith's voice was very quiet. Perhaps if they had both still been yelling, they would have resolved things differently. But Meredith took a resigned breath and said, *Okay, Connie, if that's the way you want to play it, fine. But you're making a big mistake.*

And Connie, incredulous that the Meredith she had known for over forty years, a woman she considered as close as a sister, would let their friendship asphyxiate because of money, said, *Actually, I don't think I am.*

I'll tell Freddy you want a check tomorrow, Meredith said.

Thank you, Connie said.

And they both hung up.

"And that was that?" Toby said.

"That was that," Connie said. "Weeks went by, then months, and I didn't hear from her. I kept thinking she would call to apologize."

"But you didn't call her to apologize," Toby said.

"What did *I* have to apologize for?" Connie said.

When Wolf died, Meredith sent flowers and wrote a $10,000

check to the American Cancer Society in Wolf's honor. Connie wrote to say thank you. She thought that maybe she and Meredith could mend the fence, but she didn't hear back from Meredith. Connie knew this was because of Freddy.

And then Wolf was proved right: Freddy was arrested. The Ponzi scheme was revealed.

"I'm lucky we got out when we did," Connie said. "If Wolf hadn't pulled our money, I would have been forced to sell the Nantucket house. And maybe the Bethesda house, too. I would have had nothing left."

She would have been just like Meredith.

The next day was Sunday, and as soon as Connie woke up, she called Ashlyn.

She was shuttled right into voice mail.

"Hi, honey, it's me," Connie said. "I'm still on Nantucket, and guess what? Uncle Toby is visiting!" Connie paused, as if waiting for Ashlyn to respond. For all Connie knew, Toby talked to Ashlyn on a regular basis. As desperately as Connie wanted news of her daughter, she couldn't bring herself to ask. "Anyway, call me back when you get this. I love you, Ashlyn. It's Mom."

Connie packed as carefully for their trip to Great Point as she might have for a trip to Paris. She wore a bathing suit and a sheer white cover-up that she hadn't worn since the summer Wolf was sick. Even with his failing eyesight, he'd said, *You look like an angel in that white dress, my love.* That comment alone had made Connie unwilling to wear the cover-up for anyone else. But now she saw how silly that was. The cover-up had been expensive, and it looked good on her. She would wear it. She packed her book, sunscreen, towels, and a sweater. In her overnight bag, she packed her toothbrush, face lotion, and her brush, a nightgown.

She packed food in the cooler, and a thermos of iced tea, but no wine. It would be fine. Of course, she could pack a bottle of wine and simply choose not to drink it—but who was she kidding? If the wine was there, she would be too tempted.

She heard a horn beeping outside. Dan!

"Dan, this is my brother, Toby. Toby, this is Dan Flynn."

"Dan the man!" Toby said, shaking Dan's hand.

Dan grinned. "Nice to meet you. You and Connie look alike."

"We do?" Connie said. She could see right away that everything was going to be fine. Toby was used to charming everyone he came in contact with, and Dan would be no exception. Dan and Toby were alike; they were men of the outdoors. Neither of them cared about money or prestige or about leaving behind a legacy. They cared about being free to do as they liked. They were a perfect match.

Dan kissed Meredith on the cheek. He said, "I like the way you did your hair."

Meredith was wearing a red baseball hat with sorority letters on it. It had been Ashlyn's, long abandoned to the dusty shelf of the front closet. Connie had initially been shocked to see Meredith wearing it, then she thought, *Oh, what the hell.* No more taboos. And Meredith seemed marginally more cheerful this morning.

"Thanks," Meredith said.

"I meant, no wig," Dan said.

"Wait a minute," Toby said. "Do you actually wear a wig?"

"I've been traveling incognito," Meredith said. "But not today."

Dan touched Meredith's shoulder. "You won't need a disguise today."

"Great Point!" Toby said, rubbing his hands together.

"Let's go!" Dan said.

They drove through the town of Sconset, stopping at the market for sandwiches and bags of chips, pretzels, and marshmallows. Connie had made a fruit salad, potato salad, and coleslaw, and Dan said he had the rest of their provisions covered.

The top was down on the strawberry Jeep, and the sun shone on the four of them as they drove out of Sconset along the Polpis Road, past Sankaty Lighthouse and the golf course, past the flat blue oval of Sesachacha Pond, to the Wauwinet turnoff. Here, the road grew winding and rural—there were farmhouses surrounded by open land, and then there was a thicket of green, leafy trees before they reached the gatehouse at the Wauwinet inn. Dan stopped the Jeep and hopped out to let the air out of the tires. Toby said, "Can I help?"

"I'd love it," Dan said. He tossed Toby the tire gauge and worked with the car key.

Connie was up front, Meredith directly behind her. Connie turned around and smiled at Meredith.

"You okay?" she said.

"Great," Meredith said. She had her big, dark sunglasses on, so Connie couldn't tell if this was a real "great" or a sarcastic "great."

Connie listened to the hiss of air escaping the tires. It was like a double date, she thought. Having Toby here balanced things out. She remembered her last double date with Meredith—and Wolf and Freddy—in the south of France. Freddy had arranged for a car trip to the picturesque village of Annecy. They had traveled in a 1956 Renault; they had a driver in a military-blue chauffeur cap who spoke only French. Meredith had been the one who communicated with him. Connie remembered being envious of Meredith's French and feeling angry at herself for taking four years of useless Latin. The four of them had gone to an elegant lunch at a Michelin-starred restaurant overlooking a lake. It was a place Meredith and Freddy went often; they knew the owner, a distinguished, olive-skinned gentleman in an immaculate suit. The man had reminded Connie of Oscar de la Renta; he had kissed Connie's hand and brought both her and Meredith glasses of rose champagne. Krug. The lunch must have cost five hundred euros, though no bill ever came to the table. It had been like that with Freddy and Meredith—you had these amazing experiences that just seemed to magically happen—though, of course, Freddy had paid for lunch somehow. The lunch had probably cost more like a thousand euros because there had been at least two bottles of the Krug. There had been lobster and mango salad, and microgreens with marinated artichokes that were grown at a local farm. There had been a whole poached fish with sauce on the side and these special potatoes braised in olive oil, and a cheese platter with figs and tiny champagne grapes. And then, at the end of the meal, chocolate truffles and espresso. It had been the lunch of a lifetime. Freddy, Connie remembered, had drunk only mineral water. He had sat at the head of the table, the undisputed king, ordering up this dish and that, while Connie and Wolf and Meredith grew giddy on the Krug. Freddy's tee-totaling, Connie saw now, had been a way of controlling them all. And hadn't this car trip to Annecy and this lunch occurred the day after Freddy had kissed Connie on the terrace? Yes, she remembered feeling Freddy's eyes on her during that lunch; she had felt his admiration and his desire. She had, if she could be perfectly honest, basked in it.

He had kissed her, touched her.

Connie nearly turned around to ask Meredith the name of that restaurant—it was the kind of thing one was meant to remember—but Connie decided she wouldn't bring it up. For all she knew, the owner of the restaurant had been an investor; for all she knew, the restaurant was now gone, one more casualty of Delinn Enterprises.

You are an incredibly beautiful woman, Constance.

The attendant from the gatehouse came out to check their beach sticker. He was an older gentleman with a gray buzz cut and a stern demeanor. Ex-military for sure. A retired lieutenant. That was who was needed for this job: someone who could keep the unregistered riffraff off the hallowed conservation acres of Great Point.

The attendant brightened when he saw Dan. "Hello there, young Flynn," he said. "How goes it this fine day?"

The two men shook hands.

"It goes," Dan said. He looked at Toby, then back at the Jeep. "These are some friends of mine…"

Be careful! Connie thought.

"From Maryland."

Toby, never one to shy from an introduction, offered his hand. "Toby O'Brien."

"Bud Attatash," the attendant said. He looked past Toby at the Jeep.

Don't introduce us! Connie thought.

"You ladies ready to go have some fun?" Bud asked.

Connie waved. She couldn't see what Meredith was doing.

"How is it up there today?" Dan asked. Connie thought, *Get in the car. Please, let's go.* But then she remembered that Dan's real job was to know everyone on this island and everything that went on. Clearly, he felt he had to take two minutes to chew the fat with Bud Attatash.

Bud said, "Well, it's August and the seals are finally off the point. They've made their way up the coast."

"It'll smell a lot better," Dan said.

"Got that right," Bud said. He scratched the back of his neck. His collar was as stiff as cardboard. "Hey, did you hear about a dead seal on the south shore? Murdered, they say. Dropped off special delivery for that Delinn woman."

Toby made a noise. Bud looked over.

Dan said, "Yes, I did hear about that. Awful stuff."

Connie's palms itched. Her shoulders were burning in the sun. She was afraid to turn around to check on Meredith. Toby, she saw, looked stricken. If he'd had three drinks in him, he would have socked Bud Attatash in the jaw.

"Awful is right," Bud said. "Killing an animal like that."

"Senseless violence," Dan said.

Get in the car! Connie thought. She cleared her throat. Toby read her mind and hopped into the backseat next to Meredith.

Dan took a step back with one foot but wasn't able to make the full commitment to leaving.

Bud said, "They'll never catch the guys who did it. That woman has too many enemies."

"It's a little more complicated than that, Bud," Dan said. "And if you don't believe me, you should talk to the chief about it." Even Dan seemed flustered now, and Connie felt a flash of irritation. How had he not been able to keep the conversation off this one topic? Jesus! "Well, we should be shoving off now."

"A poor, innocent sea creature," Bud said.

They pulled out onto the sand, leaving Bud Attatash in his khaki uniform staring after them at the gatehouse.

Dan said, "Sorry about that."

Nobody spoke. Connie checked on Meredith in the side-view mirror. Her expression, under the brim of the hat and behind the dark, saucer-size lenses of her sunglasses, was inscrutable.

"Bud is harmless," Dan said. "I've known him my whole life."

Again, no one spoke. Connie turned on the radio. It was a commercial, loud and grating. She pushed in the CD, thinking it would be the Beatles, but the music that came blaring out was even worse than the radio. Dan popped the CD back out with a proprietary air that made Connie feel like she shouldn't have presumed to touch the radio in the first place.

He said, "Sorry. I let Donovan borrow the car. That's his music."

Connie feared all the good karma she'd attached to this day was in danger of draining through the floorboards.

But the Jeep bounced over some bumps in the sand, and Toby whooped, and Connie was forced to grab hold of the roll bar. They drove past the last of the summer homes and headed out onto the pure sands of Great Point.

Suddenly, their silence seemed not due to the awkwardness with Bud Attatash back at the gatehouse but, rather, in deference to the stark beauty of the landscape around them. The sand up here was creamy white. The vegetation consisted of low-lying bushes—bayberry and sweet-scented *Rosa rugosa*. The ocean was a deep blue; the waves were gentler than the waves in Tom Nevers. In the distance, Connie saw Great Point Lighthouse. What was breathtaking was the purity of the surroundings. A few men were surf casting along the shore. Crabs scuttled past the seagulls and the oystercatchers.

Why had Connie never come out here before? The real answer, she supposed, was that the Flutes didn't come to Great Point; it wasn't in their repertoire of Nantucket excursions. Mrs. Flute, Wolf's mother, claimed she couldn't abide the thought of automobiles on the beach, but Wolf told Connie that what this really meant was that his parents—being stingy Yankee folk—didn't want to fork over the money for a beach sticker. (It had been seventy-five dollars back in the day; now, it was nearly twice that.)

Well, Connie thought, they had missed out. The place was a natural treasure.

Dan drove them through the sand tracks to the tip of the island. "There," he said. "You can see the riptide."

Toby stood up in his seat. "Man," he said. "Amazing."

Connie could see a demarcation in the water, a roiling, where the riptide was. This was the end of the island, or the beginning of it. The lighthouse was just behind them.

"Can we climb the lighthouse?" Meredith asked. She sounded a little closer to her normal self. Hopefully, she had chalked the encounter with Bud Attatash up to bad luck. More than anything, Connie wanted to keep Meredith happy.

"Yes, can we?" she asked Dan.

"We can," Dan said. He pulled the car around to the harbor side of the point and parked. There were sailboats scattered across the horizon.

They trudged through the hot sand toward the lighthouse. There was an antechamber with two wooden benches, but the door that led into the lighthouse was shut tight.

"You never used to know if the door would be locked," Dan said. He turned the knob.

"It's locked," Connie said. She was disappointed. She tried the knob herself.

"It's locked," Dan said. "But I have a key."

"You do?" Meredith said.

Dan pulled a key out of his pants pocket. It was the color of an old penny. "I've had this key since I was eighteen years old. Back then, the ranger out here was a man named Elton Vicar. And I dated his granddaughter, Dove Vicar."

"Dove?" Connie said.

"Dove stole this key from Elton and gave it to me, and I was smart enough to hold on to it. Because I knew it would come in handy someday."

"Are you sure it still works?" Connie said. How could a key that Dan had had for thirty years still work?

Dan slid the key into the knob. He had to wiggle it, but he fit it in and turned the knob and the door opened. "They'll never change the lock. Too much trouble. Plus, they have no reason to."

"So are we doing something illegal, then?" Meredith asked. She sounded nervous.

"Relax," Dan said. "The crime was committed long ago, by Dove Vicar, who is now Dove Somebody Else, living somewhere in New Mexico."

"But aren't we breaking and entering?" Meredith said.

"We have a key!" Dan said, and he stepped inside.

Connie had never been inside a lighthouse before, but this one was about what she expected. It was dark and dingy with a sandy concrete floor; it smelled like somebody's root cellar. In the middle of the room was a wrought-iron spiral staircase and Dan began marching up. Connie followed, thinking, *I am dating the only man on Nantucket with a key to the Great Point Lighthouse.* Meredith was behind Connie, and Toby brought up the rear. Connie watched her step; the only light was filtering down in dusty rays from above.

At the top of the stairs, there was a room of sorts—a floor and windows and a case that held the reflecting light, which was powered by solar panels.

Toby was impressed. "How long ago was this built?"

"Originally in seventeen eighty-five," Dan said. "Reconstructed in nineteen eighty-six."

There was a narrow balcony that encircled the top. Connie and Meredith stepped out and walked around the outside. Connie could see all the way across Nantucket Sound to Cape Cod. To the south, the island was spread out before them like a blanket— the houses and trees and ponds, sand dunes and dirt roads. Connie had been coming to Nantucket for twenty years, but today might have been the first day she truly saw it.

Dan parked the Jeep on the harbor side, and they unfolded chairs and laid out towels.

"This," Connie said, "is a breathtaking spot. Isn't it breathtaking, Meredith?"

Meredith hummed. "Mmmhmmm."

Dan opened a beer. "Does anybody want a drink?"

Connie said, "Toby, I brought iced tea."

Toby held up a hand. "I'm fine right now, thanks."

Dan said, "Meredith, how about you?"

"I'm all set."

"Connie?" Dan said. "Can I pour you a glass of wine?"

"I brought iced tea," she said.

"Really?" he said. "No wine?"

"Really," Connie said. She put on a wide-brimmed straw hat that she'd bought to keep the sun off her face but that she never bothered to wear. Time to start taking care of herself. Wear a hat, leave the chardonnay at home. "I'll have an iced tea."

"Okay," Dan said. He sounded surprised.

Toby said, "Meredith, do you want to go for a walk?"

Meredith said, "Connie, do you want to go for a walk?"

Connie said, "Not just yet. You two go."

Meredith didn't move. She said, "I'll wait for Connie."

Toby said in a very adult, very serious voice Connie couldn't remember ever hearing him use before, "Meredith, come for a walk with me. Please."

Meredith sat, still as a stone. "No," she said.

Connie thought, *Is today going to be a total disaster?*

Toby walked off in silence. Connie watched him go. Then, a few seconds later, Meredith got to her feet, and Connie thought, *Oh, thank God.* But Meredith took off in the opposite direction.

Dan settled in a chair next to Connie. He had a copy of *The Kite Runner* in his lap. "So, do I dare ask? What's their deal?"

"Oh, God," Connie said. "I have no idea."

"You have no idea?"

When Connie looked at Dan, she was overwhelmed by how little she knew him—and she was overwhelmed by how little he knew her. How did it happen, getting to know someone? It took time. It took days spent together, weeks, months. The thought of all the effort it would take to get to know Dan and to have Dan know her suddenly seemed exhausting. Why had she not just brought the wine? Everything was so much easier with wine.

"Meredith and Toby dated in high school," Connie said.

"Ah," Dan said, as if this explained everything. But how could he possibly understand?

"They were madly in love," Connie said. "It was irritating."

Dan laughed. "Irritating?"

"Well, you know, he was my brother; she was my best friend…"

"You felt left out?"

"Sort of, yes. At first, I was really bothered by it. I nearly put an end to it—I had the power to do that, I think, at least with Meredith. But I grew used to the idea, and I had boyfriends, too, always…"

"That doesn't surprise me," Dan said.

"So we used to double date. We went to the movies and to

dances at Radnor High School, where Toby went. We went roller skating." Connie laughed. It *was* funny thinking about her and Meredith and Toby and Matt Klein at the roller rink with the disco ball spinning, creating spots of multicolored light. They skated to Queen and Lynyrd Skynyrd and Earth, Wind & Fire. Connie and Meredith skated backward—they had spent hours practicing this in Meredith's basement—and Toby and Matt rested their hands on the girls' hips. Connie and Meredith both had feathered hair; they kept plastic combs in the back pockets of their designer jeans. Between skates, the four of them would sit at the plastic tables in the snack bar and drink suicides and eat bad nachos. "But, I don't know, my boyfriends were always just guys to pass the time with. Meredith and Toby were different. They were in love. They were very vocal about that, very smug about it."

"Irritating," Dan agreed.

"And then once I'd pretty much embraced the fact that they were probably going to get married and have five kids, Toby broke up with her."

"Did something happen?"

"He was nineteen years old, going off to college, and he wanted his freedom. Meredith was a wreck. I was surprised by that. She was always so tough, you know, so cool, and...impervious, like nothing could affect her. But when Toby broke up with her, she crumbled. She cried all the time, she leaned on her parents a lot, she was very close with her father...I remember right after it happened, I tried to take her mind off him, and it backfired."

Dan leaned forward. "Really? What happened?"

"I had been invited to this party at Villanova, and I convinced Meredith to go with me. I had to beg her, but she agreed, and once we got there, she started drinking this red punch. Kool-Aid and grain alcohol."

"Oh, God," Dan said.

"And the next thing I knew, everyone else in the room was jumping up and down to the Ramones, and Meredith was slumped over on the couch. Passed out. Dead weight." What Connie didn't say was that there was a minute or two when Connie had feared Meredith was actually dead. Connie had screamed until someone shut off the music. And then another partygoer, who claimed he was pre-med, determined that Meredith was breathing and had a pulse. Then the music was cranked back up, and it became Connie's responsibility to get Meredith out of there. "The problem was that we had walked to the party," Connie said. For the preceding two years, Toby had been their ride everywhere. Connie had failed her driver's test three times, and Meredith was still learning how to drive from her father, but Meredith spent more time crying than driving. "So my options were to call my parents for a ride, call Meredith's parents for a ride, or try to get Meredith home on my own."

"So...?" Dan said.

So, Connie's parents were always drunk themselves and could offer no assistance. And Connie hadn't wanted to call the Martins because they truly believed that Meredith hung the moon, and Connie couldn't stand the thought of being the one to inform them that their daughter was a human being, an eighteen-year-old girl with a broken heart and some pretty typical self-destructive impulses. And she couldn't call Toby.

"I carried her home," Connie said. "On my back."

Dan hooted. "You're kidding me."

Yes, it sounded funny—anyone who heard the story always laughed—but it hadn't been funny at the time. It had been sad—a sad, difficult, poignant night in Connie and Meredith's shared experience of growing up. Connie had managed to rouse Meredith enough to get her to cleave onto Connie's back. Connie held Meredith's legs, and Meredith wrapped her arms around Connie's neck, and rested the hot weight of her head on Connie's shoulder. How many times had they stopped so that Meredith could throw up? How long and loudly had Meredith cried because of Toby? And Connie thought, *Why do you need Toby when I'm right here?* But she held her tongue. She rubbed Meredith's back.

I know, I know it hurts, I know.

Connie knew where the Martins kept their extra key, and she knew the alarm code for the house. She got Meredith upstairs into her own bed without waking up Chick or Deidre. Connie filled the bathroom cup with water and put three Excedrin on Meredith's nightstand, where, Connie saw, Meredith still kept a picture of herself and Toby from Toby's prom at Radnor. Connie turned the picture facedown and whispered to Meredith's sleeping form that everything was going to be fine.

The epilogue to that story, which Connie didn't like to think about now, was that the following January, Meredith sent Connie a letter from Princeton. The letter said, *Guess what? You were right. I am going to be fine! I've met an amazing guy. His name is Fred.*

Meredith returned from her walk with a handful of shells that she set in a row along the edge of her towel like a prepubescent girl.

She gave Dan a teensy smile. "It's lovely here. Thank you for bringing us."

Dan said, "Meredith, you're welcome."

Connie thought, *Things are improving.*

Toby returned a little while later with an armload of driftwood, which he dropped in a noisy pile a few inches from where Meredith lay.

"For a fire," he said. "Later."

"Great!" Connie said.

Toby nudged Meredith's shoulder with his big toe. "You missed a great walk," he said.

"No, I didn't," Meredith said. "I took a great walk. I went that way."

Toby eyeballed her a second, then shook his head.

Connie closed her eyes and thought, *Things are not improving.* She thought, *Okay, the two of you don't have to fall back in love, no one expects that, but can't you be friends? And if you can't manage to be friends, could you at least be civil?*

Meredith stood up. "I'm going for a swim."

"Me, too," Toby said.

Meredith whipped around. "Stop it, Toby," she said.

Toby laughed. "The ocean is big enough for both of us."

"No," Meredith said. "I don't think it is." She waded in, and when the water was at her hips, she dove under. She was as natural to the water as a porpoise. Toby dove in after her, and Connie thought, *God, Toby, leave the woman alone.* But he swam right up to her and snapped the strap of her black tank suit, and Meredith splashed him in the face and said, "Get some new tricks."

And he said, "What's wrong with my old tricks?"

Meredith said, "What's *wrong* with your old tricks? Do I really need to answer that?" But if Connie wasn't mistaken, her voice was a little more elastic, and that was all Toby would need to wiggle into her good graces. Meredith swam down the shoreline, and Toby took off after her, undeterred.

"That looks like fun," Dan said. He stood up to join them, and Connie followed, although she hated being pressured into the water. But the water here was warm and shallow. Connie floated on her back and felt the sun on her face. Dan encouraged her out a little deeper where he cradled her in his arms and sang a James Taylor song in her ear. "Something in the Way She Moves." He had a wonderful voice—he was good enough to be a real singer—and Connie loved the buzz in her ear. When he finished, she said, "You are the man with the key."

"The key to what?" he said.

The lighthouse, silly! she nearly said. But instead, she said, "The key to my heart."

He seemed pleased by this. "Am I now?" he said.

She nodded. Then she felt guilty. Wolf! Wolf was the man with the key to her heart. It was foolish to believe she could love anybody else like that.

She swam back to shore.

*   *   *

After lunch, Meredith curled up on her blanket and fell asleep. Toby leaned forward in his chair and watched the sailboats in the distance. Connie wondered if he was thinking about *Bird's Nest.* Of course he was. She had been more than a boat; she had been, for Toby, a home. As Connie was studying him—she wanted to say something, though she wasn't sure what—she saw him cast his eyes at Meredith. He gazed at her for a long couple of seconds, and Connie thought, *Oh, boy.*

Dan pushed himself up out of his chair. "I'm going to fish for a little while. Connie?"

"I'll pass."

Toby hopped to his feet. "I'd love to join you."

Connie watched her lover and her brother amble down the beach with their fishing poles. Meredith's breathing was audible; she was fast asleep. Connie wondered what she was dreaming about. Did she dream about her sons or Freddy or Connie or her attorney or the angry woman at the salon? Did she dream about Toby, and if so, was it Toby at eighteen, or Toby now, at fifty-one? Connie's eyes drifted closed. She heard Dan singing a song without words, she felt the breeze lift the brim of her straw hat, she wondered if seals went to heaven and decided they probably did.

When she woke, it was because Toby was shouting about a fish. Dan yelled up the beach, "It's a keeper!" Connie squinted at them. Meredith was still asleep. Connie decided to walk over and be impressed. She recognized the dark markings on the scales—a striped bass. Big one.

Dan said, "Now *that's* a beauty."

Toby said, "The sea has always provided for me."

Connie looked at Dan. "Are we going to eat it?"

"I brought my filet knife," he said. "And a bottle of olive oil and my Lawry's seasoned salt. I knew we'd catch something. We'll cook it over the fire."

Connie smiled and kissed her brother on the cheek. "Hunter-gatherer," she said. "Meredith will be so impressed."

They played horseshoes, and Dan won handily. They played Wiffle ball, and Connie hit the ball over everyone's heads into the eelgrass and they couldn't find it again. Although this ended their game prematurely, Dan was impressed by the hit, and Connie beamed.

Toby said, "You should have seen her play field hockey. She was a killer."

Connie and Dan went for a walk and stopped to kiss, which got so heated at one point, Connie thought they might...there was no one around, so...but Dan pulled away. He said, "If Bud comes driving around and sees us, he won't like it."

"Does Bud come driving around?" Connie asked.

"Oh, sure," Dan said, and he nibbled on Connie's ear.

The sun was setting. When Connie and Dan got back to the camp, Toby had dug a pit with a shovel he'd found in the back of Dan's Jeep. He piled in the wood and used the paper from their sandwich wrappings to start a fire. He was a man with survival skills. Two failed marriages, a lifelong battle with alcohol, a little boy he didn't see enough of. Connie had buried a husband and lost a daughter; Dan had buried a wife and lost a son. Meredith — well, Meredith had experienced difficulty the likes of which Connie couldn't begin to imagine. And yet, despite all of this collective suffering, the four of them gathered around the growing heat and light of the bonfire, and let it warm them.

God, human beings are resilient, Connie thought.

We are resilient!

Dan filleted the bass, and Connie set out cheese and crackers on a plate. Toby and Meredith were sitting side by side on the blanket, not touching, not talking, but they were definitely coexisting more peacefully now. Or was she imagining this?

It was high school over and over and over again.

There was a noise. Connie looked up to see a forest-green pickup truck coming their way. Although it had been a nearly perfect day, they had seen very few people—a couple of lone fishermen on foot, a handful of families in rental Jeeps who approached their spot then backed up, for fear of infringing. But this truck drove toward the camp, then stopped suddenly, spraying sand on Toby and Meredith's blanket. There was white writing on the side of the truck. *Trustees of the Reservation.* A man poked his head out the window. He was wearing a green cap. It was Bud Attatash.

He stepped out of the truck. "You folks doing all right?"

Dan was monitoring the progress of the striped bass on the grill. He said, "We're doing great, Bud. Couldn't have asked for a better day."

"I'll agree with you there," Bud said. He stood with his hands in his pockets, an uncomfortable air about him. He hadn't come to talk about the weather. Was he upset about the grill? Or about the fire? Dan had gotten a fire permit; it was in the glove compartment of the Jeep. Was he going to scold them for having an open container? One open beer?

"You headed home?" Dan asked. He had explained that, as ranger, Bud Attatash spent the summer living in a cottage out here on the point.

"Yep," Bud said. "I just wanted to stop by and see how you folks were doing."

"We're cooking up this striped bass," Dan said. "It was legal, half inch over."

"They've been big this summer," Bud said. He cleared his throat. "Listen, after you folks headed out, I got to thinking about what you said about that dead seal on the south shore being a more complicated issue than it appeared. So I called up Chief Kapenash, and he told me about it. He said that you, Dan, were a part of that whole thing." Here, he looked, not at Dan, but at Meredith, whose face had gone scary blank. "And I realized that I said some inappropriate things." He nodded at Meredith. "Are you Mrs. Delinn?"

Meredith stared. Toby said, "Please, sir, if you don't mind..."

"Well, Mrs. Delinn, I just want to apologize for my callous words earlier. And for perhaps sounding like I cared more about a dead seal than I did for your welfare. What those people did was inexcusable. No doubt, you've been through enough in your private life without these hooligans trying to scare you."

Meredith pressed her lips together. Toby said, "That's right, you're right, she's been through enough."

"So if anyone ever bothers you again, you let me know." He gazed out over the dark water at the twinkling lights of town. "Nantucket is supposed to be a safe haven."

Dan came over to shake Bud's hand. "Thanks, Bud. Thank you for coming all the way out here to say that. You didn't have to."

"Oh, I know, I know," Bud said. "But I didn't want any of you to get the wrong idea about me. I'm not coldhearted or vindictive."

"Well, thanks again," Dan said. "You have a good night."

Bud Attatash tipped his cap at Meredith and then again at Connie, and then he climbed into his truck and drove off into the darkness.

"Well," Meredith said after a minute. "That was a first."

They ate the grilled fish with some sliced fresh tomatoes that Dan had gotten at Bartlett's Farm. Then they each put a marshmallow on a stick and roasted it over the fire. Meredith went back in the water, and Toby stood to join her, but Meredith put a hand up and said, "Don't even think about it." Toby plopped back down on his towel. "Yeah," he said. "She wants me." Connie climbed into Dan's lap and listened to the splashing sound of Meredith swimming. Dan kissed her and said, "Let's get out of here."

Yes! she thought.

She and Dan started breaking down the camp and packing everything up. Meredith emerged from the water with her teeth chattering, and Connie handed her the last dry towel. She collected the trash and stowed everything in the coolers. She folded up the blankets and the chairs while Dan dealt with the cooling grill and doused the fire. Toby put away the fishing poles, and Meredith collected the horseshoes. A seagull landed for the remains of the striped bass. Connie found the plastic bat in the sand and tucked it into the back of the Jeep. The Wiffle ball was still out there somewhere, Connie thought, tucked into the eelgrass like a seagull's egg, a memento of one of the small triumphs of the day.

The days zipped by. Connie spent nearly every night at Dan's house. She left a toothbrush there, and she bought half-and-half for her coffee (Dan, health nut, had only skim milk) and kept it in the fridge. She had met both of Dan's younger sons—Donovan and Charlie—though they had little more to say to her than "Hey." Dan relayed the funny things they said to him after Connie left.

Donovan, who was sixteen, had said, "Glad you're getting laid on a regular basis again, Dad. Can I borrow the Jeep?"

Charlie, the youngest, said, "She's pretty hot for an older lady."

"Older lady!" Connie exclaimed.

"Older than him, he means," Dan said. "And he's fourteen."

On the days that Dan had to work, Connie and Meredith and Toby walked the beach and then sat on the deck and read their books and discussed what they wanted to do for dinner. These were the moments when Toby acted like an adult. But more and more often, there were moments when Toby acted like an adolescent. He would mess up Meredith's hair or throw stones at the door of the outdoor shower while she was in there, or he would steal her glasses, forcing her to come stumbling blindly after him.

"Look at you," he'd say to her. "You're *chasing* me."

Connie said to Dan, "I can't tell if that's going to happen or not."

Toby asked if he could stay another week.

"Another week?" Connie said. "Or longer?"

"I don't start at the Naval Academy until after Labor Day," he said.

"So what does that mean?" Connie asked. "You'll stay until Labor Day?"

"Another week," Toby said. "But maybe longer. If that's okay with you?"

"Of course, it's okay with me," Connie said. "I'm just wondering what I did to deserve the honor of your extended presence?" What she wanted him to say was that he was staying because of Meredith.

"This is Nantucket," Toby said, "Why would I want to be anywhere else?"

MEREDITH

On the morning of the twenty-third of August, Meredith was awakened by the phone. Was it the phone? She thought it was, but the phone was in Connie's room, far, far away, and Meredith was in the grip of a heavy, smothering sleep. Connie would answer it. The phone kept ringing. Really? Meredith tried to lift her head. The balcony doors were shut tight—even with Toby across the hall, she didn't feel safe enough to sleep with them open—and her room was sweltering. She couldn't move. She couldn't answer the phone.

A little while later, the phone rang again. Meredith woke with a start. Connie would get it. Then she remembered that Connie wasn't home. Connie was at Dan's.

Meredith got out of bed and padded down the hall. Toby probably hadn't even heard the phone; he slept like a corpse. Meredith liked to believe this was a sign that he had a clean conscience. Freddy had jolted awake at the slightest sound.

Connie didn't have an answering machine, and so the phone rang and rang. *It's probably Connie,* Meredith thought, *calling from Dan's house with some kind of plan for the day—a lunch picnic at Smith's Point or a trip to Tuckernuck in Dan's boat.* Meredith's heart quickened. She had fallen in love with Nantucket—and yet in a few weeks, she would have to leave. She was trying not to think about where she would go or what she would do.

The caller ID said, NUMBER UNAVAILABLE, and Meredith's brain shouted out a warning, even as she picked up the phone and said hello.

A female voice said, "Meredith?"

"Yes?" Meredith said. It wasn't Connie, but the voice sounded like she knew her, and Meredith thought, *Oh, my God. It's Ashlyn!*

The voice said, "This is Rae Riley-Moore? From the *New York Times?*"

Meredith was confused. Not Ashlyn. Someone else. Someone selling something? The paper? The voice sounded familiar to Meredith because that was how telemarketers did it now; they acted like you were an old friend. Meredith held the phone in two fingers, ready to drop it like a hot potato.

"I'm sorry to bother you at home," Rae Riley-Moore said.

At home. This wasn't Meredith's home. If this was a telemarketer, she wouldn't have asked for Meredith. She would have asked for Connie.

Meredith said nothing. Rae Riley-Moore was undeterred.

"And so early. I hope I didn't wake you."

Meredith swallowed. She looked down the hall to the closed door of Toby's room. He would still be fast asleep. But a few days ago, he'd said, *If you need to come into this room for any reason, just walk right in. I am here for you, Meredith. Whatever you need.*

At the time she had thought, *Here for me? Ha!*

Meredith said, "I'm sorry. What can I do for you?"

"I'm calling about the news that broke this morning?" Rae Riley-Moore said. "In regard to your husband?"

Meredith spoke without thinking. "Is he dead?" Suddenly, the world stopped. There was no bedroom, no old boyfriend, no beautiful island, no $50 billion Ponzi scheme. Meredith was suspended in a white-noise vacuum, waiting for an answer to come through the portal that was the phone in her hand.

"No," Rae said. "He's not dead. And he's not hurt."

Things came back into focus, though Meredith was still disoriented. This wasn't Ashlyn, and it wasn't a telemarketer trying to sell her a subscription. This was something about Freddy. Meredith sat down on the smooth, white cotton of Connie's bed. There, on the nightstand, was Connie's clock radio, its blue numbers said 7:16. Certainly, Meredith knew better than to answer the phone. If the phone rang at seven o'clock in the morning, it was for a terrible, awful, disturbing reason.

"What then?" Meredith asked. "What is it?"

"Federal investigators have found evidence of an affair between your husband and a Mrs. Samantha Deuce. Your interior designer?"

Decorator, Meredith thought automatically. Samantha wasn't certified in interior design.

"And at two a.m. this morning, Mrs. Deuce made a statement to the press confirming the affair. She said that she and your husband had been together for six and a half years."

Meredith gagged. She thought, *Oh, God, it's true.* She thought, *It's true, it's true, Samantha and Freddy, Samantha confessed, it's true!* She thought, *Hang up!* But Meredith couldn't bring herself to hang up.

"Is this news to you?" Rae asked.

Was it news to her? It was. And it wasn't. "Yes," Meredith whispered. Her lips were wet with saliva.

"I'm sorry," Rae said. And she did, Meredith had to admit, sound sorry. "I didn't realize... I thought you knew."

"Well, now I hope it's clear," Meredith said. She cleared her throat. "I hope it's clear... that I knew *nothing* about what Freddy did behind closed doors."

"Okay," Rae Riley-Moore said. "So it's fair to say you're shocked and hurt."

Shocked. Could she honestly say *shocked?* Hurt, yes. And nothing about this was fair.

"You're telling me Samantha *confessed* to this?" Meredith said. "You're telling me she said they'd been together for six and a half *years?*"

"Since the summer of 2004," Rae said.

Summer 2004: Meredith rummaged. Cap d'Antibes? No, Sam had never been with them to France, though she'd dropped hints, hadn't she? Southampton? Yes, Samantha had come to their house in Southampton all the time—she and Trent had a place in Bridgehampton. Samantha, it now seemed to Meredith, had always been around. She had decorated three of the Delinns' four homes, down to the teaspoons, down to the hatbox toilets. Samantha had been their tastemaker, their stylist. She and Meredith used to go shopping together; Samantha picked out clothes for Meredith and clothes for Meredith to buy Freddy. She had insisted on the Yankees memorabilia and the antique piggy banks for Freddy's den.

Meredith had *seen* them together in his den; Meredith had *seen* Freddy's hand on Samantha's lower back. But Meredith had turned a blind eye, thinking, *No, not Freddy. Never.*

"Were they... are they... in *love?*" Meredith asked. She couldn't believe she was asking a total stranger, but she had to have the answer. She tried to remember: Had Samantha been at the indictment? No. Had she been at the sentencing? Meredith wasn't sure, since she herself hadn't attended the sentencing. Meredith hadn't heard from Samantha when the news broke—not a phone call, not an e-mail—except for an invoice for a small piece of artwork that arrived after Freddy was already in the city jail. Meredith had handed the invoice over to her attorneys. She didn't have the money to pay for it; it was something for Freddy's office. It was, she remembered now, a photograph of an Asian city that Meredith hadn't recognized.

"Malacca," Freddy had said. Meredith had been visiting Fred at the office a few weeks before the collapse. She had noticed the photograph hanging behind his desk, and she'd asked about it. "It's the cultural capital of Malaysia."

The invoice had been for twelve hundred dollars.

Twelve hundred dollars, Meredith thought now. *For a photograph of a place we've never been.*

Meredith had thought the invoice might have a note written on it, an expression of sympathy or concern. But no.

"Did she say they were in love?" Meredith asked again, more forcefully. "Mrs. Deuce. Samantha. Did she say that?"

Down the hall, the door to Toby's room opened, and Toby stepped out. He stood, in boxers and a T-shirt, looking at her.

Meredith held up a finger. She needed to hear the answer.

"She said she was writing a book," Rae Riley-Moore said.

Meredith hung up the phone. She walked toward Toby, and Toby walked toward her, and they met in the middle of the hallway.

Toby said, "I have some bad news."

The bad news was that Toby had been awoken by a commotion outside. There were news vans lining the road at the edge of Connie's property.

"I assume they're here for you?" Toby said.

"Oh, my God." Meredith couldn't have felt more exposed if they'd caught her stepping out of the shower. How did they know where she was staying? The police dispatcher, maybe. Or someone at the salon. Or they'd been tipped off by the wretched person who was terrorizing her.

"Do you know what it's about?" Toby said.

Meredith peered out the window. "Oh, my God," she said. "I can't believe this. I can't believe it."

"Did something happen?" Toby asked. "Who was on the phone?"

"A reporter from the *New York Times*," Meredith said.

Toby stared at her.

"Freddy had an affair with our decorator, Samantha, for six and a half years." Meredith said these words, but she didn't believe them. She understood they were, most likely, the truth, but she didn't *believe* them.

Toby reached out for her. Meredith closed her eyes. Toby smelled like warm sleep. If she were brutally honest with herself, she would admit that she'd been wanting Toby to hold her like this for days. She'd been pushing him away, scorning him at every opportunity— he was still a teenager in so many ways, he had never grown up— but the truth was, she yearned for a little piece of what they'd had back then. But now, with this news, the only man she could think about was Freddy. Was it possible that she still loved Freddy? And if that wasn't possible, then why did she feel this way?

"The guy is a bastard, Meredith," Toby said.

Right, Meredith thought. That was the predictable answer. Freddy had cheated so many people, why would he not cheat Meredith? He was a liar; why would he not lie to Meredith? Mmm, impossible to explain.

Meredith had believed that Freddy had adored her. Worshipped her.

The idea that she might have been wrong about that—so very, very wrong—made her dizzy and nauseous. She pulled away from Toby and bent at the waist, bringing her head to her knees. The pike position in diving. She thought, *Okay, this is where I crumble, where I dissolve. I fall to the floor and I ... I cry.*

But no, she wouldn't. She took a breath and stood up.

"What do we do about the reporters?" she asked. "How do we make them leave?"

"Call the police?" he said.

"Are they breaking the law?" she asked.

"If they set foot on the property, they're trespassing."

"They won't set foot on the property," Meredith said. "Will they?"

"Call the police anyway?" Toby said, "Or...you could give them what they want. Give them a statement."

Right. They wanted a statement. They wanted Meredith to decry Freddy, call him a bastard, a liar, a cheater. She looked at Toby's face uncertainly, although it wasn't Toby's face she was seeing; it was Freddy's face. Just as Freddy had been unable to give Meredith certain things, so now Toby would be unable to give her the answer to...why.

Why? Had Meredith done something wrong? Was Samantha Deuce better than Meredith in some way? Was she able to give Freddy something Meredith couldn't give him? Meredith had given him everything. Everything.

Toby said, "I'll call the police anyway. And I have to call Connie. She'll want to know that there are barbarians at the gate. Okay?"

Meredith nodded. Toby went for his cell phone. Meredith went into her bathroom, where she retched into the toilet until there was nothing left inside of her.

Toby brought Meredith a mug of coffee that she couldn't even look at, much less drink, and his cell phone. He had Connie on the other line.

Meredith said, "Hello?"

Connie said, "Oh, honey. I'm so sorry."

Meredith was in the kitchen. She was in a bright, sunny room with a pack of wolves at her back. "It's a beautiful day," Meredith said. "You and Dan should do something fun. You should avoid the house until we figure out what to do about all these reporters."

"Dan called Ed Kapenash," Connie said. "They're sending someone out to disperse the crowd."

"I hope that works," Meredith said.

"Is there anything I can do?" Connie asked. "For you?"

Take me back to yesterday, Meredith thought. "No," she said. Everything that had to be done, she had to do herself.

"You don't even sound angry," Connie said. "Aren't you *angry*, Meredith?"

Angry, Meredith thought.

"You're not going to let him off the hook for this, too, are you?" Connie said.

"I haven't let him off the hook for any of his actions, Connie," Meredith said. She heard something confrontational in her voice. She didn't want to fight. She didn't want to feel. She wanted to *think.* She wanted to *know.* She said, "I'll call you later, okay?"

"Okay," Connie said. "I love you, you know."

Meredith had been waiting all summer to hear Connie speak those words. Meredith hoped she was sincere and not saying them out of pity. "I love you, too."

She managed to wash her face and change into clothes. She put on a very comfortable white skirt and a soft pink T-shirt. She brushed her hair and her teeth. But something about all of these simple actions felt final, as though she were doing them for the last time. How could she go on?

Toby knocked at the door. He poked his head in. "How are you doing? Are you okay?"

She wanted to be left alone. But she was terrified of being left alone. She said, "They're still out there?"

"Yes, but the police are coming any minute. I'm going down to wait for them. Will you be okay?"

Okay? she thought.

Meredith tried to be calm and rational. Unlike the eighth of December, when she was forced to deal with a situation of such enormous proportions her mind could scarcely comprehend it, today was simple. Today was a man cheating on his wife. She, Meredith, was the wife.

She didn't feel any pain yet; she was suspended in a kind of breathless shock. Why shock? She had seen Samantha and Freddy together in Freddy's den. She had caught Freddy with his hand on Samantha's back. Meredith had witnessed them together, but she had dismissed it. It was a piece of dandelion fuzz that she'd blown off her palm into the wind. And why? If she ignored it, then it wasn't real? What she didn't know couldn't hurt her? Was that true, also, of Freddy's heinous crimes? Hadn't she been staring them right in the face but been refusing to see?

Toby was still downstairs. Meredith crept along the hall, to Connie's master suite. She opened the door to Connie's bathroom.

The pills were there. Six amber bottles in a line. Meredith checked the label of each one, as though she'd forgotten the exact names of the drugs or the exact order she would find them in or the exact heft of each bottle in her hand. Connie hadn't been taking the pills.

Meredith wanted the Ativan. And, yes, it occurred to her to take the whole bottle and end her life right there in Connie's room. If what Samantha had told the press was true, if she and Fred had been *lovers*—at the thought of this word, Meredith gagged again—then what choice would Meredith have but to end her life?

She counted out three Ativan. She already had two, in a pill box in her bathroom. If she took all five, would that be too many? Maybe. She would save the two that she had and take three right here, right now. She knew what she was after: Something more than sleep, something less than death. She wanted to be knocked out, unconscious, unaware, unreachable, untouchable.

She made it back to her bedroom, shut the door, checked that the balcony doors were secure, climbed into bed, and buried her face in the sweet pink covers. It was too bad, she thought. It was such a beautiful day.

They had met Samantha when they bought the penthouse apartment at 824 Park Avenue. Samantha had seemed to come with the building. She was decorating three other apartments, and so her presence had been nearly as steady as that of Giancarlo the doorman. Meredith and Freddy kept bumping into Samantha in the elevator. Either she was holding great big books of fabric swatches, or she was accompanied by plasterers and painters. They bumped into her in the service elevator carrying a pair of blue and white Chinese vases once, and an exquisite Murano glass chandelier another time.

It was finally Freddy who said, "Maybe we should have that woman decorate our place."

Meredith said, "Who?"

"That blonde we keep seeing around here. I mean, our place could use some help."

What year would that have been? Ninety-seven? Ninety-eight? Meredith had tried not to take offense at Freddy's comment. She had "decorated" the penthouse much the same way she'd "decorated" the other apartments they'd lived in, which was to say, eclectically. Meredith wanted to achieve the look of an apartment in a Woody Allen film—lots and lots of books crammed on shelves, a few pieces of art, a ton of family photographs, old worn furniture in leather and suede and chintz, most of which had been inherited from her mother and grandmother. Meredith liked Annabeth Martin's silver tea service on a half-moon table next to a hundred-year-old Oxford dictionary that she'd found in a back room at the Strand. She liked a mishmash of objects that displayed her intellectual life and her broad range of tastes. But it was true that, compared to the apartments of the people the Delinns now socialized with, their penthouse seemed bohemian and cluttered. Unpolished. Undone. Meredith knew nothing about window treatments or fabrics or carpets or how to layer colors and textures or how to display the artwork they did have. As soon as Freddy suggested they hire a decorator, Meredith realized how pathetic her efforts had been in presenting what they owned. No one else had so many tattered paperback books on shelves; no one else had so many photographs of their children—it seemed immodest all of a sudden.

Furthermore, now that they had the penthouse, there were more rooms—whole rooms, in fact, that Meredith had no idea what to do with. The room that was to be Freddy's personal den had walnut library shelves with nothing on them but his and Meredith's matched framed diplomas from Princeton.

"It looks like a dentist's office," Freddy remarked.

And so, Meredith set out to introduce herself to this woman they kept seeing around, the decorator whose name (Meredith had discovered from eavesdropping) was Samantha Deuce. Meredith approached her one afternoon as she was standing under the building's awning in the rain, waiting for Giancarlo to hail her a cab. Meredith introduced herself—Meredith Delinn, the penthouse—and asked if Samantha would be willing to come up to the apartment sometime so they could talk about the decorating.

Samantha had made a wistful face—not a hundred percent genuine, Meredith didn't think—and said, "I wish I could. But I'm so slammed that I can't, in good conscience, take on another project. I'm sorry."

Meredith had immediately backpedaled, saying yes, of course, she understood. And then she'd retreated—shell-shocked and dejected—back into the building.

That night at dinner, she told Freddy that Samantha, the ubiquitous decorator, had turned her down.

"Turned you *down?*" Freddy said. "Who turns down a job like this? Were you clear, Meredith? Were you clear that we want her to do *the whole apartment?*"

"I was clear," Meredith said. "And she was clear. She doesn't have time for another project." There had been something about the look on Samantha's face that bugged Meredith. Her expression had been too *prepared,* as though she knew what Meredith was about to ask, as though she knew something about Meredith that Meredith had yet to figure out herself. Had Samantha heard unsavory things about the Delinns? And if so, what were those things? That they were nouveau riche? That they were without taste? That they were social climbers? Meredith and Freddy hadn't known anyone else in the building at that time; there was no one to speak for or against them.

"I'll talk to her," Freddy said, and Meredith remembered that his decision to step in had come as a relief. She was used to Freddy taking care of things. Nobody ever said no to him. And, in fact, two weeks later, Samantha was standing in their living room, gently caressing the back of Meredith's grandmother's sofa as though it were an elderly relative she was about to stick in a home. (Which was true in a way: Samantha relegated nearly all of Meredith's family furniture to storage first, and then, when it became clear that it would never be used, to the thrift shop.)

Meredith said brightly, "Oh, I'm glad you came up to see the apartment after all."

Samantha said, "Your husband convinced me."

Meredith thought, *He talked you right out of your good conscience?*

And now, it was clear that he had.

Samantha Champion Deuce was a brassy blonde, nearly six feet tall. She towered over Meredith. She had broad shoulders and large breasts and hazel eyes and a wide mouth. She wore lipstick in bright colors: fire-engine red, fuchsia, coral. She wasn't a beauty, though there were beautiful things about her. She captivated. She was always the dominant personality in the room. She had a sexy, raspy voice like Anne Bancroft or Demi Moore; once you heard it, you couldn't get enough of it. She would say to Meredith, "Buy this, it's fabulous." And Meredith would buy it. She would walk into a room and say, "We're going to do it this way." And that was how the room would be done. She never asked for Meredith's opinion. The few times that Meredith expressed disapproval, Samantha turned to her and said, "You mean you don't *like* it?"

Not as though her feelings were hurt, but as though she couldn't imagine anyone in the world not liking it.

Hmmpf, she'd say. As if Meredith's response had stumped her.

Samantha moved through her life with extreme self-confidence. It was so pronounced that Meredith was drawn to studying Samantha's mannerisms: her wicked smile, the way she swore to great, elegant effect ("fucking Scalamandré, I fucking love it!"), the way she shimmered in the presence of every man from Freddy Delinn to the Guatemalan plaster guy ("José, you are a beast and a god. I could *eat* you").

As Meredith got to know her better, she learned that Samantha had been raised with four older brothers in Dobbs Ferry, New York. Her family was middle-class royalty. The four brothers were the best high-school athletes the town had ever seen; they all received Division I athletic scholarships. Samantha herself had played basketball all the way through Colby College. She married her college sweetheart, the preppy, handsome, and completely underwhelming Trent Deuce. They had lived downtown on Great Jones Street until their first child was born, when they moved to Ridgewood, New Jersey. Trent had worked for Goldman Sachs, but he'd been canned after 9/11. He then worked for a buddy who had a smaller brokerage firm — really, the details of Trent's career were always presented vaguely by Samantha, though Freddy had gathered enough information to conclude that Trent Deuce was a loser and would be better off at a car dealership in Secaucus selling used Camaros. (Freddy rarely spoke badly of *anyone,* so hearing him say this was flabbergasting. Now, Freddy's dismissal of Trent made perfect sense.)

Somewhere during the course of Trent's peripatetic career, Samantha had deemed it necessary to go back to work. She decorated a friend's house in Ridgewood. (Here, it should be noted that Meredith and Freddy had never once been invited to Samantha's home in Ridgewood, and Meredith had been grateful for that. Who wanted to make the trip from Manhattan to the Jersey suburbs?

No one. In Meredith's mind, Ridgewood was soccer mom/Olive Garden hell.) After the success of the Ridgewood friend's home, Samantha decorated the Manhattan apartment of the Ridgewood friend's mother, who happened to be fantastically wealthy, have millions of friends, and entertain often and lavishly. This set Samantha's career on its way. By the time Meredith met Samantha, she was a wealthy woman in her own right.

But not quite.

There was a subtle class distinction between Samantha and the Delinns—always. On the surface, Samantha told Meredith and Freddy what to do and they did it. But there was the underlying fact that she worked for them.

The Yankees memorabilia, the antique piggy banks. A certain lavender Hermès tie, Freddy's favorite tie, had also been one of Samantha's picks. Even the pink and tangerine palette of the Palm Beach house—which Meredith had bucked against—Freddy had defended. Pink and tangerine? Seriously? Samantha had used a pair of Lilly Pulitzer golf pants as her inspiration.

She's the expert, Fred said.

Samantha had something that Freddy valued. A knowledge, a perspective. He was a rich man. They, Freddy and Meredith, were a rich couple. Samantha was the one who showed them how to be rich. She had shown them how to spend. Nearly every extravagance that Meredith indulged in, Samantha Deuce had introduced her to.

Six and a half years. The summer of 2004. Had Fred and Samantha been in love? *Think, Meredith! Remember!*

She remembered Samantha in Southampton, decorating the house in whites and ivories, despite Meredith's protests that she had two teenage boys who also lived in the house, and Meredith wanted Leo and Carver and their friends to be comfortable dragging sand in, or sitting on the sofa in damp bathing suits. But the Southampton house had been done to Samantha's specifications, in whites and ivories, including a white grand piano that Meredith found tacky. ("Don't you think a white grand piano just screams Liberace? Or bad Elton John?" Meredith said. Samantha's eyes widened. "You mean you don't *like* it?")

Fred and Meredith used to meet Trent and Samantha for dinner at Nick and Toni's; inevitably, Freddy and Samantha would be seated on one side of the table, and Meredith and Trent on the other. Meredith struggled with conversation with Trent. She tried to remember to read the sports section of *USA Today* before they all went out, so she would at least have that to fall back on. More and more often, Samantha showed up alone, claiming that Trent was stuck in the city "working," or that she'd left him at home to care for the kids, because he absolutely never saw them during the week. Trent was always dismissed in this way, and so there had been many nights where it was just the three of them—Meredith, Freddy, and Samantha. Freddy used to say, "I'm going out with my wife and my girlfriend." Meredith had laughed at this; she had found it innocent and charming. She had occasionally been suspicious of dark, exotic beauties—women who resembled Trina or the lovely Catalan university student—although, really, Meredith was so certain of Freddy's undying devotion that these worries had flickered, and then extinguished.

It was around 2004 when Freddy had started to take care of himself again. Like everyone else, he stopped eating carbs for a while, but that was too hard, especially since he couldn't resist the focaccia or the ravioli with truffle butter at Rinaldo's. But he ate more vegetables. He had salads for lunch instead of reubens and omelets. He started working out at the gym in their building. The first time he'd told Meredith he was going downstairs to work out, Meredith said, "You're going to do *what?*" Freddy had never been much of an athlete or an exerciser. His tennis game was adequate and he could swim, but he didn't have time for golf. He didn't even like tossing the lacrosse ball with the boys. Meredith could no sooner see him lifting weights than she could see him break dancing with the Harlem kids in Central Park. But he went at the workout regimen with a vengeance; he hired a personal trainer named Tom. Some days he spent more time with Tom than with Meredith. He lost weight, he developed muscles. He had to have a whole new set of suits made on his next trip to London. He let his hair grow longer. It was really gray by then, more salt than pepper, and his beard was coming in gray, and some days he went two or three days without shaving so he would have a scruff that Meredith found sexy but that she suspected was raising eyebrows at the office. She said, "Did you have a fight with your razor?" Freddy said he wanted to try something different. He grew a goatee.

Samantha had loved the goatee, Meredith remembered. She used to stroke it like a cat, and Meredith had found this funny. She had wanted Samantha to join her in teasing Freddy. *That's his midlife crisis,* Meredith said.

Could be worse, Samantha had said.

When Samantha was around, Freddy was looser, he laughed more, he occasionally had a glass of wine, he occasionally stayed out past nine thirty. Once, the three of them had even gone dancing at a nightclub. Samantha had been immediately absorbed by the crowd. When Meredith and Freddy found her, she was dancing with a bunch of the gorgeous, emaciated Bulgarian women whom Meredith had seen around town—working behind the counter at the fancy food store or babysitting the art galleries— and their hulking boyfriends. They all abandoned the dance floor for the bar, where they did shots of Patrón. Freddy had followed them to the bar, he magnanimously paid for ten shots of Patrón, and then he tried to convince Samantha to leave the club with him and Meredith. Nope, she didn't want to go.

Meredith said, *Come on, Freddy. We'll go. She can stay. She's going back to Bridgehampton tonight anyway.*

But Freddy didn't want Samantha to stay. He had words with her that turned into an argument. Meredith couldn't hear what they were saying to each other, though she did see Freddy take Samantha's arm and Samantha pull her arm back. Now, of course, it was clear that it had been a lover's spat. Freddy didn't want Samantha to stay with this group of young, Eastern European hedonists. She might do drugs, she might participate in group sex and find a younger, hotter lover. But at that time, all Meredith thought was that it was a good thing she and Freddy had never had a daughter. Freddy's concern for Samantha that night had struck Meredith as avuncular, bordering on fatherly, even though Samantha was only seven years younger than Meredith and nine years younger than Freddy.

They had left Samantha at the club. Freddy had been fuming. Meredith had said, *Come on now, Fred. She's a big girl. She can take care of herself.*

What an idiot Meredith had been!

Was the summer of 2004 when the nickname had surfaced? At some point, Freddy had started calling Samantha "Champ," a shortened form of her maiden name, Champion. Meredith had noticed the sudden use of the nickname, and she thought, *Hmmm, I wonder what precipitated that?* But she'd never asked. Samantha was a part of their lives; after the decorating was done, she became their lifestyle consultant. She was always around — in their homes, in Fred's office, on the phone. Meredith had assumed the nickname came about organically from some conversation between Freddy and Samantha.

Does the word "champ" mean anything to you?

When had they met for this affair? And where? Six and a half years. Safe to say they had met hundreds of times then, right? But in Meredith's mind, Freddy had spent every night in bed beside her. He had been in bed by nine thirty, asleep by ten, awake by five, in his home office until six thirty when he left for the office-office. Had Meredith and Freddy spent nights apart from each other? Well, yes: Freddy had to travel. He went to London to do business with the office there, and that was where he'd gotten his suits tailored. Had Samantha met him in London? It would be safe to say yes. She had probably introduced Freddy to the tailor whose name he would not disclose. That tailor probably thought Samantha was Freddy's wife. There were times when Meredith was in Palm Beach when Freddy had to fly back to New York. Lots of times—especially in recent years. Had he seen Samantha then? Yes; of course, the answer was yes. Where did they meet? (Why did Meredith have to know this? Why torture herself with the details? What did it matter now?) Did they meet at a hotel? If so, which hotel? Did they meet in Ridgewood? Certainly not. Did they meet in Meredith and Freddy's apartment? Did they have sex in Meredith and Freddy's *bed?* Meredith could see how awful and insidious this was going to get.

Did they rendezvous on the yacht *Bebe?* There had been plenty of times when Freddy had flown to "check out" one problem or another with *Bebe*—when the yacht was in the Mediterranean, and when she was in Newport or Bermuda. But *Bebe* had a crew and a captain. If Freddy had been on board with Samantha, certain people would have known about it.

So certain people knew about it. Billy, their captain knew, and Cameron, the first mate knew. They were complicit.

Samantha said she'd always wanted to see their property in Cap d'Antibes, but this may have been a smoke screen. She may have been quite familiar with the property.

As Meredith awoke from her stupor—someone was calling to her from the bottom of a deep hole, or she was the one in the deep hole and someone was calling to her from the top—she flashed on the photograph that Samantha had selected for Freddy's office. A photograph of Malacca, in Malaysia. As far as Meredith knew, Freddy had never been to Malaysia; he'd never been to Asia at all, except for his trip to Hong Kong before they were engaged. Or was Meredith wrong about that? Had Freddy and Samantha been to this place, Malacca, together? The photograph had been hanging right behind Freddy's desk. What had hung there previously? Meredith tried to think. Another photograph.

Toby had her by the shoulder. The room was dark; there was a light on in the hallway behind him and she could see the outline of Connie standing there.

"What time is it?" Meredith asked.

"Nine o'clock," Toby said. "At night. You slept all day."

Meredith was relieved. It was nighttime. She could go back to sleep. She closed her eyes. But the dark was terrifying. She was unmoored, in danger of floating away. She opened her eyes.

"Toby?" she whispered.

"Yes?"

She wanted to ask him something, but she didn't have to. She already knew the answer. Veronica's funeral had been in July of 2004. Meredith had been on Long Island, and Freddy had arranged for a helicopter to take Meredith to New York and then a private car to drive her down to Villanova. Meredith had asked Freddy to come with her. And what had he said? "I never met the woman, Meredith. This is your chance to be with Connie. Go be with Connie. I'll stay here and hold down the fort."

Hold down the fort?

"Never mind," Meredith said to Toby now.

Meredith felt Toby staring at her, then he retreated to the hallway and pulled the door closed.

Meredith awoke in the morning, dying of thirst. She slipped downstairs to the kitchen and poured herself a tall glass of ice water. She drank deeply and thought about how there were times when you were just grateful for cold, clean water, and this was one of those times.

Connie appeared in the kitchen, floating like a ghost or an angel in a white nightgown and robe. Meredith figured that Dan must be upstairs.

Connie hugged Meredith.

"Oh," Connie said. "I'm sorry." She pulled away. She had tears in her eyes. "I am so, so sorry."

Meredith nodded. It hurt to move her head. Everything hurt.

She hadn't thought that anything could hurt again after what she'd been through, but yes, this hurt. This hurt differently. God, she couldn't believe she was even thinking this: it hurt worse.

Connie said, "You slept for nearly twenty-four hours."

Meredith exhaled. She said, "I took three of your Ativan."

Connie hugged her again. "Oh, honey."

"I think maybe you'd better hide the rest of the pills. It did occur to me to take them all."

"Okay," Connie said. "Okay."

"I thought you'd be mad," Meredith said. "I snooped around your bathroom when I first got here. I've snuck five Ativan altogether and two Ambien. I stole them."

"I don't care about the pills," Connie said. "I care about you."

"I don't know what to do," Meredith said.

"What do you want to do?" Connie asked.

Meredith pulled away and eyed her friend. "I want to talk to Fred."

"Oh, honey, you're kidding."

"I'm not kidding. That's all I want. I don't want to read about their love affair in her book. I want to hear about it from my husband. I want him to confess to me. I want to hear the truth from him."

"What makes you think Freddy would tell you the truth?" Connie said.

Meredith had no answer for this.

A little while later, both Toby and Dan came downstairs. Connie made coffee. Meredith thought, miraculously, that the coffee smelled good. She was back to counting each small blessing: cold water, hot coffee with real cream and plenty of sugar.

Dan and Toby were concerned about the practical problem they faced.

"The reporters are still out there," Toby said. "In fact, they seem to have multiplied overnight."

Dan looked at Meredith apologetically. "I called Ed Kapenash yesterday morning, and by noon, the reporters were all gone. We could have gotten you out of here for a little while. But now they're back. I could call Eddie again, but..."

"Or we could try Bud Attatash," Toby said. "He seems like the type of guy who owns a shotgun and isn't afraid to use it."

"It's okay," Meredith said. She was embarrassed that Dan had to ask personal favors from the chief of police on her behalf. She sat down at the table with her coffee. Three months ago, she had been all alone. Now she had friends. She had a team. She added this to her list of things to be grateful for. "I'm going to enjoy this coffee, and then I have some phone calls to make."

"I'll make French toast," Connie said.

Upstairs, in the privacy of her bedroom—balcony doors still shut tight—Meredith called Dev at the office, while praying a Hail Mary.

The receptionist answered, and Meredith said, "This is Mrs. Delinn, calling for Devon Kasper."

And to Meredith's shock, the receptionist said, "Absolutely, Mrs. Delinn. Let me get him for you."

Dev came to the phone. "Holy shit, Meredith."

"I know."

"Once you gave me the name, the Feds did the rest. It was all right there. All over his date book, his planner..."

"Stop," Meredith said. "I didn't know they were having an affair."

"What?"

"I knew that 'champ' was Samantha. That was what Freddy called her. But I didn't know they were sleeping together."

"Meredith."

"Devon," Meredith said. "I didn't know that my husband and Samantha Deuce were having an affair."

There was silence. Then Dev said, "Okay, I believe you."

"Thank you." She sighed. "There are reporters all over the front lawn."

"Good," Dev said. "You should make a statement."

"No," Meredith said.

"Meredith," Dev said gently. "This could help you."

"The fact that my husband was betraying me, not honoring our vows, *for six and a half years,* could help me? I can see you know nothing about marriage. I can see you know *nothing* about the human heart."

Dev, wisely, changed tactics. "The information about the star was good information."

"Did you find the account?" Meredith asked. "Did you find Thad Orlo?"

"The Feds are still working on it," Dev said. "I can't tell you what they've uncovered."

"Even though it was my information to begin with?" Meredith said.

"Even though," Dev said. He paused. "Do you think this Champion woman knew what was going on with Fred and the business?"

"You'd have to ask her that," Meredith said. She wondered how she would feel if it turned out that Samantha *had* known about the Ponzi scheme. Would Meredith feel betrayed? Would Freddy have shared his biggest secret with Samantha, but not with his wife? Then again, wasn't *not* knowing its own kind of gift? But Meredith was the one who had lost everything. Samantha was still out walking around, still running a decorating business, still driving her children to Little League and dance, still cozy at home with her underwhelming husband, her community, and her friends. Samantha Deuce wasn't under investigation, her home wasn't being vandalized, she wasn't being stalked. She might be now, with this admission. Samantha must have had no choice. The Feds must have had ironclad evidence; they must have had phone records or eight-by-ten glossies or a video. Or, perhaps, Samantha had been so overwhelmed by her love for Fred that she decided to talk. Or an $8 million book deal sounded good.

"There's something else I want to tell you about," Meredith said. "There's a framed photograph in Freddy's office. It's a street scene in an Asian city. Freddy said the city is called Malacca. It's in Malaysia. It's the cultural capital of Malaysia."

"And this is relevant because..."

"Because to my knowledge, Freddy has never been to Malacca. Or Malaysia at all. And yet this was a photograph that Samantha bought for Fred's office. The invoice came after he went to jail: twelve hundred dollars. Freddy hung the photograph right behind his desk." At that instant, Meredith remembered. The street scene in Malacca had replaced a grainy photograph of Freddy with his brother, David: the two of them bare chested in cutoff shorts, standing in front of a Pontiac GTO that David had restored. It was the only surviving picture of the two brothers together, and Freddy had replaced it with Malacca? "This photograph had a secret meaning for Freddy, I think. I'm sure of it now."

"Like it was a place he trysted with the Deuce woman?" Dev said.

"Just find the photograph," Meredith said.

"Okay. I'll do that. Your instincts are good."

"And Dev?"

"Yes."

There was one last thing. The most important, vital thing. But she was having a hard time thinking of how to ask.

"I need to talk to Fred."

"Fred," Dev said flatly.

"I need to talk to him," Meredith said. "About this and about other things. Can I call him, or do I have to travel to Butner?"

"Traveling to Butner would be a waste of your time," Dev said.

Part of her was relieved to hear this. The thought of leaving Nantucket was debilitating enough. She couldn't imagine traveling to North Carolina in the brutal heat of August, or of suffering the dust and filth and indignity in order to visit the prison's most infamous inmate. There would be reporters everywhere like buzzards on fresh roadkill.

"Really?" she said. "A waste?"

"There's been no change in his demeanor," Dev said. "He won't speak to anyone. Not even the priest. It's unclear if he *can't* speak or if he's choosing not to speak."

"He might choose to speak to me, though," Meredith said. "Right?"

"He might," Dev said. "But it's a gamble."

"Can I call him?" Meredith asked.

"He's permitted one phone call a week."

Meredith swallowed. "Has he...? Has he taken any other phone calls?" What she wanted to know was if Freddy had talked to Samantha.

"No," Dev said. "No phone calls. He speaks to no one."

"Can you help me set up a phone call?" Meredith asked.

Dev sighed. It was the sigh of a much older man. Meredith was aging him. "I can try. Do you want me to try? Really, Meredith?"

"Really," Meredith said.

"Okay," Dev said. "I'll contact the prison and see what I can do."

"Thank you," Meredith said. "It's important to me."

"Make a statement, Meredith," Dev said. "Save yourself."

She had spent the whole summer wondering how to save herself, and now, she found, she didn't care. *Goddamn you, Freddy!* she thought (zillionth and seventh). She didn't care if she lived or died; she didn't care if she was dragged off to prison. She would, like Fred, fold herself into an origami beetle. She wouldn't speak to another human being as long as she lived.

And was that what Fred had wanted all along? Had he meant for them to be ruined together? Had he asked her to transfer the $15 million so that she would go to prison?

Save herself? For what?

Brilliant and talented. That girl owns my heart.

Mommy, watch me!

Sail on Silvergirl. Sail on by. Your time has come to shine. All your dreams are on their way.

Meredith sat on her bed and took a stab at writing a statement. She pictured herself marching out to the end of Connie's driveway to face the eager reporters; this would be the juiciest news since OJ drove off in the white Bronco. She imagined her face and graying hair on every TV screen in America. She couldn't do it.

But she wrote anyway.

I have been informed that my husband, Fred Delinn, who is serving one hundred and fifty years in federal prison for his financial crimes, had been conducting an affair with our decorator, Samantha Champion Deuce, for over six years. This news has come as a profound shock. I had no idea about the affair, and I am still ignorant of the most basic details. Please know that I am hurting, just the way that any spouse who discovers an infidelity hurts. My husband's financial crimes were a public matter. His infidelity, however, is a private matter, and I beg you to respect it as such. Thank you.

Meredith read her statement over. It was...minimalist, nearly cold. But would anyone be surprised by this? She had an opportunity here to say that she'd known nothing about Freddy's financial dealings. Should she add a line? *Clearly, my husband kept many secrets from me.* But that felt too confessional. *I knew nothing about Freddy's Ponzi scheme and nothing about this affair.* I didn't know Freddy was stealing everyone's money and I didn't know he was romancing Samantha Deuce, our best friend.

I didn't know Freddy.

"Jesus!" she said, to no one.

*   *   *

She took the statement down to the kitchen where Connie and Dan and Toby were still gathered around the table, finishing up plates of golden brown, cinnamony French toast.

"The *Post* is going to have a field day with this," Connie was saying. Then she saw Meredith and clammed up.

Meredith waved the paper at them. "I wrote a statement," she said.

"Read it," Connie said.

"I can't read it," Meredith said. "Here."

Connie read the statement, then passed it to Toby. Toby read it, then passed it to Dan. When they finished, Meredith said, "Well?"

"You're too nice," Connie said.

"The guy's a bastard," Toby said. His face was bright red—from the sun or from anger, Meredith couldn't tell. "Why don't you just align yourself with the rest of America and come right out and call the guy a bastard? If you aren't tougher on him, people are going to think you were conspiring with him."

"Is that what *you* think?" Meredith asked.

"No . . ." Toby said.

"I've been holding my tongue because that was how I was raised," Meredith said. "I don't feel like spilling my guts all over the evening news. I don't want the *details* of my *marriage* popping up across the Internet. I don't even want to make this statement. I think it's crass."

"Because you're a repressed Main Line snob," Toby said. "You're just like your parents, and your grandmother."

"Well, it's true my parents never battled it out on the front lawn," Meredith said. "They didn't hurl their wedding china at one another. But, for the record, I'm not 'repressed.' You know damn well I'm not 'repressed'! But I also didn't spread my love and affection around the way you've apparently spent your life doing. And the way my husband did."

"Hey, now," Connie said. She put a hand on Meredith's arm.

Toby lowered his voice. "I just think you need to sound angrier."

"At who?" Meredith said. "You know what I thought when I met Freddy Delinn? I thought, here's a guy who's rock solid; this guy isn't going to ditch me so he can go off sailing in the Seychelles. You, Toby, you made Freddy look like a safe bet."

"Oh, boy," Dan said.

"But I never lied to you, Meredith," Toby said. "You have to give me that. I was insensitive when I was nineteen years old. I was possibly even worse than insensitive when I saw you a few years ago. I know I hurt you and I'm sorry. But I never lied to you."

Meredith stared at Toby, then at Connie and Dan. "You're right," she said. "He's right."

"The statement is what it is," Connie said. "It's a statement. It's classy and discreet, worthy of Annabeth Martin." Connie cut her eyes at Toby. "And that is a *good* thing. So, are you going out there to read it now?"

"I can't," Meredith said.

"You can't?"

"I want *you* to read it," Meredith said.

"Me?" Connie said.

"Please," Meredith said. "Be my spokesperson. Because I can't read it."

Connie got a strange expression on her face. In high school, every time Meredith had been sick, or at early diving practice, Connie had jumped at the chance to do the readings at morning chapel. She had been sick with jealousy when Meredith gave her salutatorian's speech at graduation. Something like 90 percent of Americans were afraid of public speaking—but not Connie.

"Me?" she said. "Your spokesperson?"

"Please," Meredith said. It would be better to have beautiful, serene, red-haired Connie read the statement. America would love Connie. People would see that Meredith did have someone who believed in her. But most important, Meredith wouldn't have to do it herself.

"Okay," Connie said, standing up.

"You're not going out like that?" Dan asked. Connie was still in her filmy nightgown and robe.

"No," Connie said. "I'll wear clothes."

A few minutes later, Connie was dressed in a pair of white linen pants and a green linen shirt and flat sandals. She looked like an ad for Eileen Fisher. With the paper in hand, she walked straight out to the end of the driveway, for the weirdest press conference ever. Flashbulbs started going off. Meredith closed the front door behind her.

Meredith wanted to watch Connie from the window, but she was certain she would be photographed if she did. So she sat at the oval dining table with Toby and Dan, and waited. She imagined all of the people across the country who would hear Meredith's words come out of Connie's mouth.

Well, for starters, Ashlyn would see Connie on TV. Had Connie thought of this? Leo and Carver would see Connie. Gwen Marbury would see Connie, Amy Rivers, Connie's friend Lizbet, Toby's ex-wife in New Orleans, Dustin Leavitt, Trina Didem, Giancarlo the doorman, Julius Erving. Everyone in America would watch the footage. Samantha herself would watch it. Possibly even Freddy would watch it, on a TV in prison.

And what would he think?

A few minutes later, Connie stepped back into the house. The reporters, far from dispersing, were yelling things. What were they yelling?

Connie looked pink and winded, as if she had just finished a foot race. She was perspiring.

Dan said, "How'd it go?"

Toby said, "Water, Con?"

Connie nodded. "Please."

They all trekked into the kitchen, where Toby fixed his sister a glass of ice water with lemon.

"Why are they yelling?" Meredith asked.

"Questions," Connie said. "They have questions."

Meredith thought, They *have questions?*

Connie said, "Mostly, they want to know if you're going to divorce him."

"Divorce him?" Meredith said.

"Leave him."

"Leave him?" Meredith didn't get it. Or she thought maybe the reporters didn't get it. The man was in jail for 150 years. He was never getting out. Maybe people thought Meredith would move to North Carolina, would visit him every week, would lobby her congressman and pray and wait for ten or twelve years for possible conjugal visitation rights. Meredith and Freddy making love in some tin-roofed trailer. Maybe that was what Meredith had envisioned for herself. But no—Meredith had envisioned nothing of the sort. The present was so overwhelming, she'd had no energy or imagination for any kind of future, with or without Freddy.

Would she divorce him?

She didn't know.

She was Catholic, she believed in the sacrament of marriage, she believed in the vows—till death do us part. Her parents had remained married, and her grandparents. She and Freddy would never live together as husband and wife again, so what would be the point of getting divorced?

Across the kitchen, she and Toby locked eyes.

The point of getting divorced was that Meredith would be free to get an annulment and marry again. Start over.

The notion was exhausting.

"I can't answer any of those questions," Meredith said. "I don't know what I'm doing."

Connie hugged Meredith so hard, Meredith nearly tipped over.

"It's going to be okay," Connie said. "I think the statement worked, or it will work, once they realize it's all they're going to get."

"So you didn't say anything else?" Meredith said. "You didn't answer for me?"

"It was hard," Connie said. "But I just stood there with a plastic smile on my face. "

"We should see what it looks like on TV," Toby said.

Connie jumped at this idea, and Meredith couldn't blame her, though Meredith didn't want to see the statement broadcast on TV; she wanted three more Ativan and a dark bedroom. She wanted to talk to Freddy; her throat ached with the need. *Tell me everything. Tell me who you really were.*

Toby and Dan and Connie went into the sitting room and turned on the television. Meredith lingered in the hallway, not committing to watching, not committing to hiding upstairs. She was dangerously close to the front door; anyone might see her through the sidelights. She stepped into the sitting room. She heard Connie reading her words: *Please know that I am hurting...* She saw Connie on the screen, looking natural and calm and poised. The channel was CNN. The banner at the bottom of the screen read: *Meredith Delinn spokesperson, Constance Flute, responds to the news of love affair between Freddy Delinn and the couple's decorator, Samantha Deuce.*

In the background, Meredith could see Connie's house.

The banner changed to read: *Meredith Delinn seeking refuge on Nantucket Island.*

It was her they were talking about, her life. That was her best friend speaking her words. They showed the house—this very house where they were now watching TV. It was weirdly reflexive.

Connie said, "I look awful."

Toby said, "It's not really about you, Con."

Dan said, "You look great."

Meredith needed to thank Connie for going out there on her behalf and reading the statement, but she couldn't find the words.

And then the phone rang.

*　　*　　*

Toby answered. He said, "May I ask who's calling?"

Meredith started to shake. She clung to the soft material of her skirt.

Toby put a hand over the receiver. "It's your attorney."

Meredith took the phone upstairs to her room. She reminded herself to breathe. She was light-headed; the caffeine from the coffee darted through her like lightning bolts. She felt a pressure in her bowels. But not now, with Dev on the phone. She lay down on her bed.

"Two things," Dev said. He sounded more chipper than he had earlier. Maybe his coffee had kicked in, too. "I just saw the statement on TV."

"Already?" Meredith said.

"We have a twenty-four-hour news feed in the office," Dev said. "Everyone does these days."

"And...?" she said.

"You could have said more," he said. "And you could have said it yourself."

Meredith nodded, though of course he couldn't see this. "I couldn't..."

"Because you know what people's response will be. Is already."

"What?"

"That you hired someone to do it for you. A spokesperson."

"I didn't *hire* Connie. She's my friend. I didn't have the guts to do it myself. She offered."

"I'm just telling you the perception. What people will think."

"I don't care what people think," Meredith said.

"You do, though," Dev said.

Meredith thought, *He's right. I do.*

Taking pity on her, he said, "But it was better than nothing. You communicated *something*. That's what matters."

"The second thing?" Meredith said. The caffeine high was fading. She was suddenly exhausted.

"I spoke to the warden at Butner," Dev said.

Her bowels squelched. She put a hand to her abdomen.

"He's looking into it for you," Dev said. "The phone call."

Dan had to leave the house to go to work. He asked if anyone was up for steaks that night at his house.

Toby said, "Not tonight, man."

Meredith said nothing. She was now the fun-sucker Dan had feared she would be.

Connie said, "Maybe. Call later."

"You guys should go," Meredith said. Dan was leaving soon for a three-day camping trip to New Hampshire with his sons. And by the time he returned, there would be less than a week left before Labor Day. It was all going to end; there was nothing Meredith could do to stop it.

Connie and Meredith and Toby retreated to the back deck. It was hot; Meredith wanted to swim, but she was afraid if she tried to swim, she would drown. Her limbs felt light and useless. She was a husk. She was a bladder filled with the hot, stinking air of anxiety.

Toby said, "You should divorce him, Meredith."

"Leave her be, Toby," Connie scolded. Then a few seconds later, she said, "You *should* divorce him. I'll pay for it."

Meredith laughed a sad, dry laugh. She hadn't even considered cost.

Toby swam. Meredith moved in and out of consciousness. She felt sluggish, then jumpy; the Ativan were exacting revenge. Toby became Harold, Harold had been brutally killed, and it was Meredith's fault. It was like Meredith had a hex on her, why not blame her for everything, the oil spill in the Gulf, the bloodshed in the

Middle East. Why, oh why, had Samantha spoken? Everyone would hate Samantha now, too, her life would be ruined. She must have loved Freddy, must love him still if she was going to allow him to destroy her life. She still had young kids, one of them only ten. Her business would go kaput, or maybe not. Maybe infidelity boosted a decorator's cachet. What did Meredith know? Samantha was writing a book. Meredith could write a book, should write a book, but what would that book say? *I wasn't paying attention. I was moving blithely through my days. I accepted what Freddy told me as the truth. I had never been exposed to lying or liars growing up; I didn't know what to look for.*

Connie said, "What are you thinking about?"

Meredith said, "Nothing."

The phone in the house rang. Meredith nearly leapt out of her chair at the sound. She knew she shouldn't answer it, but she hoped it was Dev calling back with an answer from the warden. She checked the caller ID: *NUMBER UNAVAILABLE.* Meredith couldn't help herself: she picked up.

A woman's voice said, "Meredith?"

Meredith felt like someone's hands were around her neck. She felt like she had a golf ball stuck in her throat, or one of the gobstoppers the boys used to buy at the candy store in Southampton.

"It's Samantha," the woman said, though of course Meredith knew this.

"No," Meredith said.

"Meredith, please."

Please what? What did Samantha want? Did she expect to bond with Meredith now that she had been exposed as Freddy's lover? Did she think that she and Meredith would be sister-wives, do the blended family thing the way Toby was so content doing? Meredith as some sort of ersatz aunt to Samantha's children? Meredith and Samantha joining forces to appeal Freddy's sentence?

"No," Meredith said, and she hung up.

*   *   *

The phone rang again an hour and six minutes later. Meredith was hyperaware of time passing. She thought of Samantha stroking Freddy's goatee. He had grown the goatee for Samantha, he had started going to the gym for Samantha. Everything had been for Samantha.

Meredith believed that it had all started when she went to Veronica's funeral. Or shortly after. Because Freddy sensed something, because Meredith came back addled and distracted. Freddy had asked her how the funeral was, and she had said, "Oh, it was fine," though it hadn't been fine; it had been an emotional sweat bath, but Meredith had stayed true to Freddy. She had stayed true, but not Freddy. He had stepped out of bounds. He had called Samantha, or something had sparked between the two of them in person. Meredith understood that. Because of what had happened between her and Toby at the funeral, she understood. But when you're married, you smother those sparks. You step on them, you extinguish them.

Meredith felt like she was going to vomit again. When she checked the caller ID, it gave the name of the law firm.

"Hello?" Meredith said.

"Meredith?" It was Dev.

"Yes," she said.

"Boy, do I have news for you," he said. "Sit down and fasten your seatbelt."

Meredith didn't like the way this sounded. At all. She said warily, "What is it?"

"Listen to this: There were four numbered accounts at the bank in Switzerland where Thad Orlo was most recently employed that looked like they might have links to Delinn Enterprises. Each of the accounts had the same numbers and letters as the one on your supposed NASA certificate, only in a different order. These accounts were all "managed" by Thad Orlo, and each account contained either a little over or a little under a billion dollars. But these were holding accounts; there was no action on them."

Meredith said nothing. She hated to say it, but she no longer cared about Thad Orlo or the missing money. Still, she had the wherewithal to ask, "Whose accounts were they?"

"All four accounts were under the name of Kirby Delarest."

Meredith gasped.

Dev said, "Wait, it gets better."

"But you know who Kirby Delarest is, right?" Meredith asked. "He lived near us in Palm Beach. He was an investor."

"Not an investor," Dev said. "He was Freddy's henchman. He was the one responsible for hiding the money and moving it around."

"He's dead," Meredith said. She thought of Amy Rivers, her lip curled in disgust. "He killed himself."

"He killed himself," Dev said, "because he was in so deep. Because he was afraid he was going to get caught. But Meredith…" Here, Dev paused. Meredith could picture him pushing back his floppy bangs or adjusting his glasses. "He was not only investing with Thad Orlo. He *was* Thad Orlo."

"What?" Meredith said.

"Kirby Delarest and Thad Orlo were the same person. He held two passports—one American, Kirby Delarest, and one Danish, Thad Orlo. Thad Orlo had an apartment in Switzerland where he worked for the Swiss bank and managed four accounts, which contained a total of four billion dollars. Kirby Delarest of Palm Beach, Florida, owned three large condo buildings in West Palm as well as a P.F. Chang's restaurant and a couple of rinky-dink strip malls. His real action, though, was overseas. He hid Freddy's clients' money and kept it safe. Four billion dollars. Can you believe it?"

Meredith reminded herself to breathe. She saw Connie coming up the stairs from the beach rubbing her wet hair with a towel, and she prayed that Connie wouldn't come inside and ask if Meredith wanted a turkey sandwich for lunch. Meredith needed to process what she'd just heard; she felt like she was torn between two worlds. There was this world, Nantucket, with the ocean and the outdoor shower and lunch on the deck, and then there was the world of international banking and double identities and lies. Kirby Delarest was Thad Orlo. Kirby had been tall and blond and lean, and he'd had that accent, which he'd claimed he'd acquired growing up in Wisconsin. Meredith knew something was wrong with that answer, but she hadn't questioned him. What had Freddy always said? Midwesterners were the most honest people on earth. Ha! Kirby Delarest had been in cahoots with Freddy. His daughters always wore those beautiful matching Bonpoint dresses. Meredith thought of the afternoon when she had discovered Freddy and Kirby Delarest by the pool, the bottle of Petrus consumed by two men on a Wednesday afternoon to celebrate the fact that they were robbing the whole world blind. Kirby Delarest had shot himself in the head rather than face Freddy's fate.

Meredith's eyes burned like she was in the desert. The account numbers had all been variations on the phony NASA star. These were Silver Girl accounts. Did that implicate her further? Please, she prayed, no.

"So you found the money, then?" she said. "Four billion? That's a lot of money."

"No, no," Dev said. "The money was withdrawn last October. All of it — gone, vanished. Moved, most likely in cash, to another location."

"When in October?" Meredith asked, dreading the answer.

"October seventeenth."

Meredith shut her eyes. Connie tapped on the glass door. Meredith opened her eyes. Connie mouthed, *Are you okay?*

"That's..." Meredith said.

"What?" Dev said.

"You're sure it was the seventeenth?" Meredith said. "The seventeenth of October?"

"What is it?" Dev said. "What is the seventeenth of October?"

"Samantha Deuce's birthday," Meredith said.

"Okay," Dev said. "Okay, okay, okay. Could be a coincidence. But probably not. Let me call you back."

"Wait!" Meredith said. "I have to know…Have you heard from the warden? At Butner? Can I speak to Fred?"

"Fred?" Dev said, as though he wasn't sure who Meredith meant. Then he said, "Oh. No, I haven't heard back."

"I really need to…"

"I'll let you know if I do," Dev said. "When I do." And he hung up.

Meredith lowered herself onto a chair. She thought about Kirby Delarest, his wife Janine, those little blond girls, as perfect and precious as the von Trapps. She thought of Kirby Delarest's brains splattered all over his garage. Meredith remembered Otto, the folk sculpture in Thad Orlo's Manhattan apartment with his gray cottony hair and the piece of wire twisted to make spectacles. She remembered how carefully she had watered the Norfolk pine, terrified it would turn brown and lose its branches in their custody. She had never met Thad Orlo, though she had lived among his things. Those fancy knives, the blond wood rocking chair. She had felt she'd known him.

The phone rang at ten minutes past six.

The evening news, Meredith thought. America was now watching the evening news.

Connie was there to check the caller ID. "Number unavailable," she said. "Should I answer?"

"I'll answer," Toby said. He had just come downstairs in fresh clothes. Meredith had been unable to tell him or Connie about the Thad Orlo/Kirby Delarest story, partly because it was so bizarre that Meredith couldn't believe it was true, though of course it was true. Freddy hadn't acted alone; he'd had helpers, *henchmen,* Dev had called them, people helping him to dig a mass financial grave—and it made sense that Meredith would know some of these people. *Kirby Delarest was Thad Orlo.* All of the things that hadn't made sense about Kirby Delarest were now explained. Meredith had been right about Thad Orlo, and she had been right about the phony NASA star, and yet she worried about just how right she had been. The $4 billion in those accounts were, however tangentially, connected to her. Had Freddy hidden the money there for her? He'd moved it on October seventeenth—*Samantha's birthday*—but what did that mean? Was it a coincidence, or was the money for Samantha?

Meredith was afraid to think any further.

She also didn't tell Connie or Toby because she wanted to keep the noxious fumes of the story out of this house. This house was Meredith's only safe place. But she couldn't keep the phone from ringing.

"*I'll* get it," Connie said, and she picked up. "Hello?"

Meredith watched Connie's face, trying to gauge friend or foe, but she couldn't tell. Connie looked surprised; her mouth formed a small, tight "o." Her eyes popped, then mysteriously, filled with tears. Were these sad tears, happy tears, angry tears, a little of each? Meredith couldn't tell.

Connie held out the phone. "It's for you," she whispered. She blinked. Tears spilled down her pretty, tanned face. Meredith took the phone, and Connie moved away with purpose.

"Hello?" Meredith said, thinking, *What has Connie just handed me?*

"Mom?"

Oh, my God. She nearly dropped the phone. It was Carver.

What did he say? What did she say? She could only remember the conversation in snippets afterwards.

"I saw the news," he said.

"Did you?" she said.

"Jesus, Mom. I can't believe it."

She didn't want to talk about this. She had her son on the phone. Her baby, her beloved child.

"How are you? What are you doing? How is your brother? Are you making it? Are you okay?" She would have said there was nothing bigger inside her than her hurt, but yes, this was bigger. Her love for her sons was bigger.

But Carver was stuck back on this other thing. "He cheated on you, Mom. Now do you see? Please tell me you see him for what he really is…a shallow, empty person who fills himself up with lies and things that he can take from other people. You get it now, right?"

"I get it," she said, though she was lying. She didn't get it. "I need to talk to him."

"Who?"

"Your father."

"No!" Carver shouted. "Forget him, leave him, divorce him, get him out of your life. This is your chance."

"Okay," Meredith said. "Yes, you're right. You're right. How are you? How are you?"

Carver's voice softened. "But he did love you, Mom. That's what blows me away about all of this. He really did love you. He revered you, like a queen or a goddess. Leo agrees with me. He knows it, too."

Leo! Meredith thought. She wanted to talk to Leo. He was such a straight arrow, such a good kid, on his hands and knees scraping wax off the hard wood floor of the church, refusing Meredith's help. There had been one time when Meredith had shot up to Choate in the middle of the week to see Leo's lacrosse game. Meredith broke the speed limit in the Jaguar, but she had made it there in time to surprise Leo, and he had scored the goal that won the game. Meredith had been there to cheer, and then afterward, she took Leo and Carver and two teammates to Carini's for pizza. She had made it back to the city before Freddy got home from work, but when he walked in, she told him what she'd done; she told him about the goal and how surprised Leo had been to see her, and how he'd kissed her through the car window before she pulled out of the gates, even though his buddies were watching.

Freddy had smiled wearily. "You're a wonderful mother, Meredith," he'd said. But his mind had been elsewhere.

"Are you okay?" Meredith asked. "Is Leo okay?"

Carver sighed. "We're doing okay, Mom."

But what did this *mean?* Was he really okay? Meredith had been picturing the two of them in a big, dusty Victorian house. She wanted to hear about the house, how they were refinishing the floors or painting the baseboards.

"We love you," Carver said. "But I'm calling to make sure you do the right thing. File for divorce. Please. Promise me."

She wanted to promise. But she couldn't promise. No one understood. She was absolutely alone. She panicked because she heard the end of the conversation encroaching in Carver's voice, and there was still so much to say. So much she wanted to know. He was going to hang up, and she didn't have a number for him. He would be lost to her again, as lost to her as Freddy was, as her father was.

"Wait!" she said. "Your number! Can I call you?"

Again, the sigh. Carver had become a sigher, like a disappointed parent.

"Julie Schwarz wants Leo to wait," he said. "Until the smoke clears a little more. Until a little more time has passed. And that goes for me, too. I shouldn't have called you now, but I had to. I had to talk to you."

"I know," Meredith said. "Thank you."

"You heard me, Mom, right?" Carver said.

"Right," Meredith whispered.

"I love you, Mom. Leo loves you, too," Carver said. And then he hung up.

Meredith said, "I love you, too. I love you, too!" She became aware that she was speaking to a dead phone, and she became aware that there were other people in the room: Toby, who was watching her, and Connie, who was watching Toby watch her.

CONNIE

She should have gone over to Dan's house for dinner. When she called him to say she was staying home, he told her he might just go out by himself. Connie pictured him eating at the bar at A.K. Diamond's, where he knew everyone and everyone knew him, where his old flames would find him, or the cute receptionist from the salon would be sitting on a neighboring bar stool. Connie desperately wanted to go with him, but she couldn't go out; her face was all over the news. Sure enough, when Connie checked her cell phone, she had missed calls from Iris and Lizbet; they had seen her on CNN. She couldn't go anywhere.

"Remember, I'm leaving for New Hampshire on Friday," Dan said.

Connie hesitated. Dan was taking Donovan and Charlie on a wilderness-survival camping trip for three days in the White Mountains. He wouldn't even be able to call her.

"I have to stay in," Connie said. She knew he was waiting for her to invite him over, but she couldn't do that, either. The emotions in this house were too raw. "Tomorrow for sure."

But now, she wished she'd gone. She watched Meredith hang up the phone. Meredith said, "That was Carver."

Connie could barely bring herself to nod. She was the one who had answered the phone, she was the one who had heard Carver say, "Hi, Aunt Connie? It's Carver. Is my mom there?" Connie had been consumed by an emotion she couldn't identify, though now she supposed it was just plain envy, concentrated envy, envy in its purest and most insidious form. Meredith's son had called her. He had heard the news and reached out. He had told her he loved her. Connie had felt both pierced and deflated. She could check her cell phone right now, but she knew that even though her face had been on TV all day, there would be no message or missed call from Ashlyn.

*   *   *

Meredith seemed a little lighter since the phone call from Carver—although she was quick to admit that Carver had barely said a word about himself. Meredith didn't know where he was living or what he was working on or if he still had friends or if he was dating anyone.

"He just called to make sure I was going to divorce Freddy," she said.

"And what did you tell him?" Connie asked.

Toby stared. Meredith said nothing.

"My offer stands," Connie said. "If you want to divorce Freddy, I'll pay for it."

Meredith said nothing. Connie could see the shine of the phone call wearing off. Meredith was very slowly slipping back down to her previous depths.

"He told me he loved me," Meredith said.

"Of course he loves you," Toby said. "He's your son."

The phone rang again, just as the sun was setting, at seven thirty. Setting sun at seven thirty? God, the summer was ending; they were running out of time. Dan was leaving the day after tomorrow for his camping trip, and when he got back, they would have a scant week left together. Last year, Connie remembered, she had been grateful for the end of summer. The sunshine and the beach and the forced cheerfulness had been trying for her. Last summer, she had been unable to look at the ocean without thinking of Wolf's ashes. So much had changed in one year; she should be happy for that.

Toby was over by the phone, checking the caller ID. "It's an unknown caller," he said. "Want me to answer it?"

"No," Connie said, but Meredith said, "Go ahead," and since Meredith's answer would always trump Connie's answer with Toby, he answered.

"Hello?" He paused. He looked at Meredith. He said, "May I

tell her who's calling?" He paused. He said, "I won't give her the phone unless you tell me who this is."

Then, to Meredith, he said, "It's her."

"Samantha?" Meredith said.

Toby nodded.

"No," Meredith said.

Toby hung up. Connie thought, *I told him not to answer.* But her insides were jumping. She hated to admit it, but it was exciting living through this kind of drama.

"Wait a minute," she said. "That was *Samantha?*"

"Samantha Deuce," Toby said.

Meredith slowly shook her head.

"You don't seem surprised," Connie said.

"She called earlier."

"She *did?*"

"I answered, and when I figured out it was her, I said, 'No,' and hung up."

"Wow," Connie said. "That woman has guts."

"Well, yeah," Meredith said.

Connie put out some crackers with bluefish pâté, but none of them ate. It grew dark in the room, and Connie thought, *I should turn on some lights,* but lights seemed too harsh, or perhaps too optimistic, so Connie lit candles, as she might have during an electrical storm. It was too bad it wasn't raining, she thought. A storm would fit the mood.

Connie wanted wine. If this had been three weeks ago, she would already be on her third glass. And Dan wasn't here, so... Connie poured herself some.

She said, "Meredith, do you want wine?"

Meredith said, "Do I want wine? Yes. But I shouldn't. I won't."

Connie shouldn't either, but she was going to anyway. She took in a mouthful, thinking, *Deliver me.* But the wine tasted sour; it tasted like a headache. She poured it down the drain. She got herself a glass of ice water with lemon. She knew they should do something about dinner. Meredith was in the armchair, folded into herself like an injured bird, and Toby was sprawled across the sofa, keeping vigil on Meredith. He loved her. It was as plain as the nose on his face.

But Meredith wouldn't divorce Freddy. The man had done despicable things, both publicly and privately, and yet Meredith still loved him. Any other woman would have left Freddy Delinn in the dust, but not Meredith.

Dinner, they needed to eat dinner, Connie thought, *something simple—sandwiches, salad, scrambled eggs, even. But she wasn't hungry.*

She said, "Meredith, are you hungry?"

Meredith said, "I'll never eat again."

At that second, Toby's cell phone rang. He said, "It's Michael," and he bounded up the stairs to his bedroom.

Meredith said, "I can't believe Samantha called here twice."

"I'm sure she wants to talk to you," Connie said.

"I'm sure she does," Meredith said.

They sat for a second, listening to the mantel clock tick. Connie could hear the strains of Toby's voice. "Hey, buddy." Everyone was talking to their children tonight, except for her.

Meredith must have heard Toby, too, because she said, "It was good to talk to Carver. It was magical to hear his voice, just to hear him call me 'Mom,' you know? Just to hear him say he loves me. I can't see him, I can't touch him, but at least I know he's alive out in the world somewhere. Thinking of me."

Connie was suddenly too sad for tears. This, she realized, must have been how Meredith felt. Her sadness took on a sharp, shining edge.

She said, "Do you think Samantha was the only one?"

"What?" Meredith said.

"Well, we know Freddy did things in a big way."

"What are you saying?" Meredith asked. "That there might have been other lovers?"

"There might have been," Connie said. "I mean, you know how Freddy was."

"No," Meredith said. Her voice was cold stone. "How was Freddy?"

"He was flirtatious," Connie said. "And at times, he was more than flirtatious."

"Did he ever make a pass at you?" Meredith asked. She sat up in the armchair, her spine straight, her chin lifted as though there were a string from the top of her head to the ceiling. Meredith was so small in stature, she looked like a ventriloquist's dummy. "He did, didn't he?"

"He did," Connie said. She couldn't believe she was saying this. She had decided there would be no more taboo subjects, but really, to bring *this* up? *Stop, Connie, stop! Shut up!* But there was something inside driving her. She couldn't say what. An urge to *tell.* "He made a pass at me in Cap d'Antibes. He told me I was a beautiful woman, and then he kissed me."

"He kissed you."

"And he, sort of, touched my breast. Cupped it."

Meredith nodded once, succinctly. "I see. Where was Wolf?"

"Running."

"And where was I?"

"Shopping."

"So the two of you were alone in the house, then," Meredith said. "Did you sleep with him?"

"No, Meredith, I did not sleep with him."

"This was...when?" Meredith said. "What year?"

Connie tried to think. She couldn't think. "It was the year we had lunch at that restaurant in Annecy. Do you remember that lunch?"

"Yes," Meredith said. "So...two thousand three. Does that sound right?"

"I don't know," Connie said. "I guess so."

"Before Samantha," Meredith said. She slapped her hands against her thighs. "So maybe there were others, then. Safe to assume there were others. Dozens, maybe, or hundreds..."

"Meredith..." Connie said.

"Why," Meredith said. She shut her mouth and swallowed. "Why on earth didn't you tell me?"

God, what was the answer to that question? Freddy had made a pass; Connie had deflected it. There was, essentially, nothing to tell. Maybe she had kept quiet about it because it was a private moment between her and Freddy; he was paying her a compliment, and it had made Connie feel good. It had made her feel *desired*. She didn't want to ruin that feeling by turning it into something else. Maybe she hadn't wanted to spoil the week in Cap d'Antibes by making a mountain out of a molehill. Maybe she hadn't had access to the kind of language it would require to tell Meredith what had happened without implicating herself. It hadn't been Connie's fault. Except, she had worn the clingy patio dress that put her breasts on display. But a woman should be able to dress however she wanted. It wasn't an invitation for men to act inappropriately.

"I don't know why I didn't tell you," Connie said. "It didn't seem like a big deal."

"My husband kissed you and touched you, and you remember it all these years later, but it didn't seem like a big deal?"

"It was alarming," Connie said. "Of course it was. But I backed away. In my mind, I minimalized it. I guess because I was embarrassed."

Meredith stared. She had an arsenal of cold, scary looks. "I can't believe you."

"Meredith, I'm sorry..."

"You're my best friend. And after you, my closest friend was Samantha."

"I didn't sleep with Freddy," Connie said. "I didn't encourage Freddy or invite any further attention. I did nothing wrong."

"You didn't tell me," Meredith said.

It suddenly felt like a question pulled from a woman's magazine: If your best friend's husband makes a pass at you, do you tell her? Certainly the answer was no. But maybe the answer was yes. Maybe Connie should have told Meredith. One thing was for sure: Connie should *not* have told Meredith about it tonight. She had done so out of meanness; she had wanted to hurt Meredith, when Meredith was already hurting so badly. *Do I look like a woman who needs more surprise news?* But why? And then Connie knew: she was jealous about the phone call from Carver. Now look at the mess. If Connie had intended to keep her moment with Freddy a secret, it should have remained a secret forever.

"I'm sorry," Connie said. "I should have told you, I guess."

"You *guess?*" Meredith said. "You *guess?*" Her voice was shrill and righteous. Connie stood up. She needed a glass of wine; she didn't care if it tasted like Drano. She took a glass from the cabinet and opened the fridge.

Meredith said, "That's right. Pour yourself some wine. That'll fix everything."

Connie slammed the refrigerator door shut, then she threw the wine glass into the kitchen sink and the glass shattered. The noise was startling. Her anger and upset were unbelievable, and she knew that Meredith's anger and upset matched, if not surpassed, hers. Was there room in one house for so much agony? Connie looked at the broken glass — and she spotted a chip in her enamel sink. Her gorgeous farmer's sink, of which she had once been so proud.

Wolf, she thought. *Ashlyn.* Lost to her. Lost.

She thought, *Dan. I should have gone to Dan's.*

She said, "Well, while we're at it."

"While we're at it, what?" Meredith said.

"While we're at it, I'm not the only one who made a mistake. I'm not the only one in the wrong here."

"What are you talking about?" Meredith said.

She was standing with her hands on her hips, her graying hair tucked behind her ears, her horn-rimmed glasses slipping to the end of her nose. She had gotten those glasses in the eighth grade. Connie remembered her walking into American History class and showing off the glasses, and then in lunch and study hall, passing them around for other girls to try on. Connie had been the first one to try them on; they had turned the cafeteria into a blurry, swarming mass of color. Connie had almost vomited. And yet, she had been jealous of Meredith's glasses, and of Meredith, since childhood. Practically her entire life.

"I'm talking about the things you said about Wolf," Connie said. "The horrible things. You insinuated that we were pulling our money because Wolf had brain cancer and didn't know any better."

Meredith said, "You basically came right out and called Freddy a crook."

"Meredith," Connie said. "He was a crook."

Meredith pushed her glasses up her nose. "You're right," she said. "He was a crook." She stared at Connie. She seemed to be waiting for something. "And what I said about Wolf was ruthless. I'm sorry. I don't know how I could have been so awful."

"And you didn't come to Wolf's funeral," Connie said. "And you knew that I needed you there."

"I was on my way," Meredith said. "I was at the door of the apartment, wearing a charcoal-gray suit, I remember. And Freddy talked me out of it." She bit her lower lip. "I don't know how he did it, but he did. You know Freddy."

"Whatever Freddy told you to do, you did," Connie said.

"That's why I'm in trouble with the Feds," Meredith said. "Freddy asked me to transfer fifteen million dollars from the business to our personal account three days before he was exposed, and I did it. I thought he was going to buy a house in Aspen." She laughed. "I thought I was going to Aspen, but instead I'm going to jail."

So that was why she was under investigation, Connie thought. She hadn't been brave enough to ask. Another taboo shattered. She said, "You were supposed to come visit me here in nineteen eighty-two, but you didn't come because of Freddy. Because Freddy had sent that telegram. He'd proposed, remember? And I said, 'That's great, we can celebrate your engagement.' But you only wanted to celebrate with Freddy."

"That was thirty years ago," Meredith said.

"Exactly," Connie said. "He's been holding you hostage for thirty years."

"I still don't understand why you didn't tell me what happened in France," Meredith said. "Did our friendship mean nothing?"

"Wait a minute," Connie said. "We've both done damage to the friendship. It wasn't just me. I didn't tell you about Freddy because, at the time, my best judgment told me to let it go. I'm sorry I brought it up."

"Not as sorry as I am," Meredith said.

"I'm not Samantha Deuce," Connie said. "You're angry with Samantha. Not with me."

At that moment, Toby came downstairs. "What's going on?" he said. "Did someone break a glass?"

"Connie," Meredith said.

Toby turned to Connie. Connie could speak, but Toby wouldn't hear her. This was her house—where, it might be pointed out, both Meredith and Toby were guests—but she had no voice.

"I'm going to bed," Connie said. *Dinner,* she thought. She foraged through the pantry and selected a Something Natural herb roll, which she took a bite out of like an apple.

Meredith said, "No, the two of you stay up. *I'm* going to bed."

Old habits die hard, Connie thought. It was exactly nine thirty.

*   *   *

Connie spent the night on the living-room sofa. After growing accustomed to sleeping in a real bed, she felt that the sofa offered as much comfort as an old door laid across sawhorses, and when she woke up, Connie felt like she had fallen from a ten-story building. Her breath stank of onions from the herb roll. She had forgotten to pour herself a glass of water, and her lips were cracked. She needed lip balm. She needed to brush her teeth.

She stood up, gingerly. She decided she wouldn't think about anything else until she took care of these small tasks.

Water. Chapstick. Toothbrush.

She cleaned out the sink—carefully removing the shards of glass with rubber gloves. She made a pot of coffee. She was okay. Her heart hurt but she was functioning.

Her cell phone was there on the counter, charging, and because she couldn't help herself, she checked for missed calls or messages. She was thinking of Dan, but really she was thinking of Ashlyn. There was nothing new. The voice mails from Iris and Lizbet lingered, unheard.

The coffee machine gurgled. Connie got a mug and poured in half-and-half and warmed it up in the microwave. She poured in the coffee and added sugar. She could remember drinking coffee for the first time with Meredith and Annabeth Martin in Annabeth's fancy drawing room at the house in Wynnewood. Connie and Meredith were wearing long dresses. Connie's dress had been red gingham with a white eyelet panel down the front that was embroidered with strawberries. Connie remembered thinking, *Coffee?* That was something adults drank. But that was what Annabeth Martin had served; there was no lemonade or fruit punch. Annabeth had poured cream out of a tiny silver pitcher and offered the girls sugar cubes, stacked like crystalline blocks of ice, from a silver bowl. Connie's coffee had spilled into her saucer and Annabeth had said, "Two hands, Constance."

And then, when Connie got home and told her mother that Annabeth had served them coffee, Veronica had said, "That woman is trying to stunt your growth."

Connie smiled now, remembering. Then she felt a heaviness gather inside her. She and Meredith had been connected since her earliest memories. She didn't want Meredith to be upset with her. She couldn't lose another person.

She took her coffee out to the deck. There were a few clouds on the horizon, but the rest of the sky was brilliant blue. Nantucket was the kind of place that was so beautiful it broke your heart, because you couldn't keep it. The seasons passed, the weather changed, you had to leave—and return to the city or the suburbs, your school, your job, your real life.

Connie drank her coffee. She thought, *I can't lose anyone else.*

She turned and saw Meredith standing in the doorway, holding a cup of coffee. She was in a short white nightgown. She looked like a doll. Her hair was lighter.

Connie spoke without thinking. "Your hair is lighter."

Meredith said, "You're just saying that because I'm mad."

"I'm saying that because it's true. It's lighter. It's blonder."

Meredith took the seat next to Connie and reached for her hand. "I'm sorry," she said.

"I'm sorry," Connie said.

Meredith narrowed her eyes at the view. Her face was tanned, and she had a spray of freckles across her nose. She said, "I would have died without you."

Connie squeezed her hand. "Shhh," she said.

Later that morning, the phone rang. Toby said, "Geez, the phone has rung more in the past two days than it has in the past two weeks."

Connie threw him a look. Meredith was upstairs getting dressed. There were no reporters out front, so Connie and Meredith were going to run to the grocery store, and if that went well, to Nantucket

Bookworks to stock up on novels. Dan had called; he was taking Connie to the Pearl for dinner, so Meredith and Toby would be on their own at home.

Connie checked the caller ID. It was the law firm. Connie picked it up. The fifteen-year-old attorney asked for Meredith.

Connie said, "Just a moment, please."

Connie caught Meredith coming down the stairs. She said, "It's your counsel."

Meredith said, "I wish we'd left five minutes ago."

Connie said, "I'm going to run up and brush my teeth. We'll go when you're off the phone?"

"Okay," Meredith said. She had her wig in one hand. They were back to the wig.

Goddamn you, Freddy, Connie thought.

She climbed the stairs slowly because she wanted to listen. Toby was right there in the room, probably unabashedly eavesdropping. Connie heard Meredith say, "Hello?" Pause. "I'm doing okay. Do you have any news for me?"

Connie stopped in her tracks, but she was near the top of the stairs, and she didn't hear anything more.

MEREDITH

He wouldn't talk to her.

"I asked everyone in the system at Butner," Dev said. "Everyone gave the same answer: Fred Delinn won't take your phone call, and they can't make him. They can't even make him listen while you talk."

Meredith felt her cheeks burn. She was embarrassed. Humiliated. She was dying a living death. "Why won't he talk to me?"

"It's anyone's guess, Meredith," Dev said. "The guy is a sociopath, and he's deteriorated mentally since he's been in. Everyone at the prison knows what happened with Mrs. Deuce. They understand why you want an audience. Mrs. Briggs, the warden's secretary, personally pushed for Fred to face you on Skype and at least be forced to listen to what you have to say, but that idea was shot down. It's against prisoner's rights. They can lock him up, they can make him go to meals, they can make him go out into the yard at nine a.m. and come in from the yard at ten a.m., they can make him take his meds. But they can't make him talk, and they can't make him talk to you."

Meredith reminded herself to breathe. Toby was somewhere in the room, though she wasn't sure where. Her right knee was knocking into the table leg. "I should go down there and see him in person."

"He won't see you," Dev said, "and they can't make him. You'll go down there for nothing, Meredith. It's a romantic idea, like in the movies. I get it. You go down there, he sees you, something clicks, he offers up all kinds of explanations and apologies. That isn't going to happen. He's a sick man, Meredith. He's not the man you once knew."

She was tired of this idea, even though she knew it to be true.

"So you're telling me I can't go?"

"I'm telling you you shouldn't go," Dev said. "Because he won't see you. You can travel down there to hot and desolate Butner, you can plan on enduring a media circus, you can meet with Nancy Briggs and Cal Green, the warden, but they're just going to tell you the same thing that I'm telling you. He won't see you. He won't talk to you."

"I'm not going to yell at him," Meredith said. "I'm not going to hurt him. I'm not going to go on some kind of crazed jealous-wife rampage. I just want answers."

"You won't get answers," Dev said.

She couldn't believe what she was hearing. She had thought that perhaps the prison would make it difficult for her to talk to Fred.

But from the sound of it, they wanted to facilitate the phone call but couldn't—because Freddy refused. It was the very worst thing: He had stolen everybody's money, he had lied to the SEC and single-handedly put the nation's economy in the toilet. He had cheated on Meredith for six and a half years with a woman she considered to be their closest friend. He had lied to Meredith tens of thousands of times—fine. But what she couldn't forgive was this, now. What she couldn't forgive was this stonewalled silence. He *owed* her a conversation. He *owed her the truth*—as egregious as it might be. But the truth was going to stay locked up in Butner. It was going to stay locked up in the sooty black recesses of Freddy's disturbed mind.

"Fine," Meredith said. She slammed down the phone. She was furious. Furious! She would make a statement to the press vilifying the man. She would take down Freddy and the undisputed harlot who was Samantha Champion Deuce. (She wrote her own *Post* headlines: *CHAMPION HOMEWRECKER, CHAMPION TWO-FACED LIAR.*) Meredith *would* file for divorce, and three hundred million Americans would support her; they would raise her up. She would regain her position in society; she would hit the lecture circuit.

She turned around. Toby was standing there, and something about the look on his face made Meredith's anger pop like a soap bubble.

She said, "He won't talk to me. He refuses. And they can't make him."

Toby nodded slowly. Meredith expected him to take this opportunity to say, *He's a rat bastard, Meredith. A piece of shit. What further proof do you need?* But instead, Toby said, "Maybe he'll change his mind."

Meredith smiled sadly and headed for the front door to meet Connie in the Escalade. They were going to the store. Meredith had planned on wearing her wig, but this suddenly seemed pointless. The wig was meant to protect her, but she had just suffered the ultimate blow. Nothing anyone did could affect her now; the wig had been rendered useless. Meredith left it on the stairs. When she got home, she would throw it away.

Toby was being kind about Freddy because he could afford to be. He knew, as Meredith did, that Freddy would never change his mind.

That night, before she left for her date with Dan, Connie made dinner for Meredith and Toby. It was a crabmeat pasta with sautéed zucchini in a lemon tarragon cream sauce, a stacked salad of heirloom tomatoes, Maytag blue cheese, and basil, sprinkled with toasted pine nuts and drizzled with hot bacon dressing, and home-made Parker House rolls with seasoned butter.

Unbelievable, Meredith thought. Connie had showered and dressed. She looked absolutely gorgeous, and she had made this meal.

"I feel guilty," Meredith said. "You should have served this meal to Dan."

"I offered," Connie said. "But he really wanted to go out."

Without us, Meredith thought.

"And I wanted to cook for you," Connie said.

Because she feels sorry for me, Meredith thought. *Again.* But there was something almost comforting about reaching this point. Nothing left to lose, nothing left to care about, nothing left to want.

The outdoor table was set with a tablecloth and candles. There was a breeze off the ocean that held a hint of chill.

Fall was coming.

Connie wrapped herself up in a pashmina and said, "Bon appétit! I'm off for my date. I'll be back tomorrow morning. Dan's on the noon boat."

"This is lovely," Meredith said. "Thank you."

"And there's dessert in the fridge," Connie said.

"Have fun," Toby said, pushing her gently to the front door.

She left, and Meredith had the feeling that Connie was the parent, and she and Toby were teenagers on a date. It was supposed to be romantic—the candlelight, the delicious food, the ocean before them like a Broadway show. Meredith should have dressed up, but she was in the same clothes she'd put on that morning: a ratty old T-shirt from Choate that Carver had worn his senior year, and her navy-blue gym shorts. She knew it was possible that she would sleep in these clothes and wear them again the next day. She didn't care how she looked. She didn't even care, anymore, about her hair.

Thirty years of marriage, and he wouldn't talk to her. So many dinners at Rinaldo's she had sat with Freddy the way she was now sitting with Toby, and she had talked about her day, and Freddy had nodded and asked questions, and when Meredith asked him about work, he'd run his hands through his hair and check his BlackBerry as if a pithy answer would be displayed there, and then he'd say something about the stress and unpredictability of his business. Meredith had no idea that Freddy was printing out fake statements on an ancient dot-matrix printer, or that he was spending his lunch hours with Samantha Deuce at the Stanhope Hotel. Freddy had pretended to live in awe of Meredith, but what he really must have been thinking was how blind and gullible and stupid she was. She was like...his mother, Mrs. Delinn, who toiled at providing for Freddy and giving him love. *He'll pretend like he can get along without it, but he can't. Freddy needs his love.* And Meredith had been only too happy to take over the care and maintenance of Freddy Delinn. He was a rich man, but she was the one who rubbed his back and kissed his eyelids and defended him tooth and nail to those who said he was corrupt.

There had been one time in early December when Freddy had called out in the night. He had shuddered in bed, and when Meredith rolled over, she saw his eyes fly open. She touched his silvering hair and said, "What? What is it?"

He didn't speak, though his eyes widened. Was he awake?

He said, "David."

And Meredith thought, "David? Who is David?" Then she realized he meant his brother.

"It's okay," Meredith said. "I'm here."

And he had turned to her and said, "You're never going to leave me, Meredith, right? Promise me. No matter what?"

"No matter what," she'd said.

Freddy's eyes had closed then, though Meredith could see manic activity beneath his twitching lids. She had stayed awake as long as she could, watching him, thinking, *David. I wonder what made him dream of David?*

But now she suspected he hadn't been thinking about David at all. He'd been thinking about money, the SEC, a looming investigation, being caught, discovered, indicted, imprisoned. He had invoked his brother's name to throw Meredith off the trail of his real worries. He had known how to lie to her, even when he was only semiconscious.

No matter what, Meredith had promised. But she hadn't known what kind of "what" he was talking about.

"I don't think I can eat," Meredith said. Toby was very patiently holding his utensils in the hover position over his plate, waiting for her.

Toby's face darkened. "The guy is the biggest creep on earth," he said. "He didn't deserve you."

It was confounding hearing these words from Toby. Quite possibly, Freddy had said something similar about Toby so many years ago, when Meredith told him about how Toby broke up with her on the night of her high-school graduation. *You're better off without him. He didn't deserve you.*

Toby put a forkful of pasta in his mouth and chewed sadly, if such a thing was possible.

"You're luckier than Freddy," Meredith said. "You got me at my best. Sixteen, seventeen, eighteen. That was the best Meredith, Toby, and she was yours."

Toby swallowed and looked at her. "You're at your best right now." He fingered the fraying sleeve of her ancient T-shirt. "You're the best Meredith right now."

Meredith thought back to the day of Veronica O'Brien's funeral. Meredith had arrived at the church nearly an hour early, and the only person there was Toby. He was sitting in the back pew, and Meredith had tapped his shoulder and he turned and they looked at each other and—what could Meredith say? She hadn't seen Toby in nearly twenty years at that point, but the sight of his face brought her to her knees. He stood up and took her in his arms. It started out as a condolence hug. His mother had, after all, just died. The indomitable Veronica O'Brien was gone.

Meredith said into his chest, "I'm so sorry, Toby."

He tightened his grip on her, and she felt her body temperature rise. She thought she was imagining it. Of course, she was imagining it. She was married, married to rich and powerful Freddy Delinn. Freddy gave her everything her heart desired, so what could she possibly want from Toby now? But the human heart, as Meredith learned then, rarely paid attention to the rules. She felt Toby's arms tense around her, she felt his leg nudge up against her leg, she felt his breath in her hair.

"Meredith," he said. "My Meredith."

The next thing Meredith knew, Toby was leading her out of the church, leading her to the shady spot under a majestic tree where his car was parked. He opened the passenger-side door for her and she got in.

She stared out the windshield at the trunk of the hundred-year-old tree, and when Toby got into the car, Meredith said, "Where are we going?"

"I want to take you somewhere," he said. "I want to make love to you."

"Toby," Meredith said.

"Did you feel it back there?" he asked. "Tell me you did."

"I did."

"You did, right? Look at me, I'm shaking."

Yes, Meredith was shaking, too. She tried to think of Freddy, who had hired a helicopter and a private car to get her here, but who had not given her the most precious thing—and that was his time. He hadn't come with her.

Meredith said, "This is insane."

"I should have been more persistent at Connie's wedding," he said. "I knew then that I'd made a mistake with you."

"You broke my heart," Meredith said. "I thought we would get married."

"I want to take you somewhere."

"But the *funeral*..."

"We have time," he said. He started the engine and drove out of the churchyard

"We should turn around," Meredith said.

"Tell me you don't want me."

"I can't tell you that," Meredith said.

"So you do want me?"

She was glowing with arousal, but it wasn't just sexual. A part of Meredith had been yearning for this moment — Toby wanting her back—since she was eighteen years old.

He drove through the town of Villanova to the O'Brien house. He screeched into the driveway, and he and Meredith got out. The day was hot, Meredith was wearing a black lace Collette Dinnigan dress; it was too fancy for the Main Line, and now it was plastered to her, and itching. Toby led Meredith into the O'Briens' garage, which smelled exactly the same as it had twenty-five years earlier—like cut grass and gasoline from Bill O'Brien's riding mower. A tennis ball hung from a string over one of the bays; it had been placed there when Veronica smashed her Cutlass Supreme into the garage's back wall after too many gimlets at Aronimink. As soon as they were shut in the cool dim of the garage, Toby took Meredith's face in his hands, and he kissed her.

And oh, what a kiss it had been. It had gone on and on, Meredith *could not* get enough, it had been so long since someone had kissed her like that. Freddy loved her, but there were a hundred things more important to him than sex and romance. Money, money, money, his business, his reputation, his clients, his profile in *Forbes,* his appearance, his yacht, his suits, his early bedtime—all of those rated with him in a way that kissing Meredith did not.

"Come upstairs with me," Toby said. "To my room."

She thought of parking with Toby in the Nova. *The best of times are when I'm alone with you.* She tried to think of Freddy, but she couldn't conjure his face. So, she would go upstairs with Toby. She would have him again, just this once.

They hurried through the house, up the stairs. It was so familiar, it played tricks on Meredith's sense of time and place. She had started her day in Southampton 2004, but now it was three o'clock in the afternoon and she was in Villanova 1978. Toby's room was exactly the same—why hadn't Veronica turned it into an exercise room or a study like every other empty nester? There was Toby's lava lamp, his poster of Jimmy Page, his water bed. The heels of Meredith's Manolos got caught in the shag rug. She stumbled and Toby caught her, then somehow they both crashed onto the water bed, and this knocked Meredith back into her present self. She stared up at the ceiling, and there were the tape marks from where Toby had hung his Farrah Fawcett poster.

He started to kiss her again. She said, "Toby, stop. I can't."

"What?" he said. "Why not?"

She rolled onto her side, creating wave motion in the mattress. She looked into his green eyes. "I'm married, Toby."

"Please, Meredith," he said. "Please?" He looked like he might cry. She reached out to wipe away the first tear with her thumb.

"I'm sorry, Toby," she said. "I can't."

He watched her for a second, perhaps to see if she was bluffing. She hoisted herself up off the bed and straightened her dress.

"So that's it?" he said.

"We should go back," she said. "It's your mother's funeral."

"Is it the man you love?" Toby asked. "Or is it the money?"

Meredith stared.

"Is it the houses? Is it the place in France? Is it the behemoth boat? I saw her once, you know, in the Mediterranean. Saint Tropez."

"Toby, let's go."

"Does he make you laugh?" Toby asked.

"No," Meredith said honestly. "But you're not very funny right now, either. Let's go back."

"I can't believe you're doing this to me."

Meredith turned on him. "What am I supposed to do? Allow you to make love to me, allow the feelings to come back, and then watch you take off tomorrow for...where? Where, Toby?"

"Spain," he said. "On Tuesday."

"See?" she said.

"You wouldn't come with me even if I asked you," he said. "Because you're married to money."

Meredith shook her head. "I wouldn't come with you even if you asked me because you wouldn't ask me."

On the way back to the church, Toby wept silently, and Meredith felt bad. He had just lost his mother. But Meredith was angry, too—for so many reasons.

Connie and Wolf had been ascending the church stairs. Connie waved to Toby to hurry up; they were to follow the casket inside. She herded Meredith along, too, but Meredith demurred. She wasn't family. Connie studied her critically and said, "Did you two go somewhere together?"

Meredith kissed the side of Connie's face. She said, "I have to leave right after. I'm sorry, Con. I can't stay for the..."

"You can't stay?" Connie said.

"I have to get back," Meredith said.

Toby appeared then, over Meredith's shoulder. "Yeah," he said. "She has to get back."

Now, Meredith smiled sadly at Toby. "At your mother's funeral..."

"You did the right thing," he said. "Then."

"Yes," she said. "I suppose I did. Then."

Meredith reached a hand out to him, and he grabbed it and brought it to his mouth. They rose from their chairs and faced each other and Meredith thought, *My God, what am I doing?* And in a flash, it came back: the greedy, hungry desire for this man. Did Toby understand? Did he feel it? Toby lifted her up by the hips, and she rubbed against the length of his body. He was more powerful than Freddy; Meredith felt featherlight, no more substantial than a wish or a hope. Toby kissed her, his mouth was warm and buttery, tender at first, then fierce. She wanted fierce. She wanted fire.

She had wanted to kiss Freddy good-bye before the FBI dragged him away last December, but when she'd taken his arm, he'd looked at her in wild confusion.

Toby's hands were in her hair. It was the tree on Robinhood Road all over again; something so old it was new. She could feel him hard against her leg, an occurrence that had confused her at age fifteen and that, truth be told, confused her now. Was she finally going to make love to Toby O'Brien again? His hands shifted to her back, his hands were up inside her T-shirt, unhooking her bra. Meredith thought of Freddy with his hand on Samantha's back. Was Meredith acting out of anger, out of retribution? If so, she should stop right now. But she didn't want to stop. She was pulsing with heat and light; she was experiencing an arousal that was as cutting and bordering on painful as it had been in her new body. This was a different kind of sexual awakening. It was electrifying in its utter wrongness. *Stop!* she thought. But she had no intention of stopping. It felt like Toby was going to tear her T-shirt in two just to get at her.

She twisted and darted inside the house.

"Meredith?" Toby said. He thought she was running away.

"Come on!" she screamed.

They made love on Toby's bed amid his rumpled sheets, which smelled like him. The sex was urgent, quick, rough, and desperate. Afterward, Meredith lay panting; the inside of her elbow hurt from where Toby had pinned her. Toby touched Meredith's hair, her graying hair, she was so much older now, but there was something fountain of youth–like about this summer. Meredith felt seventeen. She grabbed Toby's hand—the thought of being touched gently unnerved her—and she brought his hand to her mouth and kissed it first, then bit it.

"Ouch!" he said.

"I'm starving," she said.

That night, she feared she might dream about Freddy or Samantha or the warden at Butner—but instead she dreamed about their dog, Buttons. In Meredith's dream, Buttons was Toby's dog. He was standing on the bow of Toby's boat, eating a striped bass. Meredith was yelling at him—*No! Please Buttons. No, you'll get sick!* Toby was dressed in a white naval cadet's uniform, with the brass buttons and flat-top hat. He tried to pull the fish away from Buttons, but Buttons fought back like a junkyard dog and Toby ended up reeling backward and falling into the water. Meredith checked over the edge, but there was no sign of him, except for his floating hat. He had disappeared.

She woke up. Toby was propped on one elbow, watching her. She had inhaled the plate of food that Connie had made her, as well as a dish of panna cotta with berries, which Toby had brought to her in bed. She had left the smeared dishes on Toby's nightstand, and she'd fallen asleep without brushing her teeth. Now, she felt louche and irresponsible. Her elbow still hurt, and there was a dull soreness between her legs.

She couldn't help wondering if Freddy had ever gazed at her like this. She wanted so badly to believe that he had, but it was probably time to admit that Freddy had only adored himself. And money. And, possibly, Samantha. Meredith almost hoped he had adored Samantha, because that, at least, would mean Freddy was human.

She said to Toby, "I dreamed I lost you."

"I'm right here," he said.

Later, Meredith tiptoed naked across the hallway to her bedroom and climbed out onto her Juliet balcony for one quick second almost daring the paparazzi to come get her. *You're the best Mere dith right now.* She nearly laughed at the thought. She could do so much better than this.

Meredith slipped on a robe and padded down to the outdoor shower. She stayed in as long as she could in good conscience, and then she went back upstairs to dress. Toby was asleep in his bed, snoring. Meredith gently closed his door.

She retreated to her room. She pulled the cardboard box out of the closet. In that box was the spiral-bound notebook that she had been taking notes in on the day that Trina Didem interrupted her anthropology class to tell Meredith that her father was dead. Meredith had kept the notebook.

It still had plenty of empty pages. Meredith lay across her bed the way she used to as a schoolgirl. She meant to write Freddy a long letter that would elicit all the answers she needed, but the only two words that came to her, which she traced over and over again until the letters were heavy and dark, were **OBLIVION** and **LOVE**.

These were her crimes.

CONNIE

Dan would be gone for three days. Four, really, because he was coming back on the late boat on Monday, so Connie wouldn't see him until Tuesday. When she said good-bye to him, she felt a sick kind of desperation, which she tried to hide.

It was Dan who said, "I can't believe how much I'm going to miss you."

"And it's only three days," Connie said. What she meant was: *Think how bad it will be a week from now when I go back to Maryland.*

But then, too, Dan was excited about his camping trip with the boys. Connie had taken a gander at all their equipment: the three-season tent, the Coleman stove, the sleeping bags and air mattresses, the fishing poles and tackle box overflowing with flies, the generator and heavy-duty flashlights, the grocery bags of ramen noodles and peanut butter and instant oatmeal.

"We're going to catch fish and fry it up," Dan said. "We're going to hike and swim in waterfalls. We are going to *survive.*"

Connie pretended to be excited for him. He would be consumed with the wilderness, leaving little time to pine for Connie.

She kissed him good-bye in his driveway — self-consciously, because the boys were in the house — and then she drove away.

She needed something to keep her mind occupied. But what? And then it came to her. She would teach Meredith to cook.

"You're going to teach me to cook?" Meredith said. "Me?"

"I'm going to teach you the basics," Connie said. "So when you're..."

"Living alone..."

"You can feed yourself," Connie said.

"Cheaply," Meredith said.

"Right," Connie said. She smiled uneasily. She wanted to ask Meredith what her plans were once Labor Day arrived, but she didn't want to cause Meredith any additional anxiety. But really, what was she planning on doing? Where would she go? To Connecticut, to live near her boys? Before the most recent development with Freddy, Connie had feared that Meredith would move to North Carolina. That wouldn't happen now, thank God. Meredith needed to *cut bait*—Dan's term—and set herself free from that man. It was Connie's opinion that, in refusing to see her or talk to her on the phone, Freddy was doing Meredith a favor. He was giving her a chance to liberate herself. Really, Freddy was acting out of kindness—either that, or he was too much of a coward to answer for his actions.

"You can stay here, you know," Connie said. The house had heat. Connie had toyed with the idea of staying here herself. What reason did she have to go back to Bethesda? The powers that be had asked her to serve on the board of directors at the VA, so she could look forward to a lifetime of meetings in the building that had been more important to Wolf than his own life. She would go back to Bethesda because that was where her life was—her friends, her Whole Foods, her UPS man. She would go back to Bethesda because that house was where Ashlyn had grown up, and Connie would keep it for her, in case she ever decided to come back. Pointless? Probably.

"I can't stay here," Meredith said. "I've imposed on you long enough."

"You know better than to say that."

"I still have time to think about it," Meredith said. "I don't have to decide today. And there's still a chance that I'll be..."

Connie held up a hand. She couldn't stand to hear Meredith say it. She turned to her cutting board. "The first thing I'm going to teach you is how to chop an onion."

They chopped onion, shallot, garlic. They sautéed the shallot in butter. Connie showed Meredith how to move the shallot around the sauté pan with a wooden spoon. They added white wine and reduced it. They added Dijon mustard. They added heavy cream, salt and pepper, and a handful of fresh herbs.

"There," Connie said. "We have just made a mustard and herb cream sauce. You can add grilled sausage and serve this over pasta. You can substitute lemon juice for the Dijon and add shrimp."

Meredith was taking notes. It was so elementary, who needed notes? But Meredith had always been that kind of student.

Connie poached some chicken breasts in water, white wine, and celery leaves. She let the chicken cool, then shredded it with two forks.

"You don't even need a food processor," Connie said.

"That's good," Meredith said. "Because I can't afford one."

"You can probably buy one on eBay for cheap," Connie said.

"And which computer will I be using when I bid on eBay?" Meredith said, "And which credit card will I use?" She smiled. "I'm only kidding. I still have some money. Very little, but some. All I need is the guts to apply for a new credit card. All I need is the courage to walk into the public library and ask to use the Internet."

"Correct," Connie said. "You're a free citizen. You can do these things, and no one—*no one,* Meredith—can stop you."

They did eggs next. Eggs were cheap. Connie mixed three eggs with a little milk and some salt and pepper. She threw some butter in the frying pan.

"Scrambled eggs," Connie said. "Low heat, slow motion. You can add any kind of cheese you want. I like cheddar or Gruyère."

"Does my future include Gruyère cheese?" Meredith asked.

"Cheddar, then," Connie said.

"Government cheese," Meredith said. She laughed. "Do you think the government would even give me cheese? If they don't indict me, maybe they will give me cheese."

Connie turned off the burner under the eggs; they were rich and creamy. She threw in a handful of fresh thyme, and the aroma enveloped them. "Do I need to worry about you?" she asked.

"Yes," Meredith said. She smiled, then she reached out to hug Connie. "This is amazing, Con. You're helping me."

"No," Connie said. "You're helping me."

They ate the scrambled eggs right out of the pan, and then they moved on to quiche. Connie used a prepared pie shell—Meredith wasn't ready to make her own pastry dough—and mixed up a basic custard of eggs, half-and-half, and salt and pepper.

"You can add anything you want," Connie said. "Bacon, sausage, chopped ham, chopped Spam, government cheese, scallions, chives, wild onions you find on the side of the road, diced tomatoes, diced zucchini, mushrooms, you name it. Then you pour it into the crust like this, and bake it at three fifty for fifty minutes."

Meredith took notes. Connie shredded some Emmental cheese and added chopped deli salami and some diced tomatoes and snipped chives. She slid the quiche into the oven. They would eat it for lunch.

Dan had been gone for only an hour. Connie wasn't sure how she was going to make it through the next three days.

"Now," she said, "I'm going to teach you the most important lesson of all."

"What's that?" Meredith said. She seemed genuinely interested, and Connie wondered how Meredith could be so focused— nearly happy—when she was doomed to read about Freddy's affair in a book written by Samantha Deuce.

Just then, Toby walked into the kitchen and said, "Something smells good." He kissed Meredith on the back of her neck and grabbed her around the waist. Meredith cast her eyes down, and Connie thought, *All right, what's going on?*

She said, "Did something happen last night?"

Meredith elbowed Toby in the ribs. "Connie was just about to teach me the most important lesson of all."

Toby said, "Dinner was delicious. When we finally ate it."

Connie glanced at her brother. He kept a straight face, then broke out into a beautiful smile. Meredith turned around and kissed Toby in a way that evoked 1979, and Connie nearly groaned. This would be a lot easier to stomach if Dan were here.

"Out of the kitchen," Connie said to Toby. "I'll call you when lunch is ready."

"But I want to learn the most important lesson," Toby said. "What is it?"

Connie felt like she should give a profound answer. What *was* the most important lesson? Was it love? Was it forgiveness? Was it honesty? Was it perseverance?

She wielded her whisk. "Vinaigrette," she said.

They ate a late lunch of quiche and perfectly dressed salad greens. After lunch, Meredith and Toby wanted to go for a bike ride— probably they wanted to be alone—but if Connie sat around the house by herself she would lose her mind, so she tagged along with them. They biked out to Sconset. The climbing roses were in their second bloom, even more lush and lavish than they had been in July—and then they decided to bike Polpis Road. This was nine miles on top of the two they had already done. Connie was in terrible shape, but the bike ride invigorated her. Her heart was pumping and her legs were warm and tingling, and she filled with a kind of euphoria from the fresh air and the endorphins. It was ideal weather—low seventies with low humidity and mellow sunshine. Autumn was coming. Maybe it was this thought that made Connie suggest that they head into town instead of home to Tom Nevers.

"Town?" Toby said. "You're sure?"

"We can get ice cream," Connie said.

They biked an additional two miles into town, at which point Connie was wiped out. She collapsed on a stool at the counter of the Nantucket Pharmacy. Meredith and Toby flanked her and the three of them ordered chocolate frappes. There were lots of other people in the pharmacy—primarily older people who had come to get their prescriptions filled and harried-looking mothers with recalcitrant children demanding jimmies, but none of them seemed to notice Meredith, and more unusual still was the fact that Meredith didn't seem to mind if she was noticed or not. She interacted with one little girl whose scoop of peppermint-stick ice cream was threatening to topple into the lap of her hand-embroidered sundress. The little girl was about six years old and had a perfect blond bob. The little girl *was* Meredith Martin at age six.

"Let me help you with that," Meredith said, and she secured the ice cream onto the cone with a spoon.

"Thank you," the girl's mother said.

Meredith smiled. To Connie, she murmured, "She looks like one of these little girls I knew in Palm Beach." Her expression darkened, the demons were encroaching, and Connie thought, *We have to get out of here while things are still okay.*

She eased back off her stool; even that made her legs ache. She said, "I'm never going to make it back home. We have to call a cab."

"Thank God you said that, Nance Armstrong," Toby said.

They called a cab that could accommodate the bikes, and rode home in exhausted silence.

It was six o'clock. They took turns in the outdoor shower, with Meredith slated to go last.

"So you can stay in as long as you want," Connie said.

"You're so good to me," Meredith said.

"Who's the little girl in Palm Beach?" Connie asked.

"Long story," Meredith said.

Connie wanted to pour a glass of wine—oh, boy, did she—and she had earned it with nearly fifteen miles of biking and Dan away and Meredith and Toby in a state of bliss, but she decided against it. She prepared pasta and served it with the Dijon shallot cream sauce that she and Meredith had made earlier, and a salad with vinaigrette, and some leftover Parker House rolls. It was a good dinner, and the three of them ate outside. After, they cleaned up, and Toby asked if they wanted to watch a movie. Meredith said yes, but Connie said she was tired and thought she would go upstairs to read.

"But reading might not last long," Connie said. "I'm beat."

"It was a good day," Meredith said.

"Dinner was delicious," Toby said. "Thank you."

Once in the master suite with the door shut, Connie thought, *I survived the first day without Dan.* But how would she make it through three more days? And how, how, *how* would she leave the island?

She loved him.

She sat on the edge of her bed. Okay, wait. She was unprepared to love anyone but Wolf Flute. So she didn't love Danforth Flynn. But God, her heart was splintering at the prospect of even three days without him. The clock radio was on the nightstand. Connie reached over to turn it on, and then she got an idea.

No, the idea was stupid. It was so cliché. But before she could stop herself, Connie had her cell phone in her hand and she was dialing. With all those hours of avid listening, she knew the number by heart.

At first, the line was busy. Of course, it was busy; Delilah had millions of listeners who all wanted to send songs out to their loved ones. Connie hit redial.

And on her sixteenth try, someone answered. Not Delilah, but a screener.

"Tell me your story," the screener said. The screener was male; he sounded as young as Meredith's attorney. Was this some college kid earning extra money by screening for Delilah? Connie found this amusing.

She thought, *My story? My story will take all night.*

She said, "My husband died two years ago of brain cancer, and I never thought I'd find love again." Here, Connie walked over to her dressing table. She pointed to herself in the mirror and thought, *You, Constance Flute, are made for Delilah!* "But this summer, I've met a wonderful man named Dan, and my life has changed. I've changed. Dan is away this weekend, on a camping trip with his sons, but I'd like to send out a song to him so he knows I'm thinking of him."

"What's the song?" the screener asked.

" 'Something in the Way She Moves' by James Taylor," Connie said. The song Dan sang in her ear up at Great Point.

"Good stuff," the screener said. "I'm going to get you on."

The next day, Connie taught Meredith how to make a cream soup from scratch.

"Once I show you the basics," Connie said, "you can do this with any vegetable: broccoli, asparagus, carrot, tomato, mushroom."

"Right," Meredith said. "But what's going to keep me from reaching for a can of Campbell's for a dollar forty-nine instead?"

"You'll see once you taste it," Connie said. "First, you sauté an onion in four tablespoons of butter until the onion is soft." She moved the onion around the stock pot as the butter foamed. Connie had done so well on the radio that now she was thinking TV, she was thinking the Food Network, her own cooking show! "Then, add three tablespoons of flour and cook for one minute. Cooking the flour a little eliminates the starchiness." If Toby could go to the Naval Academy, why couldn't Connie do the Food Network? "Add the vegetable next—in this case, four cups of *sliced summer squash*." Connie enunciated clearly, mugged for an imaginary camera, then dumped the squash into the pot. Meredith didn't notice the theatrics; she was bent over her little notebook, writing down every step. Would she really make her own soup? Connie wondered. Or was she destined for Campbell's? "Pour in six cups of chicken broth, a cup of white wine, and a teaspoon of fresh thyme. Put the top on the pot and simmer for twenty minutes."

Connie set the timer. She turned to Meredith. She was unable to hold it in any longer. "I was on Delilah last night."

Meredith's brow crinkled. "Huh?"

"I called in to Delilah and sent a song out to Dan."

"You did not."

"I did so. I was on the radio."

"Why didn't you tell us?" Meredith said. "Oh, my God, what I would have given to hear that. What song did you ask her to play?"

" 'Something in the Way She Moves.' " Connie said. "By James Taylor."

A shadow crossed Meredith's face.

Connie said, "Don't even think about it."

Meredith turned away. Connie absently stirred the squash in the pot.

"Okay, do think about it," she said. "What song would you send out to Freddy?"

"I don't know," Meredith said. " 'I Will Survive'?"

"And you will," Connie said. "You will, Meredith."

Meredith walked over to the sliding-glass doors. "I'm going to sit in the sun," she said. "You know, we only have nine days left."

Nine days. A ticking started in Connie's head, like a time bomb.

When the squash had cooked and cooled to room temperature, Connie went outside to grab Meredith. "Time to finish the soup."

Connie poured the cooled contents of the pot into her food processor. When she turned it on, the mixture became a smooth, sunny-colored liquid. Connie poured it back into the pot and added salt, pepper, and a cup of heavy cream. She lifted a spoonful for Meredith to taste, then she tasted it herself.

Sublime. It was fresh, sweet, and squashlike. This was why Meredith couldn't simply pick a can off the shelf.

"You have to promise me that you'll try this yourself," Connie said. "With some really good produce."

"I'll try," Meredith said. "But I can't promise. How can I promise?"

That evening, they ate the soup with a fresh, piping hot baguette— the crevices filled with melting sweet butter—and a green salad with vinaigrette that Meredith had made herself, as a final exam of sorts. It tasted just like Connie's vinaigrette, and Meredith was thrilled. They did a cheers with their water glasses. The cooking lessons had been a success, Meredith was a quick study, and it was a good thing because Dan would be home soon enough, and Connie would have other things to do.

In the middle of the night, Connie was awakened by a noise. At first, she thought it was the radio; she had fallen asleep listening to Delilah. But it was a rattling, coming from downstairs. It was a pounding.

The vandal, Connie thought. There had been nothing for weeks, nothing since Toby arrived, but now, yes—someone was outside. Connie slipped out of bed. She was wearing only a T-shirt and underwear. She needed shorts.

She called out, "Toby!" The man slept like the dead. She might have to splash him with cold water to wake him up.

But when she got out to the hallway, Toby and Meredith were standing at the top of the stairs.

"Someone's outside," Connie said.

"I'll take care of it," Toby said.

"It sounds like the person is trying to get in," Meredith said. "What if it's Samantha? What if she came here to confront me?"

"Is that possible?" Connie asked. Of course, it was possible, but was it likely? It did sound like the person was knocking, then shaking the doorknob, trying to force the door. What if it was the FBI, come to take Meredith away?

Toby turned on the hall light. Connie peered down the stairs at the clock. It was only five after eleven.

Toby said, "Who is it?"

Connie and Meredith were creeping down the stairs one at a time. Connie tried to look out the sidelights.

A muffled voice said, "Itzashalan."

Connie said, "It's Ashlyn!"

Toby unlocked the door, and Connie heard herself cry, "Wait, wait!" Because they had to punch in the security code first, Ashlyn's birthday, Connie did it automatically, her whole body was shaking like she had a fever, and she thought, "Is it Ashlyn? Is it?"

And they opened the door and Connie looked, and there was her baby girl.

Connie didn't know whether to laugh or cry. She did both. She was a hysterical, sobbing mess, but it didn't matter, did it? She had her daughter, her very own daughter, in her arms. Toby's eyes were brimming, and Meredith—well, Connie didn't expect tears from Meredith and she didn't find any. Meredith was smiling and nodding her head. Meredith was level-headed enough to get everyone inside and Ashlyn's luggage in and the cabbie paid. She shepherded everybody into the kitchen, and Connie sat at the table and encouraged Ashlyn to sit, but she wouldn't let go of Ashlyn's hand. No way.

Meredith said, "Ashlyn, are you hungry? Would you like some summer-squash soup? It's homemade."

Ashlyn looked at Meredith, then at Toby, then at Connie, and she burst into tears.

Connie said, "Honey, what's wrong?" She realized then that something horrible must have happened. Ashlyn wouldn't have shown up here out of the blue for Connie's sake.

"Bridget and I…" She tried to get air in. "Bridget and I…"

"Split up?" Connie said.

Ashlyn nodded. "For good this time!" she wailed and dropped her head to the table.

Oh, no. Oh, dear. Connie wasn't sure what to do. She touched the top of Ashlyn's head, the pale hair. "Oh, honey. I'm sorry."

Eventually, Ashlyn raised her head. Her nose was red and running. "We split earlier this summer…"

"When you called me before?" Connie said.

"When I called you before," Ashlyn said.

"But...?"

"But then we got back together, and I didn't feel like I could talk to you about it. Because of what happened at the funeral."

"Ashlyn," Connie said. "I'm sorry about what happened at the funeral."

"I love Bridget so much," Ashlyn said. "And she was my best friend besides." They all waited, watching Ashlyn cry, and Connie thought, *I'd do anything to make her feel better.* But there was nothing. Of course, there was nothing any of them could do.

"What happened?" Connie asked.

"I wanted a baby," Ashlyn said.

Instinctively, Connie made a noise. She pressed her lips together.

"And Bridget didn't," Ashlyn said. "I really did and she really didn't. And two months ago when she found out that I'd been to a donation center and had put myself on the list for insemination, she told me she was leaving. She moved out. Our separation lasted two and a half days, then I went to her and said I couldn't stand to be away from her, and I said I would give up the idea of having children."

"She doesn't want children right now?" Connie asked. "Or not ever?"

"Not ever," Ashlyn said. "She's on track to be the best female pediatric heart surgeon in the state of Florida. She wants to be the best pediatric heart surgeon, man or woman, in the country someday. She said she was around children enough to know that she wasn't capable of raising her own. She thinks she's too selfish, too driven."

"But lots of men are like that," Connie said. "If you agreed to stay at home..."

"She still wouldn't do it," Ashlyn said. She started crying again.

Connie squeezed Ashlyn's hand, thinking, *This is my daughter's hand. This is all I've been wishing for.*

Meredith set down a bowl of warm soup and a hunk of baguette and a glass of water. Toby cleared his throat. He said, "So then why did you break up?"

Ashlyn wiped at her red eyes. Her hair was in a messy bun. It didn't look like she'd seen the sun all summer. But she was, absolutely, the most beautiful creature Connie had ever laid eyes on.

Ashlyn said, "I'm pregnant. Due in April."

Toby jumped in surprise. Meredith said, "Oh, Ashlyn, that's wonderful."

Connie thought, *Wolf! Wolf! Did you hear that?*

Ashlyn was still crying. "And I thought news of a baby, a real live baby, would change Bridget's mind." She sniffled. Meredith brought a box of Kleenex. Ashlyn blew her nose. "But it didn't."

"So here you are," Toby said.

She crumpled the Kleenex in her hand. "So here I am." She looked at Connie with bleary eyes. "I've been a terrible daughter, and I know I don't deserve a second chance, but I came here because I didn't have anywhere else to go."

"That sounds familiar," Meredith said. She rested her hands on Toby's shoulders.

Connie thought, *What is the most important lesson of all? Perseverance? Honesty? Forgiveness? Love?*

Wolf, Ashlyn, Toby, Meredith, Dan. Ashlyn, Ashlyn, Ashlyn— Connie and Wolf's daughter, their only child, conceived so many years ago in the back of a pickup truck a few miles away, beneath a sky filled with stars. Ashlyn was going to have a baby. Ashlyn had been so angry—she had been silent and seething—but she had come back to Connie because Connie hadn't stopped loving Ashlyn even for a second. Ashlyn would soon know it herself: parents didn't stop loving their children for any reason.

Love, then, Connie decided. *The most important lesson is love.*

MEREDITH

Meredith felt like they were all graduating from college, and everyone knew what the next step was but her.

In the span of sixteen or seventeen hours, Connie's life had transformed as dramatically (almost) as Meredith's life had the previous December—only for the better. Connie would return to Bethesda the Tuesday after Labor Day. That was as planned. What was different now was that Ashlyn was putting her house in Tallahassee on the market and moving back up to Bethesda, into Connie's house. Ashlyn would live with Connie indefinitely. She would have the baby, and Connie would care for it while Ashlyn went back to work. Ashlyn had applied for a job in the ped onc department at WHC, and if she didn't get that job, she would look elsewhere.

"Lots of good hospitals in Washington," Connie said to Meredith and Toby. "And just think, next summer when we're all here, we'll have a baby!"

Next summer when we're all here: These words were a balm to Meredith. She had been invited back. It took some of the sting out of leaving, although it did nothing to help her sense of floundering, about where to go or what to do in the next ten months.

Toby was going back to Annapolis. A brand-new freshman class of cadets awaited.

"Now I wish I hadn't sold my boat," Toby said. "Now I wish I could just sail with you around the world."

Sailing with Toby around the world: it was appealing, Meredith had to admit.

"I know you," Meredith said. "You have to have your freedom."

"I'd like to share that freedom with you," he said. "Give you a little sip of it. It's the most intoxicating thing on earth."

But Meredith's freedom was still in the firm grip of federal investigators.

*   *   *

They all sat on the back deck, enjoying the sun: Connie, Ashlyn, Toby, Meredith. They had a pitcher of iced tea (decaf, for Ashlyn) and a bowl of Bing cherries, which they passed around. Ashlyn was nauseous; every half hour or so, she'd go into the house to throw up.

"I can't believe how lousy I feel," she said.

"I could tell you stories," Connie said. "About you."

Meredith squinted at the ocean. She decided to speak the words that were on everyone's mind. "I never want to leave here."

"You don't have to," Connie said. "You know you don't have to go anywhere."

The phone rang inside. The phone, the phone. Meredith's shoulders tensed. "Maybe that's Dan," she said.

"Not for another thirty-two hours," Connie said.

"I'll get it," Toby said. He heaved himself up and out of his chaise. A second later, he poked his head out and said, "Meredith, it's for you."

"Of course," Connie said.

"Is it Dev?" Meredith asked.

"I don't believe so," Toby said.

Leo, Carver, Freddy? Freddy, Freddy, Freddy? It was official: Meredith hated the telephone. The phone terrified her.

It was Ed Kapenash, chief of police. He wanted Meredith to come down to the station.

"I think we've found our man," he said. "And our woman."

Meredith and Connie went to the police station together. Although it was Meredith who was being terrorized, the property belonged to Connie. She was the only one who could press charges.

"Who do you think it is?" Connie said. "Do you think it's someone you know? Do you think it's your friend from Palm Beach?"

"I don't know," Meredith said. She was in a hazy daze. It was hot outside. She wanted to be on the deck. She wanted to go for a swim. She wanted to whip up more vinaigrette. She wanted Freddy to call. Most of all, that was what she wanted. She didn't want to be going into the police station to meet her own personal terrorist.

"Right down the hall," the secretary said. She stared grimly at Meredith for an extra second, and Meredith guessed that this was the kind of person who would dress up as "Meredith Delinn" for Halloween. "First door on the left."

Connie led, Meredith followed. The first door on the left was unmarked.

"This one?" Connie said.

"That's what the lovely woman said."

Connie knocked, and Ed Kapenash opened the door.

"Come in," he said. He ushered them in to what looked like a classroom. There was a long particleboard table, ten folding chairs, a green blackboard coated with yellow chalk dust. Two people sat at the table already, two people whom Meredith could only describe as hungry-looking. The man was beefy with a thick neck, a buzz cut of dirt brown hair, a gold hoop earring, and a T-shirt that appeared to be advertising Russian beer. He looked familiar to Meredith. She felt like she had seen that T-shirt before. Meredith got a hot, leaky feeling of fear. The woman, probably in her midthirties, had very short hair dyed jet black. She wore jeans shorts and a sleeveless yellow blouse. She had a bruise on one cheek. Meredith couldn't believe these two were just sitting at the table, as though they had arrived early for dinner.

"Mikhail Vetsilyn and Dmitria Sorchev," the chief said. "They were stopped on Milestone Road for speeding at two o'clock this morning. They said they were headed to Tom Nevers to see 'an old friend.' The van reeked of marijuana smoke. The officer on duty, Sergeant Dickson, asked them to step out of the van. He then proceeded to check the back of the van. He found three five-gallon jugs of gasoline and fourteen empty cans of electric-green spray paint. He called in reinforcements and did a full check of the van, and they found this." The chief held up a plastic bag containing a medieval-looking curved dagger, covered with blood and hair. Meredith looked down into her lap.

"Have they confessed?" Connie asked.

"They've confessed," the chief said. "Two acts of vandalism for her. That, plus the unlawful slaying of a sea mammal for him. God only knows what they were going to do with the gasoline."

"Burn the house down," the man said.

"Hey!" The chief's voice was like a whip. Meredith looked up in alarm. There was the chief, being chieflike. "I'm happy to book you with attempted arson," he said. He turned to Connie and Meredith. "I assume you want to press charges."

"Burn my house down?" Connie said. "My husband designed that house. God, yes, I want to press charges."

"But wait," Meredith said. "Who are they?" She lowered her voice, trying to convince herself they wouldn't hear her, and if they did hear her that they wouldn't understand. "Are they Russian?" Were these the assassins the Russian mob had sent? Two people who looked like they'd escaped from the gulag?

"They're from Belarus," the chief said. "Minsk."

Minsk. Meredith looked at the woman. *Like me, also from Minsk.* "Are you a housekeeper?" she said. "Do you clean houses?"

The young woman nodded.

Yes, okay. Meredith said, "Did you give your life savings to your employer to invest with Delinn Enterprises? A hundred and thirty-seven thousand dollars?"

The girl twitched her head. "Yes," she said. "How you know?"

"I met a friend of yours," Meredith said.

Connie eyed her quizzically.

"At the salon."

"Ahhh," Connie said.

Meredith studied the man. She had seen him before. *Burn the house down.* She had heard his voice before. And then she remembered: She had seen him on the ferry. He had been in line with her when she went to get coffee for her and Connie. He must have recognized her then. He must have followed Connie's Escalade out to Tom Nevers.

"We can drop the two vandalism charges on her," the chief said, "but the unlawful slaying of a sea mammal will stick with him regardless, as well as a marijuana-possession charge."

"Drop the vandalism charges," Meredith whispered.

"What?" Connie said.

"She lost her life savings."

"So?" Connie said. "It's *my* house. *My* car."

"Would you ladies like to talk about this out in the hallway?" the chief asked.

"No," Meredith said. She smiled at Connie, then whispered, "She lost a lot of money, Con. She lost everything."

Connie shook her head, unconvinced.

"And here's the other thing," Meredith said. "If they hadn't spray painted the house, you wouldn't have met Dan."

"Oh, come on," Connie said.

"You should be *thanking* them," Meredith said.

Connie rolled her eyes. She turned to the chief. "Okay, we're out of it. You'll punish him for killing Harold? And you'll make sure neither one of them does anything like this again?"

"That's our job," the chief said.

Meredith and Connie stood to leave. Meredith approached the woman, Dmitria Sorchev, and said, "I want you to know how sorry I am. I'm sorry about your money. Your savings."

The young woman pulled her lips back to reveal grayish teeth. "Fuck Freddy Delinn."

Meredith sighed and looked at Connie over the top of her glasses. Connie smiled. She liked the girl a little better now.

Connie turned to the chief. "Thank you for calling us."

"I'm glad we settled this," the chief said. He escorted the ladies out to the hallway. "There will be paperwork for you to sign, probably sometime tomorrow."

Connie and Meredith shook his hand. The secretary, thankfully, had left for lunch. Meredith stepped outside into the sun.

"I'm going to take you up on your offer," Meredith said as they
climbed into the Escalade. About eight weeks earlier, Meredith
had climbed into this car for the first time, running through a
dark alley, dodging the flash of the hidden photographer. "I'm
going to stay on Nantucket this winter."

"Atta girl," Connie said. And she started the engine.

No sooner had Meredith and Connie settled into their chaise
lounges on the deck next to Toby and Ashlyn than the phone rang
again.

"You answer it," Connie said. "I want to tell these guys what
happened with Boris and Natasha."

"Did anything happen here?" Meredith asked. She didn't want
to answer it.

"Just napping and puking," Ashlyn said. But she seemed marginally more cheerful.

Anything but a ringing phone. *Leo, Carver, Freddy. Freddy,
Freddy, Freddy! Goddamn you, Freddy!* she thought (zillionth and
eighth). That poor girl, her gray teeth, her life's savings; she might
as well have poured gasoline on the money and set it on fire herself.

Meredith dragged her feet for so long that the phone stopped
ringing. She exhaled. Then it started ringing again. The starting
up again was worse: whoever it was really wanted to talk to her.

But maybe the call wasn't for her. Maybe it was Bridget, calling
for Ashlyn.

Meredith checked the display. It was the law firm.

Meredith picked up the phone, saying a Hail Mary in her head.
Now that she had decided to stay on Nantucket, the most devas-
tating thing she could think of was for someone to take her away.
Please don't take me away. "Hello?"

"Meredith?"

"Dev?"

"Thank *God* you answered," he said. "I tried a second ago and no one answered."

"I just walked in," she said.

"We found the money!" Dev said. He sounded amped up, triumphant; he was *crowing.* "And you were right! It was in a bank in Malaysia—nearly four billion dollars in Samantha Champion's name. That money had been transferred from the four numbered accounts in Switzerland on Mrs. Champion's birthday last October."

"Four billion dollars," Meredith said. For Samantha, on Samantha's birthday, which was exactly one week before Meredith's birthday.

"The word 'champ' was all over Freddy's confidential papers, and so, thanks to you, the Feds brought Mrs. Deuce in. And when the Feds questioned her, she copped to the affair. I think she thought if she confessed to the sexual stuff that we'd be thrown off the trail of her financial involvement. But the information you gave us really helped."

"Great," Meredith said, but her voice was flat. On the one hand, she no longer cared about money. On the other hand, she couldn't believe Freddy had transferred $4 billion to Samantha on Samantha's birthday and had left Meredith with nothing.

"And we found eight billion dollars in other accounts at the same bank... in the name of David Delinn."

David Delinn.

"His brother," Meredith said.

"His brother."

"But his brother *is* dead, right?" Meredith said. God, what if Freddy had been lying from the very beginning? From their first walk together, their first conversation?

"His brother was shot and killed in a training exercise outside of Fort Huachuca in nineteen seventy-eight. Freddy used an existing account of David's from the nineteen sixties. Freddy had been depositing money into that account for decades. He was listed as trustee. The money was transferred out in nineteen ninety-two, then, apparently, transferred again. It was a web that was almost impossible to untangle."

Meredith shut her eyes. It was a web of lies involving David, Samantha, Kirby Delarest, and Thad Orlo, but not her. Not her. They knew that, right? Not her.

"So, that twelve billion dollars was recovered," Dev said, "largely thanks to you. This is going to help out a lot with the restitution to investors."

"Right," Meredith said. She wondered if Amy Rivers would get any money back. Or the poor girl from Minsk, who would need it now for her comrade's legal fees.

"The Feds are going to issue a statement at five o'clock today," Dev said. "And they will include mention that information provided by Meredith Delinn was instrumental in the investigation."

"So I'm not in trouble anymore?" Meredith said. "I can call my children?"

"The SEC is going to be sifting through the rubble of this for years, Meredith," Dev said. "But for now, the Feds are satisfied that you had no knowledge of the Ponzi scheme. They now believe what you said in your deposition: Freddy asked you to transfer the fifteen million dollars, and you transferred it. You were his pawn, but that's not a crime. So, yes, you can call your children."

"Thank you," Meredith whispered. She took a huge breath. She was getting her kids back! Leo! Carver! As soon as Meredith hung up, she would call Carver's cell phone. It would ring in the pocket of his Carhartt overalls. Meredith imagined him standing on a ladder leaning against the great big beautiful old house that he was restoring. He would answer the phone, and it would be Meredith. And after she'd told him about what had happened, she would ask to speak to Leo. Carver would call out, "Hey, Leo? It's Mom." He would toss the phone down to Leo, and Leo would grin, and he would say, "Hey, Mom."

* * *

In the days that remained of the summer, news of Freddy Delinn and the spoils of his kingdom hit the front page of every paper in the country. All reports mentioned that Meredith Delinn had been working with federal investigators to help locate the missing money.

Dennis Stamm, the head of the SEC's investigative team, was quoted as saying, "We couldn't have found this money without salient bits of information provided by Mrs. Delinn. She showed herself to be a truly great citizen with the effort she put forth in cracking the code and recovering this money for Mr. Delinn's former investors."

Meredith fully expected the reporters to reappear, but they didn't. Maybe because Ed Kapenash was an effective police chief who had finally learned how to protect the island's most notorious summer resident, or maybe because the *Post* only followed trails of blood. Girl Scouts didn't make the front page.

Meredith didn't want to waste the final days of summer watching reports about the rediscovered money on TV, and luckily, she didn't have to. She and Toby went kayaking in the Monomoy creeks, where the only sounds were the water lapping against their paddles and the cries of seabirds. When they got home, they found Connie and Ashlyn sitting together on the sofa, Ashlyn weeping, Connie rubbing Ashlyn's feet.

"Everything all right with the baby?" Meredith asked quietly later.

"Everything's all right with the baby," Connie said. "She misses Bridget."

And Meredith thought about how it felt to yearn for something that you absolutely knew you weren't going to get — in her case, a phone call from Butner. "Yes," Meredith said. "I bet she does."

They managed to get Ashlyn out of the house the next day. Dan took everybody on an expedition to Smith's Point, where Toby and Dan caught eight inedible bluefish — so they ended up having fish tacos on the outdoor deck of Millie's as the sun went down. The next morning, Meredith and Toby and Connie and Dan biked to Bartlett's Farm and found themselves on a road that cut through two resplendent fields of flowers. As far as the eye could see, there were snapdragons and zinnias and marigolds and lilies, a palette of color upon color such as Meredith hadn't seen since she viewed the Pissarros during her private tour of the Musée d'Orsay.

Meredith stopped her bike and inhaled. It was an intoxicating sip of freedom.

On their final afternoon, Meredith and Connie sojourned into town. Meredith bought two novels, which she would read after the others had left the island, and Connie bought a white baby blanket that had the word "Nantucket" embroidered across the bottom in navy thread. Then Connie wanted to zip into the kitchen store, and Meredith took the opportunity to light candles at the church.

The interior seemed brighter than it had the last time; muted light shone through the stained glass windows. Meredith stuck ten dollars into the slot, a small fortune, for despite all that had happened, she still believed.

She lit a candle for Connie first, then Toby, then Dan. She lit candles for Leo and Carver. Then she lit a candle for heartbroken Ashlyn and one for the baby inside her. Then Meredith lit a candle for her mother and her father. She had one candle left. She thought about lighting it for Dev or for Amy Rivers or for Samantha. She considered lighting it for herself. Of everyone she knew, she needed a candle the most. One thing was for sure: she was *not* going to light a candle for Freddy.

She pushed the button and thought, *For Dev.* He had been so good to her.

She slipped through the double doors into the vestibule, but she couldn't bring herself to leave the church. She rummaged through her purse for another dollar bill and went back and lit another candle—for Freddy.

Because that was how she was. She couldn't seem to abandon him.

No matter what.

Out in the sunny world, Connie waited on a bench.

Connie said, "Did that go okay?"

Meredith said, "I lit candles." She didn't tell Connie that she'd lit a candle for Freddy—but who was she kidding? Connie already knew.

"I got you something," Connie said. She handed Meredith a big white shopping bag with cord handles from Nantucket Gourmet. "Sorry it's not wrapped."

Meredith peered inside. It was an eleven-cup Cuisinart food processor. "Of course you can use the one in my kitchen," Connie said. "But this is one of your very own. A graduation present"

Meredith was so overwhelmed by the perfection of the gift that she closed her eyes. She thought back to the cruel summer weeks right after Toby had broken up with her. Connie had dragged her to a party at Villanova, and Meredith had drunk too much, and Connie had carried Meredith home on her back. This summer was like that night times fifty billion (this was the largest real number Meredith could think of). This summer, Connie had carried Meredith on her back once again. She had carried Meredith all the way to safety.

"I almost lit a candle for myself in there," Meredith said, nodding at the church. "But then I realized I didn't need to."

Connie put a hand up. "Don't say it, Meredith. You'll make me cry."

Meredith said, "Because you, Constance—you are my candle."

Connie sniffed; tears leaked out from beneath her sunglasses. Meredith pulled her to her feet, and they crossed the cobblestone street to Connie's car.

Endings were like this. You could see them coming from far away, but there was one more thing (dinner at Le Languedoc) and one more thing (ice cream at the Juice Bar) and one more thing (a stroll down the dock to see the yachts) and one more thing (an hour with Toby out on the deck, looking at the stars, knowing, finally, that not a single one of them was especially for you) and one more thing (lovemaking, tender and bittersweet) and one more thing (watching the sunrise on the Juliet balcony) and one more thing (a trip to the Sconset Market for snickerdoodle coffee and peach muffins, only they didn't have peach anymore; fall was coming, they'd switched to cranberry) and one more thing...

Endings, when anticipated, took forever.

And one more thing: Toby and Meredith sat on the floor of Meredith's room, sifting through the possessions in her one cardboard box. Downstairs, Connie and Ashlyn were packing, and Dan was helping them load the car, which was going back to Hyannis on the noon boat. Dan was taking Toby to the airport at eleven. Toby's sky-blue duffel bag was packed fat, waiting at the top of the stairs. Meredith was torn between wanting the ending to be over with—just everyone go—and wanting to squeeze the life out of every remaining second.

The first thing out of Meredith's box were the photographs, which Meredith placed facedown. Too painful. Next, were the boys' yearbooks and Meredith's favorite paperbacks—*Goodbye, Columbus* and *The Heart Is a Lonely Hunter.* There was her record album, *Bridge Over Troubled Water.* And finally, her anthropology notebook. Meredith paged through the notebook, ogling her eighteen-year-old handwriting. There was so much knowledge here, completely forgotten.

Toby studied the Simon and Garfunkel album. He pulled out the record sleeve and read her father's note. "Wow," he said. "No wonder you kept this."

Stay with me, Meredith almost said. *Live here with me for the winter.* It was ironic that Toby would have been free to do that in the past, but now he had a steady job. And, of course, his son. Toby promised he would bring Michael to Nantucket for

Thanksgiving, along with Connie and Ashlyn. Dan would come, too, with his sons.

"And when you realize that you can't live without me," Toby had said the night before, "you can come and live with me in Annapolis. It's not Park Avenue and it's not Palm Beach, but we will live an honest life."

"Dunbar's number," Meredith said, reading from her anthropology notebook. "It says here that human beings can have stable social relationships with a maximum of one hundred and fifty people. One hundred and fifty is Dunbar's number."

"Stable social relationships?" Toby said.

Meredith said, "My own personal Dunbar's number is four. On a good day, seven. You, Connie, Dan, Ashlyn, Leo, Carver, and..."

The phone rang in the house.

Meredith heard Ashlyn cry out, "I'll get it!" Meredith knew that Ashlyn would be hoping and praying it was Bridget.

A second later, Ashlyn called out. "Meredith?"

Was there any doubt? Meredith looked at Toby, and Toby pulled her to her feet. Out in the hallway, Ashlyn offered up the phone, a look of crushed disappointment on her face.

"Thank you," Meredith whispered. And then, into the phone, "Hello?"

"Meredith?"

It was Dev. He sounded excited again. Another insidious discovery? More money uncovered? Hidden with the jihadists perhaps, in the Middle East?

"Hi, Dev," Meredith said. He was her seventh stable social relationship.

"Somehow this woman, Nancy Briggs? At the prison? At Butner?"

"Yes?"

"Somehow she worked it out. Her and the priest. Or her through the priest—maybe that's what it was, since I'm sure the warden's secretary doesn't have any contact with the actual prisoners. But she convinced the priest, and the priest convinced Freddy, and he's agreed to take your call."

"He's agreed to take my call," Meredith said.

"He'll take your call," Dev said. He paused. "That was what you wanted, right? That was what you asked me for?"

"It was," Meredith said. Toby squeezed her hand, and then he left the room. He knew that there were some things that Meredith had to deal with alone.

Freddy would take her call. What did that mean? That meant he would sit in a room, and someone would hold the phone to his ear or he would hold the phone himself, and Meredith would speak. She would go down her list of eighty-four questions, as though she were giving Freddy a test. Where? When? How? Why? Why? Why? Why?

She was never going to get the answers she was looking for. Freddy wouldn't tell her the truth, or he would tell her the truth and she wouldn't believe him. There was no truth with Freddy. Freddy's own personal Dunbar's number was zero. It had always been zero.

"Oh, Dev," she said.

"Don't tell me," he said. "You've changed your mind."

"I can't believe it," Meredith said. "I'm sorry."

"You don't want to talk to Freddy."

"That's right," Meredith said. "In fact, I don't want any news of Freddy at all, from this point on. Unless, well, unless he dies. You can call me when he dies." Meredith fidgeted with her grand-mother's engagement ring. This was the ring that she had given Freddy to give to her, a strange transaction in its own right, but now, more than anything, Meredith wanted it off her finger.

Dev said, "Okay, Meredith, are you sure? You want me to call the people at Butner back and tell them to forget about it?"

Was that what she wanted? She imagined prison officials saying to Fred, *You know what? Your wife doesn't want to talk to you, after all*. What would Freddy think? Meredith didn't care what he thought. She was going to save herself. She was going to swim to shore.

"I'm sure," Meredith said.

"Fine," Dev said. He paused, and then he added. "Good for you."

"Thanks, Dev," Meredith said, and she hung up. Downstairs, she heard Ashlyn and Connie and Dan and Toby talking about taking a picture before they all left. Who had a camera? It was one more thing, and Meredith was grateful.

She hurried downstairs to join them.

EPILOGUE

Autumn on Nantucket was serene and shockingly beautiful. Meredith was able to swim until the twenty-fifth of September. She kept hoping for the company of another seal—a brother of Harold's, perhaps, or a son or daughter, or a friend or lover—but none came.

Dan Flynn, whose real job it was to know everyone on Nantucket and everything that was happening, found Meredith a beat-up Jeep for $2,000 cash.

"The thing will probably leave a trail of sand all the way down the Milestone Road," he said. "But at least you'll be able to get around."

Meredith loved the Jeep much more than she had loved any of her other, fancier vehicles. It made her feel younger, wilder, freer; it made her feel like a person she had never been. She had taken taxis until she was twenty-eight; then, she and Freddy bought a Volvo wagon, which was quickly traded in for a BMW and so on and so on.

The Jeep already had a beach sticker, so Meredith packed herself a lunch—chicken salad that she'd made herself, a ripe, juicy pear, and a whole-wheat baguette from the Sconset Market—and she headed up to Great Point on a sparkling Thursday afternoon. The foliage on the Wauwinet Road was burnt orange and brilliant yellow. Meredith wanted to internalize the colors of the leaves, much like the flower fields of Bartlett's Farm. She wanted to keep the beauty, even as she knew that it was, and only could be, ephemeral. Time would pass, the leaves would fall, children would grow up. Thinking this made Meredith feel unspeakably lonely.

But there, at the gatehouse, was Bud Attatash. He peered at Meredith and the derelict Jeep suspiciously. Then, once he recognized her, he saluted.

Meredith slowed to a stop and shifted into first gear. "Hello, Mr. Attatash."

"Bud, please. You make me feel like I'm a million years old."

Meredith smiled at him. He was checking out the car.

"You're sure that's going to make it?" he said.

"If you don't see me by sundown, you'll come out and get me?"

"That I will," Bud said. He cleared his throat. "Young Flynn tells me that you're staying on island through the winter, and that you're looking for a job. Something out of the public eye?"

"That's right," Meredith said. She needed a job—for the money, certainly, but also as a reason to get out of the house.

"Well, my wife is looking for someone to shelve books after-hours at the Atheneum. They had plenty of help this summer, but everyone has gone back to school."

"Really?" Meredith said. "I'd love to do it."

"It doesn't pay a fortune," Bud said.

Meredith blushed. "Oh," she said. "I don't need a fortune."

And so, Meredith worked Tuesday through Saturday from 5 to 9 p.m., shelving books at the Nantucket Atheneum. She worked alone; most times, the only other person in the echoing historic building was the Salvadoran janitor.

Louisa, Meredith's housekeeper and cook, had been from El Salvador. Flashes of Meredith's previous life surprised her like this.

One day, she read a collection of Gwendolyn Brooks poems before she shelved it. *My God,* she thought.

Her favorite thing about the job was everything. She liked the quiet hush of the building; she liked its dusty museum smell. She loved the Great Hall upstairs — its volumes of Nantucket whaling history, its old New England cookery books. She loved handling books, putting them back where they belonged, in their indisputable proper place. When her workload was light, she would sit and read a chapter or two of books she'd read years before, and they seemed brand-new to her. She always poked her head into the children's section, which was dark and calm, the wooden trucks put away in their garages, the picture books fanned open on display. Children still read *Goodnight Moon,* they still read Carver's favorite, *Lyle Lyle Crocodile.* There was a colorful area rug and huge, plush chairs in the shape of zoo animals. Meredith wondered if she would have grandchildren someday.

Those grandchildren would never know Freddy. Thoughts like this haunted her.

She talked to Leo and Carver several times a week. Meredith asked Leo if he wanted Annabeth Martin's diamond ring, and he said yes. He was planning to propose to Anais sometime in the spring. The house that Meredith had been imagining them in had been sold for profit, and the boys had put a bid on a dilapidated Victorian in Saratoga Springs. They had promised they would come to Nantucket to see Meredith at Thanksgiving.

Meredith bought butternut squash at Bartlett's Farm and made soup, with Connie on the phone as a consultant. Meredith froze what she couldn't eat. She met Dan every Monday night at A.K. Diamond's, and he introduced her to his year-round friends, the carpenters and firemen and insurance agents, and whereas Meredith imagined that his friends would be interested in her lurid back story, most of them just wanted to know how she liked driving that funky Jeep.

The larger world began to open its doors to her once again. Notes arrived at Dev's office from people who had received their restitution checks, and Dev forwarded these letters to Meredith, though Meredith would sometimes let them sit for as long as a week without opening them. It was difficult to accept praise or thanks when so many people had lost so much. Meredith received a letter from an elderly woman in Sioux City, Iowa, who had received a check for a quarter of a million dollars, only 60 percent of what she'd invested—but still the woman was grateful to Meredith, and at the end of the note, told her to hold her head high. *You did the right thing,* she said.

What right thing was that? Meredith wondered.

A letter came from Michael Arrow in Broome, Australia, saying that the US government had promised him restitution of $1.3 million. It wouldn't be enough to buy back his family's pearl farm, but with the favorable exchange rate, it would be plenty to buy a holiday home somewhere in the south—maybe in Geraldton, maybe in Margaret River. The letter was friendly and informative; at the end of the letter, he invited Meredith to come visit him in Western Australia "anytime."

She folded the letter back up, baffled. Where had Michael Arrow been before the restitution was promised, when Meredith was living in the dark and didn't have a friend in the world?

There was no communication from Amy Rivers.

Through Dev, Meredith was informed of interview requests from Diane Sawyer and Meredith Vieira. The manager who had once handled Oliver North wanted to put Meredith on the lecture circuit. Big bucks to be made there, this manager told Dev.

Meredith turned everything down. She didn't want to make a single penny from her connection to Freddy.

A book offer came in. Undisclosed millions. More than the advance that Samantha had gotten, because Meredith was the wife

No.

Her passport arrived in the mail. She could go anywhere in the world.

But she didn't want to be anywhere else.

*   *   *

Meredith talked to Toby on the phone, she talked to Connie. She and Dev discussed how to go about changing her name back to Meredith Martin. It was easier than she thought it might be— fifty dollars, a stack of paperwork at the town clerk's office, five minutes in front of a very sympathetic judge. Once Meredith had shed the name Delinn like a diseased skin, she thought she might feel like a different person.

But she didn't. She felt the same. Although she had decided not to talk to Freddy, she sometimes found herself talking to him in her mind.

I let go of your name, she said. Like it was a balloon that she'd sent soaring up into the air.

Meredith was lonely some nights, and sadness cropped up in her like a virus. It made her sick, it went away, it made her sick again. On cold nights, she lit a fire and she tried to read—she would always have reading—but she wanted someone beside her. *Goddamn you, Freddy,* she thought (zillionth and ninth, tenth, eleventh). One particularly bad night, she checked in Connie's bathroom for the pills, but Connie had taken them all with her.

Meredith felt like she was waiting for something. She thought perhaps she was waiting for Freddy to die. He would be murdered by the Russian mob, or he would do the job himself by eating rat poison or slicing his wrists with a shiv. Prison officials would find a scrap of paper next to his bed with a single letter on it. The letter M.

And then, one afternoon, there was a thump on the front porch, and Meredith, who was on the sofa in front of the fire reading a Penelope Lively novel, sat straight up.

Call 911? she thought. Or Ed Kapenash's cell phone?

She tiptoed to the front of the house. The sun was hanging low in the sky, casting a mellow autumn glow across the front porch.

A package.

Meredith was suspicious. *Bomb,* she thought. *Crate of rattle- snakes. Raw sewage.* She stepped out onto the porch and, without touching the box, looked at the label.

It was from Toby. And then, Meredith realized that it was October twenty-third, and that the next day was her birthday.

She lugged the package inside. She knew she should save it for the following day, but her life had been devoid of small, happy surprises like this one for so long that she went ahead and opened it.

It was a record player. A pearlescent blue Bakelite record player with a black rubber turntable and an extension cord snaking out the back. It had a grooved white plastic knob, off/on, volume one through ten. She plugged it in. Would it work? Meredith ran upstairs and grabbed her Simon and Garfunkel album, which until that moment had been as useful as a pocketful of Confederate money. She dashed downstairs and put the record on the turntable. She turned the knob and a tiny red light came on and Meredith lowered the arm until the needle fit in the groove of the first song.

The song filled the house; the music had that crackling, staticky sound that Meredith remembered from childhood. Meredith turned the music up as loud as it would go, which was, surprisingly, pretty darn loud. Meredith braced herself against Connie's beautiful kitchen counter. As the operatic strains of the song progressed through the verses, she felt something happening to her chest, her head, her face.

> *Sail on Silvergirl,*
> *Sail on by*
> *Your time has come to shine*
> *All your dreams are on their way*

There was a slow burning in her eyes, a buzzing in her nose, and then, her cheeks were wet.

She was astonished. She felt like she was standing at the refrigerator watching herself. *Look, Meredith's crying!* Then she let go. She sobbed and wailed and gasped for breath. She took off her glasses and set them on the counter. She didn't care how out of control she was; no one was around to hear her. She thought of Ashlyn's swollen belly, and she thought that these tears had been gestating in her for a long, long time.

> *See how they shine*
> *Oh, if you need a friend, I'm sailing right behind*
> *Like a bridge over troubled water*
> *I will ease your mind*

Meredith Martin Delinn was crying. Her tears were coming from someplace old and far away. They were coming from the beginning of this story—the uneaten lobster roll, the weekly poker games, the driving lessons in the Villanova parking lot. Meredith was crying because she missed her father. It was the pain that never went away.

Tomorrow was her fiftieth birthday.

When the song was over, Meredith did the only thing she could do. She picked up the arm of the record player, and she started the song again.

ACKNOWLEDGMENTS

Some books are tougher than others; this one was very tough. I have to start by thanking my editor, Reagan Arthur, for her wise direction in revising this novel. Also, the brilliant and compassionate team at Inkwell Management, led by two of my favorite men in all the world, Michael Carlisle and David Forrer. Thanks also to Lauren Smythe and Kristen Palmer, whose input was invaluable.

I wouldn't have gotten a word written without my nanny, Stephanie McGrath, who covered for me in all ways with my three kids, and who bestowed her radiant smile on our household. Thank you, again, to Anne and Whitney Gifford for use of the house on Barnabas, my refuge, and to my mother, Sally Hilderbrand, for allowing me to come home and live like a moody teenager in my childhood bedroom while I revised this novel. Thank you to Anne Fitzgerald and Laurie Richards for always making me look good.

For shining their light on my life in any number of different ways, I'd like to thank Rebecca Bartlett, Elizabeth and Beau Almodobar, Richard Congdon, Wendy Hudson and Randy "Mankills" Hudson, Shelly and Roy Weedon, Evelyn(!) and Matthew MacEachern, Jill and Paul Surprenant (couldn't have done Little League without you!), Wendy Rouillard and Illya Kagan, Mark,

Eithne, and Michaela Yelle, Jennifer and Norman Frazee, John Bartlett, Rocky Fox (for constantly replacing my gold card)), and Heidi and Fred Holdgate (the pool is my happy place). To my darlings whom I don't see nearly enough: Margie and Chuck Marino, Debbie Bennett (33!), Manda and West Riggs, David Rattner and Andrew Law, John and Nancy Swayne, Tal and Jonnie Smith (who taught me a lobster dinner should always be followed by blueberry pie), Fred and Irene Shabel, Tim and Mary Schoettle, Bob and Mindy Rich (Happy 70th, Bubba!), Catherine Ashby, and Sean and Milena Lennon (Freo forever!).

Among other things, this book is about my late father, Robert H. Hilderbrand Jr. I'd like to thank those people in my family who keep his laughter and loving memories alive: my stepmother, Judith Hilderbrand Thurman, my brothers Eric Hilderbrand and Douglas Hilderbrand, my stepbrother Randall Osteen, and my best friend in all the world whose over-the-top joyful energy and belief in me keep me going, my stepsister, Heather Osteen Thorpe. A huge hug goes out to Duane Thurman for captaining the ship and keeping us on course.

Last, I'd like to thank my husband, Chip Cunningham, who skillfully and compassionately dealt with the parts of author-under-stress-of-deadline that no one else sees, and my three children who are the coolest people I know: Maxwell, Dawson, and Shelby.

ABOUT THE AUTHOR

ELIN HILDERBRAND lives on Nantucket with her husband and their three children. She grew up in Collegeville, Pennsylvania, and is an enthusiastic Philadelphia Eagles fan. She has traveled extensively through six continents, but loves no place better than Nantucket, where she enjoys jogging, cooking, and watching her sons play Little League Baseball. Hilderbrand is a graduate of Johns Hopkins University and the graduate fiction workshop at the University of Iowa.

"But where have you been all the time?" Mama asked. "We sent Marie to the *Maison Commune*, but it was closed and the porter said there was no one there, only Albitte's secretary. Great heavens, Eugenie, to think that you walked through the town alone, at this time of night! The things that might have happened to you!"

Mama picked up her little silver bell and rang it. "Bring the child her soup, Marie!" she said.

"But I wasn't alone," I said, "Albitte's secretary was with me."

Marie gave me my soup, but before I could begin Suzanne burst out:

"The secretary? That rude fellow at the door?"

"No, he was only a messenger. Albitte's secretary is a charming young man who knows Robespierre personally. At least, he says he does. By the way, I have——"

But they would not let me finish. Etienne cut me short: "What is his name?" he asked.

"It's a difficult name, and I didn't catch it properly— Boonapat or something like that. He's a Corsican. By the way, I have——"

"And you came alone, at night, with this stranger?" Etienne shouted, playing the stern father. First they had fussed because I had come home alone, and now because I hadn't.

"He is not a stranger, he introduced himself to me," I said. "His family are in Marseilles. They are refugees from Corsica. By the way, I have——"

"Go on with your soup, or it will be cold," said Mama.

"Refugees from Corsica?" said Etienne contemptuously. "Probably adventurers. Adventurers, that's what they'll be!"

I put down my spoon to defend my new friend. "He has a very respectable family," I said. "And his brother is a General. By the way, I have——"

"What is his brother's name?"

"I don't know. I suppose it's Boonapat too. By the way, I——"

"Never heard the name," Etienne growled. "But the officers are being appointed indiscriminately, and the Generals are nobodies!"

"By the way," I got in at last, "I wanted to say——"

"Go on with your soup!" Mama insisted.

But I refused to be interrupted any longer. "By the way," I repeated, "I have invited them both for to-morrow."

Then I started quickly on my soup, because I knew how they were all looking at me in horror.

"Whom have you invited, my child?" Mama asked.

"Two young gentlemen. *Citoyen* Joseph Boonopat or whatever it is, and his young brother the General."

"That has got to be stopped," Etienne shouted, banging the table. "We don't want a couple of escaped Corsican adventurers we know nothing about!"

"And it's not proper," said Mama, "for you to invite a chance acquaintance in a Government office. That is not the way to behave. You are no longer a child, Eugenie!"

"That is the first time anyone," I exclaimed, "has told me I'm no longer a child!"

"Eugenie, I am ashamed of you," said Julie.

"But these Corsican refugees have so few friends in the town," I ventured. I hoped Mama would sympathise.

"What do we know of them? Out of the question!" Etienne grunted. His recent experiences had set his nerves on edge. "You are a disgrace to the family!" he shouted.

"Etienne, she's only a child, and doesn't realise what she has done," said Mama.

That upset me entirely. "Please understand," I said, "once for all, that I am neither a child nor a disgrace!"

There was a moment's silence. Then Mama said with all the imitation sternness she could put on: "Go to your room at once, Eugenie!"

"But I'm still hungry, I've only begun my meal," I protested.

Mama's silver bell rang again. "Marie, please serve Mademoiselle Eugenie's meal in her room," she said. Then she turned very kindly to me: "Go along, my child, have a good rest, and just think about the way you have been behaving. It has distressed your mother and your good brother. Good-night, my child."

Marie brought my supper up to the bedroom, and sat on Julie's bed.

"What's amiss? What's upset them all?" she asked sympathetically.

When we are alone Marie always calls me *tu*; she is my friend and not a servant. After all, she came to us years ago to be my wet-nurse, and I believe she loves me as much as her own natural son, Pierre, who is being brought up somewhere in the countryside.

I shrugged my shoulders. "It's all because I've invited two young men for to-morrow."

Marie nodded thoughtfully. "Very clever of you, Eugenie. It's time Mademoiselle Julie met some young men."

Marie and I always understand each other.

32

"Shall I make you a cup of chocolate?" she whispered. "From our private store?" For Marie and I have a private store of delicacies which Mama doesn't know about. Marie gets the things from the larder, without asking.

After I had drunk the chocolate, when I was alone, I began to write it all down. Now it's midnight and Julie is still downstairs. It's horrid of them to leave me out.

Julie has just come in and is beginning to get undressed. Mama has decided to receive the two gentlemen to-morrow. The invitation could hardly be cancelled. So Julie told me, as if it was nothing. "But I've been told to tell you that it will be their first and last visit."

Julie standing in front of the mirror rubbing cream on her face. The cream is called Lily Dew. Julie read somewhere that even in prison the Dubarry always used Lily Dew. But Julie will never be a Dubarry. Now she is asking whether he is handsome.

"Who?" I asked, pretending to be stupid.

"This gentleman who brought you home."

"Very handsome by moonlight. Very handsome by lantern light. But I've not yet seen him by daylight."

That's all I could tell her.

MARSEILLES, at the beginning of Prairial. (*The lovely month of May, says Mama, is almost over.*)

His name is Napoleone.

When I wake in the morning and think of him, my heart lies like a heavy lump in my breast, from sheer loving. (I lie with my eyes shut, so that Julie shall think I'm still asleep.) I didn't know you could really *feel* love—I mean, bodily. With me it's like something tugging round my heart.

But I had better tell it all just as it happened, starting from the afternoon when the two Buonapartes came to see us. As I had arranged with Joseph Buonaparte, they came the day after my failure to see Deputy Albitte. They came late in the afternoon. Etienne is not usually home by then, but he had shut up the shop and was waiting in the parlour with Mama, so that the young men should see at once that our home is not without a male protector.

Nobody had spoken more than a few words to me during the day, and I could see they were still vexed with my *bad behaviour*.

After dinner Julie had disappeared into the kitchen; she had decided to make a cake. Mama said there was no need; she was still full of Etienne's idea of 'Corsican adventurers'.

I went into the garden for a bit. Spring was in the air already, and I found the first buds on the lilac trees. Then I asked Marie for a duster and did some dusting in the summer-house—in case, I thought. When I went in with the duster I saw Julie in the kitchen. She was taking a cake-tin out of the oven; her face was burning and her forehead damp with perspiration, and her hair was just ruined.

"You're going the wrong way about it, Julie," I blurted out.

"Why? I kept exactly to Mama's recipe, and you just see if our guests don't like it."

"I didn't mean the cake," I said, "I meant your face and your hair. You'll smell of the cooking when the gentlemen come, and——" I paused——"for heaven's sake give it up, Julie, and go and powder your nose. That's more much important."

"What do you think of that, Marie?" said Julie, irritated.

"If you don't mind my saying so, Mademoiselle Julie, I think it's quite right," said Marie as she took over the cake-tin.

In our room Julie did her hair and carefully put on some rouge, while I stood at the window and looked out.

"Aren't you changing?" Julie asked in surprise. But I didn't see any real need for it. Of course I quite liked Monsieur Joseph, but in my mind I had already betrothed him to Julie. As for his brother the General, I could not imagine him taking any notice of me. Nor had I any idea what you talk about to a General. I was only interested in his uniform, though I hoped he would tell us about the fighting at Valmy and Wattignies. 'I do hope,' I was thinking all the time, 'that Etienne will be courteous and amiable; and that it will all end well.' As I looked out of the window I got more and more troubled about it. Then I saw them coming! They were having a lively discussion as they came along. And I was inexpressibly disappointed!

Well, there! He was a little man, shorter than Monsieur Joseph, and Joseph himself is only middle-sized. And he had nothing striking on at all, not a single star, or ribbon of any order. Only when they reached the gate did I see his narrow gold epaulettes. His uniform was dark green, and his top-boots were not polished and not even a good fit. I couldn't see his face because it was hidden by an enormous hat, with nothing on it but the cockade of the Republic. I didn't dream that a General could look so drab. I *was* disappointed.

"He looks very poverty-stricken," I murmured.

Julie had joined me at the window, but she kept behind the curtain. I suppose she didn't want the two citizens to see how curious she was.

"Why do you say that?" she said. "He looks very handsome! You can't expect a secretary at the *Maison Commune* to be very spick and span."

"Oh, you mean Monsieur Joseph? Yes, he looks quite elegant; at all events someone seems to brush his boots regularly. But look at his young brother, the General!" I sighed and shook my head. "Such a disappointment! I had no idea that there were such undersized officers in the army."

"What did you think he would be like?" Julie asked.

I shrugged my shoulders. "Why, like a General. Like a man who gives you the feeling that he can really command."

.   .   .   .

To think that all that happened only two months ago! It seems an eternity.

When Julie and I went into the parlour, the two brothers jumped up and bowed almost too politely, not only to Julie but to me too. Then we all sat, stiff and strained, round the oval mahogany table. Mama was on the sofa, with Joseph Buonaparte next to her. On the other side of the table sat the poverty-stricken General, on the most uncomfortable chair in the house, with Etienne next to him. Julie and I were between Mama and Etienne.

"I have just been thanking *Citoyen* Joseph Buonaparte," said Mama, "for his kindness last night in seeing you home, Eugenie."

At that moment Marie came in with liqueur and Julie's cake. While Mama filled the glasses and cut the cake, Etienne tried to make conversation with the General. "Is it indiscreet, *Citoyen Général*," he asked, "if I inquire whether you are in our city on official business?"

Joseph answered at once for the General: "Not at all. The army of the French Republic is a people's army, and is maintained by the citizens' taxes. Every citizen, therefore, has the right to know what is being done by our army. Am I not right, Napoleone?"

The name Napoleone sounded very foreign. We couldn't help all staring at the General.

"You may ask anything you like, *Citoyen* Clary," the General replied. "I, at all events, make no secret of my plans. In my opinion the Republic is only wasting its resources in this endless defensive warfare on our frontiers. Wars of defence merely

35

cost money and bring in neither glory nor the means of replenishing our exchequer. Thank you, Madame Clary, thank you very much." Mama had handed him cake on a plate. He turned back to Etienne: "We must go over, of course, to offensive warfare. It will help the French finances, and will show Europe that the people's army has not been defeated."

I had been listening, but without understanding. His face was no longer concealed by his hat, and though it's not a handsome face, it seems to me more wonderful than any face I have ever seen or dreamt of. And suddenly I understood why I had been attracted the day before to Joseph Buonaparte. The brothers resemble each other, but Joseph's features are not so strong or compelling as Napoleone's. They only suggest the stronger face for which I was longing. Napoleone's face carries out that suggestion.

"Offensive warfare?" I heard Etienne ask in dismay. We all sat in dead silence, and I realised that the young General must have said something startling. Etienne was looking at him open-mouthed. "Yes, but, *Citoyen Général*, has our army, with its very limited equipment, as we are given to understand——"

The General waved his hand and laughed. "Limited? *That's* not the word! Our army is a beggars' army. Our soldiers at the frontiers are in rags; they march into battle in wooden shoes. And our artillery is so wretched that you might suppose that Carnot, our Minister of War, thinks he can defend France with bows and arrows."

I bent forward and looked hard at him. Afterwards Julie told me my behaviour had been *dreadful*. But I couldn't help it. Especially I was waiting to see him laugh again. He has a thin face with tightly drawn skin, very sunburnt, and surrounded by reddish-brown hair. His hair comes down to his shoulders; it is not dressed or even powdered. When he laughs his drawn face suddenly becomes very boyish, and he looks much younger than he really is.

Then I started: someone was saying to me: "Your health, Mademoiselle Clary." They had all raised their glasses and were sipping the liqueur. Joseph had put his glass close to mine; his eyes were sparkling, and I remembered what we had said the day before: "Oh," I had told him, "call me Eugenie as the others do." Mama raised her eyebrows in annoyance, but Etienne was too wrapped up in his conversation with the General to hear.

"And on what front could an offensive operation be carried out with advantage?" he was asking.

36

"On the Italian front, of course. We shall drive the Austrians out of Italy. A quite inexpensive campaign. Our troops will easily supply themselves in Italy. Such a rich, fertile country!"

"And the Italians themselves? I thought they were loyal to the Austrians?"

"We shall set free the Italian people. In all the provinces we conquer we shall proclaim the Rights of Man." Though the subject seemed to interest the General, I could see that Etienne's objections bored him.

"Your garden is wonderful," Joseph Buonaparte said to Mama, looking through the glass door.

"It's too early yet," Julie ventured, "but when the lilac is out, and the climbing roses round the summer-house—"

She stopped in confusion. I could see she was losing her composure, for lilac and rambler roses do not come out together.

"Have the plans for an offensive operation on the Italian front taken definite shape?" Etienne asked. He would not drop the subject; it seemed to fascinate him.

"Yes. I have almost completed the plans. At present I am inspecting our fortifications here in the south."

"So Government circles are determined on an Italian campaign?"

"*Citoyen* Robespierre personally entrusted me with this tour of inspection. It seems to me to be indispensable before our Italian offensive begins."

Etienne clicked his tongue, a sign that he was impressed. He nodded. "A great plan," he said, "a bold plan." The General smiled at Etienne, and that smile seemed to captivate my brother, though he is such a hard-headed business man. Etienne said eagerly, stammering like a schoolboy: "If only that great plan succeeds, if only it succeeds!"

"Have no fear, *Citoyen* Clary, it will succeed," the General replied, getting up.

"And which of the two young ladies would have the kindness to show me the garden?" asked Joseph.

Julie and I both jumped up. And Julie smiled at Joseph. I don't know just how it happened, but two minutes later we four found ourselves in the leafless garden, without Mama and without Etienne.

It is only a narrow gravel path that leads to the summer-house, so that we had to go two by two. Julie and Joseph went in front, and Napoleone and I followed. I was racking my brains for anything I could say to him, I was so eager to make a good impression on him. But he seemed too buried in thought to notice our silence. And he walked so slowly that Julie and his brother got farther from us. I began to think he was deliberately dawdling.

All of a sudden he said, "When do you think my brother and your sister will be married?"

I thought at first that I must have misheard him. I looked at him in astonishment, and I could feel that I was flushing.

"Well," he repeated, "when will they be married? Soon, I hope."

"Yes, but," I stammered, "they have only just met. And after all we have no idea——"

"They are just made for each other," he declared. "You know that too."

"I?" I looked wide-eyed at him.

"Please don't look at me like that!" he said.

I was so upset that I could only look down. And I was becoming furious with him.

"But," he persisted, "you yourself were thinking last night that it would be a good thing for your sister to marry Joseph. After all, she is at the age at which young ladies generally become betrothed."

"I didn't think anything of the sort, Citizen General!" I declared. Then I had the feeling that in some way I had compromised Julie. I was no longer angry with Napoleone, only with myself.

He stood still, and turned to face me. He was only half a head taller than I, and he seemed pleased to have found somebody he didn't have to crane up to.

It was getting dark, and the grey spring twilight was dropping like a screen that shut us off from Julie and Joseph. The General's face was so close to mine that I could still see his eyes; they were sparkling, and I was surprised to find that men, too, have long eyelashes.

"You must never have any secrets from me, Mademoiselle Eugenie. I can see deep into the hearts of young ladies. Besides, Joseph told me last night that you had promised to introduce him to your elder sister. You told him, too, that your sister is very pretty. That was not true, and—you must have had a good reason for your little fib."

"We must go on," I said to that, "the others will be in the summer-house already."

"Shall we not give your sister a chance to get better acquainted with my brother before she becomes betrothed to him?" he asked softly. His voice sounded very gentle, almost—yes, almost like a caress. His accent seemed foreign much less often than his brother's.

"Joseph will very soon be suing for your sister's hand," he

told me quite simply. It was so dark now that I could only see his face dimly, but I could tell that he was smiling.

"How do you know that?" I asked, puzzled.

"We talked about it last night," he replied, as if that were the most natural thing in the world to do.

"But last night your brother had never seen my sister," I retorted, outraged.

Then he very gently took my arm, and the contact sent a thrill all over me. We went slowly on, and he talked with such tender intimacy that we might have been friends for years.

"Joseph told me of his meeting with you, and he mentioned that your family are very well-to-do. Your father is no longer alive, but I assume that he must have left considerable dowries for you and your sister. Our people are very poor."

"You have sisters too, have you not?" I remembered that Joseph had mentioned sisters of my age.

"Yes, three young brothers and three young sisters," he said. "And Joseph and I have to provide for Mama and all of them. Mama has a small pension from the State, because she was treated as a persecuted patriot after her flight from Corsica. But the pension does not even pay the rent. You have no idea, Mademoiselle Eugenie, how dear everything is in France."

"So," I said, freeing my arm, "your brother only wants to marry my sister for her dowry?" I tried to speak without heat, but I was hurt, and my voice shook with disgust.

"Why, how can you say that, Mademoiselle Eugenie! I think your sister is a very charming young lady, so kind, so modest, with such lovely eyes—I am quite sure that Joseph likes her very much. The two will be very happy together."

He began to walk faster, as if we had exhausted the subject. But I warned him that I should tell Julie what he had just admitted.

"Of course," he said. "That is why I have told you everything so carefully. Yes, tell Mademoiselle Julie, so that she shall know that Joseph will soon be suing for her hand."

I was horrified. 'How shameless,' I thought, and I imagined Etienne sneering 'Corsican adventurers!' "May I ask," I said coldly, "why you are so concerned about your brother's marriage?"

"Sh! Don't shout! You will realise, Mademoiselle Eugenie, that before taking up my command-in-chief in Italy I should be glad to see my family rather better settled. With his experience as politician and political writer, Joseph may forge ahead if he no longer has to work as a subordinate employee. As soon as I have gained my first victories in Italy, of course I shall look after all my family." He paused. "And—believe me, Mademoiselle, I shall look well after them."

We had come to the summer-house. "Where have you been, General," Julie asked, "with the child all this time? We have been waiting for you and Eugenie." But we could see that she and Joseph had forgotten all about us. They were sitting close together on a little bench, though there were plenty of chairs there. Besides, they were holding hands; I suppose they thought we wouldn't notice it in the dusk.

We all went back then to the house, and the two brothers said they must be going. But at that Etienne spoke up. "My mother and I would be very pleased if the Citizen General and Citizen Joseph Buonaparte would stay to supper with us. It is a long time since I had an opportunity of so interesting a talk." As he said that he looked quite appealingly at the General; he seemed to be ignoring Joseph.

Julie and I ran up to our room to do our hair. "Thank goodness," she said, "they have made a good impression on Mama and Etienne."

"I must tell you," I said, "that Joseph Buonaparte will soon be suing for your hand. Principally because," I added, but I had to stop, my heart was beating so, "because," I said when I could finish the sentence, "because of the dowry!"

"How can you say such a hateful thing!" said Julie, with her face flaming. "He told me how poor his family are, and of course," she added, tying a couple of little black velvet bows in her hair, "he could not marry anyone without means, as he has only a small salary and has to help his mother and the children. I think that is very noble of him—Eugenie!" she exclaimed, breaking off, "I won't have you using my rouge!"

"Has he told you already that he wants to marry you?"

"Whatever put that idea into your head? Why, all he talked about, of course, was just things in general, and his young brothers and sisters."

On our way down to the dining-room, where they were all crowded round our two guests, Julie suddenly put her arm round my shoulder and pressed her face against mine. Her cheek was very hot. "I don't know why," she whispered, kissing me, "but I am so happy!" She's surely in love, I said to myself.

As for me, I was quite calm. But I did have that curious tugging round my heart. 'Napoleone,' I thought—'a strange name.' So that's how you feel when you're in love. Napoleone!

All that was two months ago. And yesterday I had my first kiss; and yesterday Julie was betrothed. The two events belong together somehow, for while Julie and Joseph were sitting in the summer-house Napoleone and I were standing by the hedge at the bottom of the garden, so as not to disturb those two. Mama has told me always to spend the evenings in the garden with Julie and Joseph, because Julie is a young lady of good family.

Since that first visit the two brothers have been to see us almost every day. It was Etienne's doing—who could have believed it? Signs and wonders will never cease, and it was he who invited them to come. He can never have enough of his talks with the young General. Poor Napoleone, how terribly they bore him! Etienne is one of those people who value a person according to his success. When I revealed that the two Buonapartes were Corsican refugees, he refused to have anything to do with them, and called them 'adventurers'. But ever since Joseph showed him the cutting from the December *Moniteur* in which his brother was gazetted Brigadier General, Etienne has raved over Napoleone.

Napoleone had driven the English out of Toulon. That is how it happened. The English are always meddling with our affairs, and they are indignant at our condemning our King to death, though Napoleone says it is scarcely a century and a half since they did just the same to their own King. And now they, the English, had formed an alliance with the Royalists of Toulon, and had occupied the town. So our troops laid siege to Toulon. Napoleone was ordered there, and in no time he did what his seniors had been trying in vain to do: Toulon was stormed, and the English fled. Then it was that the name Buonaparte appeared for the first time in the Army Orders, and Napoleone was promoted Brigadier General. Etienne, of course, pestered him to tell him the whole story of the victory at Toulon, but Napoleone says there was nothing in it. It was only a matter of a few cannon, and he, Napoleone Buonaparte, knew perfectly well where to put cannon and which way to point them.

After his success at Toulon, Napoleone went to Paris, to try to see Robespierre. Robespierre is the most powerful man in the Committee of Public Safety. That committee is our Government. To get to the great Robespierre he had first to see the lesser Robespierre, the great man's brother. Robespierre—the real one—thought Napoleone's plans for a campaign in Italy were excellent; he discussed them with the Minister of War, Carnot, and asked him to entrust Napoleone with the preparations for the campaign. Napoleone says that Carnot falls into

D.—2*   41

a rage whenever Robespierre interferes with his Ministry, because it is no concern of Robespierre's. But nobody dares to contradict Robespierre, for he has only to sign a warrant and anyone is sent straight to the guillotine. Consequently Carnot received Napoleone with a show of friendliness, and took over the Italian plans from him.

"First," said Carnot, "go and inspect our fortresses in the south; I will give your ideas careful attention, *Citoyen Général*." But Napoleone is quite sure that his plans lie pigeon-holed somewhere in the Ministry. Robespierre, however, will soon arrange, Joseph thinks, for Napoleone to be given the supreme command in Italy.

Etienne and all our friends hate that man Robespierre. But they do not say so aloud, it would be too dangerous. It is said that Robespierre has made the members of the Revolutionary Tribunal give him secret reports on the attitude of all the officials in the State service. Even the private life of every single citizen, they say, is watched. Robespierre has declared that every genuine Republican has a duty to live a moral life and to despise luxury. Recently he actually had all the brothels in Paris closed. I asked Etienne whether brothels are a luxury, but he said angrily that I mustn't talk about such things. And no dancing is allowed in the streets any longer, though that was a pleasure everybody enjoyed on public holidays. Etienne has absolutely forbidden us ever to criticise Robespierre in front of the two Buonapartes.

Etienne talks to Napoleone of scarcely anything but the Italian plans. "It is our sacred duty," says Napoleone, "to instil into all the European peoples the ideas of Liberty, Equality, and Fraternity. And if necessary we must do it with cannon!" I always listen to these talks, so as to be with Napoleone, though they weary me terribly. The worst is when Napoleone begins to read the Handbook of Modern Artillery to my brother. That happens sometimes, and Etienne, the stupid, thinks he understands it all.

But when we are alone he never talks about cannon. And we are very often alone together. After supper Julie always says: "Don't you think we ought to take our guests into the garden for a bit, Mama?" Mama says "Go along, children!" and we four, Joseph and Napoleone and Julie and I, disappear in the direction of the summer-house. But before we get there, Napoleone generally says: "Eugenie, what do you say to a race? Let's see which of us can get first to the hedge!" Then I lift up my skirt and Julie cries "Ready—steady—go!" Then Napoleone and I set off hot-speed for the hedge. While I run to it with my hair flying and my heart beating wildly and a stitch in my side, Joseph and Julie disappear into the summer-house.

Sometimes Napoleone wins the race, and sometimes I do, but then I know that Napoleone lets me. The hedge is just up to my breast. Generally we lean close together against the foliage; I rest my arms on it and look up at the stars, and then Napoleone and I have long talks. Sometimes we talk about *The Sorrows of Werther*, a novel by an obscure German writer named Goethe, which everybody has at present on the dressing-table. I had to hide the book, because Mama won't let me read love-stories. But I was disappointed with it. It's the story, sad beyond belief, of a young man who shoots himself because the young lady whom he loves marries his best friend.

Napoleone is quite enthusiastic about the book. I asked him whether he could imagine himself committing suicide because he was crossed in love. "No," he replied, laughing, "because a certain young lady whom I love won't be marrying someone else." But then he looked sad and gazed earnestly at me, so I hurriedly changed the subject.

But often we just lean against the hedge and look at the quiet meadow beyond. The less we talk, the nearer together we seem. Then I imagine that we can hear the grass and the wild flowers breathing. Now and then a bird sings somewhere in melancholy tones. The moon hangs in the sky like a yellow lantern, and while I look at the slumbering meadow I think: 'Dear Lord, let this evening last for ever, let me go on for ever leaning against him.' For although I have read that there are no supernatural powers, and the Government in Paris has set up an altar to Human Reason, I always think 'Dear Lord' when I am very sad or very happy.

Yesterday Napoleone suddenly asked, "Are you never afraid of your destiny, Eugenie?" When we are alone with the sleeping meadow, sometimes he uses the familiar *tu*, although not even betrothed lovers or married people do that nowadays.

"Afraid of my destiny? No," I said, "I am not afraid. We don't know what the future holds in store for us. Why should we be afraid of what we don't know?"

"It is a strange thing that most people declare that they do not know their destiny," he said. His face was very pale in the moonlight, and he was looking into the distance with wide-open eyes. "For myself, I think I do. I know my destiny. My star."

"And are you—afraid of it?" I asked.

He seemed to be reflecting. Then he said quickly, "No. I know I shall do great things. I am the sort of man who will build up States and guide their course. I am one of the men who make world history."

I stared at him, amazed. I had never dreamed that people could think or say such things. Suddenly I began to laugh. At that he shrank back and his face was distorted. He turned quickly to me.

"Are you laughing, Eugenie?" he murmured. "Laughing?"

"Please forgive me," I said. "It was only because I was afraid of your face, it was so white in the moonlight, and—so aloof. When I'm afraid, I always try—to laugh."

"I don't want to give you a shock, Eugenie," he said, tenderly. "I can understand your getting frightened. Frightened—of my great destiny."

We were silent again for a while. Then a thought occurred to me. "Well, I too shall make world history, Napoleone!"

He looked at me in astonishment. But I persisted, trying to express my thought. "World history consists, after all, of the destinies of all people, doesn't it? Not only men who sign death warrants or know just where to place cannon and which way to fire them. I am thinking of other people. I mean those who are beheaded or shot at, and in fact all men and women who live and hope and love and die."

He nodded slowly. "Quite right, my Eugenie. But I shall influence all those millions of destinies of which you speak. Do you believe in me, Eugenie? Do you believe in me, whatever happens?"

His face was quite close to mine, so close that I trembled and involuntarily closed my eyes. Then I felt his lips pressed tightly on mine, until suddenly—I don't know how it happened, it was certainly not what I meant to do—my lips parted.

That night, long after Julie had snuffed out the candle, I could not get to sleep. Then Julie's voice came out of the dark: "Can't you sleep either, little one?"

"No. It's so hot in the room."

"I've something to tell you," Julie whispered. "A very great secret; you mustn't tell anyone. Anyhow, not till to-morrow afternoon. Will you promise?"

"Yes, I promise," I said, wildly excited.

"To-morrow afternoon Monsieur Joseph Buonaparte is coming to talk to Mama."

Was that all? "To Mama? What about?"

"Gracious, aren't you stupid! About us, of course, about him and me. He wants—well, what a child you are! He wants to sue for my hand!"

I sat up in bed. "Julie! That means you are betrothed!"

44

"Sh! Not so loud! To-morrow afternoon I shall be betrothed. If Mama makes no objection."

I jumped out of bed and ran across to her, but I bumped into a chair and hurt my toes. I cried out.

"Sh, Eugenie! You'll be waking everybody." But I had got to her bed. Quickly I snuggled under the warm eiderdown and excitedly shook her shoulder. I could not think how to show her how glad I was.

"Now you are a bride, a real bride! Has he kissed you already?"

"You can't ask that, child. A young lady does not let herself be kissed until her Mama has agreed to the betrothal."

"Why," I said, "he must have done."

Julie was nearly asleep. "Perhaps," she murmured.

Then I made my head comfortable on Julie's shoulder and went to sleep too.

. . . .

LATER

I think I'm tipsy. Just a little tipsy, very nice, very pleasant. Julie has become betrothed to Joseph. Mama sent Etienne down to the cellar for champagne. It's champagne that Papa bought years and years ago, to be kept for Julie's betrothal. They are all sitting on the terrace still, discussing where Julie and Joseph shall live. Napoleone has just gone to tell his mother all about it. Mama had invited Madame Letitia Buonaparte and all the children for to-morrow evening. Then we shall get to know Julie's new family. I do hope Madame Letitia will like me; I hope—no, I mustn't write it, or it won't happen! Only pray for it and secretly believe it.

We ought to have champagne often. Champagne tingles on your tongue and tastes sweet, and after the very first glass I couldn't stop laughing. After my third glass Mama said, "Nobody must give the child any more!" Suppose she knew I had already been kissed!

This morning I had to get up very early, and till now I had no chance to be alone. So as soon as Napoleone went away I ran up to my room, and now I am writing in my book. But my thoughts are running about and bumping into each other, each of them, like so many ants, carrying a little load. Ants drag along pine needles, twigs, or grains of sand; my thoughts each carry a little dream of the future. But they keep dropping them, because I have been drinking champagne and can't concentrate.

I don't know why it is, but I had quite forgotten that our

45

Swede, that Monsieur Persson, was going away to-day. Since the Buonapartes have been coming to see us I have not had much time for him. I don't think he likes Joseph and Napoleone. When I asked him what he thought of our new friends, he only said that he found it difficult to catch what they said, because they spoke so quickly, and besides that their accent was different from ours. That showed me that the Corsican accent is too difficult for him.

Yesterday afternoon he told me that he had packed everything and was going by the mail coach to-day. I determined, of course, to see him off, for I really like his equine face, and besides it is fun going to see the mail coach off. You always see different people there, and sometimes ladies in Paris gowns. But then, of course, I forgot Persson and his preparations, because, after all, I had my first kiss to think about.

Luckily I remembered Persson's departure the moment I woke up this morning. I jumped out of bed, put on my shift and my two petticoats, scarcely gave myself time to tidy my hair, and ran down to the dining-room. There I found Persson having his farewell breakfast. Mama and Etienne were hovering round him and doing all they could to make him have a good breakfast.

The poor man has a frightfully long journey ahead of him. First to the Rhine and then through Germany to the Hansa city of Lübeck, and from there by boat to Sweden. I don't know how many times he has to change coaches to get to Lübeck. Marie had given him a picnic-basket with a couple of bottles of wine and a roast chicken and hard-boiled eggs and cherries.

Etienne and I went with Monsieur Persson to the mail coach. Etienne carried one of the travelling-bags and Persson struggled with a big parcel, the other bag, and the picnic-basket. I begged him to let me carry something, and at last he reluctantly gave me the parcel, saying that it contained something very precious: "The most beautiful silk," he confided to me, "that I have ever seen in all my life. It is silk which your poor papa bought and intended for the Queen at Versailles. But events prevented the Queen——"

"Yes, really royal silk," said Etienne. "And in all these years I have never offered that brocade to anyone. Papa always said that it was only suitable for a court dress."

"But the ladies in Paris still go about elegantly dressed," I objected.

"The ladies in Paris are no longer ladies!" Etienne retorted. "Besides, they prefer quite transparent muslins. Do you call

46

that elegant? No, heavy brocade is no longer worn in France to-day."

"Well," said Persson to me, "I have ventured to buy the silk. I have been able to save a great part of my salary from Messrs. Clary, and I am glad that I have been able to spend it on this material. It will remind me——" he gulped in his emotion—"it will be a reminder of your dead Papa and of the firm of Clary."

I was surprised at Etienne. He cannot sell this heavy brocade in France. It is certainly very valuable, but at present it is quite out of fashion, so that he cannot sell it, and he has worked it off on Persson. Naturally, for a great deal of money; the firm of Clary has certainly made a good profit out of this deal.

"It was not easy for me to dispose of this material," Etienne said candidly. "But Monsieur Persson's country possesses a royal court, and Her Majesty the Queen of Sweden will need, I hope, a new State robe, and will appoint Monsieur Persson a Purveyor to the Court."

"You must not keep brocade too long, silk goes to pieces," I told Monsieur Persson, as a well-informed daughter of a silk merchant.

"This material will not," Etienne declared. "There are too many gold threads woven in."

The parcel was quite heavy, and I held it in my two arms, pressed against me. Although it was still early, the sun was hot, and my hair was sticking damply to my temples when at last we reached the mail coach. We had come rather late, and so could not spend long in farewells. The other passengers had already taken their seats in the coach. Etienne, with a sigh of relief, lifted in the travelling-bag he had been carrying and set it down on the toes of an elderly lady, and Persson almost dropped the picnic-basket as he shook hands with Etienne. Then he entered into an excited discussion with the postillion, who had placed his luggage on the roof of the coach. Persson told him that he would not let the big parcel go out of his sight and would keep it on his knees all the time. The postillion objected, and in the end the coachman lost patience and shouted: "Take your seats!" The postillion jumped up to the box and sat next to the driver and blew his horn. At last Persson got awkwardly into the coach with his parcel. The coach door was slammed to, but Persson opened it again. "I shall always hold it in honour, Mademoiselle Eugenie," he shouted. Etienne, shrugging his shoulders, asked, "Whatever does that mad Swede mean?"

"The Rights of Man," I replied, surprised at myself, because my eyes were brimming. "The broadsheet on which the Rights of Man are printed." As I said it I thought how pleased Persson's parents would be to see his equine face once more, and I thought that a man was passing for ever out of my life.

Etienne went into the shop, and I went with him. I always feel quite at home in the silk shop. I always did feel entirely at home. As a little girl I had often gone there with Papa, and he had always told me where the different rolls of silk came from. I can also distinguish the various qualities, and Papa always said that it was in my blood because I am a true silk merchant's daughter. But I think it is just because I so often watched Papa and Etienne passing a piece of material between their fingers, apparently crumbling it and then looking with their eyes screwed up to see whether it would crush easily, whether it was new or old material, and whether there was any danger of the material soon becoming brittle.

Although it was early in the morning, there were already customers in the shop. Etienne and I greeted them courteously, but I noticed at once that these were not important customers, only citizenesses who wanted muslin for a new fichu or cheap taffeta for a coat. The ladies from the great houses in the environs, who in the past had given big orders to our firm at the opening of the Versailles season, are no longer to be seen. Some of them have been guillotined, many have fled to England, but most have gone 'underground', that is to say they are living under false names in some place in which they are not known. Etienne often says that it is a great disadvantage for all craftsmen that the Republic does not arrange balls or receptions. For that the terribly stingy Robespierre is to blame.

I went to and fro in the shop for a while, helping the customers to feel the various materials and persuading them to buy bright green silk ribbons, because I had the feeling that Etienne wanted to get rid of them. Then I went home, thinking as always of Napoleone, and wondering whether he would put on a gala uniform for our celebration of Julie's betrothal.

When I got home I found Mama very excited. Julie had confessed to her that Joseph was coming in the afternoon to talk to her. And now she felt unequal to the situation. At last, in spite of the heat, she went into the town to consult Etienne. When she came back, she had a headache, lay on her sofa, and asked to be called as soon as Citizen Joseph Buonaparte had come.

Julie, on the other hand, was behaving as if she was crazy. She was going up and down the drawing-room, groaning. Her face, too, was quite green, and I knew she was ill. Julie always suffers from stomach-ache when she is very excited. In the end

48

I took the restless soul into the garden with me, and we sat in the summer-house. The bees were humming in the rambler roses, and I felt sleepy and very contented. Life is so simple, I thought, when you really love a man. Then you belong only to him. If I were forbidden to marry Napoleone, I should just run away with him.

At five o'clock there arrived a gigantic bouquet, with Joseph hidden behind it. The bouquet and Joseph were taken into the drawing-room by Marie; then Mama was informed, and the door of the drawing-room closed behind the two. I put my ear to the keyhole to try to catch what Joseph and Mama were murmuring. But I could not make out a word.

"A hundred and fifty thousand francs in gold," I said to Julie, who was leaning against the door with me. She shuddered.

"What do you mean?"

"Papa left a hundred and fifty thousand francs in gold for your dowry, and a hundred and fifty thousand for mine. Don't you remember that the lawyer read that when Papa's will was opened?"

"What does that matter?" said Julie peevishly, pulling out her handkerchief and wiping her forehead. Heavens, what a comic picture is a bride-to-be!

"Well, are we to congratulate you?" said someone behind us, laughing. Napoleone! As soon as he had come he leaned against the door with us. "May I, as a future brother-in-law, share the intolerable suspense?"

Julie's patience broke down. "Do what you like, but leave me in peace!" said she, sobbing. At that Napoleone and I went on tiptoe to the sofa and sat down silently. I was fighting against hysterics, the whole situation was so idiotically absurd. Napoleone poked me gently in the side. "A little more dignity, I should like to suggest, Eugenie!" he whispered, pretending to be cross.

Suddenly Mama was standing in the doorway, saying with a shaky voice, "Julie, please come in."

Julie rushed into the drawing-room like mad, the door closed behind her and Mama, and I—threw my arms round Napoleone's neck and laughed and laughed.

"Stop kissing me," I protested, because Napoleone had at once seized his opportunity. But in spite of that I did not let him go—until I thought of the gala uniform. I got a little away from him, and looked reproachfully at him. He had on the same threadbare green uniform as usual, with its shiny back.

"You might have put on your gala uniform, General," I

49

said. But I was sorry at once for saying that. His tanned face grew quite red. "I have none, Eugenie," he confessed. "So far I have never had enough money to buy one for myself, and all we get from the State is a tunic—the field-uniform I am wearing. We have to pay for the gala uniform with our own money, and you know——"

I nodded eagerly. "Of course, you are helping your Mama and the children! And a second uniform would be quite superfluous, wouldn't it?"

"Children, I have a great surprise, a very great surprise for you!" Mama stood in front of us, laughing and crying at the same time. "Julie and Joseph——" Her voice quivered. Then she regained composure. "Eugenie, fetch Suzanne at once! And go and see whether Etienne has come home yet. He promised me that he would be here punctually at half-past five."

I rushed up the stairs and told the two of them.

And then we all drank champagne. It was getting dark in the garden, but Joseph and Julie no longer bothered about the summer-house but just talked about the home they would set up in one of the suburbs. Part of Julie's dowry was to serve for buying a nice villa. Napoleone went away to tell his mother all about it. And I came up to my room to write it all down.

Now my nice little bit of tipsiness is all gone. I am just tired, and a little sad. For now I shall soon be alone in our room, and I shall never be able to use Julie's rouge again and surreptitiously read her novels. But I don't want to be sad, but to think about something cheerful. I must find out what day is Napoleone's birthday. Perhaps the pocket-money I have saved up will be enough for a uniform. But—where do you buy a gala uniform for a General?

MARSEILLES, mid-Thermidor. (Mama calls it the beginning of August.)

NAPOLEONE has been arrested. Since last night I have been living in a nightmare.

Meanwhile the whole town has been wild with joy; there is dancing in front of the Town Hall, and band after band of musicians are marching past. The Mayor has arranged the first ball for two years.

Robespierre and his younger brother were outlawed and arrested by the other Deputies on the ninth of Thermidor, and dragged next morning to the guillotine. Everybody who had been associated with him in any way is now in terror of arrest. So far ninety Jacobins have been executed in Paris. Joseph has already lost his position, which he owed to Napoleone's friendship with Robespierre's brother. Etienne says he will never forgive me for bringing the two Buonapartes into our house.

Mama wants Julie and me to go to the Mayor's ball. It would be my first ball, but I'm not going. I cannot laugh and dance when I don't even know where they have taken Napoleone.

Until the ninth of Thermidor—no, really until the tenth— Julie and I were very happy. Julie was working hard on her trousseau, embroidering hundreds of letter B's on cushion covers, tablecloths, sheets, and handkerchiefs. The wedding is due to take place in about six weeks. Joseph came every evening to see us, and often brought his mother and the children. When Napoleone was not inspecting a fortress somewhere, he would look in at any time of the day, and sometimes his two handsome A.D.C.s, Lieutenant Junot and Captain Marmont, came with him.

But I was not a bit interested in the interminable talk about the political situation, so that I have only now learnt that some two months ago Robespierre decreed that Deputies could be arrested like other people by any member of the Committee of Public Safety. They say that many Deputies are very frightened because they have grown rich on bribes. The Deputies Tallien and Barras are said to have become millionaires.

Suddenly Robespierre had even the beautiful Marquise de Fontenay arrested, the lady whom Deputy Tallien set free some time ago and who since then has been his mistress. Nobody knows why she was arrested; perhaps it was just to annoy Tallien. People think Tallien and Barras were afraid of being arrested for taking bribes; at all events, they organised a big conspiracy with a man named Fouché.

At first, this news was simply not believed in Marseilles. But when the newspapers arrived from Paris there were wild excitement. Flags were hung out, the shops were shut, and everybody made a round of visits. The Mayor did not even wait for confirmation, but at once released all the political prisoners. At the same time, the fanatical Jacobins were quietly arrested.

Napoleone and Joseph were terribly agitated when they came to see Etienne; they went into the parlour with him. After they left, Etienne was very bad-tempered: he told Mama that those 'Corsican adventurers' would be getting us all into prison. Napoleone stayed with me for hours in the summer-house, and told me that he would have to change his profession. "You can't expect an officer," he said, "in whom Robespierre took an interest to be retained in the army." I noticed for the first time that he took snuff.

Junot and Marmont came every day to meet Napoleone secretly at our house. They could not believe that he would simply be struck off the army list. But when I tried to comfort him and told him what Marmont and Junot had said, he shrugged his shoulders and just said, "Junot is an idiot. He's a faithful soul, but he's an idiot."

"But you always say he's your best friend!"

"Of course he is—absolutely faithful and devoted; he would go to his death for me. But he hasn't any sense—he's an idiot."

"And Marmont?"

"Marmont is very different. Marmont sticks to me because he is sure that my Italian plans will bring success in the end. Bound to!"

But everything has happened differently from what we expected. Last night, when Napoleone was at supper with us, we heard the approach of men on the march. Napoleone jumped up and rushed to the window; he never sees a squad of soldiers but he must find out what regiment they belong to, where they have come from, where they are going, and what is the sergeant's name.

The tramping stopped in front of our house; we heard shouting, and then the crunching of the gravel in the front garden; finally there came a hammering at the front door.

We all sat as if turned to stone. Napoleone had come away from the window and was looking at the door, with a pale drawn face. He had crossed his arms.

Then the door was flung open, and Marie and a soldier burst into the room together.

"Madame Clary!" Marie began, but the soldier cut her short. "Is General Napoleone Buonaparte in this house?" he shouted.

Napoleone calmly went up to the soldier, who clicked his heels, saluted, and said, "Warrant of arrest against Citizen General Buonaparte!"

He handed a paper to Napoleone. Napoleone held it close to his eyes.

"I'll bring a light," I said, jumping up.

"Thank you, my love," said Napoleone, "I can read the order quite well."

Then he put down the paper, looked hard at the soldier, and went up to him and tapped him on the button below the collar.

"Even on hot summer evenings," he said, "the sergeant's uniform is required to be buttoned up. What stupidity!"

While the soldier fingered his uniform in embarrassment, Napoleone turned to Marie.

"Marie," he said, "my sword is in the ante-room; will you please be so kind as to hand it to the sergeant."

Then, bowing toward Mama, he said, "Please forgive this disturbance, *Citoyenne* Clary!"

Napoleone's spurs clinked as he went out. Behind him tramped the sergeant. We did not move. Again we heard the crunching of the gravel in the garden; then the soldiers marched away. Not till then did Etienne break the silence.

"Let us go on," he said, "there's nothing we can do."

He picked up his spoon.

When we came to the joint he remarked, "What have I told you from the first? He is an adventurer, sponging upon the money of the Republic!"

And when we came to the dessert he added, "Julie, I regret having given my consent to your betrothal to that man."

After supper I slipped away through the back door. Although Mama had had the whole of the Buonaparte family here several times, we had never been invited by Madame Letitia to go there. I had a good idea why that was. The family live in the poorest quarter of the town, just behind the fish market, and Madame Buonaparte may well have been ashamed to let us see her poor refuge. But now I wanted to see her. I must tell her and Joseph what had happened, and talk about how to help Napoleone.

I shall never forget that journey through the dark narrow lanes round the fish market. At first I ran like mad; I felt that I must not lose a moment; I only slowed down when I was coming to the Town Hall square. My hair was all damp, and my heart was thumping painfully.

There was dancing in front of the Town Hall, and a tall man with his shirt-collar open caught me by the shoulder and roared with laughter when I pushed him away. One person after another tried to stop me; sticky fingers touched my arms, and suddenly a girl exclaimed, "Look, there's the little Clary girl!"

It was Eliza Buonaparte, Napoleone's eldest sister. Eliza is only seventeen, but that evening, painted and powdered and with dangling earrings, she looked much older. She was hanging on the arm of a young man whose fashionable high collar hid half of his face.

"Eugenie!" she called after me, "Eugenie, won't you let my partner give you a drink?"

53

But I ran on, into the narrow unlit lanes leading to the fish market. There I was in the midst of a darkness filled with a giggling and shrieking throng. A hubbub of love-making and quarrelling came out of all the doorways and windows, and courting cats were miauling in the gutter.

I breathed more freely when I reached the fish market; there were a few lights there, and I began to get the better of my timidity. Soon I was ashamed of it, and also of the fine white villa with the lilac trees and rambler roses that was my home. I crossed the fish market, and asked where the Buonapartes lived.

I was directed to the dark entrance of a lane: the house was the third on the left. Joseph had once told me that they had a basement dwelling.

I came to some narrow steps that led down to a basement, stumbled down, reached a door, and found myself in Madame Buonaparte's kitchen.

It was a big room, lit only by a candle in a broken saucer. The smell was dreadful.

Joseph was sitting at the table, in a crumpled shirt, without a neckerchief, reading newspapers by the light of the candle. Opposite him, the nineteen-year-old Lucien was bending over the table, writing. Between the two was a dish with the remains of a meal. At the back, in the dark, clothes were being washed; somebody was scrubbing hard, and water was splashing. The heat was unbearable.

"Joseph!" I said, to attract his attention. He jumped up.

"Has somebody come?" asked Madame Buonaparte, in broken French. The scrubbing stopped, and Napoleone's mother came into the light, wiping her hands on a big apron.

"It's me, Eugenie Clary," I said.

At that Joseph and Lucien started up. "For heaven's sake, what has happened?" Joseph asked.

"They have arrested Napoleone."

For a moment there was deathly silence. Then Madame Buonaparte cried out, drowning Joseph's voice:

"Holy Virgin, Mother of God! I saw it coming, I saw it coming!"

"Terrible," exclaimed Lucien.

They gave me a rickety chair to sit on, and I told them what had happened.

Then Louis came in from another room: he is seventeen and very fat. He listened apathetically.

I was interrupted by loud howls; the door flew open, and little Jerome, Napoleone's ten-year-old brother, burst in; behind him ran twelve-year-old Caroline, shouting at him the most picturesque quayside curses and trying to get something he was cramming into his mouth. Madame Buonaparte gave Jerome a box on the ear, and screamed at Caroline in Italian. She took away Jerome's tit-bit. It proved to be a stick of marzipan; she broke it into two and gave half each to the combatants. Then she shouted:

"Quiet! We have a visitor!"

That drew Caroline's attention to me, and she exclaimed:

"Oh la la, one of the rich Clarys!"

She came up to the table and sat on Lucien's knee.

'What a dreadful family,' I said to myself, and then I was sorry for saying it. They cannot help being so many or so poor. And they have nothing but their kitchen to live in.

Joseph asked question after question. "Who arrested Napoleone? Were they really soldiers? Not police?"

"No, soldiers," I replied.

"Then he won't be in prison, but under military arrest somewhere," said Joseph.

"What difference does that make?" groaned Madame Buonaparte.

"A tremendous difference," Joseph explained. "The military authorities will not let a General be simply executed; first they will court-martial him."

"You have no idea, Signorina," said Madame Buonaparte, "how dreadful this is for us." She brought a kitchen stool and sat down close to me, and put her damp work-worn hand on my arm. "Napoleone is the only one of us who is earning regularly, and he always worked so hard, and saved every centime and gave me half his pay for the other children. It is dreadful, dreadful."

"Anyhow, now he can't make me go into the army," growled fat Louis. He was quite triumphant.

"Shut your mouth," Lucien shouted.

The fat boy was now seventeen, and he had never done any work. Napoleone wanted to make him a soldier, so that there should at least be one mouth less for his mother to feed. I cannot imagine how Louis could march with his flat feet, but perhaps Napoleone meant to put him into the cavalry.

"But why," Madame Buonaparte asked, "why have they arrested him?"

"Napoleone knew Robespierre," Joseph murmured. "And he had let his plans be transmitted to the Minister of War by Robespierre."

"Always those politics," Madame Buonaparte complained. "I tell you, Signorina, politics have been the ruin of my family!

My children's poor Papa was always mixed up with politics, and he was always losing his clients' cases, and he left us nothing but debts. And what did my sons talk about all day long? About getting acquainted with prominent people, getting to know Robespierre, getting an introduction to Barras—they go on like that all the time. And look at the result!" She banged the table in vexation.

I looked down. "Your son Napoleone, Madame, is a genius," I said.

"Yes—unluckily," she retorted, looking at the flickering candle.

I looked up at her and Joseph. "We must find out where Napoleone is," I said, "and then we must try to help him."

"But we are so poor, and we don't know anybody with influence," Madame Buonaparte moaned.

"The Military Commandant of Marseilles," said Lucien, "must know where Napoleone has been taken." The family look upon Lucien as a poet and an unpractical dreamer, but it was from him that the first useful suggestion came.

"Who is the Commandant of Marseilles?" I asked.

"Colonel Lefabre," said Joseph. "And he cannot bear Napoleone. Quite recently Napoleone told the old Colonel what he thought about the fortifications here: they are in shocking disrepair."

"To-morrow," I heard myself saying, "I'll go to see him. Madame Buonaparte, would you get together some underclothing, and perhaps some food, and do it up into a parcel and send it to me early to-morrow? I'll ask the Colonel to give it to Napoleone. And then——"

"Thank you so much, Signorina," said Madame Buonaparte excitedly, "*tante grazie!*"

At that moment we heard a splash, a shriek and a long howl, and Caroline cried out happily, "Mama, Jerome has fallen into the wash-tub."

As Madame Buonaparte lifted the boy out of the tub and cuffed him, I got up to go. Joseph disappeared to get his coat and see me home. Lucien murmured, "It is very good of you, Mademoiselle Eugenie; we shall never forget it."

I felt rather frightened at the prospect of going to see that Colonel. As I said good-bye to Madame Buonaparte, she told me that she would send Polette to me with the parcel next morning. She started at the name. "Polette!" she said. "Where is she? She went out with Eliza to a friend over the way, and was going to be back in half an hour. And the two girls have been out the whole evening!"

I remembered Eliza's rouged face. No doubt she was enjoying herself with her partner in some tavern. But what about Polette? She is just my age.

Joseph and I went silently through the town. I was thinking of the evening when he first saw me home. Was that really four months ago? That was when it all began. Until then I had been a child, although I thought I was grown up. To-day I know that you are not really grown up till you fall in love.

"They can't possibly guillotine him," said Joseph, as we came to the villa. "The most they will do is to shoot him."

"Joseph!"

So that was what he had been thinking about on our long silent walk. 'He doesn't love him,' I said to myself, 'he actually hates him.'

"But we belong together," he said, "Napoleone and I and the others. We stick together."

"Good-night, Joseph!"

"Good-night, Eugenie!"

I slipped in without being noticed. Julie was in bed already, but the candle was burning on her bedside table. She had been waiting for me.

"I suppose you were with the Buonapartes!" she said.

"Yes," I replied, as I undressed. "They live in a cellar, and Madame Letitia was washing shirts at that late hour, and Jerome, that dreadful imp, fell into the wash-tub. It looks as if the two girls, Eliza and Polette, go out at night with men. Good-night, Julie—sleep well!"

At breakfast Etienne told us that Julie must put off her wedding, as he was not going to have a prisoner's brother as a brother-in-law. It would be a humiliation for the family, and very bad for the firm's reputation.

"I'll never let my wedding be postponed!" said Julie, in tears. Then she locked herself in our room.

Nobody spoke to me about the affair, because nobody but Julie has any idea that I belong to Napoleone. Except Marie; I feel sure she knows everything.

After breakfast Marie came into the dining-room and beckoned to me, and I followed her into the kitchen. Polette was there with the parcel.

"Quick, let's go before anybody sees us," I said to her. Etienne would have had a fit if he had known I was going with a parcel for Napoleone.

I have lived all my life in Marseilles, and Polette only came here a year ago, but she knows her way about much better than

I do. She knew exactly where to go to find the Colonel Commandant. She talked all the way. Her hips swayed so that her scanty blue dress swung to and fro. She walked very erect, and thrust out her breast; it is much bigger than mine, though we are of the same age. She kept passing the tip of her tongue over her lips, to keep them damp and shiny. Polette has the same narrow nose as Napoleone; her dark hair is twisted into a thousand little curls and tied up with a blue ribbon; her eyebrows are thinned and picked out with charcoal. I think Polette is lovely, but Mama doesn't like me to be seen with her.

Polette talked all the time about the Marquise de Fontenay, the new Madame Tallien. "The Parisians are all wild about her and call her Notre-Dame de Thermidor; she was brought away in triumph from the prison on the ninth of Thermidor, and Deputy Tallien married her there and then, and just imagine——" Polette opened her eyes wide, breathless with excitement—"just imagine, she is wearing dresses without any petticoat! She goes about in a quite transparent dress, and you can see everything! Everything, I tell you!"

"Where did you hear that?" I asked, but Polette took no notice.

"She has raven-black hair and raven-black eyes, and she lives in a house in Paris called the Thatched Cottage. The walls inside are covered with silk. There she receives all the famous politicians every afternoon, and I have been told that if you want anything from the Government all you need do is to tell her. I have been talking to a gentleman who only arrived yesterday from Paris, and this gentleman——"

"And this gentleman?" I repeated, in suspense.

"I made his acquaintance. The way you do make people's acquaintance, don't you? He was looking at the Town Hall, and I happened to be passing, so we got into conversation. But not a word about it—do you swear you'll say nothing?"

I nodded.

"Good," said Polette. "You swear to it by all the saints in heaven. Napoleone cannot bear my talking to strange gentlemen. He is a regular old maid on that subject. Tell me, do you think your brother Etienne would give me some material for a new dress? Something pink and transparent. That's the Command Office. Shall I come in with you?"

"I think I had better see him alone. Wait for me, won't you? Promise!"

She nodded gravely, and crossed the fingers of her right hand over the thumb. "I'll say a Paternoster. It can't do any harm."

I went in with the parcel. In the Command Office I heard myself asking the orderly to announce me to Colonel Lefabre. My voice sounded hoarse and strange.

The Colonel was sitting at a big desk in a big, bare room. At first, in my agitation, I could not speak a word. The Colonel had a red-faced cube of a head, with a stubbly grey beard, and he wore an old-fashioned perruke. I laid the parcel on the desk, and gulped in desperation. I just could not think what to say.

"What is that parcel, *Citoyenne*? And who exactly are you?"

"Pants, *Citoyen* Colonel Lefabre, and my name is Clary."

His pale blue eyes looked me up and down. "A daughter of the late silk merchant François Clary?"

I nodded.

"I've played cards with your Papa. Very respectable man, your Papa." He kept his eyes on me. "And what am I to do with the pants, *Citoyenne* Clary?"

"The parcel is for General Napoleone Buonaparte. He has been arrested. We don't know where he is. But you, Colonel, will know. I think there's a cake in the parcel. Underclothing and a cake."

"And what has the daughter of François Clary to do with the Jacobin Buonaparte?" the Colonel asked slowly and solemnly.

I flushed up. "His brother Joseph," I said, "is betrothed to my sister Julie."

"But why does not his brother Joseph come here? Or your sister Julie?" His pale blue eyes looked gravely at me. I felt sure he knew everything.

"Joseph is afraid. The families of arrested persons are always afraid," I managed to say. "And Julie now has other troubles. She is crying because Etienne, our big brother, has decided not to allow her to marry Joseph Buonaparte. All," I said with indignation, "all because you have arrested the General, *Citoyen* Colonel!"

"Sit down," was all he said.

I sat on the edge of a divan by his desk. The Colonel took snuff, and looked out of the window. He seemed to have forgotten me. Then suddenly he turned back to me.

"Listen, *Citoyenne*," he said. "Your brother Etienne is quite right. Of course he is. A Buonaparte is no match for a Clary, for a daughter of François Clary. A very respectable man he was, your poor Papa."

I said nothing.

"I don't know this Joseph Buonaparte. He's not in the army, is he? As for the other man, that Napoleone Buonaparte——"

59

"*General* Napoleone Buonaparte," I said, looking straight at him.

"As for that General, it was not I who arrested him; I only obeyed an order from the Ministry. Buonaparte has Jacobin sympathies, and all officers of his way of thinking—I mean all extremists—have been arrested."

"What will they do to him?"

"I have no information as to that."

The Colonel seemed to consider that the interview was over, so I got up. "The underclothing and the cake," I said, pointing to the parcel. "Could you give them to him?"

"Nonsense! Buonaparte is no longer here. He has been taken to Fort Carré, near Antibes."

I was not prepared for that. They had taken him away, and I could not get to him.

"But he must have a change of underclothing," I insisted.

The Colonel's face swam before my eyes; I wiped away the tears, but others came. "Can't you send the parcel to him, Colonel?"

"Now tell me, little lady, do you imagine that I have nothing to do but look after the underclothing of a scamp who is allowed to call himself General?"

I began to sob. He took snuff again; the scene seemed to upset him a good deal. "Do stop crying," he said.

"No," I sobbed.

He came away from his desk and stood in front of me. "I told you to stop crying," he roared.

"No!" I sobbed again. Then I wiped the tears away and looked at him. He was standing close to me, in obviously sympathetic perplexity. That made me cry again.

"Stop!" he shouted, "stop! Well, as you won't leave me in peace, and as you—very well, I'll send one of my men to Fort Carré with the parcel, and ask the Commandant to give it to that Buonaparte. *Now* are you satisfied?"

I gave him a tearful smile.

I was just going out when it occurred to me that I had not thanked him. I turned round. The Colonel was looking doubtfully at the parcel.

"Thank you very much, Colonel," I whispered.

He looked up, cleared his throat, and said, "Listen, *Citoyenne* Clary. I'll tell you two things, in confidence. To begin with, this Jacobin General won't have his head chopped off. Secondly, a Buonaparte is no match for a daughter of François Clary. Good-bye, *Citoyenne*."

Polette came back part of the way with me. She poured

out a flood of trivial talk. Pink silk she wanted, transparent. Madame Tallien, they said, was wearing flesh-coloured silk stockings. Napoleone would enjoy the cake. It had almonds in it. Did I like almonds? Was Julie really getting such a huge dowry that she could buy a villa for herself and Joseph? When should I be talking to Etienne about the silk, and when would she be able to go to the shop to fetch it?

I hardly listened. What the Colonel had told me was running in my head like a jingle.

> 'A Buonaparte has no right at all
> To wed a daughter of François Clary.'

When I got home I learned that Julie had got her way. Her wedding is not to be put off. I sat with her in the garden and helped her to embroider monograms on serviettes—a prettily curving B.

MARSEILLES, end of Fructidor. (Middle of September.)

I DON'T know how Julie spent her wedding night. Anyhow, the night before was terribly exciting, for me at any rate.

Julie's wedding was to be very quiet, with nobody present but our family and all the Buonapartes. Mama and Marie had been busy, of course, for days, making cakes and fruit creams, and on the night before the wedding Mama nearly broke down, she was so afraid things might go wrong. Mama is always worried before a party, but they have always been a great success.

It was decided that we should all go early to bed, and that Julie should have a bath. We have baths much more often than other people, because Papa had such modern ideas, and Mama makes sure that we go on doing what he wanted. So we have a bath almost every month, in a tremendous wooden wash-tub which Papa had made for the purpose in the laundry cellar. And as it was the night before Julie's wedding, Mama shook some jasmine scent into the bath water, and Julie felt like the late Madame Pompadour herself.

We went to bed, but neither Julie nor I could sleep, and so we talked about Julie's new home. It is outside Marseilles, but no more than half an hour's drive from us.

Suddenly we kept quiet and listened. Under the window somebody was whistling *"Le jour de gloire est arrivé!"*

I sat up. It was the second verse of our Marseilles song. And after it came at once Napoleone's signal. When he came to see us he always gave me that signal when he was still a long way off.

I jumped out of bed, pulled back the curtains, threw the window up, and leant out. It was a very dark night, sultry and oppressive. There was a storm brewing.

I screwed up my lips and whistled. There are very few young ladies who can whistle; I am one, but unluckily people don't approve of the gift, thinking it is ill-bred.

"Le jour de gloire——" I whistled.

"——est arrivé!" came from below.

A figure that had been standing close to the wall of the house moved out of the darkness and stepped on to the gravel path.

I forgot to shut the window, forgot to put on my slippers, forgot to put something round me, forgot that I had only my nightdress on, forgot what is proper and what isn't proper! I ran like mad down the stairs, opened the front door, and felt the gravel under my bare feet.

Then I could feel somebody's lips on my nose. It was so dark, and in the dark it's no good trying to see where to kiss.

There was thunder in the distance.

He pressed me to himself and whispered:

"Aren't you cold, *carissima*?"

"Only my feet," I replied, "I haven't any slippers on."

At that he lifted me up and carried me to the steps leading up to the front door. There we sat, and he wrapped his cloak round me.

"How long have you been back?" I asked.

"I have not got back yet, I am only on my way," he said. I leaned against him, and felt the roughness of his uniform on my cheek. How happy I was!

"Was it very horrid?" I asked.

"No, not at all. How good of you to take the parcel!" he said, stroking my hair with his lips. "It reached me with a covering note from Colonel Lefabre. He told me he had only sent it for your sake. I demanded to be brought before a court-martial, but I was not allowed that right."

"A court-martial! But that would have been dreadful!"

"Why? I should have been able then to explain to some senior officers what it was really all about. I could have told them of the plans I had left with that ass, Carnot, the Minister of War. They would at least have taken notice of that. Instead of that—" He moved away a little, and rested his head on his hands. "Instead of that, my plans are gathering dust in some pigeon-hole. And Carnot rests content with a precarious defence of our frontiers!"

"What are you going to do now?"

"They have set me free, because there is nothing against me. But those gentlemen at the Ministry don't like me. They will send me to the dullest sector of the front, and——"

"It's raining," I said, interrupting him. Big drops were falling on my face.

"No matter," he said, surprised at my mentioning it, and he told me of the horrid things they do to a General they want to be rid of. I drew in my legs and wrapped the cloak closer round me. It thundered, and a horse neighed.

"My horse, I tied it up to your garden fence," he said.

It began to rain more heavily. There was a flash and a clap of thunder alarmingly close, and the horse neighed desperately. Napoleone shouted something to it.

A window opened above us. "Who's there?" Etienne shouted.

"Come into the house," I whispered to Napoleone, "we shall be soaked."

"Who's that?" roared Etienne.

Then we heard Suzanne's voice:

"Shut the window, Etienne, and come over to me, I'm frightened!"

"There's somebody in the garden," Etienne replied, "I must go down and see what he's up to."

Napoleone went under the window. "Monsieur Clary, it is I, Napoleone."

There came another flash. I saw for a moment his thin slight figure in his scanty uniform. Then it was pitch dark again, there was a crash of thunder, and the horse tugged at the reins. Now it poured in torrents.

"Who is that?" Etienne shouted into the rain.

"General Buonaparte," Napoleone shouted back.

"But you are in prison!" Etienne retorted stupidly.

"I have been set free," Napoleone explained.

"But what are you doing here, General, at this hour?"

I jumped up, caught up the cloak, which came down to my ankles, and joined Napoleone.

"Don't stop here, it will be the death of you," Napoleone whispered.

"Who are you talking to?" Etienne shouted. The rain had abated, and now I could tell how his voice was shaking with fury.

"He's talking to me!" I called back. "Etienne, it's me, Eugenie!"

The rain had stopped. A very pale moon came out timidly between the clouds, and showed us Etienne in his nightcap.

A hiss came from the nightcap: "General, you owe me an explanation!"

Napoleone shouted up to him. He had put his arm round my shoulder. "I have the honour," he said, "Monsieur Clary, to request the hand of your younger sister."

"Eugenie, come in at once!" Etienne ordered. Behind him we could see Suzanne's head. It looked rather funny in its countless curlers.

"Good-night, *carissima*," said Napoleone, kissing me on my cheek, "until to-morrow's wedding breakfast." His spurs rattled as he went along the gravel path. I slipped indoors, forgetting to give him back his cloak.

Etienne was standing at his bedroom door in his nightshirt, holding a candle. I slipped past him barefooted and wearing Napoleone's cloak.

"What would Papa have said!" Etienne growled.

Julie was sitting up in bed. "I heard it all," she told me.

"I shall have to wash my feet, they are all gritty," I said, taking the jug and pouring it into the basin. When I had finished I got back into bed, spreading the army cloak over the counterpane. "It's his cloak," I said to Julie. "I shall have such lovely dreams under it."

"*Madame la Générale* Buonaparte," murmured Julie thoughtfully.

"If I'm lucky, he will be thrown out of the army," I said.

"Gracious! that would be awful!"

"Do you think I want a husband spending all his life at the front? No, let them dismiss him! Etienne can make use of him in the firm."

"You'll never get Etienne to do that!" said Julie, snuffing out the candle.

"I suppose you're right," I said. "What a pity! But Napoleone is not likely to take any interest in the silk trade. Good-night, Julie."

    •   •   •

Julie was almost late at the registrar's office. We could not find her new gloves anywhere, and Mama declared that you can't get married without gloves.

When Mama was young everybody was married in church, but since the Revolution people have had to go for the ceremony to the registry, and very few couples trouble to go on to a church or find one of the few priests who have sworn allegiance to the Republic. Julie and Joseph, of course, had no intention of bothering about that. Mama has been talking for days about the bridal veil she had; she would so have liked Julie to wear it. She told us, too, about the organ music you heard at a proper wedding when she was young.

Julie has put on a pink dress with real Brussels lace and red roses, and Etienne got a Paris business friend to hunt for some pink gloves for her and send them to him. Now we couldn't find those gloves anywhere. The wedding was to be at ten o'clock, and it was not till five minutes to ten that I found the gloves under Julie's bed. Julie rushed off with them, followed by Mama and the two witnesses.

Julie's witnesses are Etienne and Uncle Somis. Uncle Somis is one of Mama's brothers, and he comes to all the funerals and weddings. They found Joseph and his witnesses, Napoleone and Lucien, waiting at the registrar's office.

I simply had not had time to get dressed, as I had had all the hunt for the gloves. I stood at our window and called out "Good luck!" to Julie, but she didn't hear. The carriage was covered with white roses from the garden, rather faded; it did not look at all like an ordinary hackney coach.

I had given Etienne no peace till he brought me home some sky-blue satin from the shop for a new dress. Then I insisted that Mademoiselle Lisette, our dressmaker, should not cut the skirt too full. But I'm sorry to say it's not as close-fitting as in the Paris fashion-plates, and I'm laced round the waist and not close up under the breast like Madame Tallien in the pictures showing her as 'Madame de Thermidor,' the goddess of the Revolution. Still, I think my new dress is wonderful, and I feel like the Queen of Sheba, when she was tricked out for King Solomon. After all, I am a fiancée too, though Etienne seems to look upon that as nothing but a troublesome midnight rumpus.

They arrived before I was really ready, I mean the guests. Madame Letitia was in dark green; her hair was simply combed back, and bunched on her neck like a countrywoman; there is not a single white hair to be seen in it.

Eliza had thick paint on her face, and looked as garish as a tin soldier; she was wearing all the ribbons she had been able to wheedle out of Etienne in the last few weeks. Polette looked very pretty in a dainty little pink muslin dress. (Heaven only knows how she got Etienne to give her that material, the most modern there is!) Louis had untidy hair and obviously felt like a fish out of water. Caroline had had her face washed, and her hair was actually in order. That dreadful child Jerome began asking for something to eat the moment he arrived. Suzanne and I gave liqueurs to those over fourteen.

Madame Letitia said she had a surprise for us all. "A wedding present for Julie?" asked Suzanne, for Madame Letitia had not given Julie anything. She is dreadfully poor, but she might at least, I thought, have made something by hand.

Madame Letitia shook her head, smiled mysteriously, and said, "Oh no!" We wondered what she could have brought. Then it came out: yet another of the Buonapartes! He was her step-brother, an uncle named Fesch, only thirty years old, an ex-priest. But there is nothing of the martyr about this uncle Fesch, and so in these anti-clerical days he has retired from religion and gone into business.

"Is he doing well?" I asked. Madame Letitia shook her head. She hoped Etienne might persuade him to enter the firm of Clary.

Uncle Fesch came in a few minutes; he had a round jolly face, and was wearing a clean but shabby coat; he kissed Suzanne's hand and mine, and praised our liqueur.

Then they all came in from the registry. The first to appear was the carriage with the faded white roses, and Julie and Joseph and Mama and Napoleone got out. In the second carriage were Etienne, Lucien, and Uncle Somis. Julie and Joseph ran up to us; Joseph threw his arms round his mother's neck. The rest of the Buonapartes crowded round Julie; then Uncle Fesch put his arm round Mama, who had no idea who he was. Our Uncle Somis gave me a resounding kiss on my cheek and then patted Eliza. Then all the Clarys and all the Buonapartes formed such an excited cluster that Napoleone and I had a chance of a good long kiss—till somebody next to us coughed in disgust. Etienne, of course!

At the breakfast the bride and bridegroom sat between Uncle Somis and Napoleone, while I found myself squeezed in between Uncle Fesch and Lucien. Julie's cheeks were flaming with excitement and her eyes were sparkling, and for the first time in her life she looked really pretty.

Immediately after the soup, Uncle Fesch tapped his glass, because as a former priest he felt he really must make a speech. He spoke for a long time, very solemnly and very tediously, and as he considered it politically inadvisable to mention God he gave praise to 'Providence'. We owed to Providence, he said, this great happiness and this good meal and this harmonious gathering; we owed them all entirely to the great and beneficent rule of Providence.

66

Joseph winked at me and then smiled at Julie; Napoleone began to laugh. Mama's eyes were brimming more and more the longer Uncle Fesch preached; she turned them on me, full of emotion. Etienne, too, looked at me, but wrathfully, because the Providence that had brought Joseph and Julie together, and had so intimately united the Clary and Buonaparte families, was, without any question—I, Eugenie.

After the toast, Etienne made a speech; it was brief and bad. After that we left Julie and Joseph in peace.

We had just come to Marie's wonderful marzipan cakes with crystallised fruits on them, when Napoleone jumped up. Instead of politely tapping his glass, he thundered:

"Attention for a moment!"

We all sat up, coming to attention like startled recruits, and Napoleone told us, in short little sentences, how happy he felt to be able to take part in that family celebration. But he owed that good fortune not to Providence, but to the Ministry of War in Paris, which had suddenly, without any explanation, released him from arrest. Then he paused, and looked at me, and I knew what was coming—and I was very worried about what Etienne migh t do.

"So I will take this opportunity," he resumed, "when the Clarys and the Buonapartes are joined together in a family celebration, to tell you all that—"

His voice had dropped, but we were all so quiet that it was easy to tell that it was shaking with emotion.

"—that last night I sued for the hand of Mademoiselle Eugenie, and that Eugenie agreed to become my wife."

There came a storm of congratulations from the Buonapartes, and I found myself being hugged by Madame Letitia. But I looked across at Mama. Mama seemed to have had a shock; she was not at all glad. She looked away and turned to Etienne, and Etienne shrugged his shoulders.

At that moment Napoleone went up to Etienne, holding his glass, and smiled at him. It is wonderful what power Napoleone has over people; for Etienne's thin lips parted, and he grinned and clinked glasses with Napoleone.

Polette hugged me and called me 'sister'. Monsieur Fesch shouted something in Italian to Madame Letitia, and she replied happily "*Ecco!*" I think he had asked her whether I was to have as big a dowry as Julie.

Amid all the excitement and emotion nobody had been watching Jerome, and the imp had been able to stuff into his mouth whatever he could find room for. Suddenly I heard Madame Letitia cry out, and she dragged away a green-faced

67

Jerome. I took the two on to the terrace, and there Jerome surrendered all his ill-gotten gains. He felt better then, but it was quite impossible for us to take coffee on the terrace as we had intended.

Soon Julie and Joseph said good-bye to us all, and got into their decorated carriage to drive to their new home. We all went with them to the garden gate, and I put my arm round Mama's shoulder.

"Don't cry, dear Mama," I said.

Then came more liqueur and cakes, and Etienne gently told Uncle Fesch that he could not take another assistant into the firm, as he had already promised to take in Joseph and probably Lucien. Finally all the Buonapartes left, except Napoleone.

We walked round the garden, and Uncle Somis, whom we only see at weddings and funerals, asked me when I was going to be married. At that Mama turned to Napoleone, with tears in her eyes.

"General Buonaparte, will you promise me one thing?" she said. "Will you put off the wedding till Eugenie is sixteen? Will you?"

"Madame Clary," Napoleone replied, smiling, "that is not for me to say, but for you yourself, and Monsieur Etienne and Mademoiselle Eugenie."

But Mama shook her head. "I don't know how it is, General Buonaparte," she said, "you are so young, and yet I have the feeling—"

She broke off and looked at him with a wry smile. "I have the feeling," she resumed, "that [people always do what you want. They do at all events in your family, and, since we have known you, in my family as well. So I turn to you. Eugenie is still so young; do please wait till she is sixteen!"

In reply to that, Napoleone silently lifted Mama's hand to his lips. And I knew that that was a promise.

. . . . .

On the very next day Napoleone received orders to proceed at once to the Vendée to take up the command of an infantry brigade under General Hoche. I sat on the grass in the warm September sunshine and watched him tramping to and fro, pouring out his indignation at that shabby treatment. The Vendée! To hunt Royalists hiding there! A few starving aristocrats with their fanatically loyal peasants!

"I'm an artillery specialist, not a gendarme!" he exclaimed. Up and down he went, with his hands behind him. "They deny me the triumph of a court-martial, and now they propose

68

to bury me in the Vendée, like a Colonel on the eve of retirement! They are keeping me away from the front, to commit me to oblivion!"

When he was full of wrath there was a yellow gleam in his eyes.

"You could resign," I said softly. "I could buy a little house in the country with the money Papa left for my dowry, and perhaps some land with it. If we manage carefully and—"

He stood still and looked at me.

"But if you do not care for that," I continued, "you might perhaps join Etienne."

"Eugenie! Are you mad? Or do you seriously think I could settle in a farmhouse and keep fowls? Or sell ribbons in your brother's shop?"

"I did not want to hurt you, I was only thinking what we could do."

He laughed heartily. "What we could do! What the best General of Artillery in France could do! Don't you know that I am France's best General?"

Then he began walking silently up and down. In a few moments he said:

"I'm riding away to-morrow."

"To the Vendée?"

"No, to Paris. I'm going to talk to the people at the Ministry."

"But isn't that—I mean, in the army don't you have to do exactly what is ordered?"

"Yes, yes indeed. If one of my soldiers disobeys an order, I have him shot. They may have me shot when I get to Paris—I shall take Junot and Marmont with me."

Junot and Marmont, his A.D.C.s since Toulon, are still in Marseilles, without employment. They regard his future as their own.

"Can you lend me any money?"

I nodded.

"Junot and Marmont cannot pay for their lodgings. Like me, since my arrest they have received no pay. I must settle their bill at the inn. How much can you lend me?"

I had been saving up for a gala uniform for him. There were ninety-eight francs lying under the nightdresses in my chest-of-drawers.

"Give me all you can," he said, and I ran up to my room and collected the money.

He put the notes in his pocket. Then he pulled them out again and carefully counted them.

"So I owe you," he said, "ninety-eight francs."

Then he put his arms round my shoulders and embraced me. "You will see that I shall persuade all Paris: they must give me the Command-in-Chief in Italy. They have got to!"

"When will you be starting?"

"As soon as I have paid my A.D.C.s' bill. Don't forget to write to me often; at the Ministry of War in Paris; the letters will be posted on to me at the front. Don't fret."

"I shall have lots to do. I have all the monograms to embroider on my trousseau."

He nodded eagerly. "B, B, B, *Madame la Générale* Buonaparte."

Then he untied his horse, which, to Etienne's annoyance, he had tied again to our garden fence, and rode away into the town. The slim horseman in the quiet road between the villas looked unimposing and very solitary.

PARIS, twelve months later: Fructidor, Year III. (I've run away from home!)

THERE'S nothing more disagreeable than running away from home. I haven't seen a bed for two nights now, and my back aches because I've been sitting in the mail coach for four days without interruption. I feel sure I'm black and blue all over; stage coaches are so horribly badly sprung. And I haven't any money for the return journey either. But I don't need that. After all, I've run away from home and I've no intention of going back.

It's only two hours since I reached Paris. It was getting late, and in the dusk the houses all looked the same, grey houses with no front gardens, houses, houses, nothing but houses. I had no idea that Paris was so big.

I was the only one in the coach who had never been to Paris before. That wheezing M. Blanc who got into the coach two days ago, going to Paris on business, took me to a hackney coach, and I showed the driver the slip of paper on which I had written Marie's sister's address. All the money I had left went on the fare, and then the driver was rude because I couldn't give him a tip.

The address proved right, and, thank God, Marie's relatives, Clapain by name, were at home. They live in the outbuildings of a house in the Rue du Bac. The Rue du Bac can't be far from the Tuileries; we drove past the Palace and I recognised it from the pictures. I kept pinching myself to make sure I wasn't dreaming but was really in Paris and had really run away from home.

Marie's sister, Madame Clapain, was very kind to me. At first she was quite overcome at seeing the daughter of Marie's mistress. But then I told her I had come in secret, to settle some business, and I had no money; Marie had said that perhaps—

At that Marie's sister stopped being overcome and said I could stay with her. Was I hungry? And how long did I want to stay?

I said I was very hungry, and gave her my bread ration card because, on account of the bad harvest, bread is strictly rationed and food of any sort is dreadfully dear. As for how long I was going to stay I had no idea, perhaps a day or two, perhaps—

She gave me something to eat, and then Monsieur Clapain came home. He told me that their rooms were part of the outbuildings of a former aristocratic mansion. The mansion had been confiscated by the Government, but because of the housing shortage the municipality had divided the outbuildings up into small dwellings and let them to big families.

The Clapains are an enormously big family. Three small children were crawling about the floor, and two more came running in for something to eat. The kitchen where we had our meal was so full of babies' nappies hanging up to dry that it was like being in a tent.

Immediately after the meal Madame Clapain said she was going for a walk with her husband. She could hardly ever do that, she said, because of the children. But now I was there she could put the children to bed and go out for a bit. When the children were all in bed, Madame Clapain put on a little hat with an ostrich feather rather the worse for wear, Monsieur Clapain scattered a whole little bag of powder over his almost bald head, and off they went.

All of a sudden I felt dreadfully alone in this huge town and so I rummaged in my travelling-bag, just for the company of my familiar possessions. At the last moment I had put in the diary, and now I took it out and turned the pages over, and read how everything had happened. After that I set to work, with a splayed quill which I found on the kitchen cupboard next to a dust-covered inkbottle, on this account of my running away from home.

It is a whole year since my last entry. But then, so very little happens to a grass widow—or rather to a grass fiancée, with her husband-to-be away in Paris. Etienne found me some cambric for handkerchiefs and nightdresses, damask for tablecloths, and linen for bedclothes, and took the cost out of my dowry. I stitched innumerable finely curved B's, pricking my fingers times without number, and sometimes I visited Madame Letitia in her cellar dwelling, and sometimes Julie and Joseph in their charming little villa. But Madame Letitia could only talk about the way everything got dearer and dearer and how Napoleone hadn't sent her any money for ages. And Julie and Joseph never did anything but look deep into each other's eyes, and say things I could never understand, and giggle—evidently very happy but a bit idiotic. All the same, I went there quite often because Julie always wanted to know what Napoleone had written to me and gave me Napoleone's letters to Joseph to read.

Unfortunately, Napoleone didn't seem to be doing at all well in Paris. A year ago he arrived there with his two A.D.C.s and Louis—he had taken that fat youngster with him at the last moment to help Madame Letitia. And of course there had been a tremendous fuss at the War Ministry because he hadn't gone to the Vendée as he had been ordered to. He just talked about his Italian projects until, simply to get rid of him, the Ministry sent him to the Italian front, but only as an Inspector, not as Commander-in-Chief. To the Italian front he went, only to be cold-shouldered by most of the generals or told not to interfere. At last he fell ill with malaria and returned to Paris. When he turned up again at the Ministry, the War Minister raged at him and showed him the door. After that Napoleone was on half pay for some months and then he was simply dismissed from the Service without a pension.

A dreadful situation! We just couldn't imagine what he was living on. He pawned his father's watch, but that couldn't have lasted him longer than three days. He couldn't keep Louis any more, and forced him to enter the army. At times Napoleone did some casual work in the War Ministry, drawing maps and damaging his eyesight. His torn trousers were a great worry to him and he tried to patch them up himself, but the seams kept on bursting. He applied for a new uniform, but the Government would not allot one to a dismissed General. In despair he went where everyone goes nowadays who wants something: to the 'Chaumière', the 'thatched cottage' of the beautiful Madame Tallien.

At the moment we have a Government called the Directory, nominally a council of five Directors. But Joseph maintains that only one of our Directors really counts—Director Barras.

Whatever happens in the country, Barras comes to the top.

(Like filth floating in the harbour, I sometimes feel. But perhaps one shouldn't talk like that about the Head of the Nation, or at any rate one of our five Heads.) This man Barras is an aristocrat by birth, but he managed to turn Jacobin in good time, and so he has been none the worse. Then, together with Tallien and a Deputy called Fouché, he overthrew Robespierre and saved the Republic from the 'tyrant'. And after that he moved into an official residence at the Luxembourg Palace and became one of our five Directors. A Director has to see all the important people, and as he isn't married Barras has asked Madame Tallien to throw open her house every afternoon to his guests, or, which comes to the same thing, to those of the French Republic.

A business friend of Etienne's told us that at Madame Tallien's champagne flows very freely indeed, and that her salon is always full of men who have grown rich through the war, and of speculators who buy up cheaply all the aristocratic mansions which the State has confiscated and then sell them at a huge profit to the *nouveaux riches*. There are also many entertaining ladies there, friends of Madame Tallien's, said this man, but by far the most beautiful women are Madame Tallien herself and Josephine de Beauharnais.

Madame de Beauharnais is Barras' mistress, and she wears a narrow red ribbon round her neck to show that she is related to a 'victim of the guillotine'. That is no longer a disgrace but a high distinction. This Josephine is the widow of the General de Beauharnais who was beheaded, and that means that she is a former countess.

Mama asked Etienne's friend whether there were any decent women left in Paris at all, and he answered:

"Oh yes. But they are very expensive!"

He laughed, and Mama sent me to the kitchen for a glass of water.

One afternoon Napoleone called at Madame Tallien's and introduced himself to Madame Tallien and Madame de Beauharnais. They both thought it dreadful that the War Minister would not give him a new command or even a new pair of trousers, and they both promised to get him the new trousers at all events. But first he would have to change his name a bit. Napoleone sat down at once and wrote to Joseph.

"By the way, I have decided to change my name and I advise you to do likewise. No one in Paris can even pronounce Buonaparte, and from now on I am calling myself Bonaparte. And of course Napoleon instead of Napoleone! Please address my letters accordingly and tell the family of my decision. After all, we are French citizens, and I want my name to go down as a French name in the Book of History."

So he was no longer Buonaparte but Bonaparte. His trousers were still torn, his father's watch was pawned, but he still thinks of making history.

Joseph, like the ape he is, must needs change to Bonaparte as well, and so did Lucien, who got a post in St. Maximin in charge of a military depot and has begun to write political articles. Joseph sometimes goes off as a commercial traveller for Etienne and brings home some good orders, which, Etienne said, should put some fat commission into Joseph's pocket. But Joseph doesn't like being called a traveller in silk goods.

During the last few months Napoleon's letters to me have become rare, though Joseph gets one twice a week. Yet at long last I have been able to send him the portrait he wanted. It is a dreadfully bad painting, I must say. It gives me a snub nose, and I don't believe for a moment that mine is really like that. But I had had to pay the painter in advance, and so I took the painting and sent it to Paris.

He didn't even thank me. His letters have become quite empty now. They still begin with *Mia Carissima* and end with a hug. But as to our wedding date, not a word! Not a word about my being almost sixteen! Meanwhile he writes pages and pages to Joseph about the fine ladies in Madame Tallien's salon. 'I have come to realise,' he wrote in one letter, 'the important part that really distinguished women play in a man's life, women of experience, women of understanding, women of the great world.' . . . Oh, how that hurt me!

A week ago Julie decided to join Joseph on a long business tour. Mama cried a lot because one of her children was going away on a real journey, so Etienne sent her to stay for a month with Uncle Somis, to give her a change. Mama packed seven travelling-bags, and I took her to the stage coach for her four hours' journey to Uncle Somis' place. At the same time Suzanne found she felt rather 'run down', and badgered Etienne into taking her to a spa. Thus it came about that Marie and I were left alone in the house.

One afternoon I was sitting with Marie in the summer-house: that was the afternoon of decision. It was one of those autumn days when the roses are all gone and the leaves are etched sharply against the pale blue sky, and you feel that something is fading away, dying. Perhaps that is why not only silhouettes are so sharp and clear but thoughts are too: anyhow, as I was stitching another 'B' on a napkin I suddenly dropped it and said:

"I must go to Paris. I know it's mad and the family would never hear of it. But I must go."

"If you must, then go," said Marie, who was shelling peas. She didn't even look up.

Without taking it in, my eyes followed a green and golden insect crawling over the table.

"What could be simpler?" I said. "We're alone in the house. I could take the mail coach to Paris to-morrow morning."

"You've got enough money, anyhow," said Marie, and exploded a thick pod of peas with her thumbs. The little crack of the explosion did not disturb the insect on its way across the table.

"Well, it'll probably be enough for the journey if I stay only two nights at a hotel. The two other nights I might be able to spend in the parlours of the coaching inns. They might even have a bench or a sofa."

Marie looked up at me for the first time.

"I thought you had more money than that," she said, "under your nightgowns in the chest."

I shook my head. "No, I—I lent most of it to someone."

"And where are you going to stay in Paris?"

The insect had reached the edge of the table. I turned it round carefully and watched it crawling back the way it had come.

"In Paris?" I pondered. "I really hadn't thought of that. It depends, doesn't it?"

"You have both promised your mother to wait for the wedding till you are sixteen. And in spite of that you want to go to Paris now?"

"Marie," I blurted out, "if I can't go now, it may be too late and there may be no wedding at all!"

For the first time I had said right out what until then I had hardly dared to think.

Marie went on bursting pea pods. Then she asked:

"What's her name?"

I shrugged my shoulders. "I don't know, really. Perhaps it's Madame Tallien, perhaps it's the other one, Barras' mistress, Josephine, who used to be a countess. I really couldn't say. But, Marie, you mustn't think any the worse of him for that. You see, he hasn't seen me for ages. But—let him set eyes on me again!"

"Yes," said Marie, "you're right. You've got to go to Paris. Long ago my Pierre joined up and he never came back to me. And there I was with Little Pierre and no money at all, and so I had to go to the Clary family as a wet nurse. I wrote

75

to Pierre and told him everything, and he didn't even bother to answer. Yes, I should have tried to go and see him."

I knew all about Marie's sad story, she has told it to me so often.

"He was too far away," I said, "you couldn't have got to him."

The green and golden insect had reached another edge of the table.

"You go to Paris," said Marie. "You could spend the first few nights with my sister, and then we'll see."

"Yes, we'll see," I said, and getting up I put the insect down on the lawn. "I'm going to town now to ask about the mail coach to-morrow morning."

The family had taken all the good travelling-bags and I only found an old and very shabby one. I packed it in the evening, and did not forget to put in the blue silk gown which I had been given for Julie's wedding. It is my most beautiful frock. I'll put it on, I thought, when I am going to call on Madame Tallien to see him again.

The next morning Marie went with me to the coach. I passed along the familiar road to town as in a dream, a very beautiful dream in which I knew I was doing the right and only possible thing.

At the last moment Marie gave me a big medallion made of gold. "I have no money," she murmured, "I need my wages for Little Pierre. Take the medallion, it's real gold. It's from your mother, the day I weaned you. You can easily sell it, Eugenie."

"Sell it? Whatever for?"

"For the return journey," Marie said, and turned away quickly.

And so, for one, two, three, four endless days my bones were shaken in that wretched coach, along a never-ending dusty road, past fields and woods, through villages and towns. Every three hours there came a sudden jolt that threw me against the bony shoulder of the lady in mourning on my right. The jolt meant a change of horses. Then on and on again. And all the time I was thinking of how I would go to Madame Tallien's and ask for General Bonaparte. And then I would say, 'Napoleon, I know you haven't the money to come to me, so I've come to you, because we belong together!'

This strange kitchen, Marie's sister's, is full of unfamiliar shadows. I haven't seen the furniture by daylight, that's why.

Will he be glad? Of course he will! He'll take my arm and introduce me to his fine new friends, and then we'll go away to be alone, walking about since we have no money to sit in a coffee-house. And perhaps he may know someone where he can put me up till we've had Mama's consent to the wedding. And then we'll get married, and then—

Ah, they are coming home, Monsieur and Madame Clapain. Let's hope they have a reasonably good sofa on which I can stretch myself, and to-morrow—to-morrow, to-morrow, how I am looking forward to to-morrow!

PARIS, twenty-four hours—no, an eternity later!

It's night-time, and I'm sitting once again in Madame Clapain's kitchen. Once again? Perhaps it isn't 'again', perhaps it's just 'still', and I haven't been away at all from this house and the whole of this day was nothing but a bad dream and perhaps I may yet wake up. But did not the waters of the Seine close over my head? It was so near, I remember, the lights of Paris danced a minuet on the waves and in their dancing seemed to beckon me on, and I did bend over the cold stone side of the bridge and maybe I did die and float down the river, floating, floating and no longer feeling any more. Oh, if only I could die!

But no, I'm sitting at an unsteady kitchen table and my thoughts go round and round. Every word and every face comes back to me now whilst outside the rain beats against the windows.

It has been raining all day long. Before I had reached Madame Tallien's house I was soaked through already. I had put on the beautiful blue silk gown. But walking through the Gardens of the Tuileries and then on along the Rue Honoré I discovered that by Parisian standards it was quite old-fashioned. Here the women wear dresses that look like shirts and are held together under the bosom by a silk ribbon. They don't wear fichus either although it's autumn now, and they only drape a flimsy scarf around their shoulders. My tight sleeves, which come down to the elbows and have laced edges, look quite impossible. Apparently one no longer wears sleeves, only shoulder-clasps. I felt ashamed because I looked like a real provincial.

It was not difficult to find the 'Chaumière' in the Rue des Veuves. Madame Clapain had told me exactly how to get there, and although in spite of my impatience I kept stopping and looking into the shop windows of the Rue Honoré I reached my goal within half an hour. To look at it from outside the house gives a rather modest impression. It's hardly bigger

77

than our villa at home, built in rural style and thatched. But through the windows you can see the sheen of brocade curtains.

It was early yet in the afternoon, but I wanted to have my surprise ready in good time and to be waiting in one of the reception rooms by the time Napoleon would arrive. I knew that Napoleon went there almost every afternoon, so that this was the best place to meet him. And I also knew that anybody could enter here where Madame de Thermidor keeps open house, because he wrote so to Joseph.

Outside the house a lot of people were hanging about who stared with critical eyes at everybody approaching the 'Chaumière'. I looked neither left nor right but went straight to the gate, opened it, entered and ran right into the arms of a lackey. He wore a red silver-buttoned livery and looked exactly like any of the lackeys in the pre-Revolutionary aristocratic houses. It was new to me that the dignitaries of the Republic were allowed lackeys in livery. Which reminds me, by the way, that Deputy Tallien himself used to be a servant.

This fine flunkey then looked me up and down and asked in an arrogantly nasal voice:

"What do you want, citizeness?"

This question was the last thing I had expected, and so I only managed to stammer:

"I should like to—to go inside!"

"I can see that," said the lackey. "Have you an invitation?"

I shook my head. "I . . . I thought that—well, that anybody might come in here."

"You did, did you?" the fellow grinned, his eyes becoming more and more insolent. "The Rue Honoré and the Arcades of the Palais Royal are good enough for the likes of you, dearie!"

I felt myself turning puce in the face. "What—whom do you think you are talking to, citizen?" I managed to bring out, nearly overcome with shame. "I've got to get inside because I've got to see someone in there."

But he simply opened the gate and pushed me out. "Order from Madame Tallien: ladies not allowed in except when accompanied by gentlemen. Or perhaps you claim to be a personal friend of Madame's?" he added in his most contemptuous voice, pushing me out on to the street and banging the gate.

And there I was, among the curious mob on the pavement.

Meanwhile the gate opened and closed all the time; but some girls had forced themselves in front of me so that I couldn't see who the guests of Madame were.

"It's a new arrangement," said a girl with a thickly rouged face to me, and winked. "Only a month ago we were all allowed in without the slightest difficulty. But then some foreign paper wrote that Madame Tallien's house was no better than a brothel. . . ." She bleated rather than laughed and her mouth showed more gaps than teeth between purple-painted lips.

"It's all the same to her, but Barras said that one had to keep up appearances," said another one from whom I shrank back in horror because of the awful pus-filled sores in her chalk-white powdered face. "You are a new one, aren't you?" she asked me, looking pitifully at my old-fashioned dress.

"Barras! Don't talk about Barras!" Purple Lips bleated once more. "Two years ago he had to be satisfied with Lucille at twenty-five francs a night. To-day he can afford the Beauharnais! That old she-goat! Rosalie, who got in there"—her pointed chin jerked towards the house—"the day before yesterday with her new friend, wealthy Ouvrard, told me that that Beauharnais woman is having an affair now with a real youngster, an officer who knows how to press her hand and look deep into her eyes. . . ."

"Fancy Barras standing for that!" marvelled Pustule Face.

"Barras? Why, he doesn't mind, he even wants her to sleep with the officers! All he cares for is to be on good terms with the Army people because some day he may have to depend on them. Besides, he's probably sick of her already. Josephine, always in white, and nothing but white. That old bitch with grown-up children. . . ."

A young man intervened here: "Her children are twelve and fourteen years of age. Not much grown-upness there. By the way, Theresa spoke in the Assembly to-day."

"You don't say, citizen!" The two girls at once turned their whole attention on the young man. But he bent over to me and asked:

"You're not from Paris, citizeness? But you probably read in the papers that lovely Theresa is the first woman ever to have addressed the National Assembly. To-day she talked about the necessary reforms in the education of young girls. Are you interested in all that, citizeness?"

He smelled abominably of wine and cheese and I withdrew a bit from him.

"It's raining, let's go into a coffee-house," said Purple Lips, looking encouragingly at the young man with the abominable smell. But he stuck to me.

"It's raining, citizeness," he said.

Yes, it was raining. My blue frock was all wet and, besides, I felt cold. The young man touched my hand as if by accident, and at that moment I knew that I couldn't stand it any longer.

79

Just then another cab drew up by the gate. With both elbows I forced my way out of the group of loiterers, ran like mad towards the cab and right into a man wearing an army officer's greatcoat. He had just got out of the cab, a dreadfully tall man, so tall that I had to raise my eyes in order to see his face. But since he had pulled his three-cornered hat down over his eyes I saw nothing but a gigantic nose.

"Please forgive me, citizen," I said to the giant, who shrank back in astonishment from my attack, "please forgive me, but I should like to go with you."

"You would like what?" he asked, taken aback.

"Yes, I'd like to go with you for a moment. Ladies are only allowed into Madame Tallien's house if they are in the company of gentlemen. I've got to get in there, you see, I've got to— and I have no gentleman to escort me in."

The officer looked me up and down and didn't seem to like the prospect. Then, suddenly coming to a decision, he offered me his arm and said:

"Come on, citizeness!"

The lackey in the hall recognised me at once. He looked at me with indignation and then bowed deeply to the giant and took his greatcoat whilst I inspected myself in a tall mirror. Wet strands of hair were hanging into my face, and as I rearranged them I found that my nose was shiny. But there was no time to powder it because just then the giant said impatiently:

"Well, are you ready, citizeness?"

He was wearing a beautifully tailored uniform with thick gold epaulettes. When I lifted my face to see him properly I noticed that the small mouth under his striking nose was curled in disapproval. Quite obviously he was annoyed because he had given in and taken me along. And now it occurred to me that most likely he took me for one of the prostitutes outside the gate.

"Please forgive me," I murmured, "I didn't know what else to do."

"Conduct yourself decently in there and don't let me down," he said severely, made a stiff little bow and once again offered me his arm.

The lackey opened a white double door and we entered a big room crowded to the walls with people. Another lackey seemed to shoot out of the floor in front of us and looked at us questioningly. My escort turned to me abruptly:

"What's your name?"

I didn't want anybody to know of my presence, and so I only whispered my Christian name, "Désirée."

"Désirée who?" he asked, annoyance in his voice.

I shook my head. "Please, please, just Désirée."

So he told the lackey curtly, "Citizeness Désirée and Citizen General Jean-Baptiste Bernadotte."

"Citizeness Désirée and Citizen General Jean-Baptiste Bernadotte!" the lackey announced into the room. The people standing near us turned round, and a dark-haired young woman in a gown that seemed to consist of yellow veils at once left her group and glided towards us.

"How lovely to see you, Citizen General! What a marvellous surprise!" she twittered and stretched out both her hands to the giant. A searching glance of her great dark eyes ran over me from top to bottom and stopped for a fraction of a second at my dirty shoes.

Meanwhile the giant bent down over her hands and kissed—no, not her hands but her white wrists. "You are too kind, Madame Tallien," he said. "As always when Fortune allows a poor soldier from the front a sojourn in Paris, my first call is here at Theresa's magic circle!"

"As always the poor soldier from the front deigns to flatter. And he's lost no time in finding company either, I see . . ." Her dark eyes scrutinised me once more. I attempted a little bow, but its only result was that Madame Tallien lost every shred of interest in my poor little person and calmly interposed herself between the General and me.

"Come on, Jean-Baptiste," she said, "you'll have to say how-do-you-do to Barras. He is sitting in the garden-room with that horrible Germaine de Staël—you know, old Necker's daughter who scribbles novels all the time—and we've got to relieve him. He'll be delighted at your . . ."

And then I saw nothing but my giant's back and the yellow veils over her otherwise naked shoulders. Other guests came between us, and there I was quite by myself in Madame Tallien's glittering salon.

I took refuge in a window niche and surveyed the room. But I couldn't see Napoleon anywhere. There were a lot of uniforms there, but not one as shabby as that of my fiancé.

The longer I stayed the deeper I crept into the protecting window niche. Not only was my dress impossible but my shoes too appeared quite ridiculous to me. The ladies here didn't wear proper shoes at all, just soles without heels, tied round the feet with narrow gold or silver straps so that the toes were left free, and the toe-nails were painted pink or silver.

I could hear a violin playing in one of the adjoining rooms. Servants in red uniforms moved among the guests balancing trays full of enormous bowls, glasses and snacks. I gobbled a smoked salmon roll, but the taste was lost on me because of my excited state. Then two gentlemen came into the window niche and stood near me talking without paying any attention to me. They talked about the people of Paris who wouldn't put up much longer with the rise of prices and would riot soon.

"My dear Fouché," one of them said, taking snuff with a bored air, "if I were in Barras' place I'd shoot the mob to bits."

"For that you'd first have to find someone ready to do the shooting," the other one remarked.

Thereupon the first man, between two snuff sneezes, jerked out the sentence that he had just seen General Bernadotte among the guests.

The other one, the man called Fouché, shook his head. "Bernadotte? Never in your life. But what about that little wretch who keeps hanging round Josephine these days?"

At that moment someone clapped his hands, and over the general murmur I heard the twitter of Madame Tallien's voice:

"Everybody to the green room, please! We have a surprise for our friends."

I went along with the crowd into an adjoining apartment where we were so tightly packed that I couldn't see what was going on. All I could take in was the green-and-white striped silk covering the walls. Then champagne was handed round and I too was given a glass. We had to press together still more closely to let the lady of the house make her way through. Theresa passed quite close to where I stood, and I saw that she had nothing on under the yellow veils. The dark red nipples of her bosom showed quite clearly. How indecent it was!

She had taken the arm of a gentleman whose purple frock-coat was embroidered with gold all over. He was holding a lorgnette to his eyes and gave an impression of extraordinary arrogance. Someone murmured, "Good old Barras is getting fat," and I realised that I was in the presence of one of the five masters of France.

"Form a circle round the sofa please!" Theresa called out.

Obediently we arranged ourselves in a circle. And at that moment I saw him!

Where? On the little sofa. With a lady in white.

He still wore the old down-at-heel boots, but his trousers were new and immaculately pressed and new too was his uniform jacket, a jacket without either badges of rank or medals. His lean face was no longer tanned but almost sickly pale. He sat there stiffly and stared at Theresa Tallien as if the salvation of his soul depended on her. The woman by his side was leaning against the back of the sofa, her arms stretched out and her small head with its tiny curls thrown backwards. Her eyes were half closed, the lids painted silver, the long neck shining up provocatively white out of a narrow dark-red velvet ribbon. And then I knew who she was: the widow Beauharnais. Josephine!

A mocking smile played round her closed mouth, and we all followed the glance of her half-open eyes: she was smiling at Barras.

"Has everybody got champagne?" asked the voice of Madame Tallien.

The small figure in white stretched out her hand, someone gave her two glasses and she held out one towards Napoleon: "General, your glass!"

She was smiling at him now, a very intimate, somewhat pitying smile.

"Citizens and citizenesses," came Theresa's voice loud and shrill, "I have the honour to make an announcement to our friends which concerns our beloved Josephine."

Theresa obviously enjoyed the scene. She was standing quite close to the sofa, holding her glass high, while Napoleon had got up, looking at her in great embarrassment. Josephine, however, had once more thrown back her childlike curly head with its painted eyelids.

"Our beloved Josephine," Theresa continued, "has decided to enter again the holy state of matrimony. . . ." A suppressed titter sprang up somewhere and Josephine absent-mindedly fingered the red velvet ribbon round her neck. ". . . to enter again the holy state of matrimony and . . ." Here Theresa made an eloquent pause and looked across to Barras who nodded to her. ". . . and engaged herself to Citizen General Napoleon Bonaparte."

"No!"

I heard the scream exactly as everybody else did. Shrilly it seemed to cut the room in two and to hover for a moment in the air, followed by an icy silence. Not till a second later did I realise that it was I who had screamed.

The next moment I found myself in front of the sofa, saw Theresa Tallien shrink away terrified, smelled her sweetish scent and felt on me the stare of the other one, the woman in white on the sofa. But consciously I saw only Napoleon. His eyes were like glass, transparent and expressionless. A vein was quivering on his right temple.

We faced each other for what seemed to be an eternity. But perhaps it was no more than the fraction of a second. Only then I turned my eyes to the woman.

I saw her silvery eyelids. I saw the tiny wrinkles round the corners of her eyes. I saw her lips painted deep red. Oh, how I hated her! With one sudden lunge I threw my glass of champagne at her feet.

The champagne splashed on to her frock. She screeched hysterically. . . .

I found myself running for all I was worth, running and running, along a rain-drenched street. I had no idea how I had got out of the green room, the white room and the hall, past the guests who recoiled from me in horror, past the servants who tried to seize me by the arm. I only knew that suddenly a wet darkness enveloped me, that I ran along a row of houses, that I turned into another street, that my heart was thumping like mad and that like an animal, instinctively, I was running in the direction I wanted. And then I reached a quay, stumbling and slipping on the wet stones all the time till a bridge loomed up before me. The Seine, I thought, the Seine, oh good, good! And then I stopped running, walked slowly across the bridge, leant over and saw thousands and thousands of lights dancing on the water, up and down with the waves. How merry it looked! I bent forward over the parapet, the lights danced up towards me, the rain pattered. Never before in my life had I been so alone.

I thought of Mama and Julie and how they would forgive me once they knew the whole story. In any case Napoleon was probably going to report his engagement this very night to Joseph or his mother.

That, I suddenly realised, was the first clear thought in my brain. It hurt so much that I couldn't stand it. So I put my hands on the edge of the parapet and tried to pull myself up and——

Yes, and at that moment someone gripped me hard by the shoulder and pulled me back. I tried to shake off the strange hand and shouted, "Leave me alone, leave me alone!" But I was seized by both arms and dragged away from the parapet. I struggled as hard as I could to tear myself free, but it was no use. It was so dark that I couldn't even see the face of the man who dragged me off. For sheer despair I sobbed and panted and I loathed the sound of the man's voice which I heard over the noise of the rain, shouting:

"Quiet now, quiet. Don't be a fool! Come, here is my cab."

There was a chaise standing on the quayside.

I continued to struggle desperately, but the stranger was far stronger than I and pushed me into the cab. He sat down by my side and called to the coachman:

"Drive off, never mind where. Just drive."

I sat as far away as possible from the stranger. But then I noticed that my teeth were chattering with the wet and the excitement and rivulets were streaming from my hair across my face.

A hand, a big warm hand came towards me and searched for my fingers.

I sobbed. "Let me get out! Let me, please. . . ." At the same time I clung to this strange hand because I felt so wretched.

"But you asked me yourself to be your escort," the voice came out of the dark of the carriage. "Don't you remember, Mademoiselle Désirée?"

I pushed his hand away. "I—now—I, I want—to be alone."

"Oh no, you asked me to accompany you to Madame Tallien's. And now we'll stay together till I see you home."

His voice was very quiet and really very agreeable.

"Are you this General—this General Bernadotte?" I asked. And then everything came back to me with perfect clarity and I shouted:

"Do leave me alone. I hate Generals. Generals have no heart."

"There are Generals and—Generals!" he said, and laughed.

I heard something rustling in the dark and a coat was laid across my shoulders.

"Your coat will be soaked," I said. "I am wet from the rain, wet through."

"Never mind," he said. "I was expecting that. Wrap yourself up well."

A memory seared through me like fire, a memory of another General's coat, of another rainy night. That night Napoleon asked for my hand. . . .

The carriage rolled on and on. Once the driver stopped and asked a question, and the strange General answered:

"Go on, never mind where."

And so we rolled on, and I kept sobbing into the strange coat. Once I said:

"What a coincidence that you happened to pass over the bridge just then."

"Not a coincidence at all. I felt responsible for you because I brought you among those people. And when you ran away so suddenly I followed you. Only, you ran so fast I preferred to hire a cab and keep on your track. But I wanted to leave you alone as long as possible."

"And why were you so awful then and didn't leave me alone?"

"Because it was no longer possible," he said calmly, and put his arm round my shoulders. I was dead tired and weary and didn't care any longer what happened. Driving on, just driving on, I thought, and never to have to get out again, never to see again, to hear again, to speak again, I thought. . . . And so I put my head on his shoulder and he pulled me closer to him.

I tried to remember what he looked like, but I couldn't disentangle his face from all the many faces I had seen that night.

"Do forgive me," I murmured, "that I let you down so badly at Madame Tallien's."

"That doesn't matter in the least," he said, "I am only sorry—for your sake."

"Do you know," I confessed, "I deliberately splashed the champagne over her white frock. It leaves stains." Suddenly I started crying again. "She is so much more beautiful than I . . . and such a great lady. . . ."

He held me very tight and with his free hand pressed my face against his shoulder. "Yes, cry, my child, cry. It'll do you good."

I wept as I had never wept before. I just couldn't stop. I wept and sobbed and moaned, and all the time I pressed my face into the rough cloth of his uniform.

"I shall ruin your shoulder-padding with my crying," I said once, sobbing.

"Yes, you'll do that all right," he answered. "But don't let that trouble you. Cry if you feel like it."

We must have been driving through the streets of Paris for hours and hours, and all the time I cried so much that in the end I could cry no longer.

"I'll take you home now. Where do you live?" he asked.

The Seine came back to my mind and I said: "Drop me here. I'll walk home."

"Oh! Walk home? In that case we'd better drive on," he said dryly.

I took my head from his shoulder. It felt no longer comfortable because I had cried too much on it and it was too wet now. A question occurred to me.

"Do you know General Bonaparte?" I asked.

"No. I've only seen him once before in the War Minister's ante-room. I didn't like him."

"Why not?"

"Don't know why. These things, likes and dislikes, can't be explained. You, for example, I like."

We fell silent again after that. The cab rolled on through the rain which in the light of a street lantern made the pavement shine with many colours. My eyes hurt and I closed them and let my head rest against the back of the seat. Then I heard myself say:

"I believed in him more than I have ever believed in anybody in the world. More than in Mama. More than in, or rather different from the way in which I believed in Papa. I just can't understand. . . ."

"There are many things you don't understand, my girl!"

"We were to be married in a few weeks' time. And he never so much as mentioned that. . . ."

"He would never have married you, my little girl, never! You see, he has been engaged for years to a wealthy silk merchant's daughter in Marseilles."

I gave a start, and at once his hand closed warmly and protectively round my fingers again.

"You didn't know that either, did you?" he continued. "The Tallien told me this afternoon. She said that our little General abandoned a big dowry in order to marry Barras' ex-mistress. Bonaparte's brother is married to the sister of this fiancée from Marseilles. But, as things are now, a former countess with good connections in Paris is more important to him than a dowry in Marseilles. You see, little one, you'd have been the last girl in the world for him to have married."

Evenly and almost comfortingly his voice came through the dark. At first I didn't understand what he was driving at and I asked him:

"What are you talking about?"

Frantically I tried to get my thoughts into some sort of order, at the same time clinging for dear life to his hand, which, at this moment, was the only warm thing in my life.

"My dear little girl, I am sorry that I have to hurt you so much. But it is better that you should know everything. I know exactly how it feels, but—it can't get worse now. That's why I told you what the Tallien told me. First there was a rich middle-class girl and now there is a countess with excellent connections deriving from her amorous past associations with one of the heads of our State and two gentlemen of the Supreme Command of the Army. But you, my dear, you have neither connections nor a big dowry."

"How do you know?"

"One can see that. You are only a little girl and a very good girl. You don't know how the great ladies behave and what goes on in their salons. And you haven't got money either, otherwise you'd have slipped a note to Madame Tallien's lackey and he'd have let you through. Yes, you are a decent little thing and . . ."

He stopped. And then, quite unexpectedly, he burst out, "And I want to marry you."

"Let me get out, at once. I won't let you make fun of me," I said, and knocked on the window. "Driver, stop! Stop!" I shouted, and the cab stopped.

But the General shouted even louder, "Drive on at once!" and the carriage immediately got going again.

"Perhaps I didn't express myself properly," the General's voice came somewhat hesitantly out of the dark. "Please forgive me. I never have a chance of getting to know young girls like you. And—Mademoiselle Désirée, I really would like to marry you."

"In Madame Tallien's salon there are plenty of ladies who have a preference for Generals," I said. "I haven't."

"You don't believe, do you, that I would marry cocottes—sorry, Mademoiselle, ladies like that?"

I was too tired to answer, too tired to think. I still didn't understand what this man Bernadotte, this giant of a man, really wanted from me. In any case, what was the good? My life, I felt, was finished. The cold of the night made me shudder in spite of his big coat, and my silk shoes, soaked and heavy, hung like lead on my feet.

"Without the Revolution I shouldn't be an officer now, Mademoiselle, let alone a General. You are very young, but perhaps you remember that before the Revolution no one not belonging to the aristocracy could get beyond the rank of captain. My father was a lawyer's clerk and the son of a very humble artisan, Mademoiselle, and I had to work my way up. I joined the Army when I was fifteen, was nothing but a sergeant for many years, and then step by step—well, anyway, I am a Divisional General now. But perhaps you think I am too old for you?" . . .

What was he saying? 'You'll believe in me whatever happens, won't you?' Napoleon asked me once. A great lady with connections and painted eyelids! Of course, I thought, I understand you, Napoleon, I do. But it'll break me . . .

"I asked you an important question, Mademoiselle."

"I am sorry, I didn't hear it. What did you ask, General Bernadotte?"

"I asked whether, perhaps, I am too old for you?"

"But I don't know how old you are. And what does it matter, anyway?" I said.

'It matters a great deal indeed. I may really be too old for you. I am thirty-one."

"I'm going to be sixteen shortly. But I am so tired. I should like to go home now."

"Of course. Forgive me, I am so inconsiderate. Where do you live?"

I gave him the address and he told the cabman.

"Won't you think over what I asked you?" said the General. Then his voice came more hesitantly through the dark, "I shall have to be back in the Rhineland in ten days' time. Perhaps you could give me an answer by then?" And quickly he added, "My name is Jean-Baptiste. Jean-Baptiste Bernadotte. For years I have saved up part of my salary. I could buy a little house for you and the child."

"Child? What child?" I asked involuntarily. The things he said were quite beyond my comprehension.

"Our child, of course," he said eagerly, and felt for my hand again, but I withdrew it quickly. "I want a wife and a child," he continued, "have been wanting them for years, Mademoiselle."

At that my patience gave out.

"Do stop," I said, "you don't know me at all."

"Oh yes, I do," he said and it sounded very sincere. "I believe I know you better than your family knows you. I have so little time for myself, I am always at the front, you see, and therefore I can't visit your family for weeks at a time and—well, I can't take you out for walks and all that sort of thing, the things you are supposed to do before you propose. I have to decide quickly and—I have decided!"

Oh God, he means it, he means it! He wanted to use his leave to get himself married, to buy a house and . . .

"General Bernadotte," I said, "in any woman's life there is room for only one great love."

"How do you know?"

"Well, I . . ." Yes, how did I know? "You can read it in all the novels, and it is certainly true," I said.

At that moment the brakes screeched. We had arrived at the house of the Clapains in the Rue du Bac. He opened the door and helped me out.

There was a lantern over the house door. As at the gate of Madame Tallien's house, I raised myself on my toes to see his face. He had beautiful white teeth and a strikingly big nose.

I gave him the key borrowed from Madame Clapain and he unlocked the door.

"You live in a noble house," he remarked.

89

"Oh, only the servants' quarters," I murmured. "And now, good-night and many thanks, many thanks for—everything."

But he did not move.

"Do go back to your cab," I said. "You'll be wet through. And you can make your mind easy, I'll stay at home all right."

"Good girl," he said. "And when may I come for your answer?"

I shook my head. "In any woman's life—" I began saying, but he raised his hand. Then I broke off and said instead, "Really, General, it won't do! Really it won't! Not because I'm too young for you but, you can see for yourself, because I'm far too small!" And with that I rushed into the house and banged the door to behind me.

When I reached the kitchen of the Clapain family I was no longer tired, only numb. I couldn't sleep now, I'd never be able to sleep again, never . . .

And therefore, at this moment, I'm sitting at the kitchen table, writing, writing, writing. The day after to-morrow this Bernadotte fellow will come here and ask for me. I certainly shan't be here any more. Where I shall be forty-eight hours hence I don't know. . . .

MARSEILLES, three weeks later.

I HAVE been very ill: a cold, sore throat, a high temperature and what the poets call a broken heart. Illness enough.

I sold Marie's gold medallion in Paris and got enough money for it to get home. And at home Marie at once put me to bed and sent for the doctor because of my temperature. The doctor of course couldn't understand why I had got a cold because there hadn't been any rain in Marseilles for days. Marie also sent for Mama, who returned without delay to nurse me. Up till now no one has found out that I was in Paris.

At the moment I am lying on a sofa on the terrace. They wrapped me up in countless blankets and said that I was looking pale and dreadfully thin. Joseph and Julie, who came back yesterday, are expected to visit us to-night. I hope they'll allow me to stay up.

Now Marie comes running on to the terrace waving a paper in her hand. How excited she seems!

General Napoleon Bonaparte has been appointed Military

Governor of Paris. Riots in the capital have been suppressed by the National Guard.

At first I couldn't read at all, the paper trembled badly in my hand. But then it steadied and I could read in comfort. Napoleon, the paper said, has been made Military Governor of Paris. An infuriated mob wanted to storm the Tuileries and to tear the Deputies to pieces. Driven into a corner, Director Barras handed over command of the National Guard to General Napoleon Bonaparte, the man who had been sacked by the Army. On his appointment he demanded *carte blanche* from the Assembly and got it. After that he ordered a young cavalry officer by the name of Murat to collect some guns, and these he placed along the northern, western and southern sides of the Tuileries so that they covered the approaches along the Rue Saint-Roche and over the Pont Royal. The mob was not deterred by the sight of the artillery and kept on advancing till a voice with an edge as sharp as a knife ordered, 'Fire!' A single cannon-shot sufficed to drive the mob back. Now everything was quiet again, and the Directors Barras, Lareveillière, Letourneur, Rewbell and Carnot expressed their gratitude to the man who had saved the Republic from new disorders and appointed him Military Governor of Paris.

I tried to think it all over. A conversation in the window niche of Madame Tallien's house came back to my mind: 'If I were in Barras' place I'd shoot the mob to pieces, my dear Fouché.' 'For that you'd first have to find the man ready to do the shooting.'

One cannon-shot was enough, then, and it was Napoleon who did the shooting. He gave the order for the guns to fire, at whom? At the rioting mob, the paper said. Who were the rioting mob? Probably the wretches who were living in cellars and couldn't pay the inflated price of bread. As to cellars, Napoleon's mother, too, was living in one. 'Your son is a genius, Madame Buonaparte.' 'Yes, unfortunately,' she answered.

Someone interrupted me, and so I am now writing in my room.

As I was still pondering over the news I heard Joseph and Julie come into the living-room. They arrived far earlier than expected, and through the terrace door, which wasn't quite shut, I overheard Joseph saying:

"Napoleon sent a courier with a long letter and plenty of money for Mama, and I asked Mama through a messenger to meet us here. You don't mind, Madame Clary, do you?"

Oh no, Mama didn't mind at all, on the contrary, she said, she'd be very glad to see her. And meanwhile wouldn't they like to say how-do-you-do to me out there on the terrace? I was, Mama added, still very poorly.

But Joseph seemed to hesitate and Julie started to cry and to tell Mama that Napoleon had written to Joseph of his engagement to the widow of General de Beauharnais. And there was also, I heard Julie say, a message for me that he always wanted to remain friends with me.

"Oh God, oh God!" Mama exclaimed, "the poor child!"

At that moment I heard Madame Letitia, Eliza and Polette enter, and everybody talked at once, till Joseph's voice started to read out something. That must have been the letter of the new Military Governor of Paris.

Later he and Julie came out on to the terrace and sat down with me. Julie stroked my hand whilst Joseph in obvious embarrassment said something about how autumnal the garden looked already.

"May I congratulate you on your brother's success, Joseph?" I said, pointing to the letter which he was nervously crumpling between his fingers.

"Thank you, thank you," he said. "I'm afraid I have some news for you, Eugenie, which Julie and I regret. . . ."

"Never mind, Joseph, I know," and when he looked puzzled I added, "You see, the door to the living-room was open and I heard everything."

I had hardly finished my sentence when Madame Letitia happened on the terrace, looking very bellicose.

"A widow with two children," she exclaimed, "a widow with two children and six years older than my boy! And that is the kind of daughter-in-law Napoleone dares to bring me!"

I remembered Josephine in that room at Madame Tallien's house: silver-painted eyelids, babyish curls, sophisticated smile. And here was Madame Letitia with red calloused hands and the scrawny neck of a woman who had spent her life washing her children's clothes and preventing them from getting into mischief. Her bony fingers were closed round a wad of bank-notes. Aha, I thought, the Military Governor of Paris has lost no time in sending his mother a part of his Governor's salary.

A little later I was put on the divan in the living-room and heard them discuss the great events. Etienne brought out his best liqueur and emphasised how proud he was to be related to General Bonaparte. But Mama and Suzanne bent their heads over their needlework and said nothing.

"I am quite well again, really," I said. "Couldn't you let me have one of my napkins which I had started to embroider for my trousseau? I want to get on with my monograms."

The serviettes were brought and I started another series of B's which made them all feel awkward when they noticed it. Suddenly I had the feeling that one phase of my life had come to an end, and so I said into the silence that had fallen on us:

"I don't want to be called Eugenie any longer. My name is Bernadine Eugenie Désirée and I like Désirée best of all. Couldn't you call me Désirée?"

They looked at each other with concern. I felt sure they thought I had gone out of my mind.

ROME, three days after Christmas in the Year V. (Here, in Italy, they still go by the pre-Republican calendar and say: Dec. 27th, 1797.)

THEY'VE left me alone with the dying man. His name is Jean Pierre Duphot, a General on Napoleon's staff. He arrived in Rome to-day in order to propose to me, and then, two hours ago, a bullet hit him in the stomach. There was nothing he could do, the surgeon said, and so we put him on the sofa in Joseph's study.

Duphot has lost consciousness. His breath sounds like so many little sobs, and a thin trickle of blood comes from a corner of his mouth, so that I have to fold a serviette round his chin. His eyes are half open, but they see nothing. From the adjoining room I can hear the murmuring voices of Joseph, Julie, the doctor and two Embassy secretaries.

Joseph and Julie left the room because they don't like seeing a man die, and the doctor went with them. This Italian doctor thinks it far more important to be introduced to His Excellency the Ambassador of the French Republic in Rome and brother of the conqueror of Italy than to attend some unimportant staff officer on his deathbed.

I don't know why, but I have the feeling that Duphot will regain consciousness once more although I realise like the others how far gone he is already. Therefore I have fetched my diary and have begun writing in it once again after all these years. I shan't be quite so alone now. My pen scratches away on the paper, and that at any rate means that the sobbing death-rattle from the sofa is no longer the only sound in this room.

Since I saw Napoleon—only his mother now calls him

Napoleone, the rest of the world speaks of him as Napoleon Bonaparte and speaks of hardly anything else—well, since I saw him that time in Paris I have never set eyes on him again. To this day no one in my family knows of that encounter. He married Josephine in the spring of the next year with Tallien and Director Barras as his witnesses at the ceremony, and as soon as he was married Napoleon paid all the widow Beauharnais' dressmakers' bills. Two days later he went off to Italy—as Commander-in-Chief! And within the next fortnight he had won six battles!

The sound of the dying man's breathing has changed: it has become quieter. And his eyes, instead of being only half open, are wide open now. I called his name. But he did not hear me.

Yes, within a fortnight Napoleon had won six battles and the Austrians evacuated Northern Italy.

I can't help remembering our evening talks by the hedge. So Napoleon has really founded States. The first he founded he called Lombardy, the last the Cisalpine Republic. He made Milan the capital of Lombardy and appointed fifty Italians to administer the State in France's name. Overnight there appeared on all public buildings the words: 'Liberty, Equality, Fraternity'. Then the people of Milan had to hand over a big sum of money, three hundred horses and their most beautiful works of art, and all that Napoleon sent to Paris, but of course not without deducting the pay of his troops which the Directors in the past had always left unpaid. Messrs. Barras and Co. in Paris didn't know whether they were on their heads or their heels. Money in the exchequer, Italy's most beautiful horses drawing their carriages, and valuable paintings in their reception rooms! There was one painting in particular to which Napoleon drew the attention of Paris. It's called 'La Gioconda' and its painter was a certain Leonardo da Vinci: there is a woman in it, Mona Lisa they say is her name, and this woman smiles with her lips closed. Her smile reminds me of Josephine's. Perhaps Mona Lisa had bad teeth just like the widow Beauharnais.

At the end of it all something happened which no one had thought possible. As one knows, the French Republic had separated itself from the Church of Rome, and as a result the Roman Catholic clergy beyond our frontiers have always cursed the new France from their pulpits. But then suddenly the Pope approached Napoleon in order to conclude a peace treaty with France. When that came out people crowded into Etienne's shop to listen to his story of how Napoleon years ago had confided to him his great plans. For he, Etienne, was not only

General Bonaparte's brother-in-law but also his very best friend. . . .

       .   .   .

I have been sitting with Duphot again for a while and held up his head a bit. But it's no use. It doesn't make his breathing any easier and he keeps on fighting for breath. I have wiped a drop of bloodstained foam from his mouth and I notice that his face is waxen yellow. The doctor whom I called in told me in broken French that it was an 'interior hæmorrhage' and then went back to Joseph and Julie. They, for all I know, may be talking about to-morrow's reception. . . .

Apparently even before the treaty with the Vatican had been concluded the Government in Paris had become uneasy. Why? Because Napoleon drafted and signed all agreements with the Italians whom he had 'liberated' himself without ever bothering to ask the Government whether the conditions he imposed were acceptable to it. That exceeded, so the Directors seem to have grumbled, the powers of a Commander-in-Chief, it had no longer anything to do with the conduct of the war but fell under the heading of 'Foreign Policy' and was of such import- ance that they would have to send professional diplomats out to his headquarters to advise him. . . . At that Napoleon wrote out a list of names of men whom, he suggested, they should give the title and powers of an Ambassador of the Republic and despatch to Italy. The list was headed by the name of his brother Joseph. And that was how Joseph and Julie came to be here.
At first they had gone to Parma, then as Ambassador and Madame Bonaparte to Genoa, till at last they arrived in Rome. And, by the way, they had come here not directly from Marseilles but from Paris. For hardly had Napoleon become Military Governor of Paris than he wrote to Joseph that the capital offered him far better chances than a mere provincial town.
I can see now that whatever happens Napoleon will always find some profitable job or other for Joseph. At first it was the modest position of a secretary of the *Maison Commune* in Mar- seilles. Then, in Paris, he introduced him not only to Barras and his lot of politicians but also to army contractors and those newly rich who had made their money in property deals, and so Joseph too began to join this particular racket. He bought confiscated aristocratic mansions auctioned off cheaply by the Government, and re-sold them at several times their purchase price. Etienne explained to me that this type of business is

flourishing now because of the housing shortage. Within a short time Joseph had made enough money to buy a little house for himself and Julie in the Rue du Rocher.

When news of the victories in Italy came—the victories of Millesimo, Castiglione, Arcola and Rivoli—Joseph's standing in Paris at once improved tremendously. After all, wasn't he the elder brother of that General Bonaparte whom the foreign papers call 'the strong man of France' and our own the 'liberator of the Italian people', of that man whose lean face now adorns coffee cups, flower vases and snuff-boxes in all the shop windows? On one side of these cups, vases and boxes you can see him in glossy paint, partnered on the other side by the French flag. No wonder that the Government at once acceded to the request of its most successful general and appointed Joseph Ambassador!

Joseph and Julie moved into their first Italian marble palace. Julie was very wretched there and wrote in despair to ask if I couldn't come and join them, and Mama agreed. And since then I have been moving round the country with them from one palace to another, living in dreadfully high-ceilinged rooms with floors of black-and-white tiles and sitting about in pillared courts full of innumerable fountains whose curious bronze figures squirt their water from all sorts of apertures.

The *palazzo* we inhabit at present is called the Palazzo Corsini. All the time we are surrounded by clanking spurs and rattling sabres because Joseph's staff consists of nothing but officers. And to-morrow is the day of the biggest reception which Joseph has given so far, a reception for the 350 most important citizens of Rome. For the last week Julie has not been able to sleep; her face is as white as a sheet and there are black rings under her eyes. Julie, you see, belongs to the type of women who are all of a dither if they have only four guests for dinner. But every day we are at least fifteen at table now, and on top of that Joseph arranges receptions for hundreds of people every few seconds. Although a whole battalion of flunkeys, cooks and chambermaids buzzes through the house Julie feels solely responsible for the whole affair and hangs round my neck at short intervals sobbing and moaning that most certainly everything would be in a sorry mess. In that respect she's Mama's true daughter.

Duphot has moved again. For one second I had hoped that he would regain consciousness, for in that one second he looked at me with clear eyes. But almost immediately after they clouded over once more, and now he is fighting for breath again, spitting blood and sinking deeper and deeper into the pillows. What wouldn't I give, Jean Pierre Duphot, if I could help you! But I can't.

In spite of battles and victories and peace treaties and the making of new States, Napoleon found time to keep an eye on his family. From the very beginning of his Italian campaign his couriers brought money and letters to Madame Letitia in Marseilles. He made her move into a better house and send Jerome, that street urchin, to a decent school. For Caroline he found a very exclusive girls' boarding-school in Paris, the very school where his stepdaughter Hortense de Beauharnais receives her education. Well, well, how the Bonapartes have gone up in the world! And how furious Napoleon was because his mother had allowed his sister Eliza to marry a certain Felix Bacciochi! Why this hurry, he wrote, and why, of all men, this lazy hopeless wastrel of a music student, this Bacciochi?

Eliza had been going about with Bacciochi for a long time, always hoping that he would marry her. At last, after the news of the first victories in Italy, Bacciochi proposed and was promptly accepted. After the wedding Napoleon began to fear that Polette too might bring someone into the family whom he thought unsuitable, and therefore he insisted that Madame Letitia and Polette should pay him a visit at his headquarters in Montebello. And immediately after their arrival there he married Polette off to a General Leclerc whom none of us had ever heard of.

What I did not understand and what I found rather disagreeable was the fact that Napoleon, in the middle of all the world history he was making, had not forgotten me either. He seemed to have taken it into his head that he had to make amends to me for something or other. And so in complicity with Julie and Joseph he sent men along as candidates for my hand in marriage. The first to arrive was Junot, his former adjutant in his Marseilles days. One day Junot, tall, fair and charming, arrived in Genoa, steered me into the garden and clicked his heels. "I have the honour," he said, "to ask you to marry me." "No, thank you," I answered. "But it was Napoleon's order," he good-naturedly insisted, and I remembered what Napoleon had thought of Junot: "a loyal man, but stupid." I shook my head and he rode back to headquarters.

The next candidate was Marmont, whom I had also known in Marseilles. Marmont did not ask me directly but hinted at it with delicacy. Again I remembered what Napoleon had said about his friends. This one, he judged, wanted to be in on his, Napoleon's, career. There Joseph Bonaparte's sister-in-law would certainly serve this purpose well, I thought. It meant being a member of Napoleon's family, even doing Napoleon a service and incidentally marrying a handsome dowry. I answered Marmont's delicate hints with a 'no' just as delicately embroidered. But after he had gone I complained about it to Joseph. Couldn't he write to Napoleon and tell him to spare me the marriage proposals of his staff officers?

"Don't you understand," said Joseph, "that Napoleon considers it a distinction for one of his Generals to be married to his sister-in-law's sister?"

"I am not a medal to be awarded to a deserving officer," I objected, "and if this sort of thing doesn't stop I'm going back to Mama."

This morning Julie and I were sitting, in spite of the cool weather, in the pillared court of our *palazzo*. For the thousandth time Julie and I were studying the names of the Italian families of the high aristocracy who were to come to the Embassy to-morrow night. Joseph joined us there. He was holding a letter in his hand and talked casually about this and that, as is usual with him whenever something that he finds unpleasant has happened. Suddenly he said:

"Napoleon has seen to it that we get a new military attaché. General Jean Pierre Duphot, a very charming young man."

I looked up. "Duphot? Didn't a General Duphot report to you once in Genoa?"

Joseph was pleased. "Of course," he exclaimed, "and he made quite an impression on you if I remember right, didn't he? Because, you see, Napoleon writes that he hopes that Eugenie—please forgive me, he still speaks of Eugenie instead of Désirée—that you would take pity on this very lonely young man. And therefore . . ."

I got up. "Another marriage candidate? No, thank you! I had thought that that was really over and done with." Going to the door I turned round to them: "Write to Napoleon at once that he is not to send this Duphot or whatever his name is on any account."

"But he's here already! He arrived a quarter of an hour ago and brought Napoleon's letter."

I was furious and banged the door to behind me. I like banging doors. In these marble palaces it sounds like an explosion.

I didn't go down for lunch, to escape Duphot. But I put in an appearance for the evening meal. It's too boring to eat by yourself in your room. Of course, they had given the young man the seat next to me. Like a slave Joseph always does exactly as Napoleon wishes.

The young man didn't get more than a few cursory glances from me. I had an impression of a man of medium height with a big mouth horribly full of white teeth. These white teeth irritated me because he kept laughing at me all the time.

Our conversation was frequently interrupted. We are used to people standing about in crowds outside the Embassy and shouting "*Evviva la Francia! Evviva la Libertà!*" all the time, with an occasional "*A basso la Francia!*" mixed in. Most Italians are enthusiastic about the ideas that our Revolution and our Army have brought to them. But the heavy costs of our occupation and the fact that all their officials are appointed by Napoleon seems to embitter many. At all events, to-night the noise outside sounded different from other nights, louder and more menacing.

Joseph told us why. Last night some Roman citizens had been arrested as hostages because a French lieutenant had been knifed and killed in a tavern brawl. And now a deputation of the Town Council of Rome was waiting outside to speak to Joseph. An enormous crowd had gathered to watch the proceedings.

"Why don't you see them?" asked Julie. "We could have waited with the meal."

Joseph explained—and the gentlemen of his staff nodded their agreement—that that was quite out of the question. He wasn't going to see anybody, because the whole affair was no business of his but that of the Military Governor of Rome and had been the Governor's from the very beginning.

Meanwhile the noise outside kept growing, and finally there were blows on the door.

At that Joseph shouted:

"My patience is at an end. I'll have the mob dispersed. Go to Military Headquarters," he told one of his secretaries, "and demand that the square outside the Embassy be cleared. I can't stand that din any longer."

The secretary left, and General Duphot called after him: "Better be careful and go out by the back door!"

We continued our meal in silence. Before we had reached the coffee stage we heard the sound of horses. So they had sent a battalion of hussars in order to clear the square. Joseph got up at once and we went with him outside on to the balcony on the first floor.

The place below looked like a witch's cauldron. There were thousands and thousands of heads, and thousands and thousands of voices clamouring stridently. We couldn't see the Council Deputation anywhere. The excited mob must have pressed it against the portico of the house. The two sentries down there were standing motionless outside their boxes, and I had the impression that at any moment the crowd would trample them into the mud. Joseph made us all go back quickly into the room, where we pressed our faces against the panes of the high windows. He was as pale as death and kept chewing his lower lip, and his hand trembled as it played nervously with his hair.

The hussars had surrounded the square. Like statues they sat on their horses, rifles at the ready, waiting for the order. But their commander was apparently still undecided about it.

"I'll go down and try to reason with the crowd," Duphot said.

"It's useless, General, don't do it," said Joseph imploringly. "Don't expose yourself to the danger. Our hussars will . . ."

Duphot smiled and showed his white teeth. "I am a soldier, Your Excellency, and used to danger. Besides, I'd like to prevent unnecessary bloodshed."

And so, his spurs clanking, he went to the door. Before he reached it he turned round and, if you please, tried to catch my eye! I turned quickly away towards the window. So that's what it was: for my sake he indulged in this piece of bravado! In order to impress me he went down to face the raging mob unarmed and alone.

'How senseless,' I thought, 'how senseless! Junot, Marmont, Duphot, what have I got to do with them?'

At that moment the door was being opened downstairs. We opened the window a fraction in order to hear better. The clamour grew weaker, but it sounded as threatening as before. Someone yelled: "*A basso . . . !*" and once more: "*A basso . . . !*" We couldn't see Duphot yet. Then the crowd withdrew some way to make room for him, and he came into view raising his hands to ask for silence. And it was then that a shot rang out, followed immediately by the first salvo from the hussars.

I rushed out of the room and down the stairs and tore the door open. The two sentries had picked up General Duphot, holding him up under the arms. His legs dangled lifelessly to the ground, his face with the twisted mouth hung to one side, and his eternal smile was frozen to a grin. He had lost consciousness. The two soldiers dragged him into the hall and his spurs clanked as his legs trailed over the marble tiles.

"Take him upstairs!" I heard myself say. "We'll have to put him somewhere upstairs." As I was saying this, white distraught faces appeared around me: Joseph, Julie, the fat Councillor to the Embassy, and Minette, Julie's chambermaid. They made room for the two soldiers to carry Duphot up the stairs. Outside all had become quiet. Two salvoes from the hussars had been enough.

I opened the door to Joseph's study, which was nearest to the staircase. There the two sentries laid Duphot on a sofa and I pushed some cushions under his head. Joseph, who was standing by my side, said that he had sent for a doctor and that perhaps it mightn't be as bad as it looked.

I saw a damp stain on his dark-blue uniform in the region of his stomach.

"Open his tunic, Joseph," I said, and Joseph obeyed with clumsy and nervous fingers. There was a light red circle of blood on his white shirt.

"A stomach wound," said Joseph.

The General's face had turned yellow and there was a jerky kind of sob coming from his wide-open mouth. At first I thought he was crying, till I realised that he was fighting for breath.

When the Italian doctor, a thin and shortish man, arrived he was even more wrought up than Joseph. It seemed to have been a great stroke of luck for him to be called to the French Embassy. He said at once that he was a great admirer of the French Republic and of General Napoleon Bonaparte and, as he was opening Duphot's shirt, he mumbled something about these regrettable incidents to-day and about irresponsible elements at the bottom of them.

I interrupted him and asked whether he needed anything. He looked up in confusion and it took him a moment or so before he remembered.

"A drop of lukewarm water, please. And perhaps a clean cloth."

He began to wash out the wound. Joseph went up to the window and Julie was leaning against a wall on the verge of being sick. I took her out of the room and told Joseph to look after her, which he did, greatly relieved that he need not stay.

"A blanket," said the doctor, "could you get me a blanket? His limbs are quite cold already. He is bleeding to death, you know. Inside him, Mademoiselle, inside him."

We spread a blanket over Duphot.

"There is nothing we can do now, Mademoiselle. How terrible! A man of such exalted position!" he said, and his eyes went over the gold braid on Duphot's uniform. And so, having done his duty, he quickly made for the door through which Joseph had disappeared. I went with him.

In the adjoining room Joseph, Julie, the Councillor and some secretaries sat together round a big table talking in whispers and sipping port. Joseph rose and offered the doctor a glass, and I could see how the Charm of the Bonapartes enveloped the little Italian in a haze of bliss. He stammered:

"Oh, Your Excellency, brother of our great Liberator . . ."

I went back to Duphot. At first I had something to occupy me: with the help of napkins I tried to wipe away the thin trickle of blood down his chin. But I gave it up soon because the blood never stopped trickling. In the end I spread the napkins round his chin over his tunic. All the time I tried in vain to catch his eye, and when I had done what there was to be done I fetched my diary and started to write.

I must have been sitting here for many hours. The candles are almost burned down. But from the next room there still comes the gentle murmur of voices. No one wants to go to bed before . . .

A moment ago he came to at last.

I heard a movement from the sofa, kneeled down by his side and put my arm under his head. His eyes rested on my face, taking it in, for a long time. Obviously he didn't know where he was.

"You are in Rome, General Duphot," I told him, "in Rome, in Ambassador Bonaparte's house."

His lips moved and spilled out blood-flecked foam. I wiped it away with my free hand.

"Marie," he managed at last to say, "I want to go to Marie."

"Quick," I said, "quick, tell me, where is Marie?"

His eyes were clear and alive now and they asked a question. I repeated therefore:

"You are in Rome. There have been riots in the streets. A bullet hit you in the stomach."

He nodded almost imperceptibly. Yes, he had understood.

I tried to think quickly. I couldn't help him, but perhaps I could help her, Marie?

"Marie, what's Marie's surname? And where does she live?" I asked in as urgent a tone as I could muster.

Fear came into his eyes. "Don't," he brought out, "don't—tell—Bonaparte."

"But if you are going to be ill for a long time we must inform Marie. There's no need to tell Napoleon Bonaparte." I smiled at him with the smile of a friendly accomplice.

"Must—marry—Eugenie, Bonaparte said, and——" The

rest of the sentence was inaudible. Then the words became clearer once more: "Be sensible, little Marie—always look after you—after you—and little George—darling, darling Marie——"

His head fell to one side, he pursed his lips and tried to kiss my arm. He thought I was Marie. He had explained to her exactly why he wanted to leave her and her little son: to marry into Bonaparte's family, which would mean promotion and undreamed-of possibilities. . . .

His head now felt as heavy as lead on my arm. I lifted it a bit. "Give me Marie's address, I'll write to her," I said, and tried to catch his eye once more. For a second his gaze became clear again: "Marie Meunier—36—Rue de Lyon—Paris," he said.

His features had suddenly sharpened, the eyes lay deep in their sockets and beads of perspiration stood on his forehead.

"We shall always look after Marie and little George," I said. But it didn't reach him any more. "I promise," I repeated.

Suddenly his eyes grew wide and his lips twisted convulsively.

I jumped up and ran to the door. At the same time a long moan came after me and then died away.

"Come, doctor, come at once!" I heard myself call.

"It's all over," the Italian said after he had bent cursorily over the sofa.

I went to the window and drew back the curtains. The grey and leaden light of dawn crept into the room. Then I put out the candles.

In the other room they were still sitting round the table. The servants had lit fresh candles, and the room with its air of festive illumination seemed like an abode in another world.

"Joseph, you must cancel the reception," I said.

Joseph started up. He seemed to have fallen asleep with his head on his chest: "What—what's that? Oh, it's you, Désirée."

"You must cancel the reception, Joseph," I repeated.

"That's impossible. I've expressly arranged that——"

"But you've got a dead man in your house," I explained.

He stared at me with furrowed brows. Then he got up hastily. "I'll think it over," he said, and went out. Julie and the others followed him.

When Julie and Joseph reached the door of their bedroom Julie stopped and asked:

"Désirée, may I lie down in your room? I am afraid of being alone."

I did not object that, after all, she had Joseph and would not be alone, but simply said:

"Of course you can sleep in my bed. I want to go on with my diary anyway."

"Diary? Do you still write your diary? How strange!" she said with a tired smile.

"Why strange?"

"Because everything is so different now. So quite, quite different!"

She sighed and lay down on my bed without taking off her clothes. She did not wake up till lunch time.

Some time during the morning I heard the sound of hammering. When I went down to find out I saw that they were putting up a stage in the big reception room. In one corner Joseph was directing the work in Italian. At long last he had found an opportunity to speak his mother tongue. When he caught sight of me he came and explained:

"This is going to be the stage. From here Julie and I are going to watch the dancing."

"Stage? For the reception to-night?" I asked in astonishment. "But you can't go on with it, you can't!"

"Not with a dead body in the house, you're right. That's why we had the—hm, the remains of the late Duphot taken away. I've had him laid in state in a cemetery chapel, in as ceremonious a state as possible because, after all, he was a General in the French Army. And we must go on with the ball as a matter of course. It's even more important now than ever, because we have to show that law and order reign in Rome. If I cancelled it the whole world would say at once that we are not masters of the situation. Whereas the whole thing was really only a minor incident, however regrettable, you understand?"

I nodded. General Duphot had left his mistress and his son in order to marry me. And in order to make an impression on me he had exposed himself rashly to a raging mob and had been killed. But of course all this was only a minor though regrettable incident.

"I have to talk to your brother, Joseph," I said.

"Which one? Lucien?"

"No, the famous one, the General. Napoleon."

Joseph tried to hide his surprise. All his family knows that up till now I've anxiously avoided meeting Napoleon.

"It concerns General Duphot's family," I explained curtly, and left the room in which the hammering of the workmen made so much noise.

Returning to my room I found Julie awake and in tears. I sat down on the edge of the bed; she put her arms round me and sobbed and sobbed.

"I want to go home," she cried, "home! I don't want to

104

live in these strange mansions. I want a home, like everybody elsel What are we doing here, in this strange country where they want to kill us? And in these awful draughty castles? And in these high rooms which make you feel you are in a church, not in a house? We don't belong here, I want to go home!"

I pressed her to me. It took the death of General Duphot for her to realise how unhappy she was here.

A bit later there came a letter from Mama from Marseilles. We read it crouching side by side on my bed. Mama wrote in her tidy slanting hand that Etienne had decided to move to Genoa with Suzanne in order to open a branch there of the firm of Clary. In these days a French business man would have particularly attractive opportunities there and, so she wrote, the silk business would always be carried on best from Italy. She, Mama, would of course not stay behind by herself in Marseilles but she would go with Etienne and Suzanne to Genoa, and she hoped that I would soon find a good husband although I should for heaven's sake not allow myself to be hustled. As to the house in Marseilles, Etienne intended to sell it. . . .

Julie had stopped crying. Deeply shaken we looked at each other.

"Then we shan't have a home any more," she murmured.

I felt a lump in my throat. "You'd never have gone back to our villa in Marseilles in any case," I said.

Julie stared towards the window. "I don't know, I don't know. No, of course, I wouldn't. But it was so lovely thinking of the house, the garden and the little summer-house. You know, in all these months that I have been moving about here from *palazzo* to *palazzo* and feeling dreadfully wretched I have always kept thinking about it, always. Never of Joseph's little house in Paris, no, always of Papa's villa in Marseilles!"

There was a knock on the door. Joseph came in, and Julie at once started weeping again. "I want to go home," she cried.

He sat down on the bed and took her in his arms. "You shall go home," he said tenderly. "To-night we get the great reception over and to-morrow we leave. For Paris! I've had enough of Rome."

He pressed his lips together and his chin down on his chest. It made it look like a double chin. Perhaps he thought he made a more impressive figure that way.

"I shall ask the Government to give me another and, maybe, more important position," he said. "Are you looking forward to our home in the Rue du Rocher, Julie?"

"Yes, if Désirée goes with us," said Julie in a voice half choked with sobs.

"I'll go with you," I said. "Where else should I go?"

She looked up at me through her tears: "Oh, we'll have a lovely time in Paris, you and Joseph and I. You can't imagine, Désirée, what a marvellous city Paris is! And such a big city, too! Those shop windows! And the thousands of lights which the Seine reflects at night, no, you simply can't imagine it because you've never been there yet!"

Julie and Joseph left the room to make the arrangements for our departure, and I fell on my bed. My eyes were burning with lack of sleep.

In my thoughts I imagined the conversation I was going to have with Napoleon, and I tried to remember his face. But all I saw with my mind's eye was the unreal glossy face which smiles at you now from every coffee cup, flower vase and snuff-box. And then this unreal face disappeared in its turn before the lights that dance on the waters of the Seine at night, those lights which I shall never be able to forget.

PARIS, end of Germinal, in the Year VI. (Old people abroad would say April 1798.)

I'VE seen him again!

We had been invited to a farewell party. He was going to embark with his army within a few days for Egypt, to unite East and West there by the Pyramids and to turn our Republic into a world-wide Empire, as he told his mother. Madame Letitia listened to him calmly and afterwards asked Joseph whether they were trying to conceal from her that Napoleon suffered at times from attacks of malaria. It seemed to her that the poor boy wasn't all there. . . . But Joseph explained to her, and also to Julie and me, that it was by the Pyramids that Napoleon would smash the English and their Empire to pieces.

Napoleon and Josephine live in a small house on the Rue de la Victoire. It used to be the house of the actor Talma, and Josephine bought it from his widow in the days when she used to glide on Director Barras' arm through Theresa Tallien's salon. At that time the street was called the Rue Chatereine; but after Napoleon's victories in Italy the City Council renamed it Rue de la Victoire in his honour.

To get back to the farewell party: it was incredible how

many people forced themselves into the small and undistinguished house, which has only two small rooms besides the dining-room. I am still confused even now when I recall all the faces and voices.

Julie had made me almost ill during the morning by asking me every few seconds with tender concern if I was excited and if I still felt anything for him. I was excited, naturally, but I really couldn't say whether I still felt anything for him. 'When he smiles,' I thought to myself, 'he has me in the hollow of his hand,' and therefore I rather hoped that he and Josephine would still be furious with me because of the scene that day in Madame Tallien's house. Again and again I reflected that he'd probably hate the sight of me now and so certainly would not smile at me. I almost hoped he would hate me.

I put on a new dress, yellow with a red underslip, and I used a bronze chain which I had bought once in an antique shop in Rome, as a belt. The day before yesterday I had my hair cut short. It is the new fashion which Josephine introduced, and now all ladies of fashion copy the way she brushes her babyish curls upwards. I can't do that with my hair; it's too heavy and thick for that, and I have no elegant curls. So I put my hair up and held it together with a ribbon. 'But,' I thought, 'whatever I do, by the side of Josephine I shall always look like a little country cousin.'

The new frock was cut very low, but I no longer need handkerchiefs to stuff into my bosom. Just the opposite: I've made a resolution to eat fewer sweets, otherwise I'll get too fat. My nose, however, is still a snub nose, and that, unfortunately, it will remain to the end of my days. Which is particularly sad now, because since the conquest of Italy everybody is in raptures about 'the classic profile'!

At one o'clock, then, we drove up to the house in the Rue de la Victoire and entered the first of the two small rooms, which was already full of Bonapartes. Madame Letitia and her daughters live in Paris now, and the whole family meets quite often. Yet at every reunion the Bonapartes greet each other with kisses and embraces. I was pressed first to Madame Letitia's bosom and after that vigorously taken into Madame Leclerc's arms. Madame Leclerc was that little Polette who before her marriage declared that Leclerc was the only officer of her circle for whom she felt absolutely nothing. As Napoleon, however, thought that her many *affaires* would injure the reputation of the Bonaparte family, she had to marry him all the same. He is a short-legged, pouchy and very energetic man who never laughs, and looks as if he could be Polette's father.

Then, with her husband Bacciochi, there was Eliza, horribly painted and boasting all the time of the great position which Napoleon had found for her musical husband in one of the ministries. And Caroline, and Josephine's daughter, fair, angular Hortense, who had been allowed out of their exclusive boarding-school for the day, were there, huddled together on a fragile little chair and giggling at Madame Letitia's new dress of heavy brocade which reminded one of the dining-room curtains.

Among the noisy and excitable crowd of Bonapartes I noticed a thin, fair-haired and very young man with the sash of an adjutant round his uniform. His blue eyes stared a trifle helplessly at the beautiful Polette. I asked Caroline who he was and she, almost choking with giggles, managed to tell me at last that he was Napoleon's son!

The young man seemed to have guessed that I was asking about him. He made his way through the groups towards me and introduced himself: "Eugene de Beauharnais, personal adjutant to General Bonaparte."

The only ones who hadn't put in an appearance yet were our hosts, Napoleon and Josephine. But now a door was flung open and Josephine put her head through and called: "Do forgive me, my dears, do forgive me! We've only just got back. Joseph, would you mind coming out for a moment? Napoleon wants to speak to you. Make yourselves at home, my friends, I'll be with you in a second." The next moment she had disappeared.

Joseph followed her out, and Madame Letitia, annoyed, shrugged her shoulders. Everybody started talking again. But suddenly they all fell silent because someone in the next room seemed to be having an attack of hysterics. A fist banged a table or a mantelpiece and one could hear the smashing of glass. At the same time Josephine slipped into the room where we were standing aghast.

"How nice," she said, "to find the whole family together," and smilingly she went up to Madame Letitia. Her white gown clung tightly to her delicate figure, a dark red velvet scarf hung softly and loosely round the naked shoulders and made her girlish neck appear very white.

"Madame, you have a son by the name of Lucien, haven't you?" Josephine asked Madame Letitia.

"My third son, yes. What's the matter with him?" Madame Letitia answered. Her eyes were full of hatred for this daughter-in-law who didn't even take the trouble to remember the names of her brothers- and sisters-in-law.

"He wrote to Napoleon that he had married," said Josephine.

"I know," Madame Letitia answered and her eyes grew narrow. "Do you mean to say that my second son does not approve of his brother's choice?"

Josephine shrugged her delicate shoulders and smiled: "Sounds like it, doesn't it? Just listen how he is shouting!" The attack of hysterics next door seemed to amuse her a lot.

The door was thrown open and Napoleon stood there. His lean face was red with fury. "Mother, did you know that Lucien has married the daughter of an inn-keeper?"

Madame Letitia looked him up and down. Her eyes went from the reddish hair which fell untidily to the shoulders, over the deliberately plain uniform which, it was obvious, must have been tailored by the best uniform maker in Paris, down to the points of his highly polished, narrow and very elegant boots.

"Well, Napoleone," she said, "what is it you don't like about your sister-in-law Christine Boyer from St. Maximin?"

"You, all of you, don't you understand me? An inn-keeper's daughter, a village wench who every night in an ale-house waits on the farmers of the district? Mother, I don't understand you."

"As far as I know, Christine Boyer is a very good girl and has a very good reputation," said Madame Letitia, letting her eyes stray for a moment over Josephine's small white figure.

Suddenly Joseph's voice rang out: "After all, we can't all marry former—hm—countesses!"

At that I noticed Josephine flinch almost imperceptibly, but her smile grew wider. Her son Eugene flushed to the roots of his hair.

Napoleon swept round and stared at Joseph. One could see a little vein pulsating in his right temple. After a moment he passed his hand across his forehead, turned abruptly away from Joseph and said cuttingly:

"I have the right to expect suitable marriages from my brothers. And you, Mother, I want to write to Lucien at once to tell him to get a divorce or to have his marriage declared void. Tell him that I demand it. Josephine, can't we eat yet?"

And at that moment our eyes met! For a fraction of a second we looked at each other. There it was, the dreaded, hated and yet so badly longed-for meeting! Quickly he left the doorway, pushed the angular Hortense out of his way and took my hands:

"Eugenie! How glad I am that you accepted our invitation!"

His eyes never left my face. He smiled, and his lean features were filled with youth and the glow of life, as on that day when he promised Mama that he would wait for our wedding till my sixteenth birthday.

"How beautiful you've become, Eugenie," he said. "And you're grown up, quite grown up!"

I took my hands out of his: "I am eighteen now, after all," I said, and I thought I sounded gauche and not very sure of myself. "And we haven't seen each other for years." Well, that at any rate sounded a bit better.

"Yes, it's a long time, far too long, Eugenie, isn't it? The last time, let me see, where did we meet the last time?" He cast another glance at me and then broke out laughing. His eyes sparkled as he remembered our last meeting, finding it very funny indeed, very funny.

"Josephine, Josephine," he called, "you must meet Eugenie, Julie's sister. I've told you so much about Eugenie."

"But Julie told me that Mademoiselle Eugenie prefers to be called Désirée," Josephine said as she came nearer and stood beside Napoleon. Nothing in her Mona Lisa smile betrayed any recognition of me. "It was very kind of you to come, Mademoiselle."

"I should like to have a word with you, General," I said quickly, and his smile froze. He probably thought that I was going to make a scene, a sentimental childish scene. So I added: "It's about a rather serious matter."

Josephine hastily put her arm through his. "Dinner is ready," she announced, "do come and sit down, please!"

At the table I found myself between that boring Leclerc and shy young Eugene de Beauharnais. Napoleon talked ceaselessly and addressed himself mainly to Joseph and Leclerc. When we had finished the soup he hadn't even started it. I remembered that in his Marseilles days this desire to talk overcame him only intermittently, and when it did he spoke in jerky sentences supported by dramatic gestures. Now he was speaking very fluently and with great self-assurance and did not seem to want any objections or replies. When he began to talk about 'our arch-enemies, the British' Polette emitted a moaning: "Oh God, now he's off on that tack again!" and we were treated in great detail to all the reasons why he did not want to go on with the invasion of Britain. He had, he explained, made a comprehensive study of the coast round Dunkirk and had had the idea of building flat-bottomed invasion barges which could land in small fishing ports, as the big ports suitable for berthing men-of-war were too heavily fortified.

"Bonaparte, we've all finished our soup. Do start yours!" I heard Josephine's gentle voice. 'So,' I thought, 'she calls him Bonaparte instead of Napoleon and she doesn't "thou" him. Perhaps that is aristocratic etiquette; I wager she never called her first husband anything but *Monsieur le Vicomte*!'

Napoleon hadn't heard her admonition. He bent over the table towards Leclerc, who was sitting opposite him: "Imagine," he exclaimed, "imagine, Leclerc, by air! To be able to transport whole battalions by air across the Channel and drop them at strategic points in England! Battalions, provided even with light artillery transported by air!"

Leclerc opened his mouth to say something, but shut it again.

"Don't drink so much and don't drink so quickly, my boy," Madame Letitia's deep voice boomed across the table.

Napoleon put his wine-glass down at once and hastily began to eat. A silence fell for a few seconds, broken only by Caroline's senseless giggling. Then we heard Bacciochi, to whom the silence must have felt uncomfortable, say:

"Pity your grenadiers couldn't grow wings!"

Napoleon at once started up again and turned to Joseph: "You never know," he said, "I may yet be able to attack by air. Some inventors came to see me and showed me their plans of giant balloons capable of carrying three or four men and of keeping afloat in the air for hours. Highly interesting, full of fantastic possibilities!"

At last he had finished his soup and Josephine rang for the next course, chicken and asparagus sauce. As we were eating it Napoleon explained to Caroline and Hortense what the Pyramids were. Then he went on to tell the assembled company that, in Egypt, he was going not only to destroy Britain's colonial power but also to liberate the Egyptians.

"My first Order-of-the-Day to my troops—" bang, his chair had fallen over because in his excitement he had jumped up and pushed it back and run out of the room. Within a second he returned carrying a closely written sheet. "Here, you must hear this: 'Soldiers, forty centuries look down on you!' That," he said, turning to us, "is the age of the Pyramids. This Order-of-the-Day will be published there, under the shadow of the Pyramids. To continue: 'The people in whose midst we find ourselves are Mohammedan. Their credo runs: God is God and Mahomet is his prophet——' "

"The Mohammedans call God Allah," interrupted Eliza. She had started to read a lot of books in Paris and liked to show off the knowledge she had acquired.

Napoleon frowned and brushed her interruption aside. "I'll work the details out later," he said. "Here is the most important passage: 'Don't raise your voices against their faith. Treat them, the Egyptians, as you've treated Jews and Italians. Show the Muftis and Imams the same respect which you have shown to priests and rabbis.' " Here he paused and looked at us. "Well?"

"It's fortunate for the Egyptians that under the laws of the Republic you are to liberate them for the cause of the Rights of Man," Joseph said.

"What do you mean by that?"

"That the Rights of Man are the guiding principles of this Order-of-the-Day. And they didn't come from your brain." Not a muscle moved in Joseph's face as he said that, and I remembered for the first time in years what I had felt in Marseilles: that he really hated his brother.

"You've said that very beautifully, my boy," said Madame Letitia's voice soothingly.

"Please do eat up, Bonaparte," urged Josephine, "we're expecting a lot of people after dinner."

Obediently Napoleon crammed the good food into his mouth.

I happened to notice Hortense at this moment. This child— no, at fourteen you're no longer a child, don't I know!—well, this awkward youngster Hortense, who didn't at all resemble her lovely mother, never took her somewhat protuberant watery eyes off Napoleon, and there were hectic patches of red on her cheeks. I realised Hortense was in love with her stepfather, and I found this thought sad and depressing rather than funny. Eugene interrupted and said:

"Mama wants to drink your health."

I raised my glass to her, and smilingly, slowly, she raised hers and drank. When she put it down again she winked at me. I knew exactly what it meant: she remembered . . . the day at Madame Tallien's . . .

We went to the other room for coffee. There were a lot of people waiting there who wanted to wish Napoleon luck and God-speed. I had the feeling that all Madame Tallien's former clients were now trying to force their way into Josephine's little house. Men in uniform were quite numerous, among them my intended suitors Junot and Marmont, whom I gave a wide berth. I heard them tell the ladies laughingly that once in Egypt they would have their hair cut short. "We'd look like Roman heroes," they insisted, "and besides it'll keep the lice away." One very smart officer with wavy dark hair, sparkling eyes and a flat nose told Madame Letitia that it was Napoleon's idea.

"I don't doubt it, General Murat," she answered, "he's always full of mad ideas."

She seemed to have taken a liking to this young officer

whose blue tunic was covered with braid and his white trousers with gold embroidery. I think Madame Letitia is rather fond of colourful southern splendour.

A little later Josephine told three young people to get up from a small sofa to make room for an important guest. This was no other than Barras, one of the five Directors of the French Republic, in gold-embroidered purple uniform, and a lorgnette in his hand. Joseph and Napoleon Bonaparte at once took the seats on either side of him, and over their shoulders leaned a thin man whose peaked nose seemed familiar. Of course, he was one of the two men whom I had seen in the window niche at Madame Tallien's, a certain Fouché, I believe.

Eugene, perspiring madly, apparently thought it his job to find chairs for the guests. Without any warning he pushed fat Eliza and me down on to two chairs immediately in front of the sofa on which Barras was holding court. He also found a gilded arm-chair for 'the Minister of Police', M. Fouché. But when an elegant young man with a slight limp and an old-fashioned powdered wig approached our group Fouché immediately jumped to his feet again. "My dear Talleyrand," he exclaimed, "won't you sit down with us?"

They talked about our Ambassador to Vienna, who was on his way home. Something sensational seemed to have happened in Vienna. I gathered from the conversation that, on an Austrian national holiday, the Ambassador had flown the flag of our Republic and that thereupon the Viennese had attacked the Embassy to tear the flag down.

All that was new to me. I never have the chance to read a paper because of Joseph, who, as soon as they arrive, takes them away and reads them in his study. And if later on Julie and I want to see them we find that Joseph has cut out all the important articles and taken them to Napoleon to talk them over. So I never have an inkling of what goes on in the world. This incident had apparently happened almost as soon as we had made our peace with Austria and installed an embassy there.

"It seems to me, M. Talleyrand," said Joseph, "that you shouldn't have sent a General to Vienna as our Ambassador but a professional diplomat."

Talleyrand raised his thin eyebrows and smiled. "Our Republic does not as yet dispose of sufficient professional diplomats, M. Bonaparte. We have to call in auxiliaries from outside the diplomatic service. You yourself helped us out in Italy, didn't you?"

That went home. So Joseph was only an 'auxiliary diplomat'

in the eyes of this M. Talleyrand who, it appeared, was our Minister for Foreign Affairs.

"And in any case," I heard the nasal voice of Director Barras say, "in any case, this man Bernadotte is one of our ablest men, don't you think so, General Bonaparte? I seem to remember that at one time in Italy you needed reinforcements very urgently, and the Minister for War ordered Bernadotte to take the best division of the Rhine Army to Italy. And how did this man from Gascogne manage it? He crossed the Alps in the depths of winter with a whole division within ten hours, six for the ascent, four for the descent! If I remember correctly a letter from you, General, written at that time, you yourself were most impressed by this feat."

"No doubt Bernadotte is an excellent General," said Joseph, shrugging his shoulders, "but a diplomat? A politician?"

"I believe he was quite right in showing the flag of our Republic in Vienna. Why should the French Embassy not hoist its own standards when all the other buildings showed their flags?" Talleyrand said thoughtfully. "After the violation of the extra-territorial status of our Embassy, General Bernadotte left Vienna at once. But I feel that the apology from the Austrian Government will arrive in Paris even before he arrives. In any case, there was no one better suited than he for the post in Vienna," he concluded, examining the polished finger-nails of his small hand.

A barely perceptible smile showed on Barras' blueish, somewhat bloated face as he pronounced Bernadotte a very far-sighted man with great political acumen. Then he added, dropping his lorgnette and fixing his gaze on Napoleon, whose lips were pressed together and in whose temple the little vein was pulsating: "A convinced Republican, this Bernadotte, determined to destroy all the enemies of the Republic, both external and—internal!"

"And what will be his next appointment?" broke in Joseph with obvious jealous impatience.

Barras' lorgnette sparkled in the light as he answered: "The Republic needs reliable men. I imagine that a General who started his military career as a private soldier is bound to enjoy the confidence of the Army. And as he happens to enjoy the confidence of the Government as well it could only be natural if——"

"He were in the future to become Minister of War!" That was the voice of the man with the peaked nose, Fouché, the Minister of Police.

Before Barras could say any more Theresa Tallien, in a very

thin Venetian lace blouse, appeared before him. "Our beautiful Theresa," he smiled, and rose heavily to his feet.

Theresa motioned him to sit down again. "Don't get up, Director," she said. "And look, there's our Italian hero! Isn't it a charming afternoon, General Bonaparte, and doesn't Josephine look enchanting? I am told that you are taking little Eugene along with you to the Pyramids as your adjutant? May I introduce to you M. Ouvrard, the man who supplied ten thousand pairs of boots for your Italian Army? Ouvrard, here he is in person: France's strong man!" The rotund little man who followed in her wake bowed deeply.

Eliza dug me in the ribs: "Her latest boy friend! Army contractor Ouvrard! Not so long ago she was still living with Barras whom she had stolen from Josephine. Did you know that? But now that old fool sticks to the fifteen-year-olds. An uncouth chap I find him! His hair is dyed, of course. No one has hair as black as that."

All at once I felt I couldn't stand it any longer on this chair next to the perspiring, odiously perfumed Eliza. I jumped to my feet and pushed my way to the door in order to find a mirror outside in the small hall where I could powder my face.

The hall was half dark. Before I got to the candles flickering in front of the tall mirror I had a fright. Two figures leaning close to each other in a corner suddenly separated. One of them was in a white gown.

"Oh, I am so sorry," I said.

The white-gowned figure came forward into the light of the candle. It was Josephine.

"Sorry? Why?" she said, smoothing her babyish curls with a fugitive movement of her hand. "May I introduce M. Charles to you? Hippolyte, this is Joseph's charming sister-in-law, sister-in-law of my brother-in-law, that's our relationship, is it not, Mademoiselle Désirée?"

A very young man, certainly not more than 25 years of age, bowed slickly.

"This is M. Hippolyte Charles," continued Josephine, "one of our youngest and most successful—well, what? What do you do, Hippolyte? Oh, of course, army contractor! One of our youngest army contractors . . .!"

Josephine laughed and obviously found it all very amusing. "Mademoiselle Désirée," she added, "is an old rival of mine."

"Victorious or vanquished rival?" inquired M. Charles.

Before he got his answer we heard the clanking of spurs and Napoleon's voice from the door:

"Josephine, Josephine, where are you? All our guests are asking for you."

"I wanted to show Mademoiselle Désirée and M. Charles the Venetian mirror which you gave me in Montebello, Bonaparte," said Josephine calmly, taking him by the arm and pulling him towards M. Charles. "May I introduce to you a young army contractor? M. Charles, here at last your greatest wish will be fulfilled: you may shake the hand of the Liberator of Italy!"

Her laughter sounded enchanting, and at once the signs of exasperation in Napoleon's face vanished.

"You wanted to talk to me, Euge—Désirée?" Napoleon said to me.

Quickly Josephine put her hand on the arm of M. Hippolyte Charles: "Come along, I must go back to my guests."

We were facing each other alone in the flickering candlelight. Nervously I started fishing for something in my bag, whilst Napoleon went up to the mirror and stared at his own face. It looked hollow and full of shadows in the uncertain light.

"Did you hear what Barras said a moment ago?" Napoleon spoke abruptly. He was so immersed in his thoughts that he talked to me in the intimate manner of the happy times of the past without noticing it.

"I heard it, but I didn't understand it. I know so little of these matters."

He continued to stare into the mirror. " 'Internal enemies of the Republic,' a nice expression! It was meant for me. He knows that I could—"

He broke off, contemplated attentively the play of light and shadows on his face in the mirror and chewed his upper lip. Then he went on: "We Generals saved the Republic. And we Generals keep it alive. We might easily take it into our heads to form our own Government. . . . They beheaded the King and the Crown rolled into the gutter. All one need do is to pick it up. . . ."

He spoke like someone dreaming. And exactly as in days gone by, at first I felt fear and then a childish desire to laugh off the fear.

He swung round unexpectedly and said in an acid voice: "But I am going to Egypt. I leave it to the Directors to wrangle with the political parties, to let themselves be corrupted by army contractors, to choke the French economy with worthless money. I am going to Egypt and shall plant the flag of the Republic——"

"I am sorry to interrupt you, General," I said. "I have

116

written down here the name of a lady, and I ask you to give orders that she is to be provided for."

He took the chit out of my hand and read it close to the candles. "Marie Meunier, who is that?"

"The woman who lived with General Duphot, the mother of his son. I promised him that both should be provided for."

He dropped the chit and said with a gentle regret in his voice: "I felt sorry for you, very sorry. You were engaged to him, Désirée, weren't you?"

I felt like shouting into his face that I had had enough of this miserable comedy. But I only brought out hoarsely:

"You know quite well that I hardly knew Duphot. I don't understand why you torture me with these things, General."

"With what things, Désirée?"

"With these marriage proposals. I've had enough of them, I want to be left alone."

"Believe me, only in marriage can a woman find the fulfilment of her life," said Napoleon unctuously.

"I—I'd like to throw the candlestick at you!" I managed to jerk out, and I clenched my fists to prevent myself from really throwing things at him.

He came up to me and smiled, that fascinating smile of his which once upon a time meant everything to me. "We are friends, are we not, Bernadine Eugenie Désirée?" he asked.

"Will you promise me that Marie Meunier will be paid a pension for herself and her child?"

"Oh, here you are, Désirée! Get ready, we must be off!" That was Julie, who entered the hall at this moment with Joseph. When they saw Napoleon and me they stopped and looked at us in surprise.

"Will you promise, General?" I repeated.

"I promise, Mademoiselle Désirée." He took my hand and kissed it quickly. Then Joseph stepped between us and with a lot of back-slapping took leave of his brother.

PARIS, four weeks later.

THE happiest day of my life started for me in the same way as all the other days. After breakfast I took the small green watering-can and began to water the two dusty palm trees in the living-room which Julie had brought home from Italy. Joseph and Julie, still sitting at the breakfast table, were discussing a letter, and I only listened with half an ear to what they were saying.

"You see, Julie," said Joseph, "he has accepted my invitation!"

"For heaven's sake, I haven't prepared a thing!" said Julie. "And whom else are you going to ask in? Shall I try for some cockerels? And what about trout in mayonnaise as hors-d'œuvre? Trout is dreadfully expensive just now, but . . . You ought to have told me before, Joseph."

"I couldn't be sure whether he'd accept my invitation. After all, he's only been in Paris for a few days and is inundated with invitations. Everybody wants to hear from him in person what really happened in Vienna."

At this point I went out to refill the watering-can. When I came back Joseph was just saying:

"—had written to him that my friend Director Barras and my brother Napoleon had told me so many pleasant things about him and I should be happy if I could welcome him to a modest meal in my home."

"And strawberries with Madeira sauce as a dessert," Julie was thinking aloud.

"And so he accepted! Do you know what that means? It means that personal contact with France's future Minister of War has been established! Napoleon's most particular desire is being fulfilled. Barras makes no secret of the fact that he wants to hand the War Ministry over to him. Old Schérer was like so much wax in Napoleon's hand, but we haven't an inkling of what Bernadotte is going to do. Julie, the food must be really first-class, and——"

"Whom else shall we ask?"

I took the bowl of roses from the centre of the breakfast table and carried it into the kitchen to renew the water. On my return Joseph was just explaining:

"A small dinner in the family circle, that's it. That'll give Lucien and myself the opportunity to talk to him as much as we want. So: Josephine, Lucien, Christine, you and myself." Seeing me he added: "Yes, and of course our little one. Make yourself beautiful, Désirée, to-night you'll meet France's future Minister of War."

I am bored by all these 'small family dinners' which Joseph has been giving all the time in honour of some Deputy, General or Ambassador. They are always arranged in order to spy out political behind-the-scene secrets and to send them red-hot in endless epistles by special courier across the sea after Napoleon, who is on his way to Egypt.

Joseph so far has not accepted—or received—a new ambassadorial appointment. He seems intent on staying in Paris to be 'at the centre of things', and since the last elections he has even entered the Assembly as Deputy for Corsica, which island, since Napoleon's victories, has naturally become very proud of its Bonapartes. Lucien too, independently of Joseph, has stood for Corsica and been elected. A few days ago, almost immediately after Napoleon's departure, he moved to Paris with his wife Christine. Madame Letitia had found a small apartment for them, and there they live precariously on Lucien's pay as a Deputy.

Lucien belongs to the extreme Left. When he was told that Napoleon expected him to divorce his wife he nearly split his sides with laughing. "My military brother seems to have gone off his head!" he shouted. "What is it he doesn't like about Christine?"

"Her father's tavern," said Joseph.

Lucien laughed. "Mama's father only had a farm in Corsica, and a very small one at that!" Suddenly he became thoughtful, frowned, and said to Joseph: "Don't you think that, for a Republican, Napoleon has very peculiar ideas?"

Almost every day we read Lucien's speeches in the papers. That thin, blue-eyed, brown-haired fellow seems to be a great orator. It's impossible to say whether he really likes these 'small family dinners' which are given for the sake of good connections or whether he only comes so as not to offend Joseph and Julie.

As I was putting on a yellow silk dress Julie slipped into my room. With her usual introductory phrase: "If only nothing goes wrong! . . ." she threw herself on to my bed. "Why don't you put the brocade ribbon in your hair? It suits you," she said.

"Why!" I said, searching in my drawer among ribbons and combs, "why should I? There won't be anybody there of any interest to me."

"Joseph heard that this future Minister of War is supposed to have said Napoleon's Egyptian campaign was nothing but midsummer madness and the Government should never have allowed it," said Julie.

In a fit of bad temper I decided not to put anything at all in my hair but simply to brush my curls upwards and try to keep them up with two combs. I grumbled at Julie as I was doing my hair: "These political dinners bore me to tears."

"Josephine at first didn't want to come," said Julie. "Joseph had to explain to her how important it would be for Napoleon to be on good terms with this rising man. She's bought a country house, Malmaison, and she was going out there with some friends for a picnic."

"And she's right, too, in this beautiful weather," I said,

looking through the open window into the pale blue evening, which was full of the scent of lime trees. I almost hated the unknown guest of honour who kept me in the house. At that moment we heard the sound of a carriage driving up to the door, and Julie rushed out of the room with a last "If only nothing goes wrong!"

I didn't feel like going down and welcoming visitors. Not until I heard a babel of voices and got the feeling that they had all arrived and Julie was waiting for me did I overcome my reluctance. When I had reached the door to the dining-room and put my hand on the door-handle it occurred to me that I could have gone to bed and said that I had a headache. But it was too late then. The next moment I would have given anything for it not to have been too late and if I had really gone to bed with a headache.

A man was standing with his back to the door. But I recognised that back at once, the back of a giant of a man in dark blue uniform with big gold epaulettes and a broad sash in the colours of the Republic. Joseph, Julie, Josephine, Lucien and his wife were standing around him in a semi-circle holding liqueur glasses in their hands.

I couldn't help standing by the door like one paralysed and staring in confusion at the broad-shouldered back. But the family circle found my conduct rather strange. Joseph looked at me over the shoulders of his guest, the eyes of the others followed Joseph's, and at last the giant himself noticed that something strange was going on behind his back, interrupted himself and turned round.

His eyes grew wide in amazement. My heart beat so wildly that I could hardly breathe.

"Désirée, come on, we're waiting for you," said Julie.

At the same time Joseph came to me, took my arm and said: "This, General Bernadotte, is my wife's little sister: Mademoiselle Désirée Clary."

I never looked at him. Like someone in a daze I kept my eyes fixed on one of his gold buttons, felt vaguely that he was politely kissing my hand and heard from a long way away Joseph's voice saying:

"We were interrupted, General. What was it you were going to say?"

"I—I'm afraid I really don't remember what it was."

I would have known his voice among a thousand others! It was the voice from the bridge across the Seine in the rain, the voice out of the dark corner in the cab, the voice at the door of the house in the Rue du Bac.

"Sit down, please," said Julie.

But General Bernadotte did not move.

"Sit down, please," Julie repeated and went up to Bernadotte. At that he offered her his arm. Joseph, Josephine and all the rest of us sat down with them.

The 'small family dinner' given for reasons of political expediency took a course very different from the one Joseph had mapped out for it.

As arranged, General Bernadotte was sitting between the hostess and Josephine, and Lucien had taken Joseph's place beside Julie so that Joseph could sit exactly opposite General Bernadotte and direct the conversation. But the general seemed a little absent-minded. Mechanically he began to occupy himself with the hors-d'œuvre, and Joseph had to raise his glass twice to him, before he realised it and responded. I could tell by his face that he was thinking hard, that he was trying to remember what he had been told that day in Madame Tallien's house: about Napoleon and his fiancée in Marseilles, a young girl with a big dowry who was Joseph Bonaparte's sister-in-law, and about Napoleon's desertion of fiancée and dowry. . . . So immersed was he that Joseph had to speak to him three times before the guest realised that we all wanted to drink to him. Hastily he raised his glass.

He remembered his duties to the lady by his side and turned to her abruptly: "How long has your sister been living in Paris?"

The question came so unexpectedly that Julie at first was taken aback and did not quite understand what he was driving at.

"You are both from Marseilles, aren't you?" he asked again. "What I mean is, has your sister been living in Paris for a long time now?"

By now Julie had collected her wits. "No," she answered, "only for a few months. It's her first stay in Paris. And she likes it here very much, don't you, Désirée?"

"Paris is a very beautiful town," I said awkwardly, like a schoolgirl.

"Yes, as long as it doesn't rain," he said, regarding me intently.

"Oh yes, even when it rains," put in Christine, the innkeeper's daughter from St. Maximin, eagerly. "I think Paris is a fairyland town."

"You are quite right, Madame. Fairy tales happen even when it rains," Bernadotte said solemnly.

Joseph began to fidget. After all, he had not lured the future Minister of War into his house with all the powers of persuasion he could muster simply to discuss the weather and its influence on fairy tales. He took the initiative and said with an important air, "I had a letter from my brother Napoleon yesterday."

But Bernadotte didn't seem to be interested at all.

Joseph continued, "He writes that the journey is going according to plan and that the British Fleet under Nelson hasn't even let itself be seen yet."

"That's probably due more to your brother's good luck than to his good management," Bernadotte said good-temperedly, and raised his glass: "To General Bonaparte's health! I am very much in his debt!"

Joseph didn't know whether to be pleased or offended by this.

Bernadotte's whole conduct left no doubt that he felt himself to be the equal of Napoleon in rank. It was true, of course, that Napoleon had been Commander-in-Chief in Italy, but meanwhile Bernadotte had been an Ambassador and he knew as well as the rest of us that he was meant to be Minister of War.

Things began to happen as the cockerels were served, and Josephine of all women was the prime mover of it all. For some time I had felt her watching General Bernadotte and myself. I don't believe that there is anybody else in the world who can sense the tensions and the invisible forces working between a man and a woman to such an extent as Josephine. Up till now she had been quiet. When Julie talked about this being my first stay in Paris her thin eyebrows went up and she regarded Bernadotte with great interest. It was certainly possible that she remembered Bernadotte as having been present that after-noon at Madame Tallien's house. . . .

At last she found the opening she had wanted to replace Joseph's conversational topics, which ran on political and military lines, by something more to her liking. Inclining her head with its babyish curls, she winked at Bernadotte and asked:

"It can't have been very easy for you as Ambassador in Vienna, can it? I mean because of your being a bachelor. Haven't you often missed the presence of an Ambassadress in the Embassy?"

Firmly, Bernadotte put down his knife and fork. "Indeed I have, indeed! I really can't tell you, my dear Josephine—I may call you Josephine, may I not, as in those days in your friend Madame Tallien's house? Well, I really can't tell you how sorry I was not to be married. But," and now he turned to the whole assembled company, "but I ask you, ladies and gentlemen, what am I to do?"

Nobody knew whether he was joking or in earnest. There was an embarrassed silence round the table till at last Julie forced herself to remark with awkward politeness, "You haven't found the right one yet, General."

"But yes, Madame, I have! Only she disappeared again, and now—" He shrugged his shoulders as if he were in a kind of humorous dilemma and looked at me laughingly.

"And now you simply go and look for her and propose to her," Christine exclaimed. She did not find the conversation at all unusual but was quite at home in it. In her father's ale-house in St. Maximin the young fellows of the village used to talk to her about very much the same kind of difficulty.

Bernadotte grew serious. "You are right, Madame," he said. "I shall propose to her."

With that he got up, pushed his chair back and turned to Joseph: "Monsieur Joseph Bonaparte, I have the honour to ask you for the hand of your sister-in-law Mademoiselle Désirée Clary." He sat down again without taking his eyes off Joseph.

There was a deathly silence. A clock could be heard ticking, and perhaps, I thought, my heartbeat too echoed in everybody's ear. In desperation I stared down at the white tablecloth.

At last Joseph spoke. "I don't quite understand, General Bernadotte. Do you really mean that?"

"I do."

Again the deathly silence fell.

"I—I think you ought to give Désirée time to think over your proposal."

"I have given her time, Monsieur Bonaparte."

"But you've only just met her," Julie said, trembling with excitement.

I looked up. "I should very much like to marry you, General Bernadotte."

Was it I who said that? A chair fell over with a great clatter, curious and stupefied faces stared at me intolerably, I don't know how I escaped from the dining-room. I only know that I found myself sitting on the bed in my room, crying, crying.

After a while Julie came in and pressed me to her and tried to calm me down. "You needn't marry him, darling. Don't cry, don't cry."

"But I must cry," I sobbed, "I must. I can't help it, but I'm so happy, so happy that I simply have to cry."

Before I went down again—they were all in the living-room now—I washed my face in cold water and powdered it. But Bernadotte said at once, "You've been crying again, Mademoiselle Désirée."

He was sitting next to Josephine on a sofa. But Josephine

123

got up and said, "It's Désirée's place next to Jean-Baptiste now."

I sat down next to him, and then everybody talked at once to overcome their embarrassment. There was some champagne left over from dinner, and as the dessert had been forgotten in the agitation over the course of events we ate it now. The strawberries and Madeira sauce helped me over the first frightful moments.

Bernadotte was not in the least embarrassed but radiated good temper all round. After we had eaten the dessert he turned to Julie and asked politely, "Do you mind, Madame, if I take your sister for a drive?"

Julie nodded understandingly: "Of course not, my dear General! When is it to be? To-morrow afternoon?"

"No, I rather thought, now."

"But it's dark now!" Julie objected in dismay. No, it wasn't done for a young girl to go for a drive with a gentleman in the dark.

I got up and said with determination to Julie, "It'll only be a short drive. We'll be back soon." Then I left the room so quickly that Bernadotte didn't even find time to say good-bye properly to everybody present.

His carriage, an open one, was standing outside. We drove through a spring evening filled with the scent of lime blossom. When we got nearer to the heart of the city its lights sparkled so brightly that we couldn't see the stars any more.

All the time we hadn't spoken a word. As we were rolling along the bank of the Seine Bernadotte called to the coachman, and the carriage stopped close to a bridge.

"That's the bridge. Remember it?" said Bernadotte.

We got out, went side by side to the middle of the bridge leaned over the edge. The thousand lights of Paris were dancing up and down on the waves of the river.

"I went several times to the Rue du Bac and asked after you. But the people there didn't want to tell me anything about you!"

"Yes, they knew that at that time I was here secretly and without permission," I said.

We went back to the carriage, and he put his arm round my shoulders. My head just came up to his epaulettes.

"You told me that night that you were far too small for me," he said.

"Yes, and now I am smaller still! I was wearing shoes with high heels then and they're quite out of fashion now. But perhaps that doesn't matter."

"Perhaps what doesn't matter?"

"That I am so little."

"It doesn't matter at all. Just the opposite!"

"How do you mean 'just the opposite'?"

"I like it."

On the journey back I pressed my cheek against his shoulder. But the epaulettes scratched rather a lot.

"This awful gold stuff bothers me," I murmured crossly.

He laughed. "Yes, I know, you don't like Generals."

It struck me all of a sudden that he was the fifth General who had proposed to me. Napoleon, Junot, Marmont, Duphot: I decided to forget about them. I preferred to have my cheek scratched by the epaulettes of the fifth, named Bernadotte.

When we arrived back we found that all the guests had gone meanwhile and there were only Julie and Joseph left.

"I hope you'll come to see us here often, General," said Joseph.

"Daily——" I said, and stopped. Then, resolutely, I went on and brought out his name for the first time: "Daily, won't you, Jean-Baptiste?"

"We have decided to get married very soon. You won't raise any objection?" Bernadotte asked Joseph.

Of course, we hadn't talked about the wedding date at all. But as far as I was concerned I would have married him then and there.

"I shall start to-morrow looking for a pleasant little house," Bernadotte continued, "and as soon as I have found one to our liking we'll get married."

Something he had said and I remembered ran like a sweet little tune through my mind: 'For years I have saved up part of my salary. I could buy a little house for you and the child.'

"I shall write to Mama at once," I heard Julie say. And Joseph added, "Good-night, brother-in-law, good-night. Napoleon will be very pleased about the news."

As soon as Bernadotte had gone Joseph exclaimed at once: "I don't understand this at all. Bernadotte is certainly no man of rash decisions!"

"Isn't he a bit too old for Désirée? He's at least——"

"In the middle thirties, I should say," Joseph estimated. Turning to me he said, "Tell me, Désirée, do you realise that you are going to marry one of the most important men in the Republic?"

"The trousseau!" Julie cried, "what about the trousseau? If Désirée is really going to get married soon we'll have to do something about the trousseau."

"We don't want this man Bernadotte to say that the sister-in-law of a Bonaparte was married without a first-class trousseau," Joseph said, and looked at us solemnly.

"How long will it take you to get everything ready?"

"As far as the shopping part of it goes, that's quickly done," said Julie. "But the initials have to be embroidered on the linen."

At that point I intervened in the excited talk: "But the trousseau is all ready in Marseilles. All we need do is to send word to have it despatched here. And the initials are all on."

"Yes, yes, of course," cried Julie, with eyes as round as saucers for sheer surprise, "Désirée is right, the initials are all on, B——"

"Yes," I smiled going to the door, "B, B, and nothing but B!"

"The whole thing seems very peculiar to me," murmured Joseph with suspicion in his voice.

"If only she's going to be happy!" Julie said softly.

Happy, happy, oh how happy I am! Let me tell it to all the world, you, God in Heaven, you, lime trees in the street, you, roses in the vase, how happy I am!

PART II

THE WIFE OF MARSHAL BERNADOTTE

SCEAUX near PARIS
Autumn of the Year VI (1798).

I was married to General Jean-Baptiste Bernadotte on the 30th of Thermidor in the Year VI of the Republic at seven o'clock in the evening at the registry office in Sceaux, a suburb of Paris. My husband's witnesses were his friend Antoine Morien, a captain in the cavalry, and the Recorder of Sceaux, Monsieur François Desgranges. I for my part had no option but to ask Uncle Somis, who, as a matter of principle, never misses a family wedding, and, of course, Joseph to be my witnesses. At the last moment Lucien Bonaparte turned up at the registry office, so that I appeared with three witnesses in tow.

After the ceremony we all went to the Rue du Rocher, where Julie had prepared a magnificent feast. (I should add that everything went according to plan, but it had cost Julie three sleepless nights!) So as not to offend anybody, Joseph had asked all the Bonapartes living in or near Paris. Madame Letitia repeatedly expressed her regret that her stepbrother Fesch, who had returned to his priestly office, had been prevented from coming. At first Mama had intended to come from Genoa for the wedding. But she had been ailing a lot lately, and therefore the journey was considered too strenuous for her in the summer heat. As for Jean-Baptiste, he hates all kinds of family festivities, and as he has no relatives in Paris he only brought his old friend Morien along. My wedding therefore was completely dominated by the Bonapartes, for whom Uncle Somis, a slow, comfortable provincial, is no match. To my astonishment Joseph had asked at the last minute General Junot and his wife Laura, the daughter of a Corsican friend of Madame Letitia's whom he had married at Napoleon's wish. Junot, a member of Napoleon's staff, was in Paris for a short time to report to the Government on Napoleon's entry into Alexandria and Cairo and his victory at the Battle of the Nile.

I felt dreadfully bored during the wedding breakfast. It began very late. The late evening hours are the fashionable time now for getting married, and therefore Joseph had arranged for the ceremony to take place at seven o'clock. That made everything else late. Julie had wanted me to stay in bed the whole day before going to the registry office so that I should look as rested and as pretty as possible. But I had no time for that. I had to help Marie put away our cutlery, which we had only bought the day before. Besides there's always so much to do when one furnishes a house.

Only two days after Jean-Baptiste and I had become engaged he turned up to say that he had found a suitable house. I had to go there that very moment to look at it. It is a small house in the Rue de la Lune in Sceaux, 3, Rue de la Lune, to be exact. On the ground floor we have the kitchen, the dining-room and a small closet in which Jean-Baptiste put a writing desk and piles of books. Every day he comes along with more books and we have called the closet 'the study'. On the upper floor there are only a beautiful bedroom and a tiny chamber. Then there are two small offices, bedrooms for Marie and Fernand. Marie was imported into our ménage by me, Fernand by Jean-Baptiste.

Marie and Fernand quarrel all day long. Mama had wanted to take Marie with her when she moved to Genoa, but Marie refused. She didn't tell Mama what she was going to do but simply took a room in Marseilles and worked as a cook at family celebrations of people who were proud to have 'the former cook of Madame Clary' working for them. But I knew that, although she had never said so in so many words, she was simply waiting. The day after my engagement I wrote her a short note: 'I am engaged to General B. of the bridge of which I once told you. As soon as he's found a suitable house we shall get married, and if I know him he'll find the house in twenty-four hours. When can you come?' I never had an answer to that letter. But a week later Marie arrived in Paris.

"I only hope Marie will get on with my Fernand," said Jean-Baptiste.

"Who is your Fernand?" I asked, startled.

It came out then that Fernand came from Jean-Baptiste's home town, Pau in Gascony, went to school with him and joined up at the same time. But whereas Jean-Baptiste was being promoted all the time, Fernand only just escaped being thrown out of the Army scores of times. Fernand is small and fat, his feet hurt him when the Army starts marching, and his stomach aches horribly when the battle begins. It isn't his fault, of course, but it's very disagreeable for him. All the same he wanted to stay in the Army to be near Jean-Baptiste. He has a passion for polishing boots and knows how to remove the most persistent grease stains from tunics. Two years ago he was given an honourable discharge from the Army so that he could devote himself entirely to the boots and stains and the creature comforts of Jean-Baptiste. When he was introduced to me he defined himself as 'the servant of my General and schoolmate Bernadotte'.

As soon as Marie and Fernand set eyes on each other they started quarrelling. What about? About Fernand stealing from the larder and about Marie using his twenty-four shoe brushes and wanting to wash the General's underclothes without asking his, Fernand's, permission, and so on . . .

When I saw our little house for the first time I said to Jean-Baptiste, "I shall write to Etienne to pay over my marriage portion to you."

Jean-Baptiste sniffed contemptuously: "What do you take me for? Do you think that I am going to build our home with my wife's money?"

"But, Joseph——"

"I must ask you not to compare me with the Bonapartes," he said sharply. Then he took me laughingly by the shoulders and said, "My little one, all Bernadotte can buy you to-day is a doll's house in Sceaux. But if ever you feel like wanting a mansion——"

At that I nearly screamed: "For heaven's sake, anything but that! Promise me that we are never, never going to live in a mansion, please!"

I remembered with horror those long months in the Italian *palazzi*, and the thought came to me that people were speaking of Bernadotte as one of 'the coming men'. His epaulettes looked ominous to me. "Promise me," I implored him, "never a mansion, never!"

He gazed at me. His smile faded slowly from his face. "We belong together, Désirée," he said. "In Vienna I lived in a splendid palace. But to-morrow I may be ordered to the front and then I shall have nothing but a camp bed in the open. And the day after my headquarters may be moved to a castle, and if I asked you to join me there, would you refuse?"

We were standing under the big chestnut tree in our future garden. 'Soon we'll be married,' I thought, 'and I shall try to be a good wife and to keep everything beautiful and in apple-pie order. That's what I want, this tiny house with the chestnut tree and the overgrown flower beds.' But then the thought of what I wanted was followed by the ghastly images of high-ceilinged rooms, marble tiles and lackeys always getting in the way.

"We shall be very happy here," I said in a murmur.

But he was insistent. "Would you refuse?" he repeated.

I nestled up to him. "I shan't refuse," I said, "but I shan't be very happy in a castle."

When I was kneeling in front of the kitchen cupboard on the morning of my wedding day putting away the white china, Marie asked, "Aren't you excited, Eugenie?" A few hours later, when Julie's maid was trying to coax my obstinate hair into Josephine's babyish curls, Julie remarked, "Strange, I do believe, darling, you are not at all excited."

I shook my head. Excited? Why should I be excited? Since that fateful moment in the dark cab, when Jean-Baptiste's hand was the only bit of warmth left in my life, I have always known that I belonged to him. In a few hours' time I should put my signature on a piece of paper in Sceaux Registry Office and with that confirm what I have been certain of for so long. No, I wasn't excited at all.

After the ceremony we had the wedding breakfast, which, as I said before, was such a boring affair. Most of the talk, apart from Uncle Somis' toast to the bridal couple and some revolutionary oratory from Lucien, was about Napoleon's Egyptian campaign. Jean-Baptiste was heartily tired of this subject, but Joseph and Lucien had taken it into their heads to try to convince him that the conquest of Egypt was one more proof of Napoleon's genius.

"I think it out of the question," said Jean-Baptiste, "that we can hold Egypt permanently. And the British know it and so they don't bother to engage in a colonial war with us."

"But," Joseph put in, "Napoleon has taken Alexandria and Cairo already and won the Battle of the Nile."

"That won't disturb the British greatly; properly speaking, Egypt is not under British but under Turkish suzerainty anyway, and the British consider our troops as no more than a passing inconvenience——"

"At the Battle of the Nile the enemy suffered 20,000 killed, we not even fifty," interrupted Junot.

"Magnificent," added Joseph.

Jean-Baptiste shrugged his shoulders: "Magnificent? The glorious French Army under the leadership of its inspired General Bonaparte and with the help of modern heavy artillery killed 20,000 half-naked Africans who hadn't even boots on their feet. Really, I must say, a magnificent victory of the gun over the bow and arrow!"

Lucien opened his mouth to say something, but then hesitated. He looked sad when he said at last, "Killed, in the name of the Rights of Man."

"The end justifies the means," said Joseph. "Napoleon will

carry his conquests farther and drive the British out of the Mediterranean region."

"They wouldn't dream of challenging us on land," declared Jean-Baptiste. "Why should they? They have their fleet, and not even you will deny that it is far superior to our own navy. The moment they destroy the ships which carried Bonaparte's Army across the sea——" Jean-Baptiste broke off and looked at each of us in turn: "Don't you see what is at stake? Any moment now a French Army may find itself cut off from its base. And then your brother with all his victorious regiments will be caught in the desert like a mouse in a trap. The Egyptian campaign is an insane game of poker and the stake is far too high for our Republic."

I knew that Joseph and Junot were going to write to Napoleon that very night that my husband had called him a poker player. What I did not know, however, nor anybody else in Paris for that matter, was the fact that sixteen days before, the British under the command of a certain Admiral Nelson had attacked the whole French fleet in the Bay of Aboukir and almost completely wiped it out. Further, since that day Napoleon had been trying desperately to establish contact with France, failing which, he saw that his soldiers and himself would be bound to perish in the burning desert sands. No, nobody could possibly know that on my wedding day Jean-Baptiste Bernadotte foretold exactly what had in fact already happened.

At this stage of the discussion I couldn't help yawning, which is not a very decorous thing for a bride to do. But then, I was getting married for the first time in my life and didn't really know how to behave. Jean-Baptiste noticed it, rose and said:

"It's late, Désirée. I think we ought to go home."

There it was, for the first time, this so personal phrase, 'we ought to go home' . . .

At the bottom end of the table Caroline and Hortense looked at each other darkly and started to giggle. My comfortable Uncle Somis winked at me and patted me as I was saying good-bye to him. "Don't be afraid, little one," he said, "Bernadotte won't eat you."

We drove in the open carriage to Sceaux through a sultry late summer's night. The stars and a round yellow moon seemed to be within arm's reach, and I felt that it might be no accident that our house stood in the Rue de la Lune, Moon Street.

When we entered the house we saw the dining-room brightly lit. Tall candles were burning in the silver candelabra, a present from Josephine and Napoleon. On the table we found a bottle of champagne and glasses and a bowl full of grapes, peaches and marzipan cakes. But the house was silent and there was not a soul to be seen.

"That's Marie's work," I said, smiling.

"No," said Jean-Baptiste, "Fernand's!"

"But I know Marie's marzipan cakes," I said, and ate one.

Jean-Baptiste regarded the bottle thoughtfully. "If we drink any more to-night," he said, "we'll have a dreadful headache to-morrow morning."

I agreed and went to open the glass door leading out into the garden. The scent of roses hung in the air and the chestnut leaves glittered silvery at the edges. Behind me Jean-Baptiste extinguished the candles one by one.

Our bedroom was quite dark. I felt my way to the window and drew back the curtains to let the moonlight in. Jean-Baptiste meanwhile had gone into the little room next to the bedroom and I heard him rummaging for something. Perhaps he wanted to give me time to undress and go to bed, I thought, and felt grateful to him for his consideration. I undressed quickly, went to the wide double bed, found my nightdress spread out on the silk cover, put it on, slipped quickly under the blanket—and screamed at the top of my voice.

"For heaven's sake, Désirée, what is it?" Jean-Baptiste was standing by the bed.

"I don't know. Something pricked me horribly." I moved. "Ow, ow, there it is again!"

Jean-Baptiste lit a candle, and I sat up and threw the blanket back: roses! Roses, roses with prickly thorns!

"What idiot——?" Jean Baptiste started shouting, and then stopped as we stared at the rose-strewn bed in confusion.

I collected the roses as Jean-Baptiste held up the blanket. The bed was full of them, there seemed to be no end to roses and thorns.

"It's probably Fernand's doing," I murmured. "He wanted to give us a surprise."

But Jean-Baptiste would have none of that: "Of course it wasn't Fernand, of course it was Marie! Roses, I ask you, roses in a front-line soldier's bed!"

I put the roses on the bedside table, from which they spread their heavy scent. Suddenly I realised that Jean-Baptiste was looking at me and that I had nothing on but a night-dress. Quickly I sat down on the bed and said, " I am cold. Let me have the blanket back." Immediately he let it drop on me.

It was unbearably hot under the blanket. Yet I covered myself up to the ears and kept my eyes shut, and so I didn't notice that he had put out the candle.

Next morning it came out that Marie and Fernand for the first time had agreed on something. They had agreed to adorn our bridal bed with roses and they had, both of them, forgotten about the thorns.

Jean-Baptiste had taken two months' leave to spend the first weeks of our married life with me. But from the moment that the news of the annihilation of our fleet at Aboukir reached Paris he had to go to the Luxembourg Palace almost every morning to attend, with the Minister of War, the council meetings of the Directors.

He had hired a stable near the house and put two horses in it. Whenever I thought back to my honeymoon weeks I saw myself in the late afternoon standing by the garden gate and waiting for Jean-Baptiste. And as soon as a distant clip-clop of hooves became audible my heart would start beating madly and I would say to myself for the thousandth time that within a second or two Jean-Baptiste would round the corner on one of the horses, that he was my husband really and truly and for ever and that I wasn't dreaming, wasn't dreaming at all. . . . Ten minutes later we would sit under the chestnut tree and drink coffee, and Jean-Baptiste would tell me all the things that would be in the *Moniteur* next morning and also all the things that must not become known on any account. And all the time I would blink contentedly into the setting sun and play with the chestnuts lying about in the grass.

The defeat at Aboukir electrified our enemies. Russia was getting ready for war again, and the Austrians, who only a short time ago had apologised to our Government for the insult to our flag, yes, the Austrians too were once more on the march and nearing our frontiers from Switzerland and from Austria. The Italian states under French sovereignty which Napoleon had so proudly founded received the Austrians with open arms, and everywhere our armies were in panic-stricken flight.

On one of these afternoons Jean-Baptiste was particularly late in returning. As he jumped off his horse he told me, "They've offered me the Supreme Command in Italy. I am to stop the rot and at least attempt to hold Lombardy." We drank our coffee, as evening was falling. After that he fetched a candle and many sheets of paper into the garden and started writing.

135

"Are you going to accept the Command?" I asked once, feeling afraid, much afraid of I don't know what.

He looked up. "I beg your pardon? Oh, I see. Yes, I'll accept if they accept my conditions. I am just drafting them." And on went his pen over sheet after sheet.

Afterwards he went into the house, and there he continued writing. I put his supper on his writing desk, but he didn't notice it and went on writing.

A few days later I heard by chance from Joseph that Jean-Baptiste had handed in to Director Barras an excellent memorandum concerning the Italian front. In it he had stated exactly the number of troops he needed to hold the front and to garrison the rear areas properly.

But the Directors could not agree to his conditions. More men were conscripted, but there were no weapons or uniforms to equip them. Under the circumstances Jean-Baptiste refused the responsibility for the Italian front. So Schérer, the Minister of War, took over the Command himself.

One day two weeks later Jean-Baptiste appeared at home suddenly about lunch time. I was just helping Marie to bottle plums when I saw him, and I ran into the garden to meet him.

"Don't kiss me," I warned him, "I smell of kitchen, we're bottling plums, so many that you won't get anything but plums for the whole of the winter."

"But I shan't be here to eat your plums," he said, and went into the house. "Fernand," he shouted, "Fernand, get the field uniform ready, pack the saddle bags. We leave at seven to-morrow morning. At nine o'clock you'll take my luggage——"

I didn't hear the rest, he had disappeared into the house, and I was left paralysed by the garden gate.

The whole of the afternoon we spent in the garden. The sun had lost its warmth. Withered leaves covered the lawn. Yes, it had turned into autumn overnight. I had my hands folded in my lap and listened to his words and the sound of his voice. Sometimes he spoke to me as to a grown-up person, and then again softly and tenderly as if I were a child.

"You've always known, haven't you, that I would have to go to the front again. You've married a soldier, after all, and you are a sensible woman, you must calm yourself and be brave——"

"I don't want to be brave," I said obstinately.

"Listen, Jourdan has taken over the command of three armies, the Army of the Danube, the so-called Swiss Army and the Observation Army. Masséna is going to try with the Swiss

Army to hold back the enemy at the Swiss border. I am in command of the Observation Army and I am moving up to the Rhine, which I am going to cross at two points, near the Fort Louis du Rhin and between Speyer and Mayence. I demanded thirty thousand men for the conquest and occupation of the Rhineland and they've been promised. But the Government won't be able to keep its promise. Désirée, I'm going to cross the Rhine with a make-believe army, I shall have to beat the enemy with a make-believe army—are you listening, my little one?"

"There's nothing you cannot do, Jean-Baptiste," I said, and I was almost in tears.

He sighed. "The Government unfortunately seems to be of the same opinion as you and will let me cross the Rhine with a bunch of miserably equipped raw recruits."

"'We Generals saved the Republic and we Generals keep it alive'," I murmured, "Napoleon once said to me."

"Naturally! That's what the Republic pays its Generals for. There's nothing peculiar in that."

"The man from whom I bought the plums this morning abused the Government and the Army for all he was worth. He said, 'As long as we had General Bonaparte in Italy we won all the battles and the Austrians begged for peace. As soon as he's away to carry our glory overseas everything is upside down.' Strange, the impression Napoleon's campaign has made on simple people."

"And that Napoleon's defeat at Aboukir has been the signal for a sudden attack of our enemies seems to have escaped your greengrocer. And that Napoleon won battles in Italy but never fortified the conquered territories sufficiently seems to have escaped him too. Now we shall have to hold the frontier with ridiculously small army contingents whilst colleague Bonaparte is sunning himself with his excellently equipped Army on the banks of the Nile and everybody thinks him the strong man!"

"'A King's crown lies in the gutter, and all one need do is to pick it up'," I murmured.

"Who said that?" Jean-Baptiste almost shouted the question.

"Napoleon."

"To you?"

"No, to himself. He was looking into a mirror at the time. I was only standing next to him by chance."

After that we were silent for a long time. Darkness fell, and I could no longer see his face.

The silence was broken by Marie's furious yelling from the

kitchen. "I won't have pistols cleaned on my kitchen table. Take them away, at once!"

We heard Fernand answer in a soothing voice, "Do let me clean them here. I shall put the bullets in outside."

"Take them away, I say," Marie kept on yelling.

"Do you use your pistols in battle?" I asked Jean-Baptiste.

"Very rarely, since I've become a General," he answered out of the dark.

It was a long, long night. For many hours I lay alone in our bed and counted the chimes of the little church of Sceaux, knowing that downstairs in the study Jean-Baptiste was bending over maps and marking them with thin lines and crosses and circles. At last I must have fallen asleep, for suddenly I woke up terrified, feeling that something dreadful had happened. Jean-Baptiste was asleep by my side. My startled movement woke him up.

"What is it?" he murmured.

"I had a dreadful dream," I whispered. "I dreamt that you were riding away—riding to a war."

"I am riding to a war to-morrow," he answered, with the front-line soldier's ability to be wide awake at once as soon as he is woken up. "By the way," he continued, "I want to speak to you about something. Tell me, Désirée, what do you do during the day?"

"Do? What do I do? How do you mean? Yesterday I helped Marie with the plums. And the day before yesterday I went with Julie to her dressmaker, Madame Berthier, the one who fled to England with the aristocrats and has come back now. And last week——"

"Yes, but what do you *do*, Désirée?"

"Nothing, really," I said in confusion.

He put his arm under my head and pressed me to his shoulder. "Désirée, I shouldn't like you to have too much time on your hands when I'm away, and so I thought that you should take lessons."

"Lessons? I haven't had lessons of any kind since I was ten."

"That's why," he answered.

"I went to school when I was six, together with Julie. It was a school kept by nuns in a convent and all convents were dissolved when I was ten. Then Mama wanted to teach me and Julie herself, but it never really came to anything. How long did you go to school, Jean-Baptiste?"

"From my eleventh to my thirteenth year. Then they threw me out."

"Why?"

"One of our teachers was unfair to Fernand."

"And so you told him what you thought of him?"

"No, I hit him."

"I'm sure that was the only thing to do," I said, and snuggled as close up to him as possible. "I thought you'd gone to school for years and years because you are so clever. And the many books you are always reading. . . ."

"At first," he said, "I simply tried to make up for lost time. Then I learnt what they teach you in officers' training schools. But now I have to get to know a lot of other things as well. For instance, if you have to administer occupied territories, you have to have some idea of commerce, of law, of—but anyway, they aren't the kind of things that you need to know, little girl. I thought you should take lessons in music and deportment."

"In deportment? D'you mean dancing? But I can dance. I've danced at home in Marseilles every year on Bastille Day in the Town Hall square."

"No, I didn't mean dancing. Young girls used to learn quite a few other things besides dancing in their boarding-schools. How to bow, for example, or how to invite your guests with a motion of your hand to move from one room into another——"

"Jean-Baptiste," I interrupted him, "we've only got the dining-room! If ever one of your visitors should want to go from the dining-room to your study what need is there for me to make elaborate gestures with my hand?"

"If I am made Military Governor at some place or other then you'll be the first lady of the district and you'll have to receive innumerable dignitaries in your salons."

"Salons!" I was full of indignation. "Jean-Baptiste, are you talking again about castles and mansions?" And I bit him in the shoulder.

"Ow, stop!" he shouted, and I let go.

"You can't imagine," he said, " how, at that time in Vienna, all the Viennese aristocrats and the foreign diplomats waited for the moment when the French Ambassador would compromise his Republic. I am sure they prayed to high heaven that I would eat fish with the wrong knife. We owe it to the Republic, Désirée, to conduct ourselves impeccably." After a while he added, "It would be lovely if you could play the piano, Désirée."

"I don't think it would be lovely."

"But you are musical!"

139

"I don't know about that. I like music very much, yes. Julie plays the piano, but it sounds awful. It's a crime to play the piano badly."

"I should like you to take piano and also a few singing lessons," he said with determination. "I told you about my friend Rodolphe Kreutzer, the violin virtuoso, didn't I? He went with me to Vienna, and he brought a Viennese composer to me in the Embassy. Wait a moment, what was his name? Oh yes, Beethoven. Monsieur Beethoven and Kreutzer played to me many an evening, and I've regretted it ever since that, as a child, I was not taught to play an instrument——" he broke into laughter: "But my mother was glad if she could find the money to buy a new Sunday suit for me." He became serious again, unfortunately. "I do want you to take music lessons. I asked Kreutzer yesterday to give me the address of a music teacher. You'll find it in the drawer of my writing desk. Start on them and write to me regularly how you're getting on."

A cold hand seemed to claw at my heart. Write to me regularly, he had said, write, write, write. Nothing left but writing. . . .

A leaden grey morning light came in through the curtains. I stared at them, I could recognise their colour and pattern clearly. But Jean-Baptiste had fallen asleep again.

Someone hammered at the door. "Half-past six, *mon Général!*" That was Fernand's voice.

Half an hour later we were having breakfast, and for the first time I saw Jean-Baptiste in his field uniform. Neither ribbons nor medals nor sashes relieved its severe dark blue. Hardly, however, had I taken a sip of my coffee when the dreadful business of leave-taking began. Horses whinnied, people knocked at the house door, unfamiliar voices spoke and spurs clanked. Fernand opened the door: "The gentlemen have arrived, sir!"

"Show them in," said Jean-Baptiste, and the next moment the room was full of officers I had never seen before. Jean-Baptiste introduced them casually as 'The gentlemen of my staff,' told them that I was delighted to meet them, and then jumped to his feet: "Ready," he said, "let's go!"

He turned to me: "Good-bye, my little girl. Write often. The War Office will send your letters on to me by special courier. Good-bye, Marie! Look after your mistress!"

With that he went, and all the staff officers disappeared with him. I wanted to kiss him once more, I thought. But the room filled with the grey morning light all at once, started to swirl round me, the yellow flames of the candles on the table flickered strangely, and then all went black.

When I came to I was lying on my bed. A repulsive smell of vinegar surrounded me, and Marie's face hung close to mine.

"You've fainted, Eugenie," said Marie.

I pushed the compress with its nasty smell of vinegar away from my head. "I wanted to kiss him just once more, Marie, just to say good-bye, you know."

SCEAUX near PARIS, New Year's Eve between the years VI and VII. (The last year of the 18th century is just beginning.)

NEW Year bells have torn me out of my terrible dream, the bells of Sceaux village church and the distant ones from Notre-Dame and the other Paris churches. In my dream I was sitting in the little summer house in Marseilles and talking to a man who looked exactly like Jean-Baptiste, but I knew he was our son and not Jean-Baptiste. 'You've missed your deportment lesson, Mama, and your dancing lessons with Monsieur Montel,'' my son said in the voice of Jean-Baptiste. I wanted to explain that I had been far too tired for that. Just then the horrible thing happened: my son shrank, he got smaller and smaller and finally was only just a dwarf, not even knee-high. The dwarf, my son, clung to my knee and whispered, 'Cannon fodder, Mama, I am nothing but cannon fodder and I am ordered to go to the Rhine. I myself rarely use pistols for shooting, but the others do—bang bang!' He was shaking with laughter all the time. A mad fear seized me, I wanted to grab the dwarf to protect him. But he kept slipping from my grasp and under the white garden table. I bent down, but I was so tired, oh so tired and sad. And suddenly Joseph was standing by my side and held out his glass to me: 'Long live the Bernadotte dynasty!' and he laughed bad-temperedly. I caught his eyes, and they were the scintillating ones of Napoleon. At that point the bells struck up and I awoke.

Now I am sitting in Jean-Baptiste's study and have only just managed to find an inch of room among the tomes and maps for my diary. From the streets I can hear merry voices, laughter and tipsy singing. Why is everybody in such good humour when a new year begins? I myself am so unspeakably sad, firstly because Jean-Baptiste and I have quarrelled by letter, and secondly because I am so afraid of this new year.

Well then, let me tell you. The day after Jean-Baptiste's departure I obediently went to the music teacher whom this Rodolphe Kreutzer had recommended. He is a small very thin man who lives in a very untidy room in the Quartier Latin and has draped very dusty laurel wreaths all over his walls. The first thing this little man, whose breath smells abominably, told me was that it was only because of his gouty fingers that he was forced to give lessons. Otherwise he would devote himself entirely to his concerts. Could I pay for twelve lessons in advance? I paid, and then I had to sit down in front of a piano and learn the names of the different notes and which key belongs to which note. Going home after the first lesson I felt dizzy in the carriage and was afraid I might faint again. But I got home, and since then I have been going to the Quartier Latin twice a week. Also I hired a piano to practise at home. Jean-Baptiste wanted me to buy the instrument, but I thought it a pity to spend all that money.

Every day I read in the *Moniteur* that Jean-Baptiste is marching triumphantly through Germany. Yet although he writes almost every day he never mentions the war. On the other hand he never forgets to ask how I am getting on with my lessons.

I am a very bad correspondent, and therefore my letters are always short and I can't put in what I really want to tell him so badly, that without him I am very unhappy and that I am longing for him. He now writes like an old uncle! He stresses the importance of continuing my 'studies', and when he realised that I didn't even want to start them he wrote: 'Although I very much want to see you again I set great store by the completion of your education. Music and dancing are essential things, and I do recommend some lessons with Monsieur Montel. However, I notice that I am giving you too much advice and I finish for to-day by kissing your lips. Your J.—Bernadotte who loves you very much.'

Was that a lover's letter? I was so annoyed about it that in my next letter I didn't mention his advice at all and didn't tell him either that I was now having lessons with this Monsieur Montel. God alone knows who recommended this man to him, this perfumed ballet dancer, this cross between a bishop and a ballerina who makes me curtsey 'gracefully' to invisible dignitaries, walk up to equally invisible old ladies and conduct them to an invisible sofa whilst all the time he hops around me to check the effect. One might almost think that he was preparing me for a royal reception, me, a convinced Republican.

As I had written nothing about my lessons in deportment the

142

courier brought me one day the following letter from my Jean-Baptiste: 'You say nothing about your progress in music, dancing and other subjects. While I am so far away I hope that my little girl will make the best of her lessons. Your J.— Bernadotte.'

This letter came on a morning when I was particularly wretched and in no mood for getting up at all. I was feeling very lonely in the wide double bed, didn't even want to see Julie when she called, didn't want to think about anything at all. Then the letter arrived. The letterhead of the official notepaper which Jean-Baptiste uses for his private correspondence as well says: *République Française*, and underneath, *Liberté— Egalité*. Why, I clenched my teeth, why should I, the daughter of a worthy silk merchant from Marseilles, be educated into a 'fine lady'? Jean-Baptiste, I thought, is probably a great General and one of the 'coming men', but for all that he comes from a very humble family, and anyway, in a Republic all citizens are equal and I don't want to come into circles where you direct your guests about with affected gestures of the hand.

I got up and wrote him a long, furious letter. I cried as I wrote it and the ink ran. I hadn't married a preacher, I said, but a man of whom I thought that he understood me. And as for that man with the odious-smelling breath who made me do finger practice and that perfumed Monsieur Montel, they could go to the devil, I had had enough of them, enough, enough. . . .

Without reading the letter through I sealed it quickly and told Marie to get a cab and take it immediately to the War Office to be passed on from there to General Bernadotte. Of course, next day I was afraid that Jean-Baptiste would be really angry. I went to Montel for my lesson and afterwards practised scales for two hours on the piano and attempted the Mozart minuet with which I want to surprise Jean-Baptiste when he gets home.

I felt grey and sad and forsaken, as sad and forsaken as our garden with its bare chestnut tree. A whole week crept by till at last Jean-Baptiste's answer came. 'You have not told me,' he wrote, 'you have not told me yet, my dear Désirée, what it was that offended you in my letter. I do not at all want to treat you like a child but like a loving and understanding wife. All I said should have convinced you that——' And then he started off again on the completion of my education and told me unctuously that one gains knowledge 'by hard and persistent work'. In the final sentence he wrote: 'Write and tell me that you love me!'

This letter I haven't answered yet, for something has

143

happened meanwhile which made any further letter-writing impossible.

Yesterday morning I was, as so often before, sitting by myself in Jean-Baptiste's study twirling the globe on a little table and wondering about the many countries and continents of which I knew nothing. Marie came in and brought me some broth. "Drink that," she said, "you must eat things now that'll make you strong."

"Why? I am very well. I'm even getting fatter all the time. The yellow silk dress hardly fits me round the waist now." I pushed the cup away. "Besides, I hate greasy things."

Marie turned to go. "You've got to force yourself to eat. And you know quite well why."

I was startled. "Why?"

Marie smiled, came suddenly back to me and made to take me into her arms: "You do know, don't you?"

But I pushed her away and shouted at her, "No, I don't! And it isn't true either, I know it isn't!" With that I ran up to the bedroom, locked the door behind me and threw myself down on to the bed.

Naturally the thought had occurred to me, of course it had. But I didn't want to admit it. 'It can't be true,' I thought, 'it's quite out of the question, it—it would be dreadful if it were true. It can happen that for some reason or other one can miss a period, or even two in succession, perhaps even three. It can happen, can't it?'

I hadn't told Julie anything about it, for if she knew she'd drag me to a doctor. And I didn't want to be examined, I didn't want to be told that——

And now Marie knew it. I stared up to the ceiling and tried to think it out. It's something quite natural, I told myself, something quite natural, all women have children. There were Mama, and Suzanne, and—well, Julie has been to two doctors already because she so badly wants children and hasn't got any yet. But children are such a dreadful responsibility, one needs to know such a lot oneself in order to bring them up and explain to them the things that are right and the things that are wrong. And I know so little myself. . . .

Perhaps it would be a little boy with dark curly hair like Jean-Baptiste himself? And perhaps one day this little image of Jean-Baptiste would be killed in the Rhineland or Italy like so many of the sixteen-year-olds whom they are conscripting even now to defend our frontiers? Or perhaps he himself would use a pistol and kill other people's little boys?

I pressed my hand on my stomach. Was there really a new

little human being in there? What a preposterous thought! But at the same time it flashed through my mind that it would be *my* little human being, a little part of my own self, and for the fraction of a second I was happy. Then I tried to see it differently. *My* little human being? No, impossible, no man can be owned by another man. And was there any reason why my son should always be able to understand me? What about me and Mama, for instance? How often do I find her views old-fashioned, how often do I tell her white lies! And precisely the same thing would happen between my son and myself: he would lie to me, find me old-fashioned, be annoyed by me. You little fiend in my body, I thought angrily, *I* didn't ask for you to come.

Marie knocked on the door, but I didn't open. I heard her going back into the kitchen, heard her returning and knocking again. This time I let her in. "I warmed the soup up for you," she said.

I asked her: "Marie, at that time when you were expecting your little Pierre, did you feel very happy?"

Marie sat down on the edge of the bed. "No, of course not," she said, "I wasn't married, you see."

Very hesitantly I said: "I heard that you—I mean if you don't want children you can—there are women, I mean, who could help you."

Marie looked at me very intently. "Yes," she said slowly, "there are. My sister went to a woman like that. She has too many children as it is and doesn't want any more. Yes, and afterwards she was ill for a long time. And now she can't have any more children. And she will never be really right again either. But great ladies such as Madame Tallien or Madame Josephine, they are sure to know a proper doctor who would help. But it's against the law, you know."

She paused. I lay with eyes closed and pressed my hand to my stomach. It was flat, quite flat, my stomach.

"So you want the baby done away with?" I heard Marie ask. "No!"

I shouted it involuntarily. Marie got up and seemed satisfied. "Come, eat your soup," she said tenderly. "And then write and tell the General. He'll be pleased."

I shook my head. "No, I can't write things like that. I wish I could say it to him."

I drank my soup, dressed, went to Monsieur Montel and learned some more dancing steps.

This morning I had a great surprise. Josephine came to see me. Up till now she had only been twice, and every time together with Julie and Joseph. But from the way she behaved there was nothing to show that there was anything unusual about her sudden visit. She was magnificently dressed in a white frock of thin woollen material, a short very close-fitting ermine jacket and a high black hat with a white feather. But the light of the grey winter morning was not kind to her features: when she laughed it showed up all the many wrinkles round her eyes and her lips seemed very dry and unevenly painted.

"I wanted to see for myself how you are getting on as a grass widow, Madame," she said, and added, "We grass widows must stand by each other, must we not?"

Marie brought hot chocolate for us grass widows, and I asked politely: "Do you hear regularly from General Bonaparte?"

"No, not very regularly. He's lost his fleet and the British have cut his communications. Only now and then a small ship manages to get through the blockade."

I had nothing to say to that. Josephine looked round and saw the piano. "Julie has told me," she remarked, "that you are taking music lessons."

I nodded. "Do you play the piano?"

"Of course," said the former viscountess, "I have played since I was six."

"I'm also taking dancing lessons," I went on. "I don't want to disgrace Bernadotte."

Josephine took one of the marzipan cakes. "It's no simple matter to be married to a General—I mean a General who is away, in the war. Misunderstandings arise so easily when you are separated."

'Heaven knows she's right,' I thought, and remembered my stupid exchange of letters. "One can't write everything one wants to write," I said.

"Exactly!" Josephine agreed readily. "But there are always other people who interfere and write malicious letters. Joseph, for example, our brother-in-law." She pulled out a lace handkerchief and put it to her lips. "Joseph, let me tell you, wants to write to Bonaparte to tell him that he called on me yesterday at Malmaison and found Hippolyte Charles there—you remember Hippolyte, don't you? That charming young army contractor?—well, that he found Hippolyte there in his dressing-gown. So he wants to bother Bonaparte, who has other things to think of just now, with a trifling thing like that."

"Why in the world does Monsieur Charles want to walk about Malmaison in a dressing-gown?" I really couldn't understand why he chose this type of clothing for his visits.

"It was nine o'clock in the morning," said Josephine, "and he hadn't yet finished his toilet. Joseph's visit was a surprise, you know."

I didn't know what to say to that.

"I need company, I can't stand being left to myself so much, I have never been alone in all my life," she said, and tears came into her eyes. "And as we grass widows must stand together against our brother-in-law I thought that you might have a word with your sister. Perhaps she could influence Joseph not to say anything to Bonaparte."

So that was what she wanted. "Julie has no influence whatever on Joseph's actions," I said truthfully.

Josephine looked frightened. "You refuse to help me?"

I said that I was going to a New Year's Eve celebration at Joseph's house to-night and that I would have a word with Julie. "But you mustn't expect too much, Madame," I added.

Josephine was visibly relieved. "I knew you would not desert me, I knew! Tell me, why do I never see you at Theresa Tallien's? A fortnight ago she had a baby. You simply must come and see it." Walking towards the door she turned round once more: "Life isn't too boring for you in Paris, Madame, is it? We must go to the theatre together some time. And please, tell your sister that he can write to Bonaparte as much as he likes, only I'd rather he omitted all mention of the dressing-gown!"

I drove to the Rue du Rocher half an hour earlier than expected. Julie, in a new red frock which didn't suit her at all, fluttered in confusion across the drawing-room, arranging and re-arranging the little silver horse-shoes which she had put on the table to ensure a happy new year for all of us.

"Louis Bonaparte will be your neighbour at table," she said. "The fat fellow is so boring, I really don't know whom else I dare bother with him."

"I wanted to ask you something," I said. "Couldn't you ask Joseph not to mention the dressing-gown to Napoleon, I mean the dressing-gown of this gentleman Charles at Malmaison?"

"The letter to Napoleon has gone. Any further discussion is useless," said Joseph, entering at this moment. He went to the sideboard and poured himself a glass of cognac. "I wager Josephine came to your house to-day to ask for your good offices. Is that right, Désirée?"

I shrugged my shoulders.

"It's a mystery to me why you are on her side instead of on ours," Joseph continued indignantly.

"Whose do you mean by ours?" I asked.

"Mine and Napoleon's of course."

"You are not concerned in it at all. And Napoleon in Egypt can't undo what has been done. It would only grieve him. Is there any need for that?"

Joseph looked at me with great interest. "So you are still in love with him! How touching!" he scoffed. "I thought you had forgotten all about him!"

"Forgotten?" I was amazed. "How can you ever forget the first time you were in love? Napoleon himself, good God, I hardly ever think of him, but the wild heart throbs, the happiness and all the pain and suffering that followed it, I'll never forget those!"

"And that's why you want to save him a great disappointment now?" Joseph appeared to find this conversation amusing. He poured himself another drink.

"Yes. I know what such a disappointment feels like."

Joseph grinned. "But my letter is on its way already."

"In that case there's no sense in continuing to talk about it."

Joseph meanwhile had poured out two more drinks. "Come on, girls," he said, "now let's wish each other a happy New Year, you must put yourself into a cheerful mood. Any moment the first visitors may arrive."

Obediently Julie and I took the glasses. But I had not even touched the cognac when I suddenly felt very sick. The smell was repellent to me, and I put the glass back on the sideboard.

"What's the matter with you?" Julie exclaimed. "You're green in the face."

I felt beads of perspiration on my forehead, dropped on to a chair and shook my head. "No no, it's nothing. I feel like that so often now." I shut my eyes.

"Perhaps she is going to have a baby," I heard Joseph say.

"Impossible. She would have told me," Julie contradicted him.

"If she's ill I'll have to write and tell Bernadotte at once," said Joseph.

Quickly I opened my eyes. "Don't you dare, Joseph! You won't breathe a word. I want to surprise him."

"With what?" both of them asked at the same time.

"With a son," I said, and suddenly I felt very proud.

Julie knelt down by my side and took me in her arms. Joseph said, "But perhaps it's going to be a girl."

"No, it'll be a son," I declared. "Bernadotte is not a man for daughters." I rose from the chair. "And now I'm going home. Don't be annoyed, please, I'd rather like to lie down and sleep into the new year."

Joseph had filled the glasses again, and he and Julie drank my health, Julie with tears in her eyes.

"Long live the Bernadotte dynasty," Joseph said, and laughed.

The joke pleased me. "Yes, let's hope for the best for the Bernadotte dynasty," I said. Then I left for home.

But the bells wouldn't let me sleep into the new year. Now they've finished, and we've been in the Year VII for quite a while now. Somewhere in Germany Jean-Baptiste is celebrating the New Year with his staff. They may even be drinking my health. But I'm facing the new year alone.

No, not quite alone. Now there are two of us wandering into the future; you, my little son as yet unborn, and I, and we hope for the best, don't we? For the Bernadotte dynasty!

SCEAUX near PARIS
17th Messidor of the Year VII
(Mama would probably write July 4th, 1799.)

MY son arrived eight hours ago.

He has dark, silky hair. But Marie says he'll probably lose his first hair anyway.

His eyes are dark blue. But Marie says that all newly born children have blue eyes.

I am so weak that everything quivers before my eyes, and they would be very annoyed if they knew that Marie had given in and secretly brought me my diary. The midwife even thinks that I shan't survive, but the doctor says that he'll get me through all right. I've lost lots of blood, and they've somehow managed to raise the lower bedposts to stop the bleeding.

Jean-Baptiste's voice comes from downstairs.

My dear, dear Jean-Baptiste.

Jean-Baptiste!

My beloved Jean-Ba——.

SCEAUX near PARIS
One week later.

Now not even that giantess, my midwife, believes that I shall die in childbirth. I am sitting in bed propped up by many cushions, Marie brings me all my favourite dishes, and in the morning and evening France's Minister of War sits by my bedside and gives me long lectures on how to bring up children.

About two months ago Jean-Baptiste returned out of the blue.

After New Year's Day I had taken myself in hand and written to him again, short notes and not at all loving ones, because I did want him back so badly and at the same time was so angry with him. I read in the *Moniteur* that he had taken Philippsburg, which was defended by 1500 men, with a force of 300, and that he had taken up his headquarters near a town called Germersheim. From there he went on to Mannheim, conquered the city and became Governor of Hesse. He governed the Germans of this territory according to the laws of our Republic, prohibited flogging, put an end to the ghettoes and received enthusiastic addresses of thanks from the universities of Heidelberg and Giessen. There must be some very strange races about: as long as you don't conquer them they think themselves for unknown reasons to be cleverer and better than anybody else in the world. But once you've beaten them they're full of unimaginable weeping and gnashing of teeth, and many of them maintain that secretly they've been on the side of their enemy all the time!

After his victories Barras recalled Jean-Baptiste to Paris.

One afternoon I was sitting by the piano as usual practising the Mozart minuet which by now wasn't going too badly when I heard the door open behind me. "Marie," I said, "this is my surprise for our General, the minuet. It doesn't sound too bad now, does it?"

"It sounds wonderful, Désirée, and it is a very great surprise for your General!" said Jean-Baptiste's voice, and he took me in his arms. After two kisses it was as if he had never been away.

As I was laying the table I tried to think how to tell him about our baby coming. But his eagle eye misses nothing, and quite suddenly he asked:

"Tell me, my girl, why didn't you write that we were going to have a son?" He, too, never thought for a moment that we might have a daughter!

I put my hands on my hips, frowned and tried to look annoyed: "Because I didn't want to trouble my preacher! You'd have been desperate at the thought that I might be forced to interrupt my education!" I went up to him: "But, my dear great General, you may be easy in your mind: your son may not be born yet, but he has already started his lessons in deportment with Monsieur Montel!"

Jean-Baptiste at once forbade me to take any more lessons. If he had had his way he wouldn't have let me out of the house, so concerned was he about my health!

Although all Paris talked of nothing but the political crisis caused by the Royalists on the Right and the Jacobins on the extreme Left and feared new riots, I myself noticed very little of it. The chestnut tree blossomed white, and I sat under its broad branches sewing baby-clothes. Julie, who came every day and helped with the sewing, sat with me, hoping that I should 'infect' her: she wants a child so badly, and she doesn't mind at all whether boy or girl. In the afternoon Joseph and Lucien Bonaparte came round quite often and talked at Jean-Baptiste.

Apparently Barras made an offer to Jean-Baptiste which he indignantly rejected. Barras is the only one of our five Directors who matters, and all political parties are dissatisfied with their more or less corrupt practices. Barras had the idea of exploiting this dissatisfaction, getting rid of three of his co-Directors and then carrying on the Directorate with Sieyès, an old Jacobin. As he was afraid that his projected *coup d'état* might lead to riots he asked Jean-Baptiste to assist him as his military adviser. This Jean-Baptiste refused. Barras, he told him, should stand by the Constitution, and if he wanted a change in it he should put it before the Assembly.

Joseph thought my husband crazy. "You," he exclaimed, "with the help of your troops could be the dictator of France to-morrow!"

"Quite!" said Jean-Baptiste calmly, "and I want to avoid that. You seem to forget, Monsieur Bonaparte, that I am a convinced Republican!"

"But it might be in the interests of the Republic if in critical times a General were at the head of the Government or, at any rate, backed it up," said Lucien thoughtfully.

Jean-Baptiste shook his head. "A change in the Constitution is the business of the representatives of the people. We have two Houses: the Council of Five Hundred to which you, Lucien, belong, and the Council of Ancients to which you may one day belong when you reach the age necessary for membership. It is they who have to decide about the Constitution, but certainly not the Army or one of its Generals. However, I'm afraid we are boring the ladies. By the way, Désirée, what is that funny thing you are working on?"

"A jacket for your son, Jean-Baptiste."

About six weeks ago, on the 30th Prairial, Barras succeeded in inducing three of his co-Directors to retire. Now he, together with Sieyès, was the master of our Republic. The dominant parties of the Left demanded the appointment of new ministers. Our Minister to Geneva, a Monsieur Reinhart, replaced Talley-rand as Minister of Foreign Affairs, and our most famous lawyer and gourmet, Monsieur Cambacérès, took over the Ministry of Justice. But as we are involved in war on all our frontiers and can defend the Republic in the long run only if the Army is thoroughly reorganised, everything depends on the choice of the new Minister of War.

Early in the morning of the 15th Messidor a messenger appeared from the Luxembourg Palace to order Jean-Baptiste to go at once to see the two Directors. Jean-Baptiste rode away, and I sat the whole morning under the chestnut tree. I was annoyed with myself, because last night I had eaten a whole pound of cherries at one sitting, and now they were rumbling about in my stomach and making themselves more and more disagreeable. Suddenly I felt as if a knife were thrust into my body. The pain only lasted the fraction of a second, but after it had gone I sat there paralysed. Oh God, how that hurt! "Marie," I called out, "Marie!"

Marie came, saw me and said: "Up into the bedroom with you! I'll send Fernand for the midwife!"

"But surely, it's only last night's cherries!"

"Up into the bedroom!" Marie repeated, and pulled me up. The knife-thrust pain did not come again, and, relieved, I went upstairs. I heard Marie despatching Fernand, who had returned from Germany together with Jean-Baptiste. "At last he's of some use," she said, coming back into the bedroom with three sheets, which she spread over the bed.

"I'm sure it's only the cherries," I said obstinately. But I hadn't finished speaking when the knife thrust again and pierced me right through from the back. I screamed, and when the pain had passed I started to weep.

"Aren't you ashamed of yourself? Stop blubbering!" Marie shouted at me. But I could tell by her face that she was sorry for me.

"I want Julie, I want Julie!" I wailed. Julie would pity me, and I did so want to be pitied.

Fernand arrived with the midwife and was sent straight away to Julie.

Oh that midwife! That midwife! She had examined me a few times during the last few months, and there had always been something uncanny about her. But she appeared to me like some giantess out of a tale of horror. She had powerful red arms, a broad red face and a real moustache. The weirdest thing, however, was that this female grenadier had painted her lips heavily under the moustache and wore a coquettish white lace cap on the untidy grey hair.

The giantess looked me over carefully and, I thought, contemptuously.

"No hurry," she said, "with you it'll take a long time."

At the same time Marie said that she had hot water ready

down in the kitchen. But the giantess said: "No hurry! Better put some coffee on the fire!"

"Strong coffee, I take it? To cheer Madame up?" enquired Marie.

"No, to cheer *me* up," said the giantess.

An endless afternoon passed into an endless evening, the evening into an endless night. A grey dawn came and hung over the room for an eternity, then followed a burning hot morning which seemed to last for ever, then another afternoon, an evening, a night. But by then I could no longer distinguish the times of day. The knife thrust through me without interruption, and as from a great distance I heard someone scream, scream, scream. In the intervals between the thrusts all went black before my eyes. Then they poured brandy down my throat, and I was sick and could not breathe, sank back into blackness and was torn awake again into horrible pains.

Sometimes I felt that Julie was near. Someone kept wiping the perspiration from my forehead and face. My shift stuck to me, and then Marie said in her quiet voice: "You must help us, Eugenie, you must help us!"

Like a monster the giantess bent over me, the flickering candlelight threw her shapeless shadow against the wall. Was it the same night still or was it the next? "Leave me alone," I cried, "leave me alone," and my fists beat the air around me wildly. They all shrank back, and then Jean-Baptiste sat on my bed, held me tightly in his arms, and I put my face against his cheek. The knife was thrusting again, but Jean-Baptiste did not let go of me.

"Why aren't you in Paris in the Luxembourg Palace? They sent for you, didn't they?" I said in a strange, panting voice during a short spell of painlessness.

"It's night," he said.

"And they didn't tell you to go away to another war?"

"No, no, I am staying here now, I am now——"

I didn't hear the rest of what he said; the knife was at work again, and a wave of immeasurable pain closed over my senses.

A moment came in which I felt actually well. The pain had ceased, and I was so weak that I couldn't think. It felt like floating along on waves, floating along not seeing anything. But I heard. Yes, I heard! "Hasn't the doctor come yet? If he isn't here soon, it'll be too late!" This was spoken by a voice pitched high in excitement, a voice strange to me. But why a doctor? I was all right now, I was floating along on waves, the waves of the Seine with the many lights dancing up and down. . . .

Someone poured burning hot, bitter-tasting coffee into my mouth. My eyes blinked, and I noticed that it was the giantess who spoke in that excited high-pitched voice. "If the doctor isn't here within a minute——" I heard her say. Funny, I should have thought it impossible that such a mighty woman could have a voice like that. But why this fuss about the doctor? The worst was over now, wasn't it?

But it wasn't, it was only beginning.

I heard voices from the door. "Please wait in the living-room, your Excellency. Calm yourself, your Excellency, I assure you, your Excellency——"

Excellency, Excellency? What was an Excellency doing in my room?

"I implore you, doctor——" That was Jean-Baptiste's voice. Jean-Baptiste, Jean-Baptiste, you must not go away. . . .

The doctor gave me a camphor injection and told the giantess to prop me up by the shoulders. I had come to again and saw Julie and Marie standing on either side of the bed holding candelabra.

The doctor was a small thin man in a dark suit. I couldn't see his face, but I saw something flashing in his hands. "A knife," I screamed, "he's got a knife."

"No, only a forceps," said Marie calmly. "Don't scream, Eugenie!"

But perhaps he had had a knife after all, for once again the dreadful pain pierced my body exactly as before, only faster, faster, faster still and finally without any interruption whatever till I felt that I was torn here, torn there, torn completely to pieces. I fell into a bottomless pit, and all went black again.

Coming to, I heard the giantess's voice again, but now as coarse and indifferent as before: "She'll be finished soon, Doctor Moulin."

"She might get through, citizeness, if only we could stop the hæmorrhage."

Something was whimpering somewhere in the room. I should have liked so much to open my eyes, but the lids were like lead.

"Jean-Baptiste, a son, a wonderful small son," sobbed Julie.

And all of a sudden I could open my eyes, wide. Jean-Baptiste had a son. Julie held a little white bundle in her arms, and Jean-Baptiste was standing next to her. "I didn't know how small a small child is!" he said in amazement, turned and came to my bed. He knelt down, took my hand and put it against his cheek. It felt unshaven and wet, yes, quite wet. So Generals too could weep?

"We have a wonderful son," he said, "but he is still very small."

"They always are, in the beginning," I said with difficulty.

Julie showed me the bundle. A face as red as a lobster could be seen among its white coverings. Its eyes were closed and it had an air of being offended. Perhaps it hadn't wanted to be born?

"I must ask everybody to leave the room. The wife of the Minister of War needs rest," the doctor said.

"The wife of the Minister of War? Does he mean me, Jean-Baptiste?"

"Yes, I became France's Minister of War the day before yesterday."

"And I haven't even congratulated you on it," I whispered.

"You were busy," he said, and smiled.

Julie put the bundle into its cot. Only the doctor and the giantess were left with me in the room, and I fell asleep.

Oscar!

It was quite a new name to me. Os—car. . . . Really and truly, it didn't sound too bad. It was supposed to be a Nordic name, this Oscar, and that's what we called our son.

It was Napoleon's idea. He wanted to be godfather. The name Oscar occurred to him because he was reading the Celtic songs of Ossian in his desert tent. When one of Joseph's talkative letters to Napoleon reached him with the news of my pregnancy, he wrote back: "If it is a son Eugenie must call him Oscar. And I want to be his godfather!" Jean-Baptiste, who, as the father, had some say in the matter after all, he didn't mention at all. But Jean-Baptiste, when we showed him the letter, smiled.

"We don't want to offend your old admirer, my little girl," he said. "As far as I am concerned he can be our boy's godfather, and Julie can represent him at the christening. The name of Oscar——"

"It's a dreadful name," said Marie, who happened to be in the room just then.

"It's the name of a Nordic hero," put in Julie, who had brought Napoleon's letter.

"But our son is neither Nordic nor a hero," I said, and looked at his tiny face in my arms. It was no longer red but yellow from jaundice. But Marie insisted that most new babies get jaundice a few days after their birth.

"Oscar Bernadotte sounds good," said Jean-Baptiste, and there the matter ended as far as he was concerned. "In a fortnight's time," he added, "we shall leave here, Désirée, if you agree."

A fortnight later we were going to move into a new house. The Minister of War is obliged to live in Paris, and therefore Jean-Baptiste bought a small villa in the Rue Cisalpine, between the Rue Courcelles and the Rue du Rocher, quite close to Julie.

The new house wouldn't be much bigger than the little house in Sceaux. But at any rate it would give us, apart from our own bedroom, a proper children's bedroom, and downstairs we would have not only a dining-room but also a reception room, so that Jean-Baptiste would have somewhere to entertain the officials and politicians who often come to him in the evening. Up till now our social life has gone on in the dining-room.

I myself am now on top of the world. Marie cooks all my favourite dishes, and I am no longer so dreadfully feeble. I can even sit up in bed without any help. Unfortunately, however, I have too many visitors, and that is rather a strain. Josephine called and even Madame Tallien and that authoress with a face like a full moon, Madame de Staël, whom I only know very casually. Besides, Joseph solemnly handed me a novel he has written which makes him feel like a great writer. Its name is *Moïna* or *The peasant girl from Saint-Denis*, and it is so boring and sentimental that every time I start reading it I fall asleep. But Julie never stops asking me: "Isn't it wonderful?"

I know, of course, that all the visits are not meant for me personally nor for my son Oscar but for the wife of the War Minister. This moon-faced woman Madame de Staël, who, by the way, is the wife of the Swedish Minister but doesn't live with him, this Madame de Staël told me that France at last had found the man to put her affairs in order, and that everybody regarded Jean-Baptiste as the real head of the Government.

I read Jean-Baptiste's Proclamation which on the day of his appointment he addressed 'To the Soldiers of France!' It was so beautiful that I cried as I read it. 'I have seen your dreadful privation,' Jean-Baptiste said in it, 'and I need not ask you whether you know that I have shared it. I swear to you that I shall not give myself a moment's rest till I have found for you your bread, your clothing and your arms. And you, comrades, you will swear to me that you are going to defeat once again the dreadful coalition against France. We shall stand by the oaths we are taking.'

When Jean-Baptiste comes home at eight o'clock in the evening from the Ministry he eats his meal by my bedside, and then he goes to his study, where he dictates to his secretary till deep into the night. And at six o'clock in the morning he is on his way again to the Rue de Varennes, where the War Office is housed at the moment. I know from Fernand that the camp bed down in Jean-Baptiste's study is quite often not used at all. I think it awful that my husband is supposed to save our Republic single-handed. And to crown all, the Government hasn't even enough money to buy arms and uniforms for the

90,000 recruits whom Jean-Baptiste has in training, and there are stormy scenes between him and Director Sieyès.

If Jean-Baptiste could at least be left alone in the evenings when he wants to work at home! But there are always people coming and going. Jean-Baptiste told me only yesterday that the representatives of all the parties are doing their best to get him to support their side.

One evening, just as, weary and exhausted, he was gobbling down his evening meal, Fernand announced that 'a Monsieur Chiappe', who didn't want to say what he had come for, was waiting downstairs. Jean-Baptiste rose hurriedly and ran down to get rid of this mysterious Monsieur Chiappe. After a quarter of an hour he was back in our room, his face red with fury.

"This Chiappe," he said, "has been sent to me by the Duc d'Enghien. The cheek of it! What Bourbon impudence!"

"And who is the Duc d'Enghien, if I may ask?"

"Louis de Bourbon Condé, Duc d'Enghien. He is the ablest member of the Bourbon family, works for the British and is somewhere in Germany. If I seize power and give France back to the Bourbons they want to make me Constable of France and goodness knows what else. The impudence of it!"

"And what did you answer?"

"I threw him out. And told him to tell his chiefs that I am a convinced Republican."

"Everybody says that it's you who really governs France now. Could you overthrow the Directors and become Director yourself, if you wanted to?" I asked cautiously.

"Of course," said Jean-Baptiste calmly, "of course I could. The Jacobins even proposed something like this to me, the Jacobins and some of our Generals. I need only say the word and they would make me Director and give me much greater powers than the Directors have now."

"And you refused?"

"Naturally. I stand by the Constitution."

Just then Fernand announced Joseph, my brother-in-law. Jean-Baptiste groaned. "Really, that's the last straw! Well, Fernand, let him come in."

Joseph came in, and bent first over the cot and said that Oscar was the most beautiful baby he had ever seen. Then he wanted Jean-Baptiste to go down with him into the study. "I should like to ask you something and it would only bore Désirée," he said.

Jean-Baptiste shook his head. "I see so little of Désirée, I prefer to stay here with her. Sit down, Bonaparte, and be brief, I have plenty of work to do yet."

So they both sat down by my bed. Jean-Baptiste took my hand in his, and its light touch sent a feeling of serene confidence and strength across to me. I closed my eyes.

"It concerns Napoleon," I heard Joseph say. "What would your attitude be should Napoleon wish to return to France?"

"I should say that Napoleon could not return as long as the Minister of War had not recalled him."

"Bernadotte, let's be perfectly frank: a commander of Napoleon's importance is, at this moment, completely wasted on the Egyptian front. Since the destruction of our fleet the campaign there has more or less come to a standstill. The Egyptian campaign therefore can——"

"Be called a fiasco, which is precisely what I prophesied."

"I hadn't intended to express myself quite like that. However, as no decisive developments are to be expected in Africa, it would perhaps be possible to use my brother's abilities on other fronts to greater advantage. Besides, Napoleon is not only just a strategist. You yourself know his interest in organisation, and he could be of great help to you here in Paris in reorganising the Army. Moreover,"—here Joseph hesitated and waited for Jean-Baptiste to say something, but Jean-Baptiste remained silent. So Joseph went on: "You know that there are quite a number of plots being hatched against the Government?"

"As the Minister of War I am not quite ignorant about that. But what has that got to do with the Commander-in-Chief of our Army in Egypt?"

"The Republic needs a—needs several strong men. In times of war France cannot afford party intrigues and internal differences."

"If I understand you right you are suggesting that I am to recall your brother to deal with the different plots, are you not?"

"Yes, I thought that——"

"To deal with conspiracies is a matter for the police and for no one else."

"Quite, if the conspiracies are directed against the State. But I can tell you that influential circles are thinking of bringing about a concentration of all positive political forces."

"What do you mean by 'concentration of all positive political forces'?"

"For instance, if you yourself and Napoleon, the two ablest men of the Republic——"

Bernadotte cut him short: "Stop talking nonsense! Why don't you say simply: 'In order to free the Republic from party politics certain persons are contemplating the introduction of a dictatorship. My brother Napoleon wishes to be recalled from Egypt in order to apply for the position of dictator.' Why don't you simply say that and have done with it, Bonaparte!"

Joseph, disagreeably surprised, cleared his throat. Then he said: "I've seen Talleyrand to-day. The ex-minister thinks that Director Sieyès would not be disinclined to support a change of the Constitution."

"I know exactly what Talleyrand thinks, I also know what some of the Jacobins want, and I can even tell you that above all the Royalists have pinned all their hopes on a dictatorship. As for me, I have taken the oath to the Republic and I shall be loyal to our Constitution whatever happens. Is my answer clear enough?"

"You will appreciate that a man like Napoleon is bound to be driven to despair by his enforced idleness in Egypt. Moreover, my brother wants to settle some important private affairs here in Paris. He wants to divorce Josephine, whose unfaithfulness has wounded him deeply. If my brother in his distress decided to return without your authority, what would happen then?"

For one moment Jean-Baptiste's fingers closed round my hand with an iron grip. Then they relaxed and I heard him say calmly: "In that case I, as the Minister of War, should be compelled to court-martial your brother, and I suppose that he would be condemned as a deserter and shot."

"But Napoleon, the great patriot that he is, can no longer, in Africa——"

"A Commander-in-Chief has to remain with his troops. He led them into the desert, and he has to stay with them till they can be brought back. Even a civilian like you must realise that, Monsieur Bonaparte."

After he had finished, an uncomfortable silence reigned in the room.

At last I said: "Your novel, Joseph, is a most exciting book."

"Yes," he replied with his usual modesty, "everybody congratulates me on it."

He rose and Jean-Baptiste accompanied him downstairs.

I tried to get some sleep. In the uneasy state between sleeping and waking I recalled a little girl racing a nondescript thin officer till they stopped by a moonlit hedge. "I, for example, I know my destiny," the officer said and the young girl giggled. "You'll believe in me, Eugenie, whatever happens, won't you?"

I felt certain, suddenly, that Napoleon would return from Egypt. Some day he'd simply turn up and overthrow the Republic if he had the chance. He doesn't care for the

Republic nor for the rights of its citizens, and he just doesn't understand men like Jean-Baptiste, he never has and he never will. I remember what my father said: "My little daughter, whenever and wherever in days to come men deprive their brothers of their right to liberty and equality no one will ever be able to say of them: 'Lord forgive them for they know not what they do'."

At eleven o'clock Marie entered, took Oscar out of his cot and put him to my breast. Jean-Baptiste came up too. He knows that Oscar gets his supper at this time.

"He'll come back, Jean-Baptiste," I said.

"Who?"

"Our son's godfather. What are you going to do?"

"If I get the necessary powers I'll have him shot."

"And if you don't?"

"Then he'll take them himself and have me shot. Good-night, my girl."

"Good-night, Jean-Baptiste."

"And don't think of it any more. I was only joking."

"I understand, Jean-Baptiste. Good-night!"

PARIS, 18th Brumaire of the Year VII. (Abroad they would say November 9th, 1799. Our Republic gets a new Constitution!)

HE did come back!

And to-day he brought about a *coup d'état* and became the head of France's Government a few hours ago!

Several Deputies and some Generals have already been arrested and Jean-Baptiste said that we may at any moment expect a visit from the State Police. It would be dreadful, unimaginably dreadful for me if my diary fell into the hands of the Police Minister Fouché and of Napoleon himself. How they would laugh! Therefore I've decided to write down everything that's happened at once and then hand it over to Julie to keep for me. She, after all, is the new dictator's sister-in-law, and surely he'll never let his police search *her* house?

I am sitting in the drawing-room of our new house in the Rue Cisalpine. In the dining-room next-door I can hear Jean-Baptiste pacing the floor, up and down and up and down. "If you have any dangerous papers let me have them," I shouted to him. "I'll take them to Julie to-morrow with my papers."

But Jean-Baptiste answered: "I have no—how did you put

it?—'dangerous papers.' And Napoleon knows quite well what I think of his treasonable action."

Fernand was rummaging about the room, and I asked him whether there were still many people standing outside our house in silent groups. He said there were.

"What do these people want?" I wondered.

Fernand put a new light into the candelabrum and said: "They want to see what's going to happen to our General. I'm told that the Jacobins wanted our General to take over the command of the National Guard and——" He scratched his head thoughtfully and noisily and was obviously asking himself whether to tell me the truth or not. "Yes, and people think that our General will be arrested. General Moreau was arrested some time ago."

I am preparing myself for a long night. In the adjoining room Jean-Baptiste keeps pacing the floor, I write on, the hours pass slowly and we wait.

Yes, Napoleon returned quite unexpectedly, exactly as I had thought he would. Four weeks and two days ago an exhausted courier dismounted from his horse in front of Joseph's house and announced: "General Bonaparte, accompanied only by his secretary Bourrienne, has landed at Fréjus in a tiny freighter which slipped through the British blockade. He's hired a special coach and will be in Paris at any moment."

Joseph got dressed hurriedly, fetched Lucien, and both brothers went and took up stations in front of Napoleon's house in Rue de la Victoire. Their voices woke Josephine, who, when she heard what was happening, put on her most fashionable dress, dashed into her carriage and drove like fury through the southern suburbs to meet Napoleon. She hadn't even wasted any time on make-up, she did that in the carriage. She had only one aim, to get to Napoleon before Joseph saw him and to try at all costs to prevent a divorce. But hardly had her carriage driven off when Napoleon's chaise drove up to the house in the Rue de la Victoire. The two carriages had missed each other by a few moments. Napoleon jumped out, the two brothers ran to meet him, and there was a lot of back-patting. They went into the house and withdrew into one of the small rooms.

Round about mid-day Josephine returned exhausted from her futile journey and opened the door to the room where the brothers were in conference. Napoleon looked her up and down: "Madame," he said at last, "we have nothing more to say to each other. I shall take the necessary steps for a divorce to-morrow, and shall be obliged if meanwhile you will move into Malmaison. In the meantime I shall look round for a new house for myself."

Josephine broke into violent sobbing. Napoleon turned his back on her, and Lucien took her up to her room. After that the three brothers continued their conference for hours, and later on were joined by Talleyrand, the former Minister for Foreign Affairs.

Meanwhile the news spread quickly through all Paris that Napoleon had returned victoriously. Crowds gathered round his house, soldiers turned up and shouted *"Vive Bonaparte!"* and Napoleon showed himself at the window and waved to the crowd. All the time Josephine was sitting in her bedroom weeping wildly; her daughter Hortense tried to calm her down and gave her camomile tea.

It was not till the evening that Napoleon was left alone with his secretary Bourrienne. He dictated letters to innumerable Deputies and Generals in order to notify them of his safe return. Later on Hortense appeared, still angular, thin, colourless and timid, but already dressed like a young lady. The long somewhat pendant nose gave her an air of precociousness.

"Couldn't you go and talk to Mama, Papa Bonaparte?" she said in a whisper. He brushed her aside like a fly.

He did not send his secretary away till midnight. As he was still debating with himself where to lie down for the night—Josephine was still occupying the bedroom—he heard loud sobbing outside the door. He quickly locked it. Josephine continued to stand there, outside his door, and weep for two full hours. At last he opened. Next morning he woke up in Josephine's bedroom.

Julie, who had it from Joseph and Bourrienne, told me all this. "And do you know what Napoleon said to me?" she added. "He said to me: 'Julie, if I divorce Josephine all Paris will know that she cheated me, and I'll be the laughing-stock of Paris. If I don't divorce her, you see, all Paris will know that there is nothing to blame her for and it was all malicious talk. At the present moment I must not, on any account, make myself ridiculous.' A strange attitude, don't you think, Désirée?"

There were other things she had to tell me: "Junot, too, has come back from Egypt and so has Eugene de Beauharnais. Almost every day officers of the Army in Egypt land secretly in France. And according to Junot, Napoleon left a fair-haired mistress behind in Egypt, a certain Madame Pauline Fourès whom he called 'Bellilote'. She is supposed to be a young officer's wife who had accompanied her husband to Egypt in disguise. Just imagine! When Napoleon got Joseph's letter about Josephine—you remember the letter, don't you?—he ran up and down in front of his tent for two hours, then sent for 'Bellilote' and dined with her."

"What became of her?" I asked.

"Junot, Murat and the others say that he handed her over, together with his command of the Army, to his second in command."

"And what does he look like?"

"The second in command?"

"Don't be stupid, Napoleon, of course!"

Julie became thoughtful. "He's changed, you know. Perhaps it's something to do with the way he's doing his hair now. He had it cut short out in Egypt, which makes his face look plumper and his features less irregular. But it isn't that alone, no, I'm sure it isn't. By the way, you'll see him yourself on Sunday, you're coming to dinner at Mortefontaine, aren't you?"

Upper-class Parisians have a house in the country, and writers a garden to which they can retire. Since Joseph sees himself as an upper-class Parisian as well as a writer he bought the charming Villa Mortefontaine with the large park belonging to it, about an hour's drive from Paris. Next Sunday we were to dine there in the company of Napoleon and Josephine.

To-day's events would never have come to pass had Jean-Baptiste still been Minister of War on Napoleon's return. But a short time before that he had had another of his violent arguments with Director Sieyès, and in a fit of anger he offered his resignation. Pondering over it and remembering that Sieyès assisted Napoleon with his *coup d'état*, I think it highly probable that Sieyès had an inkling of Napoleon's intention of returning and deliberately brought about the argument in order to force Jean-Baptiste's resignation. Jean-Baptiste's successor did not dare to court-martial Napoleon, because some Generals and the circle of Deputies round Joseph and Lucien were too openly on Napoleon's side.

In those autumn days Jean-Baptiste received many visitors. One of them, General Moreau, came almost every day, and suggested that the Army ought to intervene if Napoleon really 'dared'. A group of Jacobin members of Paris City Council turned up to enquire whether, in case of riots, General Bernadotte would take over command of the National Guard. Jean-Baptiste answered that he would gladly take it over, provided the Government, that is the Minister of War, appointed him in due and proper manner. At that the Councillors departed in dismay.

On the morning of the Sunday on which we were to go to

Mortefontaine I suddenly heard a well-known voice downstairs. "Eugénie," it shouted, "I want to see my godchild!"

I ran down the stairs, and there he was, tanned, his hair cut short.

"We wanted to surprise you and Bernadotte," he said. "You are going to Mortefontaine, aren't you? So Josephine and I thought we could fetch you. Besides, I want to meet your son and admire your new house and say hullo to Colleague Bernadotte, whom I have not yet seen since my return."

"You are looking very well, my dear," Josephine, leaning gracefully against the verandah door, interposed.

Jean-Baptiste appeared on the scene now, and I ran into the kitchen to tell Marie to make coffee and serve liqueurs. On returning I saw that Jean-Baptiste had fetched Oscar and Napoleon was bending over the little bundle, tickling his chin and clucking at him.

Oscar didn't like it, and started to scream.

"Well, Colleague Bernadotte," said Napoleon laughingly to Jean-Baptiste, and amiably patted his back, "more recruits for the Army, eh?"

I rescued our son from the arms of his father, who stiffly held him away from himself and insisted that the bundle felt damp.

Enjoying Marie's bitter-sweet coffee, Josephine involved me in a conversation on roses. Roses are her passion, and I had already been told that she was planning a costly rose garden at Malmaison. She had seen a few rather miserable rose trees outside our verandah, and she wanted to know how I tended them. Therefore we didn't hear what Jean-Baptiste and Napoleon were talking about, but both Josephine and I were silenced abruptly on hearing Napoleon say:

"I am told, Friend Bernadotte, that you, had you been in office on my return, would have had me court-martialled and shot. What is it you are blaming me for?"

"I believe you know our Service Regulations as well as I do," Jean-Baptiste answered, and added, "perhaps even better, for you had the advantage of having been trained at an officers' training establishment, and of starting your active service as an officer, whereas I served for many years in the ranks, as you may have heard."

Napoleon bent forward and tried to catch Jean-Baptiste's eyes. At this moment I realised why he looked different now. His short hair made his head appear round and his lean face ampler; moreover, I had never noticed before the severely jutting, almost angular chin. However, all this emphasised the change only, it had not brought it about. What was decisive in this change was his smile, the smile which once upon a time I loved so much and later I hated so much; the smile which once upon a time had played so rarely and so fleetingly round his intense face. Now it never left his face, had become winning, had become at once begging and demanding.

But what did this uninterrupted smile demand? And for whom was it meant? For Jean-Baptiste, of course! He was to be won over, to be turned into a friend, a confidant, an enthusiastic follower.

"I have returned from Egypt," he was now saying, "in order to put myself once more at the disposal of our country, as I consider my mission in Africa to have come to an end. You are telling me now that France's frontiers are secure and that you during your term as Minister of War had tried to put 100,000 infantry and 40,000 cavalry into the field. The few thousand men whom I left behind in Africa can therefore be of no importance to the French Army, whose strength you increased by 140,000 men, whereas a man like me in the present desperate position of the Republic——"

"The position is not at all desperate," said Jean-Baptiste calmly.

Napoleon smiled. "Isn't it? Since the moment of my return I have been told by all and sundry that the Government is no longer in control of the situation. The Royalists are on the move again in the Vendée region, and certain people in Paris are quite openly in contact with the Bourbons in England. The Manège Club, on the other hand, is preparing for a Jacobin revolution. I suppose you know that the Manège Club intends to overthrow the Directory, Colleague Bernadotte?"

"As for the Manège Club," Jean-Baptiste said slowly, "you are certainly much better informed about its aims and intentions than I. Your brothers Joseph and Lucien founded it and preside over its meetings."

"In my opinion it is the duty of the Army and its leaders to gather together all the positive forces, to guarantee law and order and to contrive a form of government worthy of the Revolution and all it stands for," said Napoleon imploringly.

I found the conversation boring and therefore turned back to Josephine. But to my amazement her eyes were riveted firmly on Jean-Baptiste, as if his reply were of decisive importance.

"Any intervention of the Army or its leaders in order to secure a change in the Constitution I am bound to consider as high treason," was his answer.

The winning smile did not wane on Napoleon's face. But

Josephine, at the words, 'high treason', raised her thin brows. I poured out fresh coffee.

Napoleon continued: "If I were, let us say, being approached universally—and I emphasise: universally!—and if it were suggested to me to bring about a concentration of all positive forces and, with the help of sincere patriots, to work out a new Constitution which would give expression to the true desires of the people, if that happened, Friend Bernadotte, would you stand by me? Could the circle of men who intend to realise the ideals of the Revolution count on you? Jean-Baptiste Bernadotte, may France rely on your help?"

Napoleon's grey eyes, charged with emotion, drilled like gimlets into Jean-Baptiste.

"Listen, Bonaparte," said Jean-Baptiste, and put his cup down firmly, "listen, if you've come to persuade me to commit high treason over a cup of coffee I must ask you to leave my house."

Napoleon's eyes went dull and his eternal smile looked uncannily like a mechanical trick. "Am I to take it, then, that you would oppose by force of arms those of your colleagues to whose hands the country entrusted the rescue of the Republic?"

Jean-Baptiste suddenly broke out into laughter, deep, cordial, uncontrollable laughter, which made the tension snap: "My dear Bonaparte, when you were sunning yourself in Egypt it was suggested to me not once but three or four times that I should play the strong man, and, backed by the Army, bring about something like—what do you and your brother Joseph call it?—ah, yes, a 'concentration of all the positive forces'. But I refused. We have two Chambers of Deputies full of people's representatives, and if they and those whom they represent are dissatisfied they can bring in all the acts they want to change the Constitution. As far as I am concerned, I am of the opinion that the existing Constitution is quite sufficient to keep law and order and to defend our frontiers. But if the Deputies think fit to adopt a different form of government without having been forced into it at the point of a gun, then that is no business of mine or of the Army's."

"But if the Deputies were forced to a change of the Constitution at the point of the gun, Colleague Bernadotte, what attitude would you adopt then?"

Jean-Baptiste got up, went to the door of the verandah and looked into the greyish autumn sky outside. Napoleon's eyes followed him, and there was silence in the room as we waited for the answer.

Abruptly Jean-Baptiste came back into the room towards

Napoleon and put his hand heavily on his shoulder. "Bonaparte," he said, "I fought under your command in Italy, I know something of your generalship, and I realise that France has no better commander than you. But the things the politicians suggest to you are unworthy of a General of the Republican Army. Don't do it, Bonaparte, don't do it!"

Napoleon looked attentively at the embroidered tablecloth and not a muscle of his face moved.

Jean-Baptiste took his hand from Napoleon's shoulder and went back to his chair. "If, however, you do attempt it after all, I shall oppose you by force, provided——"

Napoleon looked up: "Provided what?"

"Provided that the lawful Government orders me to do so!"

"How obstinate you are!" murmured Napoleon. Then Josephine thought it time to set off for Montefontaine.

Julie's house was full of visitors. Talleyrand was there, and Fouché, and of course Napoleon's personal friends, Generals Junot, Murat, Leclerc and Marmont. They showed themselves agreeably surprised at seeing Jean-Baptiste arrive with Napoleon.

After dinner Fouché remarked to Jean-Baptiste: "I didn't know you and Napoleon were friends."

"Friends? At any rate we are relatives."

Fouché smiled: "Some people are very careful in the choice of their relatives."

"Choice? God knows, these relatives are not of my choosing," Jean-Baptiste answered good-humouredly.

In the days that followed this Sunday the whole of Paris talked of nothing else but whether Napoleon would dare or not. Once I drove by chance through the Rue de la Victoire and saw a whole crowd of adolescents shouting in chorus "*Vive Bonaparte!*" up towards the closed windows. Fernand had it that these fellows were paid for their services. Jean-Baptiste, however, said that many of them found it difficult to forget the immense sums of money which Napoleon squeezed out of the defeated Italian States and sent to Paris.

Yesterday morning, on entering our dining-room, I knew at once: to-day is the day! Joseph was there, button-holing Jean-Baptiste and talking at him for all he was worth. He wanted to persuade him to go to Napoleon with him that very moment.

"At least you ought to hear him," Joseph said, "so that you can see for yourself that all he wants is to save the Republic."

"I know his plans," said Jean-Baptiste, "and I know that they have nothing to do with saving the Republic."

"For the last time, do you refuse to help my brother?"

"For the last time, I refuse to participate in any kind of high treason."

Joseph turned to me: "Désirée, can't you make him see reason?"

"Can I get you a cup of coffee, Joseph? You are so excited," I said.

Joseph said no and left, and Jean-Baptiste went to the verandah door to stare into the garden.

An hour later General Moreau, Monsieur Sazzarin, the former secretary of Jean-Baptiste, and other members of the War Office staff swept into the house like an avalanche. They demanded that Jean-Baptiste should put himself at the head of the National Guard and bar Napoleon's way to the Council of the Five Hundred.

But Jean-Baptiste insisted: "I can't do it without the Government's order."

Some City Councillors, the ones who had been before, arrived in the middle of it and made the same demand. To them Jean-Baptiste explained that he couldn't act on the City Council's orders. He needed the authorisation of the Government, or, if the Directors were no longer in office, that of the Council of the Five Hundred.

Late that afternoon I saw Jean-Baptiste for the first time in civilian clothes. He wore a dark red jacket which looked a bit on the tight as well as on the short side, a funny high hat and a very elaborately knotted yellow scarf. My General looked like someone who had disguised himself.

"Where are you going?" I asked.

"Oh, just for a stroll," he said.

His stroll took him a good few hours, and when in the evening Moreau and his friends turned up again they had to wait for him. It was pitch-dark when he came back at last. Naturally we were curious to know where he had been all this time.

"At the Tuileries and the Luxembourg," he said. "There are troops everywhere, but all is quiet. I think the soldiers were mostly from the former Army in Italy. I recognised some faces."

"Napoleon is sure to make them plenty of promises," said Moreau.

Jean-Baptiste smiled wryly. "He's done so already, through their officers. They're all back again in Paris, Junot, Masséna, Marmont, Leclerc, the whole Bonaparte circus."

"Do you think these troops are ready to oppose the National Guard?" wondered Moreau.

"They wouldn't dream of it," said Jean-Baptiste. "I talked for a long time to an old sergeant and some of his men who took me for an inquisitive civilian. They believe that Bonaparte would be given command of the National Guard. Their officers told them that."

"That's the dirtiest lie I've ever come across," exploded Moreau. But Jean-Baptiste said calmly:

"I think it very likely that Napoleon will demand the command of the National Guard from the Deputies to-morrow."

"And we insist that you share this command with him," Moreau shouted. "Are you prepared to do that?"

Jean-Baptiste nodded: "Yes. What you could do is to put it to the War Minister that if Bonaparte is entrusted with the command of the National Guard, Bernadotte is to share it with him as the representative of the Minister of War."

For the whole of the night I could find no sleep. All the time the voices from downstairs drifted up into the bedroom, the voices of Moreau, Sazzarin and all the rest of them.

That was yesterday. Heavens, to think that it was only yesterday!

During the course of to-day messengers kept coming all the time. Mostly they were officers. But finally a young soldier rode up, bathed in sweat. He jumped from his horse and shouted: "Bonaparte is First Consul! First Consul!"

"Sit down, man," said Jean-Baptiste, without showing any excitement. "Désirée, give him a glass of wine."

Even before the young man had had time to collect himself to tell the tale a young captain rushed into the room, shouting: "General Bernadotte, Consular Government has just been proclaimed. Bonaparte is First Consul."

And now we heard the whole story. During the morning Napoleon had first gone to the Council of Ancients and asked for a hearing. The Ancients, mainly venerable and somnolent lawyers, had listened to him in the semi-coma of boredom as, excitably and confusedly, he talked about a plot against the Government and demanded unlimited powers to cope with the emergency. The chairman of the Council then told him in a tortuous speech that he should talk to the Government about it, and so, accompanied by Joseph, Napoleon had set off for the Council of Deputies. There the mood had been a very different one. Although every single Deputy knew what the appearance of Napoleon meant, they had at first gone on with the agenda in a spirit of forced equanimity. Suddenly, however, the President of the Council, the young Jacobin Lucien Bonaparte, had pushed his brother on to the rostrum, announcing that General Bonaparte had something to say of decisive importance to the Republic. Napoleon at once had started to speak amidst the "Hear, hear!" of his friends and the whistles and catcalls of his enemies, and all witnesses agreed in saying that he had stumbled and fumbled through his speech, in which he talked about a plot against the Republic and against his own life, that the agitation had grown louder and louder till he became inaudible and that at last he had had to stop altogether.

By now the agitation had become an indescribable tumult. The followers of Bonaparte forced their way to the rostrum, their opponents, belonging to all parties, made for the doors, which they found barred by troops. No one knows as yet how the troops had got there 'to protect' the Deputies. At any rate, Polette's husband, General Leclerc, was there at their head, and the National Guard, whose task it is to ensure the safety of the Deputies, made common cause with Leclerc's troops. The whole place looked like a witches' cauldron. Lucien and Napoleon stood side by side on the rostrum, and then a voice had shouted "*Vive Bonaparte!*", a dozen others chimed in, then thirty, then eighty, and the gallery, where Murat, Masséna and Marmont had appeared among the journalists, roared it too. In the end the rest of the Deputies, seeing nothing but rifles and uniforms, had screamed in desperation "*Vive Bonaparte, vive . . . vive. . . . !*"

After that the last act had begun. The soldiers had withdrawn into the corners of the hall, the Minister of Police, Fouché, had appeared, accompanied by a few gentlemen in civilian clothes, and discreetly invited those Deputies who might disturb the new dispensation of law and order to follow him. The Council, reassembling to debate a new Constitution, showed considerable gaps. The President moved the proposals for the formation of a new Government to be headed by three Consuls, General Bonaparte was unanimously elected First Consul and the Tuileries, at his desire, put at his disposal as his official residence.

In the evening Fernand brought us the special editions of the papers. The name of Bonaparte stood out in enormous letters in each of them.

"You remember, Marie," I said to her in the kitchen, "you remember the special paper at home, in Marseilles, the one you brought me out on the terrace, 'Bonaparte appointed Military Governor of Paris'?"

Marie went on filling the feeding-bottle for Oscar.

"And to-night," I continued, "he'll move into the Tuileries. Perhaps he'll even sleep in the King's former bedroom."

"Shouldn't wonder," growled Marie. "It would be like him."

I went to the bedroom and fed Oscar, and Jean-Baptiste came up and sat with us. A moment later Fernand entered and handed him a slip of paper.

"Sir," he reported, "a strange woman left this a moment ago."

Bernadotte looked at it and then showed it to me. On it was written in a trembling hand: 'General Moreau has just been arrested'.

"A message from Madame Moreau which she sent by her kitchen maid."

Oscar fell asleep, we went downstairs, and ever since then we have been waiting for the police.

I started writing in my diary.

Some nights are long, so long that they never seem to end.

Suddenly there was the noise of a carriage stopping in front of our house. Now they're coming for him, I thought, got up quickly and went into the drawing-room. Jean-Baptiste was standing there, rigid, in the middle of the room, listening tensely. I went up to him and put my arm round his shoulders. Never before in my life had I felt so close to him.

The door knocker banged, once, twice, three times. "I'll go and see," said Jean-Baptiste, and freed himself from my arm. At the same time we heard voices, a man's voice first and then a woman's laughter. My knees went weak, I fell into the nearest chair and wiped the tears from my eyes: it was Julie, thank God, it was only Julie!

They came into the salon, Joseph, Lucien and Julie. My hands shook as I put new candles into the candelabrum. A bright light filled the room.

Julie was wearing her red evening gown. Obviously she had had too much champagne. Small feverish spots were burning on her cheeks and she giggled so much that she could hardly speak.

They had all come from the Tuileries. Napoleon had been in conference all night, had worked out the details of the new Constitution and drafted a provisional list of ministers. In the end Josephine, who, meanwhile, had unpacked her trunks in the former Royal apartments, had insisted on a celebration, had sent the State equipages to fetch Madame Letitia, Julie and Napoleon's sisters, and had one of the great ballrooms in the Tuileries festively illuminated.

"We drank such a lot," babbled Julie, "but it is such a great

171

day, isn't it? Napoleon will govern France, Lucien is Minister of the Interior, and Joseph is going to be Minister of Foreign Affairs—at any rate he is down on the list, and, and—you must excuse our waking you. But as we were driving past your house I said, why not say good-morning to Désirée and Jean-Baptiste——"

"You didn't wake us up, we haven't been to sleep yet," I said.

"——and the three Consuls," I heard Joseph say, "will be assisted by a Council of State composed mainly of experts. I suppose that you, Bernadotte, will be one of the Councillors."

"Josephine is going to refurnish the Tuileries," Julie babbled on. "I don't blame her, I don't. Everything's so full of dust and so old-fashioned. She wants her bedroom all white. And imagine, Napoleon wants her to have a real court like a Queen, with ladies-in-waiting and all. Just imagine! He wants other countries to see that the wife of our new Head of State knows how to represent——"

"I insist that General Moreau be set free," Jean-Baptiste's voice broke through Julie's patter, followed by Lucien's, who declared that Moreau's arrest was only a protective custody, a protection against mob excesses. "One never knows what the people of Paris in their enthusiasm for Napoleon and the new Constitution——"

At that moment a clock struck six.

"Good God, we must be off," exclaimed Julie. "She is waiting for us in the carriage outside. We only wanted to say good-morning."

"Who's waiting in the carriage?" I asked.

"Madame Letitia. She was too tired to get out. We promised to take her home."

I felt the need to speak to Madame Letitia and ran out of the house. It was misty outside, and a few shadows slipped away into the mist when they saw me. Apparently some people had waited in front of our house all night.

Opening the door of the carriage I peered into the dark interior. "Madame Letitia," I called out, "it's me, Désirée. I want to congratulate you."

The figure in the corner shifted. But it was so dark inside that I couldn't see the face. "Congratulate? On what, my child?"

"On Napoleon becoming First Consul and Lucien Minister of the Interior and Joseph——"

"The boys shouldn't meddle so much with politics," her voice came out of the dark.

'Madame Bonaparte will never speak French properly,' I

thought. 'She speaks to-day exactly as she did when I first met her in Marseilles. And what an awful-smelling cellar they lived in then! And now they are having the Tuileries refurnished.'

"I thought you'd be very pleased, Madame," I said awkwardly.

"No. The Tuileries are no place for Napoleone. It is not proper," the voice in the dark carriage said firmly.

"But we live in a Republic," I said.

"Call Julie and the two boys. I am tired. You will see, he will get into mischief in the Tuileries, into very great mischief."

At last Julie, Joseph and Lucien came out of the house. Julie embraced me and pressed her hot cheek against my face. "It's so marvellous," she whispered, "so marvellous. Come to lunch with me. I must talk to you."

Jean-Baptiste joined us in the street to see our visitors off. On his appearance the strange shadows I had seen slipping away before emerged again out of the mist and a trembling voice shouted: *"Vive Bernadotte!"* It was taken up by three or four other voices: *"Vive Bernadotte, vive Bernadotte!"* and it seemed a bit ridiculous to me that they made Joseph start.

The morning is grey and rainy. A moment ago an officer of the National Guard arrived with the message: "By order of the First Consul, General Bernadotte will report to him at the Tuileries at eleven o'clock."

I close my book and lock it. Later on I shall take it to Julie.

PARIS, March 21st, 1804. (Only the Authorities keep to the Republican calendar now and call it 1st Germinal of the Year XII.)

I WAS crazy to drive in the dead of night to the Tuileries to see Napoleon. I knew I was crazy, have known it from the very beginning, and yet I got into Madame Letitia's carriage, trying to think what I was going to say to him.

Somewhere a clock struck eleven. The carriage was rolling along by the banks of the Seine, and in my imagination I saw myself passing along the vast empty corridors of the Tuileries, entering his room, going up to his desk and starting my explanation.

Down there was the river. In the course of the years I have come to know most of the bridges. There is one particular bridge, however, which, every time I pass it, makes my heart beat faster. I was passing it now, and I stopped the carriage, and got out and went to the bridge. *My* bridge!

It was a night in early spring, a bit chilly still, but the air felt sweet and balmy. After a day's rain the clouds were breaking up and stars appeared in the gaps.

'He couldn't have him shot,' I thought as I leaned over the edge of the bridge and saw the lights of Paris dancing on the waves, 'he couldn't.'

Couldn't he? Of course he could. He could do anything. Slowly I began to walk the length of the bridge, backwards and forwards.

My thoughts went back to all the past years through which I have lived in a whirl of events, big and small. There were the weddings I danced at, the receptions at the Tuileries I attended, the victories I celebrated, the dresses I wore and the champagne I drank: they were the small things. And there was Oscar's first tooth and Oscar's first 'Mummy' and Oscar's first toddle, holding my hand, from the piano to the chest-of-drawers: they were the big ones. All these memories flooded through my mind, and they seemed to persuade me to delay the moment when I should continue on my way to the First Consul.

Only a few days ago Julie gave me back my diary.

"I cleared out that old chest-of-drawers, you know, the big one from our house in Marseilles, to make room for the children's things. They are growing, they need a bit of extra space. So I put it in the nursery, cleared it out and found your diary. I needn't keep it for you any longer now, need I?"

"No, you needn't," I said, "or, at any rate, not at the moment."

"There are lots of things for you to write down now," said Julie and smiled. "I'm sure you haven't even entered that I have two daughters."

"No, how could I? I handed the book over to you the night after the *coup d'état*. But now I shall record that you went to Plombières Spa regularly every year with Joseph, and that Zenaïde Charlotte Julie was born two and a half years ago and Charlotte Napoleone thirteen months later. And I shall also record that you read fiction as enthusiastically as ever and that a story about a harem so entranced you that you called your poor elder daughter Zenaïde."

"I hope she'll forgive me for it," said Julie remorsefully.

I took the book home. 'Above all,' I thought, 'I must note down Mama's death.' Last summer, when Julie was sitting with us in our garden, Joseph came with a letter from Etienne. He wrote that Mama had died after a heart attack in Genoa.

"Now we are quite alone," said Julie.

174

"But you have me," said Joseph.

He didn't understand what Julie meant. Julie belongs to him and I to Jean-Baptiste, but after Papa's death only Mama could tell us what things had been like when we were children.

On the evening of that day Jean-Baptiste told me: "You know that we are all subject to the laws of nature. They determine that we should survive our parents. It would be unnatural if it were the other way round. All we can do is to obey the laws of nature."

That was his way of consoling me. Every woman who in childbirth suffers almost unbearable pain is told that she is only sharing the fate of all mothers. But that, I think, is small consolation.

From my bridge I could see Madame Letitia's carriage standing there, dark in the darkness, like a threatening monster. Meanwhile on Napoleon's desk there was a death sentence waiting to be signed, and I was going to say to him—well, what was I going to say to him? One could no longer talk to him as one talks to ordinary people, one couldn't even sit down if he didn't allow it. . . .

The floodtide of my memories was not diverted by the sight of that monstrous black carriage. There was the morning after that endless night during which we were expecting Jean-Baptiste's arrest, when Napoleon had ordered Bernadotte to appear in the Tuileries.

"You have been called into the Council of State, Bernadotte," said Napoleon to him. "You will represent the Ministry of War."

"Do you believe that I have changed my convictions in the course of one night?" answered Jean-Baptiste.

"No. But in the course of this one night I have become responsible for the fate of the Republic, and I cannot afford to do without one of its ablest men. Will you accept, Bernadotte?"

A long silence fell, so Jean-Baptiste told me later, a silence in which he looked attentively round the room, at the ceiling, at the desk, through the windows: a silence in which he watched the soldiers of the National Guard below in the courtyard; a silence in which he pondered the legal position of the Consular Government which had been recognised by the Directors before their resignation; a silence in which he came to the conclusion that the Republic had delivered itself into this man's hand to avoid a civil war.

"You are right, Consul Bonaparte," he said at last, "the Republic needs every one of its citizens. I accept."

On the very next day Moreau and all arrested Deputies were

set free, and Moreau was given a new command. Napoleon prepared for a new Italian campaign and appointed Jean-Baptiste Supreme Commander of the Western Army. In this capacity Jean-Baptiste guarded the Channel coast against British attacks; his command stretched all the way to the Gironde. He had set up his headquarters in Rennes and was not at home at the time that Oscar had whooping cough. Later Napoleon won the battle of Marengo and Paris nearly convulsed itself with victory celebrations. Our troops occupied half Europe now, because of the many territories ceded to France in Napoleon's peace treaties, and these territories all needed garrisoning.

There are more lights dancing on the waves of the Seine now than at that time long ago, I thought. Then I believed that nothing in the world could be more magnificent and exciting than Paris. But Jean-Baptiste maintained that our present-day Paris is a hundred times more splendid than the Paris of that time and that I had no real basis of comparison.

One thing Napoleon did was to allow the fugitive aristocrats to return. And so once more plots and intrigues abounded in the mansions of the Faubourg St. Germain, confiscated property was handed back to its former owners and torchbearers ran alongside the calashes of the Noailles, the Radziwills, the Montesquieus and the Montmorencys. These former ornaments of the Court of Versailles themselves, however, moved once more with measured, graceful steps through the great state rooms of the Tuileries, bowing to the Head of State of the Republic and bending low over the hand of the ex-widow Comtesse de Beauharnais, who had never fled abroad and never gone hungry but had her bills paid by Monsieur Barras and danced with the ex-lackey Tallien at the ball of the 'Association of Guillotine Victims'. Once more, too, the royal courts from all the quarters of the globe sent their most distinguished diplomats to Paris. Sometimes my poor head buzzed in confusion when I wanted to remember the names of all these princes, counts and lords who were introduced to me.

Memories, memories, there was no end to them!

"I'm afraid of him, he has no heart. . . ." That was Christine's voice calling to me in the early spring night on my bridge, Christine, the peasant girl from St. Maximin, the wife of Lucien Bonaparte. Innumerable witnesses saw Lucien push his brother on to the rostrum and heard him force the first "*Vive Bonaparte!*" from their reluctant lips. A few weeks later the walls of the Tuileries resounded with the furious arguments of the two brothers and told just as many witnesses what Lucien Bonaparte, Minister of the Interior, and Napoleon

Bonaparte, First Consul, were shouting at each other. First they argued about the press censorship introduced by Napoleon, then about the exiling of authors, and every now and then about Christine, the innkeeper's daughter who was never received in the Tuileries.

Lucien did not remain Minister for long, nor did Christine cause family strife for any length of time. The well-set-up girl from the country with the apple cheeks and the dimples began to cough blood after a damp winter.

One afternoon I was sitting with her and we talked about spring and looked at fashion magazines. Christine wanted a gold-embroidered dress she saw illustrated.

"In a dress like that," I said, "you'll go to the Tuileries and be introduced to the First Consul, and you'll be so beautiful that he'll envy Lucien."

Christine's dimples disappeared. "I'm afraid of him, he has no heart," she said.

In the end Madame Letitia succeeded in persuading Napoleon to receive Christine, and a week later he said casually to his brother:

"Don't forget to bring your wife along to the opera to-morrow night and introduce her to me."

"I am afraid," answered Lucien, "my wife is not in a position to accept your most flattering invitation."

Napoleon's lips at once tightened: "This is not an invitation, Lucien, but an order from the First Consul."

Lucien shook his head: "My wife cannot even obey an order from the First Consul. My wife is dying."

At Christine's burial everybody noticed the inscription on the most expensive of the wreaths: 'To my dear sister-in-law Christine—N. Bonaparte.'

After Christine the widow Jourberthon!

The widow Jourberthon had red hair, a full bosom and dimpled cheeks which reminded one a bit of Christine. She had been married to a petty bank clerk. Napoleon demanded that Lucien should marry a daughter of one of the returned great noblemen. Instead one day Lucien arrived at the registry office with Madame Jourberthon, whereupon Napoleon at once signed a decree banishing the French citizen Lucien Bonaparte, former member of the Council of Five Hundred, ex-Minister of the Interior of the French Republic, from the country.

Before Lucien left for Italy he came to us to say good-bye.

"On that day in Brumaire," he said, "I only wanted everything to be for the best for the Republic. You know that, Bernadotte, don't you?"

"I know," said Jean-Baptiste, "I know. But you made a great mistake, on that day in Brumaire!"

Then there was Hortense.

Two years ago Hortense broke out into such weeping and screaming that the sentries in the courtyard of the Tuileries looked up to her windows in fright. Napoleon had ordered the engagement of his stepdaughter to his brother Louis, fat, flat-footed Louis who cared nothing for the colourless Hortense and preferred the actresses from the Comédie Française. But Napoleon was not going to tolerate another *mésalliance* in his family and so ordered his engagement to Hortense. As a result Hortense had locked herself in her bedroom and screamed the house down. When she refused to let her mother in, Julie was sent for.

Julie hammered on Hortense's door till the girl opened.

"Can I help you?" Julie asked.

Hortense shook her head.

"You love someone else, don't you?"

Hortense's sobbing ceased and her face became rigid.

"You love someone else," repeated Julie.

This time Hortense nodded almost imperceptibly.

"I shall speak to your stepfather," said Julie. But Hortense stared hopelessly at the floor.

"Does this other man belong to the First Consul's circle? Could your stepfather consider him a suitable candidate?"

Hortense did not move. Only her tears continued to stream down her cheeks.

"Or perhaps this other man is married already?"

Hortense's lips opened, she tried to smile, instead of which she suddenly burst into laughter, loud, shrill, uncontrollable laughter which made her shake like someone possessed by demons.

Julie grabbed her by the shoulders: "Stop it! Control yourself! If you don't I'll fetch the doctor."

But Hortense couldn't stop. She went on laughing crazily till my patient sister Julie lost her patience and slapped her face. That made her stop.

Hortense shut her wide-open mouth and breathed deeply a few times. Then she said very quietly and almost inaudibly: "But I love—him!"

"Him? Napoleon?" This possibility had never entered Julie's mind. "Does he know?"

Hortense nodded. "There are few things he does not know. And those few the Minister of Police Fouché ferrets out for him."

How bitter it sounded!

"Marry Louis," said Julie, "marry him. It's the best thing to do. After all, Louis is his favourite brother." . . .

A few weeks later they got married. Polette had been held up as an example to Hortense. How she had fought against her marriage to General Leclerc! Napoleon had almost had to force her into the match. And how she had wept because Napoleon ordered her to accompany Leclerc on his journey to San Domingo! In San Domingo Leclerc died of yellow fever, and then Polette had been so inconsolable that she cut off her honey-coloured hair and put it in his coffin. This the First Consul kept citing as conclusive proof of Polette's great love for the dead man. But I told him:

"Just the opposite! It proves that she never loved him. Because she never loved him she wanted to do something special for him once he was dead!"

Polette's hair grew again; it grew in curls down to her shoulder, and now Napoleon insisted that she should put them up with the help of the most precious combs in the world: the pearl-studded combs of the Borghese family. The Borghese family belongs to the oldest families of Italy and is related to almost all the royal houses of Europe. The then head was the knock-kneed, shaky Prince Camillo Borghese, and into the arms of this elderly prince Napoleon put his favourite sister Polette. Her Highness, the Princess Polette Borghese! Yes, Her Highness Polette, little Polette with the patched dress who had street corner *affaires* with men. . . .

Yes, how they have changed, all of them!

For the last time I looked down to the water where the lights of Paris were dancing up and down as before. Why, I thought, why do they say that I am the only one who could succeed in this task?

I went back to the carriage. "To the Tuileries!"

On the way I sorted out one by one the points of this desperate task. The Duc d'Enghien, a Bourbon who has been said to be in the pay of the British and who for a long time threatened to reconquer the Republic for the Bourbons, had been captured. But this capture took place not on French soil but in a little town in Germany called Ettenheim, outside the French frontiers. Four days ago Napoleon all unexpectedly ordered three hundred dragoons to attack this little town. They crossed the Rhine, kidnapped the Duc in Ettenheim and dragged him away into France. Now he was a prisoner in the Fortress of Vincennes, awaiting the verdict. To-day a military tribunal condemned him to death for high treason and an attempt on the life of the First Consul.

The death sentence has been put before the First Consul for confirmation or commutation. The aristocrats who are now daily guests at Josephine's implored her, naturally enough, to ask Napoleon for mercy on the prisoner's behalf. They went to the Tuileries in force and the foreign diplomats laid siege to Talleyrand. Napoleon, however, saw no one. At table Josephine tried to take up the matter, only to be cut short by Napoleon's "Please, Madame, the matter is closed." Towards evening Joseph tried his hand and asked his brother for an interview. Napoleon enquired through his secretary what Joseph wanted to see him about, and when Joseph told the secretary it was about 'a matter of justice' the First Consul refused to see him.

During dinner that evening Jean-Baptiste was unusually quiet. But suddenly he banged the table with his fist: "Do you realise," he said, "what Napoleon's been doing? With 300 dragoons he's kidnapped a political adversary on foreign territory, brought him to France and put him before a military tribunal! For anyone with the slightest sense of justice that is a blow in the face."

"And what is going to happen to the prisoner? He couldn't have him—shot!" I said in horror.

Jean-Baptiste shrugged his shoulders. "And to think that he took the oath to the Republic, to defend the Rights of Man!"

We dropped the subject. But I couldn't help thinking all the time of the death sentence which, we had heard, was waiting on Napoleon's desk for his signature.

The silence at table grew oppressive. Finally, in order to break it I said: "Julie told me that Jerome Bonaparte has agreed to divorce his American wife."

Jerome, that dreadful boy of the days in Marseilles, had become a naval officer and on one occasion had very nearly been captured by the British. He only escaped by landing in a North American port, where he met and married a Miss Elisabeth Patterson. It caused Napoleon another fit of fury, and so Jerome, now on his way home, had given way to his great brother and agreed to divorce the former Miss Patterson. The only objection he dared to raise in his letter was: 'But she has a lot of money.'

"The First Consul's family affairs," remarked Jean-Baptiste, "are of no interest to me."

Outside we heard a carriage draw up. "It's gone ten o'clock," I said, "a bit late for calls."

Fernand came in and announced Madame Letitia Bonaparte.

That was a surprise indeed. Madame Letitia as a rule did

not visit without a previous appointment. And there she was already heaving herself into the room behind Fernand with a "Good-evening, General Bernadotte, good-evening, Madame."

Madame Letitia has grown younger rather than older during recent years. Her former hard and careworn face looked fuller, the wrinkles round her mouth seemed smoothed away. But there were a few grey strands in her dark hair, which she still wears in the Corsican peasant women's manner, tied in a knot on her neck; a few fashionable curls falling down over her forehead seem rather out of harmony with her whole personality.

We took her into the drawing-room, where she sat down and slowly stripped off her pearl-grey gloves. Looking at her hands with the big cameo ring—a present from Napoleon from Italy—I remembered the red, chapped skin of her fingers in that cellar dwelling, the fingers which had to wash clothes all day long.

"General Bernadotte, do you think it possible that my son will condemn this Duc d'Enghien to death?" she asked without any further preliminaries.

Jean-Baptiste answered cautiously: "It was not the First Consul but a military tribunal that condemned him."

"The military tribunal judges according to my son's wishes. Do you think it possible that he will have the sentence carried out?"

"Not only possible but probable. Otherwise, why should he have given the order to seize the Duc on foreign territory and put him before a court-martial?"

"I thank you, General Bernadotte." Madame Letitia looked at her cameo ring. "Do you know my son's reasons for this step?"

"No, Madame."

"Have you any ideas about them?"

"I should not like to put them into words."

She fell silent again. Sitting on the sofa bent forward and with knees slightly apart, she had the air of a very tired peasant woman who wanted a moment's rest.

"General Bernadotte, do you realise what the carrying out of this sentence means?"

Jean-Baptiste did not answer. I could see how embarrassing the conversation was for him.

Madame Letitia raised her eyes to meet his and said: "Murder, that is what it means, foul murder!"

"You should not excite yourself, Madame——"

She raised both her hands and cut him short: "Not excite myself, you say? General Bernadotte, my son is about to commit a foul murder, and I, his mother, I am not to excite myself?"

I went and sat down by her side and took her hand. It trembled. "Napoleon may have political reasons," I murmured.

"Hold your tongue," she said, and turned back to Jean-Baptiste. "There is no excuse for murder, General! Political reasons are——"

"Madame," said Jean-Baptiste, "many years ago you sent your son to a military academy and made him an officer. Perhaps, Madame, as an officer he may judge the value of an individual human life differently from you."

She shook her head. "General, this is not the question of the value of an individual human life in battle. This is a question of a man who has been dragged by force into France, there to be killed. With this killing France will lose her greatness. I will not have my Napoleone turning into a murderer, you understand, I will not have it!"

"You should go and talk to him, Madame."

"No, no, Signor——" Her voice became uncertain and her lips twitched. "It would be no use. He'd just say 'Mama, you don't understand these things. Go to bed. You want me to raise your allowance?' No, Signor, *she* must go, she, Eugenie!"

My heart stopped beating. I shook my head in desperation.

"Signor General, you don't know, but at that time when my Napoleone had been arrested and we were afraid that they might shoot him, she, little Eugenie, went to the Authorities and helped him. Now she must go to him, must remind him of it and ask him——"

"I don't believe that that would make any impression on the First Consul."

"Eugenie—I am sorry, Signora Bernadotte, Madame—you do not want your country to be called a murderous Republic by the rest of the world? You do not, do you? I have been told—oh, many people came to me to-day on behalf of this Duc—I have been told that he has an old mother and a fiancée and—oh, Madame, have pity on me, help me, I will not have my Napoleone——"

Jean-Baptiste had got up and paced restlessly up and down the room. Madame Letitia kept on:

"General, if your boy, your little Oscar, were about to sign this death sentence——"

"Désirée"—Jean-Baptiste said it gently but very firmly—"Désirée, get ready and go to the Tuileries!"

"You are coming with me, Jean-Baptiste, aren't you?"

"You know quite well, my girl, that would destroy the Duc's last chance." Jean-Baptiste smiled wryly and took me in his arms: "No, you will have to go alone. I fear it will be useless, but, darling, you must try." His voice was full of pity.

Still I did not give in: "It looks bad if I go to the Tuileries by myself at night. Too many women——" I hesitated a moment, but then went on regardless of whether Madame Letitia heard it or not——"too many women come late at night to the First Consul by themselves."

"Put on a hat, take a cape and go," was all Jean-Baptiste answered.

"Take my carriage, Madame. And if you don't object I should like to wait here for your return." I nodded and then heard her add: "I shall not disturb you, General. I shall sit here by the window and wait."

Since on Christmas Eve four years ago a bomb exploded behind the First Consul's equipage, and almost every month a new plot on the First Consul's life is being discovered by Fouché, it is impossible to enter the Tuileries without being stopped every ten yards or so by guards wanting to know your business. In spite of that everything was far simpler than I had thought. Whenever I was stopped I simply said "I want to see the First Consul", and was allowed to pass on. Nobody asked either my name or the purpose of my visit. The National Guards suppressed a smile and stared at me impertinently. I felt dreadfully embarrassed.

At last I reached the door which is supposed to lead to the First Consul's offices. I had never been here before. The few family parties to which I had gone in the Tuileries had taken place in Josephine's apartments.

The two guards in front of this door did not ask me any questions at all. So I just entered. Inside, a young man in civilian clothes was sitting at a desk, writing. I had to clear my throat twice before he heard me. He shot up from his seat in surprise: "Mademoiselle?"

"I should like to see the First Consul."

"I am afraid, Mademoiselle, you have mistaken the room. This is his office."

I didn't know what the young man was driving at. "He hasn't gone to bed yet?" I asked.

"The First Consul is still working."

"Why, then, take me to him."

"Mademoiselle——" The young man, who, in his dilemma, had not dared to take his eyes from his boots, now looked up and faced me for the first time: "Mademoiselle," he said, blushing, "Constant, the valet, surely must have told you that he would expect you at the back door. These rooms here are—are the offices."

"But I want to speak to the First Consul, not to his valet. Go to him and ask him if I may disturb him for a moment. It is very important."

"Mademoiselle!" the young man said imploringly.

"Don't call me Mademoiselle but Madame. I am Madame Jean-Baptiste Bernadotte."

"Mademoi—I am so sorry—Madame—so sorry——" He looked at me as if I were a ghost. "So sorry," he murmured.

"All right. But would you mind announcing me now?"

The young man disappeared and returned almost immediately. "Madame, may I ask you to follow me? Some gentlemen are with the First Consul at the moment, and he asks you to wait just one second."

He took me into a small waiting-room where dark-red velvet chairs were grouped round a marble table. But I didn't have to wait long.

A door opened. Three or four men carrying piles of documents under their arms appeared, bending low and saying good-night to someone invisible to me, and went out towards the ante-room, whilst the secretary darted past them and into the First Consul's room. Next moment he shot out again and announced solemnly:

"Madame Jean-Baptiste Bernadotte, the First Consul will see you now."

"This is the most charming surprise for years," said Napoleon as I entered. He was standing close by the door, and he took my hands and put them to his lips, kissing first my right and then my left. I withdrew them quickly and didn't know what to say.

"Sit down, my dear, sit down. And tell me how you are. You are getting younger, younger every time I see you."

"Oh no," I said, "time flies. Next year we'll have to look round for a tutor for Oscar."

He pressed me into the easy-chair next to his desk. He himself, however, didn't sit down. Instead, he kept wandering round the room, and I had to crane my neck not to lose sight of him.

It was a very big room with a number of small tables standing about in it, all loaded with books and documents. But on the big writing desk the documents were arranged in two neat piles resting on wooden boards. Between the two piles, directly in front of the desk chair, lay a single sheet with a dark red seal affixed to it. A big fire roared in the fireplace. The room was hot to suffocation.

"You must see this," he said, and held out a few sheets closely printed in tiny letters with paragraph signs standing out in the margin, "the first copies fresh from the printers! It is the new Civil Law, the *Code Civil* of the French Republic! The laws for which the Revolution strove, here they are: worked out, written down and printed. And in force, for all time! I have given France its new Civil Law!"

Year after year, I knew, he had closeted himself with France's greatest lawyers and worked out the new code of law. And now, here it was, in print and in force.

"The most humane laws in history!" he said. "Just look here, for instance, concerning children: the first-born has no more rights than his younger brothers and sisters. And here: all parents are compelled to look after their children. And see here——" He fetched some more sheets from one of the small tables and began to explain their contents: "See here, the new marriage laws. They make possible not only divorce but separation. And here——" He fished out another sheet. "This concerns the nobility. Hereditary titles are abolished."

"The man in the street already calls your *Code Civil* the *Code Napoléon*," I said. This was perfectly true, but besides, I wanted to keep him in good humour.

He threw the sheets back on the mantelpiece and came up to me. "I am sorry," he said, "this must be very boring for you. Do take off your hat, Madame!"

"No, no," I said, "I am only going to stay for one moment, I only wanted——"

"But it doesn't suit you, Madame, really. May I take it off?"

"No. Besides, it is a new hat, and Jean-Baptiste said it suited me excellently."

He drew back at once. "Of course, if General Bernadotte says so——" He began pacing up and down again behind my back.

'Now I've annoyed him,' I thought, and quickly undid the ribbon holding my hat.

"May I ask," he said somewhat sharply, "how I came to have the honour of your visit at this hour?"

"I've taken the hat off," I said.

He stopped at once, and then came back to my chair touching my hair very lightly with his hand. "Eugenie," he said, "little Eugenie." It was the voice of that rainy night, the night when he and I got engaged.

I bent my head quickly to escape his hand. "I wanted to ask you a favour," I said in a trembling voice.

185

He went away across the width of the room and leaned against the mantelpiece. The flames from the fire were mirrored in his polished boots. "Of course," was all he said.

"Why 'of course'?" I said.

"I realise that you would not have come to see me without some ulterior motive," he said pointedly. Stooping to throw a log into the fire he continued: "Almost everybody who comes to me asks for some favour or other. One gets used to that in my position. Well now, Madame Jean-Baptiste Bernadotte, what can I do for you?"

His jeering was more than I could bear: "Do you imagine," I said in a fury, "that I'd have come to you in the middle of the night if it had not been for something particularly urgent?"

He seemed to enjoy my anger. Amusedly he rocked from his heels to his toes and back again. It struck me that apart from his short hair and his immaculately cut uniform he looked hardly different from the man who came to us in our garden in Marseilles.

"No," he said, "I should hardly think so, Madame Bernadotte, though perhaps, at the bottom of my heart, I may have hoped so. There is always room for hope, Madame, is there not?"

'That's the wrong way,' I thought in despair, 'I can't even get him to take me seriously.' My fingers started to play nervously with the silken rose on my hat.

"You are ruining your new hat, Madame," he said.

I didn't look up. A lump came into my throat, and I felt a hot tear running down my cheek. I tried to lick it up with the tip of my tongue.

"What do you want me to do, Eugenie?"

There he was again, the Napoleon of the old days, the gentle and candid one.

"You say that many people come to you to ask you favours. Do you usually do what they ask of you?"

"If it can be done, of course."

" 'Can be done'? But surely you are the most powerful man in France, aren't you?"

"I must be able to do it with a good conscience, Eugenie. What is your wish?"

"I am asking you to spare his life."

He did not answer at once, and the roar of the fire was the only sound.

"You are talking about the Duc d'Enghien?"

I nodded.

Tensely I waited for his answer, but he took his time. Meanwhile I tore the silken rose on my hat to pieces.

"Who has sent you with this request, Eugenie?"

"What does that matter? Many people are making this request, and I am one of them."

"I want to know who sent you," he said sharply.

I only shook my head.

"Madame, I am used to having my questions answered."

I looked up. He had pushed his head forward, his mouth was twisted and little flecks of foam appeared at the corners of his mouth. "You needn't shout," I said, "I am not afraid of you." And it was quite true, I wasn't afraid of him any longer.

"Yes, I know. You are very fond of acting the courageous young lady. I remember the scene at the house of Madame Tallien," he said between his teeth.

"I am not courageous at all, I am really rather a coward. But when there is much at stake I try to pluck up my courage."

"And," he said, "at that time, at Madame Tallien's, there was a lot at stake for you?"

"Everything," I said, and waited for some cynical remark from him. It did not come. I looked up and tried to catch his eye. "But there had been one occasion before that when I had had to pluck up my courage. That was at the time when my fiancé—you know, I was engaged once, long before I met General Bernadotte—when my fiancé had been arrested after the fall of Robespierre. We were afraid that he might be shot. His brothers thought it very dangerous, but I went with a parcel of underwear and a cake to the Military Commandant of Marseilles and——"

"Yes. And that is why I must know who it was that sent you to-night."

"What has that got to do with it?"

"Let me explain, Eugenie. The person or persons who sent you obviously know me very well. They really have found the one chance to save Enghien's life. Mind you, I am only saying 'chance'. But I am interested to find out who it is who possesses such exact knowledge of me, who uses this chance so cleverly and at the same time tries to oppose me politically. Well?"

I couldn't help smiling. The complications he saw in everything, the political problems!

"Do try, Madame, to see the situation for once through my eyes. The Jacobins blame me for allowing the *emigrés* to return and even for favouring them socially. At the same time they are busy spreading the rumour that I am selling the Republic to the Bourbons. Selling our France, this France which I created, France of the *Code Napoléon*, doesn't that sound crazy?"

As he was speaking he went up to the desk and took up the sheet with the dark red seal. He stared at the few words on it, threw it down on to the desk and turned back to me.

"By having this man Enghien executed I shall prove to the whole world that I consider the Bourbons as nothing but a gang of traitors. Do you understand, Madame? When I've finished with Enghien, however," here he started swaying backwards and forwards on his heels again, heel to toe, heel to toe, and an air of triumph appeared on his face—— "the turn of the others will come, the rioters, the malcontents, the pamphleteers and those confused dreamers who call me a tyrant. I shall eliminate them from the ranks of the French people and protect France against its internal enemies."

Internal enemies . . . where had I heard that before? Yes, Barras had said it once, a long time ago, and he had looked at Napoleon as he said it.

The golden clock on the mantelpiece showed the time: one o'clock. I rose. "It's getting very late," I said.

But he made me sit down again. "Don't go yet, Eugenie," he said. "I am so glad that you came to see me. And the night is long yet."

"You'll be tired yourself."

"I am a bad sleeper, I——" A hidden door which I hadn't noticed opened a few inches on the far side of the room. Napoleon didn't notice it.

"Someone's opened the door over there," I said.

Napoleon turned round. "What is it, Constant?"

A lackey, small and gesticulating ridiculously, appeared. Napoleon went over to him. The little man whispered agitatedly "——doesn't want to wait any longer." "Tell her to get dressed and go home," I heard Napoleon say. The lackey disappeared.

That was probably Mademoiselle George from the Théâtre Français, I thought. All Paris knows that Napoleon had had an *affaire* with the singer Grassini, and that she was succeeded by 'Georgina', this sixteen-year-old actress Mademoiselle George.

"I won't keep you any longer," I said, and got up.

"Now that I have sent her away you can't leave me to myself," he answered, and again I had to resume my seat. His voice grew tender: "You have asked me a favour, Eugenie. For the first time you have asked me for something."

I shut my eyes, weary. His constant change of mood exhausted me, and the heat in the room was stifling. Also, the man radiated a feverish restlessness which made me feel dizzy.

Strange, strange, that after all these years I could still echo every mood and every sentiment of this man. I knew without a doubt that, at this moment, he was trying to come to a decision, he was at odds with himself. No, this was not the moment to go; if I stayed he might give way, he might, he might.

"But, Eugenie, you don't know what you are asking. It is not the person of this Enghien that matters, no, what matters is to show all these Bourbons, to show the whole world what France feels. The French people itself will choose its ruler——" Here I pricked up my ears, as Napoleon continued: "Free citizens of a free Republic will go to the poll."

Was he reciting poetry, rehearsing a speech?

He went to the desk once more and took up the document. The dark red seal hung down from it like a gigantic drop of blood.

"You asked me," I said very loudly, "who had sent me to you to-night. I will answer that question before you make your decision."

"Well? I am listening," he said without looking at me.

"Your mother."

Slowly he put the document down, went to the fireplace and put on another log. "I did not know," he said in low tones, "that my mother occupied herself with politics. Most likely she has been pestered and plagued——"

"Your mother does not consider the death sentence as a political matter."

"But as?"

"Murder."

"Eugenie! You have gone too far now!"

"Your mother asked me so very urgently to speak to you. God knows, it's no easy matter!"

The ghost of a smile flitted over his face, and he began to rummage among the piles of documents and files on the small tables. At last he had found what he wanted, a big sheet of drawing paper which he unrolled and held out to me. "How do you like this? I have not shown it to anybody yet."

The top of the sheet showed the sketch of a big bee, and a square in the middle showed a number of small bees at regular intervals from each other. "Bees?" I asked in amazement.

"Yes, bees." He nodded, gratified. "So you know what they stand for?"

I shook my head.

"It is an emblem."

"An emblem? Where are you going to use it?"

He made a sweeping gesture. "Where? Everywhere. On

189

walls, carpets, curtains, liveries, court equipages, the coronation robe of the Emperor——"

I sat up, startled. It made him stop and look at me. His eyes held mine as he said slowly: "Do you understand—Eugenie, little fiancée?"

I felt nothing but my heart racing in my body. Already he was unrolling another sheet. It contained lions, lions in all sorts of positions, lions rampant, lions puissant, lions couchant. Across the top of the sheet Napoleon's hand had written: 'An eagle with outspread wings.'

"I commissioned the painter David to design the coat of arms." He dropped the lions to the floor and handed me the sketch of an eagle with wings spread. "This is my choice. Do you like it?"

It was so hot in the room, I could hardly breathe. The outlines of the eagle blurred before my eyes. It seemed to grow to alarming proportions.

"My coat of arms. The arms of the Emperor of the French."

Had I dreamed these words or had I really heard them? I pulled myself together. The sketch trembled in my hands. I hadn't noticed that he had given it to me.

Napoleon was back at his desk, standing there rigidly, his mouth a thin hard line, his chin jutting out, staring at the document with the red seal. Beads of perspiration ran down my forehead, but my eyes were as if riveted to his face.

He bent forward now. He seized the pen. He wrote a single word on the paper and sanded it. Then he rang the handbell, a bell on the top of which was fixed the brass figure of an eagle with outspread wings.

The secretary arrived within a second. Napoleon folded the document carefully and gave it to him. "Seal it!" he said and watched the secretary do so. "Go at once to Vincennes," he ordered, "and hand it to the Commanding Officer himself. I'll hold you responsible for placing it in the Commanding Officer's hands."

The secretary bowed himself out of the room. In a hoarse voice I asked: "I should like to know what you have decided."

Napoleon stooped down to collect from the floor the leaves of the silk rose from my hat. "You have ruined your hat, Madame," he said, and passed me the handful of bits.

I rose, put the sketch of the eagle on one of the tables and threw the bits into the fire.

"Don't take it to heart," he said. "The hat did not suit you anyway."

Napoleon accompanied me through the empty corridors. Bees, I thought, as we went along, bees will be on all the walls here.

He took me right down to the carriage.

"Your mother is waiting for the answer. What am I to tell her?"

He bent over my hand but did not kiss it. "Give her my best wishes. And many thanks to you, Madame, for your visit."

I found Madame Letitia where I had left her, in the armchair by the window. The light of dawn was spreading over the sky and the first birds twittered in the garden. Jean-Baptiste was working at his desk.

"I am sorry that I have been so long," I said. "He would not let me go. He talked about all sorts of things." My head felt like bursting.

"Has he made his decision?" Madame Letitia asked.

"Oh yes. But he didn't tell me what it was. And I am to give you his best wishes, Madame."

"Thank you, my child." Madame Letitia got up and went to the door. There she turned round again and said: "Thank you, thank you—whatever happens."

Jean-Baptiste carried me up to the bedroom. He undressed me. I was too tired to do anything at all. "Do you know," I said, "that Napoleon wants to be Emperor?"

"I have heard the rumour, probably spread by his enemies. Who told you?"

"Napoleon himself."

Jean-Baptiste stared at me, then turned away abruptly and went into the dressing-room. I heard him walking up and down there for hours, and I could only fall asleep after he, at last, had come to bed and I could put my head on his shoulder.

I slept very late next morning and had awful dreams of a white sheet of paper over which blood-red bees kept crawling. Marie brought me my breakfast and a late morning edition of the *Moniteur*. There, on the front page, it said that at five o'clock this morning at the Fortress of Vincennes the Duc d'Enghien had been executed by a firing squad.

A few hours later Madame Letitia left to join her exiled son Lucien in Italy.

"Her Imperial Highness, the Princess Joseph!" Fernand announced. And my sister Julie swept into the room.

"*Madame la Maréchale,* and how are you this morning?" said Julie, and the corners of her mouth twitched, with laughter or with tears?

"Thank you, Your Imperial Highness," I said, and bowed low, exactly as Monsieur Montel had taught me in days gone by.

"I've come a bit earlier, so that we can have a few moments in the garden," said my sister, Her Imperial Highness, Princess of France.

Our garden is small, and in spite of Josephine's advice the rose trees haven't done too well, and there is no tree to equal the beautiful chestnut tree in Sceaux. But when the lilac and the two little apple trees, which Jean-Baptiste planted on Oscar's first birthday, are in bloom there is no lovelier place for me anywhere on earth than this garden in the Rue Cisalpine.

Julie dusted the garden seat carefully before sitting down in her light blue satin frock. Marie brought us some lemonade and looked critically at Julie. "Imperial Highness ought to put a bit of rouge on," she said. "*Madame la Maréchale* looks much prettier."

Julie threw back her head angrily: "*Madame la Maréchale* hasn't got my troubles. I am so bothered, Marie. We are moving into the Luxembourg Palace."

"The beautiful house in the Rue du Rocher doesn't seem to be good enough for Princess Julie," said Marie acidly.

"Marie, you are unfair. I hate castles, I hate them. But we must move there because the Heir to the Throne of France and his wife must live in the Luxembourg Palace."

Julie, wife of the Heir to the Throne of France, looked very miserable. But Marie did not change her tune. "The late Monsieur Clary would not have approved of it, indeed he wouldn't," she said, putting her hands on her hips. "Your late papa was a Republican, you know!"

Julie made a despairing gesture. "It isn't my fault," she moaned.

"Leave us alone for a bit, Marie," I asked. When Marie had gone I said to Julie: "Don't listen to that old dragon."

"But really, it isn't my fault," she wailed. "Moving is no fun, God knows, and all these ceremonies make me ill. Yesterday, during the parade for the Marshals, we had to stand for three whole hours, and to-day, in the Dôme des Invalides——"

"To-day we're going to sit down," I assured her. "Drink your lemonade."

The lemonade had exactly the same kind of taste as the one that these last days had left on my tongue, bitter-sweet. They had been sweet because we had been inundated with congratulations on Jean-Baptiste's promotion to Marshal of France.

The Marshal's rank is every soldier's dream whether he is a private or a General. And now this dream has come true for my husband, but so differently, so very differently from the way we had imagined.

Shortly after my visit to the Tuileries the leader of the Royalists, George Cadoudal, had been captured. After the Duc d'Enghien's execution no one had any doubt as to what was going to happen to him. But I grew nearly sick with anxiety for Jean-Baptiste when suddenly General Moreau, General Pichegru and other officers were arrested as Cadoudal's accomplices. At any moment we expected the police. Instead of that, however, Jean-Baptiste, as once before, was called to the Tuileries to the First Consul.

"The French people has decided for me. Are you going to oppose the will of the people?"

"I have never opposed the will of the people, and I cannot imagine myself ever doing it," Jean-Baptiste answered calmly.

"We shall promote you to the rank of Marshal."

"We?" asked Jean-Baptiste.

"Yes, We, Napoleon the First, Emperor of the French."

Jean-Baptiste was speechless, and Napoleon, seeing his speechless stupor, slapped his knee and danced about the room in merriment.

General Moreau was found guilty of high treason but not condemned to death, only banished. He went to America in the uniform of a French General and with his sword, on which were engraved all the names of the victorious battles he had fought, dangling from his belt.

After that things happened in quick succession. The day before yesterday the First Consul went hunting near St. Cloud. There he allowed himself to be surprised by the decision of the Senate to elect him Emperor of the French. Yesterday, during an elaborate military parade he handed the Marshal's baton to eighteen of the most famous Generals of the French Army. A week before that Jean-Baptiste had been told in strict confidence to order a Marshal's uniform according to a drawing which reached him from the Tuileries. After they had received their batons each of the new Marshals made a short speech. All eighteen of them addressed Napoleon as 'Your Majesty'. During Murat's and Masséna's speeches Napoleon kept his eyes half shut; one could tell how these last days had exhausted him. When Jean-Baptiste started his speech, however, a tense expression came into Napoleon's face, which finally changed into a smile, that winning spell-binding smile of his. He walked up to Jean-Baptiste, shook his hand and told him to consider him 'not only his Emperor but also his friend'. Jean-Baptiste stood to attention and did not let an eyelid flicker.

I witnessed all this from a stand erected for the wives of the eighteen Marshals. Oscar was with me, although it had been hinted that this would not be desirable. "Just imagine, *Madame la Maréchale*," some master of ceremonies had moaned, "just imagine how awful it would be if your infant interrupted His Majesty's speech by his crying!" But I wanted Oscar to be present when his papa was made a Marshal of France. When the many thousands of spectators cheered Napoleon because he was shaking Jean-Baptiste by the hand, Oscar in excitement waved the little flag which I had bought for him.

Julie was in a different stand, that of the Imperial family. Since an Emperor has to have an Imperial family Napoleon made his brothers—with the exception of Lucien, of course—Imperial Princes and their wives Imperial Princesses. Joseph is regarded as the heir apparent so long as Napoleon himself has no son. Madame Letitia's title caused Napoleon a lot of headaches. He could not well call her 'Empress Mother,' since she had never been an Empress, only the wife of the modest Corsican lawyer Carlo Buonaparte. But he and his brothers and sisters usually talk about her as '*Madame Mère*', and so he hit on the idea of introducing her to the nation as just that: *Madame Mère*. *Madame Mère*, by the way, is still in Italy with Lucien. As for Hortense, wife of the flat-footed Prince Louis, and Eugene her brother, they too were promoted to Imperial rank.

Napoleon's sisters had very rashly got themselves gowns embroidered all over with bees. Yet the *Moniteur* had nothing to say about any promotion of theirs to Princess. Caroline, who had married General Murat shortly after the *coup d'état* in Brumaire, became a *Madame la Maréchale* like me. According to the *Moniteur* a Marshal of France has a right to be addressed as 'Monseigneur', and Caroline, having taken her place next to me on the stand, asked me seriously whether I was going to address my husband in future as 'Monseigneur' in public. Such a stupid question, I thought, merited a very stupid answer, and so I said: "No. I call him Jean-Baptiste when there are other people about. Only in our bedroom do I call him Monseigneur."

After the ceremony we, the eighteen Marshals and their wives, dined with the Imperial family in the Tuileries. The walls, the carpets, the curtains were covered with embroidered bees. Many hundreds of women must have been working day and night to get them all embroidered in time.

At first I couldn't think of what this bee design reminded me. But as the evening went on and I had more and more champagne the bees seemed to be standing on their heads. And suddenly I knew: the lily! Napoleon's bee was the Bourbon lily upside down! 'That can't be an accident,' I thought, and I wanted to ask Napoleon about it. But he was sitting too far away from me. I sometimes heard him laugh loudly, and once, when there was a moment's silence, I heard him address his youngest sister Caroline as '*Madame la Maréchale*'.

"I don't know how it is all going to end," I said to Julie as we were sitting now on our garden seat.

"But it has only just started," said Julie in low tones, and held a smelling-bottle to her nose.

"Aren't you feeling well?" I asked her, frightened.

"I can't sleep at all now," she said. "Imagine, if the Emperor really has no son and Joseph does succeed him and I——" She began to tremble violently and threw her arms round my neck. "Désirée, you are the only one who understands me. Désirée, I am only the daughter of the silk merchant Clary, how can I——"

Gently I took her arms from my neck. "You must pull yourself together, Julie. Show them who you are, show Paris, show the whole country."

"But who am I, Désirée, who am I?" She trembled more violently than ever.

"You are the daughter of the silk merchant François Clary," I said with great emphasis. "Don't you forget that, Julie Clary! Aren't you ashamed of yourself?"

Julie got up and I took her to my bedroom. Her hair was disarranged and her nose red from tears. I helped her to put herself straight again. In the middle of it I couldn't help laughing out loud. "No wonder, Julie, that you feel tired and worn. Ladies belonging to a noble house are always most delicate, and Princess Julie of the noble family of the Bonapartes is therefore bound to be less robust than *Citoyenne* Bernadotte."

"You are making a great mistake, Désirée, if you don't take Napoleon seriously," said Julie.

"You forget that I was the very first person ever to take him seriously," I told Julie. "But let's hurry up now. I want to see the procession of the Senators on our way to the Dôme."

In Julie's carriage we reached the Luxembourg Palace and there heard Napoleon proclaimed Emperor of the French. The proclamation procession arrived with a battalion of dragoons at its head, followed, on foot, by twelve perspiring City Councillors. Obviously it could have been no fun for these pouchy gentlemen to march in slow procession right across Paris. Behind them appeared the two Prefects in dress uniform, and, announced by the roaring laughter of the crowd, old Fontanes, the President of the Senate, on horseback. The horse, a very gentle bay, was led along by a groom. In spite of that the President looked most precarious in his saddle. In his left hand he held a parchment roll, whereas his right clung to the horse's neck for dear life. All the members of the Senate followed their President, and then a band came in sight playing a vigorous march which frightened Fontanes on his horse even more. The highest officers of the Paris garrison and four cavalry squadrons brought up the rear.

The procession stopped in front of the Luxembourg Palace. A trumpeter sounded a signal in all four directions, old Fontanes drew himself up solemnly and read from his parchment something which—as I read later in the papers—said that the Senate had resolved to elect the First Consul General Napoleon Bonaparte to be Emperor of the French. The crowd listened in silence to the trembling voice of the old man, and when he had finished a few voices shouted "*Vive l'Empereur!*" The band played the Marseillaise and the procession went on its way to repeat the proclamation at other places.

Julie and I went on from there to the Dôme des Invalides. We were taken to the gallery which was reserved for the Empress, the Imperial ladies and the wives of the Marshals. We only just arrived in time.

Below there was a sea of uniforms. Seven hundred pensioned officers and two hundred pupils of the Polytechnic filled the seats. In front of them, on eighteen gilded chairs, sat the Marshals in blue and gold uniforms. They were conversing eagerly and were not, like the ex-officers and the future technicians, overpowered by the solemnity of the occasion.

Now the cardinal approached the altar, and as he knelt down in silent prayer the Marshals, too, fell silent. At the same time trumpets outside and the sound of innumerable voices shouting "*Vive l'Empereur, vive l'Empereur*" announced the arrival of Napoleon.

The cardinal rose and, followed by ten priests of high rank, went slowly towards the entrance. Here he received the Emperor of the French.

The Emperor entered accompanied by Joseph, Louis and his ministers. The two Princes wore peculiar uniforms which made them look like flunkeys on the stage of the Théâtre Français. The column of great secular and clerical dignitaries shimmered in all the colours of the rainbow as it moved up towards the altar with Napoleon and the cardinal at its head. But Napoleon's uniform, alone amidst all the glitter of the rest, was of an inconspicuous dark green and showed no medals at all.

"He's mad," whispered Caroline, "he's only put on a colonel's uniform without any medals."

Hortense, her neighbour, dug her elbows into Caroline's ribs and hushed her.

Slowly Napoleon ascended the three steps leading up to the throne on the left of the altar. At any rate, I thought that it was a throne, never having seen one before. And there he sat, a small lonely figure in a colonel's field uniform.

I strained my eyes in order to make out the emblem on the high back of the throne. It was an N, a big N surrounded by a laurel wreath.

The rustle of satin gowns around me made me realise that Mass had begun and that I had to kneel. Napoleon had got up meanwhile and descended two steps. I heard Caroline whisper into Polette's ear that he had refused to make his confession, although Uncle Fesch had tried hard to get him to change his mind. Hortense hissed at her and Caroline grew silent. Josephine had put her folded hands in front of her face and she looked as if she were deep in prayer.

Uncle Fesch, yes, Uncle Fesch! The rotund abbot who during the Revolution had preferred to become a commercial traveller, and had asked Etienne for a job with the firm of Clary, had long ago returned to his clerical garb. From the day on which French troops had entered Rome and General Bonaparte had dictated the terms of peace to the Vatican, there had never been any doubt that a cardinal's hat was waiting for Uncle Fesch. And there he was now down below in a cardinal's crimson robe, holding aloft the monstrance.

Everybody was kneeling: the Marshals, the ex-officers who in the hour of the Republic's need had defended its frontiers at the head of peasants, workmen, fishermen, clerks and raw recruits, the young pupils of the Polytechnic, Josephine, the first Empress of the French, and the whole Bonaparte family by her side, and all the priests, high or low. Only Napoleon was on his feet, standing on the first step to the throne and politely inclining his head.

The last tone of the organ died away. Absolute silence reigned, as if the thousand people filling the Cathedral had stopped breathing.

Napoleon had taken a paper from his tunic and started speaking. But he never looked at his notes; he spoke freely and effortlessly. His voice floated through the nave with a metallic hardness and purity.

"He's taken lessons from an actor," whispered Caroline again.

"No, an actress, Mademoiselle George," giggled Polette under her breath.

"Hush!" said Hortense.

As Napoleon came to the end of his speech he descended from the last step of his throne, went before the altar and raised his hand, saying: "And lastly you swear that, with all the strength at your disposal, you will guard liberty and equality, the principles on which all our institutions are based. Swear!"

All hands flew up, and mine with them. In unison the congregation shouted, "We swear!" The mighty shout rose up to the cupola and ebbed away.

The organ intoned the 'Te Deum'. Napoleon returned to his throne with measured steps, sat down and looked at the assembly. The sound of the organ filled the Cathedral.

Accompanied by his eighteen Marshals in their resplendent uniforms, Napoleon, an inconspicuous spot of green among the golden glitter, left the Dôme. Outside he mounted a white horse and rode back to the Tuileries at the head of the officers of his Guard regiments. The crowd went delirious with joy; one woman held up her baby to him and shouted: "Bless my son, bless him!"

Jean-Baptiste was waiting for me by our carriage. On the journey home I asked him, "You've been sitting right in front close to him. Did his face show any signs of emotion as he sat there on his throne?"

"He smiled. But only his face, not his eyes."

He didn't say any more, and stared silently in front of him.

"What are you thinking of?" I asked.

"Of the collar of my uniform. The regulation height is awful, I can't stand it. Besides, the collar is too tight."

I studied his get-up more closely: a white satin waistcoat, a dark blue tunic embroidered with oak leaves in gold thread. The blue velvet greatcoat was lined with white satin and bordered with gold, and gigantic golden oak leaves were strewn along the edges.

"Your one-time fiancé is making it easy for himself. He squeezes us into this strangulating outfit, yet he himself puts on the comfortable field officer's uniform," Jean-Baptiste said, disgruntled.

Leaving the carriage in front of our house we found ourselves surrounded by some shabbily dressed young men. *"Vive Bernadotte!"* they shouted, *"vive Bernadotte!"*

Jean-Baptiste eyed them for a fraction of a second and answered: *"Vive l'Empereur!"*

Later on, as we faced each other at table, he remarked casually: "You'll be interested to know that the Emperor has given his Chief of Police the order to keep watch not only over the private life of his Marshals but also over their private correspondence."

I thought this over and said after a little while: "Julie told me that he is having himself crowned properly in the winter."

Jean-Baptiste laughed. "Crowned by whom? By his Uncle Fesch in Notre-Dame perhaps?"

"No, he wants the Pope to crown him."

He put the glass of wine which he had just taken up back on the table with such vehemence that the wine spilled out all over the tablecloth. "That is, that is——" He shook his head. "No, Désirée, I think that that is out of the question. Do you think that he'd go on a pilgrimage to Rome to have himself crowned there?"

"Oh no. He wants the Pope to come here for the coronation."

Jean-Baptiste found this unbelievable. He explained to me that the Pope to the best of his knowledge had never yet left the Vatican for coronations abroad.

I put salt on the wine stains so that they could be more easily removed in the laundry, and said: "Joseph thinks that Napoleon is going to force the Pope to come."

"God knows, I hold no brief for the Holy Church of Rome—you wouldn't expect it of an old sergeant in the Army of the Revolution, anyway—but I don't think it right to force the old gentleman to a journey from Rome to Paris over these miserable roads."

"They've dug up an old crown somewhere, a sceptre and an orb, and everybody is going to have a part in the ceremony," I said. "Joseph and Louis are having costumes made in the Spanish court manner. Louis in particular, with his corporation and his flat feet, will look smart."

Jean-Baptiste pondered and then said: "I shall ask him to

give me some administrative job somewhere as far as possible away from Paris. A really responsible job for some territory, not only just a military one but one that involves civil authority as well. I have thought out a new licensing system and Customs law, and I think I could do something to raise the prosperity of the country of which I should be put in charge."

"But then you would have to go away again!"

"I should have to do that in any case. Bonaparte will never give us permanent peace, you know. We Marshals shall be for ever crossing Europe till——" He paused for a moment, then continued, "till we have ruined ourselves with our victories."

During these words Jean-Baptiste had started to undo his collar. "This Marshal's uniform is too tight for you," I said.

"True, my little girl. The Marshal's uniform is too tight for me. And that's why Sergeant Bernadotte is going to leave Paris soon. Come, drink up, let's go to bed."

PARIS, 9th Frimaire of the Year XII.
(*November 30th, 1804, according to the Church calendar.*)

THE Pope did come to Paris after all to crown Napoleon and Josephine!

And Jean-Baptiste made a dreadful scene because he had suddenly turned jealous—of Napoleon, not of the Pope.

This afternoon in the Tuileries we rehearsed the coronation procession of the Empress. My head is still heavy from it. Besides, I am feeling desperate because of Jean-Baptiste's jealousy. So, what with one thing and another, I can't go to sleep and I'm sitting at Jean-Baptiste's big writing desk with his many books and maps on it and writing in my diary. Jean-Baptiste himself has gone out, I don't know where.

In two days' time the coronation will take place, and for months past Paris has been talking of nothing else. It will be the most magnificent spectacle of all time, Napoleon said. He forced the Pope to come to Paris to let the whole world, and in particular the adherents of the Bourbons, see for themselves that the coronation in Notre-Dame is the real thing.

Most of the former grandees of the Court of Versailles—all of them pious Roman Catholics—had secretly laid bets against the Pope's coming. Hardly one of them thought he would. And lo and behold, who arrived a few days ago with a suite of six cardinals, four archbishops, six prelates and a whole host of physicians, secretaries, Swiss bodyguards and lackeys? His Holiness Pope Pius VII!

Josephine gave a banquet in his honour in the Tuileries, from which the Pope retired and in high dudgeon because she wanted to amuse him with a ballet performance afterwards. Oh yes, she had meant well. "Seeing that he is in Paris anyway. . . ." she tried to explain to Uncle Fesch. But Uncle Fesch, every inch a cardinal now, was much annoyed and cut her short.

The members of the Imperial family have been rehearsing the coronation ritual for weeks, alternately at Fontainebleau and in the Tuileries. This afternoon we too, the wives of the eighteen Marshals, were ordered to the Tuileries to rehearse the Empress's coronation procession. I went there with Laura Junot and Madame Berthier, and we were taken to Josephine's white room. We arrived there in the middle of a furious argument between various members of the Bonaparte family.

The responsibility for the conduct of the ceremony falls on Joseph, but all the details are in the hands of the Master of Ceremonies, Monsieur Despreaux, who is to receive a fee of 2400 francs for his work. He therefore is actually in charge, assisted by this dreadful Monsieur Montel who, years ago, gave me lessons in deportment.

We Marshals' wives huddled together in a corner and tried to find out what the argument was about.

"But it is His Majesty's explicit wish!" shouted Despreaux at this moment, in despair.

"And even if he throws me out of France as he did poor Lucien, I'm not going to do it," vituperated Eliza Bacciochi.

"Carry the train? Me carry the train?" shouted Polette indignantly.

Joseph tried to calm them down: "But Julie and Hortense have to do it too, and they don't refuse although they are Imperial Highnesses."

"Imperial Highnesses indeed!" hissed Caroline. "Why haven't we, the Emperor's sisters, been made Highnesses, may I ask? Are we less than Julie, the silk merchant's daughter, and——"

I felt my face grow red with rage.

"—and Hortense, the daughter of this—of this——" Caroline fumbled for a suitable word of abuse for Her Majesty Empress Josephine.

"Ladies, ladies, please!" implored Despreaux.

"It's about the coronation robe with that enormous train,"

whispered Laura Junot into my ear. "The Emperor wants his sisters and the Princesses Julie and Hortense to carry it."

"Well, can we start the rehearsal?" It was Josephine who had entered by a side door. She looked very peculiar in two sheets sewn together over her shoulder to represent the coronation gown, which apparently was not ready yet. We sank into a deep curtsey.

"Please take your places for Her Majesty's procession," Joseph called out.

"And if she stands on her head, I am not going to carry her train," said Eliza Bacciochi once more.

Despreaux came over to us. "Hm," he said, "the eighteen Marshals' ladies are only seventeen, I see. *Madame la Maréchale* Murat as the Emperor's sister is carrying the train."

"She wouldn't dream of it," shouted Caroline across the room.

"I don't quite see," meditated Despreaux, "how seventeen ladies, two by two—— Montel, can you tell me how to group seventeen ladies in nine couples to proceed ahead of Her Majesty?"

Montel danced towards us and frowned heavily. "Seventeen ladies—in couples—not one must go by herself——"

"May I assist you in the solution of this strategic problem?" asked a voice close to us. Startled we spun round, and immediately sank into another curtsey.

"I suggest that only sixteen of these ladies open the procession of Her Majesty. Then Securier, as arranged, with the ring of the Empress, Murat with her crown and finally one of these ladies with a—with a cushion with one of Her Majesty's lace handkerchiefs on it. It will give it a very poetic flavour."

"Magnificent, Your Majesty," murmured Despreaux, and bowed deeply, as did Montel by his side.

"And this lady carrying the lace handkerchief——" Napoleon paused and with apparent thoughtfulness his eyes glanced round us, from Madame Berthier to Laura Junot, from Laura Junot to the ugly Madame Lefébvre.

But I knew his decision. Firmly I avoided looking at him. I wanted to be one of the sixteen, just the wife of Marshal Bernadotte, neither more nor less. I certainly didn't want an exceptional position, I certainly didn't want——

But Napoleon spoke: "We ask Madame Jean-Baptiste Bernadotte to take over this task. Madame Bernadotte will look charming. In sky-blue, don't you think so?"

"Sky-blue doesn't suit me," I jerked out, remembering the pale blue silk frock I had worn in Madame Tallien's salon.

"Yes, sky-blue, I think," the Emperor, who no doubt remembered that frock too, repeated, and turned away.

As he went over towards his sisters, Polette opened her mouth and said: "Sire, we don't want——"

"Madame, you are forgetting yourself!" Napoleon's voice came cuttingly across the room. Of course, no one may speak to the Emperor without permission.

Napoleon turned to Joseph: "More difficulties?"

"The girls don't want to carry the Empress's train."

"Why not?"

"Sire, the Ladies Bacciochi and Murat and the Princess Borghese are of the opinion that——"

"In that case the Princesses Joseph and Louis Bonaparte will carry the train by themselves," Napoleon decided.

Here Josephine intervened.

"The train is far too heavy for two," she said.

"If we don't get the same rights as Julie and Hortense," said Eliza, "we shall do without the same duties."

"Hold your tongue!" Napoleon turned to Polette, of whom he is quite fond. "Well, what exactly do you want?"

"We have the same claim to Imperial rank as those two," said Polette, pointing with her chin in Julie's and Hortense's direction.

He raised his eyebrows. "Indeed! One would think that I had inherited our father's Imperial crown and was cheating my brothers and sisters out of their rightful inheritance! They seem to forget that every distinction conferred is nothing but a proof of goodwill on my part, a goodwill so far entirely unearned, surely?"

In the silence following his words Josephine's voice came sweetly: "Sire, I beg of you that you, in your gracious kindness, may see fit to raise your sisters to the rank of Imperial Highness."

She is looking for allies, it occurred to me, she is afraid. Perhaps it was true what people were saying, that he was thinking of divorce. . . .

Napoleon laughed. He seemed to find it all very amusing, and I saw now that the whole thing had been amusing him from the very beginning. "All right," he said, "if you promise to behave I shall confer on you——"

"Sire!" shouted Eliza and Caroline in joyous surprise, and Polette said breathlessly: "*Grazie tante*, Napoleone!"

"I should like to see the rehearsal of the coronation procession," said Napoleon, turning to Despreaux. "Please start!"

Someone played a solemn hymn on a piano. It was meant to indicate the organ. Despreaux divided up the Marshals' ladies into eight couples, and Montel showed them how to walk gracefully and at the same time solemnly. But the ladies were quite unable to do it because of the presence of the Emperor, who with a stony face kept staring at their feet. Dreadfully embarrassed and awkward, they stumbled through the room, and Polette put her hand to her mouth to prevent a fit of laughter. At last Securier and Murat were called in. They joined the parade of ladies, gravely carrying a cushion from a divan on their outspread palms. After them I had to do the walking by myself, likewise carrying an ordinary cushion. Finally it was Josephine's turn, and the freshly promoted Imperial Highnesses, with Julie and Hortense, carried her dragging bed-sheets without the slightest objection.

Four times we walked up and down the room. We stopped only when Napoleon turned to go. We curtseyed as he left. But Joseph ran after him shouting, "Sire, I implore you, Sire!"

Impatiently Napoleon said, "I have no more time to spare."

"Sire, it concerns the virgins," Joseph explained, and beckoned Despreaux to come.

Despreaux came and repeated, "The virgins, Sire. They are a difficult problem. We cannot find any."

Napoleon suppressed a smile. "For what do you need virgins, gentlemen?"

"It may have escaped Your Majesty's memory, but the chronicle about the medieval coronation ritual in Rheims, according to which we are to proceed, states that, after the anointing of Your Majesty, twelve pure virgins have to go up to the altar, a candle in each hand. We thought of a cousin of Marshal Berthier's and one of my mother's sisters, but——" Despreaux stammered, "but, but both ladies are—are not——"

"They are virgins but too old," Murat's voice trumpeted across the room. Murat, the cavalry officer, had momentarily forgotten his courtier's dignity.

"I have repeatedly stressed my desire to allow France's traditional nobility to take part in the coronation ceremonies, which are the concern of the whole of France. I am convinced, gentlemen, that among the families of the Faubourg St. Germain you will find some suitable young ladies." With that he finally disappeared.

Refreshments were handed round, and Josephine sent one of her ladies-in-waiting to ask me to join her on the sofa. She wanted to show her pleasure at the distinction Napoleon had conferred on me. She sat between Julie and myself and emptied a glass of champagne in hasty gulps. The delicate face seemed to have shrunk during the last few months, the eyes under their make-up looked unnaturally big, and the magnificent layer of paint on her cheeks showed tiny cracks. Two fine lines ran from her nostrils down to the corners of her mouth, and her forced smile made them show up considerably. But her babyish curls, brushed upwards as usual, still had their old spell of touching youthfulness about them.

"Le Roy won't be able," I remarked, "to let me have a sky-blue gown within two days."

Josephine, exhausted by hours and hours of rehearsal, forgot that she must no longer bring up her past and said: "Paul Barras once gave me some sapphire ear-rings. If I can find them I shall gladly lend them to you to go with your blue gown."

"Madame, you are too kind, but I believe——"

Here I was interrupted by a very agitated-looking Joseph.

"What is it now?" Josephine asked.

"His Majesty asks Your Majesty to see him at once in his study."

Josephine arched her eyebrows. "New difficulties about the coronation, my dear brother-in-law?"

Joseph could no longer contain his malicious joy and, bending forward, he said: "The Pope has just told the Emperor that he refuses to crown Your Majesty."

An ironical smile curled round Josephine's lips. "And what reason does the Holy Father give for his refusal?"

Joseph looked round the room with affected discretion.

"You may speak. Except for Princess Julie and Madame Bernadotte nobody can hear us, and these two ladies are members of the family, are they not?"

Putting on an impressive air Joseph said: "The Pope has learnt that His Majesty and Your Majesty did not contract their marriage in church, and he has stated that he could not— I apologise, but these are the words of the Holy Father—that he could not crown the concubine of the Emperor of the French."

"And where did the Holy Father learn so suddenly that Bonaparte and I were married in a registry office only?" Josephine inquired calmly.

"We do not know yet," Joseph answered.

"And how, do you think, is His Majesty going to answer the Holy Father?" Josephine looked thoughtfully at the empty glass in her hand.

"His Majesty will naturally enter into negotiations with the Holy Father."

"There is a very simple way out." Josephine smiled, rising

to her feet and pressing the champagne glass into Joseph's hand. "I shall talk to Bona—, to the Emperor about it at once. We shall get married in church, and everything will be all right."

Joseph passed the glass on to one of the lackeys and ran after her to be present at the interview if possible. Julie meditated and said: "I shouldn't be surprised if she has drawn the Pope's attention to it herself."

"Yes, otherwise she would have shown some genuine surprise," I admitted.

Julie studied her hands. "You know, I am sorry for her. She is so afraid of a divorce. And it would be so mean if he kicked her out now, simply because she can't have any more children. Don't you think so too?"

I shrugged my shoulders. "Here he is, staging this elaborate coronation farce in the style of Charlemagne and the ritual of Rheims and Heaven knows what, in order to impress on the world that he has founded a dynasty. And all that simply to make Joseph Emperor, if he survives him, or the small son of Louis and Hortense."

"But he can't just throw her into the street!" Tears came into Julie's eyes. "She got engaged to him when he was too poor to buy himself a pair of trousers. She accompanied him in his career step by step, she helped him make his way, and now that her crown has been delivered and everybody regards her as the Empress——"

"No," I said, "he can't play at Charlemagne and have himself crowned by the Pope, and at the same time, like any Tom, Dick and Harry, be involved in a divorce action. If even *I* see that, Josephine, who is a hundred times cleverer than I, sees it most certainly too. No, Napoleon is sure to insist on her coronation and therefore will hastily arrange a church marriage ceremony."

"And once their marriage has the Church's sanction a divorce will be far more difficult, won't it? And Josephine counts on that, doesn't she?"

"I'm sure she does."

"Besides," continued Julie, "he loves her, in his own way, of course, but he loves her and wouldn't just abandon her like that."

"Wouldn't he? Wouldn't he? Believe me, Napoleon would."

At that moment the Empress returned. Passing a lackey, she took a glass of champagne from him, called to Despreaux, "One more rehearsal, please," and came to us.

"Uncle Fesch is going to marry us secretly to-night in the

206

Imperial Chapel," she said, drinking with nervous haste. "Is it not funny? After having been man and wife for nine years! Well, *Madame la Maréchale*, have you thought it over, and would you like to borrow my sapphires?"

. . . .

On the way home I decided that I would not let myself be forced by Napoleon to wear pale blue. To-morrow morning Le Roy would deliver my shell-pink robe—all the Marshals' wives are to be dressed in shell-pink—and I should carry Josephine's handkerchief across Notre-Dame in shell-pink.

Jean-Baptiste was waiting for me in the dining-room, apparently in a very bad temper. "What were you doing all this time in the Tuileries?"

"I listened to the Bonapartes arguing among themselves and then took part in the rehearsal. By the way, they've given me a special part to play. I am not to walk with the other Marshals' ladies but by myself behind Murat and I am to carry a handkerchief for Josephine on a cushion. What do you say to this distinction?"

Jean-Baptiste flew out: "But I don't want you to have a special position. Joseph and this monkey, Despreaux, thought it out because you are Julie's sister. But I forbid it, you understand?"

I sighed. "That won't be any use. It's nothing to do with Joseph and Despreaux. The Emperor wants it."

I should never have thought it possible that anything could upset Jean-Baptiste as badly as this did. In a hoarse voice he brought out: "What was that you said?"

"The Emperor wants it. It isn't my fault."

"I will not have it! I will not have my wife compromised before the whole of France!" Jean-Baptiste roared so violently that the glasses on the table tinkled.

I didn't know what to make of his rage. "Why are you so furious?" I asked.

"They will point at you. His fiancée, they will say, Madame Jean-Baptiste Bernadotte, the great love of his youth whom he cannot forget, they will say, his little Eugénie to whom he wants to show special favour on the day of his coronation, now as ever his little Eugénie, that's what they will say! And I shall be the laughing-stock of all Paris, do you see?"

Disconcerted, I stared at Jean-Baptiste. Nobody knows as well as I do how his strained relationship with Napoleon tortures him, how he is haunted constantly by the thought of having betrayed the ideals of his youth, and how agonisingly he is waiting for the independent command as far away from Paris as possible, for which he has applied and for which Napoleon keeps him waiting, waiting, waiting. But that this painful waiting should have led to this scene of jealousy came to me as a shock.

I went up to him and put my hands on his chest. "Jean-Baptiste," I said, "it really isn't worth your while to get angry at one of Napoleon's whims."

He pushed my hands away. "You know quite well what he is about," he gasped, "you know it. He wants to make people believe that he is only showing favour to his little fiancée of old. But let me tell you, let me tell you as a man that he is not interested in this 'of old', he is interested in you now, at this moment, he is in love with you and wants to do something special for you so that——"

"Jean-Baptiste!"

He brushed his hand across his forehead. "I am sorry. It is not your fault," he said under his breath.

Fernand appeared and put the soup tureen on the table. We sat down, facing each other in silence. Jean-Baptiste's hand which held the spoon shook.

"I shall not take part in the ceremony at all," I said, "but go to bed and be ill."

Jean-Baptiste did not answer. After the meal he left the house.

And so I am sitting now at his desk, writing, and trying to make clear to myself whether Napoleon really loves me again or not.

That endless night in his office before the execution of the Duc d'Enghien he spoke to me in the tones of the young lover. "Do take off your hat, Madame . . ." and a little later "Eugenie, little Eugenie . . ." He sent Mademoiselle George away. Perhaps because he remembered that night by the hedge in our garden in Marseilles, perhaps because he remembered the fields and the stars of that night? Isn't it strange that the little Buonaparte of that night in two days' time will be crowned Emperor of the French? Isn't it quite unimaginable that there was a time in my life when I did not belong to my Bernadotte?

The clock in the dining-room strikes midnight. Perhaps Jean-Baptiste has gone to see Madame Récamier. He speaks about her so often, Juliette Récamier, the wife of an old and wealthy banker, who reads all the books that are published and even some that are not, and lies on a sofa all day long. She fancies herself as the muse of all the famous men but will have herself touched by none, least of all, according to Polette, by her own husband. Jean-Baptiste often talks to this muse about books and music, and sometimes she sends me boring novels, 'masterpieces' which she asks me to read. I hate her, and I admire her.

It's half-past twelve now. Napoleon and Josephine are at this moment most likely on their knees in the chapel of the Tuileries, and Uncle Fesch is marrying them according to the canon of the Church. How easy it would be for me to explain to Jean-Baptiste why Napoleon does not forget me, but it would only annoy him. I am a part of Napoleon's youth, that is the explanation, and no man ever forgets his youth even if he thinks of it only rarely. If I turn up in blue at the coronation I shall be for Napoleon no more than a memory come to life. Of course, it is possible that Jean-Baptiste is right and that Napoleon wants to revive his old feelings. A declaration of love from Napoleon would be like balm on a wound that doesn't need balm any longer because it healed long ago. To-morrow I shall stay in bed with a heavy cold, and the day after to-morrow as well. His Majesty's Memory in Blue has a cold and sends her apologies. . . .

I fell asleep over my diary and woke up when someone took me gently in his arms and carried me to the bedroom. The metal braids of his epaulettes scratched my cheeks as they so often do. Sleepily I murmured: "You've been to see your muse. I'm very offended."

"I have been to the opera, my little girl, and on my own. To hear some decent music. I sent the carriage away and walked home."

"I love you very much, Jean-Baptiste. And I'm very ill, I've a cold and a sore throat and I can't go to the coronation."

"I shall apologise to the Emperor for Madame Bernadotte." After a little while he added: "You must never forget, my little girl, that I love you very much. Do you hear me, or are you asleep again?"

"I am dreaming, Jean-Baptiste, I'm dreaming. What do you do if suddenly someone wants to pour balm on a wound that healed long ago?"

"You laugh at him, Désirée."

"Yes, let's laugh at him, the great Emperor of the French. . . ."

IT was very solemn, the coronation of my ex-fiancé as Emperor of the French, and once or twice it was funny too. Yes, I was there, it turned out very differently from what I expected.

The day before yesterday Jean-Baptiste explained to the Master of Ceremonies, Monsieur Despreaux, that, to my infinite distress, a high temperature and a heavy cold were making it impossible for me to attend the coronation. Despreaux couldn't understand it; the other ladies, he thought, would willingly rise from their death-bed to get to Notre-Dame. Couldn't I make it possible to attend after all? But Jean-Baptiste pointed out that my sneezing would drown the organ music.

I did stay in bed all next day. Julie, who had heard about my illness, came about lunch time and made me drink hot milk and honey. I dared not tell her that I wasn't ill at all.

However, yesterday morning I was so bored lying in bed that I got up, dressed and went into the nursery. We played merrily, but always careful not to make a mess for fear of Marie, who gets more severe with us every day.

In the middle of our playing Fernand appeared and announced Napoleon's physician. Before I had a chance of telling him that I would be ready to see Dr. Corvisart in my bedroom within five minutes this fool of a Fernand had shown him into the nursery. Dr. Corvisart put his black bag on the saddle of Oscar's rocking-horse and bowed politely.

"His Majesty," he said, "has commissioned me to inquire after *Madame la Maréchale's* health. I am glad to be able to report to his Majesty that you have quite recovered."

"But, Doctor, I am still feeling very weak," I said, in despair.

Dr. Corvisart raised his funny triangular eyebrows and said: "I believe I can say, with a good conscience as a doctor, that you will be sufficiently strong to carry Her Majesty's handkerchief in the coronation." Without the ghost of a smile he bowed once more, saying: "His Majesty's instructions have left no doubt in my mind."

I had a lump in my throat. It occurred to me that Napoleon could demote Jean-Baptiste with a stroke of his pen, that in fact we were completely in his power.

"If you really advise me to, Doctor——" I said.

Dr. Corvisart bent over my hand. "I advise you most

210

urgently, Madame, to attend the coronation." He took his black bag and left.

In the afternoon Le Roy sent my shell-pink robe and the white ostrich feathers for my hair. Round about six o'clock I was terrified by a sudden volley of artillery which shook the windows. I ran into the kitchen and asked Fernand what was going on.

"From now till midnight there will be a salvo every hour," he said, polishing Jean-Baptiste's gilded sword with great zeal. "At the same time there will be fireworks in all the public squares. We ought to take Oscar to see them."

"It's snowing too hard," I said, "and Oscar was coughing this morning."

I went up to the nursery, sat down by the window and took Oscar on my knee. It was quite dark in the room but I didn't put on the light. Oscar and I watched the snowflakes dancing through the light of the big street-lamp in front of our house.

"There is a town where every winter the snow stays lying in the streets for many months, not just for a few days as here," I said.

"And then?" Oscar asked.

"Then? Nothing."

Oscar was disappointed. "I thought you were going to tell me another story."

"It isn't a story. It's true."

"What town is that?"

"Stockholm."

"Where is Stockholm?"

"Far, far away. Near the North Pole, I believe."

"Does Stockholm belong to the Emperor?"

"No, Oscar, Stockholm has a King of its own."

"What is his name?"

"I don't know, darling."

The guns thundered again and made Oscar jump. Frightened, he pressed his face against my neck.

"You mustn't be afraid," I said, "they are only shots in honour of the Emperor."

Oscar raised his head. "I am not afraid of guns, Mama. I want to be a Marshal of France some day, like Papa."

The snowflakes continued to dance. I didn't know why, but out of the past the rhythm of the falling snow brought the horse-face of Persson back to my mind.

"Perhaps you will be a good silk merchant like your grand-father," I said.

"But I want to be a Marshal. Or a sergeant. Papa told me

that he had been a sergeant. And so was Fernand." Something important seemed to have occurred to him. "Fernand told me that I may go to the coronation with him to-morrow."

"Oh no, Oscar. Children must not be taken into the church. Papa and Mama did not get a ticket for you."

"But Fernand wants to be outside the church with me. Fernand says we can see the whole procession from there. The Empress and Aunt Julie and—and, Mama, the Emperor with his crown. Fernand promised me that."

"It's far too cold, Oscar. You can't stand outside Notre-Dame for hours. And there will be such a crowd that a little man like you would be trampled under foot."

"Please, Mama, please, please!"

"I shall tell you later exactly what it was like, Oscar."

He put his little arms round me and gave me a sweet and rather wet kiss. "Please, Mama, if I promise to drink all my milk every night?"

"No, really, Oscar, it's impossible. It's so cold and you've got a cough. Be sensible, darling."

"But, Mama, if I drink the whole bottle of nasty cough cure, Mama, may I go?"

"In this town of Stockholm," I began, "close to the North Pole there is a big lake with green ice-floes——" But he was no longer interested in Stockholm.

"Mama, Mama, I want to see the coronation, please, please, Mama!" He was sobbing now.

"When you are grown up, then you may go and see the coronation."

Sceptically Oscar asked: "Is the Emperor going to be crowned again later?"

"No—o—o. We shall go to see another coronation, Oscar, you and I, I promise you that. And it'll be a much more beautiful coronation than the one to-morrow."

"*Madame la Maréchale* is not to talk nonsense to the boy!" came Marie's voice out of the dark behind us. "Come on, Oscar, drink up your milk and cough medicine." She lit the lamp, and the snowflakes became invisible in the dark outside.

Later on, when Jean-Baptiste came up to say good-night to Oscar, he started complaining again. "Mama won't let me go with Fernand to-morrow to see the Emperor with his crown."

"Nor will I," said Jean-Baptiste.

"Mama says that she'll take me to another coronation later on when I'm grown up. Are you coming too, Papa?"

"Whose coronation is that?" asked Jean-Baptiste.

"Mama, whose coronation is that?"

I didn't know how to extricate myself. So I put on a very mysterious air and said: "I'm not telling now. It'll be a surprise. Good-night, darling, sweet dreams."

Jean-Baptiste carefully tucked him up and extinguished the light.

For the first time for I don't know how long I prepared our evening meal myself. Marie, Fernand and the kitchen maid had gone out, probably to one of the free shows that were running in all the theatres of Paris. Yvette, my new personal maid, had disappeared long before the others. I had had to engage Yvette because Julie insisted that the wife of a Marshal of France must neither do her hair nor her sewing herself. Before the Revolution Yvette had been lady's maid to some duchess or other and so, naturally, she thought herself several rungs above me in the social ladder.

After the meal we did the washing up and Jean-Baptiste put on Marie's pinafore and helped me dry. "I always used to help my mother," he said with a smile.

Turning serious he went on: "I heard from Joseph that you had a visit from the Emperor's physician."

I sighed. "In this town everybody knows everything about everybody else."

"No, not everybody. But the Emperor knows a lot about a lot of people. That's the way he governs."

Falling asleep I heard the guns thunder once more. Dreamily it went through my head that I would have been very happy in a country cottage near Marseilles raising chickens. But neither Napoleon, Emperor of the French, nor Bernadotte, Marshal of France, would have been interested in chicken-farming.

I woke up to find Jean-Baptiste shaking me by the shoulders. It was still quite dark. "What is it? Is it time to get up?"

"No," said my husband, "but you were crying so bitterly in your sleep that I had to wake you up. Did you have a bad dream?"

I tried to recall my dream, and slowly in the telling it came back to me. "I went to a coronation with Oscar, and we had to get into the church at all costs. But there were so many people outside that we couldn't get to the doors and were pushed and shoved and jostled. The crowd grew bigger and bigger, I held Oscar by the hand and all of a sudden the thousands of people turned into chickens which got under our feet and cackled for all they were worth."

"And that was so dreadful?" he asked soothingly, tenderly.

"Yes, dreadful," I said, snuggling up to him, "dreadful.

The chickens cackled like—like—yes, like people when they are curious and agitated. But that wasn't the worst. The worst was the crowns."

"The crowns?"

"Yes. Oscar and I were wearing crowns, and they were awfully heavy. I could hardly keep my head up; I knew all the time that my crown would fall down the moment I bent my head the slightest little bit. And Oscar too had a crown which was much too heavy for him. I could see how he stiffened his neck to keep his head straight, and I was so afraid the child might collapse under the weight of the crown. And then, thank God, you woke me up. It was such an awful dream."

He put his arm under my head and kept me close to him. "It is quite natural that you should have dreamt of a coronation. In two hours' time we shall have to get up and get ready for the ceremony in Notre-Dame. But however did the chickens get into your dreams?"

I didn't try to answer that, I tried to forget the nasty dream and go to sleep again——

It had stopped snowing. But it was much colder than last night. Yet in spite of that the people of Paris had started collecting outside Notre-Dame and lining the streets through which the gilded equipages of the Imperial family were to pass from five o'clock onwards.

Jean-Baptiste and I were to go to the Archbishop's palace, where the procession would be formed. While Fernand was helping Jean-Baptiste with his uniform Yvette arranged the white ostrich feathers in my hair. I thought I looked dreadful in this headgear, like a circus horse.

Every two seconds Jean-Baptiste called from his corner, "Are you ready, Désirée?" But the ostrich feathers refused to stay put on my head.

Marie burst into the middle of my dressing difficulties with a little parcel which, she said, had just been delivered by a lackey of the Imperial Household. Yvette placed it before me on the dressing-table. Under Marie's watchful eyes I stripped off the paper cover and a casket made of red leather appeared. Jean-Baptiste came up and stood behind me, and our eyes met in the mirror over my dressing-table. Without a doubt, I thought, Napoleon has thought of some more terrible things and Jean-Baptiste will be furious. My hands shook so badly that I couldn't open the casket. At last Jean-Baptiste said, "Let me do it," pressed a little lock and the casket opened.

"Oh!" sighed Yvette, and Marie muttered admiringly "Mhm!" The casket showed a box of gold, glittering gold with an eagle with outspread wings engraved on its top. Uncomprehendingly I stared at it.

"Open it," said Jean-Baptiste.

I fumbled awkwardly with the top of the box. At last it came off. The box was lined with red velvet, and what shone out at me from among the velvet folds? Gold coins!

I turned round to Jean-Baptiste. "Do you understand?"

Jean-Baptiste didn't answer. He stared indignantly at the coins. His face had turned pale.

"They are gold francs," I said, and absent-mindedly I took out the top layer of coins and spread them on my dressing-table, around and between hair brushes, pieces of jewellery and my powder bowl. In doing so I heard a slight rustle and discovered a folded piece of paper among the coins. I pulled it out and opened it and recognised at once Napoleon's writing, his big untidy letters.

'*Madame la Maréchale*,' it said, 'in Marseilles you were so very kind as to lend me your personal savings to make the journey to Paris possible for me. This journey turns out to have been a journey into good fortune. On this day I feel the need to pay my debt and to thank you. N.' A postscript added 'The sum involved at that time was 98 francs.'

"Ninety-eight francs in gold, Jean-Baptiste," I said, "but I only lent him paper money at the time, *assignats*." I noticed to my relief that Jean-Baptiste was smiling. "I had saved up my pocket money to buy a decent uniform for the Emperor; his field uniform was too shabby. But then he needed the money to pay debts, and the bills for Marshals Junot and Marmont which they had run up in their hotels. Otherwise they couldn't have got away."

Shortly before nine o'clock we arrived at the Archbishop's palace. In an upper room we met the other Marshals and their wives. We drank hot coffee and watched from the windows the exciting scenes outside before the portal of Notre-Dame. There six battalions of grenadiers supported by hussars of the Guards were trying to keep order. Inside the Cathedral feverish hammering was still going on. A double row of soldiers of the National Guard kept the curious crowds at bay. Jean-Baptiste had been told by Murat, who, as Governor of Paris, was in command of these troops, that 80,000 men had been mobilised to guard the Emperor's coronation procession.

At about this time the Prefect of Police closed all streets leading to the Cathedral to vehicular traffic. Thus it came about that the ladies and gentlemen invited to attend had to walk the last stretch to Notre-Dame. What was worse, whereas we, the participants in the procession, were allowed to leave our coats in the Archbishop's palace, these other guests had to leave theirs in their coaches, and had to arrive at Notre-Dame without any overcoats. It made me shiver to see the ladies trip through the cold weather in the thinnest of silk robes.

Something funny happened. One group of these unfortunate ladies ran into a knot of red-robed High Court judges. These gentlemen gallantly opened their wide robes to grant the freezing ladies some protection in their folds. We could hear the screaming laughter of the spectators through the closed windows.

A few carriages were allowed through, however, those of the foreign Princes who were considered guests of honour. "Third-raters," said Jean-Baptiste to me, and pointed out to me the Margrave of Baden and the Prince of Hesse-Darmstadt, and immediately behind him the Prince of Hesse-Homburg, for all of whom Napoleon pays travelling and hotel expenses.

How good Jean-Baptiste is at pronouncing those impossible Teutonic names, I thought, leaving the window for another cup of coffee. Meanwhile some dispute had arisen by the door. But I became attentive only when Madame Lannes came and told me: "I believe, dear Madame Bernadotte, that the argument by the door concerns you."

True enough, it did! A gentleman in a brown jacket and a somewhat disarranged scarf was trying in vain to slip through the guards by the door. "I must see my little sister, Madame Bernadotte, I must, I must."

It was Etienne. When he caught sight of me he shouted like someone drowning: "Help, Eugenie, help!"

"Why won't you allow my brother in?" I asked one of the guards.

He mumbled something about "Strict order to admit only participants in the procession."

I pulled Etienne into the room and called Jean-Baptiste. Between us we sat Etienne, who was perspiring with agitation, in an armchair.

He had been travelling day and night to get here for the coronation. "You know, Eugenie," he said, "how close the Emperor is to me. He is the friend of my youth, the man on whom I had staked all my hopes——" he panted, a picture of misery.

"In that case, why are you so miserable?" I asked. "Your friend of your young days will be crowned Emperor any moment now, what else do you want?"

"To see it," he implored me, "to see the ceremony."

Jean-Baptiste said soberly: "You ought to have come earlier to Paris, brother-in-law. There are no tickets left now."

Etienne, who has grown very stout these last years, wiped the sweat from his forehead. "The bad weather," he said, "it held up my coach every few hours."

"Perhaps Joseph might help," I said to Jean-Baptiste in an undertone, "we can't do anything now."

"Joseph is with His Majesty in the Tuileries and can't see anybody," wailed Etienne. "I've been there."

I tried to soothe him, and said: "Listen, Etienne, you never liked Napoleon very much, you can't really be all that keen on seeing his coronation."

At that Etienne exploded. "How can you say such a thing! Don't you know that in Marseilles I was his most intimate, his best friend, his——"

"I only know that you were disgusted because I wanted to get engaged to him."

"Really?" said Jean-Baptiste, and slapped my brother's shoulder, "were you really? Did you want to forbid Désirée's engagement? Etienne, brother-in-law, you are my friend indeed, and if the church were so crowded that I had to sit you on my knee I'd take you, I'd get you in." Laughingly he turned round and shouted: "Junot, Berthier, we must smuggle Monsieur Etienne Clary into the Cathedral. Come on, we've done more difficult things than that."

From the window I watched brother Etienne, under cover of three Marshals' uniforms, disappear inside Notre-Dame. After a little while the uniforms reappeared. Etienne, I was told, had been found a seat among the members of the Diplomatic Corps, next to the green-turbaned Turkish Minister in fact.

At this moment the Papal procession came into view, headed by a battalion of dragoons and followed by Swiss Guards. Behind him came a monk on a donkey, holding aloft a cross. We heard Berthier murmur, "That donkey costs 67 francs per day to hire," and Jean-Baptiste laughed. The monk was followed by the Pope's coach drawn by eight grey horses. We recognised the coach at once as the state equipage of the Empress, which had been put at the Pope's disposal.

The Pope entered the Archbishop's palace, but we did not see him. In one of the ground-floor rooms he put on his insignia, and, leading a group of the highest Church dignitaries, he left the palace and walked slowly towards the portal of Notre-Dame. We heard someone open a window. The crowd was silent; only some women knelt down, whereas most men did not even uncover their heads. Once the Pope stopped, said a few words and made the sign of the cross over a young man who was standing, with head lifted high, in the front rank. We were told later that the Pope had let his eyes rest smilingly on this young man and those around him and said, "I don't think that an old man's blessing can do any harm." Twice more he made the sign of the cross in the air, before he disappeared inside the Cathedral. The robes of the cardinals floated after him like a red wave.

"What is happening in Notre-Dame now?" I wanted to know.

Somebody explained to me that on the Pope's entry the choir of the Imperial Church intoned '*Tu es Petrus*' and that the Pope was going to take his seat on a throne to the left of the altar. "And now the Emperor ought to be here," my informant added. But the Emperor kept them waiting for another hour yet, the people of Paris, the regiments on duty, the illustrious guests and the head of the Holy Roman Catholic Church.

At last gun salvoes announced the approach of the Emperor. I don't know why, but suddenly everybody fell silent. In silence we prepared to leave the palace, and when I put a last dab of powder on my face I noticed to my surprise that my hands shook.

"*Vive l'Empereur! Vive l'Empereur!*" At first it sounded like the rushing sound of wind carried over a great distance: it grew louder and louder, and finally it came roaring round the next corner.

Murat appeared first, on horseback in the gold-braided uniform of the Governor of Paris; behind him came dragoons, and heralds in purple tunics with gold bees painted on their batons. I stared, mesmerised by this purple splendour. 'That,' I thought, 'is all for the man for whom I once wanted to buy a uniform because his old one was too shabby. . . .'

Then came one gilded equipage after another, each drawn by six horses, unloading first Despreaux, then the Emperor's adjutants, then the ministers, and finally the Imperial Princesses all in white and with tiny crowns in their hair. Julie came to me and pressed my hand with her ice-cold fingers. "I hope everything will be all right," she said.

"Yes," I answered in a whisper, "but look after your crown. It's sitting on one side."

When the Emperor's carriage turned the corner it was like the sun suddenly rising over a grey winter scene, such was the splendour of its colour and its ornaments. Eight horses with white plumes drew it majestically. It came to a stop. We had gone out of the palace to form a guard of honour.

The Emperor sat in the right-hand corner of the carriage.

Dressed in purple velvet, wide Spanish knee-breeches and white stockings strewn with diamonds, he gave the effect of a stranger, a man in disguise, an operatic hero with short legs as he descended. The Empress on his left, however, looked more beautiful than ever. The biggest diamonds I had ever seen shone from her babyish curls. She smiled, a radiating, youthful, oh so youthful smile, and I could see in spite of her heavy make-up that her smile was genuine. The Emperor had married her in church, he was having her crowned. What had she to fear now?

When Joseph and Louis went past me I couldn't believe my eyes. The way they had got themselves up! All in white from top to toe! But Joseph, who, I noticed, had grown fat, strode into the palace grinning from ear to ear, whereas Louis waddled along gloomily and on flat feet.

In the palace Napoleon and Josephine put on their coronation robes. Josephine's almost bore her down, but she managed to steady herself till the Princesses had seized the train and taken the weight off her. Napoleon looked us over for the first time, as he tried to force his hands into a pair of stiff gloves. "Let us start!" he said.

Despreaux had divided the different insignia among us, and we were only waiting for his sign. But the sign didn't come. Instead, we saw Despreaux whisper something to Joseph and saw Joseph shrug his shoulders. Napoleon meanwhile had turned away and was gravely examining his image in a mirror. What would the mirror show him? Only an undersized man in splendid robes the ermine collar of which nearly reached up to his ears. It would show a man who had fished a crown out of the gutter. . . .

Our embarrassed whispering and awkward standing about reminded me of a funeral. I looked round to find Jean-Baptiste and saw him standing with the other Marshals, holding the velvet cushion with the chain of the Emperor's Legion of Honour, and gnawing his lips thoughtfully.

"What are we waiting for, Despreaux?" Napoleon sounded impatient.

"Sire, it was agreed that *Madame Mère* was to open the coronation procession and *Madame Mère* is——"

"Mama has not come," Louis said, and there was a trace of glee in his voice.

We knew that Napoleon had sent many couriers to Italy to ask his mother to be in Paris in good time for the coronation. When she could no longer resist the pressure she had said good-bye to her exiled son Lucien and set out for Paris.

"We regret it very much," said Napoleon without any expression in his voice. "We will proceed."

The fanfares trumpeted and the procession began to move slowly and solemnly. First came the heralds, then pages in green, Despreaux, the sixteen Marshals' wives stiff as marionettes, Securier and Murat. Then it was my turn. An icy current of air met me as I came out of the door carrying the cushion with the handkerchief in front of me like a sacrificial gift. From the crowd restrained by an impenetrable cordon of soldiers there came a few isolated shouts as I passed: "*Vive Bernadotte—Bernadotte!*" I kept my eyes fixed on Murat's gold-braided back and never let them stray.

I entered Notre-Dame, which was full of the roll of the organ and incense, carried the cushion the length of the nave, and came to a halt at the very end, where Murat stepped aside and the altar and the two golden thrones appeared. On the throne to the left, rigid as a statue, sat a little old gentleman in white, Pope Pius VII. He had been kept waiting here by Napoleon for almost two hours.

I took my place beside Murat and watched Josephine walk up towards the altar, her eyes wide open, a smile on her lips. She stopped in front of the first step to the double throne to the right of the altar, so that the Princesses who carried her train came to a halt immediately in front of me. Then Napoleon appeared with the paladins carrying his insignia, Jean-Baptiste among them.

The organ played the Marseillaise, as Napoleon slowly made his way to the altar till he reached the side of Josephine. Behind him stood his brothers and his Marshals.

The Pope rose and said Mass. When he had finished Despreaux gave a sign to Marshal Kellermann. Kellermann advanced and held the crown up to the Pope, whose delicate hands could hardly bear its weight. Napoleon let his purple gown slide from his shoulders; his brothers caught it and handed it to Talleyrand. Here the organ ceased.

In a clear and solemn voice the Pope pronounced the words of the blessing. He raised the heavy crown, waiting for Napoleon to incline his head. But Napoleon did not incline his head. His hands in his gold-embroidered gloves reached up and snatched the crown away from the Pope, holding it high in the air for a fraction of a second. Then he placed it slowly on his head.

A movement of startled surprise went through the ranks of the spectators. Napoleon had broken the pre-arranged crowning ritual and had crowned himself! The rest of the ceremony, the handing over by the paladins of the different insignia, went smoothly, and Napoleon ascended the steps to his throne once more. Joseph and Louis took up positions on either side of the throne. *"Vivat Imperator in æternum!"* came the voice of the Pope.

The Pope now turned to Josephine, making the sign of the cross over her and kissing her on the cheek. Murat was to hand him her crown. But Napoleon intervened, coming down from his throne and stretching out his hand, whereupon Murat handed the crown to him instead of to the Pope.

For the first time to-day I saw a smile on the Emperor's face. Very, very carefully, so as not to disarrange her coiffure, he placed the crown on her babyish curls and then put his hand lightly under her elbow to conduct her up the steps to their throne. Josephine took a step forward, swayed and very nearly fell back: Eliza, Polette and Caroline quite deliberately had let go of the train in order to make Josephine fall, to make her ridiculous in the moment of her greatest triumph. Julie and Hortense, however, held on with all their strength, and Napoleon gripped her arm and supported her. Thus she escaped the indignity of falling, she only stumbled on the first step to the throne.

Young girls of the old French nobility—the pure virgins whom Despreaux had had such difficulty in finding—approached the altar with wax candles in their hands, as the Pope and high clergy retired to the chapter house. Napoleon sat rigidly and with eyes half closed. What, I wondered, was he thinking of now?

I couldn't take my eyes off his face. Now a muscle moved in it and, believe it or not, he stifled a yawn! At the same time his eyes chanced on me, he opened them wide and for the second time to-day he smiled, a good-tempered, lighthearted smile, that seemed to have come right out of the past, out of our garden in Marseilles when we raced each other and he let me win. 'Didn't I tell you,' his eyes asked, 'that time by the hedge, and you wouldn't believe me? Didn't you want me to be thrown out of the Army to make a silk merchant of me?' Yes, there he sat with crown and ermine, and yet for one moment he was the Napoleon from the garden in Marseilles. The next moment I remembered the Duc d'Enghien, and Lucien the first of the exiles, and Moreau and all the others, great and humble, who followed them. I turned my eyes away and only looked towards the throne again when I heard the voice of the President of the Senate.

He stood in front of Napoleon unrolling a parchment. One hand on the Bible, the other raised high, the Emperor repeated the words of the oath after the President. In a voice clear and cool Napoleon vowed to preserve and guard the religious, political and civil liberties of the French people.

The clergy returned to accompany the Imperial couple out of the Cathedral. Cardinal Fesch found himself next to Napoleon, and the Emperor with boyish pleasure dug his uncle in the ribs with the sceptre. The cardinal's face expressed such horror at his nephew's spontaneous gesture that Napoleon turned away with a shrug of his shoulders. Within a few seconds of this the Emperor turned round to Joseph and called out to him: "What would our father have said if he had seen us here!"

Following Murat out of the Cathedral I managed to catch a glimpse of Étienne. He was sitting next to the green-turbaned Turkish Minister, staring open-mouthed in rapture after his Emperor long after he had disappeared from his sight.

"Does the Emperor keep on his crown in bed?" asked Oscar, when I put him to bed that night.

"No, I don't think so," I said.

"Perhaps it's too heavy for him?" he pondered.

I laughed. "Too heavy? No, darling, not in the least. On the contrary!"

"Marie says that the police pay people to shout '*Vive l'Empereur!*' in the street. Is that true, Mama?"

"I don't know. But you must never say such a thing."

"Why not?"

"Because it is——" I wanted to say 'dangerous', but I suppressed it. We want Oscar to say what is in his mind, but on the other hand the Minister of Police banishes from Paris people who say what is in their minds, for instance Madame de Staël, the authoress and great friend of Madame Récamier. "Because your grandfather Clary was a convinced Republican," I said.

"I thought he was a silk merchant," said Oscar.

Two hours later, for the first time in my life I danced the waltz. It was at a great ball which His Imperial Highness, brother-in-law Joseph, gave for all the foreign Princes and diplomats and Marshals—and Étienne, as Julie's brother, he had graciously invited too. Marie Antoinette at one time had tried to introduce the Viennese waltz at Versailles; but only those received at court ever saw it danced, and after the Revolution anything that reminded people of the Queen from Austria was taboo. But now these sweet rhythms from an enemy country have infiltrated into Paris life once more.

I remembered that Monsieur Montel had shown me some waltz steps, but I had no idea how to dance them. Jean-Baptiste, however, who had been Ambassador in Vienna, showed me how to do it. He counted 'one two three, one two three' the way a sergeant does on the barrack square, and I felt like a recruit. But gradually his voice became gentler and gentler, he held me quite close to him, his mouth was in my hair, and we pirouetted and pirouetted till the illuminations of the ball-room in the Luxembourg had coalesced into a sea of lights.

"I saw the Emperor flirt with you—one two three, one two three—during the coronation," Jean-Baptiste murmured. "I saw it, I saw it."

"I had the feeling his heart wasn't in it," I said.

"In what? In the flirting?"

"Don't be horrid! In the coronation, I mean."

"Don't forget the rhythm, my girl!"

I insisted. "A coronation ought to be something which you feel very deeply."

"Not Napoleon, my girl, not Napoleon. To him it is only a formality. He crowns himself Emperor and at the same time swears loyalty to the Republic, one two three, one two three."

Somebody shouted: "To the Emperor!" and glasses clinked.

"That was your brother Etienne."

"Let's dance on, let's dance on," I whispered. His mouth was in my hair again, the cut-glass lustres glittered with all the colours of the rainbow, the whole room seemed to pirouette and sway with us. The voices of the many guests came as from a great distance. . . .

On the way home we drove past the Tuileries. They shone in splendid illumination. Pages with torches flickering red through the night stood guard. Somebody had told us that the Emperor and Josephine had dined alone and that Josephine had to keep on her crown because he liked her so much with it. After their meal the Emperor had retired to his study to pore over maps. "He is preparing his next campaign," explained Jean-Baptiste to me as we passed. Snow had started to fall and many torches went out.

PARIS, two weeks after the coronation.

A FEW days ago the Emperor handed over the eagle standards to his regiments. We all had to put in an appearance on the Champs de Mars, and Napoleon had again put on his coronation robes and his crown.

Each regiment was given a standard with a gilded eagle and a tricolour underneath. The eagles must never be allowed to fall into the enemy's hands, the Emperor said, and promised new victories to his troops. For many hours we had to stand on a platform and let the regiments march past. Etienne, who was up there with me, shouted himself hoarse with enthusiasm.

It has started snowing again. The parade never seemed to be coming to an end and we all had wet feet. But it gave me time to think out the preparations for the ball of the Marshals in the Opéra. The Master of Ceremonies had hinted to the Marshals that they ought to give a ball in honour of the Emperor. It was to be the most magnificent ball imaginable, and therefore we had rented the Opéra.

We Marshals' wives held innumerable sessions and checked over and over again the list of people to be invited. We could not afford to forget or insult anybody. Monsieur Montel taught us how to receive the Imperial couple and how to escort Napoleon and Josephine into the hall. From Despreaux we heard that the Emperor would offer his arm to one of us whilst one of the Marshals would have to conduct the Empress to her throne. This information caused long and grave discussions as to which Marshal and which Marshal's wife were to be chosen. At last we agreed on Murat, husband of an Imperial Princess, as the suitable man to receive the Empress. As for the lady, the choice lay between Madame Berthier, the senior in age, and myself, sister to Her Imperial Highness the Princess Julie. However, I succeeded in convincing the others that fat Madame Berthier was ideally suited to welcoming the Emperor. I didn't want to do it, I was too furious with him, because he kept Jean-Baptiste waiting and waiting for the independent command which he so longed for, as far away as possible from Paris.

On the morning of the great ball I had an unexpected visit from Polette, who turned up accompanied by an Italian violin virtuoso and a French captain of dragoons. She left them both in the drawing-room and retired with me to my bedroom.

"Guess," she said, and laughed, "which of the two is my lover?" She looked charming in her glittering attire and her skilful make-up, with priceless emeralds from the jewellery of the Borghese family in her tiny ears. Her eyes reminded me of Napoleon.

"Well," she repeated, "which of the two is it?"

I said I couldn't guess it.

"Both!" she exclaimed triumphantly, sitting down before my dressing-table, on which the golden casket was still standing.

"Whoever," she asked, "was so tasteless as to make you a present of a casket with such dreadful Imperial eagles on its lid?"

"It's your turn to guess now," I said.

She thought strenuously. Suddenly she looked up: "Was it—tell me—was it——"

I didn't move an eyelid. "I owe this casket to the infinite goodness of our Imperial lord and master."

Polette whistled like a street urchin. "I don't understand it," she said, "I don't. I thought Madame Duchâtel, the court lady with the long nose, was his mistress of the moment."

I blushed. "On the day of his coronation he repaid an old debt to me from his Marseilles days. That's all."

"Of course," said Polette protestingly, "of course, my dear child, that is all." She paused, meditating on something. Then she came out with it: "I want to talk to you about Mama. She arrived here, secretly, yesterday. I don't think even Fouché knows that she's in Paris. She's staying with me and you must help them."

"Help whom?" I asked.

"*Madame Mère*, and him, Napoleone, the boy with the crown." She laughed, a rather forced laugh. "I feel rather bothered. Napoleone insists that Mama has to obey the court ceremonial and to be received in formal audience by him in the Tuileries with curtseys and all the trimmings." She stopped, and I tried to imagine Madame Letitia curtseying formally before Napoleon. "He is furious," Polette continued, "because she deliberately travelled very slowly in order to miss the coronation. And he is angry because Mama didn't want to see his triumph. Yet he is longing for her, badly, and—Eugenie, Désirée, *Madame la Maréchale*, couldn't you bring the two together? Manage a kind of accidental meeting, you know, and leave them alone at the moment of their reunion so that the court ritual doesn't matter two sticks? Couldn't you arrange that somehow?"

I sighed. "You really are a dreadful family."

Polette didn't mind my saying that. "You've always known that, haven't you? You know, by the way, don't you, that I'm the only one of us whom Napoleon really likes?"

"I'd guessed that," I said, and remembered a morning in Marseilles when Polette went with me to the Town Commandant.

"The others," said Polette, beginning to polish her nails, "the others only want to get as much as possible out of him. Incidentally, Joseph no longer seems to be considered the successor since Napoleon adopted the two little sons of Louis and Hortense. Josephine is on at him day and night to make one of her grandsons his successor. And, do you know," here Polette waxed indignant, "what is the vilest thing of all? She tries to convince him that it is his fault that they have no children! His fault, I ask you!"

"I shall bring Madame Letitia and the Emperor together," I put in quickly. "I shall arrange it at the Marshals' ball. I shall send you word through Marie, and all you have to do is so see to it that your mother comes to the private box which I shall indicate to you."

"You are a treasure, Eugenie! Heavens, I feel better now." Earnestly she started making up her face and lips. "The other day an English paper published a scandalous article about me. My violin virtuoso translated it for me. The writer of the article calls me a 'Napoleon of love'. Such nonsense! We have completely different methods, Napoleon and I: he wins his offensive wars and I—I lose my defensive battles." A wan smile flitted over her face, as she went on: "Why does he marry me to men who don't interest me in the least? First Leclerc, now Borghese. My two sisters have an easier time of it, they, at any rate, have ambitions. They're not interested in people, only in influential connections. Eliza can't forget that dreadful cellar dwelling in Marseilles, she is obsessed by fear that one day she may be a pauper again, and so she snatches possessions where she can. Caroline was so young at the time that she doesn't remember it at all, but she'd be ready for any foul deed if it could help her towards a real royal or imperial crown. I on the other hand——"

"I fear your two knights are going to be impatient," I interrupted her flow.

Polette jumped up. "You're right. I must fly. Well then, I shall expect to hear from you, and I will send our *madre* to the Opéra. Agreed?"

"Agreed."

> *"Allons, enfants de la patrie,*
> *Le jour de gloire est arrivé. . . ."*

On Jean-Baptiste's arm I slowly descended the steps to the strains of the orchestra, to welcome the Emperor of the French as the guest of his Marshals.

> *"Aux armes, citoyens!*
> *Formez vos bataillons!"*

The Marseillaise, the song of my early girlhood! Once upon a time I stood in my nightgown on the balcony and threw down roses to our volunteers, the tailor Franchon, and the bandy-legged son of our cobbler, and the Levi brothers, who went out in their Sunday suits to defend the Republic which had given them full citizenship against the whole world, that Republic which did not even have money enough to provide its soldiers with boots.

> *"Formez vos bataillons!*
> *Marchons, marchons. . . ."*

Silken trains rustled, state swords clattered, and we bowed deeply to Napoleon.

When I met Napoleon for the first time I couldn't understand that the Army accepted officers as short as he is. Now he even emphasised his short stature by surrounding himself with the tallest adjutants possible, and dressed in a plain General's uniform.

"How are you, Madame?" the Emperor addressed fat Madame Berthier and, without giving her time to reply, turned to the next Marshal's lady: "I am delighted to see you, Madame. You should always dress in Nile green, it suits you. By the way, the Nile is not really green at all but yellow. I remember it as ochre."

Feverish spots appeared on the faces of the ladies thus addressed. "Your Majesty is too kind," they breathed. 'Do all crowned heads talk like Napoleon,' I thought, 'or has he prepared these short, hammered-out phrases because he supposes that that is how monarchs converse with their subjects?'

Meanwhile Josephine bestowed her highly polished smile on the ladies. "How are you?" she inquired. "I heard your little girl had whooping cough. I was so sorry to hear it. . . ." Each one of them had the feeling that the Empress for days past had wanted nothing so much as to have a few words with her.

The Imperial Princesses followed in Josephine's wake, Eliza and Caroline with arrogance, Polette obviously a bit under the weather after a lively meal, Hortense awkward and anxious to appear friendly, and my Julie, pale and trying hard to overcome her shyness.

Murat and Josephine proceeded slowly along the ballroom with Napoleon and Madame Berthier behind them. We others followed. Here and there Josephine stopped to say a few kind words. Napoleon talked mainly to men. Among them were numerous officers as representatives of provincial regiments, and Napoleon inquired after their garrisons. He seemed to know each military barracks in France inside out. Meanwhile I tried to think how to lure him to Box 17, and decided that the first thing necessary was to get him to drink a few glasses of champagne. After that I'd risk it. . . .

Champagne was handed round. Napoleon declined. He

227

stood on the stage by his dais, with Talleyrand and Joseph talking to him. Josephine called me to her and said: "I am so sorry, I could not find the sapphire ear-rings the other day."

"Your Majesty is too kind, but I was unable to dress in blue in any case."

"Are you satisfied with Le Roy's dresses, Madame?"

I forgot to answer, because suddenly, in the crowd at the farther end of the ballroom, I discovered a ruddy squarish face which I thought I knew, a face over a colonel's uniform.

"With Le Roy's dresses, Madame?" repeated the Empress.

"Yes, yes, very," I said, and looked for that squarish face again. A woman, impossibly provincial in dress and looks, was with him. 'I don't know her,' I thought, 'but I do know him, some colonel from some provincial garrison, but where?'

A little later I managed to cross the ballroom towards that face. It annoyed me that I couldn't remember who he was, and so I tried to get near him without attracting attention. But everybody gave way politely, my name was whispered, officers bowed low and ladies smiled. I smiled back, I smiled till my mouth hurt me. But at last I got near my colonel, and I heard the provincial lady hiss into his ear: "So that's the little Clary girl!"

And then I knew him! The Commanding Officer of the Fortress of Marseilles! Without a wig now, but otherwise unchanged. The unimportant little General whom he had arrested ten years ago has meanwhile become the Emperor of the French.

"Do you remember me, Colonel Lefabre?" I asked. The provincial woman bowed awkwardly. *"Madame la Maréchale!"* she said. "François Clary's daughter," said Square Face. Both waited for what I would say next.

"I haven't been in Marseilles for many years," I said.

"It would bore Madame dreadfully, such a dull backwater!" said the lady.

"If you ever wish to be moved, Colonel Lefabre," I said.

"Could you put in a word with the Emperor for us?" Madame Lefabre asked, excited.

"No, but with Marshal Bernadotte."

"I used to know your father very well," the colonel was beginning when the orchestra struck up the polonaise.

I left the Lefabres and in the most undignified manner ran back. Murat was to open the polonaise with Julie, the Emperor with Madame Berthier and I with Prince Joseph. The dance had begun when I reached Joseph, who was standing alone on the stage waiting for me.

He was indignant. "I could not find you anywhere, Désirée."

"I am so sorry," I said, and we started off. But his indignation took a long time to disappear.

After two more dances everybody made for the buffet. Napoleon had withdrawn towards the back of the stage, talking to Duroc. I beckoned a servant to follow me with champagne and approached the Emperor, who immediately interrupted his conversation.

"I have something to say to you, Madame," he said.

"May I offer some refreshment to Your Majesty?"

Both Napoleon and Duroc took a glass of champagne. "Your health, Madame!" he said politely: he drank only the tiniest little drop and put the glass back. "Well, Madame, what I wanted to say—" Napoleon stopped and looked me over from head to foot. "By the way, *Madame la Maréchale*, have I ever told you how pretty you are?"

Duroc smiled broadly, clicked his heels and asked permission to withdraw.

"Certainly, certainly, Duroc, go and entertain the ladies!" Then his eyes returned to me, measuring me in silence. Slowly a smile began to play round his mouth.

"Your Majesty wanted to say something to me," I said, and added quickly: "If I may be so bold as to make a request I should be most grateful to Your Majesty if we could go to Box 17."

He did not trust his ears. Bending forward he raised his eyebrows and repeated: "Box 17?"

I nodded.

Napoleon looked round the stage. Josephine was making conversation with a number of ladies, Joseph appeared to be haranguing Talleyrand and his bad-tempered-looking brother Louis, and the Marshals were distributed on the dancing floor. His eyes narrowed and began to flutter. "Is it—proper, little Eugenie?"

"Sire, please do not misinterpret me!"

" 'Box 17,' there is nothing to be misinterpreted, is there?" Quickly he added: "Murat will accompany us, it looks better."

Murat, as well as all the rest of the Emperor's entourage, had watched us all the time out of the corner of his eyes. A sign from Napoleon brought him across post-haste.

"Madame Bernadotte and I are going to a box. Show us the way."

The three of us left the stage and passed along the lane of overawed people which forms at once wherever the Emperor goes. On the narrow stairs leading up to the boxes we disturbed a few couples. Young officers sprang to attention out of the arms of their ladies. I found it funny, but Napoleon remarked: "The manners of these young people are too free and easy. I shall have a word with Despreaux about it. I want unexceptionable morals in my entourage."

We found ourselves before Box 17, the door of which was closed. "Thank you, Murat!" said the Emperor, and Murat left.

"Your Majesty wanted to say something to me. Is it good news?"

"Yes. We have approved the application of Marshal Bernadotte for an independent command with extensive civil administration. To-morrow your husband will be appointed Governor of Hanover. I congratulate you, Madame. It is a great and responsible position."

"Hanover!" I murmured, without having the slightest idea where Hanover was.

"When you go to visit your husband you will reside in royal castles and you will be the First Lady of the country. Here we are, Madame. Please enter and make sure that the curtains are properly drawn."

I opened the door to the box and closed it quickly behind me. I knew quite well that the curtains were drawn.

"Well, my child?" said Madame Letitia.

"He is outside. And he doesn't know you are here."

"Don't be so nervous, child. He won't bite off your head."

'No,' I thought, 'my head is all right, but what about Jean-Baptiste's position as Governor?' "I am calling him in now," I said.

Outside I said: "The curtains are drawn." I wanted to let the Emperor go in first and then simply disappear. But without any more ado he pushed me into the little room.

Madame Letitia had risen from her chair. Napoleon stood by the door rooted to the spot. The strains of a Viennese waltz filtered through the heavy curtains.

"My boy, will you not say good-evening to your mother?" She took a step towards him. 'If only she made a bow, the tiniest bow of her head, everything would be all right,' I thought. The Emperor did not move. Madame Letitia took another step.

"*Madame Mère*, what a beautiful surprise," said Napoleon, motionless.

A last step brought Madame Letitia right up to him. She inclined her head, not to bow but to kiss him on the cheek! Without thinking of court ceremonial I pressed past him to the door, thus giving him a little push which made him land in his mother's arms.

When I reappeared down below, Murat came to me at once, his flat nose sniffing like a dog hot on the scent.

"You are back quickly, Madame!"

I looked at him in astonishment.

He grinned. "I told the Empress that Bernadotte would be glad if she had a few words with him, and I hinted to Bernadotte to be near the Empress. In that way they could neither of them pay attention to what is happening in the boxes."

"Happening in the boxes? What are you talking about, Marshal Murat?"

Murat was so hot on the scent that he completely missed the gasp of surprise that, all of a sudden, filled the ballroom.

"I mean one particular box, Madame, the one to which you conducted His Majesty."

"Oh, you mean Box 17!" I laughed. "Why must Jean-Baptiste and the Empress not know what's happening in Box 17, since the whole room knows it already?"

His face was a picture. He looked up, followed the direction of the glances from the eyes of the assembly and was just in time to see the Emperor pulling aside the curtains in Box 17. Madame Letitia was standing by the Emperor's side.

Despreaux gave a sign to the orchestra, which saluted with a mighty flourish, followed by a storm of applause.

"Caroline did not know her mother was back in Paris," said Murat, and regarded me suspiciously.

"*Madame Mère*, I believe, will always want to be with the son who needs her most. First she lived with Lucien, the exile, and now she is here with Napoleon, the Emperor."

The dance went on till morning dawned. During the last waltz I asked Jean-Baptiste: "Where is Hanover?"

"In Germany. It's the country where the British royal family comes from. The population had a very bad time during the war."

"Who, do you think, is going to govern Hanover as French Governor?"

"No idea," he said. "And for all I care——" He stopped in the middle of the sentence, in the middle of the waltz, and looked at me: "Is it true?" was all he asked.

I nodded.

"Now I am going to show them," he said, and continued the dance.

"Whom are you going to show what?"

"How to administer a country. I am going to show the Emperor and the Generals. Particularly the Generals. I shall make Hanover a contented place."

He spoke quickly, and for the first time in many years I felt that he was happy, really happy. Strange that at this moment he never thought of France, only of Hanover, a State in Germany.

"You'll have to live there in a royal castle," I said.

"I suppose so. It will probably be the best accommodation," he said, with no indication of being thrilled at all. It was then that I realised that Jean-Baptiste only thought the very best quarters just good enough for him. The English King's castle in Hanover was just good enough for the one-time Sergeant Bernadotte. Why does it all seem so monstrous to me, I wondered.

"Jean-Baptiste, I'm dizzy, I'm dizzy."

But he only stopped dancing when the orchestra started packing up their instruments and the Marshals' ball had come to an end.

Before Jean-Baptiste went to Hanover he fulfilled my wish and had Colonel Lefabre moved to Paris. The story of Napoleon's underclothing gave him the idea of appointing him to the Quartermaster-General's department where he had to deal exclusively with the troops' uniforms, boots and underclothes.

The colonel and his wife came to thank me.

"I knew your father very well, very decent chap, your father," he said.

My eyes felt watery, but I smiled. "You were right, Colonel, you remember? 'A Bonaparte is no husband for—for François Clary's daughter.' "

His wife was shocked. I had committed *lèse-majesté*. The colonel, too, looked embarrassed, but he did not flinch.

"You are right, *Madame la Maréchale*. I am certain your late father, too, would have preferred Bernadotte."

The transfers of all senior officers are regularly reported to Napoleon, and when he saw the name of Colonel Lefabre in a list, he thought hard for a moment and then laughed out loud: "My colonel of the underwear! Now Bernadotte has put him in charge of all the underwear of the Army to do his wife a favour!"

Murat saw to it that Napoleon's comment became known, and to this day everybody calls poor Lefabre 'colonel of the underwear'.

In a coach between HANOVER in GERMANY and PARIS, September 1805. (The Emperor has forbidden the use of the Republican calendar. Mama, who is dead now, would have been glad, because she could never get used to it.)

WE were very happy in Hanover, Jean-Baptiste, Oscar and I. The only arguments we had there were on account of the valuable parquet floors of the royal castle. More than once Jean-Baptiste would shake his head and say: "I can understand Oscar when he thinks that the polished ballroom floor has been made specially for him so that he can slide on it. After all, he is only a little brat of six. But you . . .!" And every time he said that there would be anger as well as amusement in his voice, and I would promise by all that was holy that I would never again slide in Oscar's company across the ballroom of the castle of the former Kings of Hanover, Marshal Bernadotte's residence as the Governor of Hanover. But however often I promised I could never resist the temptation to slide across the parquet floor. Which is really too bad of me, seeing that I am the First Lady of Hanover with a small suite of my own consisting of a reader, a lady-in-waiting and the wives of the officers of my husband's staff. But I am apt to forget that sometimes. . . .

Yes, we were very happy in Hanover. And Hanover was very happy with us. That, I feel sure, sounds strange, for Hanover was occupied country and Jean-Baptiste the commander of an Army of Occupation.

Jean-Baptiste worked from six in the morning till six in the evening and sometimes after dinner till deep into the night, and the documents on his desk never seemed to grow less in number. He began his 'government' of this Teutonic country with the introduction of the Rights of Man. In France plenty of people had shed their blood in order to bring about the equality of all people before the law. But in Hanover, conquered land, the stroke of Bernadotte's pen was enough. He abolished flogging. He abolished the ghettoes and allowed the Jews to follow whatever professions or trades they liked. The Levis of Marseilles did not march into battle in their Sunday suits in vain, after all!

An ex-sergeant, naturally, knows well what is necessary for the provisioning of troops, and the levies exacted from the citizens of Hanover for the upkeep of our Army do not hurt them very much. All the contributions they have to make are laid down in writing by Bernadotte, and no officer is allowed to collect taxes on his own authority.

The citizens of Hanover are better off than they ever were before, because Jean-Baptiste did away with the Customs frontiers. In the midst of war-ravaged Germany Hanover is now like an island of prosperity trading in all directions. As the State grew wealthier and wealthier Jean-Baptiste raised the taxes a bit and with the extra money he bought flour and sent it to North Germany, where there was a famine. The Hanoverians shook their heads about it, our officers thought him crazy, but you can't really blame someone simply because he acts unselfishly. On top of it all Jean-Baptiste advised the merchants to make friends with the towns of the Hanseatic League and earn even more money that way. This advice left the Hanoverians speechless. It's an open secret, of course, that the Hanseatic towns do not observe the Emperor's Continental Blockade very strictly, and still trade with Britain. That, however, is one thing, whereas this advice by a Marshal of France to his poor miserable enemies is quite another. . . . Once trade with the Hanseatic towns had got under way properly the exchequer of the State of Hanover flourished enormously, and Jean-Baptiste could even send big sums of money to support the University of Göttingen, where some of the greatest scholars of the day are teaching. Jean-Baptiste is very proud of 'his' university. And he is very glad when he can pore over his documents.

Sometimes I found him studying enormous tomes. "The things an uneducated ex-sergeant has to learn!" he would say then, and stretch out his hand to me without looking up. And I would go up to him and stand by his side, and he would put his hand on my cheek. "You do an awful lot of governing," I'd say then awkwardly, and he would only shake his head: "I'm trying to learn, my girl, and to do my best. It is not too difficult as long as he leaves me alone. . . ." We knew, both of us, whom he meant.

I gained weight during my time in Hanover. We didn't dance for nights on end, and didn't watch never-ending parades, at any rate never for more than two hours. For my sake Jean-Baptiste reduced the number and length of parades.

After dinner our officers and their ladies would very often sit with us in my drawing-room, where we talked over the latest news from Paris. We heard that the Emperor still had his headquarters near the Channel coast, preparing his attack on Britain, and we talked in whispers about Josephine's debts.

Sometimes professors from Göttingen would be present who tried to acquaint us, in their dreadful French, with their various theories. Once one of them read a play to us in German written by a man called Goethe, the author of the bedside novel *The Sorrows of Werther* which we used to devour as girls. During the reading I tried to signal to Jean-Baptiste to cut the torture short. Our German was too bad for this sort of thing.

Another one told us about a great doctor at Göttingen who was said to be able to make the deaf hear again. At that Jean-Baptiste pricked up his ears, for many of our soldiers have become hard of hearing because of the thunder of our own cannon, and he called out:

"I have a friend who ought to go and see this doctor. He lives in Vienna, and I shall write him and tell him that he should go to Göttingen. Désirée, you must meet him. He is a musician whom I got to know during my time in Vienna. He is a friend of Kreutzer's, you know."

This announcement frightened me. I didn't want to play to this musician. I had managed to wriggle out of my lessons in deportment and music; what I had learnt from Monsieur Montel years ago was sufficient for all my purposes, and as for music, I had very little use for that.

Well, in the end I never did play to that musician. The evening he came to see us became unforgettable to me. It began very beautifully, though . . .

Oscar's eyes shine when he can listen to music, and that day he pestered me so much that I had to let him stay up. He knew far more about the concert than I. The musician's name was—oh, I had the name down somewhere, a very outlandish name, Teutonic I should say—yes, that was it, Beethoven!

Jean-Baptiste had ordered all the players of the former Royal Court Orchestra to hold themselves at the disposal of this Beethoven from Vienna, and to rehearse with him for three mornings in the great ballroom. During these days Oscar was tremendously excited: "How long may I stay up, Mama? Till after midnight? How can a deaf man write music? Do you think that he won't even be able to hear his own music? Has Monsieur Beethoven really an ear trumpet? Does he blow it sometimes?"

Oscar fired all these questions at me when I took him for a drive, which I often did in the afternoon, along the avenue of linden trees which leads from the castle to the village of Herrenhausen.

"Papa says that he is one of the biggest men he knows. How big could he be? Bigger than a grenadier of the Emperor's bodyguard?"

"Papa doesn't mean physical bigness but intellectual. This musician is probably a genius. That's what Papa means."

Oscar pondered. "Is he bigger than Papa?" he asked at last.

I took Oscar's sticky little fist, which concealed a sweet, in my hand. "That I don't know, darling."

"Bigger than the Emperor, Mama?"

The valet, who was sitting next to the coachman in front of us, turned round and looked at me curiously.

I didn't move an eyelid as I said: "No man is bigger than the Emperor, Oscar."

"Perhaps he can't hear his own music," Oscar continued his pondering.

"Perhaps," I answered, and felt sad. 'I had wanted to bring up my son differently,' I thought, 'to be a free human being in my father's sense.' The new tutor, whom the Emperor himself had recommended to us for Oscar and who arrived here a month ago, tried to teach the child the addition to the Catechism which must now be taught in all French schools and which runs: 'We owe our Emperor Napoleon the First, the image of God on earth, respect, obedience, loyalty, military service. . . .'

I happened the other day to come into Oscar's schoolroom just as he was being taught that, and I didn't believe my ears. But the narrow-chested, rather unsympathetic young teacher, former pride of the officers' training academy at Briennes, repeated the words to me and left no doubt: "Emperor Napoleon the First, image of God on earth." . . .

"I shouldn't like my son to learn that. Leave out the addition," I said.

"It is taught in all the schools of the Empire, by law," the young man answered, adding with a blank face: "His Majesty is very interested in the education of his godchild, and he has ordered me to report regularly about his progress. After all, the pupil is the son of a Marshal of France."

I looked at Oscar, who was bending over a copybook, drawing little men, bored. 'At first nuns taught me,' I thought, 'then the nuns were jailed or driven away, and we were told that there was no God, only Pure Reason which we were to worship. Then there came a time when no one bothered about our faith and everybody could worship exactly what he wanted. Napoleon became First Consul, and the priests returned, sworn not to the Republic, but to the Church of Rome. Finally Napoleon forced the Pope to come to Paris to crown him, and made Roman Catholicism the official religion. And now he has made this addition to the Catechism. . . .'

'They fetch the peasants' sons from the fields,' I continued my train of thought, 'so that they may march in Napoleon's armies. Not many peasants have the 8,000 francs needed to buy a son off military service, and so they simply hide their sons and the gendarmes take wives, sisters and fiancées as hostages instead, whilst no one bothers about the many deserters. France has enough troops, since the defeated Princes have to put their soldiers at the Emperor's disposal to prove their loyalty to him. Jean-Baptiste complains so often that his soldiers have to be commanded by his officers with the help of interpreters. Why then does Napoleon make the young men march, march to new wars and to new victories, since France's frontiers no longer need defending? France no longer has any frontiers. Or do these new wars and victories no longer concern France but only him, Napoleon, the Emperor?'

I don't know how long I had been standing there facing the young teacher. At last I turned away and went to the door, repeating: "Leave that addition out. Oscar is too small for it yet, he doesn't know what it means."

Outside, in the empty corridor, I leaned helplessly against the wall and began to cry. 'Napoleon,' I thought, 'you pied piper of souls, because they are too small, because they don't know what it means, you make the children learn that. A whole country bled itself white for the sake of the Rights of Man, and after they had at last been established you went and put yourself at the country's head. . . .'

I don't know how I got to my bedroom. I only remember that I was lying on my bed, sobbing. These proclamations! We know them so well, they always fill the front page of the *Moniteur*, always in the same words, the words he used once by the Pyramids, the words which he read to us once during a Sunday dinner. "The Rights of Man are the guiding principles of this Order-of-the-Day," someone said to him during that meal—Joseph, the eldest Bonaparte, who hates his brother, and he had added: "They did not come from your brain." No, Napoleon, you only use them to be able to tell the peoples that you have come to liberate them, whereas in reality you subject them, you only use the words of the Rights of Man in order to shed blood in their name. . . .

Someone put his arms around me. "What is the matter, Désirée?"

"Do you know the new addition to the Catechism which Oscar is supposed to learn?" I sobbed. "But I've forbidden it. You do agree, Jean-Baptiste, don't you?"

"If you had not forbidden it, *I* should," was all he said, holding me tight.

"Can you imagine, Jean-Baptiste, that I very nearly married that man?"

He laughed, and it relieved me immeasurably to hear him laugh. "There are things, my little girl, which I just will not imagine!"

That was a few days before Oscar asked me all those questions about Beethoven on one of our afternoon drives. When the musician arrived he turned out to be a well-set-up man of medium height with the untidiest hair I've ever seen at our table. He had a round, bronzed, pock-marked face, a flat nose and sleepy eyes. But when you talked to him his eyes became keen and seemed to concentrate on the lips of the speaker.

I knew he was rather hard of hearing and therefore shouted at him how glad I was that he had come to see us. Jean-Baptiste slapped his shoulder and asked how things were in Vienna. It was merely a polite question, but the musician took it seriously.

"We prepare for war," he said. "We expect the Emperor's armies will march against Austria."

Jean-Baptiste frowned and shook his head. He hadn't wanted that answer. He diverted the conversation at once and asked: "What do you think of my orchestra?"

The stout musician shook his head and Jean-Baptiste repeated the question in as loud a voice as possible.

The musician raised his heavy eyelids, his eyes winked roguishly. "I heard you the first time, Mr. Ambassador—sorry, Mr. Marshal, that's your title now, is it not? Your orchestra plays very badly, sir."

"But you will conduct your new symphony all the same, won't you?" Jean-Baptiste shouted.

Monsieur Beethoven chuckled: "Yes, I will, because I want to know what you think of it, Mr. Ambassador!"

"Monseigneur!" shouted my husband's adjutant into the visitor's ear.

"You may call me Monsieur van Beethoven. I am no seigneur."

The adjutant was in despair: "You must address *Monsieur le Maréchal* as Monseigneur!" he shouted whilst I put a handkerchief to my mouth to suppress my laughter.

Our guest turned his eyes gravely on Jean-Baptiste: "It is so difficult to know your way with all these titles," he said. "I am grateful to you, Monseigneur, for wanting to send me to this doctor in Göttingen."

"Can you hear your own music?" a child's high-pitched voice asked behind the composer. He had heard the voice, turned round and saw Oscar. Before I had time to say something

238

to make him forget the cruel question he had bent down to Oscar and said: "Did you ask me something, my boy?"

"Can you hear your own music?" Oscar crowed as loudly as he could.

Monsieur van Beethoven nodded solemnly. "Oh yes, very well indeed. In here," he said putting his hand on his chest. "And here!" and he put his hand on his mighty forehead, adding with a broad grin: "But the musicians who play my music I can't always hear clearly. And that is sometimes a good thing, particularly when they are as bad as those of your Papa."

After dinner we all went into the ballroom. The players were tuning their instruments and turned timid eyes in our direction.

"They are not used to playing Beethoven symphonies," said Jean-Baptiste. "Ballet music is easier."

Three red silk chairs embossed with the gilded crown of the House of Hanover had been put in front of the rows of seats. Here Jean-Baptiste and I sat down, Oscar, who almost disappeared in his deep chair, between us. Monsieur van Beethoven stood in the midst of the orchestra giving them directions in German which he emphasised with quiet movements of his hands.

"What is he going to conduct?" I asked Jean-Baptiste

"A symphony which he wrote last year."

Monsieur van Beethoven came to us now and said thoughtfully: "At first I had intended to dedicate this symphony to General Bernadotte. But on second thoughts I found it better to dedicate it to the Emperor of the French. But——" He paused and stared in front of him and seemed to forget all about us and his audience. At last he remembered where he was, pushed a thick strand of hair back from his forehead and murmured: "We shall see. May we begin, General?"

"Monseigneur!" hissed Jean-Baptiste's adjutant, who was sitting immediately behind us.

Jean-Baptiste smiled. "Please begin, my dear Beethoven."

The heavy figure ascended the conductor's rostrum awkwardly. We only saw his back and the broad hand with the oddly small fingers holding the batton. He knocked on the rostrum, silence fell and he began.

I had no idea whether our orchestra played well or badly. I only knew that this stout man with the wide movements of his arms spurred it on and made it make music as I had never heard it make music before. Sometimes it sounded like an organ and then again like the sweet song of violins, jubilant yet despondent. I pressed my hand to my mouth because my lips trembled. This music had nothing to do with the Marseillaise. But the Marseillaise must have sounded like this when they went into battle for the Rights of Man and the frontiers of France, at once like a prayer and a shout of joy.

I bent forward to look at Jean-Baptiste. His face was like a face of stone, his mouth had become thin, his nose jutted out boldly and his eyes showed a strange fire. His right hand gripped the arm of his chair and held it so hard that his veins stood out.

Nobody had noticed the appearance of a courier by the door, or had seen Adjutant-Colonel Villatte get up noiselessly and take a letter from the courier. When Villatte touched my husband lightly on his arm, he looked round, startled, before he met the adjutant's eyes. He took the letter, gave him a sign, and Villatte remained behind his chair. The concert went on and the music carried me away again into other realms.

In the silence between two movements I heard the rustle of paper. Jean-Baptiste broke the seal and undid the letter. Monsieur van Beethoven had turned round towards Jean-Baptiste, who gave him a sign to continue.

Jean-Baptiste read. Once he looked up and seemed to listen to this heavenly music with a deep nostalgic longing in his eyes. But then he took a pen from his adjutant, scribbled a few words on a pad and handed them to the officer, who left at once. Another officer took up his position next to Jean-Baptiste. He left in his turn with a message, and a third one appeared, this time with a clicking of heels which broke through the sound of the Beethoven music and caused Jean-Baptiste's lips to twitch in irritation for one short moment, before he went on with yet another of his messages. Only when that had been handed over did he listen again, no longer with complete abandonment and enthusiasm as before but biting his lower lip. Only during the very last passage, the choral hymn to liberty, equality and fraternity, he once more raised his head. But I felt that this was not on account of the voice from the orchestra but on account of the voice which was speaking inside himself. I couldn't tell what this voice that spoke to the accompaniment of Beethoven's music said to him, I only saw that Jean-Baptiste smiled a bitter smile.

The end came, and great applause. I took off my gloves to be able to clap more loudly. The maestro bowed gauchely and pointed to the musicians with whom he had been so dissatisfied before.

All three adjutants had now collected behind Jean-Baptiste,

where they were waiting with tense faces. Jean-Baptiste, however, went towards the rostrum and helped Monsieur van Beethoven down as if he were an exalted dignitary. "Thank you, Beethoven," he said, "from the bottom of my heart, thank you."

The pock-marked face of the musician suddenly had an air of smoothness and restfulness about it, and even of amusement. "Do you remember, General, how, one evening in Vienna, you played the Marseillaise to me?"

"With one finger on the piano," laughed Jean-Baptiste, "that is all the playing I do."

"That was the first time I heard your hymn, the hymn of a free people." Jean-Baptiste towered above him, and Beethoven had to raise his head to be able to see into Jean-Baptiste's eyes. "I have often thought of that evening during the writing of this symphony. That was why I wanted to dedicate it to you, a young General of the French people."

"I am no longer a young General, Beethoven."

Beethoven didn't answer that. He kept staring at Jean-Baptiste so that he thought he hadn't heard him, and shouted once more: "I was saying I am no longer a young General."

Still Beethoven didn't answer. The three adjutants behind Jean-Baptiste started to make gestures of impatience.

"Somebody else came," Beethoven at last said heavily, "somebody else, and carried the message of your people across all frontiers. That is why I thought that I should dedicate the symphony to him. What do you think, General Bernadotte?"

"Monseigneur!" the three adjutants shouted almost in unison. Jean-Baptiste, angrily, motioned them to stop.

"Across all frontiers, Bernadotte," Beethoven repeated with an artless, almost childlike smile. "That night in Vienna you told me about the Rights of Man. I had known very little about them before, I am not interested in politics. But that, that, you see, had nothing to do with politics." He smiled again. "You played the Marseillaise to me with one finger, Bernadotte."

"And that is what you made of it, Beethoven," said Jean-Baptiste, deeply moved. A pause followed. One of the adjutants whispered, "Monseigneur!"

Jean-Baptiste collected himself, his hand went over his face as if to wipe away old memories. "Monsieur van Beethoven, I thank you for your concert. I wish you a happy journey to Göttingen and I do hope that the doctor there will not disappoint you."

Then Jean-Baptiste turned round to our guests, the garrison

officers and their ladies and the cream of Hanover's society. "I should like to bid you good-bye. To-morrow morning I am joining the Army in the field." Smilingly he bowed. "On the Emperor's order! Ladies and gentlemen, good-night."

Then he offered me his arm.

Yes, we were very happy in Hanover.

In the grey of a dawn eerily shot through with yellow streaks of candlelight Jean-Baptiste said good-bye to me. "You and Oscar are going back to Paris to-day," he said.

Fernand had prepared Jean-Baptiste's luggage. The gold-embroidered Marshal's uniform had been packed away carefully in the travelling bag together with table silver for twelve persons and a narrow camp bed. Jean-Baptiste wore the plain field uniform with the General's epaulettes.

I took his hand and pressed it against my face.

"My little girl, don't forget to write often! The War Ministry will——"

"Forward my letters, I know. Jean-Baptiste, will there never be an end to it? Will it always be like this, always and always?"

"Give Oscar a big kiss from me, little girl."

"I asked you, Jean-Baptiste, will it always be like this?"

"The Emperor's order: to conquer and occupy Bavaria. You are married to a Marshal of France. This should not be a surprise to you," he said in a voice which had lost all expression.

"Bavaria? And when you've conquered Bavaria, are you coming back to me in Paris or are we going to return to Hanover?"

"From Bavaria we shall march against Austria."

"And then? But there are no more frontiers to defend. France has no more frontiers, France——"

"France is Europe. And France's Marshals have to march, my child. Orders of the Emperor!"

"To think how often you have been asked in the past to assume power! If only you had at that time——"

"Désirée!" His voice broke in sharply. And in a gentler tone he continued: "My little girl, I started as an ordinary private soldier and I never went to an officers' training academy, but I would never dream of picking up a crown out of the gutter. I do not pick up things out of the gutter. Do not forget that! Do not forget that, ever!"

He extinguished the candle. The grey farewell dawn broke through the curtains.

Shortly before I got into the coach Monsieur van Beethoven appeared once more. I had just put on my hat and Oscar was proudly holding his own little travelling bag when he came in, slowly, awkwardly and with a stiff bow.

"I should like you," he fumbled for words, then went on: "I should like you to tell General Bernadotte that I cannot dedicate the new symphony to the Emperor either. Least of all to him." He paused, then said: "I shall simply call it 'Eroica', to commemorate a hope which did not find fulfilment. General Bernadotte will know what I mean," he sighed.

"I shall give him your message and I'm sure he will understand, Monsieur," I said, and gave him my hand.

"Do you know, Mama, what I want to be?" asked Oscar as our coach was rolling along the endless roads. "I want to be a musician."

"I thought you wanted to be a sergeant or a Marshal like your Papa. Or a silk merchant," I said absent-mindedly. I had my diary on my knee and was writing.

"I thought it over. I want to be a composer like Monsieur Beethoven. Or—a King."

"Why a King?"

"Because as a King one can do good to so many people. A servant told me so in the castle. Hanover used to have a King, before the Emperor sent Papa there. Did you know that?"

Now even my six-year-old son had found out how uneducated I am!

He insisted: "Composer or King!"

"Then you'd better be a King," I said. "That's easier."

PARIS, June 4th, 1806.

If only I knew where Ponte Corvo is! But I shall read about it to-morrow morning in the paper. So why bother about it now? I'd rather write down what has happened since my return from Germany.

Oscar had the whooping cough and was not allowed to go out. My friends avoided our house like the plague because they were afraid their children would catch it. I had wanted to start my piano and deportment lessons again, but even Monsieur Montel, that ballerina in trousers, was mortally afraid of infection. Anyway, I was really rather glad not to have to go to the lessons, as I was always so tired. Oscar coughed and was sick, mostly at night, and therefore I had his bed put in my room to be near him.

At Christmas time the three of us, Oscar, Marie and I, were quite alone. I gave him a violin for his present and promised him violin lessons as soon as he was well again.

Now and then Julie came to see us. During her visits she made Marie massage her feet, which were quite swollen owing to the long spells of standing about at the great receptions which she and Joseph had to give during the Emperor's absence. I kept away from her and sat in the dining-room so as not to infect her, whilst she had her massage in the drawing-room. Through the open door Julie shouted out all the news to me.

"Your husband has conquered Bavaria," she shouted one day in late autumn. "You'll read it to-morrow in the *Moniteur*. He met an Austrian army there and beat it. Marie, massage a bit harder, otherwise it's no good. Your husband is a great General, Désirée!"

In October she mentioned casually: "We've lost our whole navy. But Joseph says it doesn't really matter. The Emperor will show our enemies who is the master of Europe."

In December she appeared one day quite out of breath: "Désirée, we've won a tremendous battle, and to-morrow Joseph and I are going to give a ball for a thousand guests. Le Roy has his people working all night to get a dress ready for me. Wine-coloured, Désirée. How d'you like that?"

"But, Julie, red doesn't suit you, don't you know? What news of Jean-Baptiste? Is he all right?"

"All right? More than all right, darling! Joseph says that the Emperor is, so to speak, in his debt because he prepared everything so well. You know, five Army Corps marched into the battle at Austerlitz——"

"Austerlitz? Where is Austerlitz?"

"No idea. Does it matter? Somewhere in Germany, I think. Listen, five Army Corps, one each under Lannes, Murat, Soult, Davout and your husband. Jean-Baptiste and Soult held the centre."

"What centre?"

"How do I know? The centre of the line, I suppose, I'm no strategist. Napoleon with the five Marshals stood on a hill, and all the enemies of France are now beaten for good. Now we shall really have peace, Désirée!"

"Peace," I said, and tried to imagine Jean-Baptiste's return. "Then he's coming home at last," I shouted across the dining-room.

"They say he's on his way at this moment. We have to manage all Europe now and he'll have to think it all out," Julie called back.

"Never mind Europe, he's got to come home because Oscar keeps asking for him."

"I see, you're talking about Jean-Baptiste, but I mean the Emperor. He's on his way back, and Joseph says Jean-Baptiste can't come yet. The Emperor has ordered him to administer not only Hanover but Ansbach as well. Alternately he's to be there and in Hanover. You ought to go to him in Ansbach and have a look at things there."

"I can't," I said, somewhat subdued, "not with Oscar's whooping cough."

Julie didn't hear me. "Do you really think wine-red is wrong for me? Joseph likes me in it, he says it's a regal colour. Ow, Marie, not too hard, please. Why don't you answer, Désirée?"

"I'm unhappy," I said, "I so want to see Jean-Baptiste. Why can't he have leave?"

"Don't be childish, Désirée! How is the Emperor to hold the conquered territories if he doesn't put his Marshals in command there?"

'Yes, how is he to hold them?' I thought bitterly. 'With this new victory he's won the whole of Europe, with this and the help of eighteen Marshals. And I, I of all people, am married to a Marshal. There are millions of Frenchmen, but only eighteen Marshals. Why, why did I have to marry one of these eighteen? And I love him and want him so badly, oh so badly!'

"Drink a cup of chocolate and lie down, Eugenie," said Marie. "You never slept a wink last night, you know."

I looked up. "Where is Julie?"

"You fell asleep and she left to try on dresses, I suppose, and make arrangements for her ball and dust the Elysée Palace before a thousand guests arrive."

"Marie, is it ever coming to an end, this war-making, this taking over of other countries which have nothing to do with us?"

"Oh yes, but to a dreadful end," said Marie gloomily. She hates wars because she fears that one day her son will be called up too. And she hates all the royal castles we live in because she is a Republican. So were we all, once upon a time.

I lay down and fell into a fitful sleep from which I was awakened very soon by the sound of Oscar's coughing and panting for breath. . . .

Many weeks passed. Spring came, and still Jean-Baptiste

245

hadn't returned. His letters were short and uninformative. He was residing in Ansbach and trying to introduce there the same reforms as in Hanover. I should come to him, he wrote, as soon as Oscar was better.

But Oscar recovered very slowly. We gave him lots of milk to drink and put him outside in the garden in the spring sun. Josephine came once and said that I don't look after my roses properly. So she sent me her gardener. The gardener was awfully expensive and made such a mess of my roses that hardly anything was left of them.

People at last stopped being afraid of catching infection from Oscar, and Hortense invited him to play with her two boys. After Napoleon's adoption of their two sons Hortense and Louis Bonaparte imagine that their eldest boy will one day inherit his throne. On the other hand there is Joseph who thinks that the throne will be his. (Why Joseph should take it for granted that he would survive his younger brother, or why no one thinks it possible that Napoleon might nominate a son of his own to be his heir I don't understand. After all, there is little Léon, the son of Josephine's reader Eleonore Revel, who was born last December, and there is just a chance that the Empress may repeat her performance of her first marriage. . . . Thank God, the whole thing is no concern of mine!) As I was saying, Oscar had been invited to play with Hortense's sons, and a few days later he had a temperature and a sore throat and wouldn't eat. Now, of course, it was worse than ever before and nobody would come anywhere near our house: Oscar had got German measles.

Dr. Corvisart called and prescribed cold compresses to get Oscar's temperature down. But the compresses were no good. Oscar raved in his fever and called desperately for his father. At night he wouldn't sleep anywhere but in my bed, and I would clasp him tightly to me. There was a risk of infection, but Marie said that one rarely got this kind of illness twice. Oscar's thin body was full of little red blisters which, Dr. Corvisart said, he must not scratch.

I never saw my reader these days. Heaven knows to whom she read, certainly not to me, she was so afraid of measles. It annoyed me, though, that I had to pay her her salary all the same. Since Jean-Baptiste's promotion to Marshal we've had so many unnecessary expenses.

The days passed, one very much like the other. Then, one spring afternoon, Julie turned up surprisingly, because since Oscar's measles she had stopped coming completely and only sent her maid regularly to inquire how he was. She appeared in the drawing-room full of excitement, and when I entered the house from the garden she shouted: "Don't come near me, you'll infect me. But I want to be the first to tell you the great news. It's inconceivable——"

Her hat sat askew, little trickles of perspiration ran down her face and she was pale.

I was terrified. "For heaven's sake, what is the matter?" I asked.

"I've become a Queen, Queen of Naples," she said in a toneless voice; her eyes were wide with terror.

At first I thought she had fallen ill and was raving, that she had caught measles somewhere, though certainly not from us, and I shouted: "Marie, come quickly, Julie isn't well."

Marie appeared, but Julie declined her help. "Leave me alone, I am all right, only I can't get used to the idea yet. A Queen, me a Queen! The Queen of Naples. Naples is in Italy, isn't it? My husband, His Majesty King Joseph! And I am Her Majesty Queen Julie. Oh, Désirée, the whole thing is terrible. We shall have to go to Italy again and live in those dreadful marble palaces. . . ."

"Your father wouldn't have liked it, Mademoiselle Julie," put in Marie.

"Hold your tongue!" said Julie harshly. I had never heard her speak like that to Marie before. Marie's mouth set in a thin hard line and she left the room, slamming the door behind her. But no sooner had she gone than my companion, Madame La Flotte, appeared in her very best gown and sank into a deep curtsey before Julie as if she were the Empress. "Your Majesty, may I congratulate you?" she lisped.

Julie, whom Marie's furious exit had left in a state of near-collapse, gave a nervous start at the sight of Madame La Flotte and the corners of her mouth twitched. She collected herself quickly and her face was that of a bad actress who wants to play a Queen. "Thank you. How do you know what has happened?" she asked in a new, strange voice.

My companion was still in her deep curtsey on the carpet before Julie. "The whole town talks of nothing else, Your Majesty." Somewhat absurdly she added: "Your Majesty is too gracious!"

"Leave me alone with my sister," said Julie in her new voice. At that my companion tried to remove herself with her back to the door, an effort which I watched with great interest. When at last she had managed to get out through the door I said: "She seems to think that she is at court."

"In my presence," said Julie, "from now on one has to behave as at court. Joseph is busy this afternoon collecting a real regal suite." She shuddered, as if she were cold. "Désirée, I'm so afraid of everything."

I tried to encourage her. "Nonsense, you'll always be yourself."

But Julie shook her head and hid her face in her hands. "No, it's no good. You can't talk it away, I am a Queen now."

She began to weep, and without thinking I went up to her. She screamed at once: "Don't touch me, go away. Measles!"

I went back to the door to the garden. "Yvette!" I called.

Yvette, my maid, came, and on seeing Julie she, too, curtsied deeply.

"Bring a bottle of champagne, Yvette."

"I can't do it," said Julie, "I can't do it. More receptions, more court balls in a strange country. Away from Paris. . . ."

Yvette returned with the bottle and two glasses, and I poured out for us. Julie took her glass and at once began to drink hurriedly, thirstily.

"Your health, darling," I said, "I suppose it's an occasion for congratulations."

"It's all your doing," she smiled, "you brought Joseph into our house."

I remembered the whispers that were going round about Joseph being unfaithful to Julie. Small *affaires*, though, nothing really serious. He realised a long time ago that his talent as an author didn't amount to much but that his political talent was something to be proud of. And now brother-in-law Joseph had become a King.

"I hope," I said, "you are happy with Joseph."

"I have him so rarely to myself," she said, and stared past me into the garden. "I suppose I am happy, really. I have the children, Zenaïde and little Charlotte Napoleone."

"Your daughters will all be Princesses now, and everything will be all right," I said, and smiled. At the same time I tried to get it all into focus: Julie was a Queen, her daughters were Princesses, and Joseph, the little secretary of the *Maison Commune* who married Julie on account of her dowry, was King Joseph I of Naples.

"The Emperor, let me tell you, has decided to turn the conquered territories into independent States to be governed by the Imperial Princes and Princesses. And, of course, these States are to be linked to France by pacts of friendship. We, Joseph and I, are going to govern Naples and Sicily, Eliza has become Duchess of Lucca, Louis King of Holland and Murat Duke of Cleves."

"Good heavens, do you mean to say that the Marshals too will have to take their turn?" I asked, startled.

"No, it's because Murat is married to Caroline, and Caroline would be mortally insulted if she didn't have the revenues of a country to dispose of like the others."

I felt relieved.

"In any case," Julie went on, "someone will have to reign over the countries which we have conquered."

"Which who conquered?" I asked pointedly.

Julie made no answer but poured herself another glass, drank it hastily and said: "I wanted to be the first to tell you all that. And now I must go. Le Roy is going to do my robes of state. So much purple!"

"No," I said firmly. "You must object to that. Red just doesn't suit you, it doesn't. Have the coronation robe green, not purple."

"And all the packing I have to do!" wailed Julie. "And the ceremonial entry into Naples! You are coming with us, aren't you?"

I shook my head. "No. I have to nurse my boy, and besides, well, I am waiting for my husband. Jean-Baptiste is bound to come home some time or other, isn't he?"

From that day till this morning I heard no more from Julie. I only read in the *Moniteur* about her, about Their Majesties the King and Queen of Naples and their balls, receptions and preparations for their journey.

To-day Oscar was allowed out of bed for the first time and he sat by the open window. It has been an enchanting June day, the air was filled with the scent of lilac and roses, and the sweetness everywhere made me long more than ever for my Jean-Baptiste.

A carriage stopped outside our door. Every time a carriage draws up unexpectedly at our house there is a breathless moment when my heart waits for a miracle to happen. There was a breathless moment now, but it was only Julie who got out of the carriage. I heard her ask for me, and the next moment she came into the room. My companion and Yvette curtsied deeply, Marie, however, who had just been dusting, strode away into the garden with a stony face. She didn't want to see Julie.

Julie's regal gestures, which I am sure she owes to Monsieur Montel's tuition, swept everybody out of the room. Oscar got up and ran towards her.

"Aunt Julie," he cried, "I am well again." She took him in her arms and pressed him to her. Looking at me over his curly head she said:

"I wanted to tell you before you read it to-morrow morning in the *Moniteur* that Jean-Baptiste has become Prince of Ponte Corvo. Your Serene Highness, I offer you my congratulations!" She laughed and kissed Oscar, adding: "Congratulations, my little heir to the Principality of Ponte Corvo!"

At first I didn't know what to say, but at last I managed to bring out: "I don't understand that. Jean-Baptiste isn't a brother of the Emperor, is he?"

"But he governs Hanover and Ansbach so well that the Emperor wants to confer a distinction on him," she said in a jubilant voice, letting go of Oscar and coming close to me. "Aren't you pleased, Your Highness? Aren't you pleased, Princess?"

"I suppose——" I interrupted myself: "Yvette, champagne!" then turned back to Julie: "Champagne in the morning makes me drunk, I know. But Marie won't serve us chocolate any more since you made her furious that time. Well, now tell me: where is Ponte Corvo?"

Julie shrugged her shoulders. "How stupid of me! I should have asked Joseph. I don't know, darling. But does it matter?"

"Perhaps, if we have to go there and reign there. But wouldn't it be dreadful!"

"The name sounds Italian. Perhaps it's near Rome," Julie said. "In that case you might be quite close to us. But that," her face clouded over, "that would be too good to be true. Your Jean-Baptiste is a Marshal, and the Emperor needs him for his campaigns. No, I'm sure you'll be able to stay on here and I'll have to go to Naples without you."

"These wars must end some time, mustn't they?"

'Ruin ourselves with our victories,' who said that to me once? Jean-Baptiste did. France has no more frontiers to defend, France is Europe, and Napoleon and Joseph and Louis and Caroline and Eliza reign over it all, and now the Marshals are to take a hand too. . . .

"Your health, Your Serene Highness!" Julie raised her glass.

"To yours, Your Majesty!"

'And to-morrow we'll read it in the *Moniteur*,' I thought, as the champagne trickled sweetly down my throat. Ponte Corvo, where was Ponte Corvo? And when would my Jean-Baptiste come home?

Summer 1807, *in a coach somewhere in* EUROPE.

MARIENBURG, that was the name of the place I was making for. I had no idea where it lay, but a colonel was sitting by my side whom the Emperor had given me as my escort, and this colonel held a map on his knees from which he now and then shouted directions to the coachman. I took it therefore that we should get to Marienburg in due course. . . .

Marie, who was sitting opposite me, kept grumbling about the bad roads in which we got bogged so often. From the language which I heard people use when we stopped to change horses I guessed that we were passing through a stretch of Poland. It didn't sound Germanic to me. The colonel explained to me that we were taking a shorter route.

"We could have gone through Northern Germany," he said. "But it would have meant a detour, and Your Highness is in a hurry."

Yes, I was in a great hurry.

"Marienburg is not very far from Danzig," said the colonel.

That didn't mean anything to me either, as the whereabouts of Danzig were as unknown to me as those of Marienburg.

"A few weeks ago there was still fighting along these roads," the colonel went on. "But now we are at peace."

Yes, Napoleon had concluded another treaty of peace, this time at Tilsit. The Germans, under the leadership of the Prussians, had risen, and with the help of the Russians had tried to chase our troops out of the country. In the *Moniteur* we read all about our glorious victory at Jena. At home, however, in the secrecy of our four walls, Joseph told me that Jean-Baptiste had refused to obey an order from the Emperor, 'for strategical reasons', and that he had told the Emperor plainly that he could court-martial him if he liked. But before that could come to pass Jean-Baptiste had surrounded General Blücher and his army in Lübeck (another place I wouldn't know where to look for on the map!) and taken the town by assault.

There followed an endless winter during which I hardly got news at all. Berlin had been taken and the enemy troops were pursued across Poland. Jean-Baptiste was in command of the left wing of our Army. Near Mohrungen he won a victory over an enemy army far superior in numbers. On that occasion he not only won a decisive success against the advancing

251

foe but even managed to save the Emperor himself. This personal act of bravery made such a profound impression on the Prussian High Command that they sent his travelling bag with the Marshal's uniform in it, and the camp bed, which had already fallen into their hands, back to him.

All that, however, happened many months ago. Meanwhile Jean-Baptiste's regiments beat back all attacks on the flank of our army, the Emperor won the battles of Eylau and Jena, and dictated the conditions of peace to a Europe united in subjection to him. And one day, to everybody's surprise, Napoleon arrived back in Paris, and his lackeys in their green uniform—green is the colour of Corsica—rode from house to house to distribute invitations to a great victory ball in the Tuileries.

For this ball I put on my new robe of pale pink satin with dark roses on the bodice, and on my head I wore the diadem made of rubies and pearls which Jean-Baptiste had sent me through a courier on the last anniversary of our wedding day in August.

"Your Serene Highness is going to have a good time," said my companion jealously, staring at the golden casket with the engraved eagle in which I keep my jewellery, the casket which was given me on the day of the coronation.

I shook my head. "I shall be very lonely in the Tuileries. Not even Queen Julie will be there." No, she wouldn't be there because she was in Naples enduring in the southern heat an infinite loneliness.

The ball in the Tuileries took a course very different from the one I had expected. We foregathered in the great ballroom and waited there till the doors opened and the Marseillaise rang out. The Emperor and the Empress appeared and we curtsied deeply. They made a slow round of the guests, talking to some and making others miserable by overlooking them.

I couldn't see Napoleon properly at first because of the tall adjutants who surrounded him. Suddenly he stopped, quite close to me, in front of a Dutch dignitary, I thought, and he began:

"I am told that malicious tongues maintain of my officers that they only send their troops to the fighting line, whereas they themselves keep out. Well, is not that what they say in your country, in Holland?" he thundered all at once.

I knew that the Dutch were very dissatisfied with French overlordship in general and with their awkward King Louis and their melancholy Queen Hortense in particular. I was not surprised, therefore, about the Emperor's displeasure towards them, and didn't listen to what he said but studied his face instead. The sharp features under the short-cut hair had become ampler, the smile of his colourless mouth had changed from the winning and challenging smile of years ago to one of superiority. Besides, he had grown fatter, he looked as if he were going to burst out of his plain General's uniform, which bears no medals except that of the Legion of Honour which he himself had founded. He had a pronounced look of rotundity about him, and this rotund image of God on earth harangued with wide gestures and only now and then controlled himself and clasped his hands behind his back, as formerly in moments of great tension. He had clasped them behind his back now as if he were trying to keep a grip on those far too restless fingers of his.

His superior smile turned sneering: "Gentlemen, I believe that our great Army has proved the bravery of its officers in unique style. Not even the highest officers refrain from exposing themselves to danger. In Tilsit I received news that one of the Marshals of France has been wounded."

There was deep silence. Could the whole ballroom hear my heart beat?

"The Marshal in question is the Prince of Ponte Corvo," he added after an artificial pause.

"Is—that—true?" My voice cut through the circle of etiquette which surrounds the Emperor. At once a frown appeared on his face. One doesn't shout in the presence of His Imperial Majesty. . . . The frown disappeared from his face, and at that moment I knew that he had seen me before he spoke. So that was the way in which he wanted to inform me, in front of thousands of strangers, as if he wanted to punish me. Punish me for what?

"My dear Princess," he said, and I curtsied deeply. He took my hand and pulled me up. "I regret to have to tell you this," he said, at the same time looking indifferently away from me. "The Prince of Ponte Corvo, who has gained great distinction in this campaign and whose conquest of Lübeck we greatly admired, has been slightly wounded in the neck, near Spandau. I am told that the Prince is already on the road to recovery. I beg you not to alarm yourself, dear Princess."

"And I beg you to make it possible for me to go to my husband, Sire," I said in a toneless voice. Only now the Emperor turned his eyes on me fully. Marshals' wives do not usually follow their husbands to their headquarters.

"The Prince has gone to Marienburg to have himself looked after properly. I advise you against this journey, Princess. The roads through Northern Germany, and above all in the region round Danzig, are very bad. Moreover, these districts were battlefields only a short while ago. They are no sight for the eyes of beautiful women," he said coldly. But he examined my face with great interest.

'That's his revenge,' I thought, 'for my visit to him the night before the execution of the Duc d'Enghien, his revenge for my escape from his hands that night, his revenge for my love of Jean-Baptiste, the General whom he had not wanted me to marry.'

"Sire, I ask you from the bottom of my heart to enable me to get to my husband. I have not seen him for nearly two years."

His eyes still rested on my face. He nodded. "Almost two years. You see, gentlemen, how the Marshals of France sacrifice themselves for their country! If you want to risk it, dear Princess, you will be given a passport. For how many persons?"

"For two. I am only taking Marie."

"I beg your pardon, Princess—whom?"

"Marie. Our faithful old Marie from Marseilles. Your Majesty will perhaps remember her," I said defiantly.

At last! His face stopped being a marble mask and a smile of amusement appeared on it. "Of course, faithful Marie! Marie of the marzipan tarts!" He turned to one of the adjutants: "A passport for the Princess of Ponte Corvo and one accompanying person."

His eyes glanced round his circle and stopped at a tall colonel in the uniform of the grenadiers. "Colonel Moulin, you will go with the Princess, and you are responsible to me for her safety." Turning back to me, "When do you want to depart?"

"To-morrow morning, Sire."

"I should like you to convey my kind regards to the Prince and to take him a present from me. In recognition of his services for this victorious campaign I am presenting him with——" I saw his eyes change colour, his smile turn to a jeer; now, I felt, he was going to strike—"I am presenting him with the house of the former General Moreau in Rue d'Anjou. I bought it from his wife a short time ago. I am told the General has gone into exile in America. A pity, an able soldier but unfortunately a traitor to France, a great pity. . . ."

Curtseying deeply again, I only saw his back and his hands stiffly clasping each other behind it. General Moreau's house! That Moreau who, together with Jean-Baptiste, wanted to stand by the Republic on that 18th Brumaire and whom, five years later, in connection with a Royalist plot, they arrested and condemned to prison for two years. The ludicrousness of it, to arrest this most loyal General of the Republic as a Royalist. The First Consul subsequently commuted the sentence to exile for life. And now, as Emperor, he bought his house and gave it as a present to Moreau's best friend, the man whom he hates but can't do without. . . .

And that was how I came to travel along highways through battlefields, past dead horses with inflated bellies stretching their limbs to the sky, past little mounds surmounted by slanting crosses hastily put together. And all the time it was raining, raining, raining.

"And all of them had mothers," I said, apparently apropos of nothing.

The colonel, who had fallen asleep by my side, started. "I beg your pardon? Mothers?"

I pointed to the small mounds of earth outside in the rain. "Those dead soldiers. Are they not all mothers' sons?"

Marie pulled the curtains across the carriage windows. Puzzled, the colonel looked from one to the other. We said nothing. He shrugged his shoulders and closed his eyes once more.

"I am longing for Oscar," I said to Marie. It was the first time since he was born that I had left him. In the early hours of the morning before my departure I had taken him to Madame Letitia at Versailles, where the Emperor's mother lives in the Trianon Palace. She had just returned from early Mass when we arrived, and she promised me to look well after Oscar. "After all, I have brought up five sons," she said.

'Brought up, yes, but badly,' I thought. But one couldn't say such things to the mother of Napoleon.

"You go to your Bernadotte, Eugenie, I'll look after him," she repeated, and stroked his hair with her horny hand.

"Should we not stop at an inn?" the colonel asked.

I shook my head.

At nightfall Marie pushed a hot-water-bottle, which we had filled at a coaching inn, under my feet. The rain drummed on the roof of the coach, and the soldiers' graves and their pitiful crosses were drowned in the downpour. And on we went on our way to Marienburg.

"This really is too awful!" I said involuntarily when our coach came at last to a halt outside Jean-Baptiste's headquarters. I had slowly got used to mansions and palaces, but the Marien- burg is neither one nor the other but a medieval, grey, desolate, decayed, eerie castle.

There were crowds of soldiers outside by the gate, and great was the excitement and clicking of heels when Colonel Moulin showed my passport. Fancy, the Marshal's wife herself!

Getting out of the carriage I said: "Please do not announce me. I want to surprise the Prince."

Two officers took me through the portal into a miserably paved courtyard. The mighty ruined walls around it shocked me deeply. Any moment I expected to see knightly damsels and minnesingers. Instead I saw only soldiers of a number of different regiments.

"Monseigneur has very nearly recovered. About this time Monseigneur works and does not generally wish to be disturbed. What a surprise!" said the younger of the two officers, and smiled.

"Was it impossible to find a better headquarters than this minnesinger castle?" I couldn't help saying.

"In the field it is a matter of indifference to the Prince where he resides. And at any rate there is plenty of room here for our offices. In here, Your Highness, if you please."

He opened an inconspicuous door and we passed along a corridor. It was cold in here and the air smelt stale. At last we reached a little ante-chamber and there Fernand rushed up to me. "Madame!" he shouted.

He was so elegantly dressed that I hardly recognised him.

"Dear me, you *have* become elegant, Fernand!" I laughed.

"We are now the Prince of Ponte Corvo," he said solemnly. "Please to look at the buttons, Madame!" He pushed out his stomach to show me the gold buttons on his wine-red livery. They showed a strange armorial design. "The arms of Ponte Corvo, the arms of Madame!" he said proudly.

"At long last I am setting eyes on them," I said, and regarded the complicated engraving with interest.

"We are really quite well again. Only the new skin over the wound still itches," said Fernand. I put my finger over my mouth. Fernand understood and very quietly opened a door.

Jean-Baptiste didn't hear me. He was sitting by a desk, his chin in his hand, studying a folio. The candle near the book threw its light on his forehead, a clear and serene forehead.

I looked round. Jean-Baptiste had put a strange mixture of things into the room. The desk covered with documents and leather-bound folios stood against the fireplace, in which a big fire roared. A map of enormous size hung by the mantelpiece and the flickering flames threw a red glare over it. In the background I saw his narrow camp bed and a table with a

256

silver washing bowl and some bandaging material. Apart from that the vast room was empty.

I went nearer to him. The logs in the fire crackled and Jean-Baptiste didn't hear me. The collar of his dark blue field uniform stood open and showed a white scarf. It was loosened under the chin and I saw a white bandage. Now he turned a page of the heavy tome and wrote something in the margin.

I took off my hat. It was warm by the fireplace, and for the first time for days I felt warm and sheltered, but tired too, dreadfully tired. Yet tiredness didn't matter now, I had arrived.

"Your Highness," I said, "dear Prince of Ponte Corvo——"

He jumped to his feet. "My God, Désirée!" And the next moment he stood by my side.

"Does the wound still hurt?" I asked between two kisses.

"Yes, particularly when you put your arm on it as firmly as now," he said.

I dropped my arms at once. "I shall kiss you without putting my arms round you," I said.

"Marvellous!"

I sat on his lap and pointed to the big tome on his desk. "What is that you are reading?"

"Law. An uneducated sergeant has to learn a lot if he is to administer the whole of Northern Germany and the Hanse towns."

"Hanse towns? What are they?"

"Hamburg, Lübeck and Bremen. And·don't forget that we are still responsible for Hanover and Ansbach besides."

I shut the book and clung tightly to him. "Oscar was ill," I whispered, "and you have been away from us for so long. You were wounded and you were far away from me. . . ."

I felt his mouth on mine. "My little girl, my little girl," he said, and held me tightly.

Suddenly the door was flung open, which was rather embarrassing. I jumped down from his lap and tidied my hair. But it was only Marie and Fernand.

"Marie wants to know where the Princess is going to sleep. She wants to unpack," Fernand said in a doleful voice. I realised, of course, that he was furious because I had brought Marie.

"My Eugenie can't sleep in this place full of bugs," said Marie.

"Bugs?" Fernand shouted. "There aren't any here. It's far too cold and damp for them."

"When these two are arguing I feel I am back home in Rue

Cisalpine," said Jean-Baptiste, and laughed. As he spoke I remembered the Emperor's present, Moreau's house. 'After supper I shall have to tell him,' I thought. 'But first let's eat, and drink some wine, and then we'll see.'

"Fernand, you'll see to it that within an hour you'll have a bedroom and a drawing-room ready for the Princess," ordered Jean-Baptiste. "And don't take any of the damp furniture from the depot. Tell the Adjutant on Duty to requisition some decent furniture from the big houses in the district."

"And without bugs!" hissed Marie.

"The Princess and I want to dine alone here, in my room, in an hour."

We heard them continue their argument outside, and we laughed a lot, remembering our bridal bed full of roses and thorns. I climbed back on to his knees and talked to him about everything that came into my mind, about Julie's difficulties as a Queen, Oscar's whooping cough, his measles, and Monsieur Beethoven's message to him about the new symphony, which he could not, after all, dedicate to the Emperor but would simply call 'Eroica' to commemorate a hope which he had nourished once upon a time. . . .

Fernand laid a small table and we sat down to a delicious chicken and marvellous Burgundy.

"You have bought new cutlery, Jean-Baptiste! With the initials of the Prince of Ponte Corvo! At home I am still using our old cutlery with the simple 'B' on it."

"Have the 'B' erased and the new arms put in its place, darling. You need not economise, we are very rich," said Jean-Baptiste.

Fernand, having finished waiting on us, disappeared, and I braced myself to deliver the blow. "We are richer than you think," I said. "The Emperor has given us a house as a present."

Jean-Baptiste looked up at me. "House? What house?"

"The house of General Moreau in the Rue d'Anjou. He bought it from Madame Moreau."

"I know, for 400,000 francs. He bought it some months ago, and it caused a lot of talk among officers."

Jean-Baptiste slowly divided an orange into segments and I drank a glass of liqueur. He looked suddenly very tired.

"Moreau's house," he murmured. "Friend Moreau went into exile whilst I have become the recipient of great Imperial presents. I had a letter from the Emperor to-day in which he tells me that he is going to hand over to me estates in Poland and Westphalia which guarantee me a yearly income of another 300,000 francs. But he doesn't say a word about Moreau's house and your visit.

It is not so easy to spoil a man's joy at reunion with his wife. But the Emperor of the French manages it all right."

"He said that he admired your assault on Lübeck very much," I said.

Jean-Baptiste did not answer. A deep frown had appeared on his forehead.

"I shall furnish the new house very comfortably," I went on, feeling helpless. "You must come home. The child keeps asking about you."

Jean-Baptiste shook his head. "Moreau's house will never be my home, only a *pied-à-terre* where I shall call to see you and Oscar sometimes." He stared into the fire and a smile came into his face: "I shall write to Moreau."

"But how can you communicate with him across the Continental Blockade?"

"The Emperor wants me to administer the Hanseatic towns. From Lübeck it is easy to write to Sweden, still a neutral country from which letters go to England and America. And I have friends in Sweden."

A memory came back to me, half forgotten and yet very clear: Stockholm near the North Pole, a white sky. . . . "What do you know of Sweden?" I asked.

"When I took Lübeck," said Jean-Baptiste, returning to his livelier mood, "I found some Swedish troops, a squadron of dragoons, in the town."

"How was that? Are we at war with Sweden, too?"

"With whom are we not at war? That is to say, since Tilsit we are allegedly at peace again. Anyway, at that time Sweden had made common cause with our enemies. Its crazy young King imagined himself to be the tool of God to bring about Napoleon's destruction. Apparently some kind of religious mania."

"What's his name?"

"Gustavus. The fourth of that name, I believe. The Swedish Kings are all called Carl or Gustavus. His father, the third Gustavus, was so unpopular that he was murdered during a masked ball by a member of the Swedish aristocracy."

"How awful, how barbarous—during a masked ball!"

"When we were young," said Jean-Baptiste ironically "the guillotine used to do that kind of job. Do you think that less barbarous? It is difficult enough to judge, but more difficult still to condemn." He stared into the fire for a moment, then his good temper came back to him once more. "Well, the son of this murdered Gustavus, the fourth Gustavus, sent his dragoons into the war against France, and that was how I came to capture a Swedish squadron in Lübeck. I happen to be interested in Sweden for a particular reason, and having at last the opportunity of meeting some Swedes I asked the captured officers for a meal. And so I met Mr. Mörner——" He stopped. "Wait, I have the names somewhere." He got up and went to his desk.

"It's unimportant," I said. "Go on."

"No, it is not unimportant. I want to remember the names." He rummaged in a drawer, found a piece of paper and came back to me. "So I met Mr. Gustavus Mörner, Mr. Flach, Mr. de la Grange and the Barons Leijonhjelm, Banér and Friesendorff."

"What unpronounceable names!" I said.

"These officers explained the situation to me. Their King had entered the war against the will of the people. He thought that in this way he would curry favour with the Tsar. The Swedes have always been afraid that Russia might take Finland from them.

"Finland?" I shook my head. "Where is Finland?"

"Come, I'll show you on the map," said Jean-Baptiste, and I had to go with him to the big map by the fireplace.

Here he explained to me in great detail the merits of the geographical situation of Denmark, Sweden and Norway, the madness of King Gustavus' policy towards Russia and France, and his firm belief that the only thing to do for the Swedes was to cede Finland to Russia and try for a union with Norway, at present under the unpopular sovereignty of the King of Denmark.

"Did you explain that to the Swedish officers in Lübeck?"

"I certainly did. I also told them that we are going to despatch French troops to Denmark very soon. 'Save your country through armed neutrality, gentlemen,' I said to them, 'and, if you needs must have a federation, forget about Finland and look to Norway for your partner.'"

"And what did the Swedes answer?"

"They stared at me as if I were a seven days' wonder. Don't look at me, look at the map, I told them." Jean-Baptiste paused, smiling. "And next morning I sent them home, since when I have friends in Sweden."

"Why do you want friends in Sweden?"

"It is always useful to have friends in all sorts of places. But I wish the Swedes would stop being bellicose to Russia and France at the same time. Otherwise I shall have to occupy their country. We expect the British to attack Denmark to use it as a base against us, and that is why Napoleon wants to station French troops in Denmark. As I am to be the Governor of the Hanseatic towns I expect to be Commander-in-Chief of the troops in Denmark, and if the Swedish Gustavus does not see reason some day the Emperor will give me the order to occupy Sweden. Getting there will be easy: I shall simply cross the Öre Sound from Denmark into the southern tip of Sweden. Come, have another look at the map." And I had to take up my position in front of the map again. But this time I didn't look. I had travelled for days and nights without interruption to nurse my husband, not to listen to lectures on geography.

"The Swedes can't defend the southern part of their country; it is strategically impossible." He pointed to somewhere on the map. "I suppose they would stand and try to hold a line here."

"Tell me, did you say to these Swedish officers that you may possibly conquer their country? And that they could not hope to defend their southernmost region but would have to try to defend themselves farther north?"

"I did. And you cannot imagine how they were taken aback when I told them. Especially this man Mörner. He kept exclaiming 'Monseigneur, you are giving your secret plans away. How can you take us into your confidence?' And you know what I answered?"

"No," I said, and moved slowly across to the camp bed. I was so tired that I could hardly keep my eyes open. "What did you answer, Jean-Baptiste?"

"'Gentlemen,' I said, 'I cannot imagine that Sweden would be able to hold out if it is attacked by a French Marshal.' That was my answer. Little girl, are you asleep?"

"Almost," I said, and tried to make myself comfortable on that miserable camp bed.

"Come," said Jean-Baptiste, "I have made them get a bedroom ready for you. Everybody has gone to bed. I shall carry you across and nobody will see it," he whispered.

"I don't want to get up any more. I am so tired."

Jean-Baptiste bent down to me. "If you want to sleep here I can sit at the desk. I have so much reading to do yet."

"No-o. You are wounded. You must lie down."

Undecided, Jean-Baptiste sat down on the edge of the bed.

"You must take my shoes off and my dress. I am so tired."

"I think the Swedish officers will talk to their ministers and give them no rest till they force their King to abdicate. His successor would be an uncle of his."

"Another Gustavus?"

"No, a Charles, Charles the Thirteenth. Unfortunately this

261

uncle has no children, and he is said to be very senile. Why, darling, did you put three petticoats on?"

"Because of the cold and the rain. Poor Mörner, senile and childless."

"No, not Mörner, the thirteenth Charles of Sweden."

"If I made myself very small and moved over as far as possible we would both have room in your camp bed. We could try."

"Yes, we could try, my little girl."

I woke up some time during the night lying on Jean-Baptiste's arm.

"Are you uncomfortable, little girl?"

"No, I am very comfortable. Why aren't you asleep, Jean-Baptiste?"

"I am not tired. So many things are going through my head. You go to sleep again, darling."

"Stockholm is on Lake Mälar," I murmured, "and green ice-floes float on the Lake."

"How do you know that?"

"I just know it. I used to know a man called Persson. . . ."

I didn't return to Paris till autumn. Jean-Baptiste and his staff went to Hamburg, where Jean-Baptiste started his administration. From there he wanted to visit Denmark and inspect the coastal fortifications opposite Sweden.

The weather was good on my return journey, hot-water-bottles were superfluous. A tired-looking autumn sun shone into the carriage, on the highway and the fields which had seen no harvest this year. We saw no dead horses and only a few war graves. The rain water seemed to have levelled the little mounds and the wind had pushed over the wooden crosses. One could almost forget that one was travelling across recent battlefields, or that thousands of men lay buried here. One could, but I didn't.

Somewhere Colonel Moulin succeeded in finding an old issue of the *Moniteur*. In it we read that the Emperor's youngest brother Jerome, that naughty boy Jerome who at Julie's wedding had eaten too much and been sick, had become a King. King Jerome the First of Westphalia, a kingdom made up of some German principalities. In addition Napoleon had managed to marry the twenty-three-year-old King to Princess Catherine of Württemberg, the descendant of one of the oldest German princely families. I wondered whether Jerome still remembered Miss Patterson from America whom he so willingly divorced on Napoleon's orders.

I told Marie the news.

"Now nobody can keep him under control and he'll overeat himself every day," she said.

Colonel Moulin was shocked. It was by no means the first *lèse-majesté* he had heard from her.

I threw the old *Moniteur* out of the carriage window and the wind carried it across the battlefields.

In our new home in the Rue d'Anjou in PARIS. July 1809.

THE church bells woke me up. It was hot already although it was still very early. I pushed the blanket back, folded my arms under my head and mused. The bells of Paris. . . .

'Perhaps,' I thought, 'it's the birthday of one of the many Kings of the Bonaparte family.' Napoleon had turned every member of it into Kings and Princes. Joseph, by the way, was no longer King of Naples but of Spain, and for months, literally months, Julie had been on her way to Madrid. The Spaniards, it turned out, didn't want Joseph as their King, ambushed his troops, surrounded and defeated them, and finally the rebels instead of King Joseph entered Madrid in triumph. So the Emperor had to send more troops to Spain to deliver Joseph's people from these misguided patriots.

In Naples Murat and Caroline had taken the place of Joseph and Julie. Murat, being a Marshal of France as well as King of Naples, had to be away most of the time on some front or other, leaving Caroline to represent the royal family. But Caroline didn't bother much about her kingdom and her son but stayed mostly with her eldest sister Eliza, who reigned in Toscana, getting fatter year by year and having an *affaire* with her court musician, a man called Paganini.

Julie told me all about that. She had been in Paris for a few weeks before setting out for Spain, to have her new robes of state made here. They had to be purple, of course, at Joseph's wish.

Oh those bells! Which Bonaparte's birthday could it be to-day? It wouldn't be Jerome nor Eugene de Beauharnais, now the Viceroy of Italy. This timid young man had changed a lot since he had married a daughter of the King of Bavaria. 'Some of his timidity has disappeared,' I thought, 'and he, at any rate, seems happier.'

The bells bent on. I could distinguish the deep chime of Notre-Dame from the rest. When was King Louis' birthday? That boy was going to reach a good old age in spite of his many imaginary ailments, of which only his flat feet were real. What, by the way, was the name of the Dutch rebels who repeatedly attempted to rise against Louis? Saboteurs, that was it, saboteurs, because of their sabots, the wooden shoes which they wear like our fishermen at home in Marseilles. They hate Louis because Napoleon made him their King. If only they knew how Louis dislikes his brother! Every time a merchant ship secretly left one of his ports to sail for England Louis turned a blind eye. Louis was the Dutch saboteur-in-chief to annoy his brother. He seemed to think that the least Napoleon could have done was to allow him to choose his own wife.

Who was it who talked to me about Louis only the other day? Ah, Polette of course, the only Bonaparte who has never meddled in politics but only lived for her pleasure and her lovers. No church bells would ring for her birthday, or for Lucien's for that matter. Napoleon offered the still exiled Lucien the crown of Spain on condition that he divorced his red-haired Madame Jourberthon. Lucien, the blue-eyed idealist, refused, and tried to make his way to America. His boat was intercepted by the British, who took him as an 'enemy alien' to England. The other day he succeeded in getting a letter smuggled through to his mother in France, in which he wrote that he lived under observation—yet free! To think that it was Lucien who helped Napoleon to the Consulate in order to save the French Republic! No, there wouldn't be any church bells for Lucien either. . . .

The door opened a bit. "I thought that the bells had wakened you," said Marie. "I'll get you your breakfast."

"What's all this bell-ringing for, Marie?"

"What for? The Emperor has gained a great victory."

"Where? When? Anything in the paper?"

"I'll send you your breakfast and your reader." She bethought herself a moment. "No, your breakfast first, then the young madame who reads to you."

It's a continual source of fun to Marie that I, like the other ladies at court, have to engage a young girl of the old impoverished nobility to read the *Moniteur* to me, and novels. But I'd much rather read by myself and in bed. The Emperor insists that we Marshals' wives be attended as if we were eighty and not, as in my case, twenty-eight.

Yvette brought my morning chocolate and opened the window. Immediately sunshine and the scent of roses streamed into my bedroom. The garden—there are only three rose trees in it—is very small, which is no wonder as the house is right in the middle of the town. Most of Moreau's furniture which I found here I gave away, and bought new and very expensive furniture instead. In the drawing-room I discovered a bust of the former owner. I didn't know at first what to do with it. Certainly I couldn't leave it where I found it, as Moreau is in disgrace. But I didn't want to throw it away either. So I put it in the hall, and the obligatory portrait of the Emperor into the drawing-room.

I was fortunate in obtaining a copy of Napoleon's portrait painted when he was First Consul by Adolphe Yvon. In this painting the face of the image of God on earth is as lean and straight as it was in the days at Marseilles. The hair is shown as untidy and as long as it was at that time, and the eyes have not yet acquired their present steeliness and eerie iridescence but look dreamily yet sensibly into the distance. His mouth in the portrait is still that of the fledgling Napoleone who one summer night leaned against a hedge and spoke of men chosen to make history. . . .

Meanwhile the bells went on and on. My head felt like starting to ache any moment, although by now we ought to have got used to victory bells.

"Yvette," I asked, "where and when did we win this victory?"

"At Wagram, Your Highness, on July 4th and 5th."

"Send Mademoiselle in and Oscar."

They came in at the same time. I pulled Oscar to me on to the bed, and Mademoiselle started reading. And so we learnt that at Wagram, near Vienna, an Austrian army of 70,000 men had been completely destroyed. Only 1,500 Frenchmen had fallen, three thousand had been wounded. Among the details were the names of the Marshals present at that battle. Yet there was no mention of Jean-Baptiste, although I knew that he was in Austria with his troops, the Saxon regiments fighting with the Emperor's Army.

"I hope nothing has happened to him," I couldn't help saying.

"Is there nothing about Papa in the paper?" Oscar wanted to know.

Mademoiselle went once more through the report. "No, nothing," she said in the end.

There was a knock on the door and Madame La Flotte put her charmingly made-up face into the room. "Your Highness, His Excellency, Monsieur Fouché, the Minister of Police, asks you to see him."

The church bells stopped. Fouché, did she say? He had never been before. Perhaps I had misheard the name. "Who, did you say?"

"Monsieur Fouché, the Minister of Police," Madame La

Flotte repeated, full of agitation in spite of her obvious attempt to appear unconcerned.

"Out with you, Oscar. I must get ready quickly. Yvette, Yvette!"

Thank God, there was Yvette, holding the lilac-coloured dressing-gown ready for me. "Madame La Flotte, take His Excellency to the small drawing-room."

"I have taken him there already, Madame."

"Mademoiselle, go down and ask His Excellency to be patient a second. Tell him I'm just dressing. Or rather, don't tell him that. Hand him the *Moniteur* to read."

A smile flitted across the pretty face of Madame La Flotte. "Your Highness, His Excellency reads the *Moniteur* before it is printed. It is one of his duties."

"Yvette, there's no time to do my hair, give me the pink muslin scarf, put it round my head turban fashion."

Madame La Flotte and Mademoiselle disappeared. But I called Madame back: "Tell me, don't I look like Madame de Staël in this turban? Madame de Staël, the banished authoress?"

"Your Highness, Madame de Staël has a face like a dachshund and Your Highness could never——"

"Thank you, Madame. Yvette, where is my rouge?"

"In a drawer in the dressing-table. Your Highness uses it so rarely——"

"Yes, I know, my cheeks are too red anyway. Princesses ought to be pale-cheeked by nature. But at this moment I'm a bit too pale myself. Is it really hot outside or is it only me?"

"It is very hot, Your Highness," said Yvette.

I went slowly downstairs. Someone once called Fouché everybody's bad conscience. People are afraid of him because he knows too much. During the Revolution they called him 'bloody Fouché' because no one signed so many death sentences as Deputy Fouché. He was too bloodthirsty even for Robespierre. But before Robespierre could remove him Fouché exploded his plot against Robespierre, and Robespierre went to the guillotine, not Fouché. Under the Directory Fouché disappeared from sight. The Directors wanted to prove to the world that France was no republic of murderers. Fouché, however, knew all their secrets and they couldn't get rid of him. He attended at Madame Tallien's every day and he knew everything and everybody. When someone suggested firing at the hungry mob of Paris to quell a riot, he said: "Bernadotte will never do it. But what about that little wretch who keeps hanging round Josephine these days?"

How did it come about that bloodthirsty Fouché got a job

again after all? Director Barras used him first, sending him abroad as a French secret agent. Shortly before the overthrow of the Directors he became their most trusted support and they made him Minister of Police. The first thing he did as the new Minister was that he, the former president of the Jacobin Club, went to the clubhouse of his old comrades of the extreme Left in the Rue du Bac and closed it down for good, thus setting the official seal on the end of the Revolution. From then on he kept all ministries and offices, ministers and officials, officers and civilians of any importance under observation, an easy enough job when you have plenty of money to pay your spies. Who was his spy? Or rather, who was not his spy?

On the day the Directors feared was the one chosen by Napoleon for his *coup d'état*, they relied completely on their Minister of Police. But that very day the Minister of Police had to spend in bed with a cold. And during the night following the *coup d'état* the warrant for the arrest which Jean-Baptiste and I expected to arrive any minute would have been signed not by the First Consul but by the Minister of Police he had just appointed, by Monsieur Fouché.

'What does he want of me?' I wondered again and again before entering the small drawing-room. 'What did the mass murderer of Lyons want?' That's what people called him during the Revolution when they talked about the death sentences he imposed in Lyons. 'Stupid to remember that just now,' I thought. 'He doesn't look like a murderer, anyway,' I told myself, 'he is a very neatly dressed gentleman, strikingly pale probably because he is anæmic, and he speaks most politely and gently with half-closed eyes. . . .' The communiqué this morning did not mention Jean-Baptiste with so much as a syllable, and I felt that I knew what had happened. 'But, Monsieur Fouché, I have nothing to hide, only my fear.'

He jumped to his feet when I entered. "I have come to congratulate you, Princess. We have gained a great victory, and I read that the Prince of Ponte Corvo and his Saxon regiments were the first to get into Wagram. With seven to eight thousand soldiers your husband crushed the resistance of 40,000 men and took Wagram."

"Yes, but," I stammered as I asked him to keep his seat, "but that's not in the paper."

"I only said that *I* read it, my dear Princess, but not where I read it. No, you would not find it in the papers, only in the Order-of-the-Day from your husband to the Saxon troops in which he praised their bravery."

He paused and took a little Dresden bonbon dish from the

table between us and examined it with great interest. "Moreover, I also read the copy of a letter from His Majesty to the Prince of Ponte Corvo. In that the Emperor expresses outspoken displeasure at the Prince's Order-of-the-Day and even goes so far as to state that this Order contains a number of inaccuracies. His Majesty states for instance that Oudinot had taken Wagram and that it would therefore have been impossible for the Prince of Ponte Corvo to have taken it first. Furthermore the Saxons could not have gained any distinction under your husband's leadership simply because they never fired a single shot. For the rest, His Majesty wanted the Prince of Ponte Corvo to know that he, the Prince, had not distinguished himself in any way during the campaign."

"You, you mean that—the Emperor—wrote that to Jean-Baptiste?" I asked, completely confounded.

Fouché replaced the china bowl carefully on the table. "There is no doubt about that. A copy of the Imperial letter was added to a letter to me. I have been ordered——" he looked me full in the eyes, but with an amiable expression—"I have been ordered to supervise the person of the Prince of Ponte Corvo and his correspondence."

"But, Monsieur Fouché, that is going to be difficult. My husband is in Austria with his troops."

"You are mistaken, Your Highness. The Prince of Ponte Corvo is due to arrive in Paris at any moment. After the correspondence with His Majesty he has resigned his command and asked for leave for reasons of health. This leave has been granted him for an indefinite period. I congratulate you, Princess. You have not seen your husband for such a long time, there will be a reunion for you very soon."

"May I think for a moment?"

A smile of amusement flitted over his face. "Of what, Your Highness?"

I put my hand to my forehead. "Of everything. I am not very clever, Monsieur Fouché; please don't contradict me, I must try and make clear to myself what has happened. You say that my husband wrote that his Saxon troops had distinguished themselves, didn't you?"

"They stood like a rock. That at any rate is what the Prince wrote."

"Why then is the Emperor annoyed about the rock-like stand of my husband's regiments?"

"In a secret circular to all his Marshals the Emperor laid down that His Majesty is in personal command of all his troops and that it is solely up to him to single out some formations for

268

special praise. Besides, he wants them to be quite clear about the fact that the French Army owes its victories to French and not to foreign soldiers. Any other version the Emperor declares to be incompatible with our honour as well as with our policy."

"Someone told me only the other day that my husband had complained to the Emperor about allotting him nothing but foreign troops. Jean-Baptiste really did all he could to command French troops and to get rid of those poor Saxons."

"Why poor Saxons?"

"Because the King of Saxony sends his subjects into battles which are no concern of theirs. Why did the Saxons fight at Wagram at all?"

"They are France's allies, Your Highness. But don't you see yourself how wisely the Emperor acted in putting the Saxon regiments under the command of the Prince of Ponte Corvo?"

I gave no answer.

"They stood like a rock, Your Highness, under your husband's leadership."

"But the Emperor says it isn't true."

"No, all the Emperor said was that he alone had the right to praise individual army contingents, and that it was impolitic and incompatible with our national honour to praise foreign troops. You did not listen to what I said, Princess."

'I have to get his room ready, he's coming home,' I thought. I got up. "You'll excuse me, Your Excellency, I want to get everything ready for his reception. And thank you very much for your visit, though I don't know——"

He was standing right in front of me, a man of medium height, narrow-shouldered, a bit stooping. His long nose with its slightly distended nostrils seemed to sniff. "What is it you don't know, Your Highness?"

"What you've really come for. Did you want to tell me that you are putting my husband under observation? I can't prevent you from doing that and it is a matter of complete indifference to me, but—why did you tell me?"

"Can't you guess, my dear Princess?"

An idea occurred to me which at once made me choke with rage. But I collected my wits and said very emphatically and clearly: "If you, Monsieur Fouché, thought that I would help you to spy on my husband, you are mistaken." I wanted to raise my hand with a grand gesture and shout 'Out with you', only I am not very good at that kind of thing.

He said calmly: "If I had thought that, I should have been mistaken. Perhaps I did think it, perhaps I did not. I really do not know myself now."

'Why all this,' I asked myself, 'why? If the Emperor wants to banish us he'll banish us. If he wants to court-martial Jean-Baptiste he'll court-martial him. And if he wants reasons his Minister of Police will supply them for him. After all, France is no longer a country where justice is done. . . .'

"Most ladies owe money to their dressmaker," he said in an undertone.

"Monsieur, you have gone too far now."

"Our beloved Empress, for example. She is always in debt to Le Roy. Naturally I am at Her Majesty's service whenever she wishes."

What did he mean? What was he hinting at? That he pays the Empress? For spying? 'But that's crazy,' I thought. And yet I knew instantly that it was true.

"Sometimes it is quite entertaining to control the correspondence of a man. One experiences surprises, surprises which are, shall we say, of less interest to me than to the man's wife."

"Don't trouble," I said, disgusted. "You will find that Jean-Baptiste has been writing to Madame Récamier for years and that he receives tender letters from her. Madame Récamier is a very intelligent and cultured woman, and it is a great pleasure for a man like my Jean-Baptiste to correspond with her. And now you really must excuse me, I shall have to get his room in order," I added, thinking that, all the same, I would give a lot if I could really have a look at those clever love letters from Jean-Baptiste to Madame Récamier.

"One moment, please, my dear Princess. Would you kindly give the Prince a message from me?"

"Yes. What is it?"

"The Emperor is at Schönbrunn Castle in Vienna. It is therefore impossible for me to get news through to him in time about the massing of English troops intended for landing at Dunkirk and Antwerp. My information is that they will march straight from the Channel coast to Paris. Therefore, on my own responsibility and for the safety of the country I shall call up the National Guard. I am asking Marshal Bernadotte to take over the command of these troops for the defence of France immediately on his arrival. That, Madame, is all."

I was stunned. I tried to visualise it all: invasion by the British, attack by the British, march on Paris by the British. All the Marshals were away with the armies abroad. We had hardly any troops in the country, and at that very moment Britain attacked France.

Fouché was playing with the bonbon dish again.

"The Emperor mistrusts him," I said, "and you—you want

to give him the command of the National Guard to defend our frontiers?"

"I myself am no commander of troops, Princess. I used to be only a teacher of mathematics, not a—sergeant. Heaven sends me a Marshal to Paris, so I say thank Heaven for the Marshal! Will you give my message to the Prince?"

I nodded and accompanied him to the door. Then I thought of something. Perhaps it was all a trap? This Fouché was such a cunning man.

"But I don't know," I said, "if my husband will really take on the command if His Majesty does not know anything about it."

Fouché was standing quite close to me. "You may rest assured, Madame, if it is a question of defending the frontiers of France Marshal Bernadotte will take on the command." And, after a moment he added, almost inaudibly: "As long as he is still Marshal of France."

He kissed my hand and left.

The very same evening Jean-Baptiste arrived, accompanied only by Fernand. He had left even his personal adjutants behind.

Two days later he set out again. For the Channel coast.

Villa La Grange near PARIS.
Autumn 1809.

I HAVE not enough time now to write anything in my diary. I have to be round Jean-Baptiste all day long now to try and cheer him up.

Fouché had not exaggerated the danger on that day in July. The British really did land on the Channel coast and took Vlissingen. Within a few days Jean-Baptiste achieved the miracle of fortifying Antwerp and Dunkirk so strongly that not only were all British attacks thrown back but many prisoners and an enormous booty were captured from them. The British managed to reach their ships near Dunkirk by the skin of their teeth, and fled.

These events agitated the Emperor at Schönbrunn dreadfully. In his absence a minister had dared to call up the National Guard and appoint as Commander-in-Chief precisely the one Marshal whom he, the Emperor, had put under police super-vision. Publicly Napoleon could not but acknowledge that Fouché with the help of Jean-Baptiste had saved France. With-out the mobilisation of the National Guard and the energy of a Marshal who turned untrained peasants whose hands hadn't held a rifle for more than ten years into an army, France would have been lost. He made Fouché Duke of Otranto.

Duke of Otranto, as romantic a name as Ponte Corvo! Fouché knows his duchy as little as I our Italian principality. The Emperor himself designed Fouché's arms, a golden pillar round which a serpent is twisted.

The golden pillar caused general amusement. The former president of the Jacobin Club, who used to confiscate fortunes indiscriminately by classing their owners as anti-Republican, is now one of the richest men in the country. One of his best friends is Ouvrard, the former lover of Theresa Tallien, arms contractor and, at the same time, banker who carries out Fouché's deals on the Stock Exchange. Nobody, however, talks about the serpent round the pillar, though everybody seems to interpret it in one way only: Napoleon is indebted to his Minister of Police and uses the opportunity to tell him what he thinks of him. . . .

Everybody expected the Emperor to confer a distinction on Jean-Baptiste and entrust a new command to him. But he didn't even write him so much as a letter of thanks. When I spoke to Jean-Baptiste about it he said: "Why should he? I don't defend France for his sake."

We moved out from Paris to La Grange, where Jean-Baptiste had bought an attractive big house. As to the house in the Rue d'Anjou, Jean-Baptiste never felt at home in it. Although I had all the rooms beautifully decorated he found too many 'ghosts' lurking in all the corners.

"You agree, don't you, to my placing Moreau's bust in the hall?" I asked him when he entered the house for the first time.

Jean-Baptiste looked at me: "You couldn't have found a better place for it. There it will tell every visitor at once that we do not forget whose house this used to be. Strange, my little girl, how you always guess my unspoken thoughts."

"Why strange? I love you," I said.

I enjoyed every day of Jean-Baptiste's disgrace, which made it possible for us to live quietly in the country. Julie kept me informed about events in the Imperial family. She and Joseph came back to Paris. The Emperor had sent Junot's army to Spain to enable Joseph to enter Madrid at last. But Junot's army was almost annihilated by the Spanish patriots, who had the assistance of the British. According to Junot this defeat was due to no one but Joseph, because Joseph had insisted that he, as King of Spain, would take over the command himself, and had not listened to Junot. Imagine Joseph as a commander in the field! Of course, he only did it to prove to Napoleon that he could conduct campaigns as well as 'my little brother, the General'. I wondered whether Julie still had any illusions left about her Joseph.

If Napoleon's luck suddenly deserted him as it did that time in Marseilles, would they all desert him too? No, not all. Josephine would stand by him. And yet she is the one he wants to get rid of. He wants to divorce her, they say. I have been told that he intends to found a dynasty at last with the help of an Austrian Archduchess, a daughter of Emperor Francis. Poor Josephine, it is true she deceived him, but she would never leave him to his fate.

We had a very surprising visit yesterday. Count Talleyrand, the Prince of Benevento, called. It was a 'neighbourly' visit, said the Prince, laughing, because the Duchy of Benevento adjoins the principality of Ponte Corvo, and he was given it at the same time as we were given our present.

Talleyrand is, with Fouché, the most powerful man in the service of Napoleon, although he resigned his post as Minister of Foreign Affairs last year, after a row with Napoleon in which he warned him against new wars. But apparently Napoleon couldn't do without his diplomatic services. He appointed him 'Vice-Grand Elector' of the Empire and demanded that Talleyrand should continue to be consulted in all important foreign affairs. I've always liked this lame dignitary, a witty and charming man, who never talks about politics and wars to women, and I find it difficult to believe that he used to be a bishop. But he was, he was even the first bishop to take the oath to the Republic. That didn't help him much with Robespierre, though, because of his aristocratic descent, and he had to flee to America.

A few years ago Napoleon forced the Pope to absolve Talleyrand from his clerical vows. His intention in doing so was to force his Foreign Minister to marry and thus to stop him having so many mistresses. (Yes, Napoleon had become very virtuous, particularly where the ladies and gentlemen of his court were concerned.) But Talleyrand kept excusing himself, saying that he really couldn't get married and that he had to live in celibacy. In the long run, however, he couldn't escape and had to marry his last mistress. As soon as he had married her he was never seen with her in public again. . . .

Well, however that may be, this powerful man came to see us yesterday and asked: "How is it that I never see you in Paris now, my dear Prince?"

Jean-Baptiste answered politely: "That cannot have surprised you, Excellency, as you may perhaps have heard that I am on sick leave."

Talleyrand nodded gravely and enquired whether Jean-Baptiste wasn't feeling any better yet. As Jean-Baptiste goes out for a ride every day for hours and looks very bronzed, he had to admit that he was feeling a bit better.

"Have you had any interesting news from abroad lately?" asked Talleyrand. 'A stupid question,' I thought, 'because he knows very much better than everybody else what goes on abroad.'

"Ask Fouché," said Jean-Baptiste calmly. "He reads all the letters I get before I read them. Anyway, I have heard nothing of importance from abroad."

"Not even greetings from your Swedish friends?"

This question didn't strike me as anything out of the ordinary. Everybody knows that Jean-Baptiste had been very magnanimous in Lübeck towards some Swedish officers by sending them home instead of keeping them prisoners, and it is only natural that these people with unpronounceable names should sometimes write to him. Yet this question seemed to have a certain significance, for Jean-Baptiste looked up at Talleyrand and tried to catch his eye.

He nodded. "Oh yes, a few greetings. Did Fouché not show you the letter?"

"Monsieur Fouché has a very great sense of duty, and naturally he showed me the letter. But I should not call these greetings quite unimportant. Neither unimportant nor, as yet, important."

"The Swedes deposed their mad King in March and made his uncle, Charles the Thirteenth, their King," said Jean-Baptiste.

Here I pricked up my ears. "Really? This Gustavus who thought that he had been selected by Providence to defeat the Emperor has been deposed?"

They didn't answer me but continued to look into each other's eyes. The silence became oppressive to me. "Don't you think, Excellency," I said, to break this silence, "that this Gustavus is really mad?"

"It is difficult for me to judge from here," said Talleyrand, and smiled at me. "But I am convinced that his uncle is of the highest importance for the future of Sweden. This uncle is rather senile and ailing and has no children either, if I am not mistaken, Prince?"

"He has adopted a young relative and made him his successor, Prince Christian Augustus of Holstein-Sonderburg-Augustenburg."

"How well you pronounce these foreign names," said Talleyrand admiringly.

"I lived in Northern Germany long enough, one got used to these names there."

"You did not take an interest in the Swedish language, my friend?"

"No, Excellency, I had no cause to do that."

"You surprise me. A year ago, when you were in Denmark with your troops, the Emperor left it to your judgment whether to attack Sweden or not. I remember writing to you about it. But you confined yourself to looking from Denmark across to Sweden and did nothing. Why not? I have always wanted to ask you about it."

"You say yourself that the Emperor left it to me. He wanted to help the Tsar to take Finland. Our help was not needed. It was enough, as you remarked correctly, to look from Denmark across to Sweden."

"And the view? How did you like the view of Sweden, my friend?"

Jean-Baptiste shrugged his shoulders. "On clear nights one can see the lights of the Swedish coast from Denmark. But the nights were mostly foggy. I rarely saw the lights."

Talleyrand bent forward and tapped the golden knob of his walking cane, which he always carries with him on account of his lameness, gently against his chin. I couldn't understand what pleasure he got out of this conversation. "Are there many lights in Sweden, my friend?" he asked.

Jean-Baptiste put his head on one side and smiled. He, too, seemed to get a lot of pleasure out of this talk. "No, only a few. Sweden is a poor country, a great power of the day before yesterday."

"Perhaps also a great power of—to-morrow?"

Jean-Baptiste shook his head. "No, not politically, but perhaps in other ways. I don't know. Every nation has possibilities once it is ready to forget its great past."

Talleyrand smiled. "Every individual human being, too, has possibilities once he is ready to forget—his little past! We know examples, my dear Prince."

"It is easy for you to talk, Excellency. You are descended from a noble family and you had a good education. Everything was easier, far easier for you than for those to whom you allude."

The blow went home. Talleyrand's smile disappeared. Calmly he said: "I have deserved this reprimand, Prince. The former bishop apologises to the former sergeant." Was he waiting for a smile from Jean-Baptiste? Probably.

But Jean-Baptiste sat bent forward, his chin in his hands, and did not look up. At last he said: "I am tired, Your Excellency, I am tired of your questions, tired of the Police Minister's supervision, tired of distrust. I am tired, Prince of Benevento, very tired."

Talleyrand rose at once. "Then I shall hasten to put my request to you and go at once."

Jean-Baptiste, too, got to his feet. "A request? I can't imagine how a Marshal in disgrace could do a service to the Minister of Foreign Affairs."

"You see, my dear Ponte Corvo, it concerns Sweden. I heard yesterday that the Swedish Council of State have sent some gentlemen to Paris to negotiate about the resumption of diplomatic relations between our two countries, which resumption I take to be the main reason for their change of sovereign. These gentlemen—I don't know whether their names mean anything to you, a Monsieur von Essen and a Count Peyron—asked after you in Paris immediately on their arrival."

A deep frown appeared on Jean-Baptiste's forehead. "These names mean nothing to me. Nor do I know why they should have asked after me."

"The young officers who were your guests after the capture of Lübeck talk a lot about you. You, my dear Ponte Corvo, are considered a friend of—hm—of the European North. And these gentlemen who have come as Swedish negotiators probably hope that you will put in a good word with the Emperor for their country."

"You can see how badly informed they are in Stockholm," said Jean-Baptiste.

"I should like to ask you to receive these gentlemen," said Talleyrand in an expressionless voice.

Jean-Baptiste's frown deepened. "Why? Could I be of any use to them with the Emperor? No. Or is it your intention to tell the Emperor that I meddle in foreign affairs which are no concern of mine? I should be very grateful to you, Excellency, if you could tell me in so many words exactly what it is you want."

"It is so simple. I should like you to receive these gentlemen and say a few kind words to them. What words you are going to use I leave entirely to you, of course. Is that asking too much?"

"I believe you don't know what you are asking," said Jean-Baptiste tonelessly. Never before had I heard him speak like that.

"I do not want the Swedes to get the impression that the Emperor has, let us say, temporarily dispensed with the services of one of his most famous Marshals. It would create the impression abroad of dissension within the circles close to the Emperor. You see, the reason for my request is a very simple one."

"Too simple. Far too simple for a diplomatist such as you. And far too complicated for a sergeant such as me." He shook his head. "I don't understand you, Excellency, really I don't." He put his hand heavily on Talleyrand's shoulder. "Are you going to tell me that a former bishop's sense of duty is not as great as that of a former teacher of mathematics?"

With a graceful movement of his cane Talleyrand pointed to his lame foot. "That is a lame comparison, Ponte Corvo. As lame as my foot. The question is, you see, to whom one feels one owes his duty."

At that Jean-Baptiste laughed, relieved, laughed far too loudly for a Prince, laughed as he must have laughed as a recruit in the Army. "Whatever you do, don't you say that you owe anything to me. I should never believe that."

"Of course not. Allow me to arrange my thoughts in a some-what wider context. You know, we former bishops had no easy time during the Revolution, and I withdrew from this perilous period by going to America. My stay there taught me to think not in terms of individual countries but of continents. I feel a duty towards a continent generally, a duty to our continent, dear Ponte Corvo. To Europe in general. And, of course, to France in particular. Good-bye, my beautiful Princess, fare-well, dear friend—it was a most stimulating conversation!"

Jean-Baptiste spent the whole afternoon riding. In the evening he did sums with Oscar and made the poor boy add and multiply till he nearly fell asleep over it and I tried to drag my tired son to bed. He has become far too big now to be carried to bed.

We did not mention Talleyrand's visit any more because of a dispute we had over Fernand just before we went to bed. Jean-Baptiste said:

"Fernand complains that you are too generous with your money. Every moment you put a franc or two in his hand."

"But you told me yourself that we are rich now and that I needn't economise any more. And if I wanted to please Fernand, this old school friend of yours, this most loyal of all loyal servants, there was no need for him to complain to you behind my back and say that I am too open-handed."

"Stop your tipping! Fernand gets a monthly salary from Fouché now and earns more than he knows what to do with."

"What?" I was disconcerted. "Is Fernand stooping so low as to spy——"

"My little girl, Fouché offered to pay him for spying on me, and he accepted because he thought that it would be a pity to forgo all that nice money. But, immediately after, he came to me and told me how much Fouché was paying him and suggested that I should deduct it from his salary. Fernand is the most decent fellow under the sun."

"And what does he tell the Minister of Police about you?"

"Oh, there is something to tell every day. To-day, for instance, I did sums with Oscar, which ought to be very interesting to the former teacher of mathematics. Yesterday——"

"Yesterday you wrote to Madame Récamier, and that annoys me very much," I broke in. Now we had reached a familiar subject, and we forgot all about Talleyrand.

PARIS, *December 16th,* 1809.

IT was terrible, it was terrible and embarrassing for all those who had to be present. The Emperor had ordered all the members of his family, of his Government, of his court and all his Marshals to attend, and in their presence he divorced Josephine.

For the first time after a long interval Jean-Baptiste and I had been requested to appear in the Tuileries. We were to be there at eleven o'clock in the morning. But I was still in bed at half-past ten. I had decided that whatever happened I wasn't going to get up. The day was cold and grey, and I closed my eyes.

"Whatever does this mean? You are still in bed?" said Jean-Baptiste.

I opened my eyes and saw Jean-Baptiste in his gala uniform covered with gold braid and medals.

"I've got a cold. Please excuse me to the Lord Chamberlain," I said.

"Like that day before the coronation. You know the Emperor will send you his physician. Get up at once and get ready. Otherwise we shall be late."

"I don't think that this time the Emperor will send me his physician," I said calmly. "It might happen, might it not, that Josephine at the moment when she reads out her consent to the divorce looks round and catches sight of me. I expect that the Emperor wants to spare her that." I looked imploringly at Jean-Baptiste. "Don't you understand me? I just couldn't bear this ugly, this awful triumph."

Jean-Baptiste nodded. "Stay in bed, my girl. You have got a very bad cold. And take it easy."

He left and I closed my eyes once more. When the clock struck eleven I pulled the blanket right up to my chin. 'I too am getting older,' I thought, 'I too shall have wrinkles round my eyes and no longer be able to bear children. . . .' In spite of my eiderdown I suddenly felt chilly. I called Marie and asked her for some hot milk. After all, hadn't I got a cold?

She brought the milk, sat down on my bed and held my hand. Before the clock struck twelve Jean-Baptiste returned and brought Julie with him.

Jean-Baptiste undid his high embroidered collar and said: "That was the most embarrassing scene I have ever witnessed. The Emperor asks a bit too much of his Marshals." With that he left my bedroom. Marie left with him on account of Julie, whom she still has not forgiven although Julie is now a Queen without a country. How so? Because the Spaniards finally drove Joseph away. But no one in Paris may say so.

Julie started talking at once. "We all had to take our places in the Throne Room, each according to his rank. We, I mean the Imperial family, stood quite close to the throne. Then the Emperor and the Empress entered at the same time, behind them the Lord Chamberlain and Count Regnaud. Count Regnaud kept close to the Empress, who was in white, as always. And powdered pale, you know. To look the martyr!"

"Julie, don't be so nasty about her. It must have been frightful for her."

"Of course it was frightful for her. But I've never liked her, I've never forgiven her for what she did to you at that time——"

"She didn't know anything about me then, and it wasn't her fault," I said. "What happened then?"

"There was a deathly silence. The Emperor started to read out a document, something about only God knowing how difficult a step this was for him and no sacrifice being too great for him where the well-being of France was concerned. There was also something in it about Josephine having been the sunshine of his life, of his having crowned her with his own hands and of Josephine's right to the title of Empress of France for the rest of her life."

"What did he look like when he read that?"

"You know what he looks like now on all public occasions:

stony. Talleyrand calls it his mask of Cæsar. He put his mask of Cæsar on and read so fast that one had difficulty in following him. He wanted to get it over as quickly as possible."

"And then?"

"Yes, then it all turned so terribly embarrassing. The Empress was given her document and she began to read out. At first her voice was so quiet that I couldn't understand a word. Then, all of a sudden, she broke into tears and passed the paper to Regnaud, who had to read on for her. It was a dreadful sight."

"What did it say in her document?"

"That she herewith stated, with the permission of her beloved husband, that she was no longer able to have children. And therefore the well-being of France demanded of her the greatest sacrifice ever to have been asked of a woman. And she thanked the Emperor for his kindness and was firmly convinced that this divorce was necessary so that a direct descendant of the Emperor could reign over France in years to come. But not even the dissolution of her marriage could alter her feelings in any way. . . . All this Regnaud droned out as if it were some regulation, whilst the Empress kept sobbing most pitifully all the time."

"And then?"

"Then we, the members of the family, went to the Emperor's big study, where Napoleon and Josephine signed the document of divorce, and we signed after them as witnesses. Hortense and Eugene took their weeping mother away and Jerome said, 'I am hungry,' which earned him a vicious look from Napoleon. The Emperor turned away, saying 'I believe there will be a bite for the family in the Great Hall. Please excuse me,' and left. Everybody rushed to the buffet, and then I saw Jean-Baptiste ready to leave. I asked after you and he said you were ill and so I have come along with him." She paused for a moment.

"Your crown isn't straight, Julie!" As at all official functions, she was wearing a diadem shaped like a crown, and as always it wasn't straight.

She sat down at my dressing-table to put it right, powdered her nose and continued her chatting: "She's leaving the Tuileries to-morrow to go to Malmaison, which the Emperor has given her. He has also paid all her debts, and she is going to have an annuity of three million francs, two million from the Exchequer and one from the Emperor. On top of that the Emperor has given her another 200,000 francs for the plants she had bought for Malmaison and 400,000 francs for the ruby necklace which a jeweller is making for her."

"And Hortense and Eugene, what's going to happen to them?"

"Hortense will stay on in the Tuileries, and Eugene remains Viceroy of Italy. After all, Napoleon adopted them, didn't he? Imagine that Hortense still thinks her eldest son will be heir to the throne! She must be crazy! The Princess whom Napoleon is going to marry is a Hapsburg and that means that there will be plenty of offspring." She got up. "I must be off."

"Where?"

"Back to the Tuileries. The Bonapartes will be annoyed with me if I don't take part in their celebration. Good-bye, Désirée, get better soon."

After she had gone I lay for a long time with eyes closed. 'Julie's got used to the Bonapartes and their crowns,' I thought, 'she's changed, oh how she has changed! Wasn't it my fault? I brought the Bonapartes to our father's simple, clean and unpretentious middle-class house. But I never intended all this, Father, I didn't. . . .

I had to stay in bed all day, and fell asleep early in the evening. But I woke up with a start in the middle of the night to find Marie and Madame La Flotte by the side of my bed. "Queen Hortense asks you to see her."

"Now? What is the time?"

"Two o'clock in the morning."

"What does she want? Didn't you tell her I was ill, Madame La Flotte?"

Madame La Flotte's voice squeaked with excitement. "Of course I did. But she won't go. She wants to see you all the same."

"Hush, don't shout," I said, and rubbed the sleep from my eyes, "you're waking the whole house."

"The Queen of Holland is very agitated and is crying," said Madame La Flotte. I noticed that she wore an expensive dressing-gown with ermine trimmings on the sleeves and it struck me that Fouché was probably paying her dressmaker's bills.

"Marie," I said, "give the Queen of Holland a cup of hot chocolate, that'll soothe her. And you, Madame La Flotte, tell her that I am not well enough to receive her."

"Yvette is making the chocolate for the Queen at this moment," said Marie, "and you are getting up now. I've told the Queen that you'll see her at once. Come, I'll help you. Don't keep her waiting, she's—crying!"

"Tell Her Majesty I shall be with her in a few moments," I said to La Flotte.

281

Marie brought me a plain dress. "Better dress properly," she said. "She'll ask you to go along with her."

"Where?"

"Get dressed. I think you'll be needed in the Tuileries."

"Princess," said Hortense, sobbing when I went out to her, "my mother has sent me. She asks you to come to her at once, for pity's sake." Tears were streaming down her face, her nose was red and some of her mousy hair fell over her forehead.

"But I can't do anything for your mother," I said, and sat down by her side.

"That's what I said to Mama. But she insisted that I should ask you."

"Why me?"

"I don't know why. But it's you she wants."

"And now, in the middle of the night?"

Hortense groaned. "The Empress can't sleep anyway. And she won't see anybody but you."

"I suppose I'd better go with you, Madame," I said, and sighed. Marie, standing by the door, had everything ready, hat, coat and muff.

The rooms of the Empress were only dimly lit. But her bedroom was full of light. There were candelabra everywhere, in all the corners, on all the tables, on the mantelpiece, even on the floor. Trunks stood about, wide open and half-packed. Garments were lying on every inch of floor and over the furniture, hats, gloves, robes of state, underwear, in an impossible confusion. A jewellery box stood open, its contents disarranged, and under an armchair glittered a diadem of brilliants.

The Empress was alone. She was lying on her bed, her arms stretched wide, her slim back shaking with desperate sobs as she cried wildly into the pillow. From the adjoining room came subdued female voices. They were probably packing there. But Josephine was alone, quite alone.

"Mama, here is the Princess of Ponte Corvo," said Hortense.

Josephine did not move. She went on crying even more desperately.

"Mama," said Hortense again, "the Princess of Ponte Corvo."

I decided to act and went up to her bed, took her by her shoulders and turned her round. Now she was lying on her back and staring at me out of her swollen eyes. I took fright. 'She is an old woman,' I thought, 'she has become an old woman in this one night.'

"Désirée," she said painfully. Then the tears started flowing

282

again. I sat down and took her hands, and at once her fingers closed round mine.

I saw her now at close quarters, without any make-up, and the many candles revealed mercilessly the ravages wrought by time and the destruction brought on by the last twenty-four hours. 'Has Napoleon ever seen her without make-up?' I wondered.

Josephine spoke. "I have tried to pack," she said through her tears.

"Above all, Your Majesty must get some sleep," I said. I turned to Hortense: "Do put out all those candles, Madame!"

Hortense obeyed. Like a shadow she glided from candelabrum to candelabrum till only one tiny night-light remained.

Josephine's tears had dried up at last. In their place came short hard sobs which shook her whole body and seemed to be worse than tears.

"Your Majesty must sleep now," I repeated, and tried to rise. But her fingers would not let me go.

"You must stay with me to-night, Désirée," said her trembling voice. "You know how he loves me. He loves me, better than anybody else in the world. You know that, don't you? Don't you? Better than anybody else——"

So that's why she wanted to see me to-night. Because I knew how much he loved her! If only I could help her!

"Yes, Madame, he loves you, only you. When he met you, he forgot everything and everybody else. Me, for instance. You remember, Madame?"

An amused smile flitted round her mouth. "You threw a glass of champagne at me. They couldn't get the stains out of my frock afterwards. . . . I made you so unhappy then, little Désirée. Forgive me, I didn't mean to."

I stroked her hand and let her go on talking about the past. How old had she been then? About as old as I was now.

"Mama, you will be all right at Malmaison. You always looked upon it as your real home, didn't you?"

Josephine started, torn from her reminiscences into the present. "Hortense is staying on in the Tuileries," she said, trying to catch my eye. The smile had gone, she looked aged and tired once more. "She is still hoping that Bonaparte will make one of her sons his successor. I should never have allowed her marriage to his brother. She has had so little out of life, a husband whom she hates and a stepfather whom she——"

—whom she loves, Josephine had wanted to say. But before she could say it Hortense rushed up to the bed. Did she want to hit her mother? I held her back. At that she began to sob helplessly.

'We can't go on like this,' I thought; 'now Hortense is having hysterics and will set the Empress off again at any moment.' "Get up, Hortense, and pull yourself together," I said. Who was I to give orders to the Queen of Holland? All the same, the Queen of Holland obeyed at once. "Your mother needs rest now, and so do you. When is Her Majesty going to Malmaison?"

"Bonaparte wishes me to leave to-morrow morning," whispered Josephine. "He's already ordered the workmen to get my rooms in——"

The rest of the sentence was drowned in renewed floods of tears. I turned to Hortense.

"Did Dr. Corvisart not leave any sleeping draught for Her Majesty?"

"He did. But Mama will not take it. She thinks they want to poison her."

I looked at the crying Josephine. "He has known all along," she stammered, "all along that I could not have any more children. I told him once because I expected one and Barras ——" She broke off and then, suddenly, screamed: "And this bungler, this blunderer, this oaf to whom I was dragged by Barras ruined me completely, ruined me, ruined me!"

"Hortense, ask one of the ladies-in-waiting to bring a cup of hot tea, and then go and rest. I shall stay here till Her Majesty is asleep. Where is the sleeping draught?"

Hortense found a small bottle among the heap of bottles, flagons and tins on the dressing-table, and handed it to me. "Five drops, Dr. Corvisart said."

"Thank you. Good-night, Madame."

I undressed Josephine and put her to bed. When the tea came I emptied the whole contents of the little bottle into the cup, six drops. 'So much the better,' I thought.

Josephine sat up obediently and hastily drank the tea. "It tastes like everything in my life," she said, and smiled, bringing back in that smile a likeness of the former Josephine, "it tastes very sweet with a bitter after-taste."

She dropped back on the pillows. "You were not at the— at the ceremony this morning," she said in a tired voice.

"No, I thought you'd prefer it."

"I did." There was a little pause. I heard her breathe more regularly now. "You and Lucien were the only Bonapartes not present."

"But I am not a Bonaparte at all," I said. "My sister Julie

284

is married to a Bonaparte, and that is as far as the relationship goes."

"Don't leave him, Désirée."

"Whom?"

"Bonaparte."

The draught seemed to have set her mind adrift and soothed her at the same time. I stroked her hand evenly and without much thought, a hand with prominent veins, the hand of a frail, ageing woman.

"When he loses his power," she went on, "—and why should he not? All men I have known lost their power and some even their head like the late Beauharnais. When he loses his power——" Her lids fell and I let go of her hand. "Stay with me. I am afraid."

"I shall go and sit down in the next room and wait till Your Majesty has had a good night's rest. Then I shall accompany you to Malmaison," I said.

"Yes, to Malmai——" she said and fell asleep.

I put out the candle and went into the other room, which was in complete darkness. I felt my way to the window, drew the curtains aside and looked into a grey, gloomy winter dawn. Near the window I found a deep armchair. I took off my shoes and settled myself in the chair with my legs tucked under my body. My head ached furiously and I was tired. Utter silence reigned everywhere.

Suddenly I started. Someone had come into the room and the flicker of a candle moved along the walls towards the fire-place. I heard the subdued clanking of spurs.

I craned my neck round to try to look over the high back of the chair towards the fireplace. Who dared to enter without knocking the lounge adjoining the bedroom of the Empress?

Who? He, of course.

He was standing in front of the fireplace gazing attentively round the room. I made an instinctive movement. At once he turned his face towards the chair. "Is anybody here?"

"It is only I, Sire."

"Who is 'I'?" His voice sounded furious.

"The Princess of Ponte Corvo," I said, and tried to get my legs from under me to sit up properly and put on my shoes. But my feet had got numb and were full of pins and needles.

"The Princess of Ponte Corvo?" Incredulous, he came over to me.

"I am sorry, Your Majesty, my feet are numb and I can't find

285

my shoes. One moment, please," I stammered. At last I found my shoes, got up and made my formal curtsey.

"Tell me, Princess, what are you doing here at this time of night?"

"That's what I'm asking myself, Sire," I said, rubbing my eyes. He took my hand. "Her Majesty has asked me to keep her company to-night. She is sleeping, at last." He said nothing, and as I had the feeling that he was annoyed I added: "I should like to withdraw so as not to disturb Your Majesty. But I don't know where one can withdraw to from this room, and I don't want to wake the Empress."

"You don't disturb me, Eugenie. Keep your seat."

Meanwhile the morning had grown lighter. I sat down again, desperately fighting my tiredness.

"I could not sleep," he said abruptly. "I wanted to say good-bye to this place. The workmen are coming to-morrow, no, this morning."

I nodded. But I found it embarrassing to have to be present at this leave-taking.

"See here, Eugenie. That is she. Do you not think that she is beautiful?"

He held a snuff-box out to me, which had a portrait painted on its lid. Before I could look at it he went across to the mantel-piece, fetched a candlestick and held the box against its light. It showed a round girlish face with blue eyes and very pink cheeks. The whole face gave an impression of pinkness.

"It's so difficult for me to judge from these snuff-box minia-tures," I said. "They all look alike to me."

"I am told that Marie-Louise of Austria is very beautiful." He opened the box, took snuff and pressed his handkerchief against his face, a very elegant and well-trained way of taking snuff.

He put portrait and handkerchief away and looked at me penetratingly. "I still don't understand how you got here, Princess."

As he gave no sign of sitting down I wanted to get up again. He pushed me back into the chair. "You must be dead-tired, Eugenie. I can tell by your face. Tell me, what are you doing here at all?"

"The Empress wanted to see me. I remind Her Majesty——" I swallowed, it was such a difficult thing to say—"I remind Her Majesty of the afternoon when she got engaged to General Bonaparte. It was a very happy time in the life of Her Majesty."

He nodded. Then, without more ado, he sat on the arm of

my chair. "Yes, it was a very happy time in the life of Her Majesty. And in yours, Princess?"

"I was very unhappy, Sire. But it is so long ago and the wound is no longer there," I said in a low voice. I was so tired and so cold that I forgot who was sitting next to me. Only when my head dropped sideways and on to his arm did I realise what had happened and was overcome with fright. "Do excuse me, Your Majesty."

"Leave your head where it is. I shall not be quite so alone then." He tried to put his arms around my shoulders and to pull me towards him. But I made myself stiff and leaned my head against the back of the chair.

"I was very happy in this room, Eugenie."

I didn't move.

"The Hapsburgs are one of the oldest dynasties in the world, do you know that?" he said without any preliminaries. "An Archduchess of Austria is worthy of the Emperor of the French."

I sat up, trying to see his face. Did he really mean that? A Hapsburg Princess just about good enough for the son of the Corsican lawyer Buonaparte?

He stared in front of him and then, unexpectedly, shot a question at me: "Can you dance the waltz?"

I nodded.

"Can you show me how to do it? They told me in Vienna that all the Austrian girls dance it. But at that time in Schönbrunn I had no time for it. Show me how to dance it."

I shook my head. "Not now, not here."

His face became distorted and he shouted: "Now! And here!"

I pointed to the door to Josephine's bedroom. "Sire, you will wake her up."

He only lowered his voice. "Show it me! At once. This is an order, Princess."

I got to my feet. "It is difficult without music," I said. Then I started turning slowly, counting "One two three and one two three, that's how you dance the waltz, Your Majesty."

But he didn't look at me at all. He was still sitting on the arm of my chair staring into space.

I raised my voice a bit. "And one two three and one two three."

He looked up now. The grey morning light made his face heavy and bloated. "I was so happy with her, Eugenie."

I stopped dead and looked at him, not knowing what to do. At last I brought out: "Is it—necessary, Your Majesty?"

287

"I can't wage a three-front war. There are revolts in the south, there is the Channel coast, and Austria——" He chewed his lower lip. "Austria will leave me in peace once the Austrian Emperor's daughter is my wife. My friend, the Tsar of Russia, is arming, my dear Princess, and I shall only manage to cope with my friend, the Tsar of Russia, if Austria keeps out for good." He pulled out the snuff-box and regarded the portrait once more. "She will be my hostage, my sweet young hostage."

He got up with a jerk and looked round the room very intently. "That is what it was like here," he murmured as if he wanted to commit to memory once and for all the details of the room. When he turned towards the door I curtsied deeply. With an abrupt movement he put his hand on my hair and stroked it absent-mindedly. "Can I do anything for you, my dear Princess?"

"Yes, if Your Majesty would be kind enough to send me some breakfast. Strong coffee, if possible."

He laughed out loud, a young, carefree laugh, and left the room.

At nine o'clock in the morning I accompanied the Empress out of the Tuileries through a back door. There her carriage was waiting for us.

She wore one of the three priceless sable coats which the Russian Tsar had given the Emperor as a present when they met in Erfurt. The second he had put round Polette's shoulders. What happened to the third nobody knows. Josephine was made up very carefully, her face looked almost as sweet as ever, betraying only the slightest signs of age.

Hortense was waiting for us in the carriage. "I had hoped," said Josephine in a low voice, "that Bonaparte would come to say good-bye to me." She bent forward to see the rows of windows in the Tuileries. There were curious faces behind every one of them. The carriage moved off.

"The Emperor rode to Versailles early this morning," said Hortense. "He intends to spend a few days with his mother."

Not another word was spoken during the whole of the journey to Malmaison.

PARIS.
The end of June 1810.

SHE really looks like a sausage. Our new Empress, I mean.

The wedding festivities are over, and it is said that the Emperor spent about five million francs in furnishing Marie-Louise's room in the Tuileries.

It began in March when Marshal Berthier was sent to Vienna to ask formally for the hand of the Emperor's daughter. The wedding took place there by proxy. Afterwards Caroline was sent to the frontier to receive the Emperor's wife. On the way to Paris, near Courcelles, two disguised men on horseback stopped the coach and forced themselves inside. It was the Emperor and Murat. They broke the journey at Compiègne Castle, and next morning Napoleon had his breakfast by Marie-Louise's bedside. They had had their wedding night before Uncle Fesch repeated the wedding ceremony in Paris.

During the first few months the Empress was not allowed to hold receptions on any scale. For some reason or other Napoleon imagined that women conceive more easily if they don't overtax their strength. But at last he could delay it no longer, and yesterday all of us, Marshals, Generals, Ambassadors, Princes and dignitaries of all kinds, were asked to the Tuileries to be presented to the new Empress.

It was exactly as it had been once before. The great ballroom, the lights, the brilliant robes and uniforms, the Marseillaise, the opening of the great doors, the appearance of the Emperor and the Empress: it was a precise repetition of the coronation ball. Marie-Louise, dressed in pink satin and scented with jasmine, was far taller than the Emperor and had a full bosom in spite of her youth. She kept on smiling the entire evening. As she was the daughter of a real Emperor, who had been trained to smile graciously at two thousand people at once, it didn't seem to be any strain on her at all. When I was presented to her I noticed that she wore hardly any make-up, which gave her an air of great naturalness compared with all those highly artificial creatures at her court. Her pale blue eyes looked as if they were made of china, and they had no expression at all.

The Imperial couple took their seats on their thrones and the orchestra played a Viennese waltz. Julie joined me at this point. She was dressed in purple velvet and the crown jewels of Spain glittered all over her. But again her crown wasn't straight.

D.—10   289

"My feet hurt," she complained. "Come, let's go and sit in the next room."

At the entrance to that room we met Hortense, dressed in white as her mother used to be, and flirting with Count Flahault, her equerry. We sat down on a sofa and drank champagne.

"I wonder whether she remembers that her aunt used to live here in the Tuileries," I said, apropos of nothing.

Julie looked at me in surprise. "What are you talking about? At this Imperial court you will find no one who ever had an aunt living in the Tuileries."

"Oh yes, you will. The new Empress! She is the grand-niece of Queen Marie Antoinette."

"Queen Marie Antoinette!" repeated Julie, her eyes suddenly wide with fear.

"Yes, Julie Clary, she too was a Queen. Your health, darling, and forget about her." I drank, and remembered how many reasons Marie-Louise had for hating us. . . . "Tell me," I asked Julie, who had been with her several times already, "does the new Empress smile all the time?"

Julie nodded gravely. "All the time. And I shall bring up my daughters to do the same. It seems to be the right thing for Princesses."

I smelled the bitter-sweet scent of an exotic perfume around us and knew: Polette! Here she was, putting her arm around my shoulders.

"The Emperor thinks Marie-Louise is pregnant," she said, bursting with laughter.

"Since when?" Julie wanted to know, excited.

"Since yesterday!" said Polette, and passed on in her exotic aura.

Julie got up. "I must get back to the ballroom. The Emperor likes to have the members of his family near his throne."

I looked round for Jean-Baptiste and saw him leaning against one of the windows glancing round at the crowd with utter indifference. I went up to him. "Can't we go home?" I said.

He nodded and took my arm. Turning to go we found our way barred by Talleyrand.

"I have been looking for you, Prince," he said. "These gentlemen have asked to be introduced to you." Behind him I saw some tall officers in foreign uniform, dark blue with yellow sashes. "This is Count Brahe, a member of the staff of the Swedish Embassy. Colonel Wrede, who, as the personal representative of the King of Sweden, has brought his sovereign's good wishes to the Emperor on his marriage. And Lieutenant

Baron Charles Otto Mörner, who arrived this morning from Stockholm as a special courier with some very sad news. Baron Mörner, by the way, is a cousin of that Mörner whom you, my dear Prince, once took prisoner in Lübeck. You remember him, don't you?"

"We write to each other," said Jean-Baptiste calmly, and cast his eyes over the Swedes. "You are one of the leaders of the Union Party in Sweden, Colonel Wrede, are you not?"

The tall man bowed, whilst Talleyrand explained to me that the Union Party stood for the union of Sweden and Norway. Jean-Baptiste, meanwhile, smiled politely and, still holding my arm, turned his eyes on Mörner, a dark, thick-set man with short hair. This man looked very intently at Jean-Baptiste and said in fluent, somewhat harsh French:

"I have brought the news that the Swedish Heir to the Throne, His Royal Highness Prince Christian Augustus of Augustenburg, has lost his life in an accident."

Jean-Baptiste suddenly gripped my arm so hard that I very nearly screamed. It lasted only the tiniest fraction of a second. Then Jean-Baptiste said most calmly: "How dreadful! I should like to express to you, gentlemen, my deepest sympathy."

There was a pause, filled only by the tune of a waltz. 'Why don't we go?' I wondered. 'Surely all this is no concern of ours? What of it if the childless Swedish King has to find a new heir to his throne? Let's go,' I thought, 'let's go.'

"Has a successor to the deceased heir been designated?" asked Talleyrand casually, with polite interest. Just then I happened to look at Mörner, and it struck me as curious that he was still staring at Jean-Baptiste as if he wanted to convey something to him.

'For God's sake,' I thought, 'what do they want of my husband? He can't bring their dead Prince back to life, the accident can't possibly be of any interest to him. We have our hands full enough here in Paris, we have to be careful, we are in disgrace.'

But now I realised that this tall Colonel Wrede or something was staring at Jean-Baptiste in exactly the same way. At last Baron Mörner said:

"The Swedish Parliament will be convened for August 21st to decide the question of the succession to the Throne."

Another incomprehensible pause followed. Then I spoke up and said: "I am afraid, Jean-Baptiste, we shall have to say good-bye to these Swedish gentlemen." The officers understood and bowed.

"I ask you once again," said Jean-Baptiste, "to convey to

His Majesty the King of Sweden my sympathy and add how greatly I share his and his people's sorrow."

"Is that all I am to tell him?" Mörner ejaculated.

Half turning to go, Jean-Baptiste once more let his eyes go from one Swedish face to another. They came to rest on young Count Brahe, who couldn't have been more than nineteen years of age. Jean-Baptiste said: "Count Brahe, you belong, I believe, to one of the oldest Swedish noble families. Therefore I ask you to remind your friends and your brother officers that I have not always been Prince of Ponte Corvo or Marshal of France. I am what in your circles is called a former Jacobin General, and I began my career as a sergeant. In a word, I am—a *parvenu*. I should like you to remember that, so that you do not——" he took a deep breath and once more his fingers gripped my arm hard—"that you do not hold it against me later." And quickly he added: "Good-bye to you, gentlemen."

Strangely enough, we met Talleyrand once more before we left. His carriage was standing next to ours outside the Tuileries. We were just about to get into ours when I saw him limp towards us. "My dear Prince," he said to Jean-Baptiste, "man has been given the gift of language to conceal his thoughts. But you, my friend, use this gift in the opposite direction. No one could say of you that you concealed your thoughts towards the Swedes."

"Do I have to remind you, a former bishop, that it says in the Bible 'Let your speech be Yea yea, nay nay: and whatsoever is more than these is of the evil one'? That is how the Bible quotation runs, does it not, my Lord Bishop?"

Talleyrand bit his lips. "I had never realised that you could be witty, Prince," he murmured. "You surprise me."

Jean-Baptiste laughed heartily.

"Do not over-rate the modest jokes of a sergeant who is used to a bit of fun with his comrades round the camp fires!" He turned serious. "Did the Swedish officers tell you whom the Swedish royal house is going to propose as heir to the Throne?"

"The brother-in-law of the late heir, the King of Denmark, is going to be a candidate," Talleyrand answered.

Jean-Baptiste nodded. "Anybody else?"

"Yes, the dead man's younger brother, the Duke of Augustenburg. Besides these there is a son of the deposed King who now lives in Switzerland in exile. But as his father is considered insane the son is not held in very high esteem. Well, we shall see. The Parliament of Sweden is going to be convened and the

Swedish people themselves can make their choice. Good-night, dear friend."

"Good-night, Excellency."

At home Jean-Baptiste went at once to his dressing-room and tore open his high, richly embroidered collar.

"I have been telling you for years," I said, "that you should have your collar let out. The Marshal's uniform is too tight for you."

"Too tight," he murmured, "my dear little stupid girl never realises what she is saying. Yes, far too tight." Without paying any further attention to me he went into his bedroom.

I am writing this now because I can't go to sleep. And I can't go to sleep because I am afraid of something, something that seems to loom over me, inescapably. I am very much afraid. . . .

PART III

NOTRE-DAME DE LA PAIX

PARIS.
September 1810.

A LIGHT shone straight into my face. "Get up at once, Désirée. Get up and dress quickly."

It was Jean-Baptiste holding a candelabrum over my bed and buttoning up the jacket of his Marshal's uniform.

"Are you mad, Jean-Baptiste? It's the middle of the night!"

"Hurry up. I told them to wake Oscar as well. I want the boy to be present."

I heard voices and steps on the ground floor. Yvette slipped into the room. She had hurriedly thrown a maid's uniform over her nightdress.

"Hurry up," said Jean-Baptiste impatiently, and to Yvette: "Do help the Princess, won't you?"

"For God's sake, has anything happened?" I asked in terror.

"Yes—and no. You will hear it all yourself. But do get dressed quickly."

"What am I to put on?" I asked in confusion.

"The most beautiful dress you have, the most elegant, the most precious, you understand?"

I was furious now. "No, I understand nothing at all. Yvette, bring me the yellow silk dress, the one I wore at court the other day. Jean-Baptiste, won't you tell me——"

But he had gone already. I did my hair with shaking hands.

"The diadem, Princess?" asked Yvette.

"Yes, the diadem. Bring me my jewellery box. I am going to put on everything I have. If I'm not told what's happened I can't know what to dress for. And to wake the child, in the middle of the night!"

"Désirée, are you ready?"

"If you don't tell me, Jean-Baptiste——"

"A spot of rouge on the lips, Princess," said Yvette. I saw my sleep-drenched face in the mirror. "Yes, Yvette, rouge and powder, quickly."

"Do come, Désirée, we cannot keep them waiting any longer!"

"Whom can't we keep waiting any longer? As far as I know it's the middle of the night. As far as I'm concerned I want to go back to bed."

Jean-Baptiste took my arm. "You must keep a grip on yourself now, little girl."

"What is the matter? Won't you kindly tell me what is happening?" I said furiously.

"The greatest moment of my life, Désirée."

I wanted to stop and stare at him, but he held me firmly by the arm and led me downstairs. Outside the door of the big reception-room Fernand and Marie pushed an excited Oscar towards us. His eyes shone with excitement.

"Papa, is it war? Papa, is the Emperor coming to see us? How beautifully Mama is dressed. . . ."

They had put the boy into his best suit and brushed his unruly curls close to his head. Jean-Baptiste took him by the hand.

The reception-room was brightly lit. All our candelabra had been collected and put here. Some gentlemen were waiting for us.

Jean-Baptiste took my arm again, and with the boy on one side and me on the other walked slowly towards the group of visitors.

They wore foreign uniforms embellished with blue-and-yellow sashes and glittering medals. One of them, a young man, however, was clad in a grimy tunic, his high boots were splashed all over with mud and his fair hair hung untidily down over his face. In his hand he was holding a very big sealed envelope.

They all bowed deeply as we entered, and there was a sudden silence. Then the young man with the sealed envelope stepped forward. He had the look of a man who had been riding for days and nights without interruption. Dark circles surrounded his eyes.

"Gustavus Frederik Mörner of the Uppland Dragoons, my prisoner of Lübeck," said Jean-Baptiste slowly, "I am glad to see you again. I am very glad."

So that was that man Mörner with whom Jean-Baptiste had talked one night about the future of the North. His trembling hands held out the envelope to Jean-Baptiste. "Your Royal Highness——" he said.

My heart stopped beating.

Jean-Baptiste released my arm and calmly accepted the letter.

"Your Royal Highness," the young man continued, "as Chief Chamberlain of His Majesty King Charles XIII of Sweden I beg to report that the Parliament of Sweden has unanimously elected the Prince of Ponte Corvo to be Heir to the Throne. His Majesty King Charles XIII wishes to adopt the Prince of Ponte Corvo and to welcome him in Sweden as his beloved son."

Gustavus Frederik Mörner swayed on his feet. An elderly man, his chest full of medals and stars, quickly put his hand under Mörner's arm. "I am sorry," Mörner said in a low voice, "I have not been out of the saddle for days." Then, louder: "May I introduce these gentlemen to Your Royal Highness?"

Jean-Baptiste nodded almost imperceptibly.

"Our Ambassador Extraordinary to France, Field-Marshal Count Hans Henrik von Essen."

The elderly man clicked his heels, his face was rigid.

Jean-Baptiste nodded again. "You were Governor-General in Pomerania, Field-Marshal. You defended it excellently against me at that time."

Mörner continued. "Colonel Wrede."

"We know each other." Jean-Baptiste's eyes fell on the sheet of paper which Wrede had suddenly produced.

"Count Brahe, a member of the staff of the Swedish Embassy in Paris." The young man whom I had met at the court ball bowed.

"Baron Friesendorff, adjutant to Field-Marshal Count von Essen."

Friesendorff smiled. "Another of your prisoners at Lübeck."

Mörner, Friesendorff and young Brahe gazed at Jean-Baptiste with a fervent glow in their eyes. Wrede waited with a deep frown on his brow, and the face of Field-Marshal von Essen bore no expression whatever; only his taut lips had an air of bitterness.

It was so still that we could hear the guttering of the candles.

Jean-Baptiste took a deep breath and said: "I accept the nomination of the Parliament of Sweden." He looked across at von Essen, the man whom he had once conquered, the ageing servant of an ageing childless King, and, deeply moved, he added: "I want to thank His Majesty King Charles XIII and the Swedish people for the trust they are placing in me. I vow to do everything in my power to justify this trust."

Count von Essen bent his head, bent it deeply and bowed, and all the other Swedes bowed with him.

At this moment something strange happened. Oscar, who up till now had not moved at all, stepped forward and went over to the Swedes. There he turned round and his child's hand gripped the hand of young Brahe, who was not ten years his senior. There he stood, among the Swedes, and like the Swedes he bowed his head deeply, bowed it before his Papa and his Mama.

Jean-Baptiste felt for my hand. Protectively his fingers closed over mine. "The Crown Princess and I wish to thank you for bringing this message."

299

After that a lot of things happened simultaneously. Jean-Baptiste said: "Fernand, the bottles which have been in the cellar since Oscar's birth!" I turned round and my eyes searched for Marie. All our servants were standing by the door. Madame La Flotte in an expensive evening gown, no doubt paid for by Fouché, curtsied deeply, and so did my reader. Yvette was sobbing for all she was worth. Only Marie did not move at all. She was wearing her woollen dressing-gown over her old-fashioned linen nightdress. She had had to dress Oscar and therefore found no time to dress herself.

"Marie," I whispered, "did you hear? The Swedish people offer us their crown. It's different from Julie and Joseph. It is quite different. I am afraid, Marie, I'm afraid."

"Eugenie!" Marie's voice sounded hoarse, choked with emotion, a tear rolled down her cheek, and then Marie, my old Marie, sank into a curtsey before me.

Jean-Baptiste, meanwhile, was leaning against the mantelpiece studying the letter which Mörner had given him. That severe man, Field-Marshal Count von Essen, went up to him.

"Those are the conditions, Your Royal Highness," he said.

Jean-Baptiste looked up and said: "I presume that you yourself were informed of my selection only an hour ago. You have been in Paris during all this time. I am very sorry——"

Field-Marshal von Essen raised his brows: "Why are you sorry, Your Royal Highness?"

"That you had no time to get used to the idea. I am very sorry indeed. You defended with great loyalty and fortitude whatever policy the House of Vasa chose to adopt. That cannot always have been easy for you, Count von Essen."

"It was very difficult at times. The campaign which I had to conduct against you I lost, unfortunately."

"Together we shall rebuild the Swedish Army," said Jean-Baptiste.

"Before I forward the answer of the Prince of Ponte Corvo to Stockholm to-morrow morning," said the Field-Marshal in a tone which sounded almost menacing, "I should like to draw your attention to one point in this letter. It concerns your citizenship. It is a condition of the adoption that the Prince of Ponte Corvo becomes a Swedish citizen."

Jean-Baptiste smiled. "Did you think that I would assume the Swedish succession as a French citizen?"

An expression of incredulous surprise spread over the Count's face. But I thought I must have misheard him.

"To-morrow," Jean-Baptiste went on, "I shall address an application to the Emperor of France in which I shall ask him to allow me to renounce French citizenship for myself as well as for my family. Ah, here comes the wine. Fernand, open all the bottles!"

Triumphantly Fernand placed the dusty bottles on a table. These bottles had come with us all the way from Sceaux via the Rue du Rocher to the Rue d'Anjou.

"When I bought the wine," said Jean-Baptiste, "I was Minister of War. Oscar was born then and I told my wife 'We shall open these bottles the day the boy enters the French Army'. "

"I shall be a musician, Monsieur," I heard Oscar's high-pitched voice. He was still holding young Brahe's hand. "But Mama wanted me to be a silk merchant like Grandfather Clary." Everybody laughed, even the tired Mörner. Only Count von Essen did not move an eyelid.

Fernand poured out the dark wine.

"Your Royal Highness is going to learn the first word of Swedish now," said Count Brahe. "It is 'Skål' and means 'Your health'. I should like to drink to His Royal——"

Jean-Baptiste interrupted him. "Gentlemen, I ask you to drink with me to the health of His Majesty the King of Sweden, my gracious adoptive father!"

They drank slowly and solemnly. Someone shouted: "To the health of His Royal Highness, the Crown Prince Charles John!"

"Han skål leve, han skål leve." It sounded from all sides.

What did that mean? Could that possibly be Swedish? I was sitting on the little sofa next to the fireplace. 'They've woken me up,' I thought, 'in the middle of the night, they've told me that the Swedish King wants to adopt my husband so that he becomes Crown Prince of Sweden.' But I'd always thought that only small children could be adopted. 'Sweden, Sweden,' I mused, 'next-door to the North Pole, Stockholm, the town with the whitewashed sky. Persson will read it all in the papers to-morrow and will never guess that the Princess of Ponte Corvo, the wife of the new Heir to the Throne, is the little Clary girl of his Marseilles days. . . .'

"Mama, these gentlemen say that my name is now Duke of Södermanland," said Oscar. His cheeks were red with excitement.

"Why Duke of Södermanland, darling?"

Young Baron Friesendorff explained eagerly that it was usual in Sweden for the brother of the Crown Prince to be known by this title. "But as in this case——" He broke off, blushing.

Jean-Baptiste calmly completed the sentence for him: "But as in this case the Crown Prince does not intend to take his brother along with him to Sweden his son will take this title. My brother lives in Pau. I do not want him to change his residence."

"I thought Your Royal Highness had no brother," said Count Brahe involuntarily.

"I have. I made it possible for him to study law so that he need not be a clerk in a lawyer's office for the rest of his life like my late father. So, gentlemen, my brother is a lawyer."

At the same moment Oscar asked: "Are you looking forward to Sweden, Mama?"

Deep silence fell. Everybody wanted to hear my answer. 'What can they expect me to say?' I thought. 'After all, I'm at home here, I'm French.' Then it came back to me what Jean-Baptiste had said about renouncing our French citizenship, it came back to me that I was now Crown Princess of a country which I had never seen, a country with a nobility as old as the hills, and not a new one like ours in France. I saw how they smiled at Oscar when he said that my father had been a silk merchant, all of them but the Count von Essen, who had felt nothing but shame. . . .

"Say it, Mama, that you are looking forward to it," urged Oscar.

"I don't know Sweden yet," I said, "but I shall do my best to enjoy it."

"The people of Sweden cannot ask more than that," Count von Essen said gravely.

His harsh French reminded me of Persson. I very much wanted to be friendly and so I said: "I have an acquaintance in Stockholm, a man called Persson, a silk merchant. Perhaps you know him, Field-Marshal?"

"I regret I do not, Your Royal Highness," came the brief answer.

"Perhaps you do, Baron Friesendorff?"

"I am very sorry, Your Highness."

I tried Count Brahe. "Perhaps you know a silk merchant Persson in Stockholm, by chance?"

Count Brahe smiled: "Really, I don't, Your Royal Highness."

"And you, Baron Mörner?"

Mörner, Jean-Baptiste's oldest friend in Sweden, wanted to be helpful. "There are many Perssons in Sweden, Your Royal Highness. It is a very common middle-class name."

Someone extinguished the candles and drew back the curtains. It was day and the sun glittered over Jean-Baptiste's uniform. "I do not want to sign any party manifesto, Colonel Wrede," he was saying, "not even that of the Union Party."

Mörner, still dusty and exhausted, standing by Wrede's side, put in: "But at that time in Lübeck Your Royal Highness said——"

"I said that Norway and Sweden form a geographical unit, and we shall do our best to bring about the union. But that is the concern of the Swedish Government, not just of one individual party. And, by the way, the Crown Prince must stand above all parties. Good-night, gentlemen, or rather good-morning."

I don't remember how I got up to my bedroom. Perhaps Jean-Baptiste carried me, or Marie with the help of Fernand.

Lying on my bed with eyes closed I felt Jean-Baptiste's presence. "You must not shout at your new subjects like that," I said.

"Try to say Charles John," he said.

"Why?"

"That is going to be my name. Charles, after my adoptive father, and John for Jean, of course." He played with the words. "Charles John, Charles XIV John. 'Carolus Johannes' it will be on the coins. Desideria, Crown Princess Desideria."

I sat up with a jerk. "That's going too far. I won't have myself called Desideria. Under no circumstances, you understand!"

"It is the wish of the Queen of Sweden, your adoptive mother-in-law. Désirée is too French for her. Besides Desideria sounds more impressive. You must admit that."

I fell back on the pillows. "D'you think I can do away with my own self? Can I forget who I am, what I am, where I belong? Can I go to Sweden and play at being a Crown Princess? Jean-Baptiste, I fear I'm going to be very unhappy."

But he wasn't listening, he was still playing with the new names. "Crown Prince Desideria. Desideria is Latin and means the longed-for one. Is there a more fitting name for a Crown Princess whom a people itself has chosen?"

"No, Jean-Baptiste, the Swedes don't want me. They want a strong man, yes. But they certainly don't want a weak woman who, moreover, is the daughter of a silk merchant and whose only acquaintance is a Monsieur Persson."

Jean-Baptiste got up. "I am going to have a cold bath now, and then dictate my application to the Emperor."

I made no move.

"Pay attention, Désirée, please. I am applying on behalf of my wife, my son and myself for permission to relinquish French citizenship in order to acquire Swedish citizenship. You agree, don't you?"

I gave no answer and didn't look at him either.

"Désirée, I shall not apply if you object. Don't you hear me?"

Still I gave no answer.

"Désirée, don't you see what is at stake?"

At last I looked up at him, and I felt as if I saw him for the first time properly: the high forehead with the dark, curly hair fringing it, the bold nose jutting out, the deep-set eyes, at once inquiring and reassuring, the small yet passionate mouth. Then I remembered the leather-bound tomes in which the former sergeant studied law, and the Customs regulations in Hanover which revived that country's prosperity. . . . 'Napoleon picked a crown out of the gutter, but you, Jean-Baptiste,' I thought, 'were offered it by a whole people with the King at its head.' And as I thought it out I was filled with the miracle of it all.

"Yes, Jean-Baptiste, I know what is at stake."

"And you are coming to Sweden with Oscar and me?"

"If I am really Desideria, the longed-for one. And if you promise never to call me that?" At last I had found his hand and pressed my cheek against it. I loved him, my God, how I loved him!

"I promise I shall never call you Desideria."

"I'll come," I said.

I slept long and fitfully and woke with the feeling that something dreadful had happened. I looked at the clock on the bedside table. Two o'clock. Two o'clock in the morning or in the afternoon?

I heard Oscar's voice from the garden and a man's voice I didn't recognise. Daylight filtered through the closed shutters. How did it come about that I had slept so late? Uncomfortably I felt that something had happened. But I couldn't think what.

I rang the bell. Madame La Flotte and my reader came in together and curtsied. "Your Royal Highness desires?"

Then I remembered and I felt unhappy, desperate.

"The Queen of Spain and the Queen of Holland have asked when Your Royal Highness can see them," said Madame La Flotte.

"Where is my husband?"

"His Royal Highness and the Swedish gentlemen are in conference in his study."

"With whom is Oscar playing in the garden?"

"He is playing ball with Count Brahe."

"Count Brahe?"

"The young Swedish count," said Madame La Flotte with an ecstatic smile on her face.

"Oscar has smashed a window-pane in the dining-room," my reader added, and Madame La Flotte commented, "That means good luck."

"I am awfully hungry," I said. My reader curtsied and left at once.

"What message can I give to Their Majesties of Holland and Spain?" asked La Flotte.

"I've got a headache, and I want to eat, and I don't want to see anybody but my sister. Tell the Queen of Holland that— oh well, invent something you can tell her. And now I'd like to be alone."

La Flotte curtsied and disappeared. 'This curtseying business is going to drive me mad,' I thought. 'I'm going to forbid it.'

After the meal I got up. Yvette came in curtseying and I told her to get out. I put on my plainest gown and sat down at the dressing-table.

Desideria, Crown Princess of Sweden, I mused. Former silk merchant's daughter from Marseilles, wife of a former French General, everything I loved and was familiar with seemed to be 'former' now. In two months' time I should be thirty-one years of age. Could people tell by my face? It was still smooth and round, too round even, I would have to eat less whipped cream. There were a few wrinkles round the eyes, barely visible, perhaps only caused by smiling. When I tested them by trying to laugh they deepened.

I had never known my mother-in-law. Mothers-in-law are supposed to be a difficult problem. Would adoptive mothers-in-law be easier to deal with? I realised I didn't even know the Swedish Queen's name. And why, I wondered, why did the Swedes pick on Jean-Baptiste, of all men, for their Crown Prince?

I got up, opened the shutters and looked down into the garden.

"You are aiming at Mama's roses, Count," Oscar was shouting.

"Your Highness must catch the ball. Look out, I am going to throw," shouted young Brahe. He threw hard and made Oscar sway as he caught the ball. But—he caught it!

"Do you think I could ever win battles like Papa?"

"Throw the ball back, hard!" commanded Brahe.

Oscar threw and Brahe caught it. "A good shot," he said, and as he threw the ball back once more it landed among my yellow roses, my big yellow fading roses which I love so much.

"Mama will be very annoyed," said Oscar, and looked up to my windows. He saw me. "Mama, did you sleep well?"

Count Brahe bowed.

"I should like to speak to you, Count Brahe. Can you spare me a minute? I shall come down into the garden."

I went down and sat between the young Count and Oscar on the small bench by the espalier fruit. The gentle September sunshine flowed gently over me, and I felt very much better now.

"Could you not talk to the Count later on, Mama? We have been playing so beautifully."

I shook my head. "I want you to listen carefully." I heard voices coming from the house, and Jean-Baptiste's among them sounded determined and loud.

"Field-Marshal Count von Essen and the members of his mission are going back to Sweden to-day to convey His Royal Highness's answer," said Count Brahe. "Mörner is staying here. His Royal Highness has appointed him his aide-de-camp. A special courier has gone on ahead to Stockholm."

I nodded whilst I searched hard in my mind for a suitable starting point for my questioning. I didn't find one and therefore said straight out: "Please tell me candidly, my dear Count, how it is that Sweden should offer the crown to my husband, of all men."

"His Majesty King Charles XIII has no children, and for years now we have admired the magnificent administration, the great abilities of His Royal Highness, and——"

I cut him short. "I am told that one King has been deposed because he was believed to be insane. Is he really insane?"

Count Brahe looked away towards the espalier peaches and said: "That is what we suppose."

"Why?"

"His father, King Gustavus III, before him had been rather—rather strange. He wanted to restore Sweden's old position as a great power, and attacked Russia. The aristocracy and all the officers were against it. And in order to show his noblemen that the King alone and no one else decides on peace or war he turned to the, well—to the lower classes and——"

"To whom?"

"To the business men, the craftsmen, the farmers."

"I see. What happened then?"

"Parliament, in which only the lower classes were represented at that time, conferred wide powers on him and the King marched once more against Russia. But the country was on the verge of bankruptcy and could not pay for this continuous arming. Therefore the nobility decided to take a hand and the King was murdered during a masked ball by some men in black masks. He died in the arms of his faithful von Essen. After his death our present King, his brother, took over the regency till the murdered King's young son, Gustavus IV, came of age. Unfortunately it soon became obvious that he was of unsound mind."

"This is the King who imagines himself to be God's chosen instrument for the destruction of the Emperor of the French, isn't it?"

Count Brahe nodded and continued to look towards the espalier peaches.

"Do go on with your murder story, Count Brahe," I said.

"Murder story?" He looked at me as if I had been joking. But I did not smile, and he hesitated to go on. I repeated my request and he continued.

"So we fought first against France, and when Russia and France came to terms, against Russia as well. You know what happened. We lost Finland to the Tsar and Pomerania to your husband—I am sorry, to His Royal Highness—and if the Prince of Ponte Corvo at that time when he was in Denmark with his troops had marched across the frozen Sound there would have been no Sweden left. Your Royal Highness, we are a very old nation, we are tired and bled white in wars, but we do want to —to go on living." He gnawed his lips, then went on. "That was why our officers decided to put an end to this mad policy. So they imprisoned Gustavus IV in his castle in Stockholm, deposed him and crowned his uncle, the former Regent and now adoptive father of Your Royal Highnesses."

"And where is he now, this mad Gustavus?"

"In Switzerland, I believe."

"He has a son, hasn't he?"

"Yes, another Gustavus. He has been declared by Parliament incapable of succession."

"How old is he?"

"About as old as Oscar, Prince Oscar." Count Brahe got up absent-mindedly and picked a withered leaf from the espalier peaches.

"Come back and tell me what are the objections to this little Gustavus."

Count Brahe shrugged his shoulders. "Nothing in particular. But there is nothing in his favour either. Sweden is afraid of a diseased strain in the Vasa family. It is a very old family, Your Highness, with too much inbreeding."

"Has the present King always been childless?"

Brahe came to life again. "Charles XIII and Queen Hedvig Elizabeth Charlotte had a son, but he died many years ago. At his accession the King had to adopt a successor and he chose the Prince of Augustenburg, brother-in-law to the King of Denmark and Governor of Norway. He was very popular with the Norwegians, and we had hopes of a union between Sweden and Norway through him. After his fatal accident Parliament was convened and you know the result, Your Highness."

"I know the result, yes. But I don't know how it came about. Please tell me about that."

"Your Highness knows that the Prince—I mean His Royal Highness—at the time of the Pomeranian campaign took some Swedish officers prisoner in Lübeck?"

"Of course I do. Aren't there two of them with Jean-Baptiste at this very moment? This dusty Mörner—I hope they've given him a bath meanwhile—and Baron Frie——"

"Yes, Mörner and Friesendorff. The Prince of Ponte Corvo invited these young officers, when they were his prisoners, to dinner, and during the course of the conversation told them, realistically with maps and figures, how he sees the future of Scandinavia. When our officers returned home they reported their conversation and ever since then it has been said more and more loudly in Army circles that we need a man like the Prince to save Sweden. And that, Your Highness, is all there is to it."

But it wasn't all. When I pressed him for details Count Brahe painted a frightening picture of cliques, intrigues and murder, of poverty and decay. Between the younger officers who were enthusiastic about Jean-Baptiste's ideas, and those represented by men like Count Fersen—at one time lover of Queen Marie Antoinette, whom he had tried unsuccessfully to get out of France with King Louis XVI and her family—a man abhorrent of anything the French Revolution and men like Jean-Baptiste stood for, there was a furious tug-of-war. It was complicated by the general economic deterioration of the country, and it ended on the day of the funeral of the Prince in the murder of Count Fersen of Augustenburg, by the mob outside the Royal Castle, with Army detachments passively looking on. After his disappearance the whole of Sweden agreed to the younger officers' choice of Jean-Baptiste as successor to the King, the aristocracy because they realised that a strong man was needed, the middle and lower classes because they thought that a man who was on good terms with Napoleon might manage to keep Sweden out of Napoleon's Continental Blockade and put trade and industry on their feet again. Besides, said Brahe, the traders and peasants disliked the Vasas because they were so poor that they could hardly pay their gardeners, and when they were told that the Prince of Ponte Corvo was rich their last hesitations vanished.

Murder, intrigue, poverty, and on top of that life in a castle inside which the nobility had murdered an unpopular count:

no no, it was too much. 'No, Jean-Baptiste,' I thought, 'not that,' and covering my face with my hands I cried helplessly.

"Mama, dear Mama!" Oscar pressed his arms round my neck and clung to me.

I wiped away my tears and turned to see Brahe's grave face. Did this young man understand at all why I was weeping?

"Perhaps I should not have told you all that," he said, "but I thought, Your Highness, that it would be better if you knew."

"So the whole Swedish people chose my husband. And what about His Majesty the King?"

"The King, Your Highness, is a Vasa and a man of over sixty who has had several strokes already, is plagued by gout and not very lucid in his brain. He put up opposition to the very last, suggested one North German cousin after the other and all the Danish Princes. In the end he had to give in."

'So in the end he had to give in and adopt Jean-Baptiste as his beloved son,' I thought. "The Queen is younger than His Majesty, isn't she?"

"Her Majesty is slightly over fifty years of age now, a very energetic and intelligent woman."

"How she will hate me!"

"Her Majesty is looking forward very much to seeing the little Duke of Södermanland," said Count Brahe, unperturbed.

At the door of the house Mörner appeared, freshly washed, beaming and wearing a gala uniform. Oscar ran up to him to admire the armorial insignia on the buttons of his uniform. "Look, Mama, look!" he shouted.

Mörner paid no attention to Oscar, but, noting the traces of tears on my face and the young count's gravity, looked thoughtfully from one to the other.

"Her Royal Highness wanted me to tell her about developments in Sweden and the history of our royal family during recent years," said Brahe, embarrassed.

"Are we now members of the Vasa family too?" asked Oscar eagerly.

"Nonsense, Oscar, you stay what you are, a Bernadotte," I said sharply, and got up. "Did you want me, Baron Mörner?"

"His Royal Highness asks Your Royal Highness to come to his study."

Jean-Baptiste's study was a strange sight. Next to his desk, where as usual documents were piled high, someone had placed the big mirror from my dressing-room. In front of it Jean-Baptiste was trying on a new uniform. Three tailors were kneeling around him, their mouths full of pins. Very attentively the Swedes followed the fitting manœuvres.

I glanced at the new dark blue tunic. Its high collar did not have the heavy gold braid of the Marshal's uniform, only a plain gold trimming. Jean-Baptiste examined himself very closely in the mirror. "It pinches," he said, as grave as a judge, "it pinches under the right arm."

The three tailors shot up in a bunch, undid the seam under the armpit and did it up again.

"Can you find a fault anywhere, Count von Essen?" asked Jean-Baptiste.

Essen shook his head, but Friesendorff put his hand on Jean-Baptiste's shoulders—"Pardon me, Your Highness," he said—moved it along his back and then declared that there was a crease under the collar.

All the three tailors felt for the crease but could not spot it. Fernand finally settled the matter: "Sir, the uniform fits."

"Your sash, Count von Essen!" And before the sour-looking Count had realised what he wanted Jean-Baptiste had taken the Count's blue-and-yellow sash from him and tied it round himself. "You will have to go back to Sweden without your sash, Count. I need it for to-morrow's audience. There are none to be had in Paris. Send me three Swedish Marshal's sashes as soon as you arrive in Stockholm."

Only now he noticed my presence. "The Swedish uniform. Do you like it?"

I nodded.

"We are to go to the Emperor to-morrow morning at eleven o'clock. I asked for the audience, and I want you to accompany me. Essen, is the sash meant to be worn above the belt or to cover the belt?"

"To cover the belt, Your Royal Highness."

"Good. Then I need not borrow your belt as well. I shall wear the belt of my French Marshal's uniform. No one will notice it. Désirée, do you really think the uniform fits properly?"

At that moment Madame La Flotte announced Julie. Leaving the room I heard Jean-Baptiste say: "I shall also need a Swedish ceremonial sword."

Julie, standing by the window and gazing pensively down into the garden, looked sad and lost in the heavy folds of her purple velvet coat. "I am sorry, Julie, to have kept you waiting," I said.

Julie started. Then, stretching her neck forward and widening her eyes as if she had never seen me before, she made a solemn curtsey.

"Don't poke fun at me," I shouted furiously, "I've got enough to put up with as it is."

But Julie remained solemn: "Your Royal Highness, I am not poking fun at you."

"Get up, get up and don't annoy me. Since when does a Queen bow to a Crown Princess?"

Julie got up. "If it is a Queen without a country, whose subjects rose against her and her husband from the very first day onwards, and if it is a Crown Princess whose husband was unanimously elected by the representatives of their future subjects, then it is the right thing for that Queen to bow to that Crown Princess. I congratulate you, my dear, I congratulate you from my heart."

"But how did you get to know it all? We only learnt about it last night." I sat down with her on the little sofa.

"All Paris talks about nothing else. People like us were simply placed by the Emperor on the thrones he had conquered, as his representatives, so to speak. But in Sweden Parliament meets and voluntarily—no, Désirée, it's beyond me." She laughed. "I had lunch in the Tuileries to-day. Napoleon talked about it a lot and chaffed me dreadfully."

"Chaffed you?"

"Yes. Imagine him wanting to make me believe that Jean-Baptiste would now ask to be discharged from the French Army and to become Swedish! Oh, how we laughed!"

I stared at her in amazement. "Laughed? What is there to laugh at? I could cry when I think of it."

"But, darling, for heaven's sake, it isn't true, is it?"

I said nothing.

"But none of us has ever heard of such a thing," she stammered. "Joseph is King of Spain, but he is a Frenchman all the same. And Louis is King of Holland, but he wouldn't thank you for calling him a Dutchman. And Jerome and Eliza and——"

"That is just the difference," I said. "You yourself pointed out a moment ago the great difference there was between your case and ours."

"Tell me, are you really going to settle in Sweden?"

"Jean-Baptiste says so. As far as I'm concerned it depends."

"Depends on what?"

"I shall go, of course. But, you know," I said, dropping my voice, "they want me to call myself Desideria. That's Latin and means 'The longed-for one', 'the wanted one'. I shall stay there only if they really want me in Stockholm."

"The nonsense you talk! Of course you're wanted."

"I am not so certain of that. The old aristocratic families and my new mother-in-law——"

311

"Don't be stupid. Mothers-in-law only hate you because you take their son from them," Julie argued, thinking probably of Madame Letitia. "But Jean-Baptiste is not the real son of the Swedish Queen. Besides, there is Persson in Stockholm. He won't have forgotten how good Mama and Papa were to him, and all you need do is to raise him to the peerage and then at once you have a friend at court."

"You have the wrong idea of it." I sighed, realising that Julie did not really understand what had happened.

And, to be sure, her thoughts were off on another tack once more. "Listen, something incredible has happened. The Empress is pregnant! What do you think of that! The Emperor is beside himself with joy. The son is going to be known as the King of Rome. Napoleon, you know, has no doubt whatever that it will be a boy."

"How long has the Empress been pregnant? For the last twenty-four hours again or what?"

"No, for the last three months, and——"

There came a knock on the door. Madame La Flotte announced that the Swedish gentlemen who were leaving for Stockholm to-night asked to be allowed to take their leave of Her Royal Highness.

"Show the gentlemen in."

I don't suppose any of them could tell by my face how afraid I was of the future. I shook hands with Field-Marshal Count von Essen, the most loyal subject of the House of Vasa, and he said: "We shall meet again in Stockholm, Your Highness."

Seeing Julie out to the hall I was amazed to meet young Brahe there. "Aren't you going back to Stockholm to-night?"

"I have asked to be appointed provisionally Your Royal Highness's gentleman-in-waiting. My request has been granted. I am reporting for duty, Your Royal Highness."

Tall, slim, nineteen years of age, dark eyes shining with enthusiasm, curly hair like my Oscar, that was Count Magnus Brahe, scion of one of the oldest and proudest families of Sweden, gentleman-in-waiting now to former Mademoiselle Clary, daughter of a silk merchant from Marseilles.

"I should like Your Royal Highness to grant me the honour of accompanying you to Stockholm." I dare them to look down their noses at our new Crown Princess with a Count Brahe by her side, was the thought written all over his face.

I smiled. "Thank you, Count Brahe. But, you see, I've never before had a gentleman-in-waiting, and I really don't know what I could give him to do."

"Your Royal Highness will think of something. And

meanwhile I could play ball with Oscar—I am sorry, the Duke of Södermanland."

"Provided you don't smash any more windows!" I laughed. For the first time my anxiety about the future weakened a bit. Perhaps it wouldn't be quite so bad after all.

We were ordered to appear before the Emperor at eleven o'clock in the morning.

At five minutes to eleven we entered the ante-chamber where Napoleon keeps diplomats, Generals, foreign Princes and French ministers waiting for hours. When we entered a hush fell on the assembly. Everybody stared at Jean-Baptiste's Swedish uniform and shrank back from us, shrank back literally. Jean-Baptiste requested one of the adjutants of the Emperor to announce "the Prince of Ponte Corvo, Marshal of France, with wife and son".

Among these people we felt as if we were sitting on an island. Nobody spoke to us, nobody congratulated us. Oscar clung to me tightly. They all knew what was going on. A foreign people had, of its own accord, without any compulsion, offered its crown to Jean-Baptiste. And now in there, on the Emperor's desk, lay his application for permission to relinquish French citizenship, to be discharged from the Army. Jean-Baptiste Bernadotte no longer wanted to be a French citizen. They looked as if we were an apparition, something weird and uncanny.

Everybody at court knew that we were in for a dreadful scene in the Emperor's room, one of those scenes of Imperial hysterics which make the walls shake and everybody tremble. "Thank God,' I thought, 'that he gives you a good long waiting time outside to collect yourself.' Giving Jean-Baptiste a sidelong glance, I saw him staring at one of the two sentries by the door to the Emperor's apartments. It was the bear-skin cap which attracted his attention. He studied it as if he were seeing it for the first time, or for the last time.

The clock struck eleven. Meneval, the Emperor's private secretary, appeared and called us.

The Emperor's study is almost as big as a ballroom. His desk is at the very end of this huge room, and the way from the door to the desk seems endless. For that reason the Emperor receives his friends mostly in the middle of the room. We, however, had to cross the whole of it.

Like a statue, immovable, Napoleon sat behind his desk, stooping forward a bit as if he were lying in wait for us. Talleyrand, Prince of Benevento, and the present Foreign Minister, the Duke of Cadore, stood behind him whilst we, I in front with Oscar's hand in mine and Jean-Baptiste behind me followed by Meneval, walked up to him. When I came near enough I saw that the Emperor had affected the stony Cæsarean pose. Only his eyes seemed alive.

The three of us, Oscar in the middle, ranged ourselves before his desk. I curtsied.

The Emperor did not move but kept staring viciously at Jean-Baptiste. All of a sudden he jumped up, pushed back his chair and came out from behind the desk, yelling: "In what kind of attire dare you appear before your Emperor and Commander-in-Chief, Marshal?"

Jean-Baptiste answered in a low, rather jerky voice: "This uniform is a copy of the Swedish Marshal's uniform, Sire."

"And you dare appear here in a Swedish uniform? You, a Marshal of France?" He screamed like a madman.

"I thought it was a matter of indifference to Your Majesty what uniforms the Marshals wore," said Jean-Baptiste quietly. "I have repeatedly seen Marshal Murat, the King of Naples, appear at court in some very curious uniforms."

That went home. Napoleon's childish brother-in-law Murat loves flamboyant uniforms and the Emperor laughs at them without ever calling him to order.

"As far as I am informed my royal brother-in-law's uniforms are—his own inventions." A fugitive smile played round the corners of his mouth and vanished at once, as he stamped the floor and started screaming again: "But you dare to appear before your Emperor in a Swedish uniform!" Oscar almost crept behind me in fear. "Well, Marshal, what have you to say to that?"

"I thought it right to appear at this audience in Swedish uniform. It was not my intention to insult Your Majesty. Part of the uniform, by the way, is my own invention, too. If Your Majesty would like to see——"

He pulled up the sash to show the belt. "I am wearing the belt of my old Marshal's uniform, Sire."

"Stop these disrobing scenes, Prince! Let us get down to business!"

His voice sounded different, as if he were in a hurry now. The introductory scene which was meant to intimidate us was over. 'He acts like a prima donna,' I thought, and felt quite exhausted. Wasn't he going to offer us a chair?

He certainly wasn't. He remained standing behind his desk looking down at a document, Jean-Baptiste's application.

"You sent me a very strange application, Prince. In it you

express your intention to let yourself be adopted by the King of Sweden, and request permission to resign your French nationality. A strange document! An almost incomprehensible document if one thinks back— But you probably do not think back, Marshal of France?"

Jean-Baptiste compressed his lips in order to keep silent.

"Don't you really think back? For example to the time when you went out as a young recruit to defend the frontiers of France? Or to the battlefields where this young soldier fought first as a sergeant, then as a lieutenant, then as a colonel and finally as a General of the French Army? Or to the day when the Emperor of the French made you a Marshal of France?"

Still Jean-Baptiste was silent.

"It is not so very long ago that you defended the frontiers of your fatherland without my knowledge." His old winning smile appeared unexpectedly. "Perhaps at that time you saved France. I told you once before—it is a very long time ago, and as unfortunately you do not remember the past you will probably have forgotten that too—yes, I told you once before that I cannot do without the services of a man like you. It was during those days in Brumaire. Perhaps you remember it after all? If at that time the Government had given you the authority, you and Moreau would have had me shot. The Government of the Republic did not give you the authority. Bernadotte, I repeat, I cannot do without you."

He sat down and pushed the application a bit to one side. Then he looked up and remarked with forced casualness: "Since the people of Sweden have chosen you——" he shrugged his shoulders and smiled ironically, "you of all men, to be heir to their throne, I as your Emperor and Supreme Commander herewith give you permission to accept their offer, but as a Frenchman and a Marshal of France. That is all!"

"In that case I shall have to inform the King of Sweden that I cannot assume the succession to his throne. The people of Sweden want a Swedish Crown Prince, Sire."

Napoleon jumped to his feet. "But that is nonsense, Bernadotte! Look at my brothers, Joseph, Louis, Jerome. Has any one of them resigned his citizenship? Or my stepson Eugene in Italy?"

Jean-Baptiste didn't answer. Napoleon came out from behind his desk and began to pace the floor backwards and forwards like a madman. I caught Talleyrand's eye and he winked at me almost imperceptibly. What did he mean? That Jean-Baptiste would win through in the end? It certainly didn't look like it now.

Abruptly the Emperor stopped in front of me. "Princess," he said, "I believe you do not know that the Swedish royal family is insane. The present King is incapable of enunciating clearly a single sentence, and his nephew had to be deposed because he is a lunatic. Because he is really—cuckoo!" He tapped his forehead. "Princess, tell me, is your husband crazy too? I mean, is he so crazy that he wants to stop being a Frenchman for the sake of the Swedish succession?"

"I must ask you not to insult His Majesty King Charles XIII in my presence," Jean-Baptiste said sharply.

"Talleyrand, are the Vasas cuckoo or not?"

"It is a very old dynasty, Sire. Old dynasties are often not very healthy," Talleyrand answered.

"And you, Princess, what do you think of it? Bernadotte's request for relinquishing French citizenship applies to you and the child as well."

"It is a matter of form, Sire. Otherwise we cannot accept the Swedish succession," I heard myself say. Did I say the right thing? I looked at Jean-Baptiste, but he stared past me. I glanced across to Talleyrand, and he nodded gently.

"Next: your discharge from the Army. That is out of the question, Bernadotte, really, that is out of the question." The Emperor went back behind his desk and studied the application, perhaps for the hundredth time. "I would not dream of doing without one of my Marshals. If war breaks out again—" He stopped, then added quickly: "If Britain does not give in, war is bound to break out again and in that case I shall need you. You will be as usual in command of one of my Armies. And it will not make any difference to me whether you are Crown Prince of Sweden or not. Your Swedish regiments will simply form part of your Army. Or do you believe—" here he broke into a smile which made him look ten years younger— "or do you believe I could put anybody else in command of the Saxons?"

"Since it stated in Your Majesty's Order-of-the-Day after the battle of Wagram that the Saxons did not fire a single shot, I do not think it matters much who will command them. Why not hand the command over to Ney, Sire? Ney is ambitious and has served under me."

"The Saxons took Wagram and I most certainly will not hand over your command to Ney. I will allow you to become Swedish if you remain Marshal of France. I have much sympathy for the ambitions of my Marshals. Moreover, you are a brilliant administrator, as you have shown in Hanover and the Hanse towns. You are an excellent Governor, Bernadotte."

"I asked to be discharged from the French Army."

Napoleon's fist crashed down on the table at that. It sounded like a thunderclap.

"My feet hurt, may I sit down, Sire?" I said involuntarily.

The Emperor gazed at me. His wavering eyes became quieter, grey. Did he, I wonder, remember at this point a little girl in a garden over which evening was falling, a little girl who raced him to the hedge and whom he allowed to win? . . .

"You will have to stand for many hours when you receive your subjects as the Crown Princess of Sweden, Eugenie," he said calmly. "Please, sit down. Gentlemen, let us all sit down."

And thus we found ourselves comfortably seated round the table.

"Where were we? Oh yes, you wish to be dismissed from the Army, Prince of Ponte Corvo. Do I understand correctly that you want to join our Armies not as a Marshal of France but as an ally?"

An expression of intent interest became visible in Talleyrand's face. So that was what Napoleon was driving at, had been driving at the whole time, at the alliance with Sweden.

"If I accede to the requests which for formal reasons you consider to be necessary I shall do it because I do not want to put obstacles in the way of one of my Marshals whom an old and not very healthy dynasty wishes to adopt. I should even go further and call it an excellent idea on the part of the Swedes to express their friendship for France by the choice of one of my Marshals. If I had been asked before the selection was made I should have suggested one of my own brothers, to show clearly how much store I set by that alliance and how highly I esteem the House of Vasa. However, I have not been asked, and as I have to say what I think about this selection, such a surprising one to me, after it has been made, let me say, then, that—that I congratulate you, Prince."

"Mama, he really isn't so bad," said Oscar.

Talleyrand bit his lips to stifle a laugh, and so did the Duke of Cadore. Napoleon looked thoughtfully at Oscar and then said: "What a coincidence that I should have picked on a Nordic name for this godson of mine! And on the hot sands of Egypt at that!" He laughed as if he were going to burst and slapped Jean-Baptiste's thigh: "Is not life crazy, Bernadotte?"

He turned to me: "You have heard, Princess, that Her Majesty is expecting a son?"

317

I nodded: "I am very glad about it, Sire."

Napoleon looked once more at Oscar. "I understand that you have to become Swedish, Bernadotte, if only for the child's sake. I am told that the deposed lunatic has a son, too. You must never lose sight of this exiled son, Bernadotte, you understand?"

'Now he's mapping out our future,' I thought, 'now everything's going fine. He's accepting things now.'

"Meneval, the map of Scandinavia!"

The maps were brought. "Sit here, Bernadotte."

Bernadotte went and sat on the arm of Napoleon's chair. The Emperor unrolled the map and spread it on his knee. 'How often these two must have sat like that in their headquarters,' I thought.

"Sweden, Bernadotte, breaks the Continental Blockade. There, at Gothenburg, British goods are unloaded and secretly taken to Germany."

"And to Russia," remarked Talleyrand casually.

"My ally, the Tsar of Russia, unfortunately does not devote sufficient attention to this question. There are British goods even in my ally's country. However that may be, Bernadotte, Sweden is at the bottom of it all. You will clean up in Sweden and, if necessary, declare war on the British."

Meneval had started writing down the salient points of the conversation, and Talleyrand looked curiously at Jean-Baptiste. The Duke of Cadore nodded contentedly and said: "Sweden will complete the Continental Blockade. I believe we can rely on the Prince of Ponte Corvo."

Jean-Baptiste was silent.

"Have you any objections to raise, Prince?" the Emperor asked sharply.

Jean-Baptiste looked up from the map. "I shall serve the interests of Sweden with all the means at my disposal."

"And the interests of France?" the Emperor said pointedly.

Jean-Baptiste rose, folded up the map of Scandinavia carefully and handed it to Meneval. "As far as I know, Your Majesty's Government and the Government of Sweden are at this moment negotiating a non-aggression pact which could be extended into a pact of friendship. I believe that I am therefore in a position to serve not only Sweden but at the same time my former motherland as well."

Former motherland, how that expression hurt! Jean-Baptiste looked tired and weary.

"You are the ruler of a small territory under French suzerainty," said the Emperor coldly. "I have no option but to

318

withdraw from you the Principality of Ponto Corvo and its not inconsiderable revenues."

Jean-Baptiste nodded. "Certainly, Sire. I made a point of asking for just that in my application."

"Do you intend to arrive in Sweden as plain Monsieur Jean-Baptiste Bernadotte, Marshal of France, retired? If it is your wish you might, in view of your services, be allowed to retain the title of Prince."

"I prefer," said Jean-Baptiste, "to renounce the Principality as well as the title. Should Your Majesty, however, be so gracious as to grant me a wish, I should like to ask that a barony be conferred on my brother in Pau."

Napoleon was astonished. "But are you not taking your brother along with you to Sweden? You could make him a count or a duke there."

"I do not intend to take my brother or any other member of my family along with me to Sweden. The King of Sweden desires to adopt only me and not all my relatives as well. Believe me, Sire, I know what I am doing."

We all looked at the Emperor, probably thinking the same thing: the man who showers crowns, titles and dignities on his stupid brothers.

"I believe you are right, Bernadotte," the Emperor said slowly. He rose, and we did the same. Looking at the application for the last time, he asked, with his thoughts apparently elsewhere: "And what about your estates in France, in Lithuania, in Westphalia?"

"I am about to sell them, Sire."

"To pay the debts of the Vasas?"

"Yes, and to pay for the court expenses of the Bernadotte dynasty."

Napoleon took up a pen and looked from Jean-Baptiste to me and back to Jean-Baptiste again. "With this signature you, your wife and your son will cease to be French citizens, Bernadotte. Do you want me to sign?"

Jean-Baptiste, his eyes half-closed, his mouth a thin hard line, nodded.

"This signature also retires you from the French Army, Marshal. Do you really want me to sign?"

Again Jean-Baptiste nodded. I felt for his hand.

At that moment a trumpet signal sounded in the yard for the Changing of the Guard. Its noise drowned the scratching of Napoleon's pen.

This time Napoleon accompanied us on the long way from his desk to the door, his hand on Oscar's shoulder. In the ante-chamber diplomats, Generals, Princes and ministers bowed deeply as Meneval opened the door for his master.

"Gentlemen," the Emperor said, "I should like you to join me in congratulating Their Royal Highnesses the Crown Prince and the Crown Princess of Sweden, and my godson——"

"I am the Duke of Södermanland," cried Oscar's bright voice.

"And my godson, the Duke of Södermanland," Napoleon added.

On the drive home Jean-Baptiste sat silently in his corner. I didn't disturb him.

A small crowd had assembled in the Rue d'Anjou, and someone shouted, "*Vive Bernadotte, vive Bernadotte!*" exactly as on the day of Napoleon's *coup d'état* when some people thought that Jean-Baptiste could defend the Republic against him.

Count Brahe, Baron Mörner and some Swedish gentlemen who had just arrived from Stockholm with important messages were waiting for us at the house door.

"I must ask you to excuse us," Jean-Baptiste told them. "Her Royal Highness and I wish to be alone."

We went past them into the small drawing-room. But there was another visitor waiting for us, Fouché, the Duke of Otranto. He had fallen into disgrace recently because of his secret negotiations with the British, which had come to Napoleon's ears.

He held out to me a bunch of very deep red, almost black roses. "May I congratulate you?" he lisped. "France is very proud of her great son."

"Stop it, Fouché," said Jean-Baptiste wearily. "I have just renounced my French citizenship."

"I know, Your Highness, I know."

"Then please excuse us. We cannot see anybody just now," I said, taking the roses.

When we were alone at last we sat down side by side on the sofa, tired, very tired, as if we had come home from an endless walk. After a little while Jean-Baptiste got up, went to the piano and listlessly picked out a tune on it with one finger, the only tune he can play, the Marseillaise. Suddenly he said: "To-day I have seen Napoleon for the last time in my life." Then he continued playing, the same tune, always the same tune. . . .

AT lunch time to-day Jean-Baptiste departed for Sweden.

He had been so busy during these last days that we had seen very little of each other. The French Foreign Ministry at his request made him a list of those Swedish personalities whom it considers important. Mörner and Count Brahe told him afterwards who the people on the list were.

One afternoon Baron Alquier was announced, a man in the gold-embroidered gala uniform of an Ambassador and with an eternal court smile. "His Majesty has appointed me Ambassador in Stockholm," he said, "and I should like to call on Your Royal Highness before your departure."

"You need not introduce yourself," said Jean-Baptiste, "we have known each other for years. Let me see, you were His Majesty's Ambassador in Naples when the Neapolitan Government was overthrown and a Cabinet after His Majesty's wishes put in its place."

Baron Alquier nodded smilingly. "Magnificent country round Naples——"

"And you were His Majesty's Ambassador in Madrid and the Spanish Government was forced to resign in order to make way for a Government acceptable to His Majesty," Jean-Baptiste continued.

"A beautiful city, Madrid," remarked Alquier, "only a bit too hot."

"And now you are going to Stockholm," concluded Jean-Baptiste.

"A fine town, but very cold, I hear."

Jean-Baptiste shrugged his shoulders. "Perhaps it depends on the kind of welcome one receives. There are warm ones, and cold ones!"

"His Majesty the Emperor assured me that Your Royal Highness would welcome me very warmly. As an ex-fellow countryman, so to speak."

"When are you leaving, Excellency?"

"On September 30th, Your Highness."

"Then we shall probably get to Stockholm at the same time."

"What a fortunate coincidence, Your Highness!"

"Generals rarely leave things to chance and coincidence, Excellency. And the Emperor is first and foremost a General," said Jean-Baptiste. He rose, and Alquier had to take his leave.

Couriers from Stockholm brought news about the preparations for a magnificent reception. Danish diplomats called to report that Copenhagen was getting ready for a great welcome to the Swedish Crown Prince. And every morning the pastor of the Protestant community in Paris came to instruct Jean-Baptiste in the tenets of Protestantism, which is the State religion in Sweden. Before Jean-Baptiste reaches Sweden, at the Danish port of Elsinore, he is to be received into the Protestant faith and has to sign the Augsburg Confession in the presence of the Archbishop of Sweden.

One day I asked Jean-Baptiste: "Have you ever been to a Protestant church?"

"Yes, in Germany, twice. It looks the same as a Catholic church, but without the pictures of the saints."

"Must I become a Protestant too?"

He pondered. "I do not think it necessary. You can do as you wish. But at the moment I have no time for this nice young pastor. He can instruct Oscar instead. I want him to learn the Augsburg Confession by heart, in Swedish as well if possible. Count Brahe could help him with it."

So Oscar learnt the Confession in French and Swedish.

I've also taken an interest in those lists of important Swedes. Among the many Löwenhjelms on the list is one, Charles Axel Löwenhjelm, whose name is underlined on the list. He is to meet Jean-Baptiste in Elsinore and accompany him to Stockholm as his lord-in-waiting and to inform him on questions of Swedish court etiquette.

"I leave you the lists," said Jean-Baptiste. "Learn them by heart."

"But I can't pronounce them," I said. "How, for instance, do you pronounce 'Löwenhjelm'?"

Jean-Baptiste couldn't do it either. "But I shall learn to do it. One can learn anything if one wants to." He added: "Hurry with your preparations for the journey. I do not want you and Oscar to stay here longer than is absolutely necessary. As soon as your rooms in the castle in Stockholm are ready you must set off at once. Promise me that!"

He sounded most serious about it, and I nodded.

"By the way," he added, "I have thought of selling this house."

"No, no, Jean-Baptiste, you can't do that to me."

He looked at me in amazement. "But if you want to come to Paris later on you can always stay with Julie. It is an entirely superfluous luxury to keep up a big house like this."

"It is my home, and you can't take my home away just like that. If we still had Father's villa in Marseilles, yes. But we haven't got it any more. Please, Jean-Baptiste, please, leave me this house!" And I added: "You too are sure to come to Paris again, and then you'll be glad of this house. Or are you going to stay at a hotel or the Swedish Embassy from now on?"

It was late at night. We were sitting on the edge of the bed, his bags packed ready around us.

"If I ever return," he murmured, "it will be a sad business, it will hurt me." He stared into the candlelight. "You are right, my girl. It will be better to stay here, if ever I do come here again. We will keep the house."

At lunch time to-day the big coach drew up at the gate. Fernand, still wearing his purple livery, but with the buttons showing the insignia of Sweden, put the luggage inside and waited by the carriage door.

Baron Mörner was waiting in the hall as we came downstairs, Jean-Baptiste, Oscar and I, Jean-Baptiste with his arm round my shoulders. It was all very much as it had been so often before when he left me to go to the front or to go somewhere as Governor.

Jean-Baptiste stopped in front of General Moreau's bust and stared at it. "Send the bust to Stockholm together with my other things," he said. He embraced Oscar and me and turned to Count Brahe: "It is your responsibility to see to it that my wife and Oscar follow me as soon as possible," he said in a hoarse voice. "It may even be of the utmost importance that my family leaves France very quickly. Do you understand?"

"I do, Your Highness."

Jean-Baptiste and Mörner got into the coach, Fernand took his seat beside the coachman. A few passers-by stopped, and an invalided soldier with the medals of all the campaigns on his chest shouted, "*Vive Bernadotte!*" Jean-Baptiste closed the curtains and the coach moved off.

ELSINORE in DENMARK.
During the night of the 21st to the 22nd of December 1810.

I NEVER knew how long and how cold nights could be. Marie brought me four hot-water-bottles. But in spite of them I am still freezing. Perhaps the night will pass more quickly if I go on with my diary.

To-morrow I shall board the Swedish man-of-war that will carry us across the Sound to the Swedish port of Hälsingborg, me, the Crown Princess Desideria, and my dear little son, Oscar, the future Heir to the Throne.

I would so much like to get up and go into Oscar's room and sit quietly down by his bed and hold his hand and feel the warmth of his young life. I used to do it so often in the past when I felt lonely and his father was away at some war or other. I never thought that there might be a time when I could no longer go into his room as I please. But that time has come now. You, my son, are no longer alone in your room, for at your father's order Colonel Villatte, for many years his faithful adjutant, shares it with you till we get to Stockholm. Why? In order to protect you, my darling, from assassins, from those people who are ashamed of Sweden's choice of plain Monsieur Bernadotte and his son Oscar to be their future Kings. That is why your father demanded that Villatte should sleep in your room and Count Brahe in the one adjoining it. Yes, my darling, we are afraid of murderers now.

Marie sleeps in the room next to mine. How she snores, my God, how she snores!

We have come a long way, and for the last two days we have been held up here in Elsinore by the fog which makes it impossible to cross the Sound. And it is so cold here. But people say, "That's nothing. You wait till you are in Sweden, Highness!"

We left our house in the Rue d'Anjou at the end of October, shut it up and moved to Julie in Mortefontaine to spend the last days with her. Young Brahe and the gentlemen of the Swedish Embassy seemed hardly able to wait for my departure from France. I only learnt yesterday why they were so impatient for me to leave. But I couldn't very well go without my new court robes which Le Roy was making for me. Some of them were to be white, the colour which I never wanted to wear in Paris because Josephine always wore it. But in Stockholm where nothing would remind me of her it would be different. At last, on the first of November, they were ready and delivered, and on the third we left.

We travelled in three coaches, myself, Colonel Villatte, the physician whom Jean-Baptiste engaged for the journey, and Madame La Flotte in the first, Oscar, Count Brahe and Marie in the second and our luggage in the third. I had left my reader behind. She couldn't face leaving Paris, and in any case, as Count Brahe told me, there was a complete staff waiting for me in Stockholm which the Queen had appointed for me.

But I took Madame La Flotte, who very much wanted to come because she had fallen in love with Count Brahe.

That day of departure seems to be a long long way back in the past. But in reality it is only six weeks since we left. In these six weeks, however, we have been on the road from morning till night, and wherever we arrived there would be an official reception ceremony, in Amsterdam, in Hamburg and in places with such strange-sounding names as Apenrade and Itzehoe. We did not stop for any length of time till we reached Nyborg in Denmark, where we were to cross from the Isle of Fünen to the Isle of Zealand on which lies the capital, Copenhagen. Here a courier of Napoleon caught up with us, a young cavalry officer carrying a big parcel.

We were just going to board our boat when he arrived, tied his horse to a stanchion on the quay and ran after us with his big parcel. "From His Majesty the Emperor, with his kindest regards!"

Count Brahe took the shapeless parcel and Villatte asked him: "Any letters for Her Highness?"

The young officer shook his head. "No, only this verbal message. When the Emperor was told of Her Highness's departure he said, 'A dreadful time of the year to travel to Sweden!' He looked round, saw me and gave me the order to ride after Your Highness and deliver this parcel. 'Hurry up! Her Highness will need it very badly!' he said." The officer clicked his heels.

I gave him my hand. "Thank His Majesty for me and remember me to Paris." The cold wind made my eyes water.

In the ship's cabin we unpacked the parcel. My heart stopped beating when I saw what was in it: a sable coat. The most beautiful fur I had ever seen!

"One of the Tsar's three furs!" said La Flotte, visibly shaken. We had all heard about the three furs which the Tsar gave the Emperor. The first Napoleon presented to Josephine, the second to his favourite sister Polette, and the third—the third was here, on my knee!

A marvellous fur! But I still went on feeling cold to the marrow. The Generals' greatcoats in the days of old warmed me better than even this fur coat, Napoleon's greatcoat during the night of the thunderstorm in Marseilles, Jean-Baptiste's during the rainy night in Paris. They were not as gold-embroidered, the Generals' greatcoats of those days, as they are to-day, they were coarse and badly cut, but they were the coats of the brave young Republic.

The crossing from Nyborg to Korsör took us three hours,

and some of us, such as Madame La Flotte and the doctor, were much the worse for it. We only spent a few hours in Korsör and then continued our journey, as we had to be in Copenhagen on December 17th. The King and Queen of Denmark were preparing a great reception for us, and we had to keep to the time-table. So we crept, all of us, into one coach to keep warm, and passed our time talking about Denmark, its history and its royal family. It seemed that not only the Vasas but the Kings of Denmark as well belonged to a family which was not too healthy mentally, and I shuddered at the thought that Oscar would have to marry a Princess of old royal blood some day.

Madame La Flotte noticed my shuddering and suggested that we should stop and get some hot water for our bottles. I shook my head. My shudders didn't come from the cold alone, they came from anxiety for the future, a future which was full of the shadows caused by the twilight over the Royal Houses of the North.

The evening in Copenhagen passed like a confused dream. I saw the Royal Castle by the glare of torches, a charming small building in the rococo style, friendly and inviting. But I was stiff with cold and exhaustion. Marie massaged my feet and Yvette did my hair in preparation for the reception, and I put on one of my new white robes.

I asked after Oscar. Marie said that he could hardly keep his eyes open, and so I ordered him to bed. But a moment later Count Brahe appeared and insisted that the young Prince had to take part in the gala dinner at all costs. I was furious but had to give in, and Oscar, instead of going to bed, had to appear in the uniform of a Swedish officer cadet which Berna-dotte had had made for him.

Marie gave me a glass of champagne to cheer me up. But I didn't feel much cheered when I went to the banquet. The Danish royal couple were very kind to me. They both spoke French very well and emphasised how much they admired the Emperor of France. The King urged me to go next morning and see the devastation wrought by the bombardment of Copenhagen by the British Navy. I promised I would. During the meal the King repeated how much he sympathised with Napoleon. Britain, he said, was the common enemy.

"And yet your mother was an English Princess," I said involuntarily.

I had had no intention of being tactless, but I was so tired that I said anything that came into my mind. The mention of his mother created a painful impression on the King. All the same, catching sight of Oscar, who was almost falling asleep over his ice-cream, I added, "One should never deny one's mother, Your Majesty." Thereupon His Majesty rose very soon to end the banquet and we all went into the ballroom. . . .

.   .   .   .   .

And so we've been in this little town of Elsinore for almost three days. But for the fog one could see Sweden from here. And the sea was so rough that Count Brahe kept postponing the crossing time and time again. "Your Highness cannot arrive in Sweden in a state of seasickness," he said. "There will be an enormous crowd on the other side of the Sound wanting to catch a first glimpse of the new Crown Princess."

And so we wait and wait.

The Swedish commercial agent Glörfelt, who lives here, asked me to be godfather to his son and find a nice name for him. I agreed and called the baby Jules Désiré Oscar, Jules because I was longing for Julie so badly. Oscar and I went to Kronborg Castle, and as we crossed the moat the guns roared out a salvo in salute. La Flotte, who never loses an opportunity to show off her knowledge, told me the story of a prince called Hamlet, his murdered father, his uncle and his mother, all of whom were supposed to have lived here.

"How long ago was that?" I asked La Flotte.

She didn't know. She only knew that an English author had written a tragedy about it. It certainly was an eerie castle and I was glad that we were not going to live there. . . .

At last it has been decided: we are crossing to-morrow. The fog is still there, but the sea is calmer. Once more I am going through the list of the names of the ladies and gentlemen who will receive me to-morrow in Hälsingborg: my new ladies-in-waiting Countess Caroline Lewenhaupt and Miss Mariana Koskull, my equerry Baron Reinhold Ådelswärd, my lords-in-waiting Count Erik Piper and Sixten Sparre and finally my physician Pontin.

My candles are burnt low, it is four o'clock in the morning and I want to try and get some sleep.

Jean-Baptiste is not coming to meet me. It is only here that I learnt of Napoleon's ultimatum to the Swedish Government of November 12th. Either, Napoleon demanded, Sweden declares war on Britain within the next five days, or Sweden will be at war with France, Denmark and Russia. The Council of State was convened in Stockholm and everybody's eye was on the new Crown Prince. Jean-Baptiste, at this meeting, said: "Gentlemen, I ask you to forget that I was born in France and that the Emperor holds hostage what is dearest to me in this life. Gentlemen, I do not wish to take part in this conference in order not to exercise any influence whatever on your decisions." I understand now why the gentlemen of the Swedish Embassy in Paris demanded that Oscar and I should hurry our departure.

The Swedish Council of State decided for war with Britain and handed their declaration of war to the British Ambassador on November 17th. But Count Brahe told me that he knew the Crown Prince had sent a secret message to Britain to consider this declaration of war as a mere formality. 'Sweden', this message said, 'wishes to continue the trade in British goods and proposes that British ships bound for Gothenburg from now onwards should sail under the American flag.'

I can't make head or tail of all this. Napoleon could have kept Oscar and me in France as hostages. But he let us go and sent me a sable fur because I needed it so badly here. Jean-Baptiste, however, asked the Council of State not to take his family into account at all. Sweden was far more important than his family, it was the most important thing on earth for him. . . .

Everybody tells me how the Swedes are looking forward to our boy. Ruthlessly I have been driven through the fog and the cold to hand over my child into their keeping, and I do not know whether it will be for the best.

Are heirs to a throne meant to be happy, I wonder?

HÄLSINGBORG, 22nd December, 1810.
(To-day I arrived in SWEDEN.)

THE guns of Kronborg Castle thundered as we went on board the Swedish man-of-war. The crew stood to attention, Oscar put his little hand to his three-cornered hat, and I tried to smile. It was still very foggy and the wind was as icy as ever. So I went down into the cabin. But Oscar stayed on deck to have a good look at the cannon.

"My husband hasn't come, really?" I had asked Count Brahe again and again whenever another message came from Hälsingborg about details of the reception arrangements.

"Important political decisions make His Royal Highness's presence in Stockholm necessary. New demands by Napoleon are expected." With that answer I had to be satisfied.

I had put on a green velvet hat with a red silk rose on it, a green tight-fitting velvet coat which made me look a bit taller, and a green velvet muff. Inside the muff I crumpled up the slip of paper with the names of the members of my Swedish suite. I had tried to learn them, but it seemed hopeless.

"Your Highness is not afraid, is she?" asked Count Brahe.

"Who is looking after Oscar? I don't want him to fall into the water."

"Your own Colonel Villatte is looking after him," said Count Brahe, and I thought that his 'your own' sounded a bit sarcastic.

"Is it true Your Highness has put on woollen underwear?" Madame La Flotte asked in horror. She was fighting seasickness again and her face looked greenish under her make-up.

"Yes. Marie bought them in Elsinore when she saw them in a shop window. I think you want warm underwear in this climate, particularly when we shall probably have to stand by the quayside for hours over there and listen to speeches. Why not, anyway? No one can see what you are wearing under your skirt!"

As soon as I said it I regretted it. It's not what you expect a Crown Princess to say. My new Swedish lady-in-waiting would be horrified if she had heard it.

"The Swedish coast can be seen quite clearly now. Perhaps Your Highness would like to come on deck?" Clearly he wanted me to rush out of the cabin at once.

"I'm so cold and tired," I said, and snuggled deeper into Napoleon's sable fur.

"Of course, I am sorry," murmured the young Swede, and withdrew.

The thunder of guns made me start up. They were the guns of our ship and were answered at once by the batteries on the coast. I got ready and repaired my make-up. But there were deep shadows under my eyes, the result of sleepless nights.

"Your Highness looks very beautiful," said Count Brahe reassuringly.

But it didn't reassure me. 'I shall disappoint them,' I thought. 'Everybody expects a Crown Princess to be like a princess from a fairy-tale, and I am no fairy-tale princess, I am only the former citizeness Eugenie Désirée Clary.'

I went on deck and joined Oscar.

"Look, Mama, that is our country!" the boy shouted.

"Not ours, Oscar. It's the country of the Swedish people. Don't forget that, ever!"

The strains of military music were carried across to us from the quayside. Colourful dresses and golden epaulettes shone through the fog. I saw a bouquet of pink flowers, roses or carnations. Flowers like that would cost a fortune here in winter, I felt sure.

Count Brahe gave us his last directions. "As soon as the ship ties up at the quay I shall run down the gangway and then hold out my hand to you and help you down. I should like the Prince to keep close to Your Royal Highness and, once you are on land, to take up his position to the left of Your Royal Highness. I myself shall be immediately behind you." 'Yes,' I thought, 'my young knight will be quite close behind me to protect the daughter of the Middle Class from the derisive laughter of the Swedish nobles.'

"Have you understood, Oscar?"

"Look, Mama, all the Swedish uniforms, a whole regiment, look!"

"And where am I to stand, Count Brahe?" asked La Flotte.

I turned to her. "You keep with Colonel Villatte in the background. I fear that this reception has not been arranged for your benefit."

"Do you know," asked Oscar, as the guns were firing around us, "what Count Brahe was called in Elsinore, Mama? Admiral Brahe."

"Why that, Oscar? He isn't in the Navy, he is a cavalry officer."

"But they did call him Admiral of the Navy.* Do you understand that, Mama?"

I burst out laughing, and I was still laughing when the boat landed in Hälsingborg.

"Kronprinsessan skål level Kronprinsessan, Arveprinsen!" Many voices shouted rhythmically out of the fog from behind the cordon of soldiers. But I could only see the faces of the Swedish courtiers in front of the cordon, faces rigid and frigid that stared at us without a smile. The laughter froze on my face.

The gangway was put in position and the band played the Swedish anthem, not an inspiring battle song like the Marseillaise but rather a hymn, devout, hard and solemn.

Count Brahe ran past me on to the quay and held out his hand to me. I walked towards it quickly, not feeling very secure. But then I felt his hand under my elbow, felt the land under my feet and Oscar by my side. The bouquet of glowing roses moved towards me, and a gaunt old man in the uniform of a Swedish Marshal handed them to me.

* Translator's note: This is a play on the German meaning of the French name La Flotte, 'the navy'.

"This is the Governor General of the Province of Skåne, Count John Christopher Toll," Count Brahe introduced him.

I saw the pale eyes of an old man examining me without any sign of friendliness in them. I took the roses, and the old man bent over my right hand, and then bowed deeply to Oscar. Ladies in silk fur-trimmed cloaks curtsied, and uniformed backs bowed.

It started to snow. I shook hands with the ladies and gentlemen, who forced themselves to an artificial smile. The smile became more natural, however, as Oscar went round to shake hands with them. Count Toll, in harsh French, made a speech of welcome.

Suddenly snowflakes danced round us in thick swirls. Oscar stared at them enraptured. The anthem sounded again in its strange solemnity. The moment it stopped Oscar's voice rang out through the silence: "We shall be very happy here, Mama. Look, it's snowing!"

How is it that my son always manages to say the right thing at the right moment, exactly like his father?

The old man offered me his arm to conduct me to the waiting equipages. Count Brahe kept close behind me. I looked at the forbidding face of the old man beside me, the strange faces behind me, the bright hard eyes, the critical glances, and I said in a toneless voice: "I ask you always to be kind to my son."

These words were not in the programme, they came out on the spur of the moment, and perhaps they were tactless and contrary to etiquette. An expression of great astonishment came over their faces, at once arrogant and touched. I felt the snowflakes on my eyelids and on my lips, and nobody saw that I was crying.

That evening, as I was undressing, Marie said: "Wasn't I right? I mean about the woollen knickers? Otherwise this ceremony in the harbour might have been your death!"

In the Royal Castle in STOCKHOLM, during that endless winter of 1810–11.

THE journey from Hälsingborg to Stockholm seemed endless. We travelled by day and danced the quadrille by night. I don't know why, but the aristocracy here dance nothing but the quadrille and behave as if they were at the Court of Versailles. They asked me, didn't that make me feel at home? and I could only smile and shrug my shoulders. I know nothing about the

331

Court of Versailles, all that happened before I was born, and we never had any contact with the court.

By day we broke our journey in different towns, and we got out each time. The schoolchildren sang each time, and all the mayors made speeches in a language totally incomprehensible to me. On one occasion I sighed, "If only I could understand Swedish!"

"But," Count Brahe whispered, "the mayor is speaking in French, Your Highness!"

Maybe, I thought, but this French sounded like a very foreign language to me.

It snowed and snowed and never stopped snowing, and the temperature fell to below zero. Most of the time my new lady-in-waiting, Countess Lewenhaupt, was sitting with me, and this Countess, slim and no longer young, was intent on discussing with me all the French novels of the last twenty years. Sometimes I let my other lady, Miss Koskull, travel in my coach. She is about my age, tall and broad-shouldered like most Swedish women, with healthy red cheeks, thick dark hair done in an impossible manner and strong healthy teeth. I don't like her because she always looks at me in such a curious and calculating way.

I was told all the details of Jean-Baptiste's arrival in Stockholm. He had won over the King and the Queen immediately. The ailing King had got up from his armchair with a great effort when Jean-Baptiste entered and stretched out his trembling hand to him. Jean-Baptiste had bent down and kissed it as tears rolled down the cheeks of the old man. Afterwards Jean-Baptiste had called on Queen Hedvig Elizabeth Charlotte, who had dressed up for his reception. But on her breast she had worn, as usual, the brooch with the portrait of the exiled Gustavus IV. As Jean-Baptiste bent down over her hand I was told that he said quietly, 'Madame, I understand your feelings. All I ask you is to remember that Sweden's first King was a soldier too, a soldier who wanted nothing but to serve his people.'

Jean-Baptiste apparently spends every evening in the Queen's drawing-room, and the old King shows himself in public only with the Crown Prince by his side. During audiences, during the sessions of the Council of State, everywhere Jean-Baptiste has to be by his side and support him, a tender son to a loving father. . . .

I tried to visualise the new family idyll. What part was I to play in it? Everybody called the Queen a very intelligent and ambitious woman whom Fate had married to a prematurely senile man and deprived of her only son while still a child.

She is in her early fifties, and Jean-Baptiste was to take her son's place and—no, it was all too difficult for me.

Someone said: "No one but Miss Koskull has managed up till now to make His Majesty listen and even laugh. But now this is no longer the privilege of the beautiful Mariana alone, she has to share it with His Royal Highness." Hearing that, I reflected that perhaps His Majesty was not quite so senile after all, perhaps this Miss Koskull was his mistress. I looked at her and she laughed and showed her strong healthy teeth.

On the afternoon of January 6th we drew near to Stockholm at long last. The roads were so ice-bound that at the slightest rise of the road the horses could not draw us up the incline at all. I had to get out with the others and trot along after our carriages. The icy wind whipped me with such fury that I had to bite my lips in order to stifle a scream. Oscar, however, was not in the least disturbed by the cold. He ran alongside the coachmen leading a horse and talking to the poor creature.

The landscape around us was all white, like a winding-sheet, I thought, like a winding-sheet, Persson, and not a freshly laundered bed-sheet. Suddenly I remembered Duphot. I hadn't thought for years of the dead General who had wanted to marry me. He was the first corpse I had ever seen, his the first winding-sheet. How warm it had been in Rome at that time, how warm!

"How long does winter last with you, Baron Adelswärd?" I asked. The gale drowned my words and I had to repeat my question several times.

"Till April," he said.

In April the mimosas are in flower in Marseilles.

We got back into our carriage at last. Oscar insisted on riding outside beside the coachman on his box. "I can see Stockholm better when we arrive, Mama," he said.

"But it's getting dark, darling," I said.

It was snowing so hard that nothing could be distinguished at all through the curtain of white, and at last dusk and darkness submerged everything. Now and then one of the horses stumbled on the icy road.

Then, quite unexpectedly, our coach stopped amid the red glare of torches, and the door was torn open.

"Désirée!"

It was Jean-Baptiste, who had come in a sledge to meet me. "We are only a mile from Stockholm now," he said. "Only another few moments and you are at home, my little girl."

"Papa, may I ride in a sledge? I have never ridden in a sledge before."

Count Brahe and Countess Lewenhaupt went into another sledge and Jean-Baptiste joined me. In the dark of the coach I sat pressed tightly against him. But we were not alone. Miss Koskull sat opposite us.

I felt his hand in my muff. "What cold hands you have, my girl!"

I wanted to laugh, but all I brought out was a sob. The temperature was below zero, and this climate Jean-Baptiste already called—home!

"Their Majesties expect you for tea in the Queen's drawing-room. No need to change your dress, they only want to welcome you and Oscar without formalities. To-morrow Her Majesty will give a ball in your honour."

He spoke quickly, as if hard pressed by something or somebody.

"Aren't you well, Jean-Baptiste?"

"Of course I am well. Only a bit of a cold and too much work."

"Any trouble?"

"Mm."

"Great trouble?"

Jean-Baptiste said nothing for a moment and then broke out: "Alquier, you know, the French Ambassador in Stockholm, has handed us a new note from the Emperor. He demands that we put two thousand sailors at his disposal. Just like that, two thousand Swedish seamen to prove Sweden's friendly feelings for France!"

"And your answer?"

"Please, try to see the situation correctly: it is the question of the answer of the Government of His Majesty the King of Sweden, and not that of the Crown Prince. We refused. We told him that we cannot spare these men if France forces us at the same time to declare war on Britain."

"Perhaps that'll make Napoleon desist?"

"He desist, when he at the same time concentrates troops in Swedish Pomerania? They are ready to invade Pomerania any moment. Davout is in command of them."

Lights were appearing at intervals along both sides of the road. "We are almost there, Your Highness," said Miss Koskull out of the dark.

"Aren't you longing for the lights of Paris, Jean-Baptiste?"

His hand pressed mine inside my muff. I understood: with Swedes present I was not to speak any more about our longing for Paris.

"Are you going to defend Pomerania?" I asked.

Jean-Baptiste laughed. "Defend? With what? Do you really think that the Swedish Army in its present shape could stand up to our—— I mean to a French attack? To an attack by a Marshal of France? Never, never! I myself told the Swedes in Pomerania——" He interrupted himself, then continued: "I have started the reorganisation of the Swedish Army. Every month a different regiment is coming to Stockholm, where I myself take its training in hand. If I had two years, only two years . . . !"

The lights along the road grew more frequent. I bent towards the window and tried to look out, but I could see nothing but whirling snowflakes.

"Is that not a new fur you are wearing, Désirée?"

"Yes, just imagine, a farewell present from the Emperor sent after me by courier to Nyborg in Denmark. Strange, isn't it?"

"I suppose it was difficult to refuse it."

"Jean-Baptiste, the woman isn't born yet who would refuse a sable. It's one of the three furs which the Tsar gave to the Emperor."

"I don't know whether you have been made familiar with the court etiquette here. Have you discussed it with my wife, Miss Koskull?"

She said she had, but I couldn't remember.

"It is still a bit like——" Jean-Baptiste cleared his throat, "as it was in—in the old days, you know."

I put my head against his shoulder. "As in the old days? I wasn't born then, so I don't know."

"Darling, I mean as it was at Versailles."

"I wasn't at Versailles either," I sighed. "But I'll manage it somehow, I'll pull myself together."

Flares appeared on either side, and we drove up a ramp. The coach came to a stop. I was stiff with cold when Jean-Baptiste lifted me down to the ground. Long rows of high, brightly illuminated windows looked down at me. "The Mälar Lake, can one see the Mälar Lake from here?" I asked.

"You will see it to-morrow morning," said Jean-Baptiste. "The castle is situated on Lake Mälar."

The next moment the ground around us was full of people, gentlemen in short jackets and knee-breeches, all in black and red, appeared from nowhere. "For God's sake," I said, "this isn't a masked ball, is it?" Black masks once murdered a King, I remembered. But then I heard a woman laugh stridently.

"Darling," explained Jean-Baptiste to me, "these are no fancy-dress costumes but the uniform worn here at court. Come along, Their Majesties are waiting for you."

No, Jean-Baptiste didn't want to keep his dear adoptive parents waiting. Oscar and I were chased up the marble staircases and hardly had time to take off our coats. I looked awful, I thought, with my white face, red nose, squashed hat and untidy hair, and there was no Yvette anywhere near to help me. But at any rate I could rely on La Flotte, who gave me a comb to tidy my hair. My feet were wet in my shoes from walking behind our coaches on the snow and ice-bound roads, but that couldn't be helped now. A door opened before me, a blinding brightness crushed down on me and I found myself in a white salon.

"My wife Desideria, who wishes to be a good daughter to Your Majesty. And my son Oscar!"

At first I didn't believe my eyes, for the Queen wore her hair powdered as they did many years ago in France. 'I must tell Julie,' I thought. She had a black velvet ribbon round her neck and her light-coloured eyes were screwed up as if she were short-sighted. I bowed to her.

The stare of her eyes drilled into me like gimlets. She smiled, but it was not a smile of gladness. She was far taller than I, and in her old-fashioned pale blue velvet robes she had a royal air about her. Holding out her hand to me, probably for me to kiss, she said in measured tones: "My dear daughter Desideria, I welcome you."

I touched her hand with the tip of my nose, I didn't feel like kissing it. Then I found myself in front of an old man with watery eyes and a few strands of thin white hair on a pink skull. "Dear daughter, dear daughter . . ." this old man whimpered. Jean-Baptiste stood by his side supporting him.

The Queen came to me a moment later and said: "I should like to introduce you to the Dowager Queen." She took me to a pale thin woman in black. The theatrical black widow's hood on her powdered hair seemed to float above a completely lifeless face. "Her Majesty Queen Sophia Magdalena," said the cold measured voice.

'For heaven's sake,' I thought, 'who is that? How many Queens are there at this court? The Dowager Queen, that must be the wife of the murdered Gustavus III, the mother of the exiled Gustavus IV, the grandmother of the boy whose place Oscar is taking . . .' I bowed deeply to her, deeper even than to the Queen.

"I hope you will be happy at our court, Your Highness," the old woman said in a very low voice, hardly opening her mouth as she spoke. Perhaps she didn't think it worth her while.

"And this is Her Royal Highness, Princess Sofia Albertina, His Majesty's sister."

I saw a woman with the face of a goat, a face of quite indeterminable age, her long teeth bared in a sweetish smile. I bowed again and then made my way towards the big white china stove, the kind of stove they have here, high and round, against which I loved to lean during the breaks in my journey.

My hands and feet were still like ice. It was marvellous to lean against the hot stove. A lackey served me a glass of mulled wine. I folded my hands round the warm glass and felt a bit better. Count Brahe was standing near me, but where was Jean-Baptiste? There he was, bending down towards the trembling King, who was sitting in his armchair now, patting Oscar's cheek with a hand twisted by gout.

Suddenly I felt everybody's eyes turned on me. What did they expect of me? Through the whole of my being I felt a wave of disappointment lapping up at me. I didn't look a Queen, I was no striking beauty, no *grande dame*. No, I was propping myself against the stove, I felt and looked cold, I had a turned-up nose and my short hair stuck to my head in wet curls.

"Will you not take a seat, Madame?" The Queen sat down in an armchair in a beautifully trained, beautifully studied rustle of clothes and pointed to an empty chair by her side.

"I am sorry, but my feet are so wet. Jean-Baptiste, couldn't you take my shoes off? Or ask Villatte to do it?"

At that everybody looked horrified.

Did I say something wrong? As I was holding the warm glass in my hands I couldn't very well at the same time take off my shoes. Jean-Baptiste or Villatte have done it hundreds of times for——

I looked round the faces in the room. Silence had closed round me like an iron band. It was broken by a loud unrestrained giggle which came from Mariana Koskull. The Queen turned to her sharply, and at once the giggle changed into a cough.

Jean-Baptiste came and offered me his arm. "May I ask Your Majesties to excuse my wife? She is wet and tired out from the journey and would like to retire."

The Queen nodded. The King's mouth gaped half open as if he were still pondering on what he had heard.

I kept my eyes fixed on the floor. When I looked up again I met the bitter, sarcastic smile of the Dowager Queen. Later I was told that this was the first time she had smiled for years. Her smile seemed to say, 'How have the Vasas fallen!'

By the door I turned round to call Oscar. But he was busy examining the buttons on His Majesty's tunic. The old gentleman looked very happy. Seeing that, I said no more and left on Jean-Baptiste's arm.

Jean-Baptiste kept silent till we reached my bedroom. "I have had your suite done up completely, with Parisian wall-papers and Parisian carpets. Do you like it?"

"I want a bath, a hot bath, Jean-Baptiste."

"That is impossible. It is the only wish I cannot grant you yet."

"How do you mean? Don't people have baths in Stockholm?"

He shook his head. "No. I am the only one, I believe."

"What? The Queens, the lords and ladies, no one has a bath here?"

"No one. I told you, everything is here still as it was at Versailles in the time of the Bourbons. One does not have a bath here. I had an idea that it would be like that and therefore took my bath tub along with me, but it is only during the last week that I have managed to get hot water. The kitchen is too far away from my rooms. Now they have put up a stove somewhere near my bedroom where Fernand can heat water for my bath. I shall get you a stove like that too and try and find a tub. But you must be patient for a bit, patient in every respect."

"Couldn't I have a bath in your tub to-night?"

"Are you mad? Have a bath and then run in your dressing-gown from my rooms to yours! The whole court would talk of nothing else for weeks."

"Does that mean that I could never go in my dressing-gown—I mean that I could never go into your bedroom, that I——" Stupefied, I added: "Jean-Baptiste, does etiquette at the Swedish court forbid us——" I faltered again. "You know what I mean."

Jean-Baptiste broke into a burst of laughter. "Come here, my girl, come here. You are marvellous, you are unique! I have not laughed like this since I left Paris." He threw himself into an armchair and roared with laughter. "Listen," he said. "Next to my bedroom there is another room occupied day and night by a gentleman-in-waiting. That is part of the etiquette. Naturally I have Fernand in this room as well. We are careful, darling. We receive no men in black masks and tolerate no plots among the colonnades like Gustavus IV. So, as there is always someone in the adjoining room, I prefer, shall we say, for certain conversations of a more intimate kind with my little girl, to visit the rooms of Her Royal Highness. Do you understand?"

I nodded. "Jean-Baptiste, tell me, did I behave very badly?

Was it a real crime against etiquette that I wanted Villatte to take off my shoes?"

He stopped laughing and looked at me gravely, almost sadly. "It was bad, my little girl, really bad. But," he said, getting to his feet, "how were you to know that? And the court ought to have prepared against something like that. I warned the emissaries of the King that night when they offered us the crown."

"Offered *you* the crown, Jean-Baptiste, not us."

Marie took me to bed. She put hot-water-bottles under my feet and the Emperor's sable fur over my blanket. "All wives maintain that their mothers-in-law are terrible. But, Marie, mine really is."

The next evening we danced in the ballroom of the King and Queen till late into the night, and two days later the citizens of Stockholm gave a ball in my honour in the ballroom of the Exchange. I wore my white robes and a golden veil over my hair and shoulders. The Swedish court ladies possessed marvellous jewellery, big diamonds and dark blue sapphires and magnificent diadems. Never before had I seen such precious gems.

On the day after the ball in the Exchange Countess Lewenhaupt brought me a pair of ear-rings made of diamonds and emeralds.

"A present from the Queen?" Perhaps she thought I had looked too poverty-stricken?

"No, a present from the Dowager Queen," said Countess Lewenhaupt imperturbably. "She used to wear them often. Now she wears mourning only and never any jewellery."

I wore these ear-rings on January 26th, Jean-Baptiste's birthday. The Queen gave a party in his honour, during which a kind of pageant was acted, but unfortunately not by proper actors and actresses but by Sweden's young aristocrats. They danced a quadrille in the different regional costumes of the country, and ended up by forming a circle into which tripped so-called Valkyries, Nordic goddesses of the battlefield or whatever they are. The ladies acting them wore a kind of nightgown made of tiny pieces of metal which jingled and clanked as they moved, and they each carried a shield and a spear. Miss Koskull in golden armour was the central figure, and she smiled victoriously. The others danced around her singing, "Oh Brynhild, oh Brynhild!" Miss Koskull inclined her shield and her head and looked deeply into Jean-Baptiste's eyes. During the last figure of the dance all the Valkyries danced towards us with dainty steps in minuet rhythm, bowed before Oscar, and before we realised what was happening they had lifted him into the air and amidst the applause of the spectators carried him out of the ballroom.

All that had been an idea of beautiful Koskull, and nobody could imagine a more pleasant birthday party.

Jean-Baptiste was sitting between the Queen and myself. His eyes seemed to lie deep in their sockets and he chewed his lower lip restlessly.

"Is Davout going to attack Pomerania?" I asked him, whispering. He gave a faintly perceptible nod.

"Great anxieties?"

Again he nodded. After a pause he added: "I sent a courier to the Russian Tsar."

"But he is Napoleon's ally. Do you think anything will come of that?"

Jean-Baptiste shrugged his shoulders, then said: "Perhaps. The Tsar is arming." Then a very urgent tone came into his voice: "Désirée, when you talk to Swedes never mention Finland, never. You understand?"

"I know nothing about Finland. Is it so important to them?"

"Yes, it is a matter of national emotion. They hope they'll get the Tsar to give the country back to Sweden."

"Is he likely to?"

"No, never. Just look at the map and you will see why not."

This was the moment the Valkyries danced their minuet. It was dreadful, and I applauded enthusiastically.

The next day but one was the birthday of King Charles XIII. It was our turn now to give a party to Their Majesties. Everything had been settled before my arrival. *The Barber of Seville* was performed, and Miss Koskull sang the leading part. The childish King devoured her with his eyes and again and again raised his shaky hands to applaud. At the opening of the ball Jean-Baptiste danced the first dance with Miss Koskull. They looked a well-matched couple. She is the first woman I have seen who is almost as tall as Jean-Baptiste himself. As to me, I had the honour of being asked for the first dance by a little man in a brand-new court uniform. "May I ask you for this dance, Mama?" said the little man. It was Oscar's first court ball.

A few days later the old King had a stroke. I heard about it when I was in my new bath tub, which at one time had been nothing but a laundry tub. This tub was put at the far end of my very large bedroom behind a screen made of magnificent tapestries and from there I heard Madame La Flotte talking to Miss Koskull, but not very loudly. Marie bent over me rubbing my back.

A door opened, and I gave Marie a sign to stop. The voice

340

of Countess Lewenhaupt said: "I have just come from the rooms of Her Majesty. His Majesty the King has had a slight stroke."

"Oh!" said Miss Koskull.

"It cannot have been the first," said Madame La Flotte indifferently. "How is the King?"

"His Majesty must have complete rest for the time being. There is no danger, the doctors say, but he must be careful and may not do any work for the next few weeks. Where is Her Royal Highness?"

I moved my legs and made some splashing noises.

"The Crown Princess is having a bath and cannot see anybody at the moment."

"Of course, having a bath! She will never get rid of her cough that way."

I continued my splashing.

"Is the Crown Prince going to take over the regency?"

Hearing that I stopped splashing.

"The Chancellor suggested it to Her Majesty, because of our difficult situation. There are the secret negotiations with Russia and the threatening notes from France to take care of, and so the Chancellor wishes the Crown Prince to take over the Government as soon as possible."

"And?" asked Koskull. The breath-taking tension in her voice was quite obvious to me.

"The Queen refuses to suggest that to the King. And the King does only what she wants him to do."

"Really?" said Miss Koskull sarcastically.

"Yes, really. Even if you imagine yourself to be his favourite. Your reading to him and your laughing do no more than keep him awake, which at any rate is something. . . . By the way, you read very rarely to him now. You do not seem to set so much store by being His Majesty's ray of sunshine. Am I mistaken?"

"It is more amusing," put in Madame La Flotte, "to dance with the Prince of Ponte Corvo, oh, I am sorry, I mean it is far more amusing to dance with your Crown Prince."

"*Our* Crown Prince, Madame La Flotte," corrected Miss Koskull.

"Why? He is not *my* Crown Prince, I am not Swedish, and as a French woman I owe allegiance to the Emperor Napoleon, if it is of any interest to the ladies."

"It is not," said the Countess.

Marie was leaning against the tapestries in complete silence. We looked at each other, I moved my legs in the warm water and then slipped deeper into the tub.

"And why, if I may ask, does one not, in these weeks which are of such decisive importance to Sweden, transfer the regency to the Crown Prince?" inquired Madame La Flotte.

"Because she will never allow it as long as she is alive," whispered Countess Lewenhaupt. But she whispered it so loudly that I realised this conversation was for my benefit.

"Of course not," said Madame Koskull. "She is playing first fiddle now."

"But she was Queen before the arrival of the Crown Prince," said La Flotte.

"Yes. But the King had no power at all. That was in the hands of his ministers," was Miss Koskull's friendly explanation.

Madame La Flotte laughed. "Do you imagine perhaps that the King has any power now? He invariably goes to sleep in all the meetings of the Council of State. Do you know what happened the day before yesterday? I know because Count Brahe, who, as the Cabinet Secretary of His Royal Highness, has to be present, told me. The King was dozing away sweetly and in the intervals between the reports of the different ministers he murmured mechanically, 'I agree to the suggestion of the Council of State'. They were just discussing some death sentence or other, the Minister of Justice proposed that the King should sign it, and the King murmured his automatic 'I agree to the suggestion.' Suddenly the Crown Prince gripped the King's arm, shook him hard and waking him shouted—yes, shouted, your King is half-deaf too on top of everything else!—'Your Majesty, wake up, a man's life is at stake!' So you see how it is, and yet the Queen will not make him Regent."

"And yet the Queen will not make him Regent," said Countess Lewenhaupt clearly. "She will suggest to the King to hand over the chairmanship of the Council of State to the Crown Prince. But he is not going to be Regent, at least not as long as——"

"As long as what?" asked Madame La Flotte.

I didn't stir, and Marie stood like a statue.

"If the Crown Prince is made Regent the Crown Princess will be the Regent's Consort," Countess Lewenhaupt said cuttingly.

There was a pause, and then the Countess said casually: "The Crown Prince will preside over the Council of State and the Queen, during His Majesty's illness, will act as Regent and represent the King."

Miss Koskull laughed. "And on the arm of the Crown Prince Her Majesty his Mama, his dearly beloved Mama, will

342

show herself to the people to show them who governs Sweden. That would suit her!"

"The Queen has told the Chancellor in so many words that that would be the only possible solution," the Countess concluded.

"What reason did she give for it?" asked Miss Koskull.

"That the Crown Princess did not possess sufficient experience to fulfil the duties of representation which fall on a Regent's wife. It would be injurious, the Queen maintained, to the prestige of the Crown Prince, if Her Royal Highness let herself be seen in public too often."

"I wonder whether she will tell that to the Crown Prince," said Madame La Flotte.

"She has told him. The Crown Prince was present during this interview, as well as the Chancellor and myself."

"You were present? How is that?" asked Madame La Flotte. "As far as I am informed you are lady-in-waiting to Her Royal Highness, are you not?"

"Your information is quite correct. But I also happen to have the honour of being a friend of the Queen's."

'And so the whole thing is a message of the Queen to me,' I thought. "The towel, Marie!"

Marie gave me the towel and with her strong and loving arms rubbed me dry. "Don't put up with that, Eugenie," she said, "don't stand for it." She passed me a dressing-gown.

I came out from behind the screen. My three ladies had put their heads together and were whispering. "I should like to rest. Please leave me alone," I said.

Countess Lewenhaupt bowed. "I have come with sad news, Your Highness. His Majesty has had a slight stroke, the left arm seems paralysed to some extent. His Majesty is to take a rest——"

"Thank you, Countess. I have heard it all during my bath. I should like to be left alone now."

I wrapped myself more tightly into my dressing-gown and went to the window. It was five o'clock in the afternoon and already quite dark. Masses of snow had been shovelled away and piled high against the walls of the castle. 'They are burying me here, burying me in snow,' I thought. But that was a stupid thing to think, and it occurred to me that I had not yet done my Swedish lesson for the day. Jean-Baptiste engaged a Councillor Wallmark to teach him Swedish, and this gentleman turned up every afternoon at Jean-Baptiste's rooms in vain. Jean-Baptiste was always in some conference or other and never had time for him, and as I thought it was a pity to waste all that money on lessons which Jean-Baptiste never took, I decided to have a lesson with Councillor Wallmark every day. Oscar knows quite a lot of Swedish already, but then he has three Swedish teachers and goes skating with Swedish children of his own age.

Jag er, du er, han er, I learn, *Jag var, du var, han var* . . . *Jag er* I am, *du er* you are, *han er* he is . . . "Marie!"

"Did you call me, Eugenie?"

"You could do me a favour, Marie. There is a street here in Stockholm called Västerlånggatan or something like that. Persson's father had his shop there. You remember Persson, don't you? Perhaps you could make your way there and find out whether Persson's silk shop still exists. If it does, ask for young Persson."

"He won't be quite so young any longer."

"Tell him that I am here. Perhaps he doesn't know that the new Crown Princess is the former Eugenie Clary. And if he remembers me, tell him to come and see me."

"I don't know whether that is very wise, Eugenie."

"Wise! I don't care whether it is or not. Imagine if Persson came to see me and I had someone here who knew our house in Marseilles and our garden and our summer-house where Julie got engaged, and Mama and Papa and—Marie, someone who knows exactly what it was like once upon a time! You must try and find him!"

Marie promised she would, and at last I had something to look forward to.

On the evening of that day the Queen took the King's heavy signet-ring and put it on Jean-Baptiste's hand. That meant that the King had entrusted Jean-Baptiste with the conduct of the Government. But it did not mean that he was to be Regent.

Slowly, very slowly, with roaring floods heaving under green ice-floes, spring approached. On one of the very first spring afternoons Countess Lewenhaupt appeared with an invitation from the Queen to have tea with her in her drawing-room. Every evening after Jean-Baptiste, Oscar and I had our dinner we spent at least an hour with the Queen, whose husband's health, by the way, had considerably recovered from the effects of the stroke. But I had never been to see the Queen by myself. What was the use of it, anyway? We had nothing to say to each other.

"Tell Her Majesty that I am coming," I said to Countess Lewenhaupt, tidied myself up a bit and went across to Her Majesty's rooms over miles of cold marble staircases.

They were seated round a small table, the three of them:

Queen Hedvig Elizabeth Charlotte, my adoptive mother-in-law, who ought to love me, Queen Sophia Magdalena, who had every reason to hate me, and Princess Sofia Albertina, an old flat-chested spinster with a childish ribbon in her hair and a tasteless string of amber beads round her scraggy neck, to whom I could mean nothing and who could mean nothing to me. All three were busy embroidering.

"Sit down, Madame," said the Queen.

They continued their embroidering till tea was served. Then they dropped their frames and stirred their tea. I swallowed a few drops hastily, burning my tongue.

The Queen motioned to the servants. They withdrew. Not a single lady-in-waiting was present either. "I should like to have a few words with you, dear daughter," said the Queen.

Princess Sofia Albertina showed her long teeth in a smile full of glee, but the Dowager Queen stared indifferently down into her cup.

"I should like to ask you, my dear daughter, whether you yourself feel that you are fulfilling all the obligations resting on you as the Crown Princess of Sweden?"

Her pale short-sighted eyes drilled into my face and I knew I was blushing. "I don't know, Madame," I managed to say at last.

The Queen arched her dark, boldly curving eyebrows. "You don't know?"

"No," I said. "I can't judge about that. It's the first time I have been a Crown Princess, and I'm only just starting, too."

Princess Sofia Albertina started bleating. She really bleated like a goat.

Irritated, the Queen raised her hand. In a silky voice she said: "The Swedish people, and the Crown Prince chosen by the Swedish people, are much to be pitied that you do not know how to conduct yourself as Crown Princess." Very slowly the Queen raised her cup to her lips and, drinking, looked at me fixedly over the top of her cup. "Therefore I should like to tell you, my dear daughter, how a Crown Princess has to behave."

'So everything was in vain,' I thought, 'the lessons in deportment from Monsieur Montel and the piano lessons and my keeping quietly in the background at all the court receptions in order not to embarrass Jean-Baptiste, all was in vain.'

"A Crown Princess never goes for a drive in the company of one of her husband's adjutants without being escorted by a lady-in-waiting."

Whom did she mean, Villatte? "I—I have known Colonel

Villatte for many years. He's been with us since Sceaux and we like talking about old times," I said with difficulty.

"At court receptions the Crown Princess has to speak graciously to everyone present. You, however, stand about awkwardly and almost as if you were deaf and dumb, Madame."

"Man has been given the gift of language to conceal his thoughts," I exclaimed.

The Princess bleated loudly and the pale eyes of the Queen widened in surprise. I added quickly: "That isn't my own phrase but comes from one of our—from a French diplomatist, Count Talleyrand, Prince of Benevento. Perhaps Your Majesty has heard——"

"Of course I know who Talleyrand is," the Queen said sharply.

"Madame, if one isn't very clever and very educated, but has to conceal one's thoughts, one is forced to—keep silent."

A teacup clattered. The Dowager Queen had put her cup down with a hand that trembled suddenly.

"You have to force yourself to make conversation, Madame," said the Queen. "Besides, I do not know why you should conceal your thoughts from your Swedish friends and future subjects."

I folded my hands in my lap and let her talk. 'Everything must come to an end,' I thought, 'even this tea party.'

"One of my servants reported to me that your old maid asked him about the shop of a certain Persson. I should like to draw your attention to the fact that you will not be able to make purchases in this shop."

I looked up. "Why not?"

"This Persson is not appointed as Purveyor to the Court and will never be so. On account of your inquiry I asked for information about him. He is considered to be—well, let us say to be in favour of certain revolutionary ideas."

My eyes grew wide. "Persson?"

"This Persson was in France at the time of the French Revolution, allegedly to learn the silk trade. Since his return he has frequently surrounded himself with students, writers and other muddle-headed persons and he spreads those ideas which years ago became responsible for the misery of the French nation."

What could she mean? "I don't quite understand, Madame. Persson lived with us in Marseilles, he worked in Father's shop, in the evenings I often gave him French lessons, together we learnt the Rights of Man by heart——"

"Madame!" It sounded like a slap in the face. "I implore

346

you to forget this. It is quite out of the question that this Persson has ever taken lessons from you or—or ever had had anything to do with your father."

"Madame, Papa was a greatly respected silk merchant, and the firm of Clary is still a very solid business even to-day."

"I must ask you to forget all that, Madame. You are Crown Princess of Sweden."

A very long silence followed. I looked down at my hands and tried to think. But my thoughts got all mixed up, only my feelings remained clear. "*Jag er Kronprinsessan*," I murmured in Swedish and said awkwardly, "I have started to learn Swedish. I wanted to make a special effort. But apparently it isn't enough."

There was no answer.

I looked up. "Madame, would you have persuaded His Majesty to appoint Jean-Baptiste Regent if that had not meant that I should become the Regent's Consort?"

"Possibly."

"Another cup of tea, Madame?" asked the bleating spinster.

I shook my head.

"I should like to feel that you are going to ponder my words and act accordingly, dear daughter," said the frigid voice of the Queen.

"I am pondering them at this very moment."

"You must never for a moment forget the position of our dear son, the Crown Prince, Madame," concluded the Queen.

At that my patience gave out. "Your Majesty has just reproached me for not forgetting who and what my dead father was. Now you admonish me not to forget my husband's position. I should like you to know once and for all that I never forget anything or anybody!"

Without waiting for a sign from the Queen I got up. To the devil with etiquette! I bowed whilst the three ladies sat more stiffly than ever. "Madame, in my home town of Marseilles the mimosas are in blossom now. As soon as it is a little warmer I shall go back to France."

That went home. All three of them were startled. The Queen stared at me in fright, the goat with incredulity, and even the Dowager Queen's face registered surprise.

"You are going—back?" the Queen brought out at last. "When did you decide on that step, dear daughter?"

"At this moment, Your Majesty."

"It is politically unwise, very unwise, surely. You must speak to the Crown Prince about it," she said hastily.

"I never do anything without my husband's consent."

"And where are you going to reside in Paris, Madame?" asked the goat in agitation. "You have no palace there, have you?"

"I've never had a palace there. We kept our home in the Rue d'Anjou, an ordinary house, certainly not a castle, but very prettily furnished. I don't need a castle, I'm not used to living in castles, and, Madame, I even hate castles!"

The Queen had regained her composure. "Your country house near Paris would perhaps be a more adequate residence for the Crown Princess of Sweden."

"You mean La Grange? But we sold La Grange and all our other estates to pay Sweden's foreign debts. They were considerable, Madame."

She bit her lips, then said quickly: "Crown Princess Desideria of Sweden in an ordinary Parisian dwelling house? No, impossible. Moreover— —"

"I shall discuss it with my husband. By the way, I don't intend to travel under the name of Desideria of Sweden." I felt tears coming into my eyes. 'Oh, no tears now,' I said to myself, 'don't give them that pleasure.' Throwing back my head I said: "Desideria, the longed-for one! I should like to ask Your Majesty to find an incognito for me. May I retire now?" And I banged the door behind me so that it resounded through the marble halls, as it did once in Rome, in the first castle to which the winds of Fate had carried me. . . .

From the Queen's drawing-room I went straight to Jean-Baptiste's study. In the ante-chamber one of the lords-in-waiting barred my way. "May I announce Your Royal Highness?"

"No, thank you. I am used to entering my husband's room without previous announcement."

"But I am compelled to announce Your Highness," he insisted.

"Who compels you? His Royal Highness perhaps?"

"Etiquette, Your Highness. For centuries——"

I pushed him aside, and my touch made him start as if he had been stung. I laughed. "Never mind, Baron, I shall not prevent you from upholding etiquette much longer." I entered Jean-Baptiste's study.

He was sitting at his desk, studying documents and listening to the Chancellor Wetterstedt and two other gentlemen at the same time. A green eyeshade covered the upper half of his face. I had learnt from Fernand that his eyes had suffered because the early darkness here forces him to work most of the time in artificial light. His usual working hours were from half-past nine in the morning to three o'clock the next morning, and his eyes always looked badly inflamed. But only the gentlemen of his immediate surroundings knew of this eyeshade. It had been kept a secret from me so that I shouldn't worry. I wasn't surprised, therefore, that he took it off as soon as I came in.

"Has anything happened, Désirée?"

"No. I only wanted to speak to you."

"Are you in a hurry?"

"No. I shall sit down somewhere and wait till you've finished."

I pulled an armchair towards the big round stove and warmed myself. At first I heard snatches of what Jean-Baptiste said. "We must realise that the Swedish currency is at the present moment the weakest in Europe." And: "I will not spend our few English pounds, which we earn with such difficulty through our secret trade with Britain, on unnecessary imports." Or: "But I *am* forced to intervene, I am sacrificing my whole private fortune to stabilise the rate of exchange, I am to mobilise and yet cannot take men away from our steel mills and saw mills, and I must provide artillery, or do you believe that one can win battles with sword and shield nowadays?"

Later I began to bring order into my own thoughts, then felt quite certain that I was right and grew calm. But it made me sad, very sad.

Jean-Baptiste had forgotten my presence and put his eyeshade on again, peering at a document. It concerned an incident, I heard Jean-Baptiste point out, which he considered very important. We had arrested some British sailors in Hälsingborg and the British had arrested three Swedes just to show Napoleon that we were at war with each other, and now a British diplomatist, a Mr. Thornton, had been sent to us to settle the exchange of the prisoners with the man in charge of this affair on our side, a Mr. Engström. But Jean-Baptiste also wanted the Russian Ambassador in Stockholm, Suchtelen, to take part in these negotiations. Why that? I wondered. Did Jean-Baptiste want to bring about secretly an understanding between the Russians and the British, the enemies of France? Nominally the Tsar was still Napoleon's ally, but he had started to prepare for war, and Napoleon was massing troops in Pomerania and Poland.

"Perhaps one could use this opportunity to talk about Finland with Suchtelen," one of the gentlemen was saying now.

Jean-Baptiste sighed, irritated. "You always hark back to that. You bore the Tsar and——" He interrupted himself. "I am sorry, gentlemen. I know what Finland means to you. I shall take it up with Suchtelen and I shall mention it in my next letter to the Tsar. We shall continue to-morrow. Good-night, gentlemen."

The gentlemen bowed themselves out backwards to the door. Jean-Baptiste took off the eyeshade and closed his eyes. His face reminded me of Oscar's when he was asleep: tired and contented. He loves governing, I thought. Most likely he governs well, too.

"Well, little girl, what is it?"

"I am going, Jean-Baptiste. In summer, when the roads are better I am going home, dearest," I said very gently.

He opened his eyes. "Have you gone crazy? Here is your home, here in the Royal Castle of Stockholm. In summer we are moving to Drottningholm, a beautiful country residence with a big park. You will like it there very much."

"But I must go," I insisted. "It's the best thing to do." I repeated my conversation with the Queen word for word, and he listened in silence. The frown on his forehead grew deeper and deeper till he exploded: "What I have to listen to! Her Majesty and Her Royal Highness do not get on well with each other! Incidentally, the Queen is right, you do not always behave like a—as the Swedish court expects you to. You will learn that all right, why shouldn't you? But, God knows, I cannot possibly concern myself with these things now. Have you any idea at all what is happening in the world? And what is going to happen in the next few years?"

He rose to his feet and came towards me. "Our existence is at stake," he said in a voice hoarse with agitation, "the existence of the whole of Europe. Napoleon's European bloc is tottering, the South doesn't give him a minute's rest, in Germany his opponents have established secret alliances, while his soldiers are being ambushed almost every day, and in the North——" He broke off chewing his lower lip. "As the Emperor can no longer rely on the Tsar he is going to invade Russia. Do you understand what that means?"

I shrugged my shoulders. "He's invaded and subjugated so many countries. We know him."

Jean-Baptiste nodded. "Yes, we know him. The Swedish Crown Prince knows him better than anybody else. And for that reason the Tsar of all the Russias will come to the Crown Prince of Sweden for advice in his hour of need. And when the conquered countries unite in a new coalition under the leadership of Russia and Britain, they will come to Sweden and demand a decision from us, are we for Napoleon or against him?"

"Against him? That would mean that you——" I didn't finish the sentence.

"No, it would not. Napoleon and France are not the same thing. Have not been the same thing since the days of Brumaire, the days which neither he nor I have forgotten. That is why he concentrates troops on the frontiers of Swedish Pomerania too. If he wins the war against Russia he will simply trample Sweden under foot and put one of his brothers on the throne. But as long as the Russian campaign lasts he wants to have my support. At the moment he is bidding for it, offers me Finland and wants to put in a good word with the Tsar on our behalf. As far as appearances go the Tsar is still his ally after all."

"But you said that the Tsar will never part with Finland?"

"Of course not. But the Swedes cannot get used to that idea. However, I shall compensate them for the loss of Finland." Quite unexpectedly a smile appeared on his face. "Once Napoleon is beaten and the great cleaning up in Europe begins, Napoleon's most loyal ally, Denmark, will have to pay a price. The Tsar will suggest to Denmark the cession of Norway to Sweden. And that, my little girl, is written not only in the stars but right across the map of Europe."

"Napoleon isn't beaten yet. Besides, you are saying all the time that the fate of Sweden is at stake, and you don't want to see that for that very reason I must go back to Paris."

He sighed. "If you knew how tired I am you would not be so obstinate about this. I cannot let you go. You are the Crown Princess here, and that is the end of it."

"Here I can only do harm, but in Paris I can do a lot of good. I've thought it all out."

"Don't be childish! What can you do? Spying on the Emperor for me? I have my own spies in Paris, you can be sure of that. I could tell you, for instance, that Talleyrand corresponds secretly not only with the Bourbons but also with me."

"I don't want to do any spying. But, when the great cleaning up, as you call it, comes, all Napoleon's brothers will be chased from their thrones. France was a Republic before Napoleon made himself Emperor, and even if Talleyrand corresponds with the Bourbons, they can't force France to recall them."

Jean-Baptiste shrugged his shoulders. "You can be sure that the old royal families stick together, and they will certainly try it. But what has it to do with us, with you and me?"

"If that is so, the old royal families will also try to exclude the former Jacobin General Bernadotte from the Swedish succession. And who is going to stand by you then?"

"I cannot do more than serve the interests of Sweden with all my strength. Every penny I have saved I am putting into this country to get it on its feet, and I am thinking of nothing but of ways and means of preserving Sweden's independence. If I succeed, Désirée, then the Swedish-Norwegian union will materialise as a matter of course." He was leaning against the stove and covering his inflamed eyes with his hand. "Nobody can ask more than that of any human being. As long as Europe needs me to fight Napoleon, Europe will protect me. But does one know who is going to stand by me afterwards, Désirée?"

"The people of Sweden, Jean-Baptiste, the people only, but they are what matters. Hold on to the Swedes who called you in."

"And you?"

"I am only the wife of a man who is probably a genius and not that Desideria for whom the Swedish nobility longed. I am doing harm to your prestige. The aristocracy pokes fun at me, and the ordinary Swedes when it comes to taking sides prefer their aristocracy to a foreigner. Let me go, Jean-Baptiste. It will make your position stronger." I felt a sad smile creep over my face. "After the King's next stroke you'll be made Regent. You can pursue your policy better once you take over the Regency. It'll be easier for you without me, darling."

"It sounds very reasonable, my girl, but no, no! To begin with, I cannot send the Swedish Crown Princess to Paris to be Napoleon's convenient hostage. My decisions would be influenced if I knew you to be in danger all the time and——"

"Really? But didn't you ask the Council of State shortly after your arrival here not to be influenced in any way by consideration of what is dearest to you in this life? At that time Oscar and I were still on French territory. No, Jean-Baptiste, you must not take us into consideration. If you want the Swedes to stand by you, you must stand by them." I took his hand, pulled him down to the arm of my chair and sat close to him. "Besides, do you really believe that Napoleon would ever arrest his brother Joseph's sister-in-law? Very unlikely, isn't it? He knows you, and he knows therefore that that would lead to nothing. Didn't he give me a sable fur at the same time that he received an unaccommodating letter from the Swedish Government? No, dearest, no one takes me seriously. Let me go."

He shook his head impatiently. "I am working day and night, I am doing an endless number of jobs, and I cannot go on with them if I know that you are not near me. I need you, Désirée."

"Others may need me more. A day may come when my house is perhaps the only one to offer shelter for my sister and her children. Do let me go, Jean-Baptiste, I implore you!"

"You must not profane Swedish authority in order to help your family. I shall never tolerate that."

"I shall always profane Swedish authority if it helps someone in distress. Sweden is only a small country, Jean-Baptiste, with at most a couple of million inhabitants. Magnanimity alone can make it great."

At that Jean-Baptiste smiled. "I almost believe you take the time to read books."

"I shall take the time in Paris, dearest, when I have nothing else to do. I shall try to educate myself so that you and Oscar need not be ashamed of me later on."

"Désirée, the child needs you. Can you really envisage a separation from him for any length of time? No one knows how the situation is going to develop. It may be that you could not return here easily once you are in Paris. Europe is going to be turned into a battlefield and you and I——"

"Darling, I shouldn't be allowed to accompany you to the front in any case. And the child——" Yes, the child. All the time I had tried to push the thought of him away from me. The idea of a separation from him was like an open wound, it hurt. "The child is now Heir to the Throne, surrounded by an adjutant and three teachers. Since we came here he's had very little time for me. At first he'll miss me, but then he'll realise that an heir to a throne cannot indulge his sentiments, only his sense of duty. In this way our boy will be brought up like a Prince by birth, and nobody could ever call him later on a *parvenu* King." I put my head on his shoulder and cried. At last I pulled myself together and got up. "I think it's time to eat."

Jean-Baptiste sat on the arm of the chair without moving. Away from the stove I felt at once the icy cold of the room. "D'you know that in Marseilles the mimosas are in bloom at this time?" I said.

"The Chancellor told me spring would be here in four weeks' time, and he is a reliable man," said Jean-Baptiste in a low voice.

I walked towards the door, slowly, waiting feverishly for a word from him, for his decision. I would take it as a judgment. When I arrived by the door I stopped. Whatever his decision was, it would break me, I felt.

"And how am I to explain your departure to Their Majesties and the court?" It sounded casual, as if the whole thing were of almost no importance.

"Say that I have to go to Plombières for reasons of health to take the waters there, and that I shall spend autumn and winter in Paris because I cannot stand the raw climate here."

I left the room quickly.

DROTTNINGHOLM CASTLE in SWEDEN.
The beginning of June 1811.

THE night sky spreads like pale green silk over the park. It is midnight, but still not dark. I had dark blinds put at the windows to help me to sleep, but I didn't sleep well in spite of that. I don't know whether the green twilight or my impending departure for France to-morrow morning is responsible for my sleeplessness.

Three days ago the court moved to Drottningholm, the summer residence with an endless park. The light nights are full of sweet scents, the eerie light makes everything look unreal. One doesn't sleep, one only stares into the green space. Unreal too in this light are all the last talks and farewells, painful and yet easy to bear because I am allowed to go back home. I am turning over the pages of my diary, and I remember Papa.

On June the first the Swedish court left Stockholm for this place. Perhaps I am dreaming, I tell myself this last night in which I still call myself the Crown Princess of Sweden. To-morrow morning I shall start my journey incognito under the name of Countess of Gothland. Perhaps it's all been nothing but a dream and I shall wake up in my bedroom in Sceaux, and the next moment Marie will come in and give me Oscar. But the outlines of my trunks in the room here are very real indeed. Oscar, my boy, your mother is going away to France, but not just for health reasons, and I shall not see you again for a very long time. And when I do see you again you won't be a child any more, at least not *my* child. You'll be a real Prince instead, bred to occupy a throne. Jean-Baptiste was born to reign, you are being bred to reign. But your mother was neither born nor bred to it, and that is why in a few hours I shall leave. . . .

For weeks the court found it impossible to understand that I was really going away. They whispered and threw curiously furtive glances at me. I thought they'd be annoyed with me for it. But strangely enough they were annoyed with the Queen instead. It was said that the Queen had not been a good mother-in-law to me and, so to speak, had forced me to leave. But if they had expected feuds between Her Majesty and Her Royal Highness they were disappointed. I am leaving the scene to-morrow morning as the unknown Countess of Gothland.

I only went along to Drottningholm to see the famous summer

354

seat of the Vasas where Oscar is going to spend his summers from now onwards.

The evening after our arrival we were given an entertainment in the little theatre built by the mad King Gustavus III at enormous expense. Miss Koskull, in her blissful amateurishness, sang a few arias which the King applauded enthusiastically, but she had no response whatever from Jean-Baptiste. Yet there was one moment during that dark winter when I thought that . . . Now the tall Miss Koskull, the Valkyrie, the goddess of the battlefield, had lost all attraction for Jean-Baptiste, now that I was going. All the same, my darling, I am going whatever happens. . . .

In my honour Their Majesties gave a farewell banquet. After the meal we even danced a little. The King and Queen sat in gilded armchairs and smiled graciously, that is to say, as far as the King with his drooping mouth and uncomprehending face can smile at all.

I danced with Baron Mörner, Chancellor Wetterstedt and Foreign Minister Engström, and finally with Jean-Baptiste's youngest Cabinet Secretary, our Count Brahe. After the dance I said to him: "It is hot in here. I should like a breath of fresh air." We went outside.

"I should like to thank you, Count Brahe," I told him. "You stood by my side chivalrously when I arrived, and I know that you will see me just as chivalrously to my carriage to say good-bye. You did everything in your power to give me an easy beginning here. Forgive me for having disappointed you. This is the end of the beginning."

He hung his dark head and chewed the little moustache which he had been growing. "If Your Highness wishes——"

I shook my head energetically. "No, Count, no! Believe me, my husband is a good judge of men, and if he's made you a Cabinet Secretary in spite of your youth, then it is because he needs your services, needs them here in Sweden."

He didn't thank me for this compliment but continued chewing his moustache. But then he raised his head abruptly. "I ask Your Royal Highness not to go. I implore Your Highness!"

"The matter was settled weeks ago, Count Brahe. And I believe I am doing right."

"But no, Your Highness. I implore you once more to postpone your departure. The time does not seem to me——" He stopped, ran his fingers through his hair and then jerked out: "I am certain that the time you have chosen is wrong."

"The time is wrong? I don't understand you."

He turned his head away. "A letter came from the Tsar. More than that I cannot say."

"Then don't say it. As His Highness's Secretary you must not mention his correspondence. But I'm glad that the Tsar has written. The Crown Prince greatly values a good understanding with him, and I hope that it was a friendly letter."

"Too friendly."

I could make nothing of young Brahe's behaviour. What did my departure have to do with the Tsar?

"The Tsar has offered the Crown Prince a token of his friendship," said Brahe in despair, and he continued without looking at me: "The Tsar began his letter with the words 'My dear Cousin,' great sign of friendship, that."

Yes, a very great sign indeed, the Tsar addressing the former Sergeant Bernadotte as his cousin. I smiled and said: "That means a lot for Sweden."

"It is a question of the alliance, and we have to decide now either for Napoleon or for Russia. Both proposed an alliance to us. And that is why the Tsar wrote 'My dear Cousin, if it can be of any assistance in strengthening your personal position in Sweden I offer you——'"

"Finland, isn't it?"

"No, he says nothing about Finland. 'If it can be of any assistance in strengthening your personal position I offer you entry into my family.'" Count Brahe's shoulders seemed to sag as if under a heavy burden.

I stared at him uncomprehending. "What does it mean? Does the Tsar, too, want to adopt us?"

"The Tsar speaks only about—His Highness." At last he turned his face back to me. It had a tortured look about it. "There are other possibilities, Your Highness, for bringing about an entry into a family." Then I understood what he meant.

Oh, yes, there were other possibilities. Napoleon married his stepson to a Bavarian Princess and he himself is the son-in-law of the Emperor of Austria, and therefore related to the Hapsburgs. All one had to do was to marry a Princess. It was very simple indeed. A Government measure, a document of State such as the one that Josephine had had to read out. . . . And before my mind's eye I saw Josephine screaming, Josephine moaning with pain on her bed.

"That would indeed secure the position of His Highness," I said in a toneless voice.

"It would not, not with us in Sweden. The Tsar has taken Finland away from us, and we cannot get over this loss so quickly.

But, Your Highness, with the rest of Europe it would greatly enhance his position."

Josephine came back to my mind. But Josephine had not given him a son, had she?

"And therefore," Count Brahe concluded, "I should like to point out that this is not a favourable time for Your Highness's departure."

"Yes, it is, Count Brahe. Now even more so. One day you will understand." I gave him my hand. "I ask you very sincerely to stand loyally by my husband. We have the feeling that here they grudge us our French friends and servants. For that reason Colonel Villatte, my husband's oldest and most faithful adjutant, is returning with me to Paris. Try to take his place, Count, my husband will be very lonely. I shall see you to-morrow."

I didn't return to the ballroom immediately. Instead I walked slowly down the endless park as if in a daze. It was to this palace, to this park, that Gustavus IV had been brought as a captive after his enforced resignation. Here, in the alleys and avenues, he ran up and down with his warders running behind him, talking to himself and the lime trees in his despair and madness. And there, by the Chinese pavilion, where in his young days he used to compose his elegies, his mother would wait for him every day, the mother of a madman, the widow of a murdered man, Sophia Magdalena.

The wind of summer soughed gently in the leaves. I noticed a shadow, and then I saw that the shadow was moving towards me. I screamed, I wanted to run away but stood rooted to the spot. Immediately in front of me on the pebble path in the pale light of the moon stood the Dowager Queen in her black dress.

"I am sorry if I frightened you," she said.

"You—you were waiting here for me, Madame?" I felt ashamed because the wild beating of my heart hardly allowed me to speak.

"No, I could not know that you prefer a walk to dancing, Madame," said the flat voice. "I myself always go for a walk on fine summer nights. I do not sleep well, Madame. And this park brings back many memories."

I could hardly find an answer to that. Her son and grandson had been banished, my husband and my son had been called to their place. "I am saying good-bye to these avenues which I hardly know. I am returning to France to-morrow morning." I was glad to have found something to say.

"I did not expect ever to be able to speak to you alone. I am glad of this opportunity."

We walked along side by side. I had lost my fear of her, an old lady in black clothes. The air was full of the scent of the limes.

"I ponder often over your departure. I believe I am the only one who knows your reasons," she said.

"It's better not to talk about it," I said, and walked a bit faster. At that she reached for my arm, and the unexpected touch frightened me so much that I shrank back.

"But, my child, are you afraid of me?" Her voice had gained an unsuspected depth and sounded full of an irredeemable sadness. We stopped.

"Of course not, that is—yes. I am afraid of you, Madame."

"Of me, a sick, lonely woman?"

I nodded. "Because you hate me like all the other ladies of your family. I disturb you, I don't belong here—there's no sense in talking about it. It doesn't alter the facts. I do understand you very well, Madame. You and I attempt to do exactly the same thing."

"Do please explain what you mean by that."

I felt tears rising in my throat. This last evening with all its misery made me cry. But only one short sob came out, then I had myself under control again. "You are staying in Sweden, Madame, in order to remind everybody by your presence of your son and grandson. As long as you are here it will be impossible to forget the last Vasas. Perhaps you would have preferred to live in Switzerland with your son, who is said to live in very modest circumstances. Perhaps you would prefer to keep house for him and darn his socks instead of doing embroidery in Her Majesty's drawing-room." I lowered my voice. "But you're staying, Madame, because you are the mother of an exiled King and serve his interests by staying here. Am I right, Madame?"

She didn't stir, but stood there, gaunt and upright, a black shadow in the green twilight. "You are right," she said. "And you, Madame, why are you leaving?"

"Because by leaving I best serve the interests of the future King."

A long silence followed. At last she said: "That was exactly what I thought." A few bars of guitar music floated through the park, and the voice of Miss Koskull singing came to us for a moment. "Are you sure that your leaving would also serve your own interests?" she asked.

"Quite sure, Madame. I am thinking of the distant future and of King Oscar I," I said. Then I bowed deeply to her and went back to the castle.

It is two o'clock in the morning. The birds have just begun to twitter in the park. Somewhere here in this castle there lives an old woman who can't find sleep. Perhaps she is still wandering about in the park. She is staying, I am leaving. . . .

I have described the last evening. There's nothing more to add to it. But still, I can't escape my thoughts. Has the Tsar any daughters? Or sisters? For heaven's sake, I am seeing ghosts again.

My door opens very, very gently. Are there any ghosts walking about the castle? I could shout for help, but perhaps I am wrong. No, the door is really opening, I force myself to go on writing——

Jean-Baptiste!

In the coach during the journey from SWEDEN to FRANCE.
The end of June 1811.

MY passport is made out in the name of Countess of Gothland. Gothland is a big Swedish island. I don't know it at all. The Queen thought of it for my title. Under no circumstances was she going to allow her dear daughter, the Crown Princess, to travel through Europe in too modest a style. But on the other hand no attention was to be drawn to the fact that Desideria, the allegedly longed-for one, after a few months in her new home was already on her way back. Hence the disguise.

The Queen came to see me off. Oscar cried inconsolably but tried to hide his tears. The Queen put her hand on his shoulder; the boy, however, shook it off.

"Promise me, Madame, that you will see to it that the boy goes to bed every evening at nine o'clock," I asked her.

"I had a letter the other day from Madame de Staël. She makes some very sensible and progressive suggestions for the Prince's education," said Jean-Baptiste.

"Oh, that woman!" I murmured, and repeated, " At any rate, bed at nine o'clock!" I looked at Jean-Baptiste for the last time for nobody knows how many weeks to come. So many intelligent and educated women around him, perhaps even a Russian Grand Duchess. . . .

Jean-Baptiste put my hands to his lips. "Count Rosen will be at your side whatever happens."

Count Rosen, Count Brahe's best friend, clicked his heels. He is my new adjutant, a young man with gleaming fair hair and the adjutant's sash around his waist. Count Brahe came, but we didn't have any more conversation with each other.

"I wish you a very good journey, Madame," said the Queen, who all at once looked old. She seemed not to have slept well. The pouches under her pale eyes were swollen. Was there anybody at all who had slept well last night?

Oh yes, the Countess Lewenhaupt had! She was positively beaming now that she no longer had to be lady-in-waiting to a silk merchant's daughter. Miss Koskull, too, looked fresh and blooming, well made-up and very sure of triumph. No doubt, she saw possibilities. . . .

At the last minute everybody crowded round me so eagerly that they pushed Oscar aside. But he elbowed his way back to me. He is almost as tall as I am now, which is not saying very much. All the same, he really is tall for his age.

I took him into my arms. "May God protect you, darling!" His hair gave out a fresh fragrance, the fragrance of sun and lime blossom. He must have been out riding this morning.

"Mama, can't you stay? It is so beautiful here!"

How good that he found it beautiful here, how good!

I entered the carriage. Jean-Baptiste propped a cushion up behind my back, and Madame La Flotte took her seat next to me. Villatte and Count Rosen joined us in our coach, Marie and Yvette travelled in a second one. As the carriage started to move I bent forward and looked at the row of windows. I felt sure that at one of the windows on the first floor there would be a black figure standing. And there was! She stayed, I left.

"When we arrive in Plombières we won't have a single summer dress of the latest fashion," said Madame La Flotte. "We should go to Paris first and do some shopping there."

Fair-haired children were standing by the roadside, waving, and I waved back at them. Already I was longing for Oscar, already. . . .

PARIS. *January 1st*, 1812.

WHEN all the church bells of Paris were ringing in the New Year we were facing each other alone, Napoleon and I.

That surprising invitation came to me through Julie. "Their Majesties receive after midnight. But the family is asked for ten o'clock, and you are to come along with us at all costs," the Empress said."

When Julie told me this we were sitting as usual in the small drawing-room in the Rue d'Anjou where she tells me all her cares and worries. She seems contented with her life as the Queen of Spain whose husband has never managed to sit on his throne, contented with her life at the court in Paris where she finds the Empress a really majestic figure and the Empress's son, the blue-eyed and fair-haired King of Rome, a really adorable little baby. She couldn't understand at first why I didn't call at the Tuileries after my return. I didn't call, and I have been leading a very quiet life ever since, seeing only Julie and a few friends. That was why this invitation came as a surprise, and I couldn't rid myself of the feeling that it was an invitation for a purpose. But what purpose?

And so for the third time in my life I rode to the Tuileries with fear in my heart. The first time was the night I asked Napoleon in vain to spare the life of the Duc d'Enghien. The second time I went with Jean-Baptiste and Oscar before we went to Sweden.

Last night I wore my white and gold robe and the ear-rings from the Dowager Queen, and though I didn't feel cold, I had thrown Napoleon's sable round my shoulders. 'In Stockholm,' I thought, 'the temperature will be down to thirty degrees below freezing point.' I breathed deeply when I entered the palace. I felt at home among the dark-green liveries of the servants, the tapestries and the carpets with the bee pattern, bees, bees everywhere, exactly as he had told me that night. And there were bright lights everywhere, no half-darkness and no ghosts.

The whole family had foregathered in the Empress's salon. When I came in everybody rushed to greet me, a genuine Crown Princess now. Even Marie-Louise rose and came to meet me. She still wore pink, her eyes still looked as if they were made of china, but her smile was more effusive than ever. Her first question was about her 'dear cousin' the Queen of Sweden. Naturally a member of the Vasa family is nearer to the heart of a Hapsburg than all the Bonapartes of the world together.

I had to sit beside her on a very fragile sofa. Madame Letitia was there, too, and I was pleased to meet the old lady again, *Madame Mère* with Parisian curls and carefully manicured finger-nails. Polette, the Princess Borghese, more beautiful than ever, drank a lot, and I remembered that Julie had recently hinted at a mysterious illness Polette had contracted, a quite unmentionable illness. Of course I hadn't been able to imagine what kind of illness that might be. Then there was Joseph, too, smiling disagreeably when talking of the 'Bernadotte dynasty'.

It was past eleven o'clock and the Emperor had not yet

appeared. "His Majesty is still working," Marie-Louise explained. The champagne glasses were filled and Julie inquired when we would be shown the baby.

"At the beginning of the New Year," said Marie-Louise. "The Emperor wants to see it in with the boy in his arms."

At that moment Meneval, the Emperor's secretary, came. "His Majesty wants to speak to Your Royal Highness."

"Do you mean me?"

His face remained grave. "Your Royal Highness, the Crown Princess of Sweden."

Marie-Louise, talking to Julie, didn't seem to be surprised. I realised that she had invited me on the Emperor's order. The Bonapartes, however, fell silent.

Meneval took me to Napoleon's small study. The two former interviews had taken place in his big one. Napoleon looked up for a moment as we entered, said: "Take a seat, Madame," and then, very impolitely, continued with what he was doing. Meneval disappeared, I sat down and waited.

A file with many closely written sheets was lying in front of him. I thought I recognised the writing. Probably Alquier's despatches from Stockholm, I reflected. The clock on the mantelpiece kept ticking towards the New Year, and I sat and waited.

Suddenly I heard myself say: "There is no need, Sire, to intimidate me by keeping me waiting. I am timid by nature, and where you are concerned I am not very brave."

He still didn't look up but said: "Eugenie, Eugenie, one waits till the Emperor opens the conversation. Did Monsieur Montel not manage to teach you even that much etiquette?" Then he continued to read.

I studied his face. The mask of Cæsar was running to flesh now, the hair had thinned out. 'Strange,' I thought, 'this is the face I once loved.' It was a long time ago, but I remembered how I loved him. It was only the face I had forgotten.

My patience gave way. "Sire, you called me to examine me on questions of etiquette?"

"Among other things. I should like to know why you came back to France."

"On account of the cold climate, Sire."

He leant back, folding his arms across his chest, screwing up his mouth ironically. "Well, well, the cold climate. You were cold in spite of my sable fur?"

"In spite of your sable fur, Sire."

"And why did you not call at court? The wives of my Marshals are in the habit of calling on Her Majesty regularly."

"I am no longer the wife of one of your Marshals, Sire."

"Quite right. I very nearly forgot. We have to deal now with Her Royal Highness the Crown Princess Desideria of Sweden. But in that case, Madame, you should know that members of foreign royal families when they are visiting my capital usually ask for an audience. If only for politeness' sake, Madame!"

"I am not visiting here. I am here at home."

"Oh, I see, you are here at home." He rose slowly, came out from behind his desk and suddenly yelled at me: "And you think I accept that, do you? You are here at home, and your sister and the other ladies tell you every day what is going on at court. And you sit down and write it all to your husband. Do they think you so clever in Sweden that they sent you here as a spy?"

"No, on the contrary, I am so stupid that I had to return here."

He hadn't expected this answer. He had even held his breath to continue his yelling. Now he said in an ordinary voice: "What does that mean?"

"I am stupid, Sire, stupid, unpolitical, uneducated, and unfortunately I have not made a good impression on the Swedish court. And as it is very important that we, Jean-Baptiste, Oscar and I, become popular in Sweden I came back. It's all very simple."

"So simple that I do not believe you, Madame!" It sounded like the crack of a whip. He began pacing the room. "Perhaps I am mistaken, perhaps you are not here at Bernadotte's direction after all. In any case, Madame, the political situation is so precariously balanced that I must ask you to leave France."

I stared at him, disconcerted. Was he throwing me out? "I should like to stay here," I said in a low voice. "If I can't remain in Paris I should like to go to Marseilles."

"Tell me, Madame, has Bernadotte gone mad?" He threw this question at me out of the blue. Rummaging among the papers on his desk he pulled out a letter. The writing on it I recognised as Jean-Baptiste's. "I offered Bernadotte an alliance and his answer is that he is not one of my vassals!"

"I don't meddle in politics, Sire. And I don't know what that has to do with my staying here."

"Then let me tell you, Madame!" He banged his fist on the table, and I heard plaster drop from the ceiling. Now he was really infuriated. "Your Bernadotte dares to refuse an alliance with France! Why, do you think, did I offer him this alliance? Well, tell me!"

I kept silent.

"Not even you can be as stupid as all that, Madame. You are bound to know what everybody knows in all the drawing-rooms. The Tsar has raised the Continental Blockade and his Empire will soon cease to exist. The biggest army of all time will occupy Russia. The biggest army of all time . . ." The words seemed to intoxicate him. "On our side Sweden could reap immortal glory. It could regain its position as a great power. I offered Finland to Bernadotte, if he marches with us, Finland and the Hanseatic towns. Imagine that, Madame, Finland! And Bernadotte refuses! Bernadotte is not going to march! A French Marshal who is not taking part in this campaign!"

I looked at the clock. In a quarter of an hour the New Year would begin. "Sire, it will be midnight soon."

He didn't hear me. He was standing in front of the mirror by the fireplace staring at his own face. "Two hundred thousand Frenchmen, one hundred and fifty thousand Germans, eighty thousand Italians, sixty thousand Poles, apart from one hundred and ten thousand volunteers of other nations," he murmured. "The Grand Army of Napoleon I. The greatest army of all time. I am marching again."

Ten minutes to midnight. "Sire——" I began.

He swung round, his face distorted with fury: "And Bernadotte slights this army!"

I shook my head. "Sire, Jean-Baptiste is responsible for the well-being of Sweden. His measures serve the interests of Sweden and nothing else."

"Who is not for me is against me! Madame, if you do not leave France voluntarily I could have you arrested as a hostage."

I did not stir.

"It is rather late," he said suddenly, went quickly up to his desk and rang the bell. Meneval appeared at once. "Here, Meneval, despatch this at once by express messenger." Turning to me he said: "Do you know, Madame, what that was? An order to Marshal Davout. Davout and his troops will cross the frontiers and occupy Swedish Pomerania. What do you say now, Madame?"

"That you are trying to cover the left flank of your great army, Sire."

He laughed out loud. "Who taught you that sentence? Have you talked to any of my officers lately?"

"No, Jean-Baptiste told me that a long time ago."

His eyes grew narrow. "Is he thinking of defending Swedish Pomerania? It would be amusing to see him fighting Davout."

"Amusing?" I remembered the battlefields, the long rows

of miserable little mounds with their wooden crosses blown over by the wind. And that he thought amusing. . . .

"You realise, Madame, don't you, that I could have you arrested as a hostage in order to force the Swedish Government into an alliance?"

I smiled. "My fate would not influence in the least the decisions of the Swedish Government. But my arrest would prove to the Swedes that I am ready to suffer for my new country. Are you really going to make a martyr out of me, Sire?"

The Emperor bit his lips. 'Even a fool can stumble on to the right answer at times,' I thought. 'Napoleon was certainly not going to turn Madame Bernadotte into a Swedish national heroine. . . .'

He shrugged his shoulders. "We shall force our friendship on nobody. We are accustomed to be wooed for it."

It was three minutes to midnight.

"I expect you to persuade your husband to ask for our friendship." Putting his hand on the door handle he added: "If only for your own sake, Madame!"

He had an air of malice about him and I looked at him questioningly. At this moment the church bells rang out. Their chimes drowned my question and his answer. He let go of the handle and stared in front of him, listening to the bells like someone mesmerised. When they had finished he murmured: "An important year in the history of France has opened." I turned the handle and we went out.

In the big study adjutants and lords-in-waiting were assembled. "We must hurry. Her Majesty is expecting us," the Emperor said, and broke into a run. His gentlemen ran after him with clanking spurs. I followed slowly with Meneval, through the empty rooms.

"Did you send off the order?" I asked him.

He nodded.

"The Emperor violates the neutrality of a country. The first action of the New Year," I said.

"No, Your Highness," he corrected, "the last one of the old."

When I got back to the salon of the Empress I saw the little King of Rome for the first time. The Emperor was holding him and he cried enough to move a heart of stone. He was dressed in a lace shirt and the broad sash of an order. "Sashes instead of nappies, I must say!" lamented Madame Letitia. The Emperor with the Empress at his side tried to soothe his screaming son and tickled him tenderly. But the crush of foreign diplomats and giggling ladies round him made him more frightened than ever. Catching sight of me, Napoleon came over to me with his fleshy face beaming down on his yelling son. Without thinking what I was doing I held out my arms and took the baby from him. Madame de Montesquieu, the child's aristocratic nanny, was on the scene at once, but I held on to the child. He was wet under the shirt. I tickled his fair hair on the nape of his neck, he stopped crying and looked at me timidly. I pressed him to me, and my thoughts strayed across Europe to Oscar. 'Oscar,' I thought, 'my Oscar. . . .' I kissed the fair silky hair of the little boy and handed him back to his nurse. Someone shouted "To the health of His Majesty the King of Rome!" His Little Majesty was at this moment carried out of the room.

The Emperor and the Empress were in excellent mood and conversed—what did the Swedish Queen call it? 'graciously'—and conversed most graciously with their guests.

"Your Highness will see, the Crown Prince is going to link up with Russia. And the Crown Prince is right!" Did I dream these words or did someone whisper them into my ear? I looked round and saw Talleyrand limping away from me.

I wanted to go home, I was tired. But now the Emperor came towards me, the Empress on his arm. 'If only she didn't wear pink, with those pink cheeks of hers,' I thought.

"And here is my hostage, my beautiful little hostage," he said amiably. The groups around us broke into cultured laughter. "But, ladies and gentlemen," he said in irritation, because he sometimes dislikes people to laugh prematurely at his jokes, "you don't know what the point is. Besides, I fear Her Royal Highness will not feel like laughing. Marshal Davout has regrettably been forced to occupy a part of the Nordic motherland of Her Highness."

There was dead silence everywhere.

"I suppose the Tsar has more to offer than I have, Madame. I am told he is even offering the hand of a Grand Duchess. Can you imagine that this would attract our former Marshal?"

"Marriage to a member of an old princely family is always attractive to a man of middle-class origin," I said slowly. The faces around me grew icy with terror.

"No doubt," the Emperor smiled. "But an attraction like that could endanger your own position in Sweden, Madame. Therefore I advise you as an old friend to write to Bernadotte and persuade him to an alliance with France. In the interests of your own future, Madame!"

"My future is assured, Sire." I bowed deeply. "At least —as mother of the future King."

Astonishment covered his face. When he had recovered he thundered at me: "Madame, I do not want to see you at court again before the Swedish-French alliance has been concluded." He passed on with Marie-Louise.

Marie was waiting for me at home. Yvette and the other girls had the evening off to celebrate New Year's Eve. Marie undid the ear-rings and opened the gold clasps of the robe on my shoulders.

We had a glass of wine. "Your health, Marie. The Emperor told me he has massed the biggest army of all time and he also told me I am to write to Jean-Baptiste about an alliance. Could you tell me, Marie, how I managed to get all mixed up with world history?"

"Look, if you hadn't fallen asleep in the *Maison Commune* in your young days, that gentleman Joseph Bonaparte would not have had to wake you. If you hadn't taken it into your head that he and Julie——"

"Yes, and if I hadn't been burning with curiosity about his brother, the little General! How shabby he looked in his worn-out uniform!"

I propped my elbows on the dressing-table and closed my eyes. 'Curiosity,' I thought, 'pure unadulterated curiosity got me into all this.' But the way over Napoleon led to Jean-Baptiste. And I had been very happy with Jean-Baptiste.

"Eugenie," Marie said cautiously, "when are you travelling to Stockholm again?"

'If I hurry,' I thought, 'I might just be in time to celebrate my husband's engagement to a Russian Grand Duchess.' I felt desperate and didn't say anything.

"A happy New Year!" Marie said at last.

A happy New Year? It had only just begun, but I had an idea that it would be anything but happy.

PARIS. *April* 1812.

PIERRE, my Marie's son, arrived as a complete surprise to everybody. He had volunteered to join the biggest army of all time. Up till now I had gladly paid the 8,000 francs every year necessary to exempt him from conscription—gladly, because I've always had a bad conscience about him, as Marie had had him brought up away from her so that she could come as a nurse to our house. Pierre, a sinewy, tall fellow with a sun-tanned, cheerful face and Marie's dark eyes, was in a brand-new uniform.

Marie was stunned by his arrival. Her bony hands kept stroking his arms. "But why?" she kept asking, "why? You were so satisfied with the bailiff's job Her Highness got you."

Pierre showed his gleaming teeth. "Mama, one's got to be in on it, march with the Grand Army, overthrow Russia, occupy Moscow! The Emperor's called us to arms to unite Europe. Just think of all the chances, Mama! You can——"

"You can what?" Marie asked bitterly.

"Become a General, a Marshal, a Prince, a King and God knows what!" The words tumbled out of him, the enthusiastic volunteer about to march with the Grand Army, and, like all the enthusiasts of all the grand armies of all time, he wanted his rifle garlanded with roses. So Marie picked our roses, and we put roses in all the buttonholes of his tunic, wound them round the hilt of his bayonet and stuck one red bud into his rifle barrel.

He stood to attention and saluted as he left. "Come back safely, Pierre!" I said.

Marie took him to the door. When she came back the furrows in her face had deepened even more. She took a rag and began to polish the silver candlesticks with passionate intensity.

A regiment with drums beating was marching past just then. Villatte had joined us in the room. Since the Grand Army had begun to march a strange restlessness had come over him.

I listened to the regimental music down in the street, and thought how empty it sounded, how tinny, all drums and trumpets and nothing else. How long ago it was that I had last heard the Marseillaise without any musical accompaniment, just sung, by dock workers, bank clerks and tradesmen! Now a thousand trumpets blare out the tune whenever Napoleon shows himself. . . .

Count Rosen entered holding a despatch in his hand and saying something. I couldn't hear him because of the noise of the trumpets outside. We turned away from the window.

"I have very important news for Your Highness. On April 5th Sweden concluded an alliance with Russia."

"Colonel Villatte!" My voice went completely flat as I called Jean-Baptiste's old colleague, his loyal friend, his most trusted collaborator, our friend Villatte. . . .

"Your Highness?"

"We have just been told that Sweden and Russia have made an alliance." I couldn't turn to face him but I had to go on. "You are a French citizen and a French officer, and I suppose that this agreement with the enemies of France will make your stay in my house impossible. When we left you asked your regiment to grant you leave to make it possible for you to accompany us and to assist me. I am asking you now to consider yourself free from all obligations towards me."

It hurt, it hurt badly to have to say that.

"But, Your Highness, I—I cannot possibly leave you now," said Villatte. I bit my lips, then looked towards the fair-haired Count Rosen. "I shall not be alone."

The Count stared past me into a corner. Did he realise that I was saying good-bye to our best friend? "Count Rosen has been appointed my personal adjutant. He will protect me if necessary." I didn't mind Villatte seeing the tears running down my cheeks. I gave him both my hands. "Good-bye, Colonel Villatte."

"Has there been no letter from the Marshal, I mean from His Highness?"

"No. I received the news through the Swedish Embassy."

He looked helpless. "I don't really know——"

"But I know what you feel. You must either ask for your discharge from the French Army like Jean-Baptiste or——" I pointed towards the window through which came the sound of marching boots—"or march, Colonel Villatte."

"Oh no, not march," Villatte said indignantly, "ride!"

I smiled through my tears. "Ride, Villatte, ride with God! And come back safely."

PARIS.
The middle of September 1812.

THANK God for my diary! I should go mad if I hadn't that to write in. In all this big city I have no one now to whom to confide my thoughts, not even Julie, the wife of a Bonaparte. Nobody is left, strangely enough, but Count Rosen, who, Swedish to the core, cannot understand how the new Crown Prince could have made an alliance with the old arch-enemy of his country, Russia.

Count Talleyrand, Prince of Benevento and adviser to the Ministry of Foreign Affairs, and Fouché, Duke of Otranto and former Minister of Police, were here and only left a few hours ago. They came separately, and met by chance in my drawing-room. Talleyrand arrived first. I am not used to having visitors now. My friends are intoxicated by the Emperor's victories in Russia and avoid my house.

Talleyrand was waiting in the drawing-room, studying the portrait of Napoleon as First Consul through half-closed eyes. Before I could introduce Count Rosen to him the Duke of Otranto was announced.

"I don't understand it!" I exclaimed.

Talleyrand arched his eyebrows. "I beg your pardon?"

"It's such a long time since I had any visitors at all," I said, confused. "Show the Duke in."

Fouché was disagreeably surprised to find Talleyrand there. He lisped, "I am glad to see Your Highness in company. I was afraid Your Highness would be very lonely."

"I was very lonely till this moment." I sat down under the portrait of the First Consul, the gentlemen took their seats opposite me. Yvette brought in tea, and as Count Rosen handed the teacups round I explained to him that the second visitor was France's famous Minister of Police who had retired to his estates for reasons of health.

We talked about the Russian campaign and I remarked that the church bells had been ringing almost continuously since the capture of Smolensk.

"Oh yes, Smolensk," said Talleyrand, opening his eyes fully at last to examine Napoleon's picture more closely still, "oh yes, Smolensk. By the way, the bells are going to ring again in half an hour's time, Your Highness."

"You don't say so, Your Excellency!" Fouché exclaimed.

Talleyrand smiled. "Does that surprise you? After all, the Emperor is leading the greatest army of all time against the Tsar. So, as a matter of course, the bells are going to ring again soon. Does it upset you, Your Highness?"

"Of course not. On the contrary, I am, after all——" I broke off. I was going to say 'I am a Frenchwoman after all', but I am not a Frenchwoman any longer and my husband had concluded a pact of friendship with Russia.

"Do you believe the Emperor will win the war?" Talleyrand asked.

"He has never lost a war yet," I answered.

There was a curious pause, Fouché regarding me intently whilst Talleyrand drank the really excellent tea slowly and with great enjoyment. "The Tsar has asked for advice," he said at last, putting down his cup.

"The Tsar will sue for peace," I said, bored.

Talleyrand smiled. "That was what the Emperor expected after the victory of Smolensk. But the courier who arrived in

370

Paris an hour ago with the news of the victory at Borodino knows nothing about peace negotiations. And that in spite of the fact that this latest victory opens the road to Moscow."

"I suppose that means the end of the Russian campaign, doesn't it? Have a piece of marzipan, Excellency."

"Has Your Highness heard from His Royal Highness the Crown Prince lately?" asked Fouché.

I laughed. "Oh yes, I forgot, you no longer supervise my correspondence. Your successor would be able to tell you that I haven't heard from Jean-Baptiste for a fortnight. But Oscar has written. He is well, he——" I stopped. It would bore the gentlemen to be told about my son.

"The Swedish Crown Prince has been away from home," said Fouché, never taking his eyes off me.

Away from home? I looked at them in astonishment, and so did Count Rosen.

"His Royal Highness was in Åbo," Fouché continued.

Count Rosen gave a start. "Åbo? Where is Åbo?" I asked him.

"In Finland, Your Highness." His voice was hoarse.

Finland again! "Finland is occupied by the Russians, isn't it?"

Talleyrand drank his second cup, and Fouché said with obvious enjoyment of the situation: "The Tsar had asked the Swedish Crown Prince to meet him in Åbo."

"Say that again, very slowly," I asked.

"The Tsar had asked the Swedish Crown Prince to meet him in Åbo."

"But what does the Tsar want of Jean-Baptiste?"

"Advice," said Talleyrand in a bored voice. "A former Marshal of France who knows the Emperor's tactics thoroughly is an excellent counsellor in a situation like the present one."

"And as a result of the advice of the Crown Prince of Sweden the Tsar is not sending negotiators to the Emperor but letting our army continue to advance," said Fouché. The note of enjoyment had gone out of his voice. It sounded quite flat now.

Talleyrand looked at his watch. "The church bells will start ringing at any moment to proclaim the victory of Borodino. Our troops will be in Moscow in a few days."

"Has he promised him Finland?" Count Rosen burst out.

"Who was to promise Finland to whom?" asked Fouché.

"Finland? What makes you say that, Count?" Talleyrand said.

I tried to explain. "Sweden is still hoping to get Finland back.

371

Finland is very dear to the hearts of the—I mean to the hearts of my compatriots."

"Is it also dear to the heart of your husband, Your Highness?" Talleyrand pursued.

"Jean-Baptiste thinks that the Tsar would on no account renounce Finland. But he very much wants to unite Sweden and Norway."

Talleyrand nodded slowly. "My informant hinted at a promise made by the Tsar to the Swedish Crown Prince to support the union of Sweden and Norway. Of course, after the end of the war."

"But isn't the war finished once the Emperor has entered Moscow?"

Talleyrand shrugged his shoulders. "I do not know what kind of advice your husband gave to the Tsar."

There was another curiously heavy pause. Fouché took another piece of marzipan and smacked his lips.

"But that advice which His Royal Highness is supposed to have given to the Tsar——" Count Rosen began.

Fouché grinned. "The French Army enters villages burned by their inhabitants. The French Army finds nothing but burnt-out stores. The French Army marches from victory to victory and—starves. The Emperor is forced to bring up supplies from his base, and he had not bargained for that. Nor had he bargained for the flank attacks of the Cossacks, who never come out into the open for a pitched battle. But the Emperor hopes to find all the supplies he needs in Moscow, a rich and well-provisioned town where he is going into winter quarters with his Army. You see, everything depends on the capture of Moscow."

"Do you doubt its capture?" asked Count Rosen.

"The Prince of Benevento said a moment ago that the church bells are going to ring at any moment for the victory of Borodino. The road to Moscow is clear. The Emperor will most likely be in the Kremlin the day after to-morrow, dear Count," Fouché said, still grinning.

A great fear began to rise in me and choke me. In despair I looked at the two gentlemen. "Please will you tell me candidly what you have come for?"

"I have been wanting to call on Your Highness for a long time," said Fouché. "And since I have learnt about the important part the Crown Prince of Sweden is playing in this gigantic conflict it is my heartfelt need to assure Your Highness of my sympathy. A sympathy of many years' standing, if I may say so."

'Oh yes, of many years' standing as Napoleon's spy,' I thought.

"I don't understand you," I said, and looked at Talleyrand.

"Is it so difficult to see through a former teacher of mathematics?" said Talleyrand. "Wars are like equations. Even in wars one has to calculate with unknown quantities, and in this war the unknown quantity is a person who, since the meeting with the Tsar, is no longer—unknown. The Swedish Crown Prince has intervened, Madame!"

"And what advantage does this intervention hold for Sweden? Instead of armed neutrality there is a pact with Russia!" Count Rosen exclaimed passionately.

"I am afraid Sweden's armed neutrality does not impress the Emperor greatly. He has occupied Swedish Pomerania. You are not dissatisfied with the policy of your Crown Prince, young man, are you?" Talleyrand said amiably.

But my blond young Count didn't give in so easily. "The Russians have one hundred and forty thousand men under arms, and Napoleon——"

"Nearly half a million," Talleyrand confirmed. "But a Russian winter without proper quarters will defeat the biggest and the best army, young man."

Now I understood. No proper quarters! I certainly understood. Oh my God. . . .

At this moment Madame La Flotte flung the door open and shouted: "A new victory! We have won the battle of Borodino!"

None of us moved. The sea of chimes seemed to drown me. 'Napoleon wants to winter in Moscow,' I thought. 'What kind of advice did Jean-Baptiste give to the Tsar? Fouché and Talleyrand have spies in all the camps, they'll always be on the right side at the right moment. Their visit to-day meant that Napoleon was going to lose the war, would lose it somehow sometime whilst the victory bells were still ringing out over Paris. Jean-Baptiste had intervened and assured its freedom to a small country in the North. But meanwhile Marie's Pierre might freeze and Colonel Villatte bleed to death.'

Talleyrand was the first to take his leave. Fouché, however, sat on, eating marzipan, smacking his lips and looking very self-satisfied. With the latest victory? Or with himself for having fallen into disgrace at a convenient juncture?

He stayed till the bells had fallen silent. "The welfare of the French people is at stake," he announced, "and the people want peace. The Swedish Crown Prince and I have the same aim— peace!" He bent over my hand, but his lips were sticky and I withdrew my hand quickly.

I went out into the garden and sat on the bench. All the fear I had felt inside the house came back, redoubled. In my restlessness and anxiety I asked for my carriage, and when I went out to it I found Count Rosen waiting to open the carriage door for me. I keep forgetting that I have a lord-in-waiting around me all the time. I should have preferred to be alone now.

We drove along the banks of the Seine. Rosen was talking to me. I didn't pay any attention till he asked me about Fouché's title. He went on to tell me details Fouché had related to him about Jean-Baptiste's meeting with the Tsar in Åbo. A British emissary had taken part in it at one time, and it was rumoured that His Royal Highness was trying to engineer an alliance of decisive importance between Britain and Russia to which even Austria might secretly——

"But the Austrian Emperor is Napoleon's father-in-law," I argued.

"That means nothing, Your Highness. Napoleon forced him into this relationship. No Hapsburg would ever have voluntarily accepted this *parvenu* into his family."

The carriage rolled slowly past the towers of Notre-Dame, black against the deep blue of the evening. I told the Count about my part in the coronation of Napoleon and that I had carried a velvet cushion with a lace handkerchief on it for the beautiful Josephine. "I shall introduce you to the Empress Josephine, Count," I said. The idea had come to me suddenly. I would show this little Count the most beautiful woman in Paris, who, having cried for two days and two nights after the divorce, had become her old self again, the best-made-up woman in Paris. I would show her to him and ask her at the same time how to use make-up. If the Swedes were meant to have a *parvenu* Crown Princess they should at any rate have a beautiful one. . . .

As soon as we got home I started writing my diary. Then Marie came and asked if Colonel Villatte had written and said anything about Pierre.

I shook my head.

"After this last victory the Tsar will sue for peace," said Marie contentedly, "and Pierre will be back here before winter comes." She knelt down before me and took off my shoes. There are many white strands in her hair, her hands are coarse from the work she has had to do all through her life, and every penny she has earned she has sent to Pierre. And now Pierre was marching towards Moscow. Jean-Baptiste, what was going to happen to Pierre in Moscow?

"Sleep well, Eugenie, sweet dreams!"

"Thank you, Marie. Good-night!" Exactly as it was in my childhood days.

And who was putting Oscar to bed at this moment? One, two or even three adjutants or lords-in-waiting?

PARIS, *a fortnight later.*

ONCE again I was the black sheep of the family!

Julie and Joseph came back from Mortefontaine to Paris and gave a banquet to celebrate the entry of Napoleon into Moscow. They asked me too, but I didn't want to go and wrote to Julie that I had a cold. The very next day she was on my doorstep.

"I very much want you to come," she said. "People talk so much about you and Jean-Baptiste. Of course, your husband ought to have marched with the Emperor to Russia. Then they would have had to stop spreading rumours about Jean-Baptiste being allied to the Tsar. I want this malicious talk——"

"Julie, Jean-Baptiste *is* allied to the Tsar."

Flabbergasted, Julie stared at me. "Do you mean to say that it is all true, what people say?"

"I don't know what people say. Jean-Baptiste had a meeting with the Tsar and gave him advice."

Julie moaned and shook her head in despair. "Désirée, you really are the black sheep of the family!"

I had been called something like that before, when I asked Joseph and Napoleon Bonaparte to visit us in Marseilles. That was how it all began . . . "Tell me, Julie, which family do you mean?"

"The Bonapartes, of course."

"But I'm no Bonaparte."

"You are the sister-in-law of the Emperor's eldest brother."

"Among other things, my dear, among other things. Above all, I am a Bernadotte, the first Bernadotte, if you consider us as a dynasty."

"If you don't come they'll talk even more about you and they'll know that Jean-Baptiste Bernadotte allied himself secretly to the Tsar."

"But, Julie, it's no secret at all. Only the French papers mustn't mention it."

"But Joseph has expressly demanded your presence. Don't make trouble for me, Désirée."

I hadn't seen Julie all through last summer. Her face looked aged and miserable. A tenderness arose in me for my old Julie, now a careworn, deeply disappointed woman. Perhaps she had heard about Joseph's amorous *affaires*, perhaps he treated her badly because he himself gets more and more embittered, knowing that he owes everything to Napoleon. Perhaps she felt that Joseph had never really loved her and only married her for her dowry, a dowry which means nothing now to Joseph, who, through the money he made in property speculations and crown estates, is a very rich man. 'Why then,' I thought, 'does she not leave him? Out of love? Sense of duty? Obstinacy?'

"If I can do you a service in that way I shall come," I said.

She pressed her hand against her forehead. "I've got these dreadful headaches again. Yes, please come. Joseph wants to prove, through your presence, to the whole of Paris that Sweden is still neutral. The Empress is coming too and all the diplomatic corps."

"I shall bring Count Rosen, my Swedish adjutant."

"Your what? Oh, of course. Yes, do bring him, We're always short of men, with everybody in the Army. I am so anxious about this banquet. I only hope everything will go all right." Then she left.

The tall bronze candelabra in the Elysée Palace shone brightly. I heard people talking behind my back and felt their eyes following me as I passed. But the presence of young Count Rosen reassured me and made me ignore whispers and glances. At the entry of the Empress the orchestra played the Marseillaise. Everybody present bowed deeply. I, however, as the member of a reigning house, bowed less deeply than the rest.

The Empress—in pink, as ever—stopped and talked to me in her vague impersonal manner about the new Austrian Ambassador to Stockholm, a Count Neipperg, with whom she said she had danced the waltz at her one and only court ball before she married. I could only say that Count Neipberg must have arrived after my departure from Stockholm. Marie-Louise went on to talk graciously to someone else.

At midnight the trumpets once more blared out the Marseillaise. Joseph stepped to the place beside the Empress and holding up his champagne glass he said: "On the 15th of September His Majesty the Emperor entered Moscow at the head of the most glorious army of all time and took up residence in the Kremlin, the palace of the Tsar. Our victorious Army will spend the winter in the capital of our conquered enemy. *Vive l'Empereur!*"

I was emptying my glass slowly when Talleyrand appeared

before me. "Has Your Highness been forced to attend?" he inquired, pointing in Joseph's direction.

I shrugged my shoulders. "Whether I'm here or not is of no importance, Excellency. I know nothing of politics."

"It is strange that Fate should choose you of all people to play such a significant part, Your Highness."

"What do you mean by that?" I asked, terrified.

"Perhaps one of these days I shall turn to you with a request of the greatest importance, Your Highness. Perhaps you will grant it. I shall address this request to you in the name of France."

"Would you mind telling me what you are talking about?"

"Your Highness, I am very much in love. Don't misunderstand me, please, I am in love with France, Your Highness, with—our France." He took a sip from his glass of champagne and continued. "I mentioned to Your Highness a short time ago that the Emperor is battling no longer against an unknown quantity but a very well-known one, a very well-known friend of ours. You remember, Highness, don't you? Well, to-night we are celebrating the Emperor's entry into Msocow, where the Grand Army is taking up its winter quarters. Do you think, Your Highness, that that is a surprise to our well-known friend?"

My hand clutched the stem of the glass I was holding.

"My brother should be very comfortable in the Kremlin. The Tsar's residence is supposed to be furnished with oriental luxury," someone said close by. It was Joseph. "Magnificent," he continued, "that my brother managed to finish the campaign so quickly. Now our troops can stay the winter in Moscow."

But Talleyrand shook his head. "I am afraid I cannot share Your Majesty's optimism. A courier arrived half an hour ago with the news that Moscow is burning, has been burning for the last fortnight, including the Kremlin."

In the flickering candlelight Joseph's face looked green, his eyes were wide open, his mouth gaped with dread. Talleyrand, on the other hand, had his eyes half closed, unconcerned and unmoved as if he had been expecting for a long time this news which only arrived half an hour ago.

Moscow was burning, had been burning for a fortnight!

"How did it happen?" Joseph asked in a hoarse voice.

"Arson, no doubt. It broke out in different parts of the town at the same time. Our troops have been trying to cope with it in vain. Every time they thought they had the fire under control it started again in a different part of the city. The population is suffering terribly."

"And our troops?"

"Will have to retreat."

"But the Emperor told me that under no circumstances whatever could he march his troops through the Russian steppe during the winter months. He counts on Moscow for his winter quarters."

"I am only reporting the courier's message. The Emperor cannot billet his troops in Moscow because Moscow has been burning for the last fortnight." Talleyrand raised his glass towards Joseph. "Please act as if nothing had happened, Your Majesty. The Emperor does not want the news to become known for the time being. *Vive l'Empereur!*"

"*Vive l'Empereur!*" Joseph repeated in a voice which had lost all colour.

"Your Highness?" Talleyrand raised his glass towards me, too. But I stood paralysed. I saw the Empress dancing with a gouty old gentleman, saw Joseph wiping beads of perspiration from his forehead, and said: "Good-night, Joseph. Give my love to Julie. Good-night, Excellency." And then I left, entirely against all etiquette, before the Empress had left herself. But what did I care about etiquette? I was dreadfully tired, and dreadfully troubled.

"It was an unforgettable, a splendid ball," said the young Swedish Count on the way home.

Quite! Unforgettable. . . . "Do you know Moscow, Count Rosen?"

"No, Highness. Why?"

"Because Moscow is burning, Count."

"The advice His Royal Highness in Åbo——"

"Don't let's talk any more, please. I am very tired."

And Talleyrand's 'request of the greatest importance', what could it be? When would it be?

PARIS. *December 16th*, 1812.

JOSEPHINE at Malmaison showed me how to use make-up and powder in her own way and how to pluck my eyebrows in order to make my eyes appear much bigger. In the intervals of beauty treatment we made bandages for the wounded in the Russian campaign. Then, quite by chance, as Josephine was doing my eyebrows, I caught sight of this morning's issue of the *Moniteur*, and in it I read Napoleon's 29th Bulletin, the 29th Bulletin which told the world that the Grand Army was frozen, starved to death and buried in the snow wastes of Russia, that the Grand Army had ceased to exist.

"Have you seen that, Madame?" I asked Josephine, holding the paper out to her.

"Of course. Bonaparte's first communiqué for weeks. It only confirms what we feared: he has lost the war with Russia. I suppose he'll soon be back in Paris. Have you ever tried to use henna when you wash your hair? Your dark hair would have an auburn glint in candlelight. It would suit you, Désirée."

" 'This Army,' " I read, " 'which was still such a splendid body on the sixth, was quite different on the fourteenth. It had no longer any cavalry, any artillery, any transport. The enemy realised the calamity that had befallen the French Army and tried to put it to good account. He surrounded the columns with his Cossacks . . .' " And the bulletin went on to describe in detail and in sober language how the greatest army of all time had marched to its doom. Of hundreds of thousands of cavalrymen only six hundred were left, it said. The words 'exhaustion' and 'starvation' kept cropping up, and it ended with the words: 'The health of His Majesty has never been better.'

Looking up into the mirror my face was strange to me, so unfamiliar, so beautiful. I could look beautiful, after all. Returning to the bulletin I asked: "What's going to happen now, Madame?"

She shrugged her shoulders. "Life is full of possibilities, Désirée. He could make peace. Or he could continue to make war——"

"And France, Madame?" I shouted at her so that I made her start, but I couldn't help it.

Before my mind's eye I saw men marching through the snowy wastes in their thousands, saw them fall, saw them keeping wolves at bay till the men could move no longer, saw them torn to pieces by the beasts, shot by the Cossacks, drowning among the ice-floes of the Beresina, death, death, death in all its terror. . . . But His Majesty's health had never been better, never. "And France, Madame?" I repeated dully.

"Why? Bonaparte is not France, is he?" Josephine smiled down at her gleaming nails which she was polishing. "Napoleon the First, by the grace of God Emperor of the French. . . ." She winked at me. "By the grace of God! You and I know exactly how he got there, don't we? Barras needed someone to suppress hunger riots and Bonaparte was ready to do it. After that, Bonaparte the Military Governor of Paris, Bonaparte the Commander-in-Chief in the South, Bonaparte the Conqueror of Italy, Bonaparte in Egypt, Bonaparte the First

Consul——" She stopped, then said with pleasure in her voice: "Perhaps Marie-Louise will leave him now that his luck has turned."

"But she is the mother of his son!"

"That means little, very little. Whatever happens you must not forget what I told you about looks, Désirée. Promise me!"

Looks, Moscow, make-up, death in the Beresina, I felt so confused I could say nothing.

"Between ourselves," Josephine continued, "there are prouder dynasties than the Bernadotte family, Désirée. But the Swedes chose Bernadotte and he will not disappoint them. He knows how to govern, Bonaparte said so often enough. But you, my girl, you can neither govern nor do anything else. In that case you must do the Swedes at least the favour of looking pretty."

"But my turned-up nose?"

"You can't do anything about that. But it suits you, in your young face. You will always look younger than you are. . . . Well now, let's go down and make Theresa read the cards for us. Pity it's raining, I should have liked to show the garden to your Swedish Count."

Going downstairs Josephine stopped suddenly. "Désirée, why is it that you are not in Stockholm?"

I avoided her eyes. "Stockholm has a Queen and a Dowager Queen. Isn't that enough?"

"You are not afraid of your predecessors, are you? Predecessors are never dangerous, only successors. Frankly, I was afraid you had come because you were still in love with him—with Bonaparte, I mean."

Down in her white and yellow drawing-room Josephine's ladies and Polette were still busy with their bandages, Queen Hortense lay on a divan reading letters, and a very fat lady with an oriental scarf round her neck, which made her look like a gaudily coloured ball, was playing patience. My young Count Rosen gazed unhappily at the rain.

When we entered all the ladies except Polette got up. The gaudily coloured ball sank into a deep curtsey before me.

"Your Highness remembers Princess Chimay?" asked Josephine. It's Désirée when we are alone, it's 'Your Highness' in public, I noticed. Chimay? It was the name of one of the oldest aristocratic French families. I was certain never to have met one of its members before.

But Josephine laughed. "It's Notre-Dame de Thermidor! My friend Theresa!"

Oh, Josephine's friend Theresa, the ex-Marquise de Fontenay

who married the ex-valet and later Deputy Tallien! I invaded her house to look for my fiancé. But I had lost him there and found Jean-Baptiste instead. . . . Her reputation was worse even than Josephine's, and Napoleon, who as Emperor had become very strict, had forbidden her the court. Theresa, fat and mother of seven children, got her own back on Napoleon by marrying Prince Chimay, whom the Emperor would have liked to see at court because of his very aristocratic descent. The Prince, however, did not go because of Theresa's continued banishment from the Tuileries.

"I am glad to see you again, Princess," I said.

"See me again?" Theresa's eyes grew wide with astonishment. "I have not yet had the honour of being presented to Your Highness."

Polette interrupted us from the fireplace. "Désirée, the Empress has put her gold paint on your eyelids. It suits you. But tell me, is your adjutant there deaf and dumb?"

"No, only dumb," Count Rosen said furiously.

I realised it had been a mistake to bring the young Swede into this house. Josephine tried to mollify him by putting her hand on his arm, and at her touch I saw him give an almost imperceptible start. "When it stops raining I shall show you the garden," she said, smiling at him without showing him her bad teeth, and looking deep into his eyes. Then she turned to Hortense, whom she asked about Count Flahault, Hortense's official lover since her separation from her husband.

"He writes," said Hortense, "that from Smolensk onwards he has been marching by the side of the Emperor. The Emperor no longer has a horse because almost all the horses have been frozen to death or killed and eaten by the starving troops. The Emperor wears the fur coat which the Tsar gave him once, and a cap made of Persian lamb. He walks with a stick, accompanied by the Generals who have lost their regiments. He walks between Murat and Count Flahault."

"Nonsense, he walks with his faithful Meneval," said Josephine.

Hortense turned over the sheets of the long letter she was reading and said: "No. Meneval collapsed of exhaustion and was loaded on to a cart together with other casualties."

A great silence fell on the room. The logs on the fire crackled, yet we felt very cold.

"I shall arrange for a Service of Intercession to-morrow," Josephine said in a much subdued voice, and asked Theresa to read the cards for Bonaparte. Notre-Dame de Thermidor collected her cards gravely, remarking that Bonaparte was

King of Hearts as usual, divided them in two piles, made Josephine cut them, and began to lay the cards in the form of a big star. Josephine and Hortense looked on, breathless with excitement, Polette nestled close to me and tried to catch Count Rosen's eye. But his eyes avoided our group, he probably thought us crazy.

Theresa, having laid out her star and contemplated it in solemn silence for a long time, said at last: "It looks bad. I see a journey. A journey across water, a journey by boat." After another silence she repeated: "No, unfortunately, it does not look good."

"And I?" Josephine wanted to know.

"You? I see the usual thing, money trouble, nothing else."

"I am in debt again with Le Roy," Josephine admitted.

Theresa suddenly raised her hand importantly: "I see a separation from the Queen of Diamonds."

"That's Marie-Louise," whispered Polette.

"But I see nothing but calamity. By the way, what could the Knave of Hearts mean? He lies between him and the Knave of Clubs. The Knave of Clubs is Talleyrand——"

"The other day it was Fouché," said Hortense.

"Perhaps the Knave of Hearts is the little King of Rome," suggested Josephine. "Bonaparte returns to his child."

Theresa collected the cards and shuffled them once more to lay out a new star. "No," she said, "same thing again, the sea journey, financial troubles, desertion by——"

"By the Queen of Diamonds?" Josephine asked breathlessly. Theresa nodded.

"And I?" Josephine repeated.

"I don't understand. There is nothing between the Queen of Spades and the Emperor. All the same, he is not joining her, I don't really know why not, Josephine. And there, you see, is the Knave of Hearts again, by the Emperor's side, always by the Emperor's side. Seven of Clubs and Ace of Clubs cannot get at him because of the Knave of Hearts in between. It can't be the little King of Rome, it must be a grown-up. But who?"

She looked round helplessly. We couldn't give her any clue. She turned back to the cards, pondering. "It might be a female, a girl perhaps whom the Emperor does not treat as a woman, someone who has known the Emperor all his life and does not desert him in the hour of his need, perhaps——"

"Désirée, it's Désirée!" Polette shouted.

Theresa stared, uncomprehending. Josephine, however, nodded emphatically. "It could be," she said, "the little friend, a young girl of his early days. I really believe it is Her Royal Highness."

382

"Please leave me out of it," I said, and felt ashamed of all this in the presence of the young Count.

Josephine understood and stopped the game. "I think it has stopped raining," she said to the Count. "Let me show you my roses and the greenhouses."

In the evening we returned to Paris. It was raining again.

"I am afraid," I said, "you must have been very bored at Malmaison. But I wanted to introduce you to the most beautiful woman in France."

He answered politely: "The Empress Josephine must have been very beautiful—once."

'She lost her beauty in one night,' I thought. 'So shall I, with or without gold paint on my eyelids. But I hope I shall not lose it in one night. That, however, depends on Jean-Baptiste. . . .'

"The ladies at Malmaison are quite different from our ladies in Stockholm," said Count Rosen out of the blue. "They talk about their prayers and their *affaires*."

"One prays and loves in Stockholm just the same."

"Oh yes. But one does not talk about it."

PARIS. *19th December*, 1812.

SINCE my visit to Malmaison it has been raining without interruption. But the rain has not stopped people standing about in the streets talking about the fate of their dear ones in Russia, has not stopped them from going to the churches to attend the services of intercession.

Last night I couldn't sleep. I wandered about the lonely, big, cold house till in the end I put on Napoleon's sable fur and sat down in the small drawing-room to write a letter to Oscar. Marie and Count Rosen kept me company, Marie knitting a grey scarf for Pierre, of whose fate we know nothing, and Count Rosen reading Danish papers, as Swedish papers cannot be bought any more. Madame La Flotte and the servants had gone to bed.

I heard a carriage stop in front of my house, and the next moment loud knocks resounded on the door. Then voices came from the hall.

"I am not at home to anybody," I said, "I have gone to bed."

Count Rosen left the room and a moment later his harsh French could be heard outside.

A door opened. He escorted someone into the big drawing-room adjoining the small one.

'Is he out of his senses?' I thought. 'I told him I wouldn't receive anybody.' "Go in there at once, Marie, and tell him that I've gone to bed."

Marie immediately went into the other drawing-room. I heard her start a sentence and break off abruptly. Not a sound came from the next room. It was inconceivable to me whom they could possibly have allowed in at this time of night against my wishes. I heard the rustling of paper and the sound of logs being put in the fireplace. Quite obviously someone was making a fire. That was the only noise, otherwise there was complete silence out there.

At last the door opened and Count Rosen came in. His movements were strangely stiff and formal.

"His Majesty the Emperor!"

I started. "Who?" I thought I hadn't understood him properly.

"His Majesty has just arrived in the company of a gentleman, and wishes to speak to Your Royal Highness."

"But the Emperor is at the front," I said, confused.

"His Majesty has just returned." The young Swede was pale with agitation.

Meanwhile I had calmed down. 'Nonsense,' I thought, 'he can't intimidate me, I don't want to be forced into this awful situation, I don't want to see him again, at least not now, not alone.' "Tell His Majesty that I've gone to bed."

"I have told His Majesty that already. His Majesty insists on speaking to Your Highness."

I didn't stir. There was the Emperor, he'd lost his Army. And the first person he came to was me.

I got up slowly and smoothed my hair away from my forehead. I realised that I was wearing my old velvet dressing-gown and my sable fur over it, and probably looked a ridiculous sight. Reluctantly I went towards the door. "I am frightened, Count Rosen," I confessed.

The young Swede shook his head. "I don't think Your Highness need be frightened."

The big drawing-room was brightly lit. Marie was just placing candles in the last of the big candelabra. In the fireplace the fire flickered merrily.

On the sofa under the portrait of the First Consul sat Count Caulaincourt, the Emperor's Grand Equerry. He wore a sheepskin coat and a woollen cap which he had pulled down over his ears. His eyes were shut and he seemed to be asleep.

384

The Emperor was standing in front of the fire with his arms propped on the mantelpiece. His shoulders stooped. He seemed so tired that he had to prop himself up in order to be able to stand at all. A cap of grey Persian lamb sat aslant on his head. The man standing there looked a complete stranger to me.

Neither of the two had heard me come. "Sire," I said, stepping to the side of the Emperor.

Caulaincourt shot up, tore his cap off his head and stood to attention. The Emperor slowly raised his head.

I forgot to bow. Completely put out, I looked at his face. For the first time in my life I saw an unshaven Napoleon. Reddish stubble spread over his face, the bloated cheeks were slack and grey. Under a thin mouth his chin, which had lost its flesh, jutted out like a promontory. All the life had gone out of the eyes which were now turned on me.

"Count Rosen," I said sharply, "nobody has taken His Majesty's cap and coat."

"I am cold," Napoleon murmured, taking off his cap with a tired gesture.

Count Rosen took Caulaincourt's sheepskin out of the room. "Come back at once, Count," I told him. "Marie, cognac and glasses!" I wanted Count Rosen to be present during the conversation.

"Please sit down, Sire," I said, and took my seat on the sofa. The Emperor didn't move, and Caulaincourt stood irresolute in the middle of the room.

Count Rosen returned and Marie brought cognac and glasses. "A glass of cognac, Sire?"

The Emperor didn't hear.

I looked questioningly at Caulaincourt.

"We have been travelling for thirteen days and nights without a break," he said. "No one at the Tuileries knows that we are back. His Majesty wanted to talk to Your Highness first."

A fantastic situation! The Emperor had travelled thirteen days and nights to arrive at my house weary to death, and no one knew that he was in Paris! I filled a glass with cognac and went to him.

"Sire, drink that. It'll warm you," I said loudly.

He raised his head and stared at me, at my old dressing-gown, the sable fur which he himself had given me, and poured down the drink at one gulp. "Does one always wear a fur coat over one's dressing-gown in Sweden?" he asked.

"Of course not. I am cold, that's all. Did Count Rosen not tell you that I was in bed?"

"Who?"

D.—13   385

"My adjutant, Count Rosen. Come here, Count, be presented to His Majesty."

Count Rosen clicked his heels. The Emperor held his glass out to him. "Give me another glass. And give Caulaincourt one too. We have made a long journey."

Again he poured down the cognac in one go. "You are surprised to see me here, Highness?"

"Naturally, Sire."

"Naturally? We are old friends, Highness, are we not? Very old friends, if I remember aright. Why, then, are you surprised?"

"Because of the time of your call. And because you have come unshaven."

Napoleon felt his beard with his hand, and a trace of the young, uncaring laughter of his Marseilles days played for a fleeting moment over his grey face. "I am sorry, Highness, I forgot to shave recently. I wanted to reach Paris as quickly as possible. Tell me, what was the effect of my last bulletin?"

"Wouldn't you like to take a seat, Sire?"

"Thank you, I prefer to stand by the fire. But do not inconvenience yourself, Madame. Sit down, gentlemen."

We all sat down, Marie, myself, Count Rosen and Count Caulaincourt, who, I remember now, bore the title of Duke of Vicenza.

"May I ask, Sire——" I began.

"No, Madame, you may not ask! You may not ask, Madame Jean-Baptiste Bernadotte!" he screamed at me at the top of his voice. Count Rosen started on his chair.

Calmly I said: "But I should like to know to what I owe the honour of this unexpected visit."

"My visit is not an honour for you but an ignominy. If you had not been such a childish thoughtless creature all your life, you would realise what an ignominy this visit is to you, Madame Jean-Baptiste Bernadotte!"

"Keep your seat, Count Rosen. His Majesty is too tired to find the right tone," I said soothingly to the Count, who had jumped up, his hand on his sword. That would have been the last straw indeed.

The Emperor paid no attention to us. He came nearer to stare at the portrait of the First Consul, the portrait of the young Napoleon with the lean face, the radiant eyes, the long untidy hair. "Do you know at all where I have just come from?" he said in a monotonous yet hurried voice. "I have come from the steppes where my soldiers are buried. I have come from the wastes where my hussars are dragging themselves through the blinding snow. I have come from the bridge which collapsed under Davout's grenadiers, the bridge across the Beresina. I have come from the camps where men crawl between the corpses of their comrades at night to keep warm, I have——"

"How can I get the scarf to him, how?" It was Marie screaming. She had jumped up and fallen on her knees in front of the Emperor. "Majesty, help a mother, send a courier with the scarf——"

Repelled, Napoleon shrank back. I bent down to her quickly. "It is Marie, Sire, Marie from Marseilles. Her son Pierre is in Russia."

Marie had dug her finger-nails into his sleeve. Napoleon freed himself, his face distorted with rage.

"I have the number of his regiment," whimpered Marie. "This scarf, only this warm scarf——"

"Are you mad, woman?" Foam appeared at the corners of Napoleon's mouth. "I am to send a scarf to Russia, one scarf! Doesn't it make you laugh?" And he began to laugh, louder and louder and louder. "One scarf for my hundred thousand dead, for my frozen grenadiers, one beautiful warm scarf for my Grand Army!"

I took Marie to the door. "Go to bed, dearest, go."

Napoleon had fallen silent. Helplessly he stood in the middle of the room. Then he went with strangely stiff movements to the nearest chair and collapsed into it. "Forgive me, Madame. I am very tired."

Endless minutes passed, not one of us spoke. This is the end, I felt, the end. My thoughts went across land and sea to Jean-Baptiste.

Suddenly Napoleon spoke up in a clear hard voice. "I have come to dictate to you a letter to Marshal Bernadotte, Madame."

"I ask you to dictate this letter to one of Your Majesty's secretaries."

"I wish you to write this letter, Madame. It is a very personal letter and not at all long. Tell the Swedish Crown Prince that we have returned to Paris to prepare the final defeat of the enemies of France." The Emperor got up and began to pace the floor. "Tell him that we remind the Swedish Crown Prince of the young General Bernadotte who with his regiments came in spring, 1797, to the assistance of General Bonaparte in Italy. That crossing of the Alps in an incredibly short time, a masterpiece of organisation, decided the issue of the Italian campaign in our favour. Will you remember that, Madame?"

I nodded.

"Then remind Bernadotte of the battles in which he defended the young Republic and of the song:

"Le Régiment de Sambre et Meuse
Marche toujours aux cris de la liberté
Suivant la route glorieuse. . . .

"Tell him that I heard the song a fortnight ago in the Russian snow from two grenadiers who could go no further and sang the song as they dug themselves into the snow to wait for the wolves. Perhaps they were former soldiers of your husband's Rhine Army. Do not forget to mention this incident to him."

My finger-nails dug into the palms of my hands.

"Marshal Bernadotte advised the Tsar to safeguard the peace of Europe by capturing me during the retreat. You can tell him, Madame, that he very nearly succeeded, but only very nearly. I am here, in your drawing-room, and I shall safeguard the peace of Europe myself. In order to assure the final destruction of my enemies I propose an alliance to Sweden. Have you understood me, Madame?"

"Yes, Sire. You propose an alliance to Sweden."

"To put it plainly, I want Bernadotte to march with me once more. Tell your husband that, word for word."

I nodded.

"To defray the cost of rearming, Sweden will be paid one million francs a month besides goods to the value of six million francs." His eyes fastened on the young Count. "At the conclusion of peace Sweden will receive Finland, and of course Pomerania. Tell Bernadotte: Finland, Pomerania and," with a wide sweep of his arm, "the whole of the Baltic coast from Danzig to Mecklenburg."

"Count Rosen, get a piece of paper and note it down."

"Not necessary," said Caulaincourt, "I have a memorandum here dictated by His Majesty this morning." He handed Rosen a closely covered sheet.

"Finland?" the young Swede said incredulously.

Napoleon smiled at him, the winning smile of his young days. "We shall restore to Sweden her position as a great power. By the way, young man, you will be interested to hear that the archives of the Kremlin yielded me a description of the Russian campaign of your heroic King Charles XII. I wanted to learn from him. But I have the feeling," he said, smiling wryly, "that someone else, someone in Stockholm, has read these descriptions as well and seems to have learnt a lot from them, your—what do you call him? Charles John, my old Bernadotte!"

He shrugged his shoulders, breathed deeply and looked at me. "Madame, you will write to Bernadotte to-morrow. I must know where I stand."

So that was why he came. "You haven't told me what would happen if Sweden refused to enter the alliance, Sire."

He did not answer, but returned to his portrait. "A good picture. Did I really look like that, so—thin?"

I nodded. "And in Marseilles you were thinner still, you looked really starved then."

"In Marseilles?" His face registered keen surprise. "How do you know? Oh, of course, I had forgotten, quite forgotten. Yes, we have known each other for a long time, Madame."

I got up.

"I am so tired, so terribly tired," he said, almost inaudibly.

"Go to the Tuileries, Sire, and rest."

"No, dearest, I cannot. The Cossacks are on the move, and the coalition which Bernadotte has got together, Russia, Sweden, Britain. Do you know, Eugenie, what that means?"

He was back to calling me Eugenie now, and he even seemed to have forgotten that I was Bernadotte's wife. His head was too full. "What's the good of writing," I asked, "if the coalition is a fact?"

At that he screamed at me: "Because I shall wipe Sweden off the map if Bernadotte does not march with me." Abruptly he turned to the door. "You yourself, Madame, will bring me your husband's answer. If it is a rejection you can then take your leave at the same time. It would no longer be possible for me to receive you at court."

I curtsied. "I should no longer come to court, Sire."

Count Rosen saw the Emperor and Caulaincourt out. Slowly I went from candelabrum to candelabrum and put out the candles.

Rosen returned. "Is Your Highness going to write to the Crown Prince to-morrow?"

"Yes. And you'll help me with the letter, Count."

"Do you think, Your Highness, that the Crown Prince will answer the Emperor?"

"I am sure of it. And it will be the last letter my husband will write to the Emperor." I looked into the dying embers.

"I should prefer not to leave Your Highness alone just now," the young man said hesitantly.

"That's very kind of you. But I am going to Marie to console her."

I spent the rest of the night by Marie's bedside. I promised her to write to Murat, to Marshal Ney and to Colonel Villatte, of whom I had heard nothing for many weeks. I promised to travel with her to the Russian steppes in spring to find Pierre. I promised and promised and promised, and in her fright she was like a child and really thought I could help her.

This morning, special editions of the papers shout it out to the rest of the world that the Emperor has unexpectedly returned from Russia. His Majesty's health, they say, has never been better.

PARIS.
The end of January 1813.

AT long last a courier arrived with letters from Stockholm.

'My dear Mama,' wrote Oscar in his neat and very adult-looking handwriting—yes, in six months' time he'll be fourteen! —'My dear Mama, on the sixth of January we saw a marvellous play in the Gustavus III Theatre. Imagine, a famous French actress, Mademoiselle George, who used to be at the Théâtre Français in Paris, played the leading part. Afterwards Papa gave a dinner for Mademoiselle George, and the Queen didn't like it at all that Papa and the actress talked of Paris and the old days all the time. She kept interrupting them and calling him "Our dear Son Charles John," which made Mademoiselle George laugh a lot, and at last she exclaimed: "General Bernadotte, that I'd find you here in Stockholm and as the son of the Swedish Queen at that is the last thing I'd have imagined." That annoyed the Queen so much that she sent me to bed and withdrew with all her ladies. The actress stayed for coffee and liqueur with Papa and Count Brahe, and Miss Koskull took to her bed for a week with a cold in anger and jealousy. Papa works sixteen hours a day as a rule and doesn't look at all well. . . .'

I laughed, and cried a bit too, and felt like going to bed for a week exactly like Mariana Koskull.

That was the letter Oscar had written without his governor's supervision. In his second letter my son expressed himself somewhat more stylishly about the visit to Stockholm of Madame de Staël, the authoress whom Napoleon had banished and whom Papa received very often. He'd signed the letter 'Your ever loving son Oscar, Duke of Södermanland', whereas the other letter was signed simply 'Your Oscar'.

I looked in vain for a letter from Jean-Baptiste. He must have had my letter about Napoleon's visit and offer of alliance long ago. But all I found was a few hastily scribbled lines.

'My beloved little girl,' it read, 'I am badly overworked, I shall write at greater length next time. Thank you for your report about the Emperor's visit. I shall answer him, but I need time. My answer will be meant not only for him but also for the French nation and for posterity. I don't know why he wishes to have it handed over to him by you. However, I shall send it to you and I only regret that in doing so I shall have to make you suffer once more. I embrace you—Your J.B.'

Besides the letters the big envelope contained a sheet of music. In the margin Jean-Baptiste had scribbled: 'Oscar's first composition, a Swedish folk dance. Try to play the tune. J.B.' At once I sat down at the piano and played it, again and again. And I remembered Oscar saying in the coach that took us back from Hanover to Paris that he wanted to be a composer or a King. And thinking of Jean-Baptiste's scribbled lines about the answer to Napoleon that would be meant for the French nation and posterity as well, I also remembered Monsieur van Beethoven. 'I shall simply call my symphony "Eroica" to commemorate a hope which did not find fulfilment'. . . .

I rang the bell for Count Rosen. He, too, had had letters from Sweden. "Good news from home, Count?"

"I can read between the lines of the letters—they have to be careful, of course, because of the French Secret Police—that the allies, Russia, Sweden, Britain, intend to entrust the plans for the coming campaign to His Royal Highness. And Austria's attitude is most benevolent towards them."

So even his father-in-law, the Austrian Emperor Francis, would take the field against Napoleon.

"The occupied German territories, the Prussians above all, are preparing for an uprising. All the preparations for this greatest campaign in history are being made secretly in Sweden." The Count's voice, hoarse with excitement, had dropped to a whisper. "We shall be a great power again, and Your Highness's son, the little Duke of Södermanland——"

"Oscar's just sent me his first composition, a Swedish folk dance. I shall practise it and play it you to-night. Why do you look at me in such a strange manner? Are you disappointed in my son?"

"Of course not, Your Highness. I am surprised, that's what it is, I did not know——"

"You didn't know that the Prince is very musical? And yet you talk about Sweden regaining her great position?"

"I thought of the country that the Crown Prince will leave to his son when the time comes." The words came tumbling out of him now. "Sweden elected one of the greatest Generals of all time to be the heir to its throne. The Bernadotte dynasty will rebuild Sweden's traditional position as a great power."

"Count, you talk like an elementary reader for school-children," I said, repelled. "In the coming campaign your Crown Prince will do nothing but fight for the Rights of Man which we call Liberty, Equality and Fraternity. He has fought for them for fifteen years, Count Rosen. That was why all the old royal courts secretly called him the Jacobin General. And later, when everything is over and Jean-Baptiste has won this dreadful war on behalf of all Europe, they'll call him that again. Then——" I broke off, because I could tell that Rosen didn't understand a word I was saying. Finally I said in a very low voice: "A musician who never knew anything about politics once told me about a hope which never found fulfilment. Perhaps it will find fulfilment after all, at least in Sweden, and your small country will really be a great power again, Count, but in a way very different from the one you are thinking of. It will be a great power whose Kings no longer make war but have time to write poetry and make music. Aren't you glad that Oscar is musical?"

"Your Royal Highness is the strangest woman I have ever met."

Suddenly I felt very tired. "You only think so because I am the first middle-class woman you have come to know better. All your life you have known nothing but the court and the castles of the nobility. Now you are the adjutant of a silk merchant's daughter. Try to get used to that, will you?"

PARIS. *February* 1813.

ONE evening about seven o'clock the letter I had been expecting for so long arrived. I ordered my carriage immediately and went with Count Rosen to the Hôtel Dieu Hospital opposite Notre-Dame. The wet pavement reflected the rainbow colours of the lights of Paris.

"I have just had a letter from Colonel Villatte," I explained to Rosen. "He succeeded in getting Marie's son into a transport of wounded for the big Hôtel Dieu Hospital. I am told the hospital is overcrowded, and I should like to take Pierrre home."

"How is Colonel Villatte?"

"He couldn't come to Paris, he's been sent to the Rhineland, where they are trying to collect the remnants of his regiment."

"I am glad he is well," Rosen said politely.

392

"He isn't well, he's suffering from the effects of a wound in the shoulder. But he hopes to see us again."

"When?"

"Some time, when it is all over."

"A strange name for a hospital—Hôtel Dieu."

"Our Lord's Hostel, a beautiful name for a hospital. The only transport of wounded to reach Paris has been accommodated there, and Villatte managed to get Pierre into it."

"What is the matter with Pierre?"

"Villatte doesn't say. That's why I haven't told Marie yet. Here we are."

The gate was locked. Count Rosen rang the bell and after a while the gate opened just enough to show the doorkeeper, a one-armed invalid from the Italian campaigns, to judge by his medals. "No visitors allowed!" he said.

"But it is Her Royal Highness——"

"No visitors allowed!" The door was banged to.

"Knock again, Count."

He knocked, loud and long. At last the gate opened once more, I pushed Rosen aside and said quickly: "I have permission to visit the hospital."

"Have you got a pass?" the man asked suspiciously.

"Yes," I said, and we were allowed in. In a dark gateway the invalid looked us over by the light of a candle and asked for the pass.

"I haven't got it with me," I said. "I am the sister-in-law of King Joseph. You understand that I could have a pass at any time. But I am in such a hurry that I could not wait to ask for one. I wanted to fetch someone."

He didn't answer, so I repeated: "I am really King Joseph's sister-in-law."

"I know you, Madame. You are the wife of Marshal Bernadotte."

'Thank God,' I thought, and smiled. "Did you perhaps serve under my husband?"

Not a muscle in his face moved and he kept silent.

"Please call someone to take us to the wards," I said in the end.

Still he did not move. The man became alarming to me. "Lend us the candle. We shall find our own way," I said, feeling rather helpless.

He gave me the candle, stepped back and disappeared in the dark. But we heard him say in a sneering, croaking voice, "The wife of Marshal Bernadotte indeed!" and he spat resoundingly on the floor.

393

Count Rosen took the candle out of my hand, as it trembled badly. With painful difficulty I said: "Don't pay any attention to that man. We must search for Pierre."

We felt our way up a wide flight of stairs and came to a corridor with many doors. The doors were not properly shut, and groaning and whimpering could be heard from inside.

Quickly I pushed the first door open, and an indescribable odour of blood, sweat and excrement hit me in the face. I summoned all my strength.

The whimpering came from quite close by, close by my feet in fact. I took Rosen's candle and held it high to see. Both sides of the room were occupied by rows of beds, and down the centre of the room straw palliasses covered the floor. The other end of the room seemed a long way away. There I could see a candle on a table and a red sanctuary light. A nun was seated at the table.

"Sister!"

But my voice didn't carry far enough through the moaning of the wounded men to reach her. Cautiously I took a few paces forward and shouted again: "Sister!"

At last she heard me, took the candle and came. I saw a thin, expressionless face under a big white bonnet.

"Sister, I am looking for a wounded man by the name of Pierre Dubois."

"There are too many here," she said in a low voice, indifferently, "we do not know their names."

"But I have permission to look for Pierre Dubois. How am I to find him?" I couldn't help sobbing as I said it.

"I do not know," the nun answered politely. "If you have permission to look for him, then you must look for him. Go from bed to bed, perhaps you will find him." She turned round and went to her table.

For a moment the stench almost overwhelmed me. But I pulled myself together. "Let's go along the beds," I said to the Count.

Thus we went along from bed to bed, from palliasse to palliasse, saw men dying, men dead, men asking for water, men asking for their wives, men stammering requests to which I had no time to listen. But we didn't find Pierre.

It was the same in the next ward, with the only difference that here the nun was young and gentle and full of pity. She thought I was looking for my husband, but I shook my head silently and continued my fruitless search.

When we had left the next ward Rosen suddenly couldn't go on. He leant against the wall, and when I raised the candle to look at him I noticed beads of perspiration on his forehead. He turned away quickly, staggered a few paces and was sick. I felt sorry for him, but could do nothing but wait till he felt better.

In the distance I saw a red votive candle under a statue of the Madonna. I went up to it. It was a very naïve statue of the Mother of Our Lord in a blue and white robe, with healthy red cheeks, sad eyes and a laughing pink baby in her arms. I put my candle down on the floor, and for the first time in many years I clasped my hands in prayer, here under the flickering light with misery seeping out of all the doors around me.

I heard steps behind me and took up the candle.

"I apologise, Your Highness," said my young Swede, ashamed.

Before we went into the next ward I told him he had better stay outside.

He hesitated, then said: "I should like to see this through to the end with you, Highness."

"You shall, Count, you shall!" I answered, and went in, leaving him outside.

At the end of the ward sat an old nun reading in a small black book. She looked up at me without showing any surprise. "I am looking for a certain Pierre Dubois," I said, and could hear the hopelessness in my voice.

"Dubois? I think we have two of that name."

She took me by the hand and led me towards a palliasse in the middle of the room. I knelt down and by the light of the candle saw an emaciated face surrounded by untidy strands of white hair. It wasn't Pierre's face. Then the nun took me to the last bed on the left wall.

Yes, it was Pierre. His dark, wide-open eyes stared at me indifferently. The lips were swollen and had blood on them.

"Good-evening, Pierre!" I said.

He kept on staring.

"Pierre, don't you recognise me?"

"Of course," he murmured, "*Madame la Maréchale*."

I bent over him. "I've come to take you home, Pierre, to your mother, now."

His face remained without expression.

"Pierre, aren't you glad?"

Still no answer.

Utterly at a loss, I turned to the nun. "This is the man I am looking for. I should like to take him home to his mother. I have a carriage downstairs. Have you got anybody here to help me?"

"The porters have gone home, Madame. You must wait till to-morrow."

But I didn't want Pierre to stay here a minute longer. "Is he very seriously wounded? My adju— a gentleman is waiting outside, and he and I could support him, if Pierre could walk down the stairs and——"

The sister seized my hand and lifted it so that the light fell full on the blanket. Where Pierre's legs ought to have been the blanket was flat, quite flat.

My breath left me. At last I managed to say with difficulty: "I have a coachman downstairs who can give me a hand. I shall be back in a minute, sister."

I told Count Rosen to fetch the coachman to carry Pierre to the carriage. "Take my candle and bring all the blankets we have with us," I added.

I waited, and thought of Pierre who had lost his legs and would never be able to walk again. Yes, this was the Hôtel Dieu, Our Lord's Hostel where one person learnt to pray and another to be sick, where one began to understand that the whole world was one big Hôtel Dieu.

They came, Rosen and the coachman Johansson.

"Please help us, sister, to wrap him up in the blankets. Johansson will carry him downstairs."

The sister pulled Pierre up by the shoulders. He couldn't resist, but his eyes sparkled with hatred. "Leave me alone, Madame, leave me——" he shouted.

The nun pulled back the bed cover and I shut my eyes. When I opened them Pierre Dubois lay before me like a well-tied-up parcel.

Somebody tugged at my coat. I turned and saw the man in the next bed trying to sit up. But he fell helplessly. I bent down to him.

"*Madame la Maréchale* he called you, didn't he? Which Marshal?" the man asked.

"Bernadotte."

He motioned me to go nearer to him. A bewildered smile distorted his mouth, his feverish lips nearly touched my ear. "I thought so," he whispered, fighting for breath, "give your husband . . . in his castle in Stockholm . . . the regards of one of his men . . . who crossed the Alps with him. . . . Tell him, if we had known. . . . Tell him, he would never have got over the Alps . . . alive . . . if we had known. . . ." Small bubbles of blood and saliva trembled on his lips as he continued with increasing difficulty: "If we had known . . . that he . . . would let us die in Russia. . . . My regards . . . to him, Madame . . . from . . . an old comrade."

A protective hand, that of the nun, took my arm. "His will be done on earth and in Heaven. Let us go, Madame."

Johansson lifted the parcel which had once been Pierre, a young man who went to war with a rose bud in his rifle, and carried it through the door. Count Rosen took the candle and showed the way. But I clung to the old woman and she led me down the stairs. "But you are no longer the wife of Marshal Bernadotte," she said unexpectedly, "but the Crown Princess of Sweden, are you not?"

I lost all control of myself and sobbed loudly.

"Go with God, my child, and strive for peace with your people."

She let go my arm. The one-armed doorkeeper opened the gate in silence. When I turned round to kiss the old nun's hand she had disappeared into the dark.

Count Rosen sat on the back seat. The parcel that had been Pierre Dubois lay by my side. I felt over the blankets for his hand. When I found it it was cold and limp.

And that was how I brought Marie's son back to her.

PARIS.
The beginning of April 1813.

'In half an hour I shall see him for the last time in my life,' I thought, as I put some gold paint on my eyelids. 'After that the long acquaintance which began as my first love will be over and done with.' I finished my make-up and put on a new hat tied under the chin with a pink ribbon. A Crown Princess with gold-painted eyelids, a purple velvet costume, a bunch of pale violets on the low-cut neck of the blouse and new model hat with a pink ribbon, that is how he will remember me, I reflected.

Last night a courier brought Jean-Baptiste's answer to Napoleon. It was sealed. But Count Brahe had sent a copy of it for my information and added that the text of this letter from the Swedish Crown Prince to Napoleon had been transmitted to all papers for publication.

I got up and read my copy for the last time:

" *The sufferings of the Continent cry out for peace, and Your Majesty cannot reject this demand without multiplying ten-fold the sum total of crimes you have committed up till now. What did France receive as compensation for its gigantic sacrifices? Nothing but military glory, superficial splendour and deep misery within her own frontiers. . . . "*

And this letter I was to take to Napoleon! Things like that could happen only to me. I grew hot with fear as I read on:

"I was born in that beautiful France over which you reign, and her honour and well-being can never be a matter of indifference to me. But without ever ceasing to pray for its happiness I shall always defend with all the means at my disposal the rights of the nation which called me and the honour of the monarch who accepted me to be his son. In the fight between tyranny and freedom I shall say to the Swedes: I shall fight with you and for you, and all peoples who love their freedom will bless our arms.

As far as my personal ambition goes, let me say this: I am ambitious, very ambitious, but only in order to serve the interests of mankind and to gain and guarantee the independence of the Scandinavian peninsula."

The letter addressed to Napoleon, France and the world ended on a personal note:

"Independent of any decision you may come to, Sire, whether peace or war, I shall always cherish for Your Majesty the devotion of an old comrade of many wars."

I put the copy back on the bedside table and went out. We were to be at the Tuileries at five o'clock. Within the next few days the Emperor would take the field again with his new armies, to face the advancing Russians and the Prussians who had joined them.

Count Rosen was wearing the full-dress uniform of the Swedish dragoons and the adjutant's sash.

"You accompany me on many difficult missions, Count," I said as we passed over the Pont Royal. Since that night in the Hôtel Dieu a strange kind of affinity connected us, probably because I had been present when he was sick. These things bring people together more than one thinks.

We drove in an open carriage through the sweet-smelling dusk of an early spring day. 'A pity,' I thought, 'to have to go for an interview with the Emperor of the French instead of going for a sweet and secret rendezvous. . . .'

We were shown in at once to the Emperor's big study.

Caulaincourt and Meneval were present as well as Count Talleyrand, who was leaning against the window.

Napoleon, in the green uniform of the Chasseurs, his arms folded over his chest, refused to meet us halfway but waited for us standing behind his desk at the far end of the room, a supercilious smile on his face. I bowed and handed him the letter.

He broke open the seal, read it without a muscle in his face moving and then handed it to Meneval. "Have a copy made for the archives of the Ministry of Foreign Affairs and put the original with my private papers," he ordered. Turning to me he said: "You have dressed up nicely, Your Highness. Purple suits you. By the way, you are wearing a strange hat. Are tall hats the latest fashion?"

This sneering was worse than the violent eruption I had anticipated. I said nothing.

Napoleon turned to Talleyrand: "You know something about beautiful women's fashions, don't you, Excellency? How do you like the new hat of the Crown Princess of Sweden?"

Talleyrand kept his eyes half shut. He seemed to be infinitely bored. Napoleon turned to me. "Did you dress up for my sake, Highness?"

"Yes, Sire."

"And adorned yourself with violets"—his tone became jeering—"to bring me this scribble by the former Marshal Bernadotte? Violets, Madame, flower in quiet places and their scent is sweet. But this treason, at which all Russian and English papers exult, stinks to high Heaven!"

I bowed. "I ask to be allowed to leave, Sire."

"You are not only allowed to leave, Madame," he yelled, "I shall force you to leave. Or did you think that you could come and go here at court when Bernadotte marches into battle against me? He is going to train his guns on the regiments which he himself commanded in innumerable battles, and you, Madame, dare to appear here adorned with violets!"

"Sire, that night when you returned from Russia you urged me to write to my husband and bring you his answer. I read a copy of his letter, and I realise that I am seeing you for the last time, Sire. I put on the violets because they suit me. Perhaps they'll induce you to remember me more agreeably. May I now say good-bye to you, for the last time?"

Silence fell on us, a dreadful awkward silence. Meneval and Caulaincourt stared at the Emperor in amazement, and Talleyrand, interested, opened his eyes, because Napoleon quite unexpectedly became embarrassed and looked restlessly round the room. At last he said in a totally different voice: "Please wait here, gentlemen, I should like to have a few words with Her Royal Highness in private." He pointed to a door in the wall: "Please follow me, Your Highness. Meneval, offer the gentlemen a glass of brandy."

I entered the room where years ago I had pleaded for the life of the Duc d'Enghien. Nothing much had changed here, the same small tables, the same piles of documents and files. On the carpet in front of the fireplace I saw a number of small wooden blocks, in different colours, with prongs sticking out of them.

Involuntarily I picked up a red one. "What are these? Toys of the King of Rome?"

"Yes—and no. I use these blocks to plan out my campaign. Each block represents an army corps, and the prongs mean the number of divisions of that particular corps. The red one you have picked up is the Third Corps of Marshal Ney. It has five prongs. So Ney's corps has five divisions. The blue one is the Corps Marmont with three divisions, and so on. If I put them up on the floor I can see the order of battle quite clearly on the map. I know the map by heart."

"But do you chew these blocks?" I asked, and looked at the red one in surprise.

"No, that is the little King of Rome. When he is brought in here he gets them out to play with and chews them too."

I put the red block back on the floor. "You wanted to have a word with me, Sire? I am afraid I cannot discuss my husband with you."

He made a deprecatory gesture. "Who wants to talk about Bernadotte? No, it was not that, Eugenie, it was only——" He came close to me and stared into my face as if he wanted to commit to memory every feature of it. "No, when you said that I should remember you agreeably, because you were saying good-bye for the last time I thought——" He turned away brusquely and went to the window. "We cannot say good-bye like that when we have known each other for so long, can we?"

I stood in front of the fireplace and with the tip of my foot played with the small wooden blocks representing armies. I gave no answer.

"I said," came Napoleon's voice from the window, "one cannot leave just like that."

"Why not, Sire?"

He turned back to me. "Why not? Eugenie, have you forgotten the days of Marseilles? The hedge? The field? Our talks on Goethe's novel *Werther*? Our youth, Eugenie, our whole youth? You never realised why I came to you that night, after my return from Russia. I was cold, I was tired, I was lonely."

"When you dictated to me the letter to Jean-Baptiste you had quite forgotten that you knew me when I was still Eugenie Clary. Your visit was meant for the Crown Princess of Sweden, Sire." I felt sad. 'Even when we see each other for the last time he must lie,' I thought.

He shook his head vigorously. "Of course I had pondered over the alliance with Bernadotte on the morning of that day. But when I came to Paris I only wanted to see you, you alone. And then, I don't know how it all happened, I was so tired that night, as soon as we mentioned Bernadotte I forgot about Marseilles. Can't you understand?"

It grew dark. Nobody came to light the candles. I could no longer see his face. What in the world did he want of me?

"I brought together a new army of two hundred thousand men. By the way, did you know that Britain is paying Sweden one million pounds to equip Bernadotte's troops?"

No, I didn't know. But I made no reply to Napoleon.

"Madame de Staël is with him in Stockholm. Did you know that, Madame?"

Of course I did. It doesn't matter, why talk about it?

"Bernadotte does not seem able to get hold of more pleasant company in Stockholm."

I laughed. "Oh yes, Sire, he does. Mademoiselle George was in Stockholm a short time ago and enjoyed the benevolent patronage of His Royal Highness. Did you know that, Sire?"

"My God, Georgina, sweet little Georgina!"

"His Royal Highness will soon be united with his old friend Moreau. Moreau is returning to Europe and is going to fight under Jean-Baptiste. Did you know that, Sire?"

It was a good thing that darkness stood between us like a wall.

"It is being said that the Tsar offered Bernadotte the French crown." Napoleon's voice came slowly through the dark.

'That sounds crazy,' I thought, 'but possible.'

"Well, Madame? If Bernadotte ever as much as toyed with the idea it would be the blackest treason ever committed by a Frenchman."

"It would. Treason against his own ideals! May I go now, Sire?"

"If ever you yourself feel unsafe in Paris, Madame, I mean if the mob should ever inconvenience you, you must take refuge at once with your sister Julie. Will you promise me that?"

"Gladly. And the other way round, too."

"What do you mean, 'the other way round'?"

"That my house will always be open for Julie. That's why I am staying here."

"So you are counting on my defeat, Eugenie?" He came quite close to me. "The scent of your violets is intoxicating. I should really banish you from the country. You probably tell everybody that the Emperor is going to be beaten. Besides, I don't like it that you go for drives with that tall Swede of yours."

"But he is my adjutant. I have to take him with me."

"All the same, your Mama would not have liked it. And your very strict brother Etienne . . ." He felt for my hand and laid it against his cheek.

"At least you have shaved to-day, Sire," I said, and withdrew my hand.

"A pity you are married to Bernadotte," he said.

Quickly I felt my way back to the door.

He called out "Eugenie!"

But I had reached his brightly lit big study. The gentlemen were sitting round Napoleon's desk drinking brandy. Talleyrand seemed to have made a joke, for Meneval, Caulaincourt and my Swede were holding their sides with laughter.

"Let us share the joke, gentlemen," the Emperor demanded.

"We were just saying that the Senate had passed the measure for the conscription of another 250,000 recruits for the Army," recounted Meneval still laughing. Caulaincourt continued: "We found that this measure concerns youngsters far too young for the Army yet, children almost. It was then that the Prince of Benevento declared that there would have to be one day's armistice at least next year so that Your Majesty's new Army could go to church to be confirmed."

The Emperor laughed. But it didn't sound quite genuine. The recruits, I gathered, were of Oscar's age. "That is not funny," I said, "but sad."

Once more I bowed. This time the Emperor saw me to the door. We didn't exchange another word.

On the return journey I asked Rosen if it was true that the Tsar had offered Jean-Baptiste the French crown.

"That is an open secret in Sweden. Does the Emperor know?" I nodded.

"What else did he talk about?" he asked rather timidly.

I tried to think what else he had talked about. Suddenly I tore my bunch of violets from my decolletage and threw it out of the carriage window. "About violets, Count, about nothing but violets."

That same evening a little package came from the Tuileries for me. The servant who brought it said it was a present for the Crown Prince of Sweden. I undid it and found a chewed wooden block with five prongs. When I see Jean-Baptiste again I shall give it to him.

PARIS.
In summer 1813.

JOHANNSSON the coachman had carried Pierre into the garden. I was sitting by the window watching Marie bringing her son a glass of lemonade. When he had emptied it Marie put it down on the lawn and sat down with him, supporting his back with her arm.

His left leg had been amputated at the top of the thigh. But of the right leg a stump was left above the knee, and the doctor hoped that a wooden leg could be fastened on to it once the wound had healed. But so far the wound had refused to heal. Whenever Marie had to change the bandage Pierre screamed with pain like a child.

I gave him Oscar's room, and Marie had put her bed alongside his. 'But,' I thought, 'I must find him a room on the ground floor, it is so difficult to have to carry him up and downstairs all the time.'

Talleyrand came to visit me in the evening, supposedly to inquire whether I didn't feel too lonely.

"I should have been lonely this summer in any case," I told him. "I am used to having my husband away from me at the front."

He nodded agreement. "Yes, at the front. Which means that, in different circumstances, Your Highness would be alone but not—lonely!"

I shrugged my shoulders. We sat in the garden, and Madame La Flotte poured out iced champagne. Talleyrand told me that Fouché had been given a post, that of Governor of Illyria. Illyria is an Italian state which the Emperor created for the sole purpose of sending Fouché there.

"The Emperor cannot afford to have someone intriguing against him in Paris. And Fouché is sure to start a plot."

"And you," I said, "is the Emperor not afraid of you, Excellency?"

403

"Fouché plots to gain power or keep it. I, however, my dear Highness, desire nothing but the well-being of France."

I gazed up at the sky where the first stars had appeared.

"How quickly our allies left us!" remarked Talleyrand between two sips. "First of all the Prussians, who are now under your husband's supreme command. He has set up his headquarters in Stralsund."

I nodded. Count Rosen had told me all about it. "The *Moniteur* says the Emperor of Austria is trying to bring about an armistice between France and Russia," I said at last.

Talleyrand passed his empty glass to Madame La Flotte. "He is doing that to gain time for Austria's mobilisation."

"But the Austrian Emperor is the father of our Empress," Madame La Flotte said sharply.

Talleyrand paid no attention to her but looked at his glass. "Once France is beaten all the members of the coalition will try to enrich themselves at our expense. Austria wants to stake its claim to a share and therefore will join the coalition."

"But," I objected—my mouth was so dry that I could hardly speak—"surely the Austrian Emperor cannot go to war against his own daughter and grandson?"

"No? But he is doing it already." He smiled. "Only, you would not find it published in the *Moniteur*, Madame. The armies allied against us have 800,000 men under arms, the Emperor hardly half that number."

"But His Majesty is a genius," La Flotte said with trembling lips. It sounded like something learnt by heart.

"Quite, Madame. His Majesty is a genius. By the way, the Emperor has forced the Danes to declare war on the Swedes. Now the Crown Prince of Sweden has the Danes threatening him from the rear."

"I suppose he can cope with the situation," I said impatiently, and thought, 'I'll have to find an occupation for Pierre, that is the most important thing, a regular job for Pierre.' "Did you say anything, Excellency?"

"Only that the day is not far off now when I shall put my request to you," said Talleyrand, and rose to his feet.

"Give my love to my sister, when you see her, Excellency. King Joseph has forbidden her my house."

Talleyrand raised his narrow eyebrows. "And where, Highness, are your two faithful adjutants?"

"Colonel Villatte joined the Army a long time ago. He went with the Army to Russia. And Count Rosen told me a few days ago that as a Swedish nobleman he felt obliged to fight by the side of his Crown Prince."

"Nonsense, he is only jealous of Count Brahe," put in Madame La Flotte.

"No, he meant it. The Swedes are a very serious-minded people, Madame. 'Ride, ride with God and come back safely!' I told him, exactly what I had told Villatte before. You are right, Excellency, I *am* lonely."

I stared after him as he limped away. He limps so gracefully, so elegantly. At the same time I decided to entrust the administration of my money and my household to Pierre. I thought that a good idea.

PARIS.
November 1813.

EVERY time I fall asleep now I have the same dream. I dream I see Jean-Baptiste riding alone across a battlefield, a battlefield a fortnight after a battle, the kind of battlefield I saw once on the journey to Marienburg, full of small mounds of earth and dead horses with inflated bellies. Jean-Baptiste is on his white horse which I know from so many parades, leaning forward in the saddle. I can't see his face, but I know he's crying. The white horse stumbles over the mounds and Jean-Baptiste falls forward even more and doesn't sit up again. . . .

For more than a week a rumour has been going round Paris about a decisive battle near Leipzig, but nobody knows anything for certain. . . .

I had been dreaming again of Jean-Baptiste on his white horse when I heard it whinny. It woke me up. It was the first time that I had heard it whinny in my dream.

I opened my eyes. The night-light had burned down, the hand of the clock seemed to point to half-past four. Suddenly I heard the whinnying of a horse, outside the house. I sat up in bed and listened. Then a very gentle knock came at the door, so gentle that nobody else could have heard it.

"Who's there?" I asked.

"Villatte," one voice said, and another, "Rosen."

I pushed back the heavy bolt. "For God's sake," I said, "where have you come from?"

"From Leipzig," said Villatte.

"With the kind regards of His Royal Highness," added Rosen.

I went back into the hall and, feeling cold, pulled the dressing-gown tightly round my shoulders. Count Rosen lit one of the candelabra, whilst Villatte had disappeared, probably to put the horses into the stable. I noticed that Rosen wore the coat and bearskin cap of a French grenadier. "A strange uniform for a Swedish dragoon," I said.

"Our troops are not on French soil yet. So His Highness sent me here in this ridiculous disguise, in order to avoid difficulties for me."

Villatte returned. "We rode night and day," he said. His face was emaciated and he looked exhausted. "By the way," he said quite inconsequentially, "we lost the decisive battle."

"We won it," exclaimed Rosen passionately, "and His Highness himself took Leipzig. The moment that he entered Leipzig at one end Napoleon fled from the other. His Highness was at the head of his troops from beginning to end."

"And why aren't you with the French Army, Colonel Villatte?"

"I am a prisoner of war, Your Highness."

"Rosen's prisoner?"

The ghost of a smile went over Villatte's face. "Yes, so to speak. His Highness did not send me to a prisoner-of-war camp but sent me here to be at your side till——"

"Till?"

"Till the enemy troops enter Paris."

So that was it, that was why the lonely rider across the battle-field was crying in my dream. "Come, gentlemen, I will make some coffee."

Villatte and Rosen between them managed to make a fire and I put the kettle on. Then we sat round the kitchen table and waited. The boots, hands and faces of both men were caked with mud.

"How is Jean-Baptiste? Have you seen him, Villatte? Is he well?"

"Very well! I saw him myself, before the gates of Leipzig, in the midst of the hardest fighting, and he was very well indeed!"

"Did you speak to him, Villatte?"

"Yes, afterwards. After the defeat, Madame."

"Victory, Colonel Villatte, victory! I shall not tolerate——" Count Rosen's high-pitched voice piped.

"What did he look like, Villatte, afterwards?"

Villatte shrugged his shoulders and stared in front of him. The water boiled, I made the coffee and poured it into the inelegant cups of the servants.

"Well, Villatte, what did he look like?"

"He has gone grey, Madame."

The coffee tasted bitter, I had forgotten the sugar. I fetched

406

it and put it on the table. It took me some time to find it, and I felt ashamed that I didn't know where things were in my own house.

"Your Highness makes wonderful coffee," said Rosen.

"That's what my husband says, too. Well now, Count, tell me all you know."

"If I only knew where to start! There is so much, so much!"

Yes indeed, there was so much! Rosen began by describing how he arrived at Jean-Baptiste's headquarters at Trachtenberg Castle, where Jean-Baptiste in the presence of the Tsar and the Emperor of Austria drafted the plans for the campaign and, incidentally, overawed Their Majesties by his phenomenal memory and precision, which neither they nor their Generals could match.

"What," I wanted to know, "did His Highness say when you turned up out of the blue?"

Rosen looked uncomfortable. "To be frank, he was furious and shouted at me that he could very well win the war without my help. And—yes, I ought to have stayed in Paris to be with Your Highness."

"Of course you ought to have stayed here," Villatte agreed.

"And you? You went away too to be in it."

"No, no, not to be 'in it' but to defend France. Besides, Her Royal Highness is your Crown Princess, not mine. But that is of no importance now, is it?"

Count Rosen went on to describe Jean-Baptiste's first big battle against the French at Grossbeeren, where he stood firm against the most vicious assaults. The French Army contained the Dupas Division, the regiments of which had served for many years under Bernadotte. 'How could you bear it,' I thought, 'how could you bear it, Jean-Baptiste?'

"In the evening," Rosen went on, "His Highness rode along from regiment to regiment to thank the men. Count Brahe and I accompanied him. Near the tent of the Prussian General Bülow we saw some French prisoners. When His Highness saw them he hesitated at first but then rode slowly towards them and along their line and looked closely at each man. Once he stopped and told the nearest man that he would see to it that they lacked nothing. But the man did not answer. So His Highness rode on and suddenly seemed dead tired and he leaned forward in the saddle. He only recovered when he saw the captured French flags. The Prussians had planted them in neat rows in front of their General's tent—mind you, without having any permission to do so from His Highness, the Commander-in-Chief, and His Highness dismounted, went to the Eagle Standards, saluted them and stood to attention in front of them for a few minutes. Then he turned abruptly and went back to his headquarters. There he shut himself into his tent and gave orders that he would see nobody, not even Brahe, his Personal Adjutant. Only Fernand brought him some soup."

We were silent and I poured out some more coffee. After a little while Count Rosen continued. "At the Battle of Leipzig, on October 18th, His Highness attacked Schönefeld, just outside Leipzig. Schönefeld was defended by French and Saxon regiments under Ney."

At that I looked at Villatte, and Villatte, the tired Villatte, smiled and said: "As you see, Madame, Napoleon put his best troops against Bernadotte, the Saxons among them, of course. The Emperor had never forgotten that Bernadotte maintained the Saxons always stand like rocks. Count Rosen, how did the Saxons stand in the Battle of Leipzig?"

"If I hadn't seen it with my own eyes, Highness, I should never have believed it. It was fantastic! Before the battle began His Highness changed, for the first time during the campaign, from his field uniform into his gala uniform which everyone can see miles away, asked for his white horse, gave the order to attack, and then rode straight towards the enemy lines where the Saxon regiments were drawn up. And the Saxon regiments——"

"Stood like rocks!" laughed Villatte, "not a shot was fired!"

"Exactly, not a shot was fired! Brahe and I rode after His Highness. He halted quite close to the Saxons and they—presented arms! '*Vive Bernadotte!*' shouted one of them, and the whole line took it up: '*Vive Bernadotte!*' His Highness raised his baton, turned his horse round and rode back; the Saxons followed in perfect order, the regimental music at their head, twelve thousand of them with forty guns. His Highness told them where to take up their positions in the firing-line. Then, during the battle, he sat on his horse for hours and hours, never moving, never having to refer to maps or to use field-glasses, yet always knowing exactly what was going on. At night, when the firing had died down, he quite unexpectedly demanded the dark-blue greatcoat of his field uniform, a hat without any badges and a fresh horse, not a white one. He and Fernand rode away and only returned at dawn next morning. A sentry saw them ride past in the night and saw His Highness dismount and walk on while Fernand stayed behind to hold the horses. Another sentry saw him sit down by a fallen soldier and heard him talk. Perhaps His Highness had not realised that the man was dead. It was a French soldier, by the way."

Another silence. "And then?" I asked at last.

"Then His Highness began the attack on Leipzig. He took it and entered it at the so-called Grimma Gate the moment that Napoleon fled through the West Gate at the other end of the town. His Highness rode to the Market Place of Leipzig and waited there for his allies, the Tsar, the Emperor of Austria and the King of Prussia. At Trachtenberg Castle he had told them he would meet them on Leipzig Market Place, and so he sat there and waited. As it so happened French prisoners were led past at that moment. His Highness had his eyes half closed; I thought he wasn't looking at the prisoners at all. But all of a sudden he raised his baton and pointed to a colonel. 'Villatte,' he said, 'come here, Villatte!' "

Here Villatte took up the story. "I stepped forward. 'What are you doing here, Villatte?' he asked. 'I am defending France,' I said. 'Are you? Then I must tell you you are defending it very badly, Villatte. Besides, I expected you to stay with my wife in Paris.' 'Your wife herself sent me to join the Army,' I said. He made no answer to that. I stood next to his horse and saw my captured comrades march past. In the end I thought he had forgotten I was there and wanted to go and join the other prisoners. But as soon as I stirred Bernadotte bent down from his horse and held me by the shoulder. 'Colonel Villatte, you are a prisoner of war. I order you herewith to return immediately to Paris to my wife's house. Give me your word of honour as a French officer that you will not leave her till I come myself.' Those were his words. I gave him my word of honour."

Villatte's part of the story ended, Rosen took over again and reported the strange arrangement Jean-Baptiste made for them. Villatte was the prisoner, but on French soil, beyond the reach of the allied armies, he was to guarantee Rosen's safety and to procure him the right of asylum in my house from the authorities in Paris. To get Rosen through the French lines Villatte got him a French bearskin cap and uniform. It sounded a complicated arrangement to me. I daresay they themselves didn't know who was in charge of whom. In any case, the arrangement worked, they rode and rode day and night, and they had arrived here safely.

I heard a clock strike half-past six. "And the Emperor?" I asked.

"He hopes to defend the Rhine frontier somehow," answered Villatte, "and, if that fails, to defend at least Paris."

'The Rhine frontier,' I thought, 'the front where Jean-Baptiste became a General. . . .'

Someone came into the kitchen and said: "Damnation, who's

gone into the kitchen without my permission?—oh, I am sorry, Your Highness!"

It was my fat cook. A kitchen maid opened the windows, and the cold morning air made me shudder.

"A cup of hot chocolate, Your Highness?" suggested the cook.

I shook my head, "No, thank you," and then told Villatte and Rosen to go to their old rooms. "You'll find everything as you left it."

I asked for a duster, instead of which the maid brought me a beautifully white napkin. She probably thought that that was the right kind of duster for a Crown Princess. However, I took it and went to Jean-Baptiste's room to give it a good dusting. The room looked very inhospitable. All the things that Jean-Baptiste valued went with him to Stockholm, so there was nothing much left here to make it friendly.

I opened the window to let some fresh air in. Marie came in. "Don't stand by the open window in your dressing-gown," she said. "You'll catch a cold. What are you doing here, any-way?"

"I'm preparing the room for Jean-Baptiste. His troops are marching on Paris, he's coming home, Marie!"

"He ought to be ashamed of himself!" she hissed, not very loudly but loud enough for me to hear, and I remembered the rider of my dream, my poor, lonely rider. . . .

PARIS.
The last week of March 1814.

MARIE had just come home from the baker's, where the women shoppers were telling each other dreadful tales about the things the Cossacks had in store for the female sex, when we heard for the first time the distant thunder of the guns. That was two days ago. Since then they have never been silent.

We knew the Austrians, the Cossacks and the Prussians were in France, but that was all we knew. Now they are here on our doorstep.

I am waiting for Jean-Baptiste, but I don't know where he is. I don't get any more letters, either from him or from Oscar. Now and then a message is smuggled through to us, and that is how I know that Jean-Baptiste has refused to pursue the beaten French across the Rhine, that he gave up his command of all troops bar his 30,000 Swedes, that he was marching northwards through Hanover against the Danes and that he had written a letter to the Tsar demanding that France's frontiers should remain inviolate because Napoleon was not France and Napoleon had been beaten already anyway. . . . But the Prussians, the Russians and the Austrians invaded France all the same, whilst Jean-Baptiste continued his private war against Denmark, Napoleon's ally whom he had forced into war against Sweden.

Marshal Marmont is in charge of the defence of Paris, Marmont who once wanted to marry me. But the thunder of the guns is coming nearer and nearer hourly.

Meanwhile we had news that Jean-Baptiste had reached Kiel and sent an ultimatum to the King of Denmark from there. He demanded the cession of Norway to Sweden and offered a million *thaler* in exchange. Denmark accepted the demand for the cession of Norway but rejected indignantly the offer of money. "So you are Crown Princess of Sweden and Norway," said Count Rosen when he received the message, the last message we had had from him, about three weeks ago. Since then we have heard nothing except that he gave in to the demands of his allies and marched towards the Rhine, towards Belgium, and that he got into a carriage there—it was said together with Count Brahe— and disappeared, just disappeared.

I am writing in my diary, writing feverishly to run away from my anxiety, writing down everything. Nobody knows where Jean-Baptiste is. Some say that Napoleon secretly in his despair asked Jean-Baptiste for help. Others that he had a disagreement with the Tsar because of the Tsar's refusal to recognise France's frontiers of 1794. Meanwhile the papers in Paris write that he has gone mad, that his father had died as a lunatic and that his brother, too, was out of his mind and—no, I can't repeat that, now that Jean-Baptiste is wandering about somewhere. Marie and Yvette try to keep from me the papers which write this kind of stuff, but Madame La Flotte takes jolly good care to leave them lying about in the drawing-room.

His chamberlain Count Löwenstein managed to get two messages through to me from Liége recently. In both of them he wanted to know whether I had any idea of the whereabouts of His Royal Highness. I hadn't, I haven't now, but I can guess, and my guess is that he has come home and is somewhere in France. Perhaps, my dear chamberlain Count Löwenstein, it is better to leave him alone for the time being now that he is looking round the ruins. . . .

Yesterday, March the 29th, at half-past six in the morning,

Marie came into my bedroom. "You are to go to the Tuileries at once."

"To the Tuileries?" I asked incredulously.

"King Joseph has sent a carriage for you. You must go to Julie at once."

I got up and dressed quickly. Julie, obedient to her husband, had not been to see me for months. And now this unexpected request!

"Shall I wake one of the adjutants?" asked Marie.

"No," I said. Surely I could go to Julie without either my 'allied' or my 'prisoner-of-war' adjutant.

Shuddering with cold, I rode through empty streets where only the street cleaners were busy. I saw them sweeping together posters printed in big letters. The lackey got me one which read:

'Parisians, surrender! Do as your fellow countrymen did in Bordeaux, call Louis XVIII to the throne and safeguard peace!'

It was signed by Prince Schwarzenberg, the Austrian Commander-in-Chief.

A whole regiment of cuirassiers sitting immovably on their horses was lined up outside the Tuileries. Inside, the yard was filled with coaches, carriages, ten green State equipages and wagons of all kinds. Lackeys were carrying innumerable heavy iron chests to the wagons. 'The crown jewels and treasures of the Imperial family and its money,' I thought. The sentries looked on with expressionless faces.

I was surprised to be taken to the private rooms of the Empress. When I got there I found Joseph standing in front of the fireplace and trying very hard to look like Napoleon. He had clasped his hands behind him and spoke in a hurried voice with his head thrown back. The Empress, whom Napoleon had made Regent during his absence, sat on a sofa with Madame Letitia. Madame Letitia had thrown a scarf round her shoulders peasant fashion, and the Empress wore a travelling coat and a hat and had the air of a visitor who could hardly spare a minute to sit down. Meneval was there, some members of the Senate and King Jerome of Westphalia, now a tall slim man in immaculate uniform. Many candles lit the room brightly, their light mingled with the grey light of dawn and made the whole scene look unreal.

Joseph was just reading a letter from Napoleon. "Here it is," he said, "here: 'Do not leave my son, and remember that I would rather have him dead in the Seine than alive in the hands of enemies of France' and so on and so on."

"But we know that. You read the letter to us before, last night in the Council of State. What possibilities are there of preventing the child from falling into the river or into the hands of the enemy?" asked Jerome in the deliberate nasal drawl which he had acquired in America.

Joseph pulled another letter from Napoleon out of his breast pocket and read it aloud. It contained exact instructions as to how many men were to be posted at each gateway and how they were to be armed: fifty men with rifles and shot-guns and a hundred men with lances. Besides the troops at the gates they were to form a mobile reserve of three thousand men, armed in the same way.

"That is all very clear, Joseph," remarked Madame Letitia. "Have you carried out the orders?"

Joseph, who was responsible for the defence of the city proper, answered that he couldn't because there were neither rifles nor shot-guns left in the depots.

He, Jerome and Meneval argued for a while as to what could or could not be done with lances against guns. When they had ended Marie-Louise asked calmly and as if it were a matter of no importance: "Well? What is the decision? Am I to leave with the King of Rome or am I to stay?"

"Madame," said Jerome, planting himself in front of her, "the officers of the Guards have sworn never to surrender Paris as long as you and the King of Rome are in it. Every man capable of bearing arms will, to the last drop of his blood——"

Joseph interrupted him: "Jerome, we have nothing but lances for the men capable of bearing arms."

"But the Guards are still fully armed, Joseph!"

"Yes, but there are only a few hundred of them. However, I realise that the presence of the Regent and her son will spur on the Guards as well as the people of Paris to fanatical resistance, whereas their departure would have an unfortunate influence on the populace. I fear that in that case——" He broke off in the middle of the sentence.

"Well?" the Empress asked once more.

"I leave the decision to the Regent," said Joseph, tired. He had lost his well-studied resemblance to Napoleon; nothing was left of him but a fat, elderly, helpless man.

Marie-Louise said: "I want to do my duty and don't want to be blamed for anything afterwards." She sounded very bored.

"Madame," urged Jerome, "if you leave the Tuileries now

413

you may lose any claim to the French crown, you and your son. Stay, Madame, let the Guards defend you, entrust your fate to the people of Paris."

"Well, let's stay, then," she said amiably, and began to undo the ribbons of her hat.

"But, Madame, think of His Majesty's instructions!" moaned Joseph. "You know he wants his son dead in the Seine rather than——"

"Don't repeat that dreadful sentence!" I exclaimed. Everybody turned round to me. It was very embarrassing. I was still standing in the doorway and, bowing in the direction of the Empress, I said: "I am sorry, I didn't want to intrude."

"The Crown Princess of Sweden in the Regent's rooms? Madame, this is a challenge which cannot be left unanswered!" shouted Jerome, and rushed at me like a madman.

"Jerome, I myself asked for Her Royal Highness because of—because of Julie," Joseph said awkwardly, pointing to my sister. I followed his movement and discovered Julie with her daughters on a sofa at the far end of the room. Their outlines were blurred by the uncertain morning light.

"Please take a seat, Highness," said Marie-Louise kindly.

Quickly I went over to Julie and sat down by her side. She had put her arm round the shoulders of her daughter Zenäide. "Don't get agitated, Julie," I whispered, "you shall come to me with your children."

Meanwhile the discussion near the fireplace raged on, till Joseph came away from the group there to us.

"If the Regent and her son go to Rambouillet I shall have to accompany her," he said to Julie.

"But how can you if you are to defend the city?"

"The Emperor has told me that I am not to let his son out of my sight. The whole family is coming along. Julie, I am asking you for the last time——"

Julie, tears streaming down her face, shook her head. "No, no, please. We'll be chased from castle to castle till the Cossacks catch up with us. Please, let me go to Désirée, Joseph, her house is safe. Isn't it, Désirée?"

Joseph and I looked at each other for a long time. "You too could come to me, Joseph," I said at last.

He shook his head and forced himself to smile. "Perhaps Napoleon will be here in time to hold Paris, and in that case I shall be back with Julie in a few days' time. If not——" he bent to kiss my hand, "let me thank you for all you are doing for Julie and my children, you and your husband."

At this moment the chamberlain announced that the Prince

of Benevento requested an audience. Smilingly the Empress asked him in.

Talleyrand, tired and worn, but with his hair carefully powdered and wearing the uniform of the Vice-Grand Elector of the Empire, limped quickly towards the Empress. "Your Majesty, I have just come from the Minister of War, who is in touch with Marshal Marmont. The Marshal requests Your Majesty to leave Paris immediately with the King of Rome. He does not know how much longer he will be able to keep open the road to Rambouillet. I am disconsolate to have to be the bringer of this dreadful message."

A deep silence fell. It was broken only by the rustling of the silk ribbons of Marie-Louise's hat, which she started tying up again under her chin. "Shall I be able to meet His Majesty in Rambouillet?"

"But His Majesty is on the way to Fontainebleau and from there will go on straight to Paris," said Joseph.

"But I mean His Majesty the Emperor of Austria—my papa."

Joseph grew deathly pale, Jerome clenched his teeth, and I saw a vein on his forehead swell. Only Talleyrand smiled. He didn't seem at all surprised. Madame Letitia, however, gripped the arm of her daughter-in-law fiercely: "Come on, Madame, come on!"

By the door Marie-Louise turned round and surveyed the room. Her eyes met those of the still smiling Talleyrand. "I hope no one is going to blame me for anything afterwards!" she sighed, and went out.

But her son, the little King of Rome, didn't feel like going. He screamed and screamed and shouted: "Don't want to! Don't want to!" At long last Hortense appeared. She knew how to deal with the boy, and a moment later Napoleon's son went obediently down the stairs between his two governesses.

"Exit Napoleon II," murmured Talleyrand close to me.

"I am very uneducated," I said. "What does 'exit' mean?"

"Exit is a Latin word and means 'goes out,' 'leaves,' 'disappears.' Exit Napoleon II, therefore, stands for Napoleon II disappears from—the Tuileries? The pages of world history?" He looked at his watch. "I am afraid I have to say good-bye, my carriage is waiting."

He, like the Empress, surveyed the room thoughtfully. Looking at the curtains with the bees he said: "A pretty pattern! Pity that they will soon be removed!"

"If you hang them upside down the bees look like lilies. Like the Bourbon lilies!"

He raised his lorgnette to his eyes. "Indeed! How strange! But really, I must go now, Highness."

"No one is keeping you, Prince. Is it true you are going to follow the Empress?"

"I am. But first I shall be taken prisoner by the Russians outside the gate. That's why I must not be late. The Russian patrol is waiting for me now. *Au revoir*, Highness!"

"Perhaps Marshal Marmont will rescue you," I hissed. "You deserve it."

"Do I? But I fear I must disappoint you. Marshal Marmont is far too busy to bother about me at the moment: he is conducting the negotiations for the surrender of Paris. But keep this piece of news to yourself, Highness. We want to avoid unnecessary bloodshed and confusion." He bowed gracefully and limped away.

I drove home with Julie and her daughters. For the first time since the day Julie had become Queen, Marie spoke to her again. Like a mother she laid her arm round Julie's narrow shoulders and led her up the stairs.

"Marie, give Oscar's room to Queen Julie and Madame La Flotte's to her children. Madame La Flotte will have to move into the spare room."

"And General Clary, the son of Monsieur Etienne?" asked Marie.

"What do you mean?"

"The General arrived an hour ago and would like to stay here for the time being."

General Clary was Etienne's son Marius, who had become an officer instead of going into Papa's firm, and with the help of God and Napoleon had reached General's rank. I decided that the two adjutants could share Rosen's room and that he should have Villatte's.

"And what about Countess Tascher?"

This question only made sense to me when I entered the drawing-room. There Etienne's daughter Marceline, who is married to a Count Tascher, threw herself into my arms, crying.

"I am so frightened, Aunt, in my house. The Cossacks might come at any moment," she sobbed.

"And your husband?"

"He is somewhere at the front. Marius stayed at my house last night and we decided to come here to you for the time being——"

I let her have the spare room and thought of putting Madame La Flotte on the divan in my boudoir.

"And my children's governess?" Julie wailed. "You must give her a room of her own. Otherwise she'll give me notice. Who is having Jean-Baptiste's bed?"

'Not the governess,' I thought in fury, and fled into Jean-Baptiste's empty bedroom. There I sat down on the wide empty bed and listened into the night. . . .

At about five o'clock in the afternoon the guns had ceased firing. Villatte and Rosen, returning from a walk, reported that Blücher had taken Montmartre by storm and that the Austrians were in Menilmontant. The allies, they said, demanded unconditional surrender.

PARIS.
March 30th, 1814.

AT two o'clock this morning the capitulation was signed. When I looked out of the window I saw the Swedish flag flying over my house. Count Rosen had put it up with the help of Johansson, the Swedish coachman. A dense crowd was waiting outside. Its voice rose dully to my window.

"What do they want, Villatte?"

"There is a rumour that His Royal Highness is coming to-day."

"But what do they want of Jean-Baptiste?"

The sounds from outside grew louder and more menacing, and I stopped asking.

A carriage arrived at the gate. Gendarmes pushed back the crowd and I saw Hortense with her two sons, the nine-year-old Napoleon Louis and the six-year-old Charles Louis Napoleon, get out. The murmur of the crowd ceased. One of the boys pointed to the Swedish flag and asked a question. But Hortense quickly pulled her boys into the house.

Madame La Flotte came. "Queen Hortense asks Your Highness if the Emperor's nephews could live under the protection of Your Highness for the time being. The Queen herself is going to join her mother at Malmaison."

'Two little boys in the house,' I thought, 'there may even be some toys of Oscar's left in the attic.' "Tell Her Majesty I shall look after the boys."

Their arrival needed another rearrangment of bedrooms. I saw their mother drive away. "*Vive l'Empereur!*" the crowd shouted. Then it closed its ranks once more, and the ominous sound of its low murmur was with me all day long.

417

PARIS.
April 1814.

ON the 31st of March the allies entered Paris. The Parisians didn't have much time to bother about their conquerors, they were too busy queueing at the baker's and grocer's. The storehouses round Paris had been destroyed and the roads to the southern provinces blocked, and the result was starvation.

On April 1st a provisional Government headed by Talleyrand was formed, and negotiations started with the allied powers. Talleyrand gave a brilliant banquet in honour of the Tsar, who was staying at his palace, and the members of the old aristocratic families whom Napoleon had allowed to return took part in it.

Napoleon himself was at Fontainebleau with 5,000 men of his Guards regiments. Caulaincourt negotiated for him with the victors. On April 4th he signed his declaration of abdication. It said that since, in the view of the allied powers, his person formed the only obstacle to the restoration of peace in Europe, he was willing to renounce his throne and to leave France for the sake of his country's well-being, which was inseparable from the rights of his son, the rights of the Empress's regency and the continued validity of the Imperial laws.

Two days later, however, the Senate declared that a regency on behalf of Napoleon II was out of the question. Everywhere in Paris I suddenly saw the white flags of the Bourbons which no one bothered to remove and no one bothered to hail. In the *Moniteur* I read that only the reinstatement of the Bourbons could guarantee lasting peace. . . .

Most members of the Bonaparte family had fled to Blois with the Empress. Marie-Louise was seeing nobody. She had asked her father for protection for herself and her son, and her father, the Austrian Emperor, discarded his grandson's name Napoleon and called him Francis.

Julie had several letters from Joseph written at Blois. They were smuggled through the allied lines by young peasants who liked doing it because it was a chance for them of seeing Paris. Julie and the children were to stay with me, wrote Joseph, till the new Government and the allies had decided what to do about the Bonapartes and their property. Meanwhile Julie had run out of money and I had to lend her some to pay the governess. Joseph had taken everything, even her jewellery, she said. My

418

nephew Marius was in the same position, and I told Pierre to advance him what he needed. Then Marceline bought two new hats and had the bill sent to me. So it went on, till Pierre told me that I had no money left at all. I went to see him in his little office—I had given him the former caretaker's flat on the ground floor—and he accounted to me for all the money we had spent.

"Could Your Highness count on money from Sweden within the next few days?" he asked.

I shrugged my shoulders.

"Perhaps you could ask His Highness the Crown Prince?"

"But I don't know where he is."

"I could borrow all the money we need, of course, if Your Highness would sign a promissory note. The Crown Princess of Sweden has an unlimited credit these days. Do you want to sign?"

"No, I can't. How can I borrow money? Certainly not as the Crown Princess of Sweden. It would make a very bad impression and my husband wouldn't like it. No, really, it's impossible."

Marie came in. "You could sell some of your silver, Eugenie."

"Yes, I could do that. No, Marie, I can't do that either! All our silver has our initials on it. All Paris would know soon that we have no money and that would injure the reputation of Sweden badly."

"I could pawn some of Your Highness's jewellery," suggested Pierre. "No one would know whose it is."

"No, I have so little valuable jewellery, and what little I have I need if I have to receive the Tsar or the Austrian Emperor."

"Julie has plenty," said Marie.

"Joseph has taken all hers with him."

"But how are you going to feed all the people under your roof?"

I stared at the empty cash-box. "Let me think."

They let me think.

"Marie, the firm of Clary has always had a warehouse in Paris, at least in Papa's days, hasn't it?"

"Oh yes. It's still there. Every time Monsieur Etienne comes to Paris he goes there. Has he never told you about it?"

"No. There's never been any reason for mentioning it."

Marie raised her eyebrows. "Hasn't there? Who's inherited that half of the firm which belonged to your Mama, then?"

"I don't know——"

"According to the law you, Queen Julie and your brother Etienne own one third each of that half," explained Pierre.

"But Julie and I had our dowries."

"Yes," Marie said, "that was your share of the estate left by your father. When he died Etienne inherited one half of the firm and your mother the other. So since your mother's death you own——"

"One sixth of the firm of Clary, Your Highness," said Pierre.

'I ought to talk it over with Julie,' I thought. But Julie was in bed with migraine. How could I go to her and say that I had no money for our lunch? "Marie," I said, "let cook fetch some veal. The butcher will get his money to-night. Please get me a *fiacre* as quickly as possible."

The big drawing-room was full of life. Marius and Villatte were poring over maps and fighting the battles of the last months all over again. Julie's daughters were having a noisy argument with Hortense's sons about the contents of a *bon-bonnière* made of magnificent Sèvres, and Madame La Flotte, translating an article to Count Rosen, was in tears because this article called Napoleon a bloodhound.

I went up to Marius. "Where," I asked him, "is the warehouse of the firm of Clary?"

He blushed. "But, Aunt, you know I have nothing to do with the silk trade. I have been an officer all my life." Obviously it was embarrassing to him to talk about it in Villatte's presence.

I persisted. "But your father is a silk merchant and, surely, you remember where his warehouse is. He went there every time he came to Paris."

"But I never went with him, I——"

I watched him closely and that made him break off. Then, quickly, he said: "In a cellar in the Palais Royal, if I remember right." And he gave me the address.

The cab took me to a very spacious and elegant basement shop in the Palais Royal. Entering I found myself in a very neatly furnished office and opposite an elderly man in formal clothes who was sitting behind a writing-desk. He wore the white rosette of the Bourbons in his buttonhole. The shelves seemed nearly empty.

"What can I do for you, Madame?"

"Are you the manager of the firm of Clary in Paris?"

"I am, Madame. White satin is unfortunately sold out, but——"

"That isn't what I have come for."

"Oh, I understand, Madame wishes to purchase some dress

420

material? Till yesterday I had some brocade with the lily pattern left, but it is all sold out now, unfortunately. But velvet or——"

"Business is flourishing, Monsieur——"

"Legrand, Madame," he introduced himself, "Legrand."

"Tell me, Monsieur Legrand, these white materials, brocade with the Bourbon lily, white satin and muslin to put over the curtains, when did they arrive here? As far as I know all the roads to Paris are blocked."

He laughed heartily and loudly so that the two double chins whipped merrily up and down over his high collar. "Monsieur Clary sent all these materials months ago from Genoa. The first consignments arrived shortly after the Battle of Leipzig. Monsieur Clary, the head of the firm, is very well informed. As Madame may know, Monsieur Clary is——" he cleared his throat, smirking, "Monsieur Clary is the brother-in-law of the victor of Leipzig, the brother-in-law of the Swedish Crown Prince. Madame will realise that——"

"And so you've been selling white silk for weeks to the ladies of the old nobility?" I interrupted him.

He nodded proudly.

I gazed at the white rosette on his lapel. "I could never understand where all the white rosettes sprang from overnight. So these noble ladies whom the Emperor received at his court have all been sitting down secretly sewing white rosettes?"

"But, Madame——"

But I was furious, dreadfully furious. I understood now why the shelves were nearly empty. "And you sold white silk, one roll after the other. Whilst the French troops were still fighting to throw back the enemy you have been sitting here making money, haven't you?"

"But, Madame, I am only an employee of the firm. Besides, most of the stuff has not been paid for yet. The ladies will only be able to pay when the Bourbons have returned and when the husbands of these ladies get their big jobs——" He stopped and looked at me with suspicion. "Madame, what can I do for you?"

"I need money. How much have you got in your till?"

"Madame, I don't understand——"

"I own one sixth of the firm of Clary, I am a daughter of the founder of the firm, and I need money urgently. How much have you got in your till, Monsieur Legrand?"

"Madame, I don't quite understand. Monsieur Etienne has only two sisters, Madame Joseph Bonaparte and Her Highness the Crown Princess of Sweden."

"Quite right. And I am the Crown Princess of Sweden. How much money have you got in your till?"

Monsieur Legrand felt for his waistcoat pocket with a trembling hand, pulled out his spectacles and looked at me. After this examination he bowed as deeply as his stomach would allow. When I shook hands with him he was nearly overcome with emotion.

"I was an apprentice in your father's shop in Marseilles when Your Highness was still a child, a dear child, and so naughty!"

"You wouldn't have recognised me, would you? Not even with your glasses?" I felt like crying myself. "I am not quite so naughty now, I'm doing my best——"

Legrand rushed to the door and locked it. "We don't need any customers now, Your Highness," he said.

"I've thought and thought how to manage without making debts," I said. "A Clary can't make debts, can she? I am only waiting for my husband——"

"The whole of Paris is waiting for the triumphant entry of the victor of Leipzig," said Legrand. "The Tsar is here already, the Prussian King too, it can't be long now."

"In all these years I've not drawn out my share in the profits of the firm," I said. "Therefore I should like to take anything you have in cash."

"I have very little cash. The day before he left King Joseph asked me for an enormous sum." I opened my eyes in amazement. He went on talking without noticing my surprise. "King Joseph drew out his wife's share in our takings twice a year. What we took to the end of March by the secret sale of the white materials has been drawn out by King Joseph. There are only the outstanding debts left."

So even Joseph Bonaparte made money on the white rosettes. Whether he knew about it or not, what does it matter now?

"Here," said Legrand, and gave me a bundle of notes. "That is all we have at the moment."

"Better than nothing," I said, and put them into my bag. An idea occurred to me, and I said: "Legrand, we must at once collect all outstanding debts. People say that the franc is going to fall. My cab is waiting outside. Take it and go round all the customers. If they refuse to pay, ask for the material back. Will you?"

"But I can't leave the shop. I sent the only apprentice we have left with some samples to an old customer of ours who urgently needs some new clothes, the wife of Marshal Marmont, in fact. And Le Roy's buyer—they are working day and night for the ladies of the new court—may call at any moment."

I took off my coat. "Whilst you're going round collecting I shall see to the customers here."

"But, Your Highness——"

"What are you 'butting' about? I helped often enough in the shop in Marseilles. Don't be afraid. I know how to handle silk. Hurry up, Monsieur!"

Legrand, completely put out, stumbled towards the door.

"One moment, Monsieur. Please take off the white rosette if you call on behalf of the firm of Clary."

"But, Your Highness, most people——"

"Yes, most people, but not my Papa's former apprentices. I'll see you later."

When he had gone, I sat down behind the desk and once more felt like crying. That was because of the memory of Marseilles. A naughty child with not a care in the world whom Papa had taken in hand and taught the Rights of Man. That was a long time ago, a very long time ago.

The door-bell rang, and a man in a light blue, beautifully embroidered tail-coat and with a white rosette came in, Le Roy's buyer. He didn't know me, I had always dealt with the manageress.

"You are Le Roy's buyer, aren't you? I am deputising for Monsieur Legrand. What can we do for you?"

"I should have liked to see Monsieur Legrand himself."

"I am sorry," I said, and pulled a heavy roll of velvet from the shelf. A label affixed to it said '*Madame Mère's* order. Returned.' It was dark green, the colour of Corsica, with the bee pattern woven into it. "Here," I said, "dark green velvet with the Bourbon lily pattern," and turned the roll round so that the bees lay upside down.

The buyer held up his lorgnette and examined the velvet sceptically. "The lilies remind me of the bee," he criticised.

"That's not my fault," I said.

"Besides, dark green is out of fashion now. We saw too much of that colour during the Empire. In any case, velvet is too heavy for spring weather. Have you any pale lilac-coloured muslin?"

I looked along the shelves which had some shades of muslin. The one he wanted was on the top shelf. It would be! I found a ladder and climbed up.

Meanwhile he went on: "The Empress Josephine desires a pale lilac dress. It is a subtle indication of mourning. She needs the dress for her reception of the Tsar."

I nearly fell off the ladder. "She—she wants to receive the Tsar?"

"Yes. She very much wants to see him to talk with him about her allowances. They are still negotiating about the annuities for the Bonaparte family. It looks as if they are going to be generous to these successful nobodies. Well, have you the muslin I want or not?"

I climbed down the ladder with the material and unrolled it before him.

"Too dark," he said.

"Lilac, the new fashion," I said.

He regarded me with contempt. "What makes you say that?"

"It looks well and a bit melancholy. Just right for Josephine. By the way, we can only sell for cash at the moment."

"Out of the question just now. Our customers do not pay on delivery, either. Of course, as soon as the situation is cleared up, Mademoiselle——"

"It is cleared up. The franc is falling. We can only sell for cash on the spot."

I took the roll of cloth from the desk and carried it back to the shelf.

"Where is Monsieur Legrand?"

"I told you, not here."

His eyes scanned the half-empty shelves. "You have hardly any stock left."

I nodded. "Almost sold out. And all for cash."

He stared, mesmerised, at a few rolls of satin. "Madame Ney," he murmured.

"Shall we say light blue satin for *Madame la Maréchale* Ney?" I suggested. "It would go with her rubies and she likes light blue."

"You seem to be well informed, Mademoiselle——"

"Désirée," I said amiably. "Well? How shall we dress Marshal Ney's wife for the occasion of her presentation to the Bourbons in the Tuileries?"

"You sound so bitter, Mademoiselle Désirée. You are not by any chance a partisan of the Bonapartes at heart, are you?"

"Take light blue for Madame Ney. I'll let you have the satin at the pre-war price." The price was on a tag in Etienne's thin writing. I named it.

"I shall give you a bill of exchange," he said.

"You'll pay cash or you'll leave the material here. I have other customers."

He paid.

"And the lilac muslin?" I asked, measuring and cutting the satin as I had seen Papa and Etienne do it at home.

"But the Empress never pays promptly," he lamented.

I paid no attention to that. At last he sighed and said: "Seven and a half yards of muslin, then."

"Make it nine. She'll be wanting a scarf of the same material."

Reluctantly he paid for Josephine's melancholy dress. When he went he said: "Ask Legrand to reserve the green velvet with the gold lilies for us till to-night." I promised I would.

I attended to three more customers before Legrand returned. "Did you get it all?" I asked.

"Not all, but a part. Here it is." He gave me a leather bag full of bank-notes.

"Make a note of everything and I shall give you a receipt."

He began to write out a receipt and pushed it towards me for my signature. I thought for a moment and then signed as 'Désirée, Crown Princess of Sweden, née Clary'.

"From now onwards I shall settle the accounts regularly with my brother Etienne. And, by the way, get as much of the lilac-coloured muslin in as you can, it's the new fashion, you'll see. And reserve the green velvet which *Madame Mère* sent back for Le Roy. No, I'm not joking, he really wants it. Good-bye, Monsieur Legrand."

I got back into the cab and told the driver to take me to the Rue d'Anjou. He gave me a newspaper. It was a special edition containing Napoleon's declaration of abdication. 'Yes,' I thought, 'yes, and we'll have veal to-night, and I must keep an eye on my bag with all the money in it, and the air is full of spring already. . . .' Women were still queueing up in front of bakers' and butchers' shops, and copies of the abdication edition disintegrated on the wet pavements.

Suddenly the cab stopped. A chain of gendarmes barred the entrance to the Rue d'Anjou. The driver dismounted and opened the door. "Can't drive on," he said, "the Rue d'Anjou is cordoned off; they expect the Tsar."

"But I must get into the Rue d'Anjou, I live there."

The driver explained that to a gendarme, and I was allowed to pass, but only on foot. So I got out and paid the driver.

Gendarmes drawn up on both sides of the street formed a lane, the carriage-way was empty and made my steps resound. Just before I reached my house I was stopped by a sergeant-major of the gendarmerie on horseback. "No entry here!"

I looked up at him. His face seemed familiar. Yes, it was

the man who for years had been standing guard over our house by order of the Minister of Police. I never knew what it meant, whether honour or supervision. Napoleon had the houses of all his Marshals guarded. This sergeant-major was an elderly man in a shabby uniform and a shabby hat. His tricorn showed a darker patch, the patch where up till two days ago he had worn the blue-white-red rosette of the Empire. It was obvious that he had left that patch free by design. The white rosette of the new Government was loosely fastened alongside it.

"Let me pass, you know I live in that house over there." I nodded in the direction of my house, in front of which gendarmes were standing in a bunch.

"In half an hour's time His Majesty the Emperor of Russia is going to pay a call on Her Royal Highness the Crown Princess of Sweden. My orders are not to let anybody walk past the house," he rattled off without looking at me.

'My God,' I thought, 'that's the last straw, the Tsar visiting me!' "In that case let me pass at once," I shouted furiously. "I must change my dress!"

But the shabby sergeant-major was still looking over my head into space.

I stamped my foot. "Look at me, will you? You have known me for years. You know very well that I live in that house there."

"Sorry, my mistake! I mistook Your Highness for the wife of Marshal Bernadotte." At last he turned his eyes on me, eyes full of a malicious glint. "I apologise for the mistake. I realise now, Your Highness is the lady who receives the Tsar's call." He roared: "Clear the way for the Crown Princess of Sweden!"

I ran the gauntlet of the gendarmes. My feet were as heavy as lead, but I kept running.

They were waiting for me at home. The front door opened from inside when I reached it and Marie hauled me in. "Quick, quick," she said, "the Tsar will be here in half an hour's time."

I threw the bag with the money to Pierre and ran up to my boudoir. Marie undressed me quickly, Yvette started brushing my hair, and I shut my eyes, exhausted. Marie forced a glass of cognac on me, which I drank in one gulp. It made my throat burn.

"What will you wear?" asked Marie, and I decided on the purple velvet dress which I had worn at the last interview with Napoleon.

Just as I was putting on my gold paint and rouge I saw in the mirror that Julie had come in, dressed in one of her purple gowns and holding one of her small crowns in her hand. "Shall I wear the crown or not, Désirée?"

I turned round and looked at her, uncomprehending. She had gone so thin that the purple dress, which doesn't suit her anyway, hung round her body in loose folds. "For heaven's sake, what do you want the crown for?"

"I thought—I mean when you present me to the Tsar you would probably introduce me by my old title and——"

I turned away and spoke to her reflection in the mirror. "You really want to be presented to the Tsar, Julie?"

She nodded energetically. "Of course I do. I shall ask him to protect my interests and those of my children. The Emperor of Russia——"

"Aren't you ashamed of yourself, Julie Clary? Napoleon has only just abdicated, his family shared in his success, you accepted two crowns from him, now you must wait for what is going to be decided about you. Your interests—" I swallowed. My mouth felt dry. "Julie, you are no longer a Queen but only Julie Bonaparte *née* Clary. No more. But no less either."

The little crown fell clattering to the floor. The next moment Julie had banged the door behind her.

Yvette placed the ear-rings of the Swedish Dowager Queen in my ears, and Marie said that all day long people had been asking for me.

"What did you tell them?"

"Nothing. You've been away a long time."

"Yes. I sent the manager round to collect debts, and I had to attend to the customers while he was away."

"Five minutes to go," said Marie. "How is business?"

"Flourishing. They are selling satin and muslin for the new court dresses for the wives of Napoleon's old Marshals. Give me another glass of cognac."

Marie poured out another glass without a word, and without a word I gulped it down. It burnt my throat, but now it was rather an agreeable burning.

I looked at myself in the mirror. The last time I had worn this dress I had had a bunch of violets on my decolletage. 'A pity,' I thought, 'I haven't any to-day.'

"By the way, Eugenie, some flowers have come for you, violets. I put them on the mantelpiece in the drawing-room. You must go down now."

I don't know whether it was my tiredness or the cognac, at any rate I floated down the stairs as if in a dream. In the hall everybody had lined up, Marceline, General Clary, Madame La Flotte, Julie's daughters, Hortense's sons, Count Rosen in a

Swedish full-dress uniform, and, in the background, Colonel Villatte. As soon as I got down Villatte asked to be excused from attending, and I let him go.

"I should like you all to go into the big drawing-room and stay there. I shall receive the Tsar in the small drawing-room." I saw astonishment on all their faces. "I notice, Count Rosen, that you have found yourself a Swedish adjutant's uniform."

"His Royal Highness sent it me through a Russian adjutant."

'Jean-Baptiste,' I thought, 'never forgets the tiniest detail.'
"You will accompany me into the small drawing-room, Count."

"And we?" exclaimed Marceline.

From the door to the drawing-room I said: "I shouldn't like to ask anybody French to be introduced to the ruler of a hostile power before peace has been concluded between France and the members of the coalition. To the best of my knowledge the Emperor has only just abdicated."

Marius blushed, Marceline uncomprehendingly shook her head, Madame La Flotte bit her lips and the children asked whether they might be allowed to peep through the keyhole. The small drawing-room was in perfect order. Champagne, glasses and sweetmeats were arranged on the small table by the mirror, and on the mantelpiece stood a silver basket with violets in it, puny-looking and past their best, and against it a sealed envelope.

The sound of trumpets and horses' hooves filled the room as a carriage drew up outside. I stood, rigid, in the middle of the room.

The door opened and the Tsar strode in, a giant with a round boyish face, fair hair and a carefree smile, a giant in a brilliantly white uniform with glittering white epaulettes. Immediately behind him came Talleyrand and a host of people in foreign uniforms. I bowed and held out my hand to the young giant, who put it to his lips.

"Your Highness, it is my deeply felt need to pay my respects to the wife of the man who has contributed so largely to the liberation of Europe," said the Tsar.

My two servants crept round, offering champagne. The Tsar sat down with me on the small sofa, and Talleyrand took the chair opposite. "The Prince of Benevento was kind enough to put his house at my disposal," said the Tsar, and smiled.

'Does he always wear uniforms of brilliant white,' I wondered, 'even in battle? Nonsense, the Tsar was no leader of armies, he was a monarch waiting for news of victory from his Generals. Only Jean-Baptiste was Prince and General at the same time,' I thought, and smiled into my glass of champagne.

"It was a matter of infinite regret to me that Your Highness's husband did not enter Paris by my side," he continued with eyes suddenly narrowing. "It was something I had counted on. We exchanged a number of letters during the advance across the Rhine, a small difference of opinion concerning the future frontiers of France. . . ."

I drank and smiled into my glass of champagne.

"I should have been glad if His Royal Highness could have taken part in the discussions on the shaping of the new France. After all, Your Highness's husband is better informed about the wishes of the French people than I or our dear cousins, the Emperor of Austria and the King of Prussia. Moreover, they and their advisers are apt to pursue quite different and particular interests." The Emperor emptied his glass and an adjutant refilled it. Neither of my servants was allowed near him.

I kept smiling.

"I am awaiting with impatience the arrival of your husband, Highness. Perhaps Your Highness knows when I may expect him?"

I shook my head and drank my champagne.

"The provisional Government of France under the leadership of our friend, the Prince of Benevento"—he raised his glass to Talleyrand and Talleyrand bowed—"has informed us that France longs for the return of the Bourbons and that only their restoration can guarantee internal peace. This has surprised me. What does Your Highness think of it?"

"I know nothing about politics, Sire."

"During my frequent conversations with Your Highness's husband I had rather gained the impression that the Bourbon dynasty is not—hm, well, is not at all acceptable to the French people. Therefore I suggested to His Royal Highness——" he held his empty glass up to the adjutant without taking his eyes off me, "Madame, I have therefore proposed to your husband to persuade the French people to elect its great Marshal Jean-Baptiste Bernadotte, Prince of Sweden, as its King."

"And what did my husband answer, Your Majesty?"

"Nothing, Your Highness, quite incomprehensibly, nothing. Our dear cousin, the Crown Prince of Sweden, has not answered our letter, he has not arrived in Paris at the appointed time, my couriers can no longer establish contact with him. His Highness has—disappeared." He emptied the freshly filled glass and looked at me sadly. "The Emperor of Austria and the King of Prussia support the return of the Bourbons, and Britain is putting a man-of-war at our disposal to convey Louis XVIII across. As the Crown Prince of Sweden has not answered me

I shall conform to the wishes of the French Government and of my allies." He stared thoughtfully into his glass. "Pity," he said, "pity." And abruptly he added: "You have a charming salon, Madame."

We rose, and the Emperor went to the window and looked out into the garden. I was standing quite close to him and hardly reached to his shoulders.

"This is Moreau's old house," I said.

The Tsar, overcome by sudden painful memories, closed his eyes. "A shell smashed both his legs when he was serving as a member of my General Staff. He died at the beginning of September. Did Your Highness not know?"

I pressed my head against the cool glass of the window. "Moreau is an old friend of ours from the days when my husband still hoped to be able to preserve the Republic for the people of France." I spoke in a very low tone, and not even Talleyrand was near enough to hear us.

"And is it for the sake of this Republic that your husband will not accept my suggestion?"

I made no answer.

"No answer is answer enough," he smiled.

Then I remembered something and became very angry. "Sire," I said.

He bent down. "My dear cousin?"

"You offered my husband not only the French crown but also the hand of a Grand Duchess!"

He laughed. "It is said that walls have ears. But that even the thick walls of Åbo should possess them! . . . Do you know what your husband answered, Highness? 'But I am married already,' he said, and the subject has never been touched on again. Does that reassure you, Highness?"

"I never needed a reassurance, Sire, at least in that respect. Will you have another drink, my dear—cousin?"

Talleyrand joined us, bringing glasses, and he didn't leave us alone for another second.

"If I could do anything for you, dear cousin, you would make me very happy."

"You are very kind, Sire. But I need nothing."

"Perhaps you would like a guard of honour of Russian Guards officers?"

"For heaven's sake, no!" I exclaimed. Talleyrand smiled ironically.

"I understand," the Tsar said gravely, "of course I understand, my dearest cousin." He bent over my hand. "Had I had the honour of knowing you before I should never have made that suggestion to the Crown Prince. I mean the Åbo suggestion."

"But you meant well, Sire."

"The ladies of my family who might have been considered are very ugly. You, however, my dear, my very dear cousin . . ."

The rest of his sentence was drowned by the clicking of his spurred heels. Then he left with his entourage.

After he had gone my thoughts wandered back to Moreau who had come back from America to fight for France's liberty. He had not lived to see the return of the Bourbons and the white rosettes. . . . I caught sight of the faded violets. "Count Rosen, where did the flowers come from?"

"Caulaincourt brought them. He was on his way from Fontainebleau to Talleyrand to hand over the instrument of abdication."

I went to the mantelpiece. There was no address on the sealed envelope. I tore it open and found a sheet of notepaper with nothing on it but a scribbled 'N'. I took out a bunch of the violets. They smelled beautifully as if they were still fresh, still quite alive, yet they were half dead already.

I felt very tired. Selling satin and muslin for the firm of Clary, reading Napoleon's abdication, entertaining the Tsar of Russia, learning the news of Moreau's death, and now the violets from Fontainebleau, it was enough to make me reel with tiredness. So I told Rosen to apologise for me at table and went straight to my room.

At the bottom of the stairs Marie was waiting for me. She took me to bed, undressed me and tucked me in as if I were a child.

I woke in the middle of the night and sat up in bed with a jerk. Everything was black around me and perfectly still. I pressed my hands against my temples to remember what it was that had woken me. What had it been? A thought? A dream? No, the knowledge that something was going to happen during the night, perhaps at this hour, something that I had felt coming all through the evening, something—— Suddenly I knew. It was something to do with abdication and the violets.

I lit the candle and went into my boudoir. The special edition with the announcement of the abdication was still lying on my dressing-table. I read it through very very carefully: '. . . the Emperor declares that he renounces the thrones of France and Italy and that there is no sacrifice, not even that of his life, which he is not willing to make . . .' ran the Emperor's proclamation.

That was it, 'no sacrifice, not even that of his life. . . .' They were the words that had woken me. I knew, I knew for certain that he was going to commit suicide. That was why he had sent the violets: a man alone at the end of his life looked back to his youth, to the beginning of his journey where he found the young girl leaning against the hedge in a dreamy garden and, since she was still within reach, he sent her the last greeting, her, who had been the first.

The violets were all the proof I needed that he was going to take his life. 'I shall order Villatte,' I thought, 'to ride to Fontainebleau at once and to force his way into his bedroom. Perhaps he will be too late, but I must try it, I must.

'Why must I, why? Was there any obligation on me? Must I really?'

I slipped from the chair down to the floor, fighting hard not to lose my self-control, not to scream, not to wake anybody, fighting hard the sense of doom. It was an endless night. Not till dawn broke did I get back to my bed. My limbs ached and I felt terribly cold.

After breakfast I sent for Colonel Villatte: "Go to Talleyrand's office in the course of the morning and inquire on my behalf after the state of the Emperor Napoleon's health!"

Later I took a cab and drove with Count Rosen to the shop of the firm of Clary. I had been told that the Prussians were 'shopping' in Paris without paying for the goods. When we arrived Monsieur Legrand was just trying unsuccessfully to prevent some Prussian soldiers from carrying off our last rolls of silk. I told Rosen, whose Swedish uniform commanded respect, to deal with them, and he managed to persuade the Prussians to pay up.

When we returned an enormous crowd had assembled in front of my house. Two Russian Guardsmen were solemnly pacing up and down the length of the house. As I got out, these men, who wore enormous beards and looked altogether frightening, presented arms. "It is a guard of honour," said Count Rosen.

"But what are these people waiting for? Why are they staring up at the windows?"

"Perhaps there has been a rumour that His Royal Highness is returning to-day. After all, to-morrow is the day for the official entry of the victorious rulers and their Marshals. It seems hardly possible that His Royal Highness should not take part in the victory parade at the head of the Swedish troops."

Hardly possible, yes, hardly possible. . . .

Before the mid-day meal Colonel Villatte reported to me on his visit to Talleyrand. "At first," he said, "they hedged. But when I said that you had sent me, Talleyrand told me in strictest confidence that——" Villatte recounted what Talleyrand had told him and finished up by saying: "It is inconceivable."

The meal took place in a most depressing silence. Even the children didn't say a word. And what was the reason for it? Firstly, said Julie, because I hadn't presented any of them to the Tsar, and secondly, I had been so strange, so unapproachable to them lately that the children, who very much wanted to see the victory parade, dared not ask me to lend them my carriage with the Swedish colours on it. I told Julie that I had plenty of problems and cares, and that I slept badly and that these were sad days. But they could gladly have my carriage if they wanted to see the parade. They would be safe in it and I didn't need it. I would stay at home to-morrow. When I had said that the horizon brightened considerably. . . .

During that night, the night from the 12th to the 13th of April, I kept the candle on my bedside table burning all night. About eleven o'clock the murmur from the crowd outside died down. The Rue d'Anjou became very quiet and the steps of the two Russian sentries rang out through the lonely night The clock struck midnight. The clock struck one, the first hour of the day of the victory parade. I listened to every inexplicable forlorn creaking of the world with all the muscles of my body tensed, I listened, I listened, I listened. The clock struck two.

Suddenly the silence of the night was shattered by the sound of wheels rolling along the street, wheels grating to a standstill outside my house. I heard the sentries spring to attention and present arms, heard a loud knock on the front door, heard voices, three or four voices, but not the one I was waiting for. I lay quite still, with eyes closed.

Someone came running up the stairs. Someone tore open the door of my bedroom, kissed my mouth, my eyes, my forehead, my cheeks: Jean-Baptiste, my Jean-Baptiste!

"You must eat something, you've had a long journey," I said awkwardly, and opened my eyes. Jean-Baptiste was kneeling by my bed, his face lying on my hand.

"A long journey, a dreadfully long journey," he said tonelessly.

I stroked his hair with my free hand. It had gone quite grey, I could see it by the light of the candle, quite grey.

I sat up in bed. "Come, Jean-Baptiste, go into your bedroom and have a rest. I'll go into the kitchen meanwhile and make you an omelette, shall I?"

But he didn't move. He pressed his head against the edge of my bed and didn't move.

"Jean-Baptiste, you're at home, you're at home at last!"

Slowly he lifted his head.

"Jean-Baptiste, get up. Your room is waiting and——"

He smoothed his forehead with his hand as if he wanted to smooth away old memories. "Yes yes, of course. Can you find beds for them all?" he asked.

"All?"

"I am not alone, you know. There are Brahe and Löwenhjelm, besides Admiral Stedingk and——"

"That's out of the question. The house is overcrowded as it is. With the exception of your bedroom and your study there isn't a single free room."

"Overcrowded?"

"Yes, Julie, her children, Hortense's sons and——"

He jumped to his feet. "Do you mean to say that you offered shelter to all the Bonapartes and are feeding them at the expense of the Swedish court?"

"Only to Julie and the children and a few Clarys. The two adjutants you sent me yourself. As to feeding, the cost of the household as well as all the salaries I am paying out of my own money."

"Out of your own money?"

"Yes, money I earned by selling silk for the firm of Clary." I went into my boudoir and slipped into my pretty green dressing-gown with the mink collar. "And now I'm going to get you and your gentlemen something to eat."

Then the miracle happened: Jean-Baptiste laughed, laughed as if he were going to burst, sat on my bed and laughed and opened his arms. "My little girl, my priceless little girl, come, come to me! The Crown Princess of Sweden and Norway sells silk! Come, my girl!"

I went to him. "I don't know what there is to laugh at. I had no money left, and everything is so dreadfully expensive. You'll see!"

"A fortnight ago I sent you a courier with money."

"Unfortunately he never arrived. Listen, when your gentlemen have had something to eat we'll have to find hotel rooms for them."

He became serious again. "They can stay at the Swedish headquarters in the Rue St. Honoré." He opened the door from my bedroom into his. I held up the light.

"Everything's ready for you," I said.

But he stared round his old familiar room with the old familiar

434

furniture as if he had never seen it before. "I think, I too shall stay in the Rue St. Honoré." Once more his voice had become toneless. "You see, I shall have to receive very many people. And I can't do that here, I can't. Don't you understand, Désirée?"

"You don't want to stay here?"

He put his arm round my shoulder. "I have only come to Paris to let the Swedish troops take part in the victory parade and to see the Tsar. But one thing I can tell you, Désirée: I shall never again return to this room, never."

"But five minutes ago you wanted to stay here with the whole of your staff!"

"That was before I had set eyes on my room again. Forgive my mistake. But there is no return to where I came from." He held me close to him. "Well, let's go down now. My staff hope that you will welcome them. I am sure that Fernand has prepared something to eat."

Mention of Fernand brought me back to reality. I put on some rouge and powder, and Jean-Baptiste and I went arm-in-arm down to the dining-room. Young Brahe was there—I should have liked to kiss him but didn't dare because of Löwenhjelm—Löwenhjelm, Admiral Stedingk, a much-bemedalled man, and Fernand in a brand-new livery with gold buttons. "How is Oscar?" I asked him.

Jean-Baptiste took some letters out of his breast-pocket and said proudly: "The Prince has composed a regimental march!"

My heart gave a little leap of joy when I heard that Oscar composed music.

Fernand's coffee was bitter and sweet at the same time. 'Exactly like this homecoming,' I thought.

We sat in front of the fireplace in the big drawing-room. I noticed Jean-Baptiste gazing towards the portrait of the First Consul in the far half-dark end of the room. One by one we fell silent till at last Jean-Baptiste turned to me and asked in a sharp voice: "And——he?"

"The Emperor is at Fontainebleau waiting to learn what is decided about him. By the way," I added, "he tried to commit suicide the night before last."

"What?" they exclaimed with one voice. Only Jean-Baptiste said nothing.

"Since the Russian campaign the Emperor's always carried poison about with him," I said, not looking at the men but into the fire. "The night before last he swallowed it. But his valet had seen him and he took the necessary measures at once. Napoleon has completely recovered now."

435

"That is grotesque," said Stedingk, "tragic and ridiculous at the same time. If he wanted to make an end why didn't he shoot himself?"

Again there was silence, silence as heavy as lead. At last Count Brahe cleared his throat and said: "Your Highness, concerning to-morrow's victory parade——"

Jean-Baptiste started, then recovered himself and began in his usual precise manner: "Above all, I shall have to clear away every actual and possible misunderstanding between myself and the Tsar. He expected me, as you know, to advance with the allies into France. I did not, and I did not take part in any battle on French soil. If my allies take it amiss——" He broke off.

I looked at Brahe, who, hesitantly, answered my unspoken question: "We drove about in Belgium and France for weeks, aimlessly, Your Highness. His Highness wanted to see the battlefields."

"The villages where fighting took place are completely destroyed. That is not the way to make war," said Jean-Baptiste between his teeth.

Löwenhjelm, deciding that this was the moment, opened the brief-case he had with him and produced a bundle of letters. "Your Highness, I have here all the letters from the Tsar to you which have not been answered. They chiefly concern——"

"Don't say it!" shouted Jean-Baptiste at him. I had never before seen him lose his self-control to such an extent. He bent forward and stared into the fire. The eyes of the Swedes, I noticed, were directed to me. I seemed to be their last hope.

"Jean-Baptiste," I began. But he gave no sign of having heard me. I got up, knelt by his side and put my head against his arm. "Jean-Baptiste, you must listen to these gentlemen. The Tsar offered you the crown of France, didn't he?"

I felt his body stiffen, but I didn't give up. "You didn't answer the Tsar. And that is what has made it possible for the Count of Artois, Louis XVIII's brother, to come to Paris to-morrow and prepare everything for the return of the Bourbons. The Tsar had no option but to conform to the wishes of the other allies and the suggestions of Talleyrand."

"But the Tsar will never understand why I kept aloof from the French campaign and why I did not answer his proposal. Sweden cannot afford a disagreement with the Tsar, don't you understand?"

"Jean-Baptiste, the Emperor is very proud to be your friend.

436

And he realises that you cannot accept the French crown. I explained it all to him."

"You what?" Jean-Baptiste gripped my shoulders and stared at me.

"Yes, he was here to pay his respects to the wife of the victor of Leipzig."

I could hear them all, Jean-Baptiste and his Swedes, breathe a sigh of relief.

I got up. "And now, gentlemen, you will want to rest a few hours before the big parade. I hope that everything will be ready for you at the Rue St. Honoré."

I left the drawing-room quickly. I didn't want to see Jean-Baptiste leave his home to stay in some palace or other. But he came after me and caught up with me on the staircase, leaning on me heavily. In my bedroom he dropped on my bed, and I had to undress him as if he were a child. I put out the candle, but already the morning was creeping through the chinks of the shutters and there was little sleep for us.

"This confounded victory parade," Jean-Baptiste said. "How can I march with bands playing across the Champs Elysées at the head of the Northern Army?"

"Of course you can. Why not? The Swedes have fought bravely for European freedom, and now they want to enter Paris in triumph with their Crown Prince at their head. How long will it all take, after all? One hour, perhaps two at most. It will be much easier than—Leipzig, Jean-Baptiste."

"Tell me, Désirée, what exactly did you tell the Tsar?"

"That in France you are a Republican and in Sweden the Crown Prince. Not perhaps in those words, but the Tsar understood me all right."

"What else did you talk about, my girl?"

"About Grand Duchesses. The Tsar thought you'd better stay with me. His Grand Duchesses are not at all pretty."

"Mhm," Jean-Baptiste said.

At last he fell asleep, a short and restless sleep like that of a traveller in the bed of some indifferent hotel room.

An argument between Fernand and Marie about the big clothes-iron put an end to Jean-Baptiste's sleep. He went into his dressing-room, where Fernand helped him to dress. Meanwhile Marie brought our breakfast and grumbled: "The Marshal might have left Fernand at home."

"Where do you call home?"

"Stockholm, of course."

The door between my boudoir and Jean-Baptiste's dressing-room was not closed, and after a while I heard the voices of

437

Brahe and Löwenhjelm. They reported that Wetterstedt, the Prime Minister of Sweden, had arrived, and that our own head-quarters was being stormed.

"By the Parisians?" asked Jean-Baptiste.

"Oh no, the street has been cordoned off and the Tsar has put a Russian regiment at our disposal," said Brahe.

Jean-Baptiste's answer was given so quickly that I only caught a few words: "Swedish dragoons . . . under no circumstances Russian sentries. . . ."

Then I heard Löwenhjelm say who it was who had stormed our headquarters. Apparently Talleyrand had called in the name of the French Government, followed by the Marshals Ney and Marmont, the Personal Adjutant of the King of Prussia, the British Ambassador, a deputation of the citizens of Paris, and so on.

In the middle of this enumeration Colonel Villatte was announced. Jean-Baptiste asked him in at once. I went to join him. Fernand was just sprinkling him with eau de Cologne and handing him the Grand Cross of the Legion of Honour. Jean-Baptiste took it as usual without thinking, when suddenly he seemed to notice it and froze in the act of putting it round his neck. Löwenhjelm warned him that the time was getting short. Slowly Jean-Baptiste came to life again and put it on. "On parade, Marshal Bernadotte!" he whispered to the hollow-cheeked face that stared back at him from the mirror.

At that moment Villatte came in. Jean-Baptiste turned to him quickly, went to meet him and slapped his shoulder. "Villatte, how glad I am to see you again!"

Villatte stood to attention.

Jean-Baptiste shook him by the shoulder. "Well, old friend?"

Villatte remained immobile, his face rigid.

Jean-Baptiste's hand slipped from his friend's shoulder. "Can I do anything for you, Colonel?"

"I am told that the allied powers yesterday ordered the discharge of all French prisoners of war. I therefore request my—release."

I laughed. But Villatte did not smile. His face became very sad instead.

"Of course, Colonel, you are free to go," said Jean-Baptiste. "I should be very glad if you could stay with us as our guest for the time being."

"I thank Your Highness for the very kind offer. I regret that I cannot accept it and I ask Your Highnesses to excuse me now."

"Villatte," I said, "you have gone such a long way with us. Won't you stay with us?"

"The Emperor has released his Army from the oath of loyalty to him," Jean-Baptiste added hoarsely. "Even his Marshals are calling on me. Why will you of all people——"

"That is just why. The Marshals have not thought it necessary to say good-bye to their Supreme Commander. I am only a colonel, Your Highness, but I know what I have to do. I shall go to Fontainebleau first and then join my regiment."

He turned and the next moment he was gone. Jean-Baptiste looked very grey in the face.

Before he left I took him into my boudoir, sat him down on the stool before the dressing-table, and began to rub his grey cheeks carefully with rouge. He protested vigorously.

"You can't ride across the Champs Elysées at the head of your victorious troops looking like death itself. If you enter like a victor you must look like a victor." I examined my handiwork and noticed with satisfaction that his cheeks looked a very natural red.

But Jean-Baptiste shook his head in revulsion. "I can't. Really, I can't." It sounded almost like sobbing.

I put my hands on his shoulders. "After the parade you'll show yourself at the command performance in the Théâtre Français. You owe that to Sweden. And now, dearest, I fear you must go."

He buried his head on my breast. All the colour had gone out of his lips, they were sore and full of cracks. "I believe that during the victory parade there will be only one other man as lonely as I and that is—he!"

"Nonsense! You are not lonely. After all, I am with you and not with him! Go now, your staff is waiting."

He got up and put my hand to his lips. "Promise me not to go and see the parade."

I promised him that.

When the bells began to ring for the beginning of the parade I went and sat in the garden. Everybody had gone in my coach to be there too, and I had given the servants the day off. Hence no one was there to announce an unexpected visitor. This unexpected visitor had found the front door open, entered and wandered through the empty house into the garden. I didn't notice him because I had my eyes closed and was thinking of Jean-Baptiste at the victory parade. "Your Highness!" I heard someone shout through the ringing of the bells, and when I, startled out of my thoughts, opened my eyes, I saw Fouché

439

with his pointed nose and small eyes, and a very big white rosette on the lapel of a rather modest tail-coat. He made a deep bow.

Rather overcome, I pointed to the bench. He sat down with alacrity and at once began to talk. I couldn't hear him because of the bells. He stopped talking, smiled and waited. Then the bell-ringing came to an end.

"I am sorry to disturb Your Highness, I have come on Talleyrand's behalf to see Madame Julie Bonaparte. Talleyrand is very busy these days, whilst I unfortunately have very much time. I had in any case intended to call on you, and so I offered to take the document along. It concerns the future of the members of the Bonaparte family."

He handed me the copy of a very lengthy document.

"I shall pass it on to my sister."

"Do have a look at the list, Your Highness."

I looked and read: the mother of the Emperor—300,000 francs; King Joseph—500,000 francs; King Louis—200,000 francs; Queen Hortense and her children—400,000 francs; King Jerome and his wife—500,000 francs; Princess Eliza—300,000 francs; Princess Polette—300,000 francs.

"These are annuities, Your Highness, annuities! Our new Government is really generous."

"Where may the members of the Bonaparte family live?"

"Only abroad, Your Highness!"

So Julie, who always feels miserable away from France, will be an exile, an exile for the rest of her life! And why? Because I, once upon a time, had brought Joseph into our house in Marseilles. 'I must try to help her,' I thought, 'I must do all I can to keep her here.'

"Perhaps you could ask His Royal Highness to intervene on behalf of Madame Julie Bonaparte? Or go and see His Majesty King Louis XVIII and put in a good word for her with him?"

"King Louis. . . ." I repeated, and tried to get used to the name.

"His Majesty is expected to arrive at the Tuileries in the next few days."

"What did this King Louis do during his exile?" I wanted to have an idea what the brothers Bonaparte might do with their time in their future asylums.

"His Majesty engaged in studies. He translated a famous book into French, Gibbon's *Decline and Fall of the Roman Empire*."

'Translated history, not made it,' I thought. "Is he bringing his own court with him?"

"Yes," he said, and went on to make the astonishing request that I should mention his name to His Majesty King Louis to help him obtain a post.

"I'm sure you have not been forgotten, Monsieur Fouché," I said. "Even I, who was only a child at the time, remember clearly the many thousand death sentences you signed."

He fumbled with his white rosette. "That, Your Highness, is no longer remembered. What I should like to be remembered, however, is the fact that several times during the last few years I tried secretly to come to an arrangement with Britain. General Bonaparte called me a traitor, Your Highness, I risked my life."

I cast another glance at the document in my hand. "What are the conditions for—General Bonaparte?"

"Very favourable ones. He may go where he likes outside France. He can take with him four hundred of his men, whom he can pick himself. Besides, he may retain the title of Emperor. Very magnanimous, is it not?"

"What has he decided on?"

"I heard the Island of Elba mentioned, a charming place much like Corsica in character."

"And the Empress?"

"She will be made Duchess of Parma provided she renounces the claims of her son to the French throne. All these details are to be thrashed out at a big congress in Vienna. Reconstruction of Europe, return of the dynasties driven out by Bonaparte, and so on. I expect His Royal Highness will want to go to Vienna to maintain his rights to the Swedish throne. I am told that Austria and Prussia insist that His Highness has no legitimate claim. I shall gladly put myself at His Highness's disposal at any time to sound opinion in Vienna and——"

I got to my feet. "I don't know what you are talking about. I shall hand the document to my sister."

If he had stayed another minute I should have screamed for help!

A little later the children came back from the victory parade and told me excitedly how marvellous Uncle Jean-Baptiste had looked in his resplendent uniform and that he had sat on his horse like a marble statue without once moving. The Tsar of Russia had kept smiling, the old Emperor of Austria waving his hand, the King of Prussia made a very angry face, but Jean-Baptiste had just sat on his horse, they said.

"And what did the spectators say?" I asked.

"All sorts of things. There was so much to see, the many foreign uniforms, and the beautiful horses, and the Cossacks

441

with their whips and the Prussians with their goose step which made everybody laugh."

"And what did they say while Uncle Jean-Baptiste rode past?"

The children looked at each other. Finally Louis Napoleon said hesitantly: "Everybody was suddenly quiet. It was as quiet as the grave."

I sent them into the house to have something to eat and went to Julie with the document Fouché had brought.

"I won't go," Julie sobbed in despair, "I won't go. They can't take Mortefontaine, they mustn't take Mortefontaine from me. Oh, Désirée, you must try and get them to let me stay on at Mortefontaine, me and the children."

I stroked her thin lustreless hair. "For the time being you'll stay here with me. Later on we can try to get Mortefontaine back. But what about Joseph? If he doesn't get permission to stay, what then?"

"He's written to me from Blois. He wants to go to Switzerland and buy an estate there, and I am to follow him as soon as possible. But I'm not going, I'm not going!" Julie sat up. "Désirée, you won't leave me, will you, you'll stay with me till everything is settled, you'll stay with me here in your house, won't you?"

I nodded. 'I brought her into the Bonaparte crowd,' I thought, 'it's my fault that she is without a home now, I must help her.'

"Will you promise me?"

"I promise I'll stay with you, Julie."

     •   •   •

On the evening of King Louis XVIII's first court ball in the Tuileries I had a cold, not a real one, of course, only the kind of cold I had at Napoleon's coronation. I stayed in bed, Marie brought me milk and honey, and I read the papers. The *Moniteur* described the departure of Napoleon for Elba. He left on April 20th. Not a single one of his Marshals had been present. General Petit paraded a regiment of Guards, the Emperor kissed the regimental colours and climbed into a coach in which General Bertrand waited for him, and that, according to the *Moniteur*, had been all. In the *Journal des Débats*, however, I found an interesting article on the Crown Prince of Sweden. There I read that the Crown Prince intended to divorce his wife Désirée Clary, sister of Madame Julie Bonaparte. After the divorce the former Crown Princess would continue to live in her home in the Rue d'Anjou in Paris under the name of the Countess of Gothland. The Crown Prince, I read, would have the choice between a Russian and a Prussian Princess. The entry of the former Marshal J.-B. Bernadotte into one of the legitimate dynasties of Europe would be of the greatest importance for his future position in Sweden.

After that, milk and honey had lost their taste for me, and I didn't want to read any more papers either. I remembered that it was the night of the first court reception of the Bourbons, and I wondered whether Jean-Baptiste had accepted the invitation.

Since the night of his arrival we have hardly been alone together. I have visited him in the Swedish headquarters in the Rue St. Honoré often enough, and in his ante-chamber I found Fouché waiting every time I called, Talleyrand on three occasions, and even Marshal Ney was sitting patiently there once or twice. In Jean-Baptiste's office there seemed to be eternal conferences between Wetterstedt, the Prime Minister, and his Generals and Admirals, whilst Jean-Baptiste either pored over documents or dictated letters.

This afternoon we had a reception in the Rue St. Honoré in honour of the Tsar. To my horror the Tsar brought along the Count of Artois, brother of the new King of France. This Count, a man with a coarse and embittered face, wears a wig. The Bourbons are trying to persuade themselves that the Revolution has changed nothing. Yet Louis XVIII had to promise to take the oath of obedience to the laws of France, which meant to the *Code Napoléon*.

The Count of Artois dashed forward towards Jean-Baptiste. "Dear cousin, France will be eternally in your debt." Jean-Baptiste grew pale, but before he could say anything the Bourbon had turned to me and said: "Your Highness, you will come to-night to the reception in the Tuileries, will you not?"

Pressing my handkerchief to my nose I answered that I was suffering from a spring cold. The Tsar was very concerned when he heard that and hoped that I would soon recover.

Lying in bed I tried to imagine what was going on in the Tuileries. All the soft furnishings would have lilies instead of bees, there would be no Marseillaise, of course, Louis XVIII, an old gentleman suffering from dropsy, would stare with tired eyes at the ballroom from which they dragged his brother to his doom many years ago, and perhaps he would embrace a certain J.-B. Bernadotte, a fanatical Republican and Crown Prince of Sweden, and call him 'our meritorious cousin', perhaps . . .

My thoughts were interrupted by the sound of steps coming quickly up the staircase. Who could it be? Everybody was in bed, as far as I knew.

"I hope I did not wake you, my girl."

It was Jean-Baptiste, not in full court dress but in his blue field uniform.

"You are not really ill, Désirée?"

"Of course not. And you, Jean-Baptiste? Why aren't you at the Tuileries?"

"Because of the strange fact that a former sergeant seems to have more sense of what is fitting than a Bourbon King." There was a pause. "A pity you are in bed, I wanted to say good-bye," he went on. "I am leaving to-morrow morning."

I thought everybody in the house would hear the hammering of my heart. He was going to-morrow, to-morrow. . . .

"I have done what I came to do here. Nobody could ask for more than that. Besides, the allies have agreed to my treaty with Denmark. But imagine, Désirée, the Norwegians don't want the union with Sweden."

'So that is our farewell,' I thought. 'I am in bed, a candle flickers, he talks of Norway.' "Why don't they?"

"Because they want to be independent."

"Then let them," I said.

Jean-Baptiste pointed out to me that that was out of the question for a variety of reasons. Above all, he had promised the Swedes this union and his position depended to a great extent on the fulfilment of his promise. If he disappointed them the Swedish Parliament that had elected him to the Succession could also exclude him from it.

After he had said that he caught sight of the papers on my bedside table. Absent-mindedly he turned the pages of the *Journal des Débats*. An article, I knew well which, attracted his attention and he began to read.

"If you married a Princess, you could become a member of one of the old dynasties," I said, and my heart felt as heavy as a stone. He kept on reading the *Journal*. "Haven't you seen this article before?"

"No. I really have no time for scandal stories. Disgusting court cackle!" He threw the paper back on the table. "Pity, I have a carriage waiting downstairs and wanted to suggest— no, let's leave it, you are probably too tired."

"You wanted to say good-bye and to suggest something," I said, pulling myself together. But I couldn't prevent my voice from sounding flat and toneless. "Say it quickly, or I'll go crazy."

He stared at me in surprise. "It is not as important as all that. I only wanted to drive with you once more through the streets of Paris. For the last time, Désirée."

"For—the last time?"

"Yes, because I shall never come to Paris again."

At first I thought I hadn't heard aright. When I knew that he had said just that, I started crying, crying with relief.

"What is the matter, Désirée? Are you not feeling well?"

"I thought you were going to tell me that you wanted a divorce," I sobbed, and pushed back the bed-cover. "I'll dress quickly and we'll drive through Paris, shall we?"

The carriage, an open one, rolled along the Seine quays. I put my head against his shoulder and felt his arm holding me. When we got to 'our' bridge the carriage stopped, and we went arm-in-arm and looked over the side of the bridge into the water where the lights of Paris shone back at us. The words of our first conversation there came into my mind and without thinking I asked them again: "Do you know General Bonaparte?"

"Yes," he answered, "and I don't like him."

I went on speaking, addressing my words to the lights of Paris dancing on the waters of the Seine: "I had to work my way up. I joined the Army when I was fifteen, was nothing but a sergeant for many years. I am a Divisional General now, Mademoiselle! My name is Jean-Baptiste Bernadotte. For years I have saved up part of my salary. I could buy a little house for you and the child. . . . That's what you said at the time, you remember?"

"Of course. But I should rather like to know how you envisage your future, Désirée."

"If you think that it is necessary, for you and Oscar, to marry a Princess, then let us have a divorce," I said, fumblingly at first. But the last part came out all right. "On one condition," I added.

"And that is?"

"That you make me your mistress."

"Out of the question! I don't want to start this mistress business at the Swedish court. Besides, I couldn't afford a mistress, my girl. No, you will have to remain my wife, Désirée, whatever happens."

The murmuring of the water from below the bridge came up to me like sweet music. "Even if the worst happens and you are King?"

"Yes, darling, even if I am King."

Slowly we made our way back to the carriage.

"You could do me a favour and stop selling silk yourself," he remarked a bit later.

"I shall ask Pierre to draw my share of the profits regularly. He'll be my steward, Marius Clary my chamberlain and Marceline Tascher my lady-in-waiting. I want to dismiss Madame La Flotte."

Driving past Notre-Dame, Jean-Baptiste told the coachman to stop, and he looked at the Cathedral for a long time, as if he wanted to commit to his memory every stone and every line of it. Then we went on to have a look at our first house in Sceaux. The stars were out, lilac trees blossomed behind garden walls.

"I went this way twice daily when I was Minister of War," he said, and most unexpectedly he added: "When, do you think, may I expect Your Royal Highness in Stockholm?"

"Not yet," I said, nestling to his shoulder, "the next years will be difficult enough for you. I don't want to make them any more so. You know how unsuited I am for the life of the Swedish court."

He looked at me sharply. "Do you mean to say that you are never going to accept the Swedish court ceremonial?"

"When I come," I said with emphasis, "I shall be in a position to determine all questions of etiquette myself."

The carriage stopped in front of No. 3 Rue de la Lune in Sceaux. Strangers lived in it now. 'Up there,' I thought, 'behind those first-floor windows, Oscar was born.'

At that very moment Jean-Baptiste said: "Imagine, Oscar has to shave already. Twice a week!"

On the way back we were so close to each other that we did not speak at all. Only when the carriage was rounding the corner into the Rue d'Anjou Jean-Baptiste said sharply: "You have no other reasons for wanting to stay here? Really not?"

"Yes, Jean-Baptiste, I have. Here I am wanted, and there I am superfluous. I must help Julie."

"I have beaten Napoleon at Leipzig. Yet I can't get rid of these Bonapartes all the same!"

"It's not the Bonapartes, it's the Clarys. Don't forget that, please!"

For the last time the carriage stopped. It all happened very suddenly. Jean-Baptiste got out with me and gazed at the house, attentively, in silence. I gave Jean-Baptiste my hand, which he put to his lips. "Whatever rumours the papers spread, don't believe them, you understand?"

"A pity. I should have liked to be your mistress. Ow!" I said, because Jean-Baptiste had bitten my finger.

Unfortunately, the two sentries were watching all the time.

446

PARIS.
Whit-Monday, May 30th, 1814.
Late in the evening.

NOTHING is more disagreeable to me than having to make visits of condolence, particularly when it is a beautiful Whit-Sunday!

Last night a tear-stained ex-lady-in-waiting from Malmaison appeared to tell me that Josephine had died at mid-day the day before. She had died of a heavy cold which she had contracted a few days before during an evening stroll in the Park at Malmaison on the arm of the Tsar. "The evening was very cool," the lady reported, "but Her Majesty would not under any circumstances put on a coat. She wore her new muslin frock with a very low decolletage and only a very thin and transparent scarf round her shoulders."

'Josephine, I know that muslin,' I thought, 'not substantial enough for a May evening. Purple it was, wasn't it? A bit melancholy and so becoming. . . .'

The former lady-in-waiting gave me a letter from Hortense. 'Bring the children along, my sole comfort,' wrote Hortense with many dashes and exclamation marks. And so I went to Malmaison with Julie and the two sons of the former Queen Hortense.

I tried to make the boys understand that their grandmother had died.

"Perhaps she isn't dead at all, perhaps she is only feigning it and is secretly going to join the Emperor at Elba," said Charles Napoleon.

In the Bois de Boulogne lime blossoms floated into our carriage. It seemed impossible to realise that Josephine was no longer alive.

At Malmaison we found Hortense and Eugene Beauharnais. Eugene was sitting in front of a minute writing desk rummaging among piles of bills. Pointing to them the gauche young man, former Viceroy of Italy and husband of a Bavarian princess, sighed. "It is inconceivable to me. Nothing but unpaid bills. For dresses, hats, rose trees!"

"Mama could never manage on her allowance," said Hortense.

"The State and the Emperor between them paid her three million francs a year! And yet—" He ran his fingers through his hair, obviously at his wits' end. "I should like to know who is going to pay these debts, which go into millions."

"That will not interest the ladies," said Hortense, and asked us to sit down. We sat down stiffly, and through the open french windows the scent of Josephine's roses came in from the garden.

"The Tsar of Russia called on Mama, and Mama asked him to dinner," Hortense said. "I suppose she wanted to ask him to take an interest in my children. You know that I am divorced now, don't you?"

We nodded politely. Hortense's lover, Count Flahault, appeared, and Eugene continued to exasperate himself about his mother's unpaid bills.

"Do you want to see her?" Hortense asked in the midst of her brother's laments.

Julie shook her head, but I said "Yes" instinctively.

Count Flahault took me up to Josephine's bedroom where she lay. Tall candles burned steadily. The shutters were closed and there was an overpowering odour of incense, roses, and the heavy perfume which Josephine used. The whole room was shrouded in half-darkness. When my eyes were used to it I saw nuns like giant black birds kneeling at the end of the bed, and I heard them murmur their requiem in a monotonous undertone.

At first I was afraid to look at the dead woman. But then I pulled myself together and went to the bed. Her coronation cloak was spread over the bed in soft folds like a good warm blanket. Her ermine collar had been placed over her breast and shoulders. It shone yellow in the light of the candles, yellow like the face of the dead Josephine.

No, Josephine didn't look horrifying, nor did she make one want to cry. She was too beautiful for that, even now. Only her small nose had an air of sharpness and strangeness about it, which emphasised the smile that was still hovering round her closed mouth, and her babyish curls held the aura of youthful attraction in their strands as they had done in life.

"How charming she looks!" said someone by my side. It was an old gentleman with a bloated face and beautiful silvery hair. He seemed to have come out of some dark corner.

"My name is Barras," he introduced himself, and raised a lorgnette to his eyes. "Have I the pleasure of knowing Madame?"

"It's a long time ago," I said. "We met at General Bonaparte's house and you were Director of the Republic at the time."

He dropped his lorgnette. "This coronation robe, Madame, this coronation robe is Josephine's debt to me. 'You marry this little Bonaparte,' I told her at the time, 'I shall make him Military Governor of Paris and all the rest will take care of itself, my dearest Josephine!' And, as you know, Madame, everything else has taken care of itself." He laughed softly. "Was she a close friend of yours, Madame?"

'No, Monsieur, she only broke my heart once,' I thought, and began to cry.

"A fool, this Bonaparte, a fool!" the old man said, and smoothed out with a tender hand a fold of the purple cloak. "A fool to divorce the only woman with whom, even on a lonely island, he would never have known a moment's boredom!"

Red roses were lying on the ermine collar of the Empress of the French. The heat of the candles had made them fade and their scent was almost painful. It seemed to choke me, to make me gasp for breath, I felt my knees grow weak, and suddenly I fell down by the side of Josephine's bed and buried my face in the velvet depths of her coronation robe.

"Don't cry for her, Madame. Josephine died as she lived: on the arm of a very powerful man, who, on an evening in the month of May among the rose trees of Malmaison, promised to pay all her debts. Are you listening, dear, dear Josephine?"

When I got to my feet again the old gentleman had disappeared into his dark corner. Nothing was heard but the monotonous flow of the requiem from the lips of the big black birds. I bent my head to Josephine once more and her long eyelashes seemed to flutter lightly.

I went downstairs and straight into the garden. The sun was so strong that the air shimmered and everywhere there were roses of every colour. I came to a little pond. On the low wall enclosing it sat a small girl watching the funny little ducklings and their fat mother on the water. I sat close to her. She had brown curly hair which fell to her shoulders in corkscrew fashion, and wore a white frock with a black scarf. When she turned her head to look at me my heart almost stopped beating: a sweet oval face with long lids over almond-shaped eyes. The child began to smile. She smiled with closed mouth.

"What's your name?" I asked.

"Josephine, Madame."

She had blue eyes and beautiful pearly teeth, and golden lights sparkled from her hair. 'Like Josephine,' I thought, 'like Josephine.'

"Are you one of the ladies-in-waiting, Madame?" the child asked politely.

"No. Why?"

"Because Aunt Hortense said that the Crown Princess of

Sweden was coming, and Crown Princesses always bring ladies-in-waiting along. Of course only when they are grown-up Princesses."

"And little Princesses?"

"Little Princesses have governesses."

The child turned her attention back to the ducks. "The ducklings are so small. I think they can't have come out of their mother's stomach earlier than yesterday."

"Nonsense, ducklings come out of eggs."

The child smiled in a very superior manner. "You need not tell me fairy-tales, Madame."

"But ducklings do come out of eggs!" I insisted.

The child nodded, bored. "As you wish, Madame."

"Are you the daughter of Prince Eugene?"

"Yes. But I don't think Papa is still a Prince. If we are lucky the allies will give us a duchy in Bavaria. My grandfather, that is my mama's father, is the King of Bavaria."

"Then you at any rate are a Princess," I said. "Where is your governess?"

"I have run away from her." She put her hand into the water. Then an idea seemed to cross her mind. "If you are not a lady-in-waiting you are perhaps a governess?"

"Why?"

"Because you must be something."

"Perhaps I am a Princess too?"

"Impossible. You don't look like a Princess. I should like to know who you are."

"Would you?"

"I like you. In spite of this stupid duckling story you have been telling me. Have you any children?"

"Yes, a son. But he isn't here."

"What a pity. I would much rather play with boys than with girls. Where is he?"

"In Sweden. But you wouldn't know where that is."

"I know exactly where it is, I am having geography lessons, you know. And Papa says——"

"Josephine, Josephine!" someone shouted.

The child sighed. "My governess!" She winked at me and pulled a real street Arab's face. "A horrid woman, but don't tell anybody, Madame!"

I made my way back to the house. Only Hortense, Eugene, Julie and I were there for dinner.

"Do you know when we shall be allowed to send a courier to Elba?" he asked Julie before we left. "I should like to inform the Emperor as quickly as possible about Mama's death. And also I want to let him have the unpaid bills."

On the way back through a blue evening it occurred to me that if one had to start a dynasty it might as well be a charming one. A shooting star fell at that moment and I wished very hard on it. "The Swedes would call her Josephina," I said aloud.

"Whom are you talking about?" Julie asked, surprised.

"Oh, no one. I was only thinking of the shooting star."

PARIS.
In the late autumn 1814.

BEHIND his steward's back Oscar wrote to me from Norway. I will paste his letter into my diary so as not to lose it.

Christiania, November 10th 1814

MY DEAR MAMA,

Count Brahe is sending a courier from here to Paris and I hasten to write to you. A special reason for writing now is that my steward, Baron Cederström, is in bed with a cold. He always wants to read my letters to you to see whether they are properly styled. The old idiot!

My dear Mama, my heartiest congratulations! You have just become Crown Princess of Norway. Norway and Sweden have been linked in a union, and the Swedish King is now also King of Norway. We have just been through a campaign in which we conquered Norway. Last night I arrived with Papa here in Christiania, the capital of Norway. But I had better tell you all in proper order.

Papa's entry into Stockholm was magnificent. The whole population lined the streets through which Papa drove, and shouted with joy. His Majesty embraced Papa and cried for happiness, and Her Majesty cried too, only a bit more discreetly. The Swedes feel like a heroic nation once again as in the days of Charles XII. But Papa was tired and rather sad. Can you imagine why, Mama?

And then although the Danes had ceded Norway to us the Parliament of Norway wanted their country to be independent and just to annoy us made a Danish Prince Regent and declared they would defend their independence.

451

Our Swedish officers were enthusiastic about the campaign, and the old King asked Papa for a warship with which to go into battle. Papa said Sweden could not afford a war longer than three months and he bought the warship out of his own pocket. The old King doesn't know that.

I said that if the old King could come along I wanted to be there too and Papa did not mind. He said these Norwegians were marvellous. They had an army only half the size of ours and had hardly any ammunition at all, and yet they risked war. He was very touched and said he would give them the most liberal constitution in Europe.

But these marvellous Norwegians insisted on their independence. So Papa and his General Staff went off to the campaign and the King and Queen and the whole Royal household and I myself followed him on board the man-of-war. When we took the fortress of Kongsten there was such a lot of shooting and firing that I said to Papa, who was standing next to me: "Papa, send an officer to the Norwegians and tell him that they could be independent for all you cared. Don't keep on shooting at them with your guns." And Papa said: "Of course not, Oscar, we are only shooting at them with dummy shells." "But in that case, Papa, it is not a real campaign, is it?" "No, Oscar, only an excursion." Papa said the Norwegians would retire behind their mountains, and when I asked him if he could cross the mountains Papa said he had crossed the Alps once with an army, and when he said that he looked very sad. "In those days," he said, "I defended a young Republic's independence. To-day I am taking it away from a small freedom-loving people. That shows you, Oscar, how one outlives oneself."

The whole campaign lasted only a fortnight, and we returned to Stockholm and Papa let the old King drive in triumph through the streets. Four days later Papa and I went back to Norway, because Papa had to appear in Christiania in person to confirm the union of Sweden and Norway. We rode there on horseback and had to sleep in tents because Papa did not want to inconvenience the peasants. I enclose a little song which I call 'Song of the Rain' and which I composed during this endless ride to Christiania.

We passed through the Fortress of Frederiksten, where the Norwegians defended themselves once against the Swedish King Charles XII, the famous Swedish King who made war against the Russians and lost it and then tried to conquer Norway. As we were riding through rain and mist we suddenly came to a big wooden cross on which was written 'This is the spot on which Charles XII fell.' The Marshals Essen and Adlercreutz at once started to say the Lord's Prayer, but Papa did not join in their prayer (he never prays!), and when we went on he said to Essen and Adlercreutz: "You had better forget that man, he was Sweden's misfortune!" Adlercreutz was offended and said: "Opinions differ on that, Your Highness!" From that you can see, Mama, that you have to be very careful when talking about Charles XII, whom Papa calls 'the greatest amateur in military matters' and whom the Swedes revere as a hero.

Last night at long last we reached Christiania in an equipage which had followed us from Stockholm. The streets were pitch-black and deserted, and there was only the guard of honour to receive us outside the palace of the former Danish Governor, and the Speaker of the Norwegian Parliament and the members of the Government inside.

The Speaker addressed Papa in excellent French. Papa smiled his winning smile, shook the solemn gentlemen by the hand and said he brought the good wishes of His Majesty the King of Sweden and Norway. I had the impression that these solemn men found it difficult not to burst out laughing at that. After all, what has the old gentleman in Stockholm to do with this union? This union is exclusively Papa's work. Papa at once started a weighty speech. "Norway's new constitution defends the Rights of Man for which I have been campaigning in France ever since I was fifteen. This union is more than just a geographical necessity, it has been a deeply felt desire of my heart for a long time!"

I don't think it made any impression on the Norwegians. And I don't think either that they will ever forget that Papa beat them with dummy shells. . . .

I went with Papa to his bedroom and saw him take off all his medals and throw them on the dressing-table with a gesture of disgust. He said: "Yesterday was Mama's birthday. I hope our letters reached her in time," and then he went to bed.

Dear Mama, I am very sorry for Papa. But you cannot be a Crown Prince and a Republican at the same time. Do please write him a nice cheerful letter. We shall be home in Stockholm at the end of the month. And now I can hardly keep my eyes open and the courier is waiting. I embrace you and kiss you.

Your son

OSCAR.

PS.: Do you think you could manage to find Monsieur Beethoven's Seventh Symphony in Paris and send it to me?

453

The courier who brought Oscar's letter also brought a letter from Count Brahe to Count Rosen. It said that on all official occasions the Norwegian flag has to be flown alongside the Swedish on my house. And on the door of my coach the arms of Norway have to be painted by the side of the Swedish arms.

I asked for a map of Europe and looked for the second country of which I am now Crown Princess.

PARIS.
March 5th, 1815.

THE afternoon began to-day like so many afternoons. With the help of my nephew Marius I drafted an application to Louis XVIII to get an extension of Julie's permit to stay on as my guest. Julie sat in the small drawing-room and wrote a long and dull letter to Joseph in Switzerland. Then Count Rosen entered and announced Monsieur Fouché, the Duke of Otranto.

This type of man is quite incomprehensible to me. When in the days of the Revolution the members of the National Assembly were asked to cast their votes about the fate of Louis XVI, Deputy Fouché cast his vote for death. And now he is moving heaven and earth in order to be received graciously by the brother of the executed King and to be given a job. The man was odious to me, but I let him come in.

He was in cheerful mood. His face, the colour of parchment, had red spots. Tea was served and he stirred his tea with an expression of great pleasure.

"I hope I did not disturb Your Highness in any important occupation?"

I didn't answer. But Julie said: "My sister has just drafted an application for me to His Majesty."

"Which Majesty?" asked Fouché.

I thought that the most stupid question possible. "King Louis, of course," said Julie, irritated. "As far as I know there is no other Majesty in France."

"This morning I might have had the chance of supporting your application, Madame. You see, His Majesty has offered me the job of—Minister of Police."

"Impossible!" I said.

"And?" asked Julie anxiously.

454

"I refused." Fouché took several well-bred sips of tea.

"If the King offers you the position of Minister of Police it is a sign that he feels insecure. And there is really no reason for that," put in Marius.

"Why not?" Fouché was surprised.

"The list, the secret list on which he puts not only all Republicans but also all adherents of the Emperor, is enough to give him unlimited power," said Marius. "It is said that your name is at the top of the list, Duke!"

Fouché put his cup on the table. "The King has interrupted the compiling of the list. If I were in his place I too should feel insecure. After all, he is advancing irresistibly."

"Would you mind telling me whom you are talking about?" I asked.

"Of the Emperor, of course."

The whole room began to spin round, shadows moved before my eyes and I felt dizzy, the kind of feeling I have not experienced since the days before Oscar's birth. Fouché's voice came to me as from a distance: "The Emperor embarked eleven days ago with his troops in Elba and arrived at Cannes on March 1st."

I heard Marius say: "But that is fantastic. He only has 400 men with him," and part of Fouché's answer: ". . . have gone over to him with flags flying and are marching with him in triumph to Paris."

"And the foreign powers, Duke?"

Count Rosen's harsh French rang out for a moment: "The foreign powers——"

"But, Désirée, you are pale, aren't you feeling well?" said Julie, and Fouché added: "Quick, a glass of water for Her Highness!"

They gave me some water and the room stopped spinning round and everything became clear again, clearer even than before.

I saw the glowing face of my nephew Marius. "He has the whole Army behind him," he said. "You cannot with impunity halve the salaries of the officers of France who made this nation great. We are marching, we are marching once more!"

"Against the whole of Europe?" Marceline asked pointedly. (Her husband has not returned to her. He fell in the battles around Paris, but, to be exact, he fell into the arms of a young girl who hid him. . . .)

A servant announced another visitor, the wife of Marshal Ney. She, a very big woman, came in like a whirlwind, pressed me to her mighty bosom and shouted: "Well, what do you say to that? But he will show him, he will! He banged his fist on the table and said he would show him once and for all!"

"Sit down, *Madame la Maréchale*, and tell me who is going to show whom."

"My husband is going to show the Emperor!" Madame Ney thundered, and fell into the nearest chair. "He has just received the order to stop the Emperor at Besançon and take him prisoner. And do you know what my old Ney answered? He'll lasso him like a mad bull and put him in a cage and exhibit him round the country, that's what he said."

"Pray forgive me, Madame," lisped Fouché, "why is Marshal Ney so annoyed with his former Supreme Commander and Emperor?"

Madame Ney hadn't noticed him before she spoke, and now became strangely embarrassed. "So you are here too?" she said. "How is that? Are you not in disgrace at court? Are you not supposed to be on your estates?"

Fouché smiled and shrugged his shoulders.

At that she lost her assurance. "You don't think, do you, that the Emperor—will manage it?" she brought out in a voice that trailed away into a whisper.

"Yes," said Marius with great certainty, "yes, Madame, he will manage it."

Julie rose. "I must write that to my husband. It will interest him greatly."

Fouché shook his head. "Don't do that, Madame. The King's Secret Police will certainly intercept the letter. Besides, I feel sure that the Emperor is in contact with your husband and has informed his brothers about his plans in advance."

"You don't think, Duke, that it is a pre-arranged plan, do you?" asked Madame Ney. "Surely my husband would know that!"

Marius thundered at her: "It cannot have escaped the attention of Marshal Ney that the Army is dissatisfied because officers and men have been put on half-pay and the pensions of the veterans and invalids have been reduced."

"Nor that of the Emperor in Elba," Fouché added amiably, and took his leave.

When he had gone there was a long silence. With a jerk Madame Ney turned to me and her deep voice growled: "Madame, as a Marshal's wife you will agree——"

"You are mistaken, I am no longer the wife of a Marshal but the Crown Princess of Sweden and Norway. I must ask you to excuse me. I have a headache."

Yes, I had a headache as never before in my life. My head was full of hammering, ringing, banging noises. I lay down and said that I wasn't at home to anybody. I felt I wasn't even at home to myself, least of all myself. . . .

You can escape your servants, you can escape your family. But whatever happens you cannot escape Hortense. At eight o'clock in the evening Marie announced "the Duchess of Saint Leu, former Queen of Holland". I pulled the blanket over my head.

Five minutes later Marceline wailed outside my door: "You must come, Aunt. Hortense is in the small drawing-room and says she'll wait for you if she has to sit up all night. She has brought her sons along, too."

I gave in. "Let her come in, but only for a moment!"

Hortense came in, pushing her sons before her. "Don't refuse your protection to my children," she cried. "Take them in till everything is decided." Hortense has gone thin during the last year, her mourning dress makes her look very pale, and her hair is untidy and uncared for.

"Your children are in no danger," I said.

"But of course they are. The King may have them arrested at any moment as hostages against the Emperor. My children are the heirs to the throne, Madame!"

"The heir to the throne is called Napoleon like his father, and lives in Vienna at the moment."

"And if anything happens to this child in his captivity in Vienna? What then, Madame?" Her eyes rested lovingly on her two gangling boys. "Napoleon III," she murmured with a strangely aimless smile, and smoothed the hair of the younger one back from his forehead. "The King will not dare to pursue my children into the house of the Swedish Crown Princess. I implore you——"

"Of course," I said, "the children can stay here."

Later—I was just on the point of falling asleep—candlelight and rustling noises woke me. I sat up in bed and saw Julie rummaging in my chest. "Julie, what are you looking for?"

"My crown, Désirée, the one I dropped on the floor in your boudoir the day the Tsar called."

"It's in the bottom drawer. What do you want with it in the middle of the night, Julie?"

"Just to try it on, and perhaps polish it up again."

LAST night Louis XVIII crept out of the Tuileries by a back door and went into exile once more, this time only as far as Ghent. This morning the tricolour went up over the Tuileries, pamphlets containing a proclamation by Napoleon were distributed in the streets, and all the buttonholes and lapels, latent but gradually getting worn, showed the blue-white-red ribbon instead of the white rosette.

In the Tuileries a great scrubbing and washing started, with Hortense in command; the new curtains disappeared and the dark green ones with the bee pattern came out of the obscurity of the storehouses. All Napoleon's gilded eagles were fetched out of the vaults, dusted by Hortense herself and placed in their old positions.

My house, too, had been turned upside down. A message from the Emperor to Julie announced that he would arrive at the Tuileries at nine o'clock in the evening, and Julie prepared herself, complete with purple and crown, to receive him. She was in a dreadful state of agitation. "Imagine Hortense and me having to receive him alone! I'm so afraid of him!"

"Nonsense, Julie, it's the same Buonaparte as in Marseilles! Your brother-in-law, Julie."

"Is he really the same man? After his triumphal march from Cannes via Grenoble to Paris, with everyone going over to him, including Marshal Ney?"

Yes, it was quite true, the Army literally fell on its knees before him, including the brave Marshal Ney. "Julie," I said, "the Army may be shouting hurrah, but everyone else is silent!"

She looked blank when I said that, then borrowed the earrings of the Swedish Dowager Queen and left. 'I only hope,' I thought, 'that Joseph brings her jewellery back with him.'

Meanwhile Marie and I bathed Hortense's boys and, at Hortense's special wish, curled their hair with a pair of curling tongs. They were to go to the Tuileries later with Julie. Louis Napoleon, whom his mother had called Napoleon III, wondered whether the little King of Rome was coming back too. But I didn't answer him.

At eight o'clock in the evening a state equipage, still with the Bourbon lily on its doors, fetched Julie and the children. My house felt very quiet when they had gone.

Count Rosen, leaning out of a window, said that he would have liked to see the Emperor's arrival. I told him to change into civilian clothes and put on a tricoloured ribbon. I would come along with him, I said, and slipped into a plain coat and put on a hat.

It was difficult to get to the Tuileries. We were caught up in an almost impenetrable crowd and slowly pushed along. I hung on to my young Count's arm like grim death.

The Tuileries were brilliantly illuminated as in the days of the great receptions. But I knew that upstairs in the ballroom there would be only a handful of people, Julie, Hortense, a few children, the Duke of Vicenza, Marshal Davout and perhaps a few more Generals.

Soldiers on horseback cleared a lane, and from the distance we heard a noise, first like the soughing of wind, then growing to a gale, a typhoon, and then it was all over and around us, the one mighty roar *"Vive l'Empereur, Vive l'Empereur!"* A carriage came into view driving madly towards the Tuileries, with officers of all ranks and all regiments riding after it in a wild gallop.

Servants holding torches appeared on the steps in front of the palace, the door of the carriage opened and the Emperor stepped out followed by Marshal Ney. The crowd broke through the line of soldiers, seized the Emperor and carried him shoulder-high into the Tuileries. I saw his face illuminated by the glare of torches. It smiled with eyes closed, the face of a man who had been dying of thirst and was now at last given a drink.

Another carriage drove up. But it was only Fouché who emerged from it, wanting to welcome the Emperor and offer him his services.

I had had enough. We managed to force our way through the dense crowd and wandered home through empty streets. But from every house the tricolour was flying.

PARIS.
June 21st, 1815.

MARIE was just bringing me my breakfast in bed when the guns began to fire and the church bells rang out.

"Heavens!" said Marie, "he's won!"

As she said it I realised that we hadn't really expected that, neither we nor the others. But there were the guns and the bells! Now everything was all right again!

Julie and Joseph went back to the Elysée Palace; Madame Letitia and all her sons came back. Only, in the Tuileries Hortense was mistress now in the absence of Marie-Louise, who still hung back, in spite of all Napoleon's letters.

As soon as he came back Napoleon ordered a general election, to prove to the world how unpopular the Bourbons were. This was the first free election since the days of the Republic, and old names reappeared in the new National Assembly, Carnot, for instance, and—Lafayette! Lafayette, who first proclaimed the Rights of Man, who had fought for the freedom of the United States, who had founded the National Guard to defend our young Republic—Lafayette, of whom Papa had spoken with such enthusiasm, was back again!

But others were absent: Jean-Baptiste's Ambassador, and the Ambassadors of all the powers, had been recalled; no country would enter into diplomatic relations with Napoleon, no Prince answered his letters. They sent not Ambassadors but armies! Inexorably 800,000 men moved towards France, without any declaration of war. And Napoleon had none to send against them but one hundred thousand men of his own. He could get no more: the young men went into hiding, the officers, including my nephew Marius, sent medical certificates instead of reporting for duty, and the Marshals with the exception of Ney and Davout, retired to their country estates.

Three days ago Napoleon crossed the frontier at the head of his army, to face the allies. His Order-of-the-Day ran: 'For every brave Frenchman the time has come to win or die.' When that was published all Paris was in the utmost gloom. And then, after all, the miracle happened: the church bells rang out for victory!

I dressed and went into the garden. Then I was startled to find that the bells had stopped ringing.

The deathly silence was so oppressive that I was glad to see a stranger coming into the garden. I went to meet him: it was Lucien Bonaparte! How strange that he should return at this of all moments, after his many years of exile in England!

"You remember me, Désirée? I was present at the two betrothals, yours and Julie's."

We sat down on a bench.

"Why have you come back, Lucien?"

"Yes, why?" Lucien leaned back and looked round the garden. "How lovely, and how peaceful!"

"The victory bells have stopped ringing."

"Yes, Désirée, it was a mistake. Old Davout, whom Napoleon had left in Paris, had them rung prematurely. Napoleon had only won a little skirmish at Charleroi; the decisive battle was fought at Ligny and Waterloo, and Napoleon was beaten. Look at that beautiful blue butterfly!"

"And the Emperor?"

"He will arrive to-night, very quietly. He'll stay with Joseph and Julie, not in the Tuileries. 'For every brave Frenchman the time has come to win or die!' You read his fine phrase, didn't you? No doubt he finds it embarrassing to have done neither."

"And the Army, Lucien?"

"What army?"

"His army, the French Army!"

"There is no army left! Of his 100,000 men, sixty thousand have died. But I haven't come to tell you that. I only wanted to ask you to remember me to Jean-Baptiste Bernadotte when you write to him. I often think of him."

"Lucien, why have you chosen this moment to come back?"

"To find somewhere to spend ten minutes in peace. The Government is fully informed, and the National Assembly is in permanent session as in the days of the Revolution."

He got up. "I must go now. I am expecting further messages."

I went to the gate with Lucien, and he took my arm familiarly. "I have often regretted," he said, with his head bent, "that day in Brumaire when I spoke for him in the Council of the Five Hundred. But I still had faith in him then."

"And now?"

"Désirée, shall we wager that he is going to send me once more to the Deputies? They are going to demand his abdication, and he will ask me to defend him. Do you know what I am going to do?"

461

I smiled. "You are going to defend him. And that is why you came back, isn't it?"

After he had gone I thought for one moment that the whole thing wasn't true, that Lucien had been mistaken, not Marshal Davout, about the bells. But then I heard a carriage draw up, and Hortense came in. She begged me, with tears in her eyes, to give shelter to her defenceless children.

PARIS.
June 23rd, 1815.

I HAD just begun to read the *Moniteur* with Lafayette's speech in that decisive session of the National Assembly—"If after all these years I raise my voice again"—when the door of my boudoir was flung open, and Julie stumbled in and dropped in front of me, putting her head in my lap.

"He has abdicated!" she sobbed. "The Prussians will be here at any moment."

Bit by bit I gathered the story of last night's events. Napoleon had come back at dead of night in an old stage coach. He had lost everything, even his personal baggage. He called all his brothers and his ministers to him immediately after his arrival, but the ministers only stayed for five minutes and then went back to the Assembly. The Emperor demanded another 100,000 men and then sent poor Lucien to face the Deputies on his behalf and reproach the nation for deserting him.

"And did Lucien actually go?" I asked.

"Yes, he went—and was back in twenty minutes! He hardly managed to get a hearing, and when at last they did listen to him and he told them that the nation had deserted his brother, Lafayette jumped to his feet and shouted: 'France has sacrificed three millions of her sons to your brother. Does he want yet more?' And Lucien left the Assembly without another word."

Fouché had told her that, said Julie; Lucien himself had told her nothing.

Later Joseph and Lucien were closeted with the Emperor throughout the night. The Emperor shouted and banged the table, but his brothers could not persuade him to abdicate till Fouché brought the news of Lafayette's motion in the National Assembly that the throne should be declared forfeited if General

Bonaparte did not resign it voluntarily within the next hour. When the Emperor heard that, he signed at last, but he abdicated in favour of his son. Of course the Government would take no notice of that.

"I'm not going back to the Elysée," said Julie. "I want to stay here with the children. They can't arrest me here, can they?"

"The allied troops aren't even here yet," I said. "Perhaps they won't come at all."

"The allied troops? No, no—our Government! They've sent a General Becker to Napoleon to keep an eye on him. The Directory——"

"Directory?"

"Yes, the new Government calls itself the Directory. They are in touch with the allies. Carnot and Fouché are two of them." She began sobbing again.

Then Joseph arrived.

"Julie, you must get ready at once," he said. "The Emperor wants to leave Paris and go to Malmaison. The whole family are going with him. Come along, Julie."

Julie clung to me more than ever.

"The whole family are going to Malmaison, Julie," Joseph repeated. His face was grey. He could not have had any sleep for the last two nights.

I took Julie's hands in mine. "Julie, you must go with your husband."

But she shook her head. "The crowds are shouting 'Down with the Bonapartes'."

"That's why you must go with your husband," I said, and pulled her to her feet.

"Désirée, may we go to Malmaison in your carriage?" Joseph asked, without looking at me.

"I was going to lend it to Madame Letitia," I said. "But perhaps you can all find room in it."

"You'll help me, Désirée, you'll help me, won't you?" cried Julie. Joseph gently led her to the door.

It is now about a year since Josephine died, and when they reach Malmaison they'll find the roses in bloom.

PARIS.
The night of June 29th, 1815.

His sword lies on my bedside table, his fate is sealed, and I was the one to seal it! Everyone is talking of my great mission, but I am full of grief.

Early this morning—it sounds crazy, but it's true!—I learned that the nation wanted to speak to me.

I had been lying awake for hours. The last guns we have were rolling past my house, to attempt the hopeless defence of Paris against the Austrians, Russians, Prussians, Saxons, and English. Suddenly Yvette came to say that Count Rosen wanted urgently to speak to me. The Count rushed in after her, and said that the representatives of the nation wanted to speak to me as soon as I could see them.

"Which nation?" I asked, as the Count buttoned up the jacket of his full-dress uniform.

"The French nation," he said, finishing his buttons and standing to attention.

"Yvette, some strong coffee, please. Until I've had some coffee, Count, you'll have to speak slowly. The French nation, you say? What does it want of me?"

"They are asking for an audience. It was of immense importance, their spokesman said. That is why I have put on my full-dress uniform."

Yvette brought some very hot coffee.

"What shall I tell them?" asked the Count.

"I'll see them in half an hour."

I found that the nation was represented by MM. Fouché and Talleyrand and by a third person whom I didn't know. He was small and very thin, and was wearing an old-fashioned white wig and a faded foreign uniform. His face was wrinkled, but he was a very bright-eyed old man.

"Your Highness, may we present to you General Lafayette?" said Talleyrand.

My heart stood still. The nation had indeed come to me! I curtsied like an awkward schoolgirl.

Lafayette began to smile with such genuineness that I plucked up courage and said:

"My father always treasured the first broadsheet of the Rights of Man. I never dreamed that one day I should have the honour of welcoming its author under my own roof."

"Your Highness," began Fouché, "in the name of the French Government, represented by the Minister of Foreign Affairs and myself, and in the name of the French nation, represented by Deputy General Lafayette, we turn to you in this grave hour."

I looked at them all. Fouché, one of the five Directors now ruling France, and Talleyrand, who only returned a few days ago from the Congress of Vienna where he had represented the Bourbons, were both ex-Ministers of Napoleon, both in gold-embroidered tail-coats, much bemedalled. Between them sat Lafayette in his faded uniform, without a single medal.

"What can I do for you, gentlemen?" I asked.

"Your Highness, I anticipated a situation like this long ago," said Talleyrand, speaking very fast and in a low voice. "Perhaps Your Highness will remember that I indicated to you once that the day might come when the nation would turn to you with a very important request. Do you remember, Your Highness?"

I nodded.

"That situation has arisen now. The French nation is putting to the Crown Princess of Sweden its great petition."

"I should like to give Your Highness a picture of the situation," said Fouché. "Through the Prince of Benevento we have offered unconditional surrender to Wellington and Blücher, in order to prevent needless destruction and bloodshed."

"They have told us that they will enter into negotiations only on one condition," put in Talleyrand, "and that is——"

"That General Bonaparte leaves France immediately!" shouted Fouché.

'What do they want of me?' I thought, looking at Talleyrand. But it was Fouché who continued:

"Although we communicated to Napoleon the wish of the French Government and nation that he should leave, he has not done so. On the contrary"—Fouché's voice trembled with rage—"on the contrary, he has approached us with a monstrous proposal. He sent his A.D.C., Count Flahault, with the suggestion of a defence of Paris by the remnants of the Army under his command. In other words, he wants a general massacre. This, of course, we rejected, and repeated our demand for his departure, whereupon he transmitted to us what one can only call another challenge. He demands—demands, Your Highness! —to be given the command of the last available regiments in order to defend Paris. He takes his success for granted and assumes that it will enable us to secure better terms of peace. Only then will General Bonaparte consent to go abroad."

Fouché breathed hard and mopped his brow.

"The irony of it, Your Highness!"

I said nothing.

"We cannot capitulate and preserve Paris from destruction until General Bonaparte has left France. The allies are at Versailles. We cannot delay another moment, Your Highness. General Bonaparte must leave Malmaison to-day and go to Rochefort."

"Why Rochefort?"

"I am afraid the allies are going to insist that we shall hand over General Bonaparte to them," said Talleyrand, yawning furtively. "But on abdicating General Bonaparte demanded that two frigates of the French Navy should be put at his disposal. These frigates have been waiting for him in vain in the harbour at Rochefort."

"The British Navy has blockaded every port. I am told that the cruiser *Bellerophon* is lying at anchor alongside the frigates at Rochefort," said Fouché.

"What have I to do with it?" I asked.

Talleyrand smiled.

"You, my dear Crown Princess, as a member of the Swedish royal family, are in a position to speak to General Bonaparte in the name of the allies."

"At the same time," said Fouché, hastily pulling a sealed envelope out of his breast pocket, "Your Highness could hand the answer of the French Government to General Bonaparte."

"I am afraid the French Government will have to send one of its couriers to Malmaison with the document."

Suddenly Fouché was furious again. "And the demand to go abroad?" he shouted. "Or to put himself at the disposal of the allies, so that France may at last have peace?"

I shook my head slowly. "You are mistaken, gentlemen. I am here only as a private person."

"My child, you have not been told the whole truth." It was Lafayette who spoke now for the first time, in a deep, calm, kindly voice. "This General Bonaparte has assembled a few battalions of young men, daredevils ready for anything. Our fear is that the General will be carried away and do something that cannot possibly change the course of events but may cost yet more lives. And lives are precious, my child."

I bent my head.

The calm voice continued:

"The wars of General Bonaparte have cost Europe more than ten million lives already."

I looked up, and over the shoulders of the three men I saw

the portrait of Napoleon as First Consul. "I shall try, gentlemen," I heard myself say. Then Fouché pushed the sealed envelope into my hand, and offered General Becker as escort and a whole battalion of the Guards for my protection. I refused both. I would only take my Swedish A.D.C.; I certainly needed no protection.

Yvette gave me my hat and gloves. Talleyrand said something about being grateful and 'perhaps' granting 'special concessions to Madame Julie'. But I paid no attention to him.

"My child, if you permit I shall go and sit in your garden and there await your return," said General Lafayette.

"Even if it takes all day?"

"Even if it takes all day, and my thoughts will accompany you!"

Close behind us, as I drove with Count Rosen to Malmaison, rode a man on horseback. It was General Becker, who by order of the French Government had to keep watch on the former Emperor of the French.

Close to Malmaison the road was barricaded. The soldiers manning the barricade let us pass as soon as they saw General Becker. The entrance into the park was heavily guarded too. Becker dismounted and opened the gates for us. I was full of apprehension, and tried to tell myself that this was just another little trip to Malmaison, where I knew every garden seat and every rose tree.

Meneval and the Duke of Vicenza received me on the steps, and a moment later I was surrounded by familiar faces—Hortense, Julie, Joseph, Lucien. From the open window of the drawing-room Madame Letitia beckoned to me.

"Joseph," I said, nervously, "I should like to speak to your brother, immediately."

"How kind of you, Désirée! But you must wait a few minutes. The Emperor is expecting an important communication from the Government, and he wishes to be alone meanwhile."

"I have it with me," I said. "And I want to speak to General Bonaparte."

I saw Joseph's face pale when I said 'General Bonaparte'.

"His Majesty is sitting on the bench in the maze. You know the maze, don't you?"

"I know the park very well indeed," I answered, and turning to Rosen I said: "Wait for me. I must see this through alone."

I knew how to find my way through the maze so as to come up to the bench unobserved—that little white bench with just room for two.

There I found Napoleon. He wore the green uniform of

the Chasseurs. He was sitting with his chin in his hand, staring unseeing into the flowering hedge in front of him.

When I saw him all my fear fell away, and with it every tender memory. Before I could call to him he turned a little and caught sight of my white frock.

"Josephine," he said, "lunch time already?"

Only my silence brought him back to reality. He recognised me and said in surprise, and with evident pleasure: "Eugenie, you have come after all!"

No one heard him call me Eugenie, no one saw him move to make room for me. When I sat down he looked at me with a smile.

"It is many years," he said, "since you and I looked at a flowering hedge side by side."

I still said nothing.

"You remember, don't you?"

He smoothed an imaginary strand of hair back from his forehead.

"I am waiting for a very important message from the Government. And I am not used to waiting!"

"You need wait no longer, General Bonaparte. Here is the Government's answer," I said, handing him the letter. I did not look at him as he read it.

"How is it that you, Madame, bring the letter? Does the Government not even think it worth while to send me its answer through a minister or an officer? Why is a lady who is paying me a chance visit charged with the message?"

"I am not a chance visitor, General Bonaparte," I said, bracing myself. "I am the Crown Princess of Sweden."

"And what do you mean by that?" he said between his teeth.

"The French Government has asked me to tell you that the allies will only enter into negotiation for the surrender of Paris, and so save Paris from destruction, on condition that you leave before to-night."

"I offer the Government to beat back the enemy before the gates of Paris, and the Government refuses," he roared.

"The allied advance guards have reached Versailles," I said. "Are you going to allow yourself to be captured at Malmaison?"

"Don't trouble, Madame. I know how to defend myself."

"That's just it! The Government wants to avoid unnecessary bloodshed."

His eyes narrowed to two slits. "Indeed? What if it is necessary for the honour of a nation?"

'I could tell him of all the millions who fell for the honour of the country,' I thought. 'But he would be better at figures than I, it wouldn't be much good. No, I must just sit here and not give in.'

Napoleon had risen and wanted to pace up and down. But there wasn't room enough. "Madame," he said, standing so close in front of me that I had to throw back my head to see his face. "You say the French Government wants me to leave. And the allies?" His face was distorted.

"The allies insist on your imprisonment, General."

He looked at me for one more second. Then he turned his back on me and leaned against the hedge. "This piece of paper which you have brought me from the self-styled French Government directs my attention for the second time to the frigates at Rochefort. I am free to go where I like, apparently. Why, Madame, does the Government not hand me over?"

"Probably the gentlemen hesitate to do that."

He turned back to me. "All I need do, then, is to go on board one of these ships and tell the captain where to go, and——"

"The port of Rochefort, like all other ports, is being blockaded by the British Navy. You wouldn't get far, General."

He didn't roar, he didn't rage, he sat down quietly on the bench next to me, breathing hard.

"When I saw you just now, Madame, and recognised you, I thought for one short moment that my youth had come back. I was mistaken, Your Royal Highness!"

"Why? I remember the evenings very well when we raced each other. You were a General then, a very young and handsome General. Sometimes you even let me win. But you've probably forgotten that."

"No, Eugenie."

"And once—it was late in the evening and the field beyond our garden was quite dark—you told me that you knew your destiny. Your face was as pale as the moonlight. That was the first time I was afraid of you."

"And that was the first time I kissed you, Eugenie."

I smiled. "You were thinking of the dowry, General."

"Not only, Eugenie. Really, not only——"

After that neither of us said anything. I realised that he was giving me sidelong glances, that he had had an idea connected with me. 'Lives are precious,' I thought. 'If only I could pray!'

"And if I did not let myself be taken prisoner but surrendered voluntarily, what then?"

"I don't know."

"An island? Another island? Perhaps that rock in the sea, St. Helena, of which they talked at the Congress in Vienna?"

I could see terror in his eyes.

"Is it St. Helena?"

"I really don't know. Where is St. Helena?"

"Beyond the Cape of Good Hope, Eugenie, beyond!"

"Whatever happened, General, in your place I should never let myself be taken prisoner, I would rather surrender of my own free will."

He sat, bent, with his hand over his terrified eyes. I got up, but he didn't move.

"I'm going now," I said, and waited.

He lifted his head. "Where are you going, Eugenie?"

"Back to Paris. You have given no answer either to the Crown Princess of Sweden or to the French Government. But there is time yet, till to-night."

He laughed loudly, and so unexpectedly that I shrank back. "Shall I prevent them from capturing me? Here or in Rochefort? Shall I?" He fumbled with his sword. "Shall I spoil the fun for Messrs. Blücher and Wellington?" He pulled the sword out of its scabbard. "Here, Eugenie, take it! Take the sword of Waterloo!"

The sun glinted on the steel blade. Hesitantly I put out my hand to it.

"Careful, Eugenie, don't touch the blade!"

Clumsily I took the sword and stared at it, overcome. Napoleon had risen to his feet. "At this moment," he said, "I am surrendering to the allies. I consider myself a prisoner of war. It is customary to hand your sword to the officer who captures you. Let Bernadotte explain to you all about that."

"And your answer to the Government, General?"

"Show them my sword, and tell them that I have put myself in the hands of the allies as their prisoner. I shall leave in one— no, let us say two hours for Rochefort. From there I shall write a letter to my oldest and best enemy, the Prince Regent of Britain. What happens to me after that depends on the allies." He paused, and then added hastily: "I want the frigates to wait for me whatever happens."

"They lie alongside the British cruiser *Bellerophon*," I said. I waited for a word of farewell, but none came. I turned to go.

"Madame!"

I quickly turned back to him.

"They say that the climate of St. Helena is very unhealthy. Is it possible to hope that the British, if asked, might conceivably change my place of residence?"

"You said yourself that St. Helena is beyond the Cape of Good Hope."

He stared at the ground. "After my first abdication I tried to commit suicide, but I was saved. Have you ever been between life and death?"

"Once. On the night you were betrothed to Viscountess Beauharnais, I wanted to throw myself into the Seine."

His eyes returned to me. "You wanted to—? And how were you saved?"

"Bernadotte prevented it."

He shook his head, baffled. "Strange, Bernadotte prevented you from throwing yourself into the river, you are going to be Queen of Sweden, I hand you the sword of Waterloo! You believe in destiny, don't you?"

"No, only in curious coincidences." I gave him my hand.

"Can you find your way back through the maze by yourself, Eugenie?"

I nodded.

"Tell my brothers to have everything ready for my departure, above all a civilian suit. I want to stay here by myself for a short time. And, Eugenie, our betrothal, in Marseilles, it was not only because of the dowry . . . Go now, Eugenie, go quickly, before I regret—"

I went. The paths of the labyrinth seemed endless, the sun shone down mercilessly, there was not a breath of air, not a leaf stirred, not a bird sang. 'I'm carrying his sword,' I thought, 'all is over, I'm carrying his sword.' My gown stuck to my skin, the air was palpitating. At last I heard a window open, and Julie called out: "That's taken a long time!"

They were waiting on the steps—his brothers, Count Rosen, and General Becker. They stood there rooted to the ground, and stared at the sword, which I was carefully holding away from me.

I stopped. Count Rosen put out his hand to take the sword, but I shook my head. None of the others moved.

"General Becker," I said, "General Bonaparte has decided to surrender to the allies, and has handed his sword to me as Crown Princess of Sweden. In two hours he will leave for Rochefort."

Julie and Madame Letitia came out of the house. "Napoleone—" whispered Madame Letitia and began to cry softly. "In two hours?"

"I shall accompany my brother to Rochefort, General Becker," said Joseph calmly. 'He still hates him,' I thought, 'otherwise he would not go with him now.'

I heard one of the officers say softly to Joseph, "Two regiments are ready under His Majesty's order to——"

"That," I shouted, "is what General Bonaparte wants to spare France—civil war. Spare him that!"

"Has Napoleone had anything to eat?" wailed Madame Letitia. "Is he going a long journey?" I heard Julie sob close to me.

I managed to say that the General had asked for civilian clothes and wanted to be left alone for a little while. Then, somehow, I must have got into my carriage. I saw the open road, and the fields, and trees and bushes. A slight fragrant breeze played round us.

Count Rosen took the sword from my cramped fingers and put it in a corner of the carriage. Just then something made me throw my head back, and at that moment a very sharp stone crashed painfully on my knee.

Rosen shouted something in Swedish to Johansson, the coachman, and Johansson whipped up the horses to a gallop. The next stone only hit the back wheel. My Count's face was deathly pale.

"I swear," he said, "that the attackers shall be tracked down."

"Why? It's of no importance."

"Of no importance? An attack on the Crown Princess of Sweden?"

"But it wasn't an attack on the Crown Princess of Sweden. It was meant for *Madame la Maréchale* Bernadotte, and she no longer exists!"

Darkness was beginning to fall as we reached the suburbs. Everywhere there were clusters of people talking in murmurs. 'By now,' I thought, 'Napoleon must be on his way to the coast, on the first stage of his long voyage. And Paris is saved.'

Near the Rue d'Anjou we encountered a large crowd making its way slowly toward my street. We had to stop, someone recognised me, and a shout went up, *"La Princess Royale de Suède!"* In a moment the whole town seemed to be shouting it. Gendarmes appeared and made a way for me, and at last I reached my house. Torches were burning in front of it, the gate stood open, and we drove straight in. Behind us the gate was shut immediately.

As I was getting out of the coach I felt a violent pain in my knee. I clenched my teeth, reached for the sword, and limped into the house. The hall was brightly lit and filled with strange people.

Lafayette came forward to meet me. "In the name of France I thank you—Citizeness!" He put his hand under my elbow to support me.

"But who are all these strange people?" I asked.

"The representatives of the nation," said Lafayette, smiling.

"And *la grande nation* has many representatives, Your Highness." It was Talleyrand speaking. He came toward me followed by Fouché, who had two white rosettes in his buttonhole. The many representatives of the nation bowed low amid deep silence.

"And," I asked, "the thousands of people outside, what are they waiting for?"

"It has become known that Your Highness has tried to mediate," said Fouché. "The people of Paris have been awaiting Your Highness's return for hours."

"Tell the people that General Bonaparte has surrendered to the allies and has left Malmaison. That will make them go home."

"They want to see you, Citizeness," said Lafayette.

"See me?"

Lafayette nodded. "You are bringing us peace, capitulation without civil war. You have fulfilled your mission, Citizeness."

I shook my head. No, I didn't want to show myself. But Lafayette insisted. "Show yourself to your people, Citizeness. You have saved many lives. May I conduct you to a window?"

He took me to a window in the dining-room. The noise of the crowd rushed in from the street the moment the window was opened, and it ebbed away the moment Lafayette stepped up to it and showed himself to the people. He began to speak, and his voice sounded like a flourish of trumpets:

"Citizens and Citizenesses, peace is assured. General Bonaparte has given himself up into captivity and a woman from your midst, a simple woman whom a freedom-loving nation in the North has made its Crown Princess, has received his sword from him, the sword of Waterloo!"

The roar of the crowd redoubled as Lafayette made room for me. Remembering Josephine's advice, I had asked for a footstool so as not to be too small for a Crown Princess, and I mounted it now. With both hands I held the sword out of the window into the torch-lit darkness below. A few words were being shouted over and over again; in the end I caught them— "*Notre-Dame de la Paix! Notre-Dame de la Paix!*"

"Our Lady of Peace," they were calling me, "Our Lady of Peace!" I wept—I could not but weep.

Lafayette pushed Count Rosen toward the window, seized a candelabrum, and let its light fall on Rosen's Swedish uniform and blue and yellow sash. "Sweden, long live Sweden!" was shouted up from the street, and again "*Notre-Dame de la Paix!*"

The window was closed as I went back into the room, feeling suddenly strange and forlorn among the excited groups of

Deputies. Unfortunately they showed no sign of leaving. I put the sword on the table under the portrait of the First Consul, and decided that I must offer the Deputies something to eat and drink. But all I had apart from wine were the cherries we had meant to bottle. So Marie and I gave them to the representatives of the nation, who fairly fell on them. I remembered the people outside in the street who had had to form queues for every bit of food in recent days, and I told Marie and the chef to let them have all the flour we had stored away in the cellar.

Talleyrand was the first to notice that something was wrong with my knee. "Is Your Highness hurt?" he asked as I limped toward the door.

"No, only—a bit tired."

He raised his lorgnette to his eyes. "Our Republican friend the Marquis de Lafayette seems to be an old favourite of Your Highness!"

The tone in which he said it made me furious. "He's the only man with clean hands in this room," I said.

"Naturally, Your Highness! He has spent all these years planting cabbages in the country and so has kept his hands clean!"

"Philosophers," I said, "in quiet backwaters——"

"——Are always a dictator's best subjects!"

He listened to the noise of the flour distribution outside.

Lafayette came. "How kind you are, my child! First you secure peace, and now food!"

"How kind, and how clever!" said Talleyrand, and smiled, taking at the same time a glass of wine from a servant. "The small country of the North and its great future: to secure peace —and food! To Sweden, Your Highness!"

Just then I saw that Fouché was about to take the sword. "Oh no," I called out, and limped quickly toward him.

"But the French Government——" he urged.

For the first time I noticed the greedy glint in his eyes. "Oh no," I said, "the sword has been handed to the allies and not to the French Government. I shall keep it till General Blücher and Wellington decide what to do with it." I took it from him and, as my knee hurt badly, went up with it to my bedroom, leaving the Deputies to argue together for I don't know how long.

Marie undressed me. She shook her head at my blue and swollen knee.

The street outside had become quiet, and I started writing my diary. And over the writing of it morning has dawned.

Papa, Lafayette has grown old. And your pamphlet with the declaration of the Rights of Man is probably in Sweden now.

Only ninety days—no, about a hundred, have passed since Napoleon's return from Elba, a hundred days like so many eternities.

In the Battle of Leipzig my old Jean-Baptiste died, and young Désirée breathed her last in the maze at Malmaison. How shall these twain ever come together again?

Papa, I don't think I shall ever again write in my diary.

PART IV

QUEEN OF SWEDEN

PARIS.
February 1818.

I was at the piano, trying to play a new piece Oscar has composed, when the Swedish Ambassador was announced. I was pleased at his visit, for this dark, rainy afternoon was just right for a cup of tea in company.

But on entering he closed the door and remained standing there, with the whole room between us. As he didn't stir from the door I got up to go to meet him. Then he bowed very low, very ceremoniously, and I noticed the black band round his arm.

"Your Majesty!"

He straightened up slowly. "Your Majesty, I have come with sad news. King Charles died on February the 5th."

I stood paralysed. I hardly knew the small shaky King. But his death meant——

"His Majesty has commissioned me to inform Your Majesty of the circumstances of the King's death and to hand to you this letter."

I made no move. The Ambassador came up to me and held out a sealed letter.

Hesitantly I took the letter. "Sit down, Baron," I said, and sank into the nearest chair. My hands trembled as I opened the letter. It was a big sheet on which Jean-Baptiste had scribbled in haste: 'Dearest, You are now the Queen of Sweden. Please conduct yourself accordingly. In haste—Your J.-B.

'P.S. Don't forget to destroy this letter at once.'

I dropped the sheet and smiled—and remembered that the Ambassador was watching me. Quickly I tried to put on a face full of sad dignity. "My husband writes that I am now the Queen of Sweden and Norway," I said gravely. The Ambassador smiled, I should have liked to know why.

"His Majesty," said the Ambassador, "was proclaimed King Charles John IV of Sweden and Norway by the heralds on February 6th, and his wife Her Majesty Queen Desideria."

"Jean-Baptiste ought never to have allowed me to be called Desideria. How did His Majesty die?"

479

"His Majesty had a very easy death. He had a stroke on the first of February. Two days later it was known that the end was near. His Majesty and His Highness the Crown Prince kept vigil in the sick-room."

I tried to visualise the scene: the castle in Stockholm, the crowded sick-room, Jean-Baptiste, Oscar—Crown Prince Oscar! —the Queen, Princess Sofia Albertina—and who else? The Ambassador told me who else had been there and in the adjoining room, and he also told me how the King never took his eyes from Jean-Baptiste and how gradually his breath grew slower and fainter, till it was all over.

The Ambassador went on to tell me of Jean-Baptiste's first acts as the new ruler; he told me that the coronation was to take place on May 11th.

"Really?" I said. "May 11th?"

"Did His Majesty have a special reason for the choice of that particular day?" asked the Ambassador.

"On the 11th of May it will be exactly twenty-five years since Jean-Baptiste Bernadotte was promoted sergeant in the French Army. It was a great day in my husband's life."

"Yes, quite, Your Majesty!"

I rang for tea, which we took with Marceline, who, of course, knew nothing. When she learned the news she was so startled that she dropped her teacup.

The Ambassador left. Marceline, since dropping her cup, had stared steadily at me in awe. "Her Majesty the Queen of Sweden and Norway!" she said slowly, and continued to stare at me.

"I'll have to get some mourning dresses to-morrow," I said, and went back to the piano. Once more I looked at the music composed by Oscar, Crown Prince of Sweden and Norway, once more I touched the keys, and then I closed the lid.

"I shall never play the piano again, Marceline," I said.

"Why not, Aunt?"

"Because I play too badly for a Queen."

"Now we shall not be able to go and see Aunt Julie. You will have to go to Stockholm, I suppose. Aunt Julie was looking forward so much on your visit."

"She can still count on it," I said, and went to my bedroom to lie down.

'Julie Bonaparte,' I thought, 'away in Brussels, exiled like all those who bear the name of Bonaparte.' Ever since the Hundred Days I had been writing to ask Louis XVIII to grant Julie permission to return, and again and again I had received a very courteous refusal. And after every refusal I had gone to Brussels to console my inconsolable Julie. Joseph? He went to America under the name of Count Survillier, bought a farm near New York, and wrote contented letters in which he fondly imagined that Julie would soon be well enough to follow him. In her state of health, how could she?

And Hortense? Accompanied by Count Flahault she had managed to escape to Switzerland, darkly hinting at her departure that one of them would come back and be the Third. And when I asked who and as what, she said, "One of my sons, Madame, Napoleon—the Third!"

Not all had been lucky enough to escape like Hortense. Marshal Ney was caught, sentenced to death and executed. Many others who were on the lists of proscribed Republicans and Bonapartists suffered exile at the hands of Louis XVIII, or prison, or death. And the man who had handed the lists of proscriptions to King Louis, Fouché, what had happened to him? The King made him his Minister of Police in recognition of his services as a traitor. But when the lists of the proscribed had come to an end King Louis thought it time to exile his Minister of Police. And the rest of the Bonapartes? They lived in Italy.

But I was still here, and now I might even have to endure a visit of condolence from King Louis.

Marie came in and lit the candles. 'She'll grumble at me,' I thought, 'for lying on my bed with my shoes on.' But she only held up the light to see my face—and she looked at me in much the same way as Marceline had done.

"Don't be annoyed," I said, "I'll take my shoes off."

"Your niece has told me everything. You might have told me yourself."

"I know what you are thinking," I said. "You think that Papa wouldn't have liked it. I know that myself, without your telling me."

She undressed me.

"If you have to be a Queen, be at least a good one. When are we leaving for Stockholm?"

I took the letter. Scribbled in such haste, I noticed, full of fear that I might be unworthy of him. I held it to the candle and burned it.

"Well, when are we leaving, Eugenie?"

"In three days. That means I shan't have any time left to receive King Louis. By the way, we're going to Brussels. Julie needs me and in Stockholm I'm quite superfluous."

"But they can't have a coronation without us!"

I looked for my book, and for the first time for years I started writing my diary again.

It really has happened to me: I am Queen of Sweden!

PARIS.
June 1821.

AMONG the letters on my breakfast table to-day was one with a dark-green seal that showed clearly a coat-of-arms forbidden the world over—the Emperor's coat-of-arms. It was addressed to Her Majesty Queen Desideria of Sweden and Norway. At last I opened it, and read:

'Madame, I have been informed that my son, the Emperor of the French, died on the 5th of May this year on the Island of St. Helena. He was buried with the military honours due to a General. The British Government forbade the inscription "Napoleon" on the tombstone, and would only allow "General N. Bonaparte." I therefore gave instructions that the grave should remain without any inscription whatever.

'I am dictating this letter to my son Lucien, who often comes to see me in Rome. I am blind now.

'Lucien has begun to read me my son's memoirs, which Napoleone dictated to Count de Montholon on St. Helena. In the memoirs this sentence occurs: "Désirée Clary was Napoleon's first love." You will see from that that my son never ceased to remember his first love.

'I am told that the manuscript will soon be published, and I ask you to let us know if you wish this sentence to be left out. We realise that you in your position will have to be particularly careful, and we shall be glad to do whatever you wish.

'My son Lucien wishes to be remembered to you.

'I remain
'Yours always——'

The blind old woman had signed the letter herself. Her signature, in Italian and barely legible, ran:

'Letitia
madre di Napoleone'
(Letitia, mother of Napoleon.)

During the day I asked my nephew Marius, whom I had made my Lord Chamberlain, how the letter with the forbidden seal arrived here.

"An attaché brought it from the Swedish Embassy, where it had been sent from the Swedish Chargé d'Affairs in Rome. Why, was it an important letter?"

"It was the last letter with the Emperor's coat-of-arms on it. I should like to ask you to send some money to the British Ambassador and ask him to use it for a wreath to be laid on my behalf on the grave in St. Helena. On the grave without a name, you will have to say."

"I am afraid, Aunt, it cannot be done. There are no flowers on St. Helena. The dreadful climate of the island kills all flowers."

"Do you think, Auntie," said Marceline, "that Marie-Louise will now marry that Count Neipperg, by whom she has three children already, or so they say?"

"She married him a long time ago. Talleyrand told me so. The Pope probably declared her first marriage invalid."

"And what about the King of Rome?" said Marius hotly. "After the Emperor's second abdication he was called Napoleon II officially for a few days."

"His name is now Francis Joseph Charles, Duke of Reichstadt, son of Marie-Louise, Duchess of Parma. His father isn't even mentioned in his ducal patent. Anyone would suppose that the father was—unknown!"

"If Napoleon had had any idea of what was to happen to him!" began Marceline.

"He had," I said, as I went to my writing desk.

'An island without flowers,' I thought. The pictures of our garden in Marseilles, the field, and the flowering hedge came into my mind as I began writing to Madame Letitia.

"Aunt Julie once said something about you, or perhaps him," said Marceline hesitantly, some time later.

"You'll read all that in his memoirs," I said, as I sealed the letter. "Nothing will be left out of them."

AACHEN.
June 1822.

THIS morning, sitting at my dressing-table in the hotel, getting ready, I thought how strange it is that at forty-two I should be experiencing once more all the sweetness, the anxiety, the impatience of a first rendezvous.

"And when am I to see him?" I asked for the twentieth time.

"At half-past twelve, Auntie, in your drawing-room," Marceline answered patiently.

"But he'll be here early in the morning, won't he?"

"It was difficult to give the exact time of his arrival. That's why the visit was fixed for half-past twelve."

"And then he'll have a meal with me?"

"Yes, together with his lord-in-waiting, Charles Gustavus Löwenhjelm."

He is the uncle of my Gustavus Löwenhjelm whom they sent me a short time ago to take the place of Count Rosen, who went home. My Löwenhjelm is so pompous and formal that I hardly dare speak to him.

"The only others will be Marius and myself, Auntie, so that you can talk to him freely."

Two Löwenhjelms, Marius and Marceline? No, I said to myself, no! I sent for Löwenhjelm and told him to instruct his uncle to withdraw immediately he saw me. I felt sure that after his arrival at his hotel Oscar would go straight to the Cathedral like any other tourist. I decided to meet him there.

Of course, my Löwenhjelm was terribly upset. "The advantage of ceremonial preparations lies in the avoidance of surprises," he explained to me. But I didn't give in and in the end he agreed.

I put on my hat and a veil that covered my face, and went out by myself to the Cathedral. 'This is the last great surprise of my life,' I thought on the way; 'the first meeting with a man can mean everything or nothing. In half an hour we should know.'

I went into the Cathedral and sat down in a choir stall. Instinctively I folded my hands.

Eleven years is a long time, I reflected. Perhaps meanwhile, without noticing it, I've turned into a middle-aged lady. He, at all events, had grown up into a young man who was being sent round the European courts to look for a wife.

484

This morning innumerable tourists visited the Cathedral and crowded round the stone slab over the alleged tomb of Charlemagne. I looked at every single one of them. Was it that one? Or that other one? Or the little flat-footed fellow over there?

I don't know what a mother feels when she sees her son growing up, and notices the first faint growth of beard and the signs of his first falling in love. All that I have never known. I was waiting for a man who was to be like the one I had dreamt of all my life and had never met, my stranger son!

I recognised him at once, not because of Löwenhjelm, who had hardly changed since my Stockholm days, but because of his bearing, his walk, the movements of his head. He wore dark civilian clothes and seemed almost as tall as his father, only much thinner.

I left my seat and went toward him, without thinking how to address him. He was standing over the slab of Charlemagne's alleged tomb and bending down to read the inscription. I touched Löwenhjelm's arm. He looked up and, seeing me, withdrew without a word.

"Is that Charlemagne's tomb?" I asked in French. It was the most stupid question possible because the inscription said quite plainly that it was.

"As you see, Madame," he said without turning round.

"I know that my conduct is very unseemly, but I—I should like to make the acquaintance of Your Highness."

This time he looked up. "So you know who I am, Madame?" I saw the dark, forceful eyes of long ago and the thick curls, my curls! But he had a small ridiculously waxed moustache.

"Your Highness is the Crown Prince of Sweden," I said. "And I am a compatriot of yours. My husband lives in Stockholm, you see."

I stopped. He was looking steadily at me.

"I wanted to ask Your Highness a favour, but—but it will take a little time."

"I see," he said. Looking round for his escort he murmured, "I don't know where my companion has gone. But I have an hour to spare. If you will permit me, Madame, I should like to accompany you." Smiling, he added: "Is it permitted?"

I nodded, and I felt a lump rising in my throat. Making our way toward the door, I saw Oscar's Löwenhjelm lurking behind a pillar. Fortunately Oscar didn't notice him.

Without speaking we went out, crossed the fish market outside the Cathedral, and finally entered a narrow street. I pulled

485

the veil more tightly round my face, as I felt that Oscar was giving me sidelong glances now and then. At last we stopped at a small café with a few miserable tables outside and two dusty palm trees.

"May I invite my charming compatriot to a glass of wine?" he asked.

I looked at the dreadful shrubs with horror. 'But that won't do,' I thought, and I felt that I was blushing. 'Doesn't he see that I am a middle-aged lady? Or does he give these invitations to every chance acquaintance?' But I calmed myself with the thought that he had probably invited me because he was glad to be rid of Löwenhjelm.

"It is not very elegant here, Madame," he said, "but at least we can talk undisturbed."

To my horror he ordered champagne.

"Not now, in the morning," I said.

"Why not? Why not at any time when there is something to celebrate?"

"But there is nothing to celebrate."

"There is. Your acquaintance, Madame. Could you not put your veil aside a bit so that I could see your face? I can see nothing but the tip of your nose."

"My nose is a very unfortunate one. When I was young it used to offend me a good deal. Strange that no woman ever seems to have the nose she wants."

"My father has a really fantastic nose. Like an eagle's beak! His face is nothing but nose and eyes."

The waiter brought the champagne and poured it out.

"Skål, ma compatriote inconnue. French and Swedish at the same time—is that not so?"

"Like Your Highness," I said. The champagne was far too sweet.

"No, Madame, I am only a Swede now—and, of course, a Norwegian. The champagne is awful, don't you think so?"

"Too sweet, Your Highness."

"I am glad, Madame, that we seem to have the same taste. Most women prefer their wine very sweet. Our Madame Koskull, for instance."

I sat up sharply. "What does that mean—our Madame Koskull?"

"That is our lady-in-waiting, Mariana Koskull. First she was the late King's ray of sunshine, then Papa's favourite and, if Papa had had his way, my—mistress! What is there so surprising in it, Madame?"

486

"That you tell these things to a stranger," I said angrily.

"A compatriot! Mariana used to read to the old King, and he was so happy to be allowed to stroke her arm. Papa has simply taken over the Swedish court ceremonial as it was, perhaps in order not to offend anybody, and so he has taken over Madame Koskull as well."

I stared at him, completely put out. "Do you mean that?"

"Madame, my father is the loneliest man I know. My mother has not been to see him for many years, he works sixteen hours a day, and what spare time he has he spends in the company of a few friends from the days before his accession, such as Count Brahe, if the name means anything to you, or Madame Koskull. She brings her guitar and sings Swedish drinking songs to Papa. They are quite amusing songs, but Papa unfortunately does not understand them."

"And court balls and receptions? You can't have a court without its court functions?"

"Oh yes, Papa can. Don't forget, Madame, we are a court without a Queen!"

I emptied my glass slowly, and he filled it again. "It will all be different once you get married."

"Do you think that any young Princess will feel at ease in a huge cold castle where the King refuses to see anybody but his ministers and old friends? My father has altered strangely, Madame. A King who does not speak the language of his people is easily obsessed by the fear that he may be deposed. Do you know how far things have gone? They have gone so far that my father has prohibited journals that have published articles disagreeable to him personally. Yet the Swedish Constitution guarantees freedom of the press!"

Oscar's face had gone white with agitation. Tonelessly I asked: "You are not hostile to your father, are you?"

"No, if I were, all this would not upset me so much. Madame, my father has made Sweden great again, and prosperous; Sweden owes its liberty to him alone. Yet this same man fights every liberal tendency Parliament shows. Why? Because he imagines that liberalism leads to revolution and revolution will cost him his crown. But there is not the ghost of a chance of any kind of revolution in Scandinavia, only healthy evolution. A former Jacobin just can't see that. Do I weary you, Madame?"

I shook my head, and he went on: "It has come to this, that some people, individuals, Madame, not parties, talk of suggesting abdication to him—in my favour!"

"You must never even think of that," I said in a low tone, trembling.

Oscar bent forward. "I am tired, Madame. I wanted to be a composer, and what has come of it? A few songs, a few military marches, that's all. I have begun an opera and cannot find time to finish it, not only because of my duties at court and in the Army but especially because I have to spend so much time trying to convince my father of the necessities for changes, changes, incidentally, which the French Revolution ought to have taught him. He ought to receive the middle class at court instead of only the old nobility, and he should stop talking at every prorogation of Parliament about his deserts as a General and the sacrifice of his private fortune to pay Sweden's external debts. Papa ought to——"

I couldn't contain myself any longer, I had to interrupt him and ask: "And what about this Madame Koskull?"

"I don't think she has ever done more for him than sing songs. As for me, he seemed to have the old-fashioned idea that Crown Princes ought to be introduced to the amatory arts by ladies who were experienced campaigners. Not long ago, Madame, he sent Mistress Koskull to my room at midnight armed with her guitar!"

"Your Papa meant well, Your Highness."

"He locks himself up in his study and loses all contact with reality. What he lacks——" He broke off to pour out more champagne. A frown appeared on his forehead, reminiscent of Jean-Baptiste. "When I was a child, Madame, I badly wanted to see Napoleon's coronation. I was not allowed to, I don't know why. But I do remember my mother sitting in my room and saying that we should both go to another coronation; she promised me that, and it was to be a far more beautiful one than Napoleon's. Yes, Madame, I did go to another one, but my mother wasn't there. But, Madame, you are crying!"

"Your mother's name is Desideria, the longed-for one, the wanted one. Perhaps she wasn't wanted at the time."

"Not wanted? My father has her proclaimed Queen and she, she does not even come for that! Do you believe that a man like my father can bring himself to ask her on his knees?"

"Perhaps being a Queen is not a very congenial occupation for your mother?"

"Madame, my mother is a marvellous woman. But she is at least as obstinate as my father. I tell you that the presence of the Queen in Sweden is not only desirable but necessary!"

"If that is so, perhaps the Queen had better come," I said very softly.

"Thank God, Mama! Thank God! And now take off your veil so that I can have a real look at you. Yes, you have changed. You have become more beautiful, your eyes are bigger, and your face and— Why are you crying, Mama?"

"When did you recognise me, Oscar?"

"Recognise you? I only went to look at Charlemagne's tomb to wait there for you. I was quite curious, I must say, to know how you were going to address a strange man."

"I thought your Löwenhjelm would keep quiet about it."

"It was not his fault. I intended all along to meet you without witnesses. He noticed how I racked my brains about it and so he confessed that you had anticipated me."

"Oscar, is what you told me about Papa true?"

"It is. Only I painted it very black so that you couldn't but decide to come home. When are you coming?"

He took my hand and put it against his cheek.

"Oscar, you have a beard like a man. Come home? You don't know how they vexed me at that time in Stockholm."

"But, dear Mama, they are all dead, except Princess Sofia Albertina! Who could vex you now? Don't forget you are the Queen!"

No, I thought, how could I forget that? I'm so afraid of it.

"Mama, in the Cathedral you said something about asking me a favour. Did you say that only to start the conversation with me?"

"No, I really have a favour to ask you. It concerns my daughter-in-law."

"But there is no daughter-in-law yet. Papa has compiled a whole list of Princesses I am to look at, all horribly ugly. Papa got their portraits for me."

"I should like you to marry for love, Oscar."

"Believe me, so should I. When you get home I shall show you my little daughter, secretly. Her name is Oscara, Mama."

Heavens, I am a grandmother!

"Mama, Oscara has inherited your dimples!"

"And who is Oscara's mother?"

"Jaquette Gyldenstolpe, a charming mother!"

"Does Papa know?"

"Of course not, Mama! Promise me never to tell him!"

"But shouldn't you— —"

"Marry her? Mama, you forget who I am."

489

For some reason it irritated me to hear him say that. Oscar continued:

"Papa thought at first of a connection with the house of Hanover. But the Bernadotte dynasty is not good enough yet for the English, and I shall have to marry a Prussian Princess."

"Listen, Oscar. The arrangements were that we were going together from here to Brussels for the marriage of Aunt Julie's daughter Zenaïde to a son of Lucien Bonaparte. We expect Joseph Bonaparte back from America for the wedding. He may even stay on in Europe afterwards."

"I am sorry, Mama, but I don't like the Bonapartes. Well, the wedding. And then?"

"From Brussels I'm going on to Switzerland to Hortense—you know, Josephine's daughter. I should like you to come along too."

"Mama, I really should not like that. All these Bonapartes——"

"I want you to meet Hortense's niece."

"Who is she?"

"The daughter of Eugene de Beauharnais, former Viceroy of Italy, now Duke of Leuchtenberg. His wife is a daughter of the King of Bavaria. And the daughter is the most beautiful girl you can imagine."

"Even if she is, I still couldn't marry her. The daughter of a Duke of Leuchtenberg is no match for the Crown Prince of Sweden, Mama—for a Bernadotte!"

"No? Then let me tell you, Oscar—but give me a little more champagne first, I am beginning to like it—let me tell you: her grandfather on her father's side was the Viscount Beauharnais, a General in the French Army. Her grandmother was the Viscountess Beauharnais, the most beautiful woman of her time, the most charming and expensive of cocottes. On her second marriage she became Empress of the French. Your paternal grandfather, however, was a lawyer's clerk in Pau, and nothing at all is known about his wife, your father's mother."

"But, Mama——"

"Let me finish. Her grandfather on her mother's side is the King of Bavaria, and the Bavarian royal family is one of the oldest reigning families in Europe. Your grandfather on your mother's side was the Marseilles silk merchant François Clary."

He clapped his hands to his head. "The grand-daughter of a cocotte!"

"Yes, and an enchanting one at that! I've only seen the little

490

Josephine once, when she was a child, but she has the same smile, the same charm as the big one had."

Oscar sighed. "Mama, simply for dynastic reasons——"

"Exactly, for dynastic reasons! I want to be the ancestress of a beautiful dynasty."

"Papa will never give his consent."

"Imagine anybody asking him to marry an ugly woman! I shall handle Papa. You go and have a look at Josephine."

We left the café arm-in-arm and went to our hotel. My heart was beating with happiness and bad champagne.

"How old is she, Mama?"

"Only fifteen. But at that age I had my first kisses."

"You were a precocious child, Mama."

We came in sight of the hotel. Oscar, suddenly very serious, took my hand.

"Mama, you'll promise me, won't you, to accompany my fiancée to Stockholm?"

"Yes, I promise."

"And that you will stay on?"

I hesitated. "That depends."

"On what?"

"On myself, Oscar. I shall only stay on if I succeed in becoming a good Queen. I shall take it very seriously indeed."

"All you need, Mama, is practice. Look! There they are, your Löwenhjelm and mine, both looking anxious."

"I shall introduce some reforms at the Swedish court," I whispered into his ear. "We shall send Miss Koskull to her well-earned retirement." We looked at each other and laughed heartily.

"Mama, we are both a little drunk," said Oscar.

Well, well, is that really becoming for an illegitimate grandmother, I mean the grandmother of an illegitimate child?

At the ROYAL CASTLE in STOCKHOLM. Spring 1823.

"How beautiful our country is!" said my daughter-in-law, the Crown Princess Josefina of Sweden, in an awed voice.

We were standing near the bows of the impressive warship that had met us at Lübeck and was now nearing Stockholm. Oscar and Josephine had been married in Munich. As she is a Roman Catholic and Oscar a Protestant, she insisted on being married in a Roman Catholic church, by proxy as Oscar couldn't be there. The proper ceremonies for the wedding are to take place in Stockholm after our arrival.

We passed countless rocky islets covered with black fir trees, with green shoots showing on every branch, or birches veiled with yellow blossom.

"Our beautiful country," repeated Josephine's grand-daughter, and her shining eyes drank in the sight of the marvellous birch forests.

Marceline, Marius, and Marie and Pierre were with me, and Yvette, of course, the only one who could do my hair properly besides Julie. They were the little bit of France I had brought with me. I had appointed Marceline my chief stewardess and Marius my financial adviser, to their intense satisfaction and that of their father. I had left Julie behind in Brussels; she was far more reconciled to her exile than I had ever known her to be, and talked of joining her daughter Zenaïde, who was married and living in Florence. Joseph had come over from America, and his main topic of conversation was cattle breeding. He too talked vaguely of going to live in Italy when he was old. "And so," said Julie, linking her arm in his, "everything has turned out for the best." But she said it without conviction.

"I am so happy, Mama," whispered Josefina into my ear. "From the moment we set eyes on each other, Oscar and I knew that we were meant for each other. But I was sure that neither you nor His Majesty would allow it."

"But why not, Josephine?"

"Because, Mama, I am only the daughter of the Duke of Leuchtenberg, and I am sure you counted on a Princess from a royal family, did you not?"

"Counted? You don't count on anything where your children's happiness is concerned, you only hope for the best."

A salvo came from the coastal fortress of Vaxholm, which we were passing, and I noticed a small boat approaching our ship.

"And that is my advice to you, Josefina," I continued. "Never stand in the way of your children if they want to marry for love."

"But, Mama, what about the succession?"

"Leave that to fate and the future. But teach all Bernadottes that love is the only honourable reason for marrying."

Josefina looked horrified. "But, Mama, what if it is a commoner?"

"What of it? Aren't we commoners, we Bernadottes?"

Another salvo thundered. I put the field-glasses to my eyes and studied the little boat making for us. "Josefina, Oscar's coming on board!"

We entered the port of Djurgården. The air was reverberating with the thunder of the guns, great crowds were lining quays and streets as far as we could see, and lots of small garlanded boats danced round our ship. Oscar and Josefina were standing beside me, waving. Josefina wore a blue dress and an ermine stole that had begun to go yellow with age. Once upon a time Napoleon had given that stole to Josephine, and Hortense made a present of it to Josefina to remind her of her beautiful grandmother.

I felt my hands turn clammy as I clenched them in growing excitement. Marie touched them reassuringly with her hard hand and put the heavy mink stole over my shoulders.

"This is the end of your journey, Eugenie," she said.

"No, Marie, this is only the beginning."

The guns had stopped firing, and a band began to play.

"I composed that music for you," said Oscar to Josefina. Meanwhile I looked round through the field-glasses and found what I was looking for: a purple velvet cloak and white plumes on a hat.

The gangway was brought out and I found myself facing it alone. Everybody, even Oscar and Josefina, had gone back a few paces. The band on the quayside struck up the Swedish national anthem, and everybody froze into immobility. Then two gentlemen who had been waiting close to the purple velvet cloak rushed toward the gangway to escort me down. They were Counts Brahe and Rosen, the one smiling, the other pale with excitement. But the purple cloak came between them and me at the end of the narrow shaky gangway and I felt a familiar grip on my arm.

The crowd cheered, the guns thundered, the band played, as we walked on to the quay followed by Oscar and his Crown Princess. Under a triumphal arch made of birch branches a little girl in white handed me a giant bouquet of blue lilies and yellow tulips and recited a poem of welcome. Then, to the obvious surprise of all present, I opened my mouth to say something in return. A great hush fell on the quayside. I was almost paralysed with fear, but my voice was loud and calm as I began with the words:

"*Jag har varit länge borte——*"

I could see them holding their breath! Swedish, the Queen was speaking Swedish! I had composed the little address, Count Löwenhjelm had translated it for me, and I had learnt it

493

by heart. It was dreadfully difficult, and I felt relieved when I reached the last words: *"Länge leve Sverige!"*

We drove through the streets in an open equipage, Josefina nodding graciously left and right next to me, Jean-Baptiste and Oscar facing us. I sat stiffly upright, smiling to the crowds till my face ached. But even then I continued to smile.

"I was amazed," said Oscar, "at your speaking in Swedish, Mama. I am very proud of you."

I felt Jean-Baptiste's eyes on me, but I couldn't bring myself to look at him. Why not? Because I realised how much I was still in love with him, still or again, I don't know which.

And all the time I was chuckling a little at the thought that he was a grandfather already, without knowing it!

DROTTNINGHOLM CASTLE.
August 15th–16th, 1823.

At midnight to-night I was a ghost for the first time in my life. In my white dressing-gown I 'walked' the corridors of the castle as the 'white lady'.

We came here to Drottningholm for a rest after a strenuous summer in which Oscar and Josefina and I danced every night at some ball or other, in some castle or other, in South Sweden as well as here. And we had made Jean-Baptiste attend and dance too, in spite of all his excuses. Everything at court is new and fresh, new lords and ladies-in-waiting, new liveries, new furniture, new wallpaper and paint, and so is this régime of cheerfulness and new life and new contact with the people. But it has been strenuous! And so we have come here.

Last night I went early to bed, but I couldn't sleep. The summer nights here are so disturbingly light.

The clock struck midnight. It's the 16th of August, I remembered. I slipped into my dressing-gown and started 'walking'. I wanted to go to Jean-Baptiste. It was completely silent everywhere, only the parquet floor creaked under my steps. How I hate castles!

In Jean-Baptiste's study I very nearly collided with Moreau's white marble bust, but in the end I managed to feel my way to Jean-Baptiste's dressing-room door. I opened it and—stared straight at the barrel of a pistol! Someone hissed at me in French.

"Who goes there?"

I laughed. "A ghost, Fernand, that's all!"

"Your Majesty has given me a fright," said Fernand, offended. He was in a long nightshirt, and he still held the pistol as he bowed to me. His camp bed was pulled across Jean-Baptiste's door.

"Do you always sleep in front of His Majesty's door?"

"Yes. The Marshal is afraid."

The door was flung open, and Jean-Baptiste, his green shade pushed up on to his forehead, bellowed:

"What does this mean?"

I curtsied. "Your Majesty, a ghost requests an audience."

Fernand pushed the camp bed aside, and for the first time since our arrival in Drottningholm I stood in Jean-Baptiste's bedroom. Even there every inch of space seemed to be filled with leather tomes and files of papers. 'He's still studying,' I thought, 'as in Hanover, as in Marienburg.'

Jean-Baptiste stretched himself wearily, and asked with a smile:

"And what does the ghost want?"

"It only wants to announce its presence," I said, and sat down comfortably in an armchair. "It's the ghost of a young girl who, once upon a time, married a General and went into a bridal bed full of roses and thorns."

Jean-Baptiste sat down on the arm of my chair and put his arm round me.

"And why does this ghost announce its presence on this particular night?"

"Because it was twenty-five years ago to-night."

"Heavens!" he exclaimed, "it is our silver wedding day, is it?"

"Yes," I said, nestling close to him, "and in the whole of Sweden no one besides ourselves will think of it. No salvoes, no school-children reciting poetry, no regimental bands! Isn't it marvellous, Jean-Baptiste?"

"We have travelled a long way," he said, tired, and put his head on my shoulder. "And in the end you came back to me after all."

"You have arrived, Jean-Baptiste. Yet in spite of that you are afraid of ghosts?"

He didn't answer. His head felt heavy on my shoulder.

"Fernand sleeps across your bedroom door with a pistol in his hand. What ghosts are you afraid of?"

"The ghosts of Vasa. During the Congress of Vienna the last Vasa King, the exiled one, you know, put in his claims to the throne for himself and his son."

"But that's eight years ago. The Swedes deposed him because he was crazy. Is he really crazy?"

"His policy certainly was. The allies rejected his claims, of course. They couldn't very well do anything else after the way I, during that horrible campaign——"

"Jean-Baptiste, don't let those memories torment you. The Swedes know exactly what you did for them. They know that you made their country prosperous and rich."

"Yes, yes, but the opposition——"

"Does the opposition ever mention the Vasas?"

"No, never. But let an opposition that calls itself Liberal exist, and it is only one more step to revolution!"

"Nonsense, the Swedes know what they want. You've been proclaimed and crowned King."

"And can be killed or deposed to make room for the last Vasa. He is an officer in the Austrian Army."

I decided there and then to lay that ghost. Then he would be able to sleep at all events.

"Jean-Baptiste, the Bernadotte dynasty rules in Sweden once and for all, and you are the only one who is not convinced of that."

He shrugged his shoulders.

"But unfortunately there are people who maintain that in your fear of the opposition you don't stick to the Constitution." I turned my face away. "The Swedes set great store by their freedom of the press, dearest. And every time you suppress a paper there are one or two people who might take it into their heads to compel you to abdicate."

He winced. "Is that so? There, you see that my ghosts are not imaginary ones. The Prince of Vasa——"

"Jean-Baptiste, no one ever mentions the Prince of Vasa. The only one they mention is—Oscar, the Crown Prince!"

I heard a sigh of relief. "Is that true? Look at me, is that really true?"

"No one is dissatisfied with the Bernadotte dynasty. It has come to stay. Tell Fernand to sleep from now on in his own bedroom."

When Jean-Baptiste later drew the curtains aside from the windows the park of Drottningholm lay in bright golden light.

I went up to him by the window. "As far as Oscar is concerned," he said, gently stroking my hair, "I gave him what I never had myself, a good education, education for kingship. Sometimes I feel sad that I myself shall never see him King. Come along, let's have breakfast together as we did twenty-five years ago."

In the study we stopped before Moreau's bust. "Moreau, old friend!" said Jean-Baptiste thoughtfully, and tenderly I touched his marble face. 'They don't dust very well,' I thought, 'in these royal castles.' Then we went on, clasping each other tightly.

"I am glad," said Jean-Baptiste suddenly, "that I gave in and let Oscar marry Josefina."

"If you had had your way he'd have married some King's plain daughter, and old Miss Koskull would have been his only excursion into romantic young love, you unnatural father!"

In my boudoir a great surprise awaited us. On the breakfast-table laid for two was a fine bunch of roses, red, white, yellow, and pink. A piece of paper leaned against the vase. 'Our very best wishes to Their Majesties, Marshal J.-B. Bernadotte and wife. Marie and Fernand.''

Jean-Baptiste laughed, and I cried.

STOCKHOLM CASTLE.
February 1829.

OLD Princess Sofia Albertina, the last Vasa in Sweden, is dying. Since her brother's death the old Princess has been living in the so-called Crown Prince's Palace, and although Jean-Baptiste saw to it that she was regularly asked to the court table, Oscar was the only one who took any interest in her. He calls her Aunt, and says she used to give him sweets when he was a boy. Yesterday I heard him say that she was ill, and this morning one of her octogenarian ladies-in-waiting came to me with the message that it was Her Highness's last wish to speak to me—to the silk merchant's daughter, of all people!—in private.

When I came to her she was dressed in my honour in grande toilette, lying on a sofa, and she tried to get up as I entered.

"Don't trouble to get up," I said, horrified at the sight of her sallow, wrinkled skin, her hollow cheeks, and the dull stare of her eyes in their deep sockets.

Her drawing-room was full of pink roses embroidered on purple. The poor thing had done nothing all her life but embroider roses, and always the same pattern!

She smiled at me as I sat down, and sent her ladies away.

"I am very grateful to Your Majesty for your visit," she said. "I am told that your time is very fully occupied."

"Yes," I agreed, "we are very busy." I told her about Jean-Baptiste's full days and Oscar's promotion to Admiral of the Fleet and his plans for prison reform and the book he is writing on the subject.

"A strange occupation for an Admiral," she said.

"And for a musician," I added.

She nodded, bored. Somewhere a clock was ticking.

"Your Majesty does a good deal of hospital visiting," she said unexpectedly.

"Naturally, that is one of my duties. Besides, there's lots of room for improvement." Soon that subject was exhausted in its turn, and I heard the clock ticking again.

"I am told that you speak a bit of Swedish, Madame," she said a little later.

"I'm trying to learn it, Your Highness. Jean-Baptiste has no time to learn languages, and nobody thinks any the less of him for that. But I receive all deputations in Swedish as best I can."

The Princess seemed to be asleep and she looked as white as her powdered hair. I felt very sorry for her loneliness in her last moments. Suddenly she said:

"You are a good Queen, Madame!"

"We are doing our best, Jean-Baptiste, Oscar and I."

The ghost of the malicious smile of former days flitted over her face. "You are a very intelligent woman."

I looked at her in amazement.

"Yes," she continued, "at that time when poor Hedvig Elizabeth stigmatised you as being only a silk merchant's daughter you left the room in high dudgeon, and only returned as Queen. Hedvig Elizabeth has never been forgiven for that. A court without a young Crown Princess!" She giggled gleefully. "To the end of her life Hedvig Elizabeth had the reputation of the bad mother-in-law, he he he!"

These recollections seemed to revive her. "Oscar brought the children to see me, little Charles and the new-born baby, what's his name?"

"Oscar," I said proudly.

"Charles is very like you, Madame," she said. "I should have liked children of my own, but they never found a suitable husband for me. Oscar says you would have no objection if his children married commoners. How do you imagine that would work, Madame?"

"I've never thought about that. But Princes can renounce their titles, can't they?"

"Of course they can——" She broke off and fell into another doze. Somewhere the clock was ticking. Then she spoke again.

"I wanted to talk to you about the crown, Madame."

"Which crown?" I asked, thinking that her mind must be wandering.

"The crown of the Queens of Sweden."

Her eyes were wide open, and she spoke calmly and clearly.

"You were not crowned when His Majesty was. Perhaps you do not know that we have a crown for our Queens, a very old one, not big but quite heavy. I have held it in my hand several times. You are the mother of the Bernadotte dynasty. Why won't you be crowned?"

"Because up to now nobody has thought of it," I said softly.

"But I am doing so now. I am the last Vasa alive in Sweden and I am asking the first Bernadotte to take care of the old crown."

"I don't like these ceremonies," I said.

She opened her bloodless fingers and waited for me to give her my hand in token of consent. "I have not much time left to ask."

I could not but respond to that appeal.

I remembered that at a coronation long ago I had had to carry a handkerchief on a velvet cushion, to the ringing of the bells of Notre-Dame.

Did the old Princess guess the way my thoughts had turned? "I had the memoirs of this Napoleon Bonaparte read to me." She looked at me quizzically. "How strange that the two most important men of our time should have fallen in love with you, Madame. After all, you really are no beauty!"

Then she sighed, very softly:

"A pity I was born a Vasa. I should have preferred to be a Bernadotte and marry a commoner and have some fun in life."

When I left I bowed deeply to her and kissed the old hand. The dying Princess smiled, astonished at first and then a bit malicious. For, truly, I am no beauty.

"HIS Royal Highness regrets that it is quite impossible for him to find a free afternoon during this week." So Oscar's lord-in-waiting reported to me.

"Tell His Royal Highness that it is a question of fulfilling a wish of his mother's." After some hesitation the gentleman disappeared.

"But, Aunt, you know that Oscar is so terribly busy," said Marceline, not quite discreetly.

Oscar's lord-in-waiting returned. "His Royal Highness regrets that it is quite impossible this week."

"Then tell His Royal Highness that I am expecting him at four o'clock this afternoon. He will accompany me on an excursion."

"Your Majesty, His Royal Highness regrets——"

"I know, my dear Count, my son regrets that he is unable to fulfil my wish. Therefore tell him that it is no longer a wish of his mother but a command from the Queen."

Promptly at four o'clock Oscar was announced, together with three gentlemen of his suite. On the sleeve of his Admiral's uniform he wore the mourning band for Princess Sofia Albertina, who had died on March 17th. I myself wore mourning.

Oscar behaved very formally, to show me how furious he was. I told him to dismiss his gentlemen, I wanted to go on this excursion without any escort. I put on my hat and we left, on foot, to Oscar's surprise and dismay.

"We are going to the Västerlånggatan," I said, and Oscar led the way. He hadn't said a word yet, he was too furious with me. But that didn't prevent him from saluting and smiling to the passers-by who recognised him and bowed on meeting him. I had pulled the mourning veil over my face and was dressed so plainly and consequently looked so uninteresting that no one thought I belonged to His Highness.

"Here is the Västerlånggatan," said Oscar at last. "May I ask Your Majesty where we are going now?"

"To a silk shop belonging to a man called Persson. I have never been yet, but it shouldn't be difficult to find."

Oscar's patience broke. "Mama, I cancelled two conferences and an audience because of your command. And where are you taking me? To a silk shop! Why don't you let the man come to you?"

"Persson isn't appointed to the court. Besides, I'd like to see his shop."

"But surely you don't need me?"

"You can help me choose the material for my coronation dress. And I want to introduce you to Monsieur Persson."

Oscar was speechless. "Introduce me to a silk merchant?"

I felt sad. Perhaps it hadn't been a good idea to take Oscar along. I keep forgetting that my son is a Crown Prince.

"Persson was an apprentice in your grandfather Clary's shop in Marseilles. He even lived in our house," I said with emotion. "Oscar, don't you understand, there is a man in Stockholm who has known my father and my home!"

Oscar bent down to me quickly and pushed his arm through mine. Looking round, he stopped an elderly man and asked for Persson's shop. After a good deal of bowing and scraping the man managed to give Oscar the information.

It was a comparatively small shop. But I saw at once that the silks and velvets in the window were of excellent quality. Inside there were a lot of customers, prosperous middle-class women who were so busy fingering the silks that they paid no attention to Oscar's uniform. Consequently we were pushed around till our turn came. Behind the counter three young men were serving, one of them with an equine face and fair hair who reminded me of the young Persson of bygone days. It was this one who asked us what we wanted.

"I should like to see your silks," I said in my broken Swedish. He didn't understand me at first, and I repeated my request in French. "I'll call my father, he speaks French very well," said the young man, and disappeared.

Looking round I noticed that we were now quite alone in front of the counter, and to my horror I saw all the other customers pressed against the wall behind me, awestruck. I heard their murmur:

"The Queen!"

They had recognised me because I had put up the veil, the better to see the silks.

At that moment a side door opened, and Persson appeared, Persson from Marseilles, our Persson. He hadn't changed much. The fair hair had turned a dull grey, the blue eyes looked no longer timid but full of quiet self-confidence, and he smiled obligingly and showed his long yellow teeth.

"Madame wishes to see some silk?" he said in French.

"Your French has gone from bad to worse, Monsieur Persson. And to think of all the trouble I took with your pronunciation."

The long lean figure stiffened. He opened his mouth to say something, but his lower lip trembled and he couldn't speak a word.

"Have you forgotten me, Monsieur Persson?"

He shook his head, slowly, as if in a dream. I tried to help him and said cordially:

"Monsieur Persson, I should like to see your silk cloths."

He stroked his head in confusion, and said in his miserable French:

"You have really come to see me, Mademoiselle Clary!"

It was too much for Oscar: the crowded shop, the intently listening ladies, and old Persson stammering in French. "Perhaps you would be kind enough to take Her Majesty and me into your office and show us your goods there," he said.

We went through a side door into a little office full of ledgers on a high desk, and hundreds of samples lying about just as they used to do in Papa's sanctum, and I felt immediately at home. In a frame over the desk hung a yellowed pamphlet which I recognised as soon as I saw it.

"Yes, here I am, Persson," I said, and sat down on the chair by the desk. "I should like to introduce my son to you. Oscar, this is Monsieur Persson, who was your grandfather's apprentice in Marseilles."

"I am surprised," Oscar said, smiling, "that you have not been appointed Purveyor to the Court long ago."

"I have never asked for the honour," said Persson slowly. "In any case, since my return from France my reputation in certain circles has not been a good one. And that is the reason," he said, pointed to the framed broadsheet.

"What is that?" Oscar asked. Persson took it from the wall and handed it to him.

"That, Oscar, was the first publication of the Rights of Man. Papa, your grandfather, brought it home, and Monsieur Persson and I learned it by heart. When Monsieur Persson went home he asked me for the broadsheet as a souvenir."

Oscar made no answer, but went to the window, wiped the dust off the glass with the sleeve of his Admiral's uniform, and began to read.

Persson and I looked at each other. "And the Mälar is really as green as you always told me it was," I said. "I never could visualise green water. And now the green water runs under my windows!"

"How well you remember it all, Mademoi——Your Majesty!" he said hoarsely.

"Of course I remember it. That's why it has taken me such a long time to come to you. I was afraid you'd blame me for——"

"Blame you? What could I ever blame you for?"

"For being a Queen now. Because we both used to be Republicans."

Persson looked across at Oscar in alarm. But Oscar was too immersed in the Rights of Man to hear. That restored Persson's self-confidence and he whispered to me: "That was in France, Mademoiselle Clary. But here in Sweden we are both—monarchists!" Then, with another glance at Oscar, he added: "Provided that—you understand, don't you?"

I nodded. We were silent and thought of our villa and the shop in Marseilles. Then Persson broke the silence.

"The sword of the General Buonaparte hung in the hall every evening during the last weeks of my stay in your house. How I hated it!" Blood mounted to his grey cheeks as he spoke.

"Persson, you were not jealous, were you?"

He turned his eyes away. "If I had imagined at that time that a daughter of François Clary might take to life in Stockholm, I should——"

He left the sentence unfinished.

I was dumb with surprise. So he would have offered me a home and a shop here, within a stone's throw of the castle!

"I need a new dress, Persson," I said gently.

He turned his eyes back to me, and was his old self once more, grey and dignified. . . .

"What kind of dress?"

"For my coronation. You may have read that it is going to be on the 21st of August. Have you any silk suitable for a coronation robe?"

"I have, indeed. The white brocade, you remember?"

He opened the door and called his son: "François!" He explained to me that he had called his son after my father, and then told the young man to bring the white brocade from Marseilles. "You know which one I mean."

The brocade came, heavy silk with threads of real gold. I took it on my knees, and Oscar, putting down the broadsheet, came over to look at it.

"Marvellous," he said, "just the stuff you want, Mama! Is it not too heavy?"

"It is very heavy, Oscar. I know because I carried it to the coach for Monsieur Persson when he left."

"Your Majesty's father declared that this silk could only be used for the State robe of a Queen," added Persson.

"Why have you never offered it at court?" I wondered. "It would have pleased the late Queen immensely."

"I kept it in memory of your Papa and the firm of Clary. Moreover, the brocade is not for sale."

"Not even now?" asked Oscar.

"Not even now, Your Royal Highness," Then he called for his son again: "François, pack this brocade." And then bowed to me.

"Your Majesty, may I ask your gracious permission to offer you this brocade as a present?"

I felt a lump rising in my throat, and couldn't speak.

"I shall send it to the castle at once, Your Majesty."

I looked at the space on the wall where the framed broadsheet hung, and I looked at Persson.

"If Your Majesty could wait another moment," he said. He took the frame and wrapped it in an old piece of newspaper. "Please, Your Majesty, will you accept this too? Many years ago I promised to honour it always. And I have kept my promise."

An ironic smile appeared on his face. "I have wrapped it up so that Your Majesty can safely go through the streets with it. I myself have had trouble several times in the past."

Arm-in-arm like lovers, Oscar and I made our way back to the castle. We had nearly reached it and still I hadn't managed to say what I wanted to, I searched desperately for the right words.

"Oscar, perhaps you feel we have wasted an afternoon," I began, but stopped because we had come within hearing of the sentries. "Let's go on, Oscar, I have something to say to you." And in spite of his obvious impatience I made him go as far as the Mälar bridge.

The waters roared under the bridge. 'At this time,' I thought, 'the lights of Paris begin to dance on the waters of the Seine.'

"Listen, Oscar. I have always hoped that Persson would let me have Papa's broadsheet, and that's why I asked you to come with me."

"Are you going to lecture me now on the Rights of Man?"

"Yes, Oscar."

But Oscar was growing more and more irritated.

"Mama, the Rights of Man are no longer a revelation for me. Here they are familiar to every educated person."

"Then it's about time the less educated ones learned them by heart. But I want to tell you that——"

"That I am to fight for them, isn't that it?"

"Fight for them? No, defend them!"

I looked at the turbulent water under the bridge. A memory from my childhood rose in my mind: a severed head rolling into blood-bespattered sawdust.

"Oscar, much blood was shed for their sake before and after their proclamation, and Napoleon so profaned them as to quote them even in his battle orders. And many others continue to abuse and dishonour them. I want my son to stand up for them and bring up his children to do the same."

Oscar remained silent for some time. Then he took off the old newspaper in which the Rights of Man were wrapped, and let it flutter into the Mälar.

When we had reached our gate he suddenly broke into laughter. "Mama, that amorous chirping of your old adorer was magnificent. If Papa knew of that!"

On my Coronation Day.
(21st of August 1829.)

"DÉSIRÉE, I implore you, don't be late for your own coronation!"

I shall never forget this sentence as long as I live, because Jean-Baptiste kept shouting it out to me without interruption as Marie, Marceline, Yvette and I kept searching feverishly through my wardrobe. In between rummaging I admired Jean-Baptiste's marvellous coronation robe, his gold chains, his strange boots with the ermine trimming.

"Désirée, are you not ready?"

"I can't find them, Jean-Baptiste."

"What can't you find?"

"My sins, Jean-Baptiste. I put them all down on paper, and I've mislaid the sheet."

"Good gracious, can't you remember them?"

"No, there are too many—all little ones of course. That's why I wrote them down. Yvette, have another look."

I needed my sins because I had to go to confession before the coronation ceremonies began, and Josefina was to come with me. She and I were the only Roman Catholic members of the Protestant House of Bernadotte in Lutheran Sweden. The confession was to take place in the little chapel which Oscar had installed for Josefina on the top floor of the castle, and

505

only after the absolution would I put on my coronation robe of white and gold brocade, which Papa had once held in his hands, and drive in solemn state to the Storkyrka, the Cathedral.

Josefina came in. "Mama, it is high time." But I still couldn't find my sins. I had to call off the search for them, and we went across to the drawing-room, where Oscar was waiting for me in gala uniform.

"I had no idea," said Jean-Baptiste to Oscar, "that your Mama's coronation would be hailed with such enthusiasm. Look at the crowds down there."

They kept behind the curtains and peered through them.

"I am not surprised," answered Oscar. "Mama is enormously popular, you know."

"Really?" Jean-Baptiste smiled at me, and then his irritation returned and he said:

"Désirée, are you ready or not? Have you found your sins?"

No, I hadn't, and the family wasn't co-operating at all and no one wanted to lend me some of their own. But Oscar had a bright idea.

"You have been living in sin with a man for years. There is a really big sin for you to confess."

"What sin do you mean?"

"Did you marry Papa in church or in a registry office?"

"Only in a registry office."

"There you are! The Roman Catholic Church does not recognise marriages not solemnised in church. Now, hurry up."

We arrived at the chapel just in time, and returned in fearful haste and out of breath. I ran past innumerable curtseying ladies to my boudoir, where Marie, my old Marie, now bent with age, and Yvette set to work on me at once.

"Auntie, the Archbishop is waiting already outside the church," said Marceline before she let us begin.

If you study your face every day in the mirror you don't get a fright by discovering that you are old. You see it coming and get used to it. I am now forty-nine years old, and have laughed and cried so much that many little wrinkles have formed round my eyes. And there are two lines from the nose down to the corners of my mouth. They established themselves when Jean-Baptiste fought at Leipzig.

I put cream, powder and rouge on my face as *la grande* Josephine had taught me, and thought of the way the Swedes were reacting to my coronation—as if they had been waiting for just that and nothing else for years! Jean-Baptiste didn't know what to make of their enthusiasm. Did he really think it would be enough to be married to him in order to be the Queen? Doesn't he realise that only with this coronation I have said Yes to him, finally and for ever? Jean-Baptiste, this coronation is the promise of a bride, this time given in church and at the altar, to love and obey.

Most women when they have reached my age are allowed to stop being young. Their children have grown up and their husbands have reached their goal. They may be their own mistresses. Only I may not. I am only beginning. But then, it isn't my fault that I have founded a dynasty. I am the Queen now, and for once, just for to-day, I want to look like a Queen!

"How young you are, Désirée, not a single grey hair!"

Jean-Baptiste was standing behind me, kissing my hair. I laughed.

"Many grey hairs, Jean-Baptiste, but they've been dyed for the first time. Do you like it?"

There was no answer. I turned round and saw not my Jean-Baptiste but a man in a heavy ermine coat, with the circlet of the crown of the Kings of Sweden round his forehead, a great and strange King. King Charles John XIV of Sweden.

He was staring at the yellowed broadsheet on the wall. It was new to him. It is so long since he was last in my boudoir.

"What is that, my girl?" he asked.

"An old broadsheet, Jean-Baptiste. The very first publication of the Rights of Man."

He frowned.

"My father bought it many years ago when the printer's ink on it was still wet. And now this yellow bit of paper gives me strength, I wasn't born to be a Queen."

I felt tears coming, and had to powder my face over again.

"May I stay here?" Jean-Baptiste asked. He sat down by my dressing-table and pulled a sheet of paper out of his pocket while Yvette came along with the curling tongs.

"Is that your list of sins?" I asked him. "A long list?"

"No, this sheet only contains notes about the coronation ceremony. Shall I read them to you?"

I nodded, and he read the thousand and one details about heralds, pages, costumes, the order of the procession and so on. When he mentioned the deputation from Norway he said that the enthusiasm of Sweden had suggested to him the idea of a separate coronation in Norway.

"No," I said, "no, not in Norway."

"Why not?"

"Because here in Sweden I may now be Desideria, the wanted one, but not in Norway. Don't forget that you forced Norway into this union, which may last your time and Oscar's but certainly not much longer."

"The union was necessary. Do you know that you are talking high treason ten minutes before your coronation?"

"In a hundred years' time we shall both sit comfortably on a little cloud and watch the Norwegians declare their independence, and choose a Danish Prince for their King simply to annoy the Swedes, and both you and I will get a good deal of amusement out of it up there on our cloud."

Marceline and Marie rushed in now with my coronation robe. The gold threads in the white brocade had acquired a silvery sheen in the course of the years, I noticed. I put it on and looked at myself and realised that it was the most beautiful dress that I had ever seen.

Meanwhile Jean-Baptiste went on with the explanation of the coronation procession. I heard that my two Counts, Brahe and Rosen, were to bear the insignia of State, and I was glad because I had insisted that they should have this distinction, which ought to have gone to the highest-ranking ministers. Hadn't they thrown the weight of their ancient names into the scales at the time when the Swedes had had to get used to the silk merchant's daughter on their throne?

And who was going to follow the two Counts, bearing the crown on a red cushion? Miss Mariana Koskull! That, too, had been my choice. "You are not dissatisfied with my choice, are you?" I said. "It does not say anywhere that the crown must be carried by a virgin, as it does in that ancient French stipulation which Napoleon had such difficulties in fulfilling; you remember he had to find ten virgins? All that is required is a woman of the high aristocracy. That's why I suggested Mariana Koskull." I winked at Jean-Baptiste. "And for her services to the Vasa and Bernadotte dynasties!"

At that Jean-Baptiste showed sudden interest in my jewels and bent down to inspect them.

At last I was ready. Marie came to put the purple cloak round my shoulders, but Jean-Baptiste took it out of her hand and did it himself, very tenderly. Then we stood side by side in front of the big mirror.

"It is like a fairy-tale," I said softly, "once upon a time there lived a great king and a little queen. . . ."

I turned away quickly. "Jean-Baptiste, the broadsheet!"

He took the frame from the wall and handed it to me. I bent down and kissed the glass over the faded text of the Rights of Man. Jean-Baptiste's face went white with excitement.

The folding doors to the salon opened. Josefina was there

with the children. The three-year-old Charles made a dash toward me and then stopped dead. "That isn't Grandmama, that is a Queen," he said and stroked the purple cloak, his face full of awe. Josefina handed me Oscar, the baby. I took him in my arms. He had beautiful blue eyes, and hardly any hair as yet. 'It's for you as well,' I thought, 'for you, the second Oscar, that I'm going to be crowned.'

The dull roar I heard coming from outside reminded me of the night when the torches lit up the Rue d'Anjou. I heard Jean-Baptiste say: "Why are the windows closed?" and "What are they shouting down there in the street?"

But I knew already, it was French. My Swedes wanted me to understand them, and they remembered what they had read about that night of the many torches. They were shouting: "*Notre-Dame de la Paix!*", "Our Lady of Peace!" I handed the baby back to Josefina quickly because I had begun to tremble uncontrollably.

The rest happened as if in a dream. I went down the marble steps, I saw Brahe and Rosen carrying the insignia, and nodded to Rosen in memory of our drive to Malmaison and of Villatte. I saw Koskull in a blue dress carrying the crown on the velvet cushion and smiling happily. I saw Oscar and Josefina enter their open carriage, and then Jean-Baptiste and I entered ours, the last of all the carriages.

"I am arriving last in church, like a bride," I said, and then the jubilant acclamations of the crowd along both sides of the streets roared into my ears.

Jean-Baptiste smiled and waved, and I wanted to smile and wave too, but I couldn't. For I heard them call for me, and for me alone. "*Länge leve Drottningen—Drottningen!*" "Long live the Queen!" I heard it and I felt that I should not be able to help crying.

In front of the Cathedral Jean-Baptiste himself arranged the folds of my purple cloak and led me to the porch. There the Archbishop and all the bishops of Sweden were waiting for me.

"Blessed be she who cometh in the name of the Lord!" the Archbishop said. The organ music rose like a great wave, and I could only think again when the Archbishop put the crown on my head. 'How heavy it is,' I thought.

It is late at night, and everybody thinks I have gone to bed to prepare myself for the festivities taking place to-morrow and the day after in my honour. But I wanted to write once more in my diary. How strange that I should have arrived at the last page to-day!

Once, many years ago, it was nothing but white empty pages

and lay on my birthday table. I was fourteen years old and wanted to know what I was to write in it. Papa answered: " The story of Citizeness Bernadine Eugenie Désirée Clary."

Papa, I have written it down, all of it, and there's nothing more to be added now. The story of the citizeness has come to an end, and that of the Queen is beginning now. I shall never understand how it all came about. But I promise you, Papa, to do all I can not to bring discredit on your name, and never to forget that you were a highly respected silk merchant all your life.